INDEBTED

SERIES

4-6

Third Debt

Fourth Debt

Final Debt

Indebted Epilogue

by

PEPPER WINTERS

Indebted Series 4-7 (Third Debt, Fourth Debt, Final Debt, Indebted Epilogue)
Copyright © 2015 Pepper Winters
Published by Pepper Winters

Published: Pepper Winters 2015: **pepperwinters@gmail.com**
Cover Design: by Ari at Cover it! Designs:
http://salon.io/#coveritdesigns
Cover Design: Kellie Design Book Cover by Design:
http://www.bookcoverbydesign.co.uk/
Proofreading by: Jenny Sims: **http://www.editing4indies.com**
Proofreading by: Kayla the Bibliophile
Proofreading by: Erica Russikoff: http://www.ericaedits.com/
Proofreading by: Ellen Blackwell:
http://www.blackwellproofreading.com/
Images in Manuscript from Canstock Photos:
http://www.canstockphoto.com

*For every believer, dreamer, and fantasist
who have read my work & welcome my
words into their heart.
I'll never forget you.*

. . .

Ever.

OTHER WORK BY PEPPER WINTERS

Pepper Winters is a New York Times, Wall Street Journal, and USA Today International Bestseller.

Her Dark Romance books include:

Monsters in the Dark Trilogy
Tears of Tess (Monsters in the Dark #1)
Quintessentially Q (Monsters in the Dark #2)
Twisted Together (Monsters in the Dark #3)

Indebted Series
Debt Inheritance (Indebted #1)
First Debt (Indebted Series #2)
Second Debt (Indebted Series #3)
Third Debt (Indebted Series #4)
Fourth Debt (Indebted Series #5)
Final Debt (Indebted Series #6)
Indebted Epilogue (Indebted Series #7)

Her Grey Romance books include:
Destroyed
Ruin & Rule (Pure Corruption MC #1)
Sin & Suffer (Pure Corruption MC #2)

Her Upcoming Releases include:
2016: Indebted Beginnings
2016: Je Suis a Toi (Monsters in the Dark Novella)
January 2016: Sin & Suffer (Pure Corruption MC #2)
2016: Super Secret Series to be announced
2016: Unseen Messages (Standalone Romance)

Follow her on her website
Pepper Winters

This story isn't suitable for those who don't enjoy dark romance, uncomfortable situations, and dubious consent. It's sexy, it's twisty, there's colour as well as darkness, but it's a rollercoaster not a carrousel.

Warning heeded...enter the world of debts and payments.

(As an additional warning please note, this is a cliffhanger, answers will not be answered, the storyline won't be resolved, and character motivations won't be revealed until further on. It's a complex story that will unfold over a few volumes.)

If you would like to read this book with like-minded readers, and be in to win advance copies of other books in the series, along with Q&A sessions with Pepper Winters, please join the Facebook group below:

Indebted Series Group Read

INDEBTED #4
THIRD DEBT

INTERNATIONAL BESTSELLING AUTHOR
PEPPER WINTERS

I'D GIVEN MY heart to my enemy.

I'd fallen.

Fallen.

Fallen.

Hard.

There was no bottom to my affection. No limit to what I would do to protect it.

Jethro was mine and it was up to me....

...up to me to end this.

I was no longer trying to save myself.

I was trying to save him.

From his nightmares.

From himself.

From them.

HOW HAD THIS happened?

Where did it all go so wrong?

Jethro was supposed to love me. I was supposed to love him.

Yet he'd given me over to his family. He'd bound the ropes, blindfolded my eyes, and gifted me to his kin.

"Know what time it is, Nila Weaver?" Daniel breathed in my ear.

I jerked away. The restraints around my body meant I couldn't run, couldn't fight; I couldn't even see.

Oh, God.

Please don't let them do this.

I wanted to scream for Jethro to save me. I wanted him to put an end to this and claim me once and for all. Didn't our connection mean anything?

You know it's all different now.

Ever since I'd returned to Hawksridge Hall, things had been different— horribly, *horribly* different.

The fire crackled in the billiards room where the Hawk men had been playing poker. The air was hot and muggy and laced with cognac fumes.

Tonight, I'd had plans to end whatever changed between Jethro and me forever.

But now…those plans had changed.

Kestrel ran his fingers over my collar. "Relax, little Weaver. It will all be over soon."

Cut chuckled. "Yes, soon you can go to sleep and pretend none of this happened."

My ears strained for one other voice. The voice of the man who controlled my heart even though he'd thrown it back in my face.

But only silence greeted me.

Daniel snickered, licking my cheek. "Time to pay, Weaver."

Someone clapped and in a voice full of darkness and doom said, "It's time for the Third Debt."

Two Months Prior...

I MEANT WHAT I said before.

I meant it with every bone in my body.

Someone has to die.

I still stood by that conclusion. Only, I'd hoped it wouldn't be me.

Too bad wishes never come true.

I'd always wondered what it would feel like. How I would react, knowing that I'd failed. I'd lain awake so many nights trying to imagine how I would behave when my father finally had enough. I'd scared myself shitless fearing I wouldn't be strong enough, *brave* enough, to face the consequences I'd lived with all my life.

But none of that mattered now. I'd done what I swore never to do and revealed myself. My father knew there was no changing me—he would come for me.

But so fucking what?

She's safe.

That was all I needed to focus on.

I'd done my utmost to be the perfect son, but I'd been fighting an unwinnable battle. No matter how much I wished I could be like them—I wasn't. And it was pointless to keep fighting.

Not anymore.

I'm done.

I was done the moment Nila called me Kite and admitted she loved me.

Fuck, that isn't true.

I was done the moment I set eyes on her in Milan.

I stood looking out the window, gripping the windowsill with white fingers. The view of Hawksridge—of manicured hedges and vibrant rose bushes—was no longer in colour but black and white. Before my very eyes, the sparkle and dynamism of life left me as Nila stepped into the black sedan below.

How could the ebullience of the world suddenly disappear, leaving behind a monochromatic disaster the second she vanished?

The moment she'd left the dining room, I'd removed myself from my father's smug glare and managed to hold it together the entire three minutes it took to walk down the corridor, putting enough distance between me and the people who couldn't see me break.

I'd managed to keep walking until there was no one to see me, but then my self-control snapped. My legs had propelled into a run. I'd fucking sprinted to the bachelor wing while every step twisted my ice into daggers, making me bleed, making me care.

I hadn't stopped until I'd slammed my hands on the windowsill and looked through the wavy centuries-old glass at the procession below.

My heart lurched as a man in a suit closed the car door, barricading me from her forever. There were no flashing lights, no decals warning criminals who they were.

These policemen had come to steal what was mine with stealth. They knew they'd trespassed and broke treaties far older than their years with the force. My family had immunity, yet I'd underestimated Vaughn.

He hadn't turned to the law to help. He hadn't even enlisted mercenaries or other stupid ways that Weavers had done in the past. No, he'd been smart. Bloody bastard. He'd used social media to rally a public force. Even with our wealth and influence, we couldn't fight against the outcry of millions of people.

Fuck Vaughn.

Fuck his tampering.

My fists curled on the windowsill as the policeman tapped the side of the vehicle as if he'd fucking won. Him. Them. *The Weavers*.

They'd won.

She's ruined me.

Destroyed me.

I glared at the car, willing Nila to look up. But she didn't. Her silhouette, staring resolutely ahead, was obscured by tinted windows.

She'd obeyed me and left the dining room.

She didn't look back.

Now, I would've given anything for her to look back. To change her mind.

A terrible churning began inside.

Everything that I'd swallowed and kept deep, deep down flew to the surface. It grew and grew stronger, harder, *faster.*

My fingers dug like swords into the soft wood.

Even though I wanted to kill the police with my bare hands, I managed to stay in my wing as the engines of the three cars rumbled into gear. They pulled away from the house. The noise of their tyres on gravel didn't reach my window, but I had no trouble conjuring the sound.

It sounded like glass being crushed beneath grinding stone. It sounded exactly like what was happening inside me: every organ shattering into hell.

I held it together just long enough for the convoy to disappear over the ridge, slithering like a poisonous snake, taking what was mine.

Come back.

Never come back.

I should've known this would happen.

I was always destined to this fate.

It was inevitable.

In a way, I was grateful to Vaughn. He'd rescued her when I didn't have the fucking balls. He'd taken back his sister because he loved her enough to *fight* for her. She was better off with him, away from me and my fucked-up family.

The last of the convoy disappeared.

With a bone-deep sigh, I gave up. I let the glass inside me splinter and detonate. I permitted myself to do what I could never do. I let down my walls. My many, many walls.

I lost myself.

Bending in half, I rested my forehead on my knuckles as I suffered the worst unravelling I'd ever lived through.

See, Nila.

This is what I meant when I asked you to see me.

She thought she lived in an intense world? It was nothing compared to what I endured. Nothing compared to the condition I'd been cursed to bear.

Grief, terror, and guilt howled and roared with utmost ferocity.

I became hollow, empty—carved out by emotions. It was all too much. All I wanted to do was...*fade.* Fade away from biting words and gnawing consequences.

"Jethro."

Shit.

As easily as it'd been to drop my walls, it took a herculean effort to rebuild them. Ice brick after ice brick, I did my best to reconstruct the igloo I'd lived in all my life. But it was no use.

With a face twisted in defiance, I spun to meet my father.

He stood in the doorway, key in one hand and an implement of discipline in the other. We stared at each other. Matching eyes and Hawk blood. How could two men, bound by lineage and family, be so completely different?

"Come along. You can't run from this. Not anymore."

Clenching my jaw so hard my teeth almost turned into diamonds, I looked one last time at the emptiness outside my window. Watching her go was absolute torture, but seeing her return would be the worst punishment of all.

Stay away, Nila Weaver. Never come back.

"Jethro," he snarled. "Your disguises won't work this time."

He couldn't even give me a second to say goodbye. To imprint every last detail of Nila onto my soul so I could carry her with me to the underworld. He couldn't even give me the courtesy of being myself just *once* before it was over.

Bastard.

Absolute fucking bastard.

I glared at my father. His face was as sharp as the stones we smuggled.

"What have you done with Jasmine?" My sister was in a state. I hadn't seen her so emotional in years. "She needs someone to be there with her when you tell her what you've done."

Cut sniffed. "Kestrel is with her. And he'll stay with her as long as she needs."

At least Bonnie and Daniel weren't chosen to console her. The thought of leaving my sister disembowelled me.

Balling my hands, I forced myself to find courage.

Cut moved closer, his arms steadfast by his sides. "I was fair to you, son. I gave you more chances than you deserve."

So many options flashed before my eyes. I could beg for mercy, threaten him—even commit murder to protect myself.

But Nila had been in my life for two months.

My father had been in it for twenty-nine years.

He'd done his best with me. Through his manipulations and crazy conditioning, we'd both thought I could change. It wasn't his fault he had to do this.

It's mine.

I dropped my eyes, keeping my mask resolutely in place. "Send me away. Disown me. Do whatever you want." I kept staring at the carpet as I pleaded for leniency. "You have my word; I won't come back."

I'll run with her. Take her where you'll never find us.

Cut chuckled. The sound was like a babbling brook in hell. "I have no intention of doing this half-assed, Jet. This is what has to happen. Don't prolong it." Raising his arm, he pointed the gun at my chest.

Everything went into fucking lockdown.

My eyes zeroed in on the weapon; no amount of courage could prevent me from debating the worthiness of my life. Yes, I wasn't like him. But fuck, I'd tried. Didn't that mean anything? "I'm still your son."

He pursed his lips. "Debatable after the past few months."

"I disappointed you. I proved unworthy, but for Christ's sake, just let me go. Banish me, cast me away, make me penniless. Do whatever you want. Just don't kill me."

The word 'please' danced on my tongue, but I swallowed it back.

I'm not weak.

I wouldn't give him the satisfaction of begging.

"You've heard the tales. You've seen the proof of why we live such strict lives. You know I can't do that, Jethro. It's better for everyone this way. You're firstborn. I cannot legally grant my estate to Kestrel while you're still alive."

"I'll sign whatever you want renouncing my claim."

"Jet—" Cut growled, stepping closer, calm and resigned. "What's done is done. Time to suffer the consequences."

He discussed taking my life as if I were the household trash and not his flesh and blood.

I turned my back on him and looked out the window again, reliving the procession of cars that'd stolen Nila from my world.

She'd given me so much, yet taken more than I could bear.

It wasn't fair.

Life is never fair.

I snorted.

My life is over.

"Jethro—" His temper snapped my name in half. "Unless you want a bullet in your brain, I suggest you come with me. As terrible as you think of me, I don't *want* to hurt you."

I spun around. "What?"

My heart raced in false hope.

Moving closer, he waved the gun. "Come without a fuss. You don't want your sister to see a mess in here…do you?"

Whatever hope had gathered in my heart ruptured. I flinched at the thought of Jaz witnessing a gruesome dispatching.

"I'll come with you." Crossing the distance between us, I wrapped my hand around the muzzle of his gun. "Put it away. It's not needed."

Silence webbed around us.

Cut sighed and holstered the weapon in the back of his trousers. "Good boy." The compassion in his eyes was so wrong. He *did* care for me—more than he would admit.

Normally, my condition meant I had no choice but to listen. To feel. To understand.

Not this time.

My body shut down, already killing off sensitivity and accepting fate. Thoughts of beating him up and running filled my mind. It didn't have to end this way. But if I left Hawksridge, I would still have to live with the nightmare I'd been born with. And after falling for Nila, my reserves were empty. I wanted a rest.

I was fucking tired of everything.

Cut stood aside, waving at the door. "After you."

"No, after you. I'll follow. I gave you my word."

Cut scowled but finally nodded. Wordlessly, he made his way to the door and looked over his shoulder to ensure I obeyed.

This was it, then.

On the cusp of winning, I'd lost everything.

So be it.

I followed.

Nila

"STOP THE CAR. Please, stop the car."

The policeman shook his head, gripping the wheel and taking me further away from Jethro. "Sorry, Ms. Weaver. The next place we'll stop is London."

The sway of the vehicle sent goosebumps over my skin. Every spin of the tyres thickened my blood with dread.

What will Cut do to him?

How could I leave?

Straining in my seat, I winced. The bruises on my ribcage from CPR, the flaring heat in my throat from drowning, and the headache from confusion all competed with the fisting sensation around my heart.

I tapped the policeman on his shoulder. "Please, this is all a big misunderstanding. Take me back. I *want* to go back."

Now. Immediately. Before it's too late.

"Don't worry. Just relax. Everything is as it should be," the officer said.

I just walked away! How could I *do* that?

"No, it's not. I don't have time to explain, but I need you to take me back." Debts and death and diabolical Hawks didn't scare me anymore.

Only the thought of what Jethro would face scared me.

I wouldn't let him suffer alone.

What can you possibly do to help?

I ignored that thought and the panic it brought. I was useless, but I had to try. It was the least I could do. He cared for me. He sent me away and put himself in my place.

Damn him for sending me away!

The officer lost his cordial nature, turning stiff with annoyance. "Miss, I understand that you've lived through a great deal, but the Hawks are not a family to be trifled with. We've acted on the wishes of the media and your family, so don't say you did not wish to be rescued when the world knows what you're tangled in."

My eyes bugged. "The world knows what?" When he didn't answer, I pried, "How did my father get you to come?"

The policeman glared at me in the mirror. "Your father and brother didn't *make* us do anything. *We* went to them—we had to do something. Your sibling was out of control."

My heart hurt. My head hurt. I couldn't make sense of this mess.

Pressing my fingers against my temples, I begged, "Please, whatever you've heard, pay no attention. They have it wrong. Just—please take me back."

Take me back so I can save him. He needs me!

My soul cried for lying about my brother—the one person who had my wellbeing in mind—but my loyalties had changed. Somewhere along the way, I'd chosen Jethro over everyone. He was my curse, my challenge, my salvation, and I wasn't going to leave him when he needed me the most.

I'd forced him to notice me. I'd forced him to lean on me.

And now I've left him without any help.

The car didn't slow. We kept driving…mile after mile of rolling hills, grazing deer, and dense forest. The car remained silent.

Fear gave me palpitations. Frustration gave me shakes. I *hated* that I wasn't in control. I hadn't been in control my entire life, and this was just another instance in which men believed they knew better.

First my father. Then Jethro. Now these arseholes.

I wanted to scratch out their eyes and slam on the brakes. I wanted to scream and teach them just how capable I was.

Breathe. Calm down.

You're free!

You should be happy!

To prevent myself from combusting, I glanced out the window. Our speed blurred tussock and seedlings. Acres and acres of woodland and fences. No wonder Jethro had let me run for my freedom. I would never have made it to the boundary.

Miles already separated me from the Hall, but I couldn't stand another metre without Jethro.

Gripping the door handle, I tried to open it. "Let me out. This instant." It remained locked and impenetrable.

A cough caught me unaware, residual liquid still in my lungs.

The policeman glanced at me, eyebrow raised. "I'm afraid I can't do that, Miss."

"Why? Am I under arrest?"

The further we drove, the more my body hurt—I could no longer distinguish if it was from drowning or leaving Jethro in the hands of evil.

A smidgen of relief came unwanted. I was free. Despite everything, I'd gotten out alive—at the cost of another. *I'm safe.*

The officer smiled thinly. "You'll be fully debriefed when we get to London. I suggest you have a rest."

Every new distance, my diamond collar grew heavier, colder.

Every metre we travelled, my fingertip tattoos itched with spidery scratches.

It was as if the spell Hawksridge had over me tried to suck me back—gravity throttling me with diamonds and ink bursting from my skin to return to its master. As much as I despised being a prisoner of the Hawks, I'd found love with Jethro. I'd found myself, and every hill we ascended, I lost more and more of who I'd become.

My stomach churned as I remembered the gravesite with my family's tombstones. Voices filled my head, flitting like ghosts.

You said you'd be the last.

You promised you'd end this.

I glowered at the policeman driving.

It isn't over. Not yet.

I will go back and save him.

I will stop this!

My eyes widened, noticing the two policemen wore bulletproof vests. Why were they wearing raid gear on a simple 'rescue' mission? Were the Hawks seriously that crazy? Would they shoot men of the law?

The men remained silent as we coasted beneath the gatehouse and archway of the entrance to Hawksridge estate.

I craned my neck to look at the family sigil of hawks and a nest of women. "You're making a mistake." I pressed my hand against the window, wishing I could run back to the Hall where I'd spent the past couple of months trying to flee.

The policeman muttered, "Tell that to your brother."

The conversation faded, leaving a stagnant taste of trust and confusion. What had V done? What did the cops think happened to me?

My stomach once again somersaulted.

You're doing the right thing leaving.

You're doing the only thing you can.

Jethro knew that. It was because he cared for me that he sent me away. In his mind, it was the only solution. But in mine, it was a dreadful mistake.

He'll pay for setting me free.

And it'll be all my fault.

Sighing, I rested my forehead on the coolness of the glass.

I ached.

I burned.

I didn't even get to say goodbye.

Jethro

I FOLLOWED HIS every footstep.

Down corridors where I'd played as a little boy, through rooms I'd investigated, and past hidey holes where I'd played hide-and-seek with my brothers and sister.

The house held so many memories. Past centuries lived in its walls with births and deaths, triumphs and tragedies. I was just a speck in history, about to be obliterated.

My heartbeat resembled an inmate on death row as we made our way through the kitchen toward the cellar. The ancient door leading beneath the Hall was hidden in the walk-in pantry.

Hundreds of years ago, the cellar stored barrels of beer and freshly slaughtered meat. Now abandoned, it housed a few lonely wine racks and cases of expensive cognac resting beneath blankets of dust.

We descended the earthen steps and traded the dry warmth of the Hall for the damp chill of the catacombs.

A cool draft kissed our skin as vapours rose from exposed earth. My black jeans and t-shirt clung to my skin, growing heavy with mildew.

Cut didn't stop.

We made our way from the food storage area to a locked metal gate. The staff weren't permitted past this point. Secrets were stored down here. Deep, dark, dangerous secrets that only Hawks could know.

Electric lights flickered like candles as Cut unlocked the rusty mechanism and guided me onward. The screech of the hinges sounded like a skeleton dragging its bony fingers down the claustrophobic walls.

Just like the natural springs where I'd revived Nila, this warren system of circular tunnels and crudely hacked pathways was found by accident while renovating Hawksridge.

Why did previous generations toil so hard in pitch dark and dripping ice?

To build a crypt.

Weavers were buried on the chase, exposed to whipping winds and snow; my ancestors were entombed below the feet of the living, howling their laments and haunting the hallways of their old home.

It was morbid. Depressing. And I *despised* it down here. The stench of rotting corpses and tentacles of ghosts lurked around shadowy corners.

"Where are we—"

"Silence," Cut hissed. His voice echoed around the cylindrical chambers.

My sluggish beat turned frantic as Cut continued onward, leaving the crypt behind and stepping foot into the one place I'd avoided all my life.

The memory came thick and fast.

"Wait up!"

Kes charged ahead, hurtling down the cellar steps and disappearing into the dark underground pathways beneath the house. These tunnels went to all areas of the estate—to the stables, Black Diamond garage, even the old silos where grain was stored back in the day.

It was also dark, damp, and rat infested.

We had no torches, no jumpers. Being a hot summer's day, we'd been searching for spots of shades, only to end up getting bored and playing tag.

"Come on, scaredy cat," Kes taunted.

I couldn't see him in the inky blackness, but I kept running with my hands outstretched just in case I ran into something.

I came to an intersection and narrowly missed ploughing headfirst into dirt. Fumbling along the wall, my heart flew into my mouth. The wall surrounded me...three sides, soaring higher and tighter as claustrophobia kicked in.

The clank of heavy metal suddenly rang deep and piercing behind me.

"Kes?"

"We'll play dungeons and guards. You're the prisoner." Kes laughed as he rattled the bars he'd just slammed over the entranceway I'd stupidly entered.

It was so black.

I couldn't see a thing. But I could hear everything. My breathing. My heartbeat. My terror. So, so loud.

"What do you have to say for yourself, prisoner? Do you plead guilty?" Kes asked, his eight-year-old voice deepening with fake authority.

I moved toward his location, arms outstretched until I found the cold iron bars. "Let me out, Angus."

"Don't use that name."

"I'll use whatever name I want unless you get me out of here." My body itched for fresh air, light, freedom. It felt as if the walls were crumbling, folding in, and burying me alive. "Not funny. Let me out."

"Okay, okay. Jeez." He yanked on the bars. The awful clanging noise jangled around us.

I pressed from my side of the cell.

Nothing happened.

"Err, it's locked."

"What do you mean it's locked?" My soul scratched at my bones needing freedom. "Find a key—get me out!"

"Stay here. I'll go get help."

Kes's body heat and the sound of his breathing suddenly disappeared, leaving me all alone in the pitch black, locked in a prison cell where men had been tortured and died.

I shuddered, breaking the memory's hold.

Since that day, I'd never returned. Kes had dragged our grandfather to free me, and after he'd unlocked the cell, he'd forbidden us from returning to the dungeons past the crypts.

I'd readily obeyed. Never again did I want to step foot in a place still reeking with ancient pain and suffering.

But now my father carted me to the same place, only this time there was light illuminating the deep scratches on the walls from people burrowing for freedom and messages to loved ones who'd never see them.

It took all my strength to follow him around bends and duck where the ceiling hung too low. Scurries of vermin echoed up ahead, and it took everything I had not to break my father's neck and run.

Was I weak not wanting to kill my father? Was I a pussy or justified for being a loyal son? He'd given me life...wasn't it fair he could take it away?

My rationality couldn't temper my panic. My nostrils flared, inhaling damp air.

"Get in, Jethro." Cut came to a stop, waving at the same cell where Kes had accidently imprisoned me for two hours while our grandfather located the key.

The electric sconces glinted off new bars—not the thick, rusty ones of my childhood. My eyes fell to the lock—that was also modern with a number pad rather than an old-fashioned key.

I stepped backward. "You want me to go in there?"

Cut nodded, waving the gun threateningly. "In."

"Why?"

"No questions." He cocked the weapon, sliding a bullet into place.

Swallowing hard, I brushed past him and entered the cell. There was no bed, no facilities, no comfort of any kind. Just earth and mould and puddles.

I turned to face him. Why the hell had he brought me down here? To feed my deceased body to the rats? Or perhaps he meant to starve me to death and not waste a bullet?

Cut stood in the doorway, pointing the gun at my chest.

I sucked in a breath, fisting my hands. "Why bother bringing me here? No one would've heard the shot upstairs—not with so many rooms—and even if they did, no one would interfere." We all knew our place—Hawks and servants included. "I would've appreciated my last view to be of something enjoyable rather than this godforsaken place."

Cut narrowed his eyes. "What makes you think I want this over so quickly?"

I froze.

Footsteps echoed like doomsday percussion off the tunnel walls.

My heart beat faster. "Who else will witness this?" It wasn't Jasmine, that I could be sure—unless someone carried her.

Fuck, would he be that cruel? To make her watch me die after everything we'd done to her?

My mind ran wild with questions and regrets. There was so much I never did, so much I wanted to do.

Now, it was all over.

"What makes you think they're a witness?" Cut's cold voice sent shackles of numbness around my limbs.

Staring into the shadows, out of range of the light, we both waited for the mystery guest to arrive.

The moment a figure materialized from the gloom and golden eyes met mine, I bared my teeth. "What the fuck are you doing here?"

Daniel snickered, moving to take his place beside Cut. Equal breadth and height, they matched in their leather jackets and complementing smirks.

"I'm here to teach you a lesson, *brother*."

Fuck. All the tormenting and lording my firstborn status came back to haunt me. *This* was my true punishment. Not being shot or maimed but being disciplined by my fucking brother.

My gut churned. I had to will every cell to stay upright and stoic. In my mind, I conjured Nila. She possessed my thoughts—not in the everyday attire she'd worn around the Hall—but in the black feathered couture from Milan. Her skin was faultless. Her ebony eyes depthless. She'd been utterly perfect.

Then I'd stolen her. Degraded her. Fucked her. And ultimately loved her.

I pushed her image away as fast as I'd invoked it. It hurt too much.

"I don't understand you, Jethro." Cut entered the cell, his boot scuffing a pebble. "You were so close to throwing away, not just a fortune, but sentencing your sister to the grave as well as yourself."

My blood turned from liquid to rock. "Leave her out of this."

"You're saying you believe Jasmine doesn't deserve repentance? After all, it was *she* who convinced me you could be fixed. She's the one who gave her livelihood for yours that day...or have you forgotten?"

I breathed shallowly. "I haven't forgotten, and it's not her fault. Don't fucking touch her."

"Oh, we won't touch her...if you do everything we say." Daniel brushed past Cut, encroaching on my space. His aftershave of spice and musk overpowered me. My gullet fought to retch—to vomit right on his shiny black boots.

I glowered. Everything about this felt wrong. As if we were boys again playing games we didn't understand. "What do you want?"

Cut chuckled. "Isn't it obvious, Jet? I want a firstborn I can trust. I want a man who will oversee my empire. I want an heir who isn't some sort of fucked-up delinquent."

I straightened my spine. "Life is full of disappointment."

"Yes, but at least I can get some enjoyment out of this." Looking at Daniel, he nodded. "You're up, Buzzard. Teach him a lesson."

My eyes flashed to Daniel's. I kept my expression blank. I refused to beg for mercy or let him see the fear percolating inside.

Daniel smiled, cracking his knuckles and slinking out of his jacket. "Hear that, *Kite*? Time for a little payback. And I have to say, it's gonna taste fucking sweet."

Tossing his jacket into the corner of the cell, he clenched his fists and danced like a seasoned fighter. I instinctually raised my arms, preparing to spar. Daniel was third born—the mistake—he was also the smallest out of all of us, but he was still strong. Plus, he had something I was missing: savagery with no mercy.

"Ah, ah, ah, Jethro." Cut tapped the gun against the bars, sending a god-awful *twang* around the cell. "You aren't to fight back."

I snarled, "You expect me to let him pummel me and not defend myself?"

Daniel laughed, circling me like some rabid hyena.

"I have a deal to offer you, Jethro." Cut's words fell like stones. Everything had new meaning. That ridiculous hope swelled in my heart again.

"What deal?"

"Last chance," Daniel sneered, never stopping his aggravating circles.

Cut ran a hand through his hair. "I was fully prepared to kill you, son. Ready to put you out of your misery because—let's face it—you're not happy." Sympathy coated his features, confusing the shit out of me.

"You're saying you were prepared to put me down like some rabies-infested dog? For *my* sake?"

Cut frowned. "After everything that's happened between us, you still think I'm some kind of monster. I care for you. I care for all my children."

Bullshit.

"It's only natural that I want to help you."

Crossing my arms, I tried to ignore Daniel and understand this new development. "What do you propose?"

"It comes in stages."

"Go on."

"First, you need punishing. I won't tolerate any more disobedience." Toying with the gun, his eyes bored into mine. "Part one of this new deal is…"

"Let me beat your ass with no retaliation." Daniel laughed, socking a punch into my kidney from behind.

White-hot heat scorched my system, setting fire to every organ. I gasped, holding the throbbing bruise. Sickly sweat sprang over my skin. I sucked air between my teeth. "You can't be serious."

Cut's eyes narrowed to slits. "I'm more than serious. Fight back or try to harm your brother, and I'll put a bullet through your skull with no hesitation."

Daniel threw another punch, right into my intestines. A grunt escaped as I staggered forward, bending over to spit on the slimy floor. Only once I'd straightened, trembling with adrenaline, did Cut grant me the next part of his rehabilitation. "When you've accepted a thrashing to what I deem payable, then I'll tell you the next part of the deal."

Coming forward, he pressed the gun under my chin, holding my eyes on his. "You say you hurt. That life is a constant hardship. Well, I have news for you. It's not enough for me that your innards hurt. I want your body to scream, too. It's fitting and a worthwhile punishment for the son of a nobleman."

Transcriptions of such punishments executed hundreds of years ago came to mind. Aristocrats dealt in different conduct when a crime had to be paid. Fists were a gentleman's weapon rather than stocks or floggers.

Daniel's fist collided with my jaw, snapping my head sideways. I groaned as my equilibrium turned to shit. I stumbled sideways, fighting every instinct to defend myself.

Cut stepped back as Daniel round-housed me, planting his boot squarely in my chest. With flaring pain, I tumbled to the earthen floor. Fuck, it hurt. Every inch of me was on fire—pounding with agony.

"Take your sentence like a man, Jethro. Then we'll see if you deserve my proposition."

I scrambled to my feet.

Daniel cackled as he kicked my ankle, sending me face-planting into dirt. I braced myself on all fours, presenting a soft target of my belly in line with his boot.

He kicked me like a fucking animal, breaking a rib and hurtling me into Hades.

I would've given anything to fight back. I howled inside—handcuffed by the illusion of leniency. I took each blow, not for my downfall of being what I was, but for what I'd *done*.

Every strike was my penance for what I did to Nila.

Each kick was a purging for my disastrous behaviour.

I nursed Nila in my heart and found a strange healing, even in such unjust brutality.

My eyes watered as Daniel yanked my hair and cracked his knuckles against my cheekbone.

Cut muttered, "I want you bleeding in apology, son. Only then might you deserve another chance."

"WE'RE HERE."

Powerful buildings and iconic landmarks replaced the rugged landscape of Buckinghamshire's countryside. There were no trees or sweeping hills, no foxhounds or horses.

London.

"Bet you missed your family, Ms. Weaver." The policeman driving had tried small talk over the course of our three-hour drive. I'd ignored every topic.

Instead of focusing on grey concrete and overpasses, I thought of Jethro. Where was he? What were they doing to him?

My emotions split into an unsolvable jigsaw puzzle. I was smooth edges, crooked edges, and awkward corner edges. I was cutthroat and fierce, betrayer and deceiver, loved and lover.

Only a few hours had passed since I'd left Jethro, yet I felt as if I'd been adrift forever.

I have to go back.

I was no longer a girl who would bow to her father and submit to her brother. I wasn't content with letting others be in charge.

I was a fighter.

And I owed Cut Hawk payment for what he'd done.

A fog rolled in over the busy cog-work city of London as we journeyed through ancient streets and new.

Every streetlamp and road sign spoke of home.

My home.

My old home.

I knew this place. I'd been born here. Raised here. Trained here.

You also met Jethro when you were too young to remember here.

The car came to a halt outside my family's sweeping Victorian manor. The whitewashed bricks looked fresh and modern. The lilac windows decorated in my mother's favourite colour. It was quaintly feminine despite its three-story grandeur.

It's a dollhouse compared to Hawksridge Hall.

I missed the gothic French turrets and imposing size. I missed the richness and danger that breathed in its walls.

I missed Jethro.

The glass of my window on the second floor winked through the grey drizzle, welcoming me back.

The driver pressed the intercom on the wrought iron gate, barring the Weaver Household from the rest of society. We lived in an affluent end of town. No one asked for a cup of sugar here. Everyone guarded themselves behind camera systems and armed fences.

"Yes?"

The moment my father's voice came through the speaker, vertigo swooped in and held me hostage. The world spun.

"We're here, Mr. Weaver."

A crackle then a panicked bark, "Do you have her?"

The driver threw me a smile. "We have her."

SOMETHING HARD THUMPED against my chest.

It roused me, dragging me from the bowels of hell and back into a body sobbing with pain.

"Open your eyes, Jet."

I flinched, fearing another kick or punch. How long had Daniel punished me?

Long enough to break a couple more ribs and swell my left eye completely shut.

"He's gone." A presence squatted in front of me—a blurry figure obscured by blood and dirt.

I tried to swallow, but my throat was too dry. Incredibly, a water bottle was pushed into my lifeless hands. When I almost dropped it, Cut wrapped his warm fingers around mine, clasping the bottle tightly.

A wave of compassion and sympathy lapped around my sodden form, forcing my vision to focus. "Tha—thank you," I whispered brokenly.

Cut nodded, sitting on his haunches while I sipped from the already open bottle and slowly wrangled my body into life.

Struggling to sit upright, Cut moved so I could spread out my legs and recline against the frigid, dripping wall.

"Better?" he asked. As if he cared about my welfare only moments after beating me to a pulp.

Still alive, unfortunately for you.

I fought my sarcastic response and glared instead. "Did I pass your little test, Father?" In that second, I hated him. I fucking despised that this man was my patron and relation.

He didn't reply. Only motioned to the thing that'd landed on my chest and rolled to the side with an odd rattle. "That's the second requirement of this last chance."

I couldn't make out what it was. My eyes flickered as my system organised my pain into filing cabinets of life threatening, throbbing, and liveable.

"Pick it up."

Swallowing my groan, I slipped sideways against the wall and scooped up the small white bottle. I squinted, trying unsuccessfully to read the label.

"What—what are they?"

Cut shifted, bringing my attention to the gun resting on his knee. It still pointed at me, like it had during the beating Daniel gave me. "I told you. Your final chance."

I scowled at the gun. "And if I don't agree…to whatever you want me to do next?"

"It ends. Here and now. I put you out of your misery and life moves on."

My heart raced, dragging Nila back into existence. "If you kill me, does that void the Debt Inheritance?"

Could I somehow free Nila from this by sacrificing myself?

Cut pursed his lips, anger shading his features. "You're saying you would die for a fucking Weaver? Come on, Jethro. Be a man and accept what I'm trying to give you." He opened his arms, signalling Hawksridge. "This will be all yours. The companies, trade routes, mines…all *yours*. Is one woman worth all that?"

Silence was syrupy, its only companion the chilled dampness surrounding us.

Yes.

She's worth that and more.

"So that was a yes?" My voice croaked. I took another sip of water. "If you kill me, the debts are done. You need a firstborn. That's why there's only been seven Weavers claimed over the centuries. Things go wrong; life interferes. What did you tell me? That raising a Hawk and Weaver to age requirement without one dying, going missing, or failing in some way was a fucking miracle? Kill me—end this so-called miracle. Another generation would be safe."

Cut shot to his feet and kicked my leg. Normally, such a blow wouldn't hurt, but it landed on multiple bruises already given courtesy of Daniel.

I hissed, fisting my hands around the bottle and spilling water down my bloodied clothes.

"Ordinarily, Jethro, you would be right. With your death comes her salvation. She'd walk free. She wouldn't be claimed because the firstborn didn't survive."

The biggest wash of relief enveloped me. That was the answer then. The only way. I could avoid any more hardship and Nila could avoid death.

I can give you that, Nila. I can give you a long life free from me.

"Do it," I commanded, my voice firm with conviction. "It seems our wishes have finally aligned, Father. I wish to die. You wish to have a different heir. There's only one logical conclusion."

Gathering my threadbare energy, I somehow climbed to my feet. I used the wall as a cane and swayed like a drunkard, but I was on two feet—equal to Cut standing before me.

Cut raised the gun, pointing at my heart.

All fear was gone. I was happy with this sacrifice. I finally found a purpose for my screwed-up life, and Nila would be safe to live without being beheaded.

It's the right thing—the noble thing to do.

And thanks to Daniel's beating, perhaps I'd paid enough tax to find my way into heaven, rather than purgatory.

"You truly are twisted," Cut snarled. "How can you piss me off and make me proud all at the same time?"

I stiffened. I didn't need his mind games anymore. I needed an ending. *I want it over with.* "Just do it." I held out my hands, one clutching the water bottle and the other the white container that rattled with who knew what. "You know you want to."

Cut paced away, dragging a hand through his hair. "No, I do *not* want to! I'm not a fucking monster, Jethro. I'm trying to save your life, not end it!"

He stormed back, waving the deadly weapon in my face. "You know what? Death is too easy for someone like you. You're too damn strong, and I refuse to put an end to a man who could rule our name as it needs to be ruled. Kestrel is a good man, but he isn't steadfast like you. And Daniel—" He rolled his eyes. "He's a goddamn maniac who would whittle away our fortune in years." Tapping the gun against his chin, his eyes came alight with a plan.

My gut twisted.

Fuck.

"There's a new condition to my offer."

I'd been so close to saving her.

I fought the urge to hunch in defeat. "Spit it out."

"If you die…if you kill yourself, plan an accident, or find some other way to end it thinking you can protect that little Weaver Whore, then I'll give her to Daniel. Do you hear me?"

My temper roared. "But he's not firstborn—"

"I don't care about the rules anymore, Jet. Because of you, all of this is a complicated fuck-up. That girl *will* pay. She wears the collar. It will come off. And the Debt Inheritance will be paid—with or without you."

I didn't bother to ask how we'd sort out the media mess and get her back. My family was entirely too resourceful. Her escape was merely an interlude, and I was fucking kidding myself if I thought differently.

My heart galloped with hatred. "What are you saying?"

"If you do what I ask, you can continue to extract the debts. No one will lay a hand on her unless you command it. She'll remain yours and in your protection until the Final Debt."

My bruised hands tightened around the bottles. "And how do you propose I do that?" I laughed, the dark chuckle sounded like insects in the catacombs' echoing chambers. "Let's end the bullshit, Father. You know what I am. We both know I can't change. Why bother keeping me alive when I'll only cause more hardship? Just get it over with. Forget about the Weavers. Forget about me. Just forget all of it and put an end to this madness."

Cut grinned; the evilness I was used to overshadowed his pity for me. "I'll never forget, Jet. A true Hawk never forgets." Pointing at the white bottle in my hand, he muttered, "That will fix you. Make you my true son instead of this diseased creature before me."

I winced as if he'd struck me again. Nothing like a few kind words from a father to make a kid feel adored.

"Get yourself under control. No matter what you think of me, I *want* you to inherit."

Putting the water bottle down, I summoned strength and twisted off the lid of the small vial. I glanced inside. It was hard to see with the meagre light, but the tiny moon-shaped tablets gave me equal measure of despair and hope.

I looked up. "Drugs?"

Cut nodded. "Before this shitty debacle, you'd impressed me the past few years. You listened and obeyed. You showed such promise. I can't dispatch you when I still believe you can be cured."

I blinked. Was this my father? The man who'd threatened me all my life.

He'd had a sudden change of heart?

"You know these don't work on me. We've tried enough in the past." Nothing worked. From antipsychotics to beta-blockers and downers. They were all the same—useless.

Cut put the safety on and shoved the gun down his waistband. The cocky confidence of winning already infected him. "These are different. Not even on the market yet."

"How did you get them?"

"Doesn't matter. All you need to know is they're stronger than anything you've tried and come with a guarantee of success."

Suddenly, I had choices. Before, I had the daily toil of self-harming to give myself something to focus on. I had death to look forward to in order to save Nila. But now, I had to stay alive if I had any chance of saving her and putting an end to the Final Debt. I also had an option to help me survive in order to do that.

That same taunting hope fluttered with new wings. *Will they help?*

For a moment, I was selfish. Could it be possible after all this time? To live a normal life? To be free?

I couldn't stop the overwhelming rush of gratefulness. The past couple of months in Nila's company had been utter torture. She'd forced me to change— to grow—to look for other ways to exist.

But this…

What I held might be the end to all my problems.

"You believe them? That they'll work?"

Cut shrugged. "We can only hope." Picking up my water bottle, he held it out to me. "We won't know until you've taken a course. Five a day, every few hours. Take more if you need to. Don't worry about the side effects—not if you want to survive in order to keep Nila in your control."

The threat was there—disguised as a helping hand but still an ultimatum. Drug myself and become everything he ever wanted, play puppet master with the life of the woman I was in love with, and carry out his wishes…or perish at his hands and have her subjected to Daniel's murderous plans.

I hated all those choices.

"And you won't let me leave? Disown me and give the estate to Kes?"

Then I can have Nila and live far away from here.

"No negotiation." Cut crossed his arms. "You take the drugs and embrace your proper place, or you die and she lives a life of horror until her death. Your choice."

I stopped breathing.

"Get that bitch out of your mind and heart, son. Take the drugs, find your way back, then we'll see if you get to live."

Could I be strong enough to obey Cut all the while double-crossing him by loving Nila? Could I last to my thirtieth birthday, so I could tear up the Debt Inheritance and eradicate it once and for all?

I have no choice.

I had to try.

I tipped a tablet into my palm and tossed it onto my tongue. Locking eyes with my father, I took a swill of water and swallowed the first drug of many.

Nila had my heart.

But my father had my very existence.

THE CAR ROLLED through the gates.

The tyres inched closer to the front porch.

The front door opened.

My brother appeared.

V.

Before I could take a breath and prepare, the car door was jerked open.

He hadn't changed.

His black hair still fell roguishly over one eye. His body was fit and toned—wiry with model-perfect lines. He sported a slight beard—tight and dark—it made him seem like some modern day Robin Hood stealing me from the Hawks and returning me to my rightful place.

"V—" I wanted to say more, but my throat gave out. Tears spurted from my eyes.

Vaughn was here.

He could fix this. He could mend my defective heart. He could fight for me so I wouldn't have to.

We have to save Jethro. Before they do something terrible.

His hands captured my cheeks, holding me firm as his mirroring black eyes drank mine. "Threads." He pressed a kiss against my temple. "Threads. Fucking hell, you're here."

I sucked in a breath, fumbling with my seatbelt. I wanted to be closer to him. To let him erase my breaking pieces.

Because I was breaking.

Jethro had stolen my everything.

But this was my brother.

The brother I'd betrayed.

A sob latched onto my lungs, making me cough, making me relive what the Hawks did to me in the lake.

I coughed again. More tears fell.

V groaned under his breath, tearing off my seatbelt and dragging me into his arms.

My legs dangled as he crushed me to his chest. His heartbeat was steady and strong as I cried into his white shirt.

Steady and strong.

Jethro's heartbeat had been irregular and terrified.

I cried harder. Not just for how royally I'd screwed everything up but for leaving Jethro when I'd promised I'd stay.

Please, please let him be alright.

"It's okay, Threads. I gotcha. You're safe now. Those fucking bastards will never come near you again. You hear me? Never." His voice was harsh with promise.

He sounded so young compared to the scratch and scrawl of Jethro's immaculate eloquence. Swear words were something Jethro only resorted to when he couldn't control himself—whereas my brother used them as punctuation.

"Nila."

My body stiffened at my name…at the way my father breathed it so lovingly.

V unwound his arms. I raised my head and looked into my father's eyes. Archibald 'Tex' Weaver looked a hundred years older. His toned physique was gone, replaced by a sagging middle and even worse sagging eyes. His effortless style of slacks and shirts had been switched for baggy jeans and stained polo shirts.

His despair—the complete abandonment of everything he'd been—was better than any spoken apology. More poignant than any beg or plea for understanding.

"I'm so sorry, Nila," he choked, tears glittering.

I was livid. I was distraught. I had so many unresolved issues toward my father but we were *family*. Forgiveness was utmost.

Another sob escaped as I shuffled closer. V never let me go. Instead, Tex came to us. He wrapped his strong arms around his son and daughter and crushed us to the bone. His cheeks grew damp with sadness, and his signature smell of Old Spice tore up my nose and ripped my brain into ribbons.

Oh, God. Oh, God.

The world spun.

Faster and faster and *faster.*

In my family's joint embrace—the same embrace where I'd found such comfort before—now I only found sickness and horror.

I screeched as my ears roared; my eyes slid to the back of my head.

Round and around and around.

I suffered the worst vertigo spell in years.

I trembled so much, no one could hold me. They let me go, leaving me to suffer alone. They had experience dealing with me—they knew when I became like this, touch was the worst kind of torture.

V and my father guided me to the floor where I kneeled with my head on my knees, trying to hold on to the world that'd suddenly gone mad.

Down was up and up was down.

Their voices plaited into concern, rushing around, making the spinning worse.

Sickness became nausea which became overwhelming.

I couldn't get it under control. I was completely at the mercy of my broken mind.

I threw up.

A small, tiny voice in my head squeaked. *Vertigo or pregnant?*

I threw up again.

Never. Not possible. I couldn't be.

"Shit, Threads." Vaughn squatted beside me. His hands twitched to touch me. To rub my shoulders and tuck my hair behind my ear. But he knew to stay away. If he rocked me or tried to comfort me, my body might hurl me into another episode.

It was *me* who had to stand—me who had to heal.

My father stood over us, his scruffy jaw clenched. He used to be such a support system—such a much-needed part of my life. Now, he made me shatter. My newfound strength slowly siphoned into a cesspit of misery.

The world continued to swing like a crazy pendulum, sending my brain sloshing.

V whispered, "You're here. You're safe. Those motherfucking sons of bitches will pay for what they did. Starting with Jethro Hawk."

Don't touch him!

His voice had a duplex effect. My past personality sank into his capability and brotherly strength—grateful that he was now in charge. While the new Nila cringed from relying on anyone but herself.

I had him to thank for my freedom.

I had him to thank for my misery.

I lifted my head. Vaughn's black eyes stared into mine, and the love I felt for my twin broke through. I hated myself for my previous thoughts.

I was safe. I should be so grateful.

But every minute that ticked past, I vowed to go back. Not because I'd been brainwashed into accepting torture or pain, but because death had tried to claim me only for love to save me instead. Jethro had brought me to life. I wouldn't leave him behind.

We'll both break free. We have to.

My heart twinged thinking of Jethro. I was lucky enough to be loved and accepted by a family who cared for me, even if they never really knew me.

What did he have?

A prison cell that'd existed all his life.

A future that might destroy him.

Collapsing to my side, I wrapped my arms around myself and heaved. My throat howled from drowning. My head pounded. And through it all, all I could think was…

This would never have happened if Jethro were here.

His very soul was an anchor.

The one I needed the most.

I groaned at the horrible irony.

I was free at Hawksridge in a way I could never be free in London.

I couldn't live without him.

I didn't *want* to live without him.

I need to save him.

And soon.

Jethro

THE CURE BEGAN slowly—whispering across my thoughts.

The unravelling Nila had achieved slowly stitched itself back together. The love, the panic, the pressure…it all faded.

My intense world became shrouded. The glare of intensity diminished and, tablet by tablet, I grew delightfully numb.

I liked this new blanket.

I was grateful to my father.

Without him, I would've resorted to opening the scars on my soles and living in pain to survive. What he hadn't factored in was my conviction to save Nila. The drugs gave me strength to do that.

So I took another and another…believing they would be my salvation and her key to surviving.

How fucking stupid was I?

Seventy-two hours.

Three days since Nila left.

My injuries from Daniel's beating were stiff and mottled. I refused to look at myself in a mirror, as I couldn't stomach the yellow and purple bruised arsehole staring back at me.

Whereas my body hurt, my soul was miraculously floating. Every day the overwhelming hazards of my disease bleached further and further into a watermark rather than a vibrant stain.

Cut let me leave the dungeon under the condition of medicating myself. The choice between dank darkness and pills was no hardship.

I kept to myself. I didn't visit Jasmine to protect her from my appearance. I didn't go on shipment runs or seek out my father. I spent the days in the stable, finding solitude in Wings' silent presence and slipping deeper into the drug's embrace.

However, lying in bed at night couldn't stop my mind filling with her.

Nila.

I missed her smell, her taste…her heat.

I craved to be inside her, to hold her in silence and find the gift that she'd given me by falling in love. She'd used me to help her. She'd manipulated me in a way I couldn't refuse, but in the end, we were both losers…or winners—depending on my frame of mind. Her heart belonged to me. And my heart belonged to her.

I'd fallen for her.

I'd tried to become a better person for her.

But the drugs were so much more powerful than me.

I wanted to rejoice at finally finding something that worked. I should bow to the doctors for creating this miraculous cure. I needed everyone to know how incredible it felt to be cocooned by the gentle fog of intoxication.

Nila had obeyed me when she left—taking my heart and sanity with her. But now, I had a rare opportunity to fortify myself. I would become the man she needed, so when the time came to claim her, we would both be ready.

One hundred and twenty hours.

Five days since Nila left.

My injuries were healing—my ribs remained strapped and sore, but my face didn't look as swollen or grotesque.

Five days equated to thirty-seven tablets. I'd become attached to my rattling bottle, devouring the promised fog as if each drug was exclusive caviar.

Nothing affected me anymore. Not loud noises, overpowering scents. Not even raised tempers or malice. The fog was thicker…the insulation between them and me growing deeper by the day.

The tablets were working.

They were stealing, healing.

But they hadn't solved me completely. I still ached as if my heart had been ripped out. Every night I throbbed to slide inside Nila and have her come apart in my arms. My tattooed fingertips mocked me—reminding me she'd branded me and I'd branded her but for now…we were apart, even if we belonged to each other.

But soon I can collect her.

Soon I could save Nila, Jasmine, Kestrel, and myself.

So many futures rested on me. I couldn't let them down. So, I popped another tablet, I said goodbye to another ounce of feeling, and I prepared myself for the ultimate finale.

I should've seen it coming.

Why didn't I see it coming?

I'd begun taking my new tablet friends to save me from myself, to save Nila from a worse fate designed by Daniel, and to guard the goodness Nila had conjured inside me.

That was my goal…but I'd underestimated Cut.

I didn't pay close enough attention to my evolution as the drugs took me hostage.

It started slowly, methodically.

The man I knew slowly sank deeper and deeper inside, leaving a husk—a husk living with men like my father and brother—twisting the hologram of the man I once was.

It began like before: Cut put me back in charge of the mines and shipments. He returned my responsibilities and praised me for doing a good job. Security and finances filled my day, leading me further away from the soft tenderness Nila had nursed.

At night, I would be summoned to my father's quarters to talk about what would happen now I was back in control. He made me drink from his convoluted perception and made me eat his disgusting morals.

Slowly but surely, I became angry. And that cultivated anger was given direction.

The Weaver twin.

Vaughn was to blame for *everything*.

He stole her from me. His fucking meddling hadn't ceased. He brought shame and suspicion onto my house. His tampering couldn't be allowed.

Nila had been free for days—there was no reason to continue to spread gossip—in his mind, he'd won. I hadn't made any attempt to contact Nila under another of my father's conditions.

"Stay away until the drugs have worked."

I should've guessed then that the drugs had two targets: help me, but collar me. I could no longer remember why I wanted to help Nila. Yes, I had feelings for her…but they felt so long ago. She was a Weaver. My family's mortal enemy. Why would I deviate from my destiny when so many others relied on me?

Every breakfast, my father would turn on the news, YouTube, and every social media platform available today. Slowly, he filled my heart with hate.

He showed me disgusting lies and slander all originating from Vaughn. Twitter ran rampant with hashtags of *#BastardHawks* and *#InnocentWeavers*. Facebook hosted debates and surveys on their opinions of the Debt Inheritance.

Everyone had a hypothesis.

Everyone was wrong.

But they all had something in common.

They wanted our *blood*.

It was Vaughn who put me back into the icy blizzard I'd escaped from. His twin had thawed me, but he froze me all over again.

He'd gone to every journalist and reporter imaginable. He'd divulged ancient tales of filthy deeds and contracts and debts. He spilled our private affairs to the fucking world.

Every day the phone rang for interviews. Our sources with buyers on the black market grew wary—not enjoying the slander our family suffered—in case it smeared them, too. Our staff began whispering. Our fucking lives started to unravel.

We had money. We controlled police, Customs, and made a livelihood of manipulating those in power for our own means, but we had no clout when it came to strangers on the internet.

Vaughn Weaver harnessed this new age influence and brought a mob to our door, and in doing so, he made my family rally together. Hawk against Weaver. Just like before.

He proved we weren't untouchable, after all. Cut didn't deal with the knowledge well. He fucking raged at how little he could do to stop this storm of antagonisers. He never had to worry about social media when he had Emma

Weaver—but in today's society, it was a bigger beast than we ever anticipated.

Our empire was built on greased palms and ancient 'blind-eye' agreements. We all knew whatever contract we had giving us ownership of the Weavers was bullshit.

Nobody could own another.

Only imbeciles believed such a thing.

But I did believe in our power. Our wealth. Our status.

The tales of our rise from rags to riches had been told so many times, they'd reached phenomenon status within our family—spoon-fed the same crap since birth and believing in the power of a binding parchment that gave us *carte blanche* to do what we pleased. Not because it granted us immunity, but because it showed just how many people obeyed us now that we had control.

But what good was control when it unthreaded with a fucking rumour?

All of this was a game. Only Vaughn had changed the rules by bringing in spectators demanding answers.

I'd kill Vaughn for that.

He was already dead—just a nail in my rapidly freezing coffin as I popped pill after pill.

Hour after hour, I slowly gave in.

Day after day, I slowly felt nothing.

I was done being the man everyone thought was weak. I lived with a disease, but I wasn't a cripple.

I didn't need snow anymore. Or ice. Or pain.

I had drugs.

I was stone.

Nila

I'D LIKE TO say life returned to normal.

But I'd be lying.

I'd like to say I slipped back into my previous existence as entrepreneur, seamstress, and daughter.

But I'd be bullshitting to the highest degree.

Every day was worse than the one before it.

I was lost.

Alone.

Unwanted.

Life was a death sentence.

The press hounded me for interviews on my disappearance. My assistants pestered me with hundreds of new designs and orders. My father tried to talk to me about what happened. And my brother suffocated me with love.

It was all too *much*.

It drove me to boiling point.

In the beginning, I suffered physical healing from the Second Debt payment. I coughed often, doctors checked me for pneumonia, and the bruises on my chest took forever to fade. I used the pain as a calendar, slowly ticking off the hours Jethro left me all alone and unresponsive. I waited for a message from Kite007. I became obsessed with daydreams of him swooping in and taking me away from the mess of the press and envy of misguided people.

At night, I lay in a room that'd been mine since I was born. The purple walls hadn't changed. My unfinished designs draped on headless mannequins hadn't vanished, yet nothing was home anymore.

I felt like a stranger. An imposter. And the sensation only grew worse.

The strength and power I'd found on my own dissolved. My joy at suffering fewer vertigo attacks disappeared as I went from managing the incurable disease to suffering the worst I'd ever had.

Yesterday, I'd suffered nine.

The day before, I'd had seven.

I had more bruises on my knees, elbows, and spine in just a week of being a true Weaver again than I *ever* endured at Jethro's hands.

Every second the same questions hounded me.

How was I supposed to return to my old life?

How was I supposed to forget about Jethro?

How was I supposed to give up my strength in order for my brother to adore me?

And how was I supposed to forgive my father and be grateful to him for rescuing me?

How.

How.

How?

The answer...

I couldn't.

For a week, I tried. I slipped seamlessly into my previous world. I toiled in our Weaver headquarters, answered emails, and agreed to fashion shows two years from now. I painted on a mask and lied through my teeth.

I became a master at ignoring what my body told me. Throwing up was a bi-weekly occurrence and my dreams were full of accusations. Memories of Jethro coming inside me played on repeat—hinting at one thing:

Am I pregnant?

Or had I just escalated to vertigo-cripple?

Everywhere I turned there were magazine articles, newspaper speculations, billboards, and BBC broadcasts. I had to face banners of my dead mother and grandmother in Piccadilly Circus. I had to close my eyes as buses drove past with the Hawk family crest painted on their sides. And I had to swallow back bile as advertising for the latest 'must-have' accessory plastered park benches and taxi stands.

What was the 'must-have' jewellery?

My diamond collar.

Everyone wanted one. Everyone wanted to see mine, touch mine—ask me endless questions about the unopenable clasp and the meaning of such a beautiful but despicable piece.

I was a living specimen. Plopped into a goldfish bowl and made to perform like some circus freak. I was the 'unfortunate Debtee' and Jethro Hawk was the 'loathsome Debtor.'

Vaughn had destined us to a life of gossip about family feuds and incomprehensible contracts.

Every night when we gathered to eat in floundering silence, I wanted to stab my twin with a steak knife. I wanted to scream at him for announcing to the world how ludicrous our two families were.

People *laughed* at us.

People gawked—not only had V brought to light the evil insanity of the Hawks, but he'd also shown what a cruel, vindictive race our own bloodline had been.

It didn't seem to matter to him. He'd freed me. He'd turned a private agreement into an international affair. As far as he was concerned, I should be grateful.

I would've preferred to deal with rumours Jethro had put into play the first night he stole me: the photos of him holding and kissing me—doctored and delivered in a perfect alibi of a relationship turned elopement.

That was reasonable.

This was unbelievable.

Now everyone had those photographs—printed over tacky magazines and exposed in newspapers with headlines: '*The Man and His Toy.*' '*How Far Can Legacy Go?*' '*Multiple Murders Go Unpunished.*'

Every sordid detail of my family was unearthed and published. However, the facts on the Hawks were extremely vague. The press hadn't uncovered that a motorcycle club lived on the grounds. They didn't mention diamond smuggling or their massive wealth.

All it would take was for me to agree to a private interview and announce to the world about Cut's underworld dealing, his meticulous record keeping, the Weaver Journal, and the videos of debts extracted. That evidence would buy them a one-way ticket to jail.

But their lives belonged to *me*. I wanted to be the one to take them down. I wanted to watch them perish—not waste away in a cell where I couldn't reach them to make them pay.

That's not the only reason you're staying quiet.

I sighed. The main reason was because I was in love with a Hawk and would stay silent to protect him.

I'd gained my freedom. Jethro would, too. I would make sure of it.

Throughout the torture of the first week, Vaughn was in his element. He smiled with model good looks, wrapped his arms around me as he performed for the cameras, and showed the world the bruises on my wrists from the ducking stool.

I'd done my utmost to hide my hands from my family—keeping my tattooed fingertips from worldwide knowledge. But I couldn't hide the Weaver Wailer.

Everyone knew what it meant.

The first day I was back, my father made me sit for hours while he tried to remove it. He'd used every micro-tool available to work the hinge free. V even tried to pry the collar off with tiny pliers. But the mechanism was too well made. The diamonds too well set.

It didn't work.

Jewellers and diamond merchants put their hands up to try. They all failed.

As I lost the new Nila and stumbled with awful vertigo, my father slid deeper and deeper inside himself. After living with the constant questions and insinuations of how his wife died, he became a hermit. I no longer recognised him. We no longer had anything in common.

All of that was my life now.

I supposed I was lucky.

I supposed I should be *grateful*.

After all…

At least I was free.

Jethro

"KITE?"

I looked up from my desk. Jasmine wheeled herself into my room, her tiny hands wrapped around the stainless steel rims of her chair for propulsion.

It'd been ten days since Nila Weaver had left.

Two hundred and forty hours. Sixty-one tablets.

I was immune to everything.

Blank to everyone.

I couldn't think about my life before without shuddering in pain. How had I withstood it for so long when this was so much better?

The past ten days I'd finally, *finally* earned what I'd hoped all my life: Cut said he was proud of me. He'd been wary at first——never stopped watching—— searching for a weakness…a chink in my surrender to my new addiction.

But this wasn't a lie.

It was better this way. Easier this way. *Survivable* this way.

I had no fears of making it to my thirtieth birthday anymore.

When he saw the truth, he gave me more and more control. He praised me for my clear-headedness and ruthless behaviour.

My siblings, on the other hand, weren't pleased. They didn't understand what it was like to live with my condition, and I was done being judged. I pulled away. I put up walls and fastened locks. I stopped visiting Wings as I became too busy to ride. I ceased my visits to Jasmine and put an end to late night chats with Kes.

All I needed was silence and my little rattling bottle of pills.

Nila had done me a favour.

She'd shown me how diseased I truly was. And with her disappearance came my cure.

If I had any feelings left to be dispensed, I would still have a fondness toward her. But I was happy being empty. I was free being immune to the insanity of life.

"Go away, Jaz." I turned back to my task. Running my fingers over the paper Nila had signed the night of Cut's birthday, I shook my head at my scrambled forward thinking.

I thought I could circumnavigate the Debt Inheritance by forcing Nila to sign another binding contract. I'd planned to brandish it as a weapon the day I turned thirty and stop the Final Debt in its twilight hour.

I smirked.

Stupid idea and so much fucking work.

There was no point fighting the inevitable.

"What are you doing?" Jaz asked, wheeling closer, the swish of her chair softened by thick carpet.

Grabbing my sigil-engraved lighter, I flicked it open and held the Sacramental Pledge over the naked flame. The thick parchment crackled as I teased it with flickering heat.

"None of your business." I brought the fire closer.

Jaz slapped my desk, jerking my eyes to hers. "We need to talk. I'm worried about you."

I laughed softly as the fire suddenly caught hold, licking up the parchment. I became hypnotised as flames rapidly devoured the last of my madness.

Jaz eyed up the pledge. "What is that?"

The orange glow danced in my retinas. "Nothing."

I tensed, expecting to feel some sort of regret at destroying the one piece of assurance I had over Nila's soul. The night she'd signed this, she'd agreed to give me all rights over her—to *belong* to me. But there was never any chance of a happy ending.

Not for us.

Not for me.

Fire blazed, gathering strength the more paper it devoured. The black ink cindered to ash, falling like black petals onto the desktop.

"Stop burning it," Jasmine demanded, trying to knock my hand and dislodge my hold.

The paper continued to hiss and vanish.

I didn't look at her. I didn't argue.

I felt nothing.

Jasmine puffed out her cheeks, trying to blow out the fire, but it was too eager, too fast.

"Give it up, sister. Some things you cannot change." In a matter of moments, the contract between Nila and me was no more. My stupid planning and ideas that I could win against my father no longer infected my brain.

It was so *liberating*.

Wiping the charred remains into the rubbish bin, I finally looked at my sibling. Her cherub cheeks and sultry lips were wasted on her broken body. She was a stunning woman, yet she would forever remain a spinster ensconced in this house under Bonnie's control. "What do you want?"

Her eyes flickered in pain. Shouts and curses painted her skin, but her bluster faded before she even opened her mouth. Sighing sadly, she shook her head. "Why won't you tell me?"

"Tell you what?"

"What he did to you."

The air became stale. I pinched the bridge of my nose. "I don't have time for this."

"You have plenty of time, Jethro. Answer me." Her face flushed red. "What's happened to you? Why don't you seek me out anymore? Why are you so remote?" She reached for my hands, but I shifted quickly, scooting backward in my chair.

Anguish weighed heavily on her shoulders, but I felt no guilt. Jasmine had a rough start in life. She continued to deal with her own demons, but they were *her demons*. Not mine. I'd finally found a way to be free and I wished to *remain* free.

"Is that all you want?" Cocking my head at the paperwork of the latest machinery upgrades needed for our warehouses, I pursed my lips. "I really am busy——"

"Kite, you listen to me and you listen good." Waggling her finger in my face, she glared. "The day she left, I was so sure he would kill you. I suffered a panic attack thinking the one woman you loved—the one girl who could give you a place to hide—left you to die. But then I heard from Kes that you were alive. I waited for you. I waited *three days* for you to come to me——to ask for a fixing session or just to talk." Dropping her head, her midnight bob hid her eyes. "But you never came. Ten days and you *still* haven't come."

I remained silent.

Jaz looked up, her eyes wet with tears. "You're scaring me, Jethro. I miss my brother. I want him back. Tell me what happened, so I know how to find him again."

Poor deluded sister.

Standing, I bent and kissed the top of her head. "Nothing happened. And I don't want to be found. If you love me like you say you do, then be happy for me. I've finally found something that works and will never go back."

Tapping my pocket, the gentle rattle of my pills said hello. I relaxed knowing if life ever got too much, if the tears of another drove me to breaking point, all I had to do was swallow a tiny friend and I would be fine.

"Goodbye, Jaz."

Without waiting for her reply, I strode out the door and left my sister behind.

My phone vibrated its way across my bedside table at three in the morning.

I didn't jump or tense.

In a way, I'd been expecting this to happen for days.

Picking up the device, I swiped the screen and read the blinking message.

I'd wondered how long she would stay away. She'd lasted longer than I anticipated, but I had no doubt that was down to the circus of stories and endless hounding by reporters—not to mention, her brother would've done everything in his power to keep her from contacting me.

But just like my father had said, Nila had reached out.

Unknowingly, she'd just begun the next stage and walked right into a perfect trap.

Needle&Thread: *I've been staring at this phone for over a week, wondering what to say. I still can't find the words, so I'll stick with simple ones. Kite, I love you. I miss you. I'm here for you. I've become a prisoner in my own family. They watch me, guard me. I've traded one captivity for another. I need you to come claim me. If we work together, this can all be over. Please…I need you to fight for me like I've fought for you. I need to know you're alive and uninjured. Jethro, I want you to take me from this place. Let's leave. Let's runaway where no one will find us.*

This was the true test. The ultimate trial on the numbing fog I'd ingested for the past ten days. I waited to see if her words would make me step outside the comforting blankness I now embraced.

They didn't.

I was empty. Nothing could make me go back to the way I was. Not Nila. Not my sister. *Nothing*.

This game had turned into a fishing expedition, and as all good fishermen know, you have to let the fish nibble the bait before they swallowed the hook and sealed their own fate.

Swallow away, Nila Weaver.

Let me catch you.

Tossing the phone to the floor, I left her message unanswered.

I'D MANAGED TO last over a week before I sent him a message.

But once that boundary had been crossed, I couldn't stop myself from crossing it every day.

I lived only to send more messages, hoping that one day, he would reply.

Monday...

Needle&Thread: *Please, Jethro. I'm begging you. Don't throw me away like this.*

Tuesday...

Needle&Thread: *Are you okay? Did Cut hurt you? Please...I'm going out of my mind with worry.*

Wednesday...

Needle&Thread: *Message me, Kite. Please tell me this doesn't change what happened between us.*

Thursday...

Needle&Thread: *I tried to ditch my security detail today to come save you. But they chased me down the motorway. I can't get free. I need you to come get me if I mean anything to you at all.*

Friday...

Needle&Thread: *What did they do to you? Why won't you reply?*

Saturday...

Needle&Thread: *Answer me, Jethro! Just a simple message to let me know you're still alive. You owe me that at least.*

Sunday...

Needle&Thread: *The world thinks we're certifiably crazy. I agree with them. What your family has done is wicked. But you aren't. Don't let them take you away from me...*

No matter how many messages I sent, no matter how much I poured my heart into them, Jethro ignored me.

He'd cut me out completely.

Seventeen nights since I'd seen him.

Seventeen days since I'd talked to him.

Eighteen days since he'd loved me, cum inside me, and shown me how much I meant to him.

And now, *nothing.*

I lay in my queen-sized bed, staring at the ceiling where a purple chandelier glittered from the moonlight streaming in through open curtains.

Anger overrode my self-pity, and for the first time since I'd been home, I cursed Jethro Hawk.

"Damn you!" Staring again at my blank phone, I gave it one more moment to chime. *Come on…*

It never did.

With a wail, I tossed the device across my room. It clunked against the rug outside my private bathroom, glowing in the dark.

My room was big, but not nearly as large as my quarters at Hawksridge, and despite the strange blend of comfort and stress of being home, I couldn't find peace.

My eyes drifted over my top-of-the-line treadmill in the corner, to my overflowing walk-in closet.

This room was a part of me.

But now it was an enemy.

Everyone was an enemy. From work to strangers to family. I didn't fit in anywhere. I didn't even fit into my own thoughts.

Why was I grieving for a man destined to kill me?

Why was I so determined to return to a household of murderers?

Why did I panic every time nausea took me hostage?

I know why.

Because you're more in love than afraid.

Because you can't stand the way Tex looks at you.

And because you're afraid you might be pregnant…

My father tore apart my heart every damn second we were together. We couldn't talk anymore—not about trivial things or important things. Our awkward conversations were stilted and fake. He couldn't take his eyes off me, even though they were exhausted and ringed with shadows as deep as darkness itself. He shrunk beneath a lifetime of regret over me, over my mother.

And I hated I couldn't console him.

Why hadn't he gone after her?

Why had he let them come for me?

Those questions were never voiced, but I knew he felt them, lashing the air with contamination.

My family were adrift, and I had no clue how to fix it.

I dug my tattooed fingertips into my eyes, banishing the thoughts of my father and pressing back the tears that never seemed to leave.

I huffed, the silence rejecting any noise and swallowing my sadness. I couldn't stomach the quietness—the lifeless darkness.

I was *safe* here.

No one to hurt me, fuck me, or transform my soul with wings.

I am safe here.

And I didn't know how to cope with that anymore.

My ruby-encrusted dirk lay beside me on the silver and lace bedspread. It belonged to the Hawks…yet it was the only thing I'd brought with me. I'd left everything at Hawksridge, including my phone. My father had banned me from getting another—he blamed the press hounding us for constant interviews, but I knew the real reason.

He wanted me to be cut off, untouchable.

But it hadn't stopped me from commandeering a new one, and, like the love-struck moron I was, I knew every digit of Kite's number perfectly.

Countless times, I messaged him.

But not once did he reply.

I miss you.

I curse you.

I love you.

He left me empty and all alone.

"JETHRO."

I looked up from a small pile of diamonds on my desk and brushed overgrown hair from my eyes. My father stood in the doorway to my study; his stance was relaxed and open, a camaraderie between us evident after the past few weeks of my impeccable behaviour.

Placing the loupe onto a velvet case in front of me, I smiled. "Need something?"

Cut cocked his head toward the corridor. "Only a word. We've all been busy with preparations this last week. I think a debrief is in order, don't you?"

My mind prodded at the plans we'd made. The strict timeline when Nila would be ours again. The retaliation we'd lined up to dismiss the fading interest in my family's name. Vaughn was losing power as each day passed. Social media was a feral beast baying for blood, but it was short-lived, quickly moving onto juicier gossip.

The longer we waited, the less power the Weavers had. We'd also fortified our alliances with the local police, who ensured they would stay out of our way this time—otherwise…well, they knew what would fucking happen.

Scooping the diamonds into a soft pouch and storing them in my top drawer, I didn't worry that there were over three hundred thousand pounds worth of stones amongst ballpoint and fountain pens.

Strolling over to Cut, I tapped my pocket to make sure I had my vial of friends with me. The comforting rattle sounded, and with another smile, my father and I walked side by side through the bachelor wing, up the stone staircase, and to his office on the second floor.

My eyes flickered to Jasmine's door. I hadn't seen my sister again. I didn't like being estranged from her, but I was above silly dramatics now. I had no feelings to spare. It was her problem not mine. I wouldn't dwell on it.

The moment we were locked and secluded in his chambers, he motioned to his private stash of rare Rémy Martin cognac. "Please, help yourself to a drink."

"Want one?" I asked, moving to the small bar and uncorking the decanter. My mouth watered as a generous amount splashed into a crystal goblet.

Cut sat in his favourite black chair and placed his feet on the coffee table housing the bleached bones of Wrathbone, his dog. My fingers twitched around the bottle as I remembered the last time Nila had been in here. We'd done the

Tally; I'd inked my initials onto her body.

"Please." Cut relaxed into the leather. Our dealings with one another had become highly civilized—businessman to businessman rather than delinquent son and disappointed father. "Untether him for me, too, will you?"

Depositing my drink on the coffee table, I prowled to the window and the beautiful bird perched on its stand. "Hello, Finch." I stroked the breast of Cut's pet hawk.

The bird preened under my attention. Its autumn feathers glinted in the waning sunlight, and its beady eyes remained hidden beneath its blinding cap. A horrible life really—to spend so many waking hours in the dark.

The silkiness of Finch's feathers sent me into a trance. It was funny to think that all three of Bryan Hawk's sons had bird of prey names, yet he never used his. Being the president of the Black Diamonds meant he used his brotherhood name. However, his nickname had always scared me as a boy. I could imagine him stripping the bones of his enemy's carcass, just like his namesake: the Vulture. Bryan 'Vulture' Hawk. It was apt.

"Free him," Cut ordered.

Tugging on the little tie, I released the blinding cap and Finch immediately traded quiet stroking for violent flapping. The bell around his ankle tinkled as he tried to take off only for the tether to jerk him back.

"Steady, steady," I murmured, undoing the bow and freeing the bird. Finch had been named after his first kill. He hadn't gone for the gerbil we'd released onto the lawn. Instead, he soared high and plucked the tiny prey from the sky and ate it in a few strips.

"Finch," Cut said. "Cast off." He raised his arm, already wrapped in a supple piece of leather. No one wanted a talon through his or her forearm.

In a rustle of burnished feathers, Finch launched from the perch and soared across the room.

Cut grunted as the weight of the large raptor landed on his arm. He grinned, his lined face looking younger and carefree. Stroking the plumage of his pet, he caught the creance and wrapped the cord around his fist to keep him in place.

Heading to the small refrigerator by the wall, I opened a Tupperware container and brought back a delicacy of raw rabbit liver. Finch instantly hopped and snapped his beak as I handed the meat to Cut. He grabbed a bloody piece and tossed it at the bird.

Sitting down, I sipped my cognac.

For a few minutes, we let Finch entertain us, the occasional bell slicing through the squelch of raw liver. Finally, Cut cast off the hawk and let him navigate the room wherever he wanted.

Toasting his glass to mine, his eyes shadowed.

Finally getting to the point, Father?

Clinking glasses, I settled back, waiting.

"You know I saw everything that happened between you and Nila. I've shown you the tapes of you fucking her. The close-ups of your face when extracting the debts. I've listed all the times you disobeyed me and went behind my back. You had feelings for her."

I shrugged. Once upon a time, I might've panicked and done everything to deny such a revelation. Now, it didn't matter. I was above all that.

"All in the past, as you well know."

Cut nodded. "I know. That's why I'm bringing this up now. You've seen the light, and I think it's time you know a bit more of the legacy you're upholding."

I crossed my legs, nursing my goblet. "Go on."

"Did you ever stop to think about other Hawks and Weavers who had to pay the debts?"

My forehead furrowed. "No."

"You never thought others might've had the same issues you did?" Nostalgia shaded his face. "I won't deny I had a soft spot for Emma toward the end. She was nothing like her daughter—not insubordinate or stubborn, but she enticed me all the same."

My heartbeat kicked just the tiniest bit.

Without disrupting the conversation, I pulled the small bottle free and tipped a tablet into my palm. "I had no idea." Chasing the pill with a healthy dose of cognac, I added, "I suppose it's logical for any man and woman to have feelings if they're forced together long enough."

Cut stared into his drink. "I suppose."

He always did this. Always hinted at a topic in a roundabout way, waiting to see if I would trip up and reveal things. It might've worked in the past when I had things to hide and nervousness to feel, but now I had nothing.

Blank. Blank. Blank.

My voice was soft. "You did what you were tasked with. Just like I hurt Nila, you hurt Emma."

His eyes connected with mine. "Exactly. You made her bleed in the First Debt. And I have no doubt you're capable of carrying this inheritance to its conclusion."

A few weeks ago, there was no chance in hell I would've been able to complete the Final Debt. But things were different now.

My loyalties were to the Hawks. I would do my duty. I would inherit what was mine.

"Of course."

I would commit murder.

It was what I was born for.

Cut shook his head, almost in awe. "I wish that drug had been around years ago. I'm so happy to have you on my side after all this time. Not to mention, Bonnie is delighted that you no longer harass Jasmine from her studies."

I smiled, taking another drink. "Yes, we both know it was time for me to grow up."

Finch suddenly flew overhead; his russet feathers a rainbow of orange, brown, and taupe.

Cut sighed, running a hand through his white hair. "There is one thing I need to bring up, before we can put the past behind us." His body tightened. "You can probably guess what I'm about to say."

Could I?

I wracked my brains.

What had he hated about me the most? My inability to obey? My endless problems? Or was it the fact I'd slept with Nila with nothing barred and somehow lost a piece of myself that I would never get back—no matter how numb I was?

"You'll have to enlighten me. I have no idea what you mean."

"I must admit, you were beyond stupid. If those pills hadn't worked, I would've put you down for that infraction alone."

My eyebrow raised. "Oh? This will be interesting. Don't torture me with suspense—what did I do?"

He grinned. "I'd hoped you would be able to tell me why. Explain in your words what the fuck was going on in your screwed-up mind. But I guess that won't happen now that your insanity is cured."

Insanity.

That annoying little word. Out of everything, it still had a smidgen of power over me. I hated that label. All my life, I'd been called insane, broken. My father had sent me away as a young boy to undergo counselling and get psychiatric help. The conclusion came back stating I was demented, mentally unsound.

Every day of my childhood, Cut reminded me of my flaws. I'd come to hate those words. *Despise* those words.

Cut laughed again, dragging me back to the present. "Can I ask if you did it because you truly didn't think, or were you more clever than I gave you credit?"

A slight headache began. "I honestly have no idea what you're getting at."

What the fuck?

Until I had a guess, I wouldn't say a word. I'd learned how to hide, and those habits were hard to break.

Cut laughed—a full belly chuckle dancing with pride.

My heart swelled. I'd never get tired of having him be proud of me.

"Your balls are iron, Jet. I'll give you that. I always hoped having your own pet Weaver would fix you." Leaning forward, he clasped my knee. "I like this man before me. I'm honoured to call him my son."

Shit...wow.

Clearing my throat, I raised my glass to him. "Appreciate that, Father. More than you know."

Reclining back in his chair, Cut said quietly, "Let me give you a quick history. You've seen the tapes of what I did to Emma, so you know what is required of you. In turn, you know what *isn't* required of you." He tilted his head. "The men of our family are weak when it comes to their Weavers. They fucked them—same as you. They fell prey to their charms—same as you." His voice darkened. "However, unlike you, your forefathers saw what the Weavers were doing by enticing them into their beds. Nila is just like her ancestors. She was using sex to get to you—using her body to screw up your mind, and it fucking worked."

My glass was empty. I wanted another.

Cut grew angry—the same mask I recognised slipping into place. "I have no issues with you fucking her. But what *does* make me rage is you did it without protection."

I froze.

Conveniently, my mind had buried that titbit beneath all the other crap I'd been dealing with. No protection equals...

"Every time you sank inside that little whore, her face screamed victory. For her it wasn't lust or love for you, Jethro, it was happiness at being the winner. She used you and it worked."

Memories of her claiming to win made their way through my druggy fog. *He's right.*

Cut continued, "If your plaything is attractive, it only makes sense to use her for pleasure. As I mentioned before, Hawks are weak in that area and the Weavers somehow carry that knowledge in their bones. Didn't you think there'd been accidents? Birth control wasn't around at the start of this contract. Did you stop to wonder if there were half-breeds born of both Hawk and Weaver bloodlines? Impure abominations?"

My heart went from slow to interested. "No, I hadn't." I honestly hadn't contemplated much of our heritage or history. Would that void the contract then? Firstborn carrying both genes?

I guess not, because it's still in effect.

"What happened to them?"

Cut smiled cruelly. "Same thing that happened to their mothers."

The alcohol I'd consumed oozed through my blood.

He leaned forward. "When Nila returns, when the time comes to extract more debts, you're free to do whatever you want with her. I'll put an end to any illegitimate offspring, and as long as you teach that whore her place, then I give you my vow that on your thirtieth birthday, I will gladly hand you the keys to everything I own. It will all be yours, Jethro."

Finch majestically landed on the back of the couch, his beak sharp and deadly. Cut stroked the bird as if no threat echoed in his words.

I raised my empty glass. "Her tricks won't work again, Father. Consider my eyes open and my heart firmly aligned with the Hawks."

"Good to hear." His gaze locked on mine. "Because if you disappoint me again, there will be *two* bodies in Nila Weaver's grave. Mark my words, Jet. I love you, but I won't hesitate to kill you if you screw this up again."

Twenty-one days.

Five hundred and four hours. One hundred and twenty-seven tablets.

I hadn't relapsed. I'd taken my medicine religiously, and Cut had tested me thoroughly.

I'd passed.

I was ready.

To celebrate the next stage of our plan, my father took the brotherhood off the estate to a local pub in the village. He hired out the entire place and bought each Black Diamond member dinner along with an open bar.

The night was full of laughter and drunken idiocy. Kes remained cool but friendly, and Daniel drank far too much, as fucking usual. I enjoyed myself, growing in my role as heir and basking in the way my men watched me. They looked at me the same way they looked at Cut—with trepidation and respect.

I'd truly taken my place, and there was no mistaking I was next in line for the throne.

After a four-course dinner and plenty of crude innuendoes, Cut stood at the head of the table, clinking a knife against his half-empty beer.

The low ceilings of the 16th century pub pressed down on us with hops drying in the rafters. It was quaint and country—so different to the imposing halls and artifacts of Hawksridge.

"Attention." Cut tapped his glass again. Men continued to snicker and drink. Cut slammed his glass down, making the dirty plates rattle. "Attention!"

Silence fell; all eyes zeroed in on Cut. "Time to toast. Listen up."

A few men saluted while others sobered.

"Stand up, Jethro."

The past three weeks had changed us. His face had lost its pinched anger. I'd lost my defiant hatred. We no longer looked at each other like we wanted to kill and maim.

We were equals.

I got my wish. I found a place in my family. I became...*him*.

Cut raised his arms. "Tonight is a special night, boys. Not only have we expanded across Sierra Leone this month and done more trades than ever before, but I believe luck has finally granted us a true successor."

I'd done everything he'd asked. Put everything into place like he wished. And tonight, I'd earned his ultimate respect.

He tilted his glass to me. "The newspapers are bored with shredding my name. The black market dealers are back to buying in bulk, and our notoriety has only strengthened. The Weavers think they've won, but this is only the beginning."

I planted my heavy boots on the ancient floor, mirroring him in a toast. "Here, here."

The men followed, murmuring ascent.

We'd all seen the newspapers, the broadcasts of Vaughn Weaver telling secrets that should never be told. He thought he'd ruined us. That any moment we'd be arrested and convicted.

Stupid, stupid idiot.

Dressed in black leather with our stitched emblem of Black Diamonds on the pocket, I felt invincible. Nothing could stop us now. No one could even try.

I was untouchable. And it was fucking magical.

"To Jethro." Cut's voice softened. "To my son. To Kite. I'm so glad you've finally seen the error of your ways. I always knew you had potential and have no doubt you'll earn everything I have to give before this is over."

I nodded. "You can trust me."

The men stomped their feet, sloshing their beer onto the table.

Kestrel patted my back. "I hope you know what you're doing."

Daniel gave me a signature smirk. "Roll on the next debt, brother."

I was firstborn.

This was my legacy.

After weeks of preparation, I'd agreed once and for all to prove it.

By killing Nila Weaver.

Nila

LIFE MOVED ON.

I learned to live with a broken heart and stopped jumping at shadows.

No one came to steal me back, and the threat of destroying my family's life went unresolved. However, I had one question that never left: *Are they just biding their time?*

In my mind, I lived in a fake world of normalcy and safety. But somewhere out of sight, clouds were forming——growing heavier and more powerful every day.

I no longer trusted that the police could help or that publicity could keep me safe.

If the Hawks weren't done with me, there was nothing anyone could do.

Hour after hour, I wondered why I stayed. Why I headed into the factory to work under crazy deadlines and demanding buyers. Why didn't I just run?

The passion to create had gone.

I had no wish to sew.

I hated my listlessness.

I hated the coldness inside that no one could touch.

I lived in constant trepidation; serpents gathered in my gut, hissing with premonition. I missed Jethro with every fibre of my being. He was dazzling sunlight and now I lived in endless darkness.

I was dying without him.

But it wasn't finished.

The debts weren't done.

Vaughn wanted me to fly to Asia and hide. Father wanted me to enter witness protection and escape.

I didn't want to do any of those things and worried about all of us—about what this had done to my family. But despite my worries, my clothing brand exploded overnight.

Nila went from exclusive couture to being the most wanted garments in all major department stores. Vaughn became the face of menswear and even dabbled in design himself.

And me…

I went from Weaver Whore to a slave for the Weaver Empire. I didn't have the drive I once did but didn't have the heart to tell my family.

The only time I had to stand still was to wobble with a vertigo attack.

I was paraded before media.

I was the centre of a worldwide scandal.

I was a marionette.

All I could do was clutch my brother as my life spiralled out of control.

I missed the tranquillity of Hawksridge.

I missed the lavender-scented breeze when I sat out in the gardens and sketched.

But most of all, I missed the soul-deep connection with Jethro.

I'd continued to bombard him with messages, but he didn't text back.

Not once.

Not a single time.

My gut churned as the world laughed. Questions followed me wherever I went:

How could they get away with that?

Why didn't they tell someone?

Why didn't they run?

Even I felt that way.

Yes, the Debt Inheritance was used as a tool to wield power. Yes, it granted certain privileges to our pain. But none of that was the real reason.

There was nothing to stop Jethro or his family setting up a sniper rifle on the building opposite our home and firing rounds of ammo through our windows, slicing our lifespan in a blink.

They didn't need the Debt Inheritance to kill us.

This was something more.

A game.

Something I felt was more to do with Jethro than with me. I was just the unlucky target. Just like any employee had to prove their loyalty and skills before a promotion, I had a horrible feeling I was Jethro's final test.

Needle&Thread: *I don't know why I keep messaging you. You've cut me out of your life completely. Three weeks, Kite. Three long weeks of nothing. You've hurt me worse than anyone. I miss talking. I miss our messages. I miss…*

I pressed send before I could delete it.

I shouldn't miss him—not when he obviously felt nothing for me.

Try telling my stupid heart that.

My stupid heart fed me worry. I feared for his life. I had no way of knowing if he was alive or dead.

Waiting for a new message reminded me of the very beginning when I first started messaging him. I'd hang on a thread for one tiny response—waiting for a sliver of his attention. It seemed I'd gone full circle.

I leaned over to dump the phone into my bedside drawer when something miraculous happened.

It vibrated.

Oh, my God!

Fumbling with the lock screen, I swiped it on and stared greedily at the first text from Jethro in almost a month.

Kite007: *That's cruel, leaving the message unfinished.*

My heart thundered. Resting against my pillows, I replied:

Needle&Thread: *You're cruel, not replying to any of them.*

Kite007: *Cruel is my middle name.*

I glanced at my fingertip tattoo and its inked JKH.

Needle&Thread: *No, it's not.*

Kite007: *Believe what you want to believe.*

Needle&Thread: *What happened to you? Tell me. You seem different.*

Kite007: *I am different.*

My chest deflated, sorrow drowning my veins. He'd let them win. He'd changed.

Needle&Thread: *You might believe you're different, but I know what happened between us. It's not over because you care for me.*

Kite007: *That's in the past. But you're right. What happened between us isn't finished.*

My spine whipped straight. What did he mean?

Needle&Thread: *The world knows. I heard they questioned your father. It's only a matter of time before he's convicted. The debts are over. It means we can be together—truly with no horrible ending hovering over us.*

Kite007: *Still such a naïve little Weaver.*

Tears bruised my eyes. In a few words, he'd successfully tarnished my memories of him and made me doubt.

My hands shook as I responded.

Needle&Thread: *You said you'd tell me everything—who you are…what you suffer. I'm asking you…tell me. Don't let them win.*

I couldn't stand the thought of Jethro going to jail for what he'd done. Even though he deserved punishing—he'd been under the control of Cut. If he let me help him…he could stop his family and finally be happy…with me.

Kite007: *I'm not that man anymore. There's nothing to tell.*

My heart fell out of my chest.

Needle&Thread: *Don't do this, Jethro.*

Kite007: *It's not up to me, Threads.*

My world screeched to a halt. That nickname. It wasn't his to use.

Needle&Thread: *How do you know that name?*

Kite007: *Come on, silly girl. You think I don't know everything about you? You think the past month you've been free of me? That I'm not there…watching you?*

Goosebumps splattered across my arms. If his tone was nicer, I would've been thrilled to know he'd been watching me. That he missed me and had to stay close.

But his tone was sinister—reminding me all too much of Milan.

I tried to reply, but I had nothing left.

My silence encouraged another text from him.

The phone came alive in my hands.

Kite007: *Your time is almost up, Nila Weaver. Enjoy it. I'm coming for you.*

I'm coming for you.
I couldn't think of anything else.
I'm coming for you.

But when?

Work the next day did nothing to ease my state of mind.

I suffered three vertigo incidents before lunch, and when I finally had time to eat, I threw it all up again.

Please. Please...don't let my sickness be what I think it is.

I pressed my forehead against the cool porcelain of my private toilet in my office as more nausea tore through my system.

I couldn't ignore it any longer.

Dreadful horror crept over me.

I had unprotected sex.

Jethro came in me.

Twice.

I moaned as the room spun again.

I can't be pregnant. I can't!

Doctors had always told me I ran too much. My periods had stopped coming a year ago, and they said I'd tricked my body into believing it was in starvation mode; therefore, it wasn't strong enough to have children.

I'd been careless.

I'd been fucking stupid.

Why did I think I could ignore it?

Stumbling to my feet, I grabbed my purse and charged out of the warehouse with its steampunk vibe and countless cubicles all with private sewing machines. My bodyguards that Tex had commissioned were somewhere close by, but I didn't want them following me.

Not for this.

I didn't take a breath until I'd run down the stairs and dashed down the road to a local pharmacy. I didn't think people might witness me buying a pregnancy test, and I definitely didn't think I would bump into my twin as I came out with a little paper bag clutched in my hands. All I focused on was getting answers. Answers I should've learned weeks ago.

I can't be pregnant!

I slammed into his hard bulk.

V's dark eyes widened, his arms automatically coming out to catch me. "Threads! Been looking for you. I have a new idea for the backlog and—" His gaze dropped to my fingers, concern etching his brow. "Eh, you okay?"

My cheeks heated.

No, I'm not okay.

I nodded, backing away from him and hiding the test behind me. "Yes, I'm fine. I have to return to work. See you later, alright?"

Pushing past, I bolted across the road, summoned the lift, and flew into my office in record speed.

The moment I was safe, I locked the door and charged into the bathroom. "Please. *Please* don't let me be pregnant."

The mantra wouldn't stop echoing in my head. There was no logical way I could be pregnant. *Surely!*

It was explainable. *I'm not pregnant.*

My hands trembled as I ripped open the baby-blue box and read the instructions. I'd never had to do this before. It was almost as embarrassing peeing on the testing strip as it was making myself come by a showerhead.

My head pounded.

Was that only last month? Had I gone from writhing with fantasies of Jethro Hawk to spiralling into panic thinking he'd knocked me up?

Oh, God.

"Please, don't let me be pregnant!"

Shaking, I fumbled with what I had to do. Once done, I placed the cap back on the wet strip and tossed the test into the sink. I couldn't touch it any longer. I couldn't look.

Oh, God.

Oh, God!

I stepped away.

I stepped so far away.

I backed up against the wall, bracing myself against the cool grey tile.

I'm not pregnant.

I would know if I was pregnant.

You've been throwing up a lot.

That's explainable.

You suffer from vertigo.

You. Are. Not. Pregnant.

My inner thoughts henpecked and argued, swinging between screaming for being so stupid, to planning how to kill myself just to get this nightmare over with.

Five minutes ticked past, and I still didn't have the courage to look.

Go on.

Get it over with.

"Nila?"

Oh, my God, this couldn't get any worse. What was my brother doing in my office? I locked the bloody door!

He has a key.

Two seconds later, he rapped his knuckles on the bathroom. "Threads? You okay?"

My throat closed up. I wanted the ground to fissure and swallow me.

"Nila, answer me. I'm worried about you."

Swallowing back a sudden avalanche of tears, I pushed off from the wall to open the door.

Only the door swung wide, presenting my perfect brother in jeans and a white t-shirt. He looked as if he'd stepped off a runway, while I looked like a homeless ragamuffin.

His eyes went first to the damn pregnancy test in the vanity, then swung to me.

His dusky colouring went ashen; his eyes darkened. "Please. Please. *Please* tell me that animal didn't fucking *rape* you." Prowling forward, he seethed in the small space. His temper bounced off the tiles, ricocheting with violence. "Nila, tell me right now. Did that cocksucker fucking touch you?!"

I laughed. If only it had been that easy. That *awful*. I would have an excuse for my stupidity. This was all on me.

V's lips twisted in horror as my laugh turned into a sob.

It wasn't rape. It was glorious. It was everything I ever wanted and can never have again.

More tears erupted, giving way to the avalanche.

"Threads, hey. It's okay. We can get you help." Vaughn closed the distance and tugged me into his arms. "It's okay, sis. Honest. I've got you."

His concern was worse than his anger.

More tears.

More sobs.

I struggled. I didn't want him touching me. Not when I didn't know if I could live with myself. But his gentle warmth—so unlike Jethro's frostiness—seeped into me. I sagged. I hadn't let myself cry since the morning I'd been taken from Hawksridge. But now, I couldn't stop.

I let it all go.

Somehow amongst my tears, I stuttered, "He—he didn't ra—rape me, V."

Just admitting I'd brought this on myself filled me with another wave of shame, of remorse.

V stiffened. His arms bunched as he pulled back, looking into my eyes. "What do you mean, he didn't..." Understanding suddenly swamped his face. "Fuck, Nila! You *slept* with him?" Tearing his hands from me as if he were contaminated, he snarled, "You slept with that motherfucker—*willingly?*"

My tears dried up. I hung my head. "Vaughn, don't."

"*Don't?*" He stormed to the vanity and swiped the pregnancy test into his fist. He shoved it in my face, hiding the viewing window so I couldn't see if I'd just ruined my life by being impregnated with Hawk spawn.

"You slept with him unprotected!" He snorted. "Bet Tex will be so happy to know all his energy at keeping you sheltered was in vain. The first guy you're around and you have to fucking screw him and get pregnant!"

"I don't know if I'm pregnant yet!"

"Should we find out then?" He presented his palm, holding up the test. "I can't believe you. God, Nila!"

I didn't want to see.

I wanted to see.

The results were upside down.

V noticed at the same time I did. He rolled his fingers so the test bounced upright.

One little line.

One.

What does that mean?!

I quivered with terror. "The packet—what does the packet say?"

Vaughn looked behind him, returning to the vanity to pluck the discarded box from the bowl. Passing it to me, he threw the test into the bin and washed his hands. As he ran the water, it gave me time to figure out this mess, while he got a hold on his temper.

I flipped the box.

"Congratulations, you're pregnant if you see two blue lines."

Two.

I slithered into a puddle.

Thank you. Thank you. Thank you!

V spun around, his face losing the angry glare and melting into regret. "It's negative?"

I nodded.

No baby.

Suddenly, I didn't know how I felt about that.

I eyed the rubbish bin. I couldn't leave the test in there. I couldn't run the risk of prying staff or my father jumping to conclusions.

The moment V left, I'd take it to the bin in the park opposite our factory.

He sighed. "I'm sorry, Threads. I was out of line." He came by my side, sliding down the wall to wrap an arm around my shoulders. "You okay?"

I tilted my head, resting against his shoulder. He was so good to me. How could I resent him and Tex for saving me?

"Yes," I whispered. "I'll be fine."

V squeezed me. "Talk to me, Threads. You haven't said one word about what they did to you. Every time I bring it up, you change the subject." Sighing again, he added, "If you don't talk to me, you have to talk to someone. I can feel that you're unhappy. I'm feeding off your vibes." Nudging my shoulder with his, he smirked. "Twin link, remember? I could always tell if you were hurting."

Something about what he said tickled my brain, trying to connect dots I couldn't follow.

"I'll be okay soon. I promise."

Let me mend my broken heart in peace.

He couldn't know I'd fallen for Jethro—not after his campaign of death and destruction against the firstborn Hawk.

We sat there in silence for a few moments. V gave me quietness with no judgement, allowing me to put myself back together again. Slowly, my heart rate calmed, shoving away the panic.

V's touch was like a butterfly, whispering sweetly over my shoulder. He'd always been so gentle with me—so different to the man I'd fallen for. Jethro had been anything but gentle. He'd whipped me, fucked me, and adored me in his own dark way.

He scarred me.

I flinched to think what Vaughn would do if he saw what existed beneath my teal blouse. The scars Jethro had painted me with from the First Debt blemished me forever. V wouldn't be happy. Shit, I'd go so far as to say he'd tie up Jethro and give him the same punishment—only a lot harder.

Squeezing my eyes, I tried to push away those concerns. Vaughn would never know because I would never show him.

V stiffened, his fingers digging into my skin.

"What? What is it?" I shifted in his hold, peering into his eyes.

"Nothing. Forget it."

I paused. Normally, if V had a thought, I could pick up on his idea. We were in tune with work, with life. But this time, I had no clue.

Pinching him, I said, "Come on. You can't leave me hanging like that. Give me something else to think about other than this catastrophe."

Vaughn shook his head, looking as if he wanted to tear the thought from his brain. "I—no, you don't need to hear it."

"And you don't have to feel my sadness, yet you do." Sitting up, I untangled his arm from around me. "Tell me."

He sat taller, running a hand through his glossy black hair. "What if you *had* been pregnant?"

I froze. "What do you mean?"

He looked away. "This madness with the Hawks is over. The police are involved. The media know everything. You're as safe as I could make you by telling everyone what I know. But...what if it's not enough."

Tremors captured my limbs. Jethro's text came back to haunt me.

I'm coming for you.

"What do you mean?"

V looked at me, his eyes tight and grave. "What if you had his kid? What if you gave birth to a girl?"

My mind raced. "She'd be a firstborn girl. She'd suffer the same fate our mother and I did. I would *never* put her through that."

V shook his head. "She'd be firstborn. She'd be a girl. She'd be a Weaver." He leaned closer. "But she'd also be a Hawk."

V's epiphany changed everything.

I couldn't stop thinking about alternatives, imagining an entirely different conclusion to the Debt Inheritance, to Jethro, to our future as enemies.

Jethro said he was coming for me.

I didn't know when and I didn't know how…but what if I let him?

What if I went back with him *willingly*? Instead of saving him and running, why not do something to end the debt completely? I could *end* this—like I'd promised my dead ancestors.

Would it work?

Would my scheming of seducing him over and over again until I became pregnant be abhorrent or justified?

Did it make me a terrible person to contemplate bringing another life into this madness—all in the hope of breaking the debts hold?

Could I even stomach becoming pregnant with a firstborn of mixed blood? Would Jethro agree to something so drastic—so crazy? Would I go to hell for trapping someone that way?

My mind whirled with more and more questions.

If I *did* do all of those things—would it destroy everything? Put an end to debts being collected because the debts were now merged? Why had no one thought of it sooner?

Is it even possible?

There were dreadful flaws to my plan. Cut barely tolerated his own children. I couldn't see him decreeing the Debt Inheritance null and void just because the firstborn of both houses was *made* from both houses. I couldn't see him giving up that easily.

But Jethro…he might.

If he had something of his own…for the first time in his life…

Would he fight to protect it?

Would he finally give me his heart and choose me over them?

He could change.

He could save me.

He could save himself.

THE NIGHT BEFORE everything changed, my phone buzzed.

Two a.m., but I was still awake.

The tablets had numbed me to everything, but I still had issues sleeping.

Opening the message, a slow smile crossed my face.

Needle&Thread: *You said this isn't over. That you're coming for me. Well, I want you to come. I'm here waiting. Jethro. Hurry up.*

My cock twitched. Her message was almost perfect. Could she sense everything was in place? Could she tell that her home was here…with me…and it was time she returned?

Kite007: *I appreciate the invitation.*

She took her time replying. The longer it took, the harder I got. A side effect of the pills was my libido had dried up. But here…lying in the dark with no one to see or judge, I cupped my length and squeezed.

Needle&Thread: *It's not an invitation. It's an order. I'm waiting for you.*

I pinched the head of my cock, wondering how to reply. Another message arrived.

Needle&Thread: *I'm wet for you. Kiss me, Jethro Hawk.*

My cock jerked in my hold. Fuck.

I growled under my breath.

My father's wise words came back. *"Nila is just like her ancestors. She was using sex to get to you—using her body to screw up your mind, and it fucking worked."*

I fisted harder. Not this time. She wouldn't manipulate me again. I knew my place. I liked this new world, and I had no intention of stepping out of it.

Kite007: *You know I don't respond to orders.*

Needle&Thread: *Would you respond if I begged you?*

My hand worked harder, dragging pleasure up my shaft and radiating in my balls.

I didn't want to reply. I wanted this charade over with. If I fucked her again, it would be part of a debt—not breaking the rules like I had.

I'd been idiotic. A rebel son who didn't appreciate all that he'd been given.

In her absence, I finally saw the truth.

In my tablet fog, I finally found my home.

And it wasn't with her.

Kite007: *What would you beg for?*

If she were smart, she'd beg me to forget her. To run across continents and try to hide. But she wasn't smart, because she was still governed by inconvenient, uncontrollable emotion.

Needle&Thread: *I would beg for your tongue to kiss me deep. I would moan for your fingers to stretch me and make me wet, and I would get on my knees and suck you for the chance to have you inside me again.*

My eyes rolled back as I worked myself faster. My breathing puffed in the silence of my room.

What was she doing? Debts had dragged us together, but life had given us that magical spark that made even the simplest of touches or barest of smiles cataclysmic. It was fucking dangerous, and I had no intention of playing with fire again.

I had other things to chase. *Better* things.

Kite007: *If you're lucky, I might let you taste me again.*

Only while she was paying the Third Debt and nothing else. And I doubted she'd want anything to do with me by that point.

Needle&Thread: *All of you?*

Kite007: *Don't get greedy, little Weaver.*

My hand bruised hot flesh, jerking with violence as I crested and craved. A release grew stronger, just out of reaching distance. Picking up my pace, I thrust into my palm, driving myself toward the goal.

The residue of the last pill I'd taken five hours ago faded, letting me live in bliss for a short moment. Falling back into insanity, I typed:

Kite007: *I'm fucking myself. Are you jealous?*

Needle&Thread: *Obscenely jealous.*

Kite007: *Rub yourself. I want to hear you moan.*

Needle&Thread: *If I were in your bed, you'd hear me scream.*

Goddammit.

I gritted my jaw; my hips drove faster into my hand. My breathing accelerated until my bed creaked with my thrusts. In a few short hours, I would collect her—not because she'd 'invited me' but because it was time.

Our plan was in place. It was time for execution. *In more ways than one.*

Needle&Thread: *I'm so close, Kite. So close to coming. I need you to collect me. I want to be fucked by you again.*

I came.

I couldn't help it.

With a loud groan, ribbons of white shot through the air and splattered against my naked belly. Wave after wave, I rode through vicious pleasure. The foggy haze dispersed just long enough for me to twitch and moan with the first sensation I'd had in weeks.

Breathing hard, I typed one last message:

Kite007: *Don't go into the dark alone, little Weaver. Monsters roam the shadows, and your time is officially up.*

With a cold smile, I tucked the phone inside my drawer and wiped down my stomach with a sock. My breathing slowly steadied as I rested my head on my pillow. Taking the small bottle from its safe place beside me, I swallowed a pill and felt the change instantly.

Whereas before there was sensitivity, now there was nothing.

I was back to being blank, and the next time I saw her, she'd finally understand the errors of her ways.

She'd had me and lost me.

Now it was time to suffer the consequences.

It was cold tonight.

My breath billowed as I shrugged into my leather jacket and straddled my new Harley. My gloved hands were warm, my uncut feet toasty in my heavy boots.

I no longer had to hurt myself to stay sane.

I had something better.

Pulling out the small bottle, I popped another tablet of the best medicine in the world. I'd taken an extra dose today—just to be sure—and welcomed the familiar blanket over my thoughts.

My heart was a lump of snow, my extremities their usual ice.

I pulled down the black visor on my helmet.

I was no longer human but a black shadow.

The Grim Reaper.

A Hawk about to steal what was rightfully mine.

I left at midnight.

Leaving Hawksridge behind and driving at crazy speeds from Buckinghamshire to London, I counted the minutes until she'd be mine again.

I doubted she'd planned on this when she'd texted me last night. I couldn't wait to see her face and for her to finally understand what'd changed in the month we'd spent apart.

There were three of us on the road.

Me, Kes, and Flaw.

They flanked me and had my back—just in case the Weavers got any ideas. After all, we'd bided our time to make them complacent, but I wouldn't underestimate them again. Not after the sneaky fuck up Vaughn had created.

The entire journey, I thought about Nila's text messages.

I grew hard again, knowing that soon she would belong to me and I could once again prove to my father that his leniency toward me was justified.

Nila was nothing to me. Not anymore.

Time flew as we tore through the night with a roar of engines and smoke. The smell of gasoline filled my nostrils.

I was high on octane, and soon I would be high on thievery.

I was stealing what was rightfully mine.

I was claiming her, exterminating her.

Her fate was mine. There was never any other way. No alternative ending.

She was a Weaver.

I was a Hawk.

This is it.

I was outside her house.

I killed the engine.

Nila

I WOKE TO a dangerous darkness.

My heart rate exploded the moment my eyes tore open.

He's here.

I knew it as surely as I knew my name.

He's in my room.

I couldn't see him.

I couldn't smell him.

But I *sensed* him.

Coldness and anger and bite.

"Jethro—?"

I blinked, peering into dark corners.

He's come for me.

I knew it stronger than anything.

It's not over.

But this time…I had a plan. I wasn't the victim. I wasn't some stupid girl who'd been sheltered by her family. I'd stared death in the face—I'd been in its clutches—and I knew how to survive.

"Hello, Ms. Weaver."

His silky, icy voice whispered beneath my sheets, hardening my nipples to rocks. My core clenched, feeding off his power, getting wet on the sheer deliciousness of having him near.

Oh, God.

After so much time apart, he was visceral, mystical, *mythical* in his power over me.

He had a magic—a spell that softened me, even while fear percolated in my blood. I knew he wasn't safe, knew that I ought to scream and stab him, rather than grow wet and want him.

But I'd made a pact. *I will be the last Weaver.*

I had the strength to stand up to Jethro and his family. He was mine. I just had to make him accept it.

"I told you I would come for you."

The shadows twisted, revealing him as he stepped from the pitch black, moving closer toward my bed. He was dressed in leather and denim; an outfit I'd seen Cut and Daniel wear but never Jethro. He was no longer an aristocrat but a biker. The embroidery on his jacket glinted, and his large boots were whisper-quiet on the carpet. He looked like the devil—a deliciously dark sinner who'd come to ravage and possess me.

Another ripple of desire shot through my belly.

The closer he came, the more the past month faded. The lostness, the incessant vertigo, the lack of conviction I'd suffered ever since leaving just *disappeared*.

It was as if I'd never left Hawksridge. I couldn't imagine why I would.

I can think why.

A torrent of torture and threats filled my mind. Cut and Daniel and Kes. They were my true enemies. Did I really want to go back there? I doubted I would get a second chance to escape.

I know what I have to do.

I knew how to end this. I knew how to save Jethro. And I was prepared to do anything to make that happen.

"Hello, Kite," I murmured.

Jethro sucked in a breath, his chest expanding as he closed the final distance and towered over my bed. His heavy clothes couldn't hide his sensual bulk. Every time he breathed, a soft creak of leather filled the silence. The thread used to stitch the diamond on his front pocket glinted in the moonlight.

I'd never seen him in full motorcycle regalia.

It did terrible things to my core. I couldn't stop my craving—the heat in my blood or the wetness gathering between my legs. My mouth tingled to touch his, to bite his bottom lip and suck his tongue.

The room turned static. The hair on my arms stood up at the very thought of Jethro shrugging out of his jacket and climbing on top of me.

He swallowed, his eyes glittering dangerously. Holding up a small packet of powder, he whispered, "Do I need to drug you again, or will you come willingly?" He bent over me, his long fingers tracing my leg beneath the covers.

I trembled, frozen…desperate for him to drop the act and end the chilliness between us.

We'd been so close. *Connected.* Something sinister slipped over my thoughts. *Something's wrong.*

"I asked you a question, Ms. Weaver." His gaze dropped to my legs, his fingers tugging at the sheets. Inch by inch, he pulled, sliding the warmth down.

I didn't say a word as he revealed my camisole, black satin shorts, and legs; the same legs itching to wrap around his hips while he took me hard.

"I missed you." I couldn't look away. The night beneath Hawksridge—the way he'd touched me in the springs and brought me back to life—made my heart swell.

He hadn't said the words. But I'd felt his submission.

He'd fallen, too.

Just as hard as me.

Removing his hand from my covers, he tucked the drug packet back into his breast pocket. "Let me explain what will happen if you don't honour your invitation and come with me." His voice slipped into emotionless chill. "Vaughn and your father are asleep inside this house. They no longer have the interest of the press or media, and it would bring me great pleasure to teach your twin a lesson. Two seconds is all it would take to remove them from any future problems." He bared his teeth. "They deserve it after the mess they've caused."

Anxiety crept higher up my spine. His temper swirled around us as if we stood in the centre of a blizzard. I was used to that with Jethro. But whereas before I could sense something warm beneath his rage...now, there was nothing.

Touch him. Thaw him.

Swinging my legs out of bed, I gripped the edge of the mattress. "I said I would come with you and I meant it." I did my best to hide my building terror. "Leave them alone. This is between you and me." Taking a deep breath, I stood, bracing myself for a vertigo attack.

So many times over the past month, I would stumble whenever I stood. But this time...I remained stable.

My eyes widened, drinking in Jethro.

He does *fix me.*

He gave me too much to think about. Too much to analyse and read into. My brain was too frantic trying to see between his words to give into a useless imbalance.

"Did you come last night?" I murmured, remembering our messages.

His jaw clenched. "What happened last night or any other night no longer has any relevance in your future."

I shook my head, my heart smarting with pain. "What happened to you?" I reached for him, wanting to clutch his forearm and reassure myself that our bond was still there.

With a sneer, he sidestepped, staying out of reach. "What *happened* to me?" Smiling coldly, he made me seem as if I were some idiot child asking for the universe's secrets. "I got better. That's what happened to me."

"I don't—I don't understand. You weren't ill."

"You wouldn't understand. No one can understand another's problems. All you need to know is that I'm cured and I won't make the same mistakes again."

I took a step back, goosebumps scattering over my body. "Don't say that. I'm in love with you. Something like that cannot be undone—"

"Love is a chemical imbalance, Ms. Weaver. I am no longer imbalanced." He came closer. "Don't get cold feet on your invitation. You promised you would come, and you don't want to give me a reason to punish you so soon...do you?"

My skin pinpricked with panic. That sentence should've dripped with eroticism. But it wasn't. It was cold...lifeless...*like him.*

Snapping his fingers, Jethro held out his hand. He kept his digits curled slightly so I couldn't see the tattoo marks on the tips. "Come. I want to be back at Hawksridge before sunrise."

I eyed his hand, taking another step backward. My instincts blared that all of this was wrong. My careful planning of seducing him and carrying his baby was obsolete if he'd turned back into the monster who'd stolen me from Milan.

"What did they do to you?" I breathed. "This can't be real."

He snorted. "They?" Stalking forward, he snatched my wrist. "*They* did nothing." Yanking me forward, he slammed me against his body. "*You* did this, pretty little Weaver. Don't blame anyone else for your flaws. I no longer do. I've accepted them. I've dealt with them. And now it's time to go."

He pulled me again, knocking me off balance. Pressing a hand against the chilly zipper of his jacket, I said, "I'll come with you. I've *told* you that. But first let me write a letter to V."

Jethro sneered. "No. No more letters or scams. The whole world believes they're privy to our private business. Your family has done enough damage without telling your brother how to rescue you again."

I shook my head, my knees shaking.

What had he done?

Why is he so different?

He was scaring me and not in a good 'I want to blow you and then let you fuck me kind of way' more of a 'I'm thinking of stabbing you in the heart to see if you've misplaced it' kind of way.

"It's for those reasons that I'm leaving him a letter." Twisting my wrist, I broke his hold and beelined for my wardrobe.

I was about to leave this house, this bedroom, this world. *My* world.

For good this time.

I had no intention of coming back.

I would either win or lose.

My destiny was elsewhere. I had no urge to pack anything—most of my things were still at Hawksridge anyway. Seeing as Jethro was in leather, I assumed he'd come on his two-wheeled death machine.

Rifling through my drawers, I quickly pulled on a pair of black skinny jeans, a black sweater, and tapered leather jacket to match his ensemble. We were both creatures of the night.

Jethro crossed his arms, glaring as I slipped on a pair of knee-high boots and stomped past him. "I'm leaving a note, and then we'll go." Not waiting for Jethro to reply, I headed toward my desk and tore off a piece of paper from my sketchpad. With my scalp prickling, I selected a ballpoint and tried to concentrate.

A rustle of denim sounded as Jethro came closer. His large bulk seethed behind me, watching my every move.

I waited for that spark—the lust that was always beneath the surface. But once again, there was nothing but ice.

Sighing heavily, I wrote:

Dear V and Dad.

I love you. I hope you know that.

The past few weeks with you have been tough, but I love you both so much. I don't want to seem ungrateful for your hard work rescuing me, but this is something I have to do.

Don't come get me.

Don't worry on my behalf.

I have a plan.

If it works, then I'll see you again.

If it doesn't, then I'll forever be your Nila.

I didn't sign it. I just folded it in half and left it unaddressed on the table.

I spun to face my kidnapper for the second time in my short life. At least this time, I wasn't petrified of the unknown. I knew exactly what I'd agreed to and how hard it would be.

Jethro clenched his jaw. "What plan, Ms. Weaver?"

I suffered a mental image of him thawing and falling in love with me all over again—no hidden lies, no secrets. I imagined him holding a black-haired baby girl with a combination of his perfect white skin and my tanned heritage. A Hawk-Weaver. A new legacy that would erase the sins of her forbearers.

Am I strong enough to make that happen?

"No plan. Just a hope."

"Well, whatever hope you have, you might as well leave it here. It's useless baggage that will only upset you." Silently, he stole my wrist again and carted me from my room.

I'd thought he'd sneaked in using my window—after all, it was a fairly easy climb up the façade of the manor—but he'd been bolder. He'd used the front door.

The two servants we employed had their rooms downstairs. It was sad to think even now, in this day and age, our help was still housed in the basement. Had we learned nothing from our past transgressions?

They have an apartment down there. Private suites, a bathroom...it's not as if it's a dank cellar.

That was the truth, but it still couldn't hide that they lived below us. Below our high and mighty rank as Weavers.

Perhaps this was my karma.

For all *my* wrongdoings and not my ancestors.

Without a sound, Jethro opened the front door and guided me out. I looked one last time at my childhood home before the door clicked shut, casting me out.

Jethro didn't give me time to mourn. Dragging me down the front steps, he nodded at Kes. The front courtyard housed three bikes and two darkly dressed men.

Kestrel touched his temple in greeting, his light coloured eyes looking like moonbeams in the darkness. "Nila. Pleasure to see you again."

I smiled once, still dreadfully unsure if Kes was on my side, his brother's, or his father's.

Jethro tugged me close. Grabbing my hips, he tossed me onto the back of his bike. A small puff of air exploded out of my mouth at his rough handling. My skin tingled where he'd touched me, but he seemed unaffected.

I'll break you again, Jethro Hawk. I did it once. I can do it a second time.

And then I'll save both of us.

I swallowed hard as the reality of my pregnancy scheme slapped me with doubt. It would take nine long months to hatch. I doubted I had nine months to *live*—let alone breed in the hope it would keep us alive.

I need a back-up plan.

"We're done here," Jethro muttered, throwing a glance at Flaw before taking his helmet from the handlebars and jamming it on his head.

Flaw said, "If we're done. Let's go." His gloved fingers wrapped around his throttle.

I was back with the men who'd claimed me.

Back with my enemies.

Back in power and ready to destroy them.

DAWN.

The new sun painted the sky a glowing pink as we drove beneath the gatehouse at the entrance of Hawksridge. Kes and Flaw accelerated, pulling away and speeding up the long driveway.

I slowed down, steadying the bike and Nila's weight behind me.

Her torso plastered against my back, her hips as close to mine as possible. She was the exact opposite from the first time I'd collected her.

Back in Milan, she'd been respectful in her fear. She'd kept her distance and didn't try to break through my carefully constructed walls. Now, she was pissing me off taking liberties she was no longer entitled to. Her hands hadn't stopped roaming as I drove down motorways and country lanes. Her heat seeped through my jacket, infecting my skin below. She thought things were the same—that I secretly wanted her to touch me.

She couldn't be more wrong.

Slamming my bike to a halt, I planted my legs on the road and twisted to face her. "I'm going to give you a choice." Tearing her arms from around my waist, I held up a blindfold that I'd stuffed into my pocket.

Nila frowned, her eyes flickering up the hill where the road disappeared toward Hawksridge. "What choice?"

Rubbing the silk between my fingers, I said, "I can either blindfold you or not. It's up to you."

Cut was confident this imprisonment would be a lot smoother than her first, but he still didn't want her knowing the way off the estate—unless she gave a guarantee. I smirked. "Decide, Ms. Weaver."

"How is the choice up to me? And besides, I saw the driveway when the police took me away."

"Fair enough." I let the blindfold fall from my fingers and onto her thigh. "Are you going to try to run again? Or have you accepted that your home is now with me?"

I hadn't meant to word it like that. I'd meant to say had she accepted that she would die on this estate. That her life out there—her home in London— was over, done.

Forever.

Nila's gaze delved into mine. I felt her probing my soul, looking for answers and hope.

I didn't have to stop her or hide.

There was nothing inside that shouldn't be there. Not anymore.

I was proud of who I'd become.

And it was all thanks to the little white tablets in my pocket.

After a long minute, she replied, "My home is with you, Kite. I know that. I think I've always known that." She licked her bottom lip. "I won't run. I won't leave you. Not again. Whatever happened to you the past few weeks, I'm willing to look past it because I know what we found together is true and this…" She waved at me as if I offended her. "This is a lie that I don't buy."

My heart skipped—just a small skip—before settling into its wintry shell. Her power over me was gone. It'd just been tested and proven.

"You don't have to buy anything for it to be the truth."

She sighed. "No, but I can hope."

"Hope is as useless as love, Nila Weaver." Shoving the blindfold back into my pocket, I gunned the bike and took her the final distance home.

The underground parking garage housed thirty or so bikes for the Black Diamond brothers. We'd built the bunker especially for our MC, hidden away in case the police ever raided us, which until last month was never a possibility.

Now it might be thanks to the fucking Weavers and their lies to the local papers. Our bribes worked perfectly to keep the law on our side. But when strangers started moaning and demanding justice, it wasn't a simple matter of turning a blind eye anymore.

Luckily, we had a plan. Damage control was in full swing, and after a few weeks out of the limelight, Nila would be forgotten and the world would continue.

We also had a trump card.

The one thing Vaughn couldn't get his sister to do: a private interview.

Later today, Nila would answer all the questions the world wanted to know. She would shed her silence and feed the media a story that would put an end to the disgusting rumours in a carefully scripted pantomime, then she would go back to belonging to us. To *me*.

Plucking my captive from my bike, I discarded my helmet and jacket.

She was back where she belonged, but first there was a simple matter to attend to. One that my father had pointed out and shown me how important it was after my indiscretions.

He was wise, my father. I hoped to rule like him when it was my turn.

"Come with me." Taking her wrist again, I half-escorted, half-dragged Nila through the underground garage and into the private elevator that spat us out by the stables.

Neither of us spoke as we traversed the grass beneath the pink-silver light of dawn. The Hall loomed before us, its turrets glowing with sunrise and stained glass windows looking as if blood ran down the panes.

Flaw and Kestrel had gone—no doubt already snoring in their beds.

I hadn't slept much last night, but I wasn't tired. Far from it. I was awake and ready to prove my worth.

My fingers itched to open my tablet bottle. It wasn't time for another dose, but the way my heart skipped back at the gatehouse proved the fog needed reinforcing.

Now Nila was back in my vicinity, I would have to keep an eye on my dosage—increase the prescription to remain immune to whatever tricks she might play.

"Where are you taking me?" Nila asked as we stepped into the hushed world of Hawksridge and prowled through its sleepy corridors.

I didn't reply. She had no right to know. She would understand the moment we arrived.

It didn't take long, another few minutes before I stopped and opened a large carved door in the north wing of the house.

The space wasn't as big as many of the other rooms, but it'd been staged with the equipment required.

My lips twitched into half a smile as Nila crossed the threshold.

The moment her eyes landed on the medical table in the centre of the room, her mouth fell open in horror. "What—what is this?"

She struggled in my hold while I reached behind her and locked the door. She wasn't stupid.

She knew this wouldn't end well.

The light in her face went out. Her eyes widened in horror. I'd been right to suspect her motives. Did she not think I would see? That her messages weren't so fucking obvious?

"I'm not someone you can manipulate, Ms. Weaver." I patted her arse as I moved forward. A reclining chair suddenly swivelled around, revealing my father.

His eyes landed on Nila, glowing gold with triumph. "Ah, welcome, my dear. So glad to see you after this dreadful time apart." He raised his tumbler of cognac. "It wasn't the same without you here. Was it, Kite?"

I no longer hated my bird of prey nickname. I no longer despised my father using it. In fact, it was an honour. Before, it was a constant reminder that I was born and bred to be something I could never be—now it was a badge of distinction. I'd somehow achieved the impossible and become the perfect fucking son.

Smiling at Nila, I answered, "No. It wasn't the same without her."

If only she knew what'd happened while she was off playing seamstress with her brother. If only she knew what Cut had done to me, what I'd done in return. She wouldn't have come willingly. She would've done anything to avoid being my prisoner again.

"Jethro…" Her voice trailed off, her eyes never leaving the table. "What is the meaning of this?"

Cut laughed. "Come now, child. You can't play that card with us. You know as well as I do what you've done to deserve this."

"Please!" Nila plastered herself against the door, jiggling the doorknob with her hand. It was pointless. I had the key in my pocket. "You don't have to do this."

Cut slowly placed his empty glass on the table and stood. Undoing his cufflinks, he rolled up his sleeves, systematically and refined, never rushing. "I think you'll find, my dear, that we do."

Nodding in her direction, he ordered, "Jet, enough dallying. Grab the girl and let's get on with this."

"Be my pleasure." I advanced on Nila.

Blues and greys decorated the room. The wallpaper was an oriental silk that was so vibrant, the indigo pattern bounced off Nila's black hair.

"Stop it," Nila snarled. "Don't."

Standing in front of her, I held out my hand. "This can be easy or hard. Your choice."

"I hate it when you do that! Can't you see I don't want a choice?!"

I narrowed my eyes. What the fuck did that mean?

Cut chuckled. "You want us to take full responsibility for what's happening to you, is that right? When will you admit that you're the same as us? Doing something willingly doesn't mean you're going to hell, pretty girl. But fighting us at every step doesn't mean you'll go to heaven, either."

I waved my hand, openly revealing the tattoos on my fingertips. "Your choice, Nila. Own free will or restraints."

Nila visibly trembled. A curtain fell over her face, blocking all thoughts.

In a quick move, as if her courage would desert her, she pushed off from the door and brushed past me.

I smiled, dropping my hand. "Good girl."

"Where?" Nila snapped when she stood by the table, her body vibrating with tension.

"Climb on," Cut said.

With ferocity coating her face, Nila scooted onto the table and lay down. She lay there as if she was in a coffin. Her hands clasped tight on her lower belly, her chest rising and falling with panic.

She refused to look at either of us, glowering at the ceiling.

Cut patted her arm. "See...that wasn't so hard now, was it?"

She stiffened, her fingers turning white.

Cut stroked her gently. "I must admit. I missed your presence in my home." He smiled wider. "You're such fun to torment." He traced her collarbone. "However, these past few weeks have been rather enlightening. In fact, I'm delighted with the outcome and only have you to thank for it." Throwing a look my way, he grinned. "You gave me my son. My *real* son. And for that I will always be grateful to you, my dear."

Bending over, he pressed a soft kiss on her mouth.

Nila shuddered, twisting her head to the side.

I just stood there.

No feeling.

No jealousy.

No remorse.

"Don't fight it," Cut murmured. "Don't ruin what you've started."

Nila pressed herself deeper onto the table, no doubt trying to become invisible but not succeeding. I moved closer, taking the side opposite my father. Her eyes met mine, wide and feral. She sent a silent message, so loud and obvious I was sure my father saw.

Why are you doing this?

I thought you cared for me?

I had no intention of replying. If she opened her naïve little eyes, she would see my answer without me spelling it out for her. This was what happened to those who broke promises. She was a true Weaver. And I was finally a true Hawk.

Cut continued to drag his fingertip along Nila's throat, following the contours of the diamond collar. "As much as it's a pleasure to have you living under my roof, Ms. Weaver, I do have one requirement. I hope you don't begrudge me my small request."

Cut reached into his pocket and pulled free the single reason why we were here. He held up the item for her to see.

Gritting her jaw, her eyes popped wide.

The syringe glinted in the lowlight chandelier.

Fight and flight filled her body. "Wait. You don't have to drug me. Jethro, tell him. Tell him you don't have to drug me. I came on my own accord! I already promised I wouldn't run. I won't. I give you my word." A single tear rolled down her cheek. "I'll behave. You can trust me. God, please trust me. I'll behave now." Her breathing turned shallow and fast. "I don't want to be drugged. I don't want to be lost. Please!"

Cut laughed, hushing her spew of words. "I know all that, my pet. Calm down before you give yourself a heart attack."

Nila paused, hope lighting her gaze.

Cut smiled softly. "This isn't to subdue you."

"What—what is it then?"

"I'll let my son tell you that." Brushing some hair that'd fallen over her eyes, he pressed another kiss against her mouth. She tensed but permitted the touch, not twisting her head away.

The fear of being manipulated by a substance had well and truly subdued her. I'd have to remember that. If only she knew that some drugs were better than life—that they made existing so much more *pleasurable*.

Cut stood tall. "I'll leave you two lovers alone." Stroking between her breasts, he smiled. "You're free to do what you please for the rest of the morning, but I expect to see you dressed and presented for your meeting at noon."

Handing the syringe to me, he said, "I'm watching you."

Taking the implement, I nodded. "You don't need to. Consider it already done."

Cut stared, searching my reply. He would find no lie in my tone. No secrets in my voice. I meant what I said: it was already done. Being around her for a few hours hadn't changed me. I was stronger than that and wouldn't relapse.

He clapped me on the back. "I believe you."

And there it was. The one thing I'd wanted all my fucking life.

Trust.

Acceptance.

There was no trace of animosity or disbelief. He'd fully accepted me. I couldn't be more grateful. *I have no intention of jeopardising what I've waited so long to gain.*

Not for Nila. Not for anyone.

With a fatherly squeeze, Cut moved toward the door and left. The moment he'd gone, Nila turned her glassy black eyes on me. "Please, Jethro. Whatever he's told you to do—please don't do it. You know me. I know you. What we have—don't destroy it."

Ignoring her, I tapped the glass of the syringe, making sure there were no air bubbles.

"There's nothing between us, Ms. Weaver."

"Please!" She sat up, clutching my forearm. "You don't believe that."

My temper boiled over. Grabbing her throat, I growled, "Self-control or I will restrain you. Lie. Back. Down."

Shivering, she shook her head. "What *happened* to you?" She tried to capture my cheek, but I dodged her grasp.

"Touch me again and you won't like what happens." I snatched her bicep. "If you move, this will hurt a lot more than if you're still." I poised the needle above the fleshy part of her arm. "And to answer your repetitive question, nothing happened. I'm not doing this because he told me to. I'm doing this because *I* want to."

Piercing her skin, I pressed the plunger.

Tears fled to her eyes, twinkling like black stars. She winced as the cool liquid fled from syringe to flesh.

It only took a second to empty the injection. The moment it was gone, I withdrew the needle and tossed it into the stainless steel tray beside the table.

A small droplet of blood swelled from the puncture wound.

Plucking a tissue from the box on the sideboard, I handed it to her.

Taking it reluctantly, she asked sadly, "What is it? What did you just give me?"

I ran a hand through my hair. "Call it a pre-emptive."

Nila frowned. "Pre-emptive against what?"

"Any plans you might have."

My temper glowed as I remembered her note to her brother. Had she come to the same conclusion my father had, or was she still blindly believing I felt something for her? *Silly, girl.*

"I have no plans. I don't understand." She swung her legs over the table, rubbing her arm.

I moved closer, pressing both hands against her cheeks, imprisoning her. She shied away, but I slid my fingers behind her skull, wrapping them in the thick strands of her hair.

The touch wasn't meant to be kind or gentle. It was meant to show who was in power and it was about fucking time she learned that.

"It's pre-emptive; to make sure the Final Debt will be repaid."

Colour washed from her cheeks. "What do you mean?"

I cocked my head. "Come on. Don't continue to play me when you've already lost." Running my thumb along her bottom lip, I whispered, "You were clever, I will admit. But not clever enough. There is nothing you can do to hinder my plans."

She gasped, her soul falling from her eyes.

She finally understood. "How could you? How could you be so...*heartless?*"

Tugging her hair, I kissed her jaw. "It was you who saved me from such a stupid notion of feelings. The day you left, I thought my life was over. But then I found a new way—a better way—and I'm no longer your toy to play with." Pressing soft kisses down her throat, her pulse throbbed beneath my lips. "No more plans. No more games. It was a contraceptive, Nila. Now do you get it?"

Silence.

Her heartbeat exploded, blood gushing, heating her paper-thin skin below my threatening kisses.

"I've stolen what you hoped to steal from me, Ms. Weaver. There will be no children. No half-breeds. No saviour. I've won."

Nila

"MS. WEAVER, SO nice to meet you."

My attention snapped to the man wearing designer jeans and a cream tailored shirt. His hair was artfully coiffed, and he'd rimmed his baby-blue eyes with kohl. Thin and handsome, he was obviously gay and perfect for the role of jotting down gossip.

There will be no children. No half-breeds. No saviour. I've won.

I stared blankly, unable to do anything but listen to the echo of Jethro's voice inside my head.

"I've won. I've won. I've won."

Tears pricked my eyes for the hundredth time since I'd arrived back at Hawksridge. How could he say that? He'd lost. We *both* had. Somehow, Cut had turned Jethro into his lap dog and the connection we'd shared gurgled down a drain of despair.

What if I had been pregnant? Would the contraceptive have hurt the baby?

How could Jethro do something so terrible?

I hate it here.

I positively hate it here.

I'd *always* hated it here.

How could I return with such stupid plans? How did I think I could save Jethro and kill Cut? What an idiot!

Jethro doesn't even want saving.

Not after what they'd done to him.

"Ms. Weaver? Are you quite well?"

I shook my head, sniffing back unshed tears and doing my best to focus.

Gay Reporter's assistant smiled, her purple fluffy pen tapping her chin in concern. "Can we get you a glass of water or something?"

"She's fine," Jethro murmured in his signature soft voice. I'd forgotten how smooth and precise he was. Forgotten how rigid he held himself, how restrained and contained and arctically frigid.

I shot him a look full of venom. "Actually, I would love a glass of water."

Jethro pursed his lips as the blonde-haired woman who looked like a delicious cupcake in her pale pink dress and curves sprang from her chair.

She giggled. "I can't believe I get to play hostess in this place." Moving to the sideboard where an array of drinks and hors d'oeuvres had been set by invisible staff, she poured me a glass and came back. "Truly, it's an incredible home you have here, Mr. Hawk."

I smiled in thanks, taking the offered water.

Jethro shifted on the settee beside me, his temper gathering a tempest. "I'm so glad you like it." Clasping his hands, he glowered at the reporter. "Are we quite ready to begin? I have a few other appointments that demand my attention."

Gay Reporter nodded, sitting higher on the mirroring settee opposite us. "Yes, of course." Revealing tic-tac perfect teeth, he began his well-rehearsed speech. "First, we want to say what an honour it is to be chosen for the exclusive interview. I have no doubt that our readers at *Vanity Fair* will highly enjoy such an intriguing piece. My name is George, and this is Sylvie."

His eyes bounced between Jethro and me. "I predict the interview will go on for about thirty minutes, followed by a short tour of the grounds and anything else you wish to share with us for the article. Does that sound satisfactory?"

Sylvie scooped out a voice recorder, iPhone, and notepad and arranged her arsenal on the coffee table.

"Fine," Jethro murmured, playing with a diamond cufflink. He looked resplendent in a grey cashmere suit and open-necked white shirt. His salt and pepper hair caught the light with distinguished old-world wealth and his shiny Gucci shoes were pristine.

The sun streamed in through the windows, stencilling the carpet with happiness I didn't feel.

I was cold. Aching. Confused.

Once again, my fingers returned to the bruise on my arm. I flinched, remembering the pain of the needle piercing my flesh. The skin still stung from the contraceptive as if he'd only just done it—not a few hours ago.

How could he *do* that?

How could he obey Cut and dismiss me from his heart?

He'd shattered my dreams so damn quickly.

Why oh why did I come back here?

You know why.

To save Jethro, kill the Hawk bastards, and end this.

George's eyes darted around the lounge. Jethro and I rested on a loveseat with silver swans gilded on white satin. Purple velvet-flocked chairs encircled the seating area, lending a richness to the oriental charm of the day parlour.

The décor was feminine with its intricate jewelled music boxes enclosed in glass-domed cases and ancient grandfather clocks chiming the hour. I would've liked to relax in this room and I guessed Jasmine used it, too—judging by the faint wheel marks in the thick lavender carpet.

I was tired. Terribly tired.

For three months, my life had been anything but normal and I needed to rest. I needed to stop and get my bearings, because I no longer knew where I was. I thought I understood Jethro.

How wrong was I?

A vertigo wave danced in my brain. I moaned, pressing my fingertips against my temples.

Jethro inched closer, resting his cool hand on my thigh.

My skin reacted instantly, craving him, seeking more. I cursed myself for reacting that way. It took everything in me not to shove him away and sprint from the room.

What a traitor.

What a *bastard*.

"Ms. Weaver, you don't look entirely well." George looked at his wristwatch. "We can postpone for an hour or so if you wish. To rest?"

"No." Jethro's eyes locked on George's. "She'll be fine." His fingers tightened on my knee, biting uncomfortably. "Won't you, Nila?"

Once upon a time, my heart would've fluttered if he used my first name. Now, it tore off those wings and plummeted to hell.

Leaning into me, Jethro whispered in my ear, "You know what's expected of you. Behave and everything will remain cordial, got it?" Pulling away, he put on a show for the reporters. "I'm so worried about you, darling. For days, you've been saying how excited you are to reveal the truth to the world. You don't want to ruin your chance now, do you?"

George clapped his hands. "Yes, please don't let us down, Ms. Weaver. We are so excited to hear your tale." He picked up an expensive camera with a zoom lens. "If you feel restricted sitting down, we could always conduct the questions by the window over there. Be a great spot for some pictures."

"Oh, yes," Sylvie said. "It would be such a romantic shot with the two of you. Our readers would love it."

Another vertigo spell teased my vision. I didn't trust my legs to stand and shook my head. "Perhaps in a little bit. I'm happy to answer whatever you want here." I stretched my face into a smile, but it felt heavy, sad, *fake*.

George and Sylvie didn't notice.

But of course, Jethro did. Pinching my knee again, Jethro cleared his throat. "My apologies. My love has been rather overworked the past few weeks." He leaned forward with a conspirer's smile. "She went home to her family, you see. A bit of a disaster—as you might've heard."

Sylvie giggled, completely buying the lies Jethro spilled. "We did hear a rumour or two."

His commanding fingers stroked my thigh, looking like a caress but feeling like a punishment. "Those rumours were started to thwart our love. Her family doesn't approve of mine. They think she can do better than me and never approved—even though we were born for each other."

My heart thudded to a stop. The words could've been so perfect. So full of promise. Instead, they reeked with deceit and dripped with lies.

We were born for each other, that's true. But only for him to kill me in his quest for whatever Cut promised.

I sank further into the loveseat, wishing the swans on the fabric would come alive and fly me away from there. I missed the sanctuary of the Weaver quarters. After the awful injection, Jethro had left me to reacquaint myself with the space. I'd showered and tried not to cry over my gullible heart or naïve hopes smashing to dust in the face of Jethro's new behaviour.

I'd dressed in a blood-red A-line skirt that I'd made while here previously and shrugged into a slouchy jumper with a rose hand-stitched on the front. I hadn't bothered with makeup or my hair. The damp strands hung down my back adding to the chill in my soul that I doubted would ever thaw.

Sitting beside Jethro in his immaculate attire, I truly did feel sick. Dying cell by cell until I would be nothing but a corpse.

"Sounds like an awful predicament to love a man your family doesn't approve of, Ms. Weaver," George prompted.

This is it then.

The interview had officially begun.

Placing my hands in my lap, I struggled to think up an approved reply. When Cut came to collect me for the reporters, he'd given me strict instructions:

"Act heartbroken but happy. Paint your family as the bad guys and us as the victims. Make the Hawks shine, Ms. Weaver, or else."

I'm so sorry, Vaughn.

After everything he'd done to save me, I was about to undo it all with a few awful sentences.

Jethro suddenly wrapped an arm around my shoulders, crushing me into his body. His lips landed on my ear in a whisper-kiss. "Play the damn role. It's not hard."

Pulling away, his eyes burned into mine. *You wanted to come back. You invited me to take you. Now you have to play along if you want to survive.*

Looking away, I answered George's question. "It is hard. I love my father and brother so much, but when I met Jethro…I just knew. He was it for me, and no matter what they say or do, I can't change something that's written by fate."

My voice hovered in the room, quiet, unsure, but resonating in just the right frequency to melt George and Sylvie. Their postures changed, their interest flared, and Jethro relaxed a smidgen. "Good girl," he murmured into my hair.

I shivered as his breath warmed my nape. I wanted my words to be real. I wanted it so much.

Then make it real.

Just because Jethro was damaged again, didn't mean I couldn't win him back.

Where was my strength? My conviction? I'd come back not to wallow in misery but to *end* this.

Power shot into my blood; I sat straighter. Pinching my cheeks, I willed colour to paint my skin and dispel any sign of weakness. "True love is a curse, don't you think?" I smiled for the first time, shoving aside my worries and throwing myself into this new challenge.

You want me to play my part, Jethro Hawk?

Fine.

I would play it so well, I would have the press eating out of *my* hand—not the Hawks'.

"I agree. Falling in love can be the most dangerous thing anyone can do." Sylvie smiled.

Stealing Jethro's hand, I looped my fingers with his and brought his large palm to my lips. I kissed him. I breathed in his scent of leather and money. I grew strong again.

He didn't move. Didn't inhale or twitch.

It doesn't matter.

I'll get him back.

"So your brother felt so strongly that the Hawk family wasn't good enough for you, he spread vile rumours of debts and deaths…all to break you up?" George asked, his eyes gleaming.

Jethro faded into the background.

Please forgive me, Vaughn.

"Yes. V and I were very close growing up. I would tell him everything. But then I met Jethro, and I didn't want to share my secret. I kept our affair hidden. I suppose that was a betrayal in my brother's eyes. He felt like he lost me. And took it out on my love."

Jethro smiled like the doting partner. "I will admit, it's been hard."

"I can imagine." George grinned. Conferring to his notes, he perched higher. "How about, before we discuss other topics, we clear the confusion about those rumours. Would you mind?"

Jethro answered before I could. "By all means. We have nothing to hide." His lips stretched over his teeth in a cool smile. "It would be beneficial to clear the air on the disgusting rumours Vaughn Weaver spread."

My shoulders rolled at my twin's name. I should've listened to him—not about running away, but arming myself with weapons and fighting the Hawks with violence rather than my idiotic idea of getting pregnant.

That's over anyway.

I didn't know how long the contraceptive would work, but I remembered a staff member having the injection and saying it lasted anywhere from three to six months.

I won't be alive in six months.

Sylvie pulled an *Elle* magazine from her satchel beside her. Passing it to me, she asked, "Have you seen this particular article?"

I leaned forward, taking the glossy weight and forcing myself to remain detached as I stared at the cover. The model pouted for the camera, eerily close to my dusky colouring and black eyes. However, where I had long hair, hers was cut short—a sleek bob revealing the full impact of the heavy stones around her neck. The intricate design of the choker was missing the barely noticeable W's hidden in the rows of diamonds, and the filigree work around the stones was ordinary compared to the workmanship in mine. Plus, my diamonds were bigger.

I smiled smugly, stroking my collar as if it no longer heralded my death sentence but linked me to a man who belonged to me.

"No, I haven't seen it."

"Would you mind if you read some of it aloud, Ms. Weaver? Elaborate on a few key points?" George pointed at a Post-it note sticking from the pages. "I've bookmarked it for you."

Flipping the magazine open, I gasped as the same model from the front smouldered in a centrefold. She wore a dress very similar to the feathered couture I paraded at the Milan show.

The title blazed in diamonds:

'The Truth Behind the Weavers as told by Daphne Simons, Employee at Weaver Enterprises.'

"Do you know that employee?" Sylvie asked.

I looked up, shaking my head. "No. We hire too many people to know them all."

The room turned silent as I skimmed the ridiculous article.

Nila Weaver, the daughter of the conglomerate company Weaver Enterprises has recently been spotted back in London after a stint outside the limelight. Gossip has spread over the past few weeks that her family are victims of an age-old dispute that defies all logic and

*rationality. A world where promises are kept and oaths are never broken. Her brother,
Vaughn Weaver, recently broke his silence when his efforts to have his sister returned went
unheeded.*

*Turning the tables on the leaked photographs depicting Ms. Weaver with a young man
unknown at the time, and the rumour that she'd had a mental breakdown and run off with
her mystery lover, the world was shocked to discover the man in the photographs wasn't her
lover, but her kidnapper.*

How could they print such heresy?

*Upon Nila Weaver's return to London High Society, she's been repeatedly asked to tell
her story, but has remained silent on the matter. However, here at* Elle, *we have an exclusive
interview with one of her employees.*

Elle: *Thank you for meeting with us, Daphne. Care to tell us what you know?*

Daphne: *Well, all I know is she returned to work last month. She's always been
rather quiet. Too work focused and always stumbling into things. But now, she's even worse.*

Elle: *You mentioned she seems different? Can you elaborate?*

Daphne: *It's common knowledge about the collar. She never takes it off. She's
constantly touching it. The staff room is a buzz with conspiracies that she suffers that problem
when a captive falls for her kidnapper…you know what I mean?*

Elle: *You're saying she's in love with the man who collared her?*

Daphne: *Yep. For sure. My theory is the debt stuff is just a cover up. I reckon she's
into that freaky business…you know like S&M? Not to mention the diamond collar is an
obvious ode to belonging to a master when in those types of relationships. She's changed.*

Elle: *How do you mean?*

Daphne: *Well… she used to be sweet, shy. It's a family company, so we see the
Weavers interact a lot. But now she's shut down around her brother. Her love for the industry
has gone.*

Elle: *And you believe this is due to a Sadomasochistic relationship?*

Daphne: *I believe she's changed too much to fit in anymore. Mark my words. She
won't be in London long.*

*And there you have it; our very own textile heiress has returned bearing a collar, bruises,
and a history of intolerable cruelty. I suppose we won't get answers or know the full story until
justice has been served.*

"So, tell us," George said. "Is any of that true? Are you in an S&M
relationship?"

Jethro sat taller, chuckling under his breath. "You honestly expect us to
answer questions about our sex life?"

Sylvie laughed. "Sorry if it sounds like we're prying, but our readers love
to know that stuff."

Stroking my collar, I smiled coyly. "All your readers need to know is
Jethro completes me both in and out of the bedroom."

George laughed, slapping his thigh. "Now, that's a politically correct reply,
if I ever heard one."

Jethro reclined, spreading his arm over the back of the loveseat. "The
rumours about death and debts are complete lies. However, some parts are
indeed true."

I didn't know how he did it, but in a few short sentences, he'd enraptured
George and Sylvie.

"Oh, how so?"

"People no longer accept the idea of arranged marriages. They like to
think we're all free to do what we like, when we like, but realistically, we are all

still governed by class, income, our family tree." He ran a hand through his hair. "My family has known the Weavers for six hundred years. We've effectively grown up together, crossing paths and healing feuds, and ultimately agreeing to come together to form a strong alliance."

George frowned. "So you're saying this so-called Debt Inheritance is what? A marriage contract?"

Jethro shook his head. "Not quite. It's an agreement of debts between two houses that strive to support each other with payments in different forms throughout the years."

I blinked stupidly, unable to believe the way Jethro spun three weeks of rumours. It made people seem ridiculous—clutching at straws and jumping onto a witch-hunt they knew nothing about.

He sounded so reasonable, so *justifiable.*

His speech was too perfect not to be scripted...perhaps by Bonnie.

Bonnie.

Did she tell Jethro to come and collect me, or was she against this development? After all, she'd kicked me out. She was the one who wanted me gone.

"And you, Ms. Weaver. That's how your family sees this Debt Inheritance, too?" George pinned his baby-blues on me.

"Yes, of course. What else could it be? To think that one family owns another is completely ludicrous. We support one another. Sure, at times there's some unrest and rivalry, but for the most part, we're one big happy family."

Maids arrived with fresh tea and a three-tier cake stand with cucumber sandwiches and éclairs.

George grabbed one, jotting down a few notes. "So really...it's the age-old 'mountain out of a mole hill' kinda thing."

Jethro crossed his ankles, ignoring the finger food. "Yes. Not that it's anyone's business, but our two influential families have always prospered by linking our history. It's such a shame that after centuries of friendship, it's come down to Mr. Weaver spreading such terrible lies."

I sucked in a breath. I wanted to tell the truth but what good would it do? Would it stop the Hawks from breaking countless laws—would it save my life?

Vaughn had told the world, yet even with so much gossip, it was still his word against the Hawks. And they sounded so much more believable than him. A sure way to disband the Twitter posters and bury old Facebook shout-outs under new intrigue.

George swallowed a bite of cucumber sandwich. "Are you happy to be back? After the time away?"

This was it. My turn to lie as spectacularly as Jethro.

Swooning into Jethro's side, I snuggled against his chest and sighed dramatically. "Oh, yes. Every night we messaged each other. And every night we professed our belonging and knowledge that we wouldn't let lies come between us."

Jethro stiffened then slowly wrapped an icy arm around my shoulders.

My body trembled with the need to be hugged—for real. Having the weight of his body cloaking mine did nothing to ease the inconsolable pain inside my heart.

I wanted to hurt him as much as he'd hurt me.

I wanted him to wake up!

But how?

Then suddenly, I knew *exactly* how. How to get back at him for what he'd done to me. How to announce to Cut that his plan to steal my right to bear children wouldn't come without consequences.

Placing my hand on Jethro's chest, I sought out the flat-line and uninterested beat of his heart. "It was agony being apart." Dropping my voice to a breathy whisper, I said, "I was so homesick for Jethro; I threw up almost every day."

Jethro's heart remained steady and unaffected.

Try ignoring this, you monster.

"But it turned out I was throwing up because I was pregnant."

Jethro's heart screeched to a stop. He went deathly still.

George clapped. "Oh, that's wonderful! So if the Debt Inheritance is kind of like a marriage contract, then they have to let it take place now that you're carrying!"

I swallowed my morbid giggle.

You want *them to cut off my head?*

If only they knew what it meant.

"That's amazing. I call first dibs on coming to the wedding and baby shower!" Sylvie laughed.

Jethro never looked at me; his gaze remained locked on the other end of the room. He struggled to plant a smile on his face, nodding at the ecstatic interviewers. "Yes…it was quite a surprise. But of course…a welcome one."

Letting tears spring to my eyes, I murmured, "I was so happy. I couldn't wait to start our family and create something that was just ours. But…" I played up the hitch in my voice.

Sylvie leaned forward. "What—what happened?"

Jethro tightened his arm around me. "Yes, *Nila*. What happened?" His voice was whip-sharp.

George passed me his handkerchief. I accepted it, dabbing my dry eyes. "I lost the baby!" I sniffed loudly, making sure I sounded extra pitiful. "The stress of all the rumours made me sick, and I lost the best thing that could've ever happened to us."

George slapped a hand over his mouth, totally forgetting his notepad and pen. "Oh, that's tragically awful." Getting up, he came to squat in front of me.

Jethro glowered at him as George took my hand and kissed my knuckles. "It's okay though…that little one wasn't meant to be, but you can try again. You can have other babies." His gaze flashed to Jethro. "Can't you? You're both young. It's only natural to create your own family and make this love story complete."

"Yes, quite," Jethro muttered, tugging me away from George's caressing fingers.

I fought Jethro's hold, clutching onto George. If Jethro wanted the world to believe we were together and happy then it was his turn to play along with my farce.

Letting a sob free, I wailed, "That's the problem. Something happened…." I narrowed my eyes at Jethro, letting him see my wrath and hate for what he'd done.

You took away the one weapon I might've had to free us.

George clutched my fingers tighter, completely buying my story. "Oh no, not more bad news?"

Imbecile.

Leech.

As lovely as he seemed, I couldn't stand what he represented. He was there to make my family look like liars and the Hawks to smell like roses. They would tarnish my brother, break my father's heart even more, and make me seem as if I was a scatter-brained lovesick child completely out of her depth.

I mean to change all that.

"I was told the conception was a miracle. That I have a rare disorder that might mean I'll never conceive again. The doctor said I might die if I ever carried a child full term, but he knew I wouldn't give up. It's my ultimate dream—the one thing I have to have."

Jethro growled, "Nila, no need to tell the world our—"

"Jethro's father, Bryan Hawk, loves me like a daughter. He arranged for the doctor to give me a contraceptive, completely against my will. He said if I tried to bear the child of my soul-mate, I might die, and he couldn't have that on his soul!" I let ugly, wet sobs spew forth, hurling myself into the performance.

George went white, his face half enthralled with having a delicious story to tell and half full of heartbroken sorrow. "Oh, you poor thing. You poor, poor—"

Jethro sniffed, physically untangling George's fingers from mine and pushing him away. Pulling me into his body, he snapped, "It's been a hard time for all of us." Standing, he yanked me to my feet.

His eyes shot a warning.

What the hell are you doing?

Anger radiated, but beneath it all was the faintest shadow of horror. Did he believe my tale? How did he feel to know what he'd done when I might've been carrying his child?

Does it make you sick? I blazed my own silent message. *Does it rip out your insides to think you might've killed your own flesh and blood?*

Before I could seek answers in his eyes, he looked away.

"I'm sorry, but the interview is over." Jethro stood to his full height, his suit looking crisp compared to his ruffled exterior.

I'd come into this as a victim, but I'd stolen the show.

I felt redeemed.

They might've robbed my plans of pregnancy, but I'd just poached theirs in return.

I was no longer the meek little woman. I was the strong barren woman destined to live with a man she adored and never get pregnant. The media would direct their sympathy onto me—they would be kinder to my family, less likely to slander my last name.

And should all my scheming fail and it came time for me to pay the Final Debt, I might have some chance of rallying them to save me.

George stood up, his fingers fluttering over his camera. "Ah, can we bother you for some pictures? Before we conclude for the day?"

Jethro's nostrils flared. "No, I think my girlfriend needs to lie down. This has—"

"Now, *honey*, don't hide the truth from them." I wiped beneath my eyes, hoping he saw my challenge.

I'm not done with you yet.

Jethro's eyebrows knitted together. "We haven't hidden anything, *my love.*" He smiled thinly, pinching my arm where George couldn't see.

"Wait—what are you talking about, Ms. Weaver?" Sylvie asked.

I smiled radiantly. "I'm not just his girlfriend."

Jethro sucked in a breath.

George bounced on the spot with anticipation. "What do you mean?"

Beaming at Jethro, I said, "I'm his fiancée. We're getting married."

WHAT IN THE ever-loving fuck was she doing?

My mind scrambled; a terrible lancing pain stabbed my temples.

Was she pregnant?

Did she miscarry?

What the fuck did it mean if she *was* pregnant? What would the contraceptive do?

I shook my head, trying to get my erratic breathing under control. I couldn't think about those things—not while the reporters were here, watching our every move.

Pills.

I need another pill.

Nila suddenly nuzzled into my chest, wrapping her bony arms around my waist. Collecting her last night, I'd noticed she looked skinnier than normal. But I knew her well—I knew she would've run every night on her treadmill, knew she would've overworked herself to forget.

But what if she's telling the truth and was *sick?*

Did that become an extra issue with what my father had planned? And why did I even care? I *shouldn't* care.

Do something about it.

Shoving her away, I fumbled in my pocket and yanked out the bottle. Tapping two tablets into my palm, I threw them down my throat and swallowed them dry.

My heart raced as I tucked the bottle back into my pocket and jerked my hands through my hair. Knowing I had something that helped—that the drug's fog wisped through my blood—allowed me to regain control on the flapping mess Nila had created.

"Headache?" George asked, his eyebrow raised at my pocket.

Nila narrowed her gaze, too, incorrect conclusions filling her sniper glare. With the way she was behaving, I didn't want her anywhere near my newfound cure.

Slipping back into welcome numbness, I gathered her close and smiled for the damn journalists. "Yes, sorry. While Nila has been going through some terrible ordeals lately, I've suffered my own stress."

Sylvie came closer, her eyes pooling with sympathy. "Oh, I'm so sorry to hear that."

See, Nila, two can play at this game.

I waved it away as if I was a martyr only focused on the love of his life. "Only a few headaches, but I can't tell you how happy I am to have her home." I jostled Nila closer, planting a kiss on her forehead. "I missed you so much."

Nila squirmed, her lips thinning with frustration. "Me, too. I just wish you'd been there when I lost the baby instead of on business."

Our eyes locked—the challenge in hers made my fingers dig into her side harder than I intended.

Watch what you bloody say.

I hoped she got my message because I was at the end of my patience. Cut would be watching somewhere—making sure I didn't fucking fail. Once we were free of our audience, she had a shit-load of explaining to do.

Ignoring Nila, I smiled at George and Sylvie. "But that's all in the past, and we've dwelt too long on that already."

George looked like he might argue, but I used the same trump card Nila had. "Let's discuss something a lot more exciting." I narrowed my eyes on my target: Sylvie would help guide the conversation to safer ground. "We're getting married. Let's talk about that."

NO, LET'S TALK about those drugs you just swallowed.

Was it true he had a headache? Or was there something more sinister in that tiny bottle?

Sylvie clutched her heart, swooning a little. "It's so romantic. Star-crossed lovers reunited after lies and a miscarriage split them apart."

I let her turn my attention back to the stage-show but made a mental note to steal Jethro's pills the first chance I had. I had to know what they were.

"It's so tragically perfect." Sylvie's eyes were dreamy and dumbstruck by Jethro's undivided attention. He held the poor woman enraptured with his piercing golden gaze.

I nodded.

It *was* perfect.

Love and wealth and family.

Pity it's all a heinous lie.

"If *Vanity Fair* would be interested, you're more than welcome to an exclusive when I've finished designing my wedding gown." I hadn't even thought of saying that. My own lie snowballed, gathering faster and faster momentum.

If I had a future engagement with the magazine, it might make my untimely death more suspicious. If the debts took me, would they dig a little harder and uncover the truth? Then again, knowing the Hawks, they would spin some plausible tale, and I would be forgotten.

"Wow, that's a fantastic offer. Thank you, Ms. Weaver," George said. "We'd be delighted, of course."

"Excellent."

Jethro ground his teeth.

Despite his attempts to manipulate the conversation, he was in my shadow this morning. I had no intention of giving him the limelight. Jethro and his father had forced me to do this. But I would do it *my* way. I hadn't broken any of Cut's rules. I'd played along. I'd painted a picture for the world to eat up.

I'd just been smarter than they gave me credit for.

"When will the ceremony take place?" Sylvie spun on the spot, eying up the beautiful parlour. "Will you get married here or in a church?"

Jethro pinched the bridge of his nose, struggling to plant a smile on his lips. "It wasn't going to be announced for another few months, but I suppose it's out now, so we can spill a few of the details. We'll most likely have a garden wedding."

"I can imagine how happy you are," George said, fiddling with his camera and preparing to move from questions to pictures.

Jethro beamed, looking so young and carefree he took my breath away. "Extremely. I've never been so happy." His eyes landed on mine; a thought flew over his face. Then he grabbed me, dipped me as if we were on a dance floor, and before I could breathe, his lips slammed against mine.

The world switched off. Completely. Utterly. *Everything* disappeared.

There was no sound.

No colour.

No fear or stress or panic.

Just *him*.

Crackling, sparking, all-consuming lust. His taste, heat, smell. My skin hummed, my lips melted, my core clenched.

For weeks, I'd wanted nothing more than to kiss him. To hold him and find that combustible connection. To bind ourselves together even in the face of debts and danger.

I moaned as his tongue nudged against my lips.

I opened for him, sighing into the passionate kiss, suspended in his arms in front of the press. He didn't seem to care we had an audience. I *loved* that he didn't care.

He'd changed so much—lived through something I didn't understand. He'd become a stranger all over again. But no matter how he changed his thoughts and mind-set, he couldn't change his body. That part of him I knew. His body belonged to me as surely as my body belonged to him, and I had no doubt that would enrage and petrify him. Because no matter what distance he tried to put between us—it disintegrated whenever we touched.

With another soft moan, I slinked my fingers into his thick hair, jerking his mouth harder against mine. His tongue dived deeper, wrestling for dominance. His muscles trembled, holding me in the dip as the coolness of his mouth switched to heat and for the barest of delightful moments his teeth nipped my bottom lip.

Then sound came back.

Colour returned.

Awareness of the outside world drove a wedge between us.

The kiss was over.

Jethro swooped me back onto my feet, his mouth glistening.

It was a set-up.

My heart hardened. He'd kissed me for the reporters.

George stood with his camera, busily clicking, capturing every second of our sexy 'staged' slip-up.

Good.

At least people would have half of the story.

The part not drowning in bullshit.

There *was* love between us; there was a story about connection beneath all the fakery. If only love was enough, I could be free. Jethro could be free. It could all be over if only love was stronger than debts.

"That was some kiss. Hot with a capital H." George laughed, fanning himself. "I can see why your brother wouldn't want you anywhere near Mr.

Hawk, Ms. Weaver."

My tummy flipped. "Why?"

Jethro stiffened, paying strict attention.

George grabbed a tripod from his duffel. "I have a younger sister myself and if I saw her kissing a man like that, I would want to break them up, too."

Sylvie frowned, asking the question floating around in my head. "But why? It's a dream come true for any woman to have such a compatible partner."

George snorted, waving at Jethro and me with his camera. "Maybe women see it different, but from a guy's point of view, I know what I just witnessed, and it scares me."

Jethro cleared his throat, his natural intensity suffocating the room with power. "Explain. I'm not quite following."

George rolled his eyes. "Come on. You don't get it? Passion is incredibly dangerous if it's not respected and you two..." He shrugged. "Forget it. I'm overstepping. All I mean is chemistry like that can't be contained. It can bring great happiness but also destroy."

A shiver ran down my spine. His words sounded oddly prophetic.

Dragging his tripod over to the window bay, he clapped his hands. "Now, Ms. Weaver, if you wouldn't mind standing here. I want a picture of you with your diamond necklace in the sunshine."

For some reason, my feet remained planted on the carpet. What did he mean with his previous comment? That Jethro and I were freaks of nature governed by sex and nothing else? That we were idiots in a game we didn't understand?

George came toward me and manhandled me over to the window. "Perfect. Stand right there." His fingers slipped into my hair, fluffing the now dried strands, then brushed a powder over my brow and cheekbones that magically appeared from nowhere. "I don't know many women who look as stunning as you do without makeup."

I had no reply as he backed away and clicked a few test images, moving the tripod around until he was happy.

Passion is incredibly dangerous if it's not respected.

"If you could gather your hair to show off the choker?" George paused. "By the way, what does the choker symbolise? Were the rumours right that it portrays ownership...a wedding ring if you were?"

I opened my mouth to reply—with what, I had no idea—but Jethro jumped in. "It's a Hawk family heirloom. It's given to the woman who bewitches the first Hawk."

"Bewitches, that's an interesting word." Chuckling to himself, George turned his attention back on me.

Did I bewitch him?

My eyes drifted to Jethro as I cascaded black hair over my shoulder and angled my neck so the diamonds caught the sunlight. Instantly, rainbows drenched the carpet around my feet.

Jethro sucked in a breath, his hands fisting by his sides.

If what George said was true...did I have more power than I realised? Did that mean Jethro had more control over me than I thought? *Passion can be dangerous... I already tried to rule him with sex—but what if it works both ways?* Had I dug myself into this hole without even realising it?

Too many questions. And really, answers wouldn't help. I would still be in the same situation.

"Give me a half smile. Look mysterious," George commanded, ducking to take angled pictures.

I pouted and preened, doing my best to come across secretive and coy.

If I was running out of time, I meant to be talked about for years after my death. I wanted to be known as the woman who brought down an empire—even if I had to sacrifice my life to do it.

A macabre thought made me swallow a laugh.

I'm living a real life Romeo and Juliet saga. Montague and Capulets, fighting an ancient battle. Would it end like that tragic tale, too?

Five minutes later, George had taken a gazillion pictures and grabbed his tripod. "Before we go, we would appreciate some photographs with the two of you outside."

Sylvie packed up the gear and made her way to the exit. "We'd love a tour as well, if that would be possible?"

Jethro drifted close to me, stealing my hand. My heart stuttered. I couldn't stop the overheating prickle of his skin against mine.

"I'm afraid the Hall is undergoing some renovations currently. Very few rooms are useable."

There were no renovations. Just lots and lots of things to hide.

Smiling to soften the blow of his rejection, Jethro added, "But I'm more than happy to invite you back when Nila has finished her wedding gown and you can see it then." His fingers squeezed tighter around mine in a silent reproof at my earlier comment.

Looking down, he gave me a calculating look. "Isn't that right, *darling?*"

I nodded. "Sounds perfect."

If I'm still alive.

"Follow us to the gardens." Jethro strode past George and Sylvie, dragging me with him. His long legs ate up the corridor, putting a couple of metres between us and our entourage.

Once out of hearing distance, he whispered harshly, "You're doing very well so far, Ms. Weaver. I'm impressed. However, if I were you, I'd stop overstepping boundaries."

Leaning into him, I murmured, "What boundaries are those? I don't remember boundaries when I was last here. Oh right, yes I do. No going on the chase where my family is buried. No going on the second floor. No running away. No talking to Vaughn. However, I don't remember you ever telling me to stop touching you or telling you how I felt."

His shoulders bunched. "Don't get cocky, Nila. No more games. I'm done trying to win—"

"That's because you always lose."

Jethro's eyes flashed. "I *never* lose. Unfortunately for me, my opponent hasn't been playing fair."

"What do you mean?" My forehead furrowed. "Everything I've tried to do—"

"Was to manipulate me. I was stupid to believe otherwise, but my eyes have since been opened. Regrettably for you, I will no longer be so easy to control."

Leaving the Hall by the main entrance, we stepped down the imposing stairs and crunched onto the gravel below.

"You were never easy to control, Jethro, and it was never about that. It was about finding someone I never thought I'd find. It was about falling in love—"

He yanked me to a stop. "Don't mention love in my presence again. You don't love me, and I certainly don't love you." Grazing his knuckles over my jaw, he smiled frostily. "Never underestimate my desire to fit in with my family, Ms. Weaver. And remember that I'm now immune to your distractions. Life at Hawksridge is going to be a lot different from now on."

I wanted to shout and scream. I wanted to attack him and kiss.

"You don't know anything, Jethro Hawk."

"Ready?" George appeared with his incessant camera.

Jethro wrapped his arms around me. Our tense standoff was silenced for a moment. He gave me no choice but to liquefy in his arms, smile demurely, and pretend everything was perfect for one of the fakest photographs ever taken.

"I know more than I need to," Jethro murmured, his breath hot and enticing on my neck. "I know everything I need in order to complete my task."

George darted forward. Sylvie, with her bouncing blonde hair, checked the sunlight with handheld sensors. The day was cool but bright; a brilliant autumn backdrop for *Vanity Fair's* extravaganza.

"Perfect. Don't move," George said.

"Oh, I hadn't planned on it," Jethro whispered just for me. He rocked his hips into my arse as he cradled me in his arms. His head bowed as he nuzzled my hair. "You smell just as good as I remember."

"Oh, you remember that, do you?" I cocked my chin, glaring at Hawksridge and doing my utmost to remain unaffected by Jethro rubbing himself on my lower back. "And here I thought you'd forgotten everything to do with me."

"I haven't forgotten a thing."

"That's not true," I whispered sadly. "You've forgotten what I said to you the night you brought me back in the springs. You've forgotten that I said I was in love with you. That it didn't come with conditions or commands. That I couldn't hate you for what you did yesterday or tomorrow." I sighed, nursing the pain deep inside. "Don't you see what I'm offering you? Cut doesn't love you, Jethro. *He's* the one controlling you. Choose me. *Love* me. And we can be free together."

Jethro growled under his breath. "Stop wasting your time. It's not going to happen."

George pranced closer, clicking his camera, capturing us for eternity.

"You'll see, Kite. Eventually, you will see, and I hope for both our sakes it isn't too late."

That was the last time we talked while we became the perfect models for George. For the next hour, we were told where to stand, how to smile, what to do. Photographs were taken in front of Hawksridge, in the stables with the foxhounds threading around our feet, and beneath the apple trees in the orchard.

With each click of the shutter, my heart fell a little more. I had no doubt the pictures would turn the world from suspicion to adoration. The rumours would die. The questions would disappear. And life would move on.

Exactly as the Hawks intended.

Jethro

SCREW HER AND her conniving plans.

I wanted to fucking throw something, punch someone, and surrender to the rapidly building hailstorm inside.

You need a top-up.

I thought my dosage was perfect, but it was useless against her. The intensity she projected—the feral energy and righteous anger. It was enough to fucking cripple my walls and blow away my numbing fog.

Not going to happen.

I'd come so far. I wouldn't go back. I *couldn't*. I wouldn't survive and not just because Cut would kill me, but because I couldn't live that way any longer. I wasn't fucking built for this disease. I'd done my penance. Twenty-nine long years of it.

Pulling the small bottle from my pocket as I entered my quarters, I placed two pills on my tongue and swallowed them back.

Nila hadn't even been back a day and I'd already tripled the amount I normally took.

And when I kissed her.

Fuck!

What was I *thinking?*

To get so close to her? To taste her again?

I'd planned on an impromptu ad-lib for the article, but it fucking backfired on me.

I stormed into my bathroom and tore off the grey suit I'd worn for the *Vanity Fair* interview. Cold sweat drenched my back. Goosebumps covered my skin as I stripped the rest of my clothing and stepped into the shower.

As soon as the meeting was over, I'd left Nila in the parlour and stormed to my room. Being around George and Sylvie had been easy. Their reactions and opinions didn't lash at me nearly as much as Nila's did.

What was it about her? Why couldn't I block her out?

Hot water rained over me, burning my flesh. Instead of washing away the tension of the morning, all I could think about was Nila pleasuring herself with the showerhead a few weeks ago. The way her face had tightened and pleasure made her glow. She'd never looked so goddamn beautiful.

My cock thickened, demanding I do something about the ache.

I couldn't let her do this to me. Not again. Not after I'd had the best month of my life with my father. I'd finally found something that could work. I'd finally tasted freedom.

I just had to stay out of Nila's clutches and do what I was born to do.

Fisting my cock, I thrust into my palm.

"You won't win this time, Nila," I growled. "I want you out of my head. Out of my fucking heart."

Get out.

My quads tensed as bliss danced with pain. I was rough, punishing my cock for having the audacity to want the one thing that could destroy me. My balls tightened, delicious pleasure gathered in my belly.

Fuck, I wanted her. I wanted to be inside her.

I needed to stay far away from her.

My fingers squeezed harder.

You can't have her.

Not if I wanted what Cut promised. Not if I wanted to rule.

My mind raced. I might not be able to have her physically, but Cut would never know what fantasies I allowed inside my fractured brain.

I could have her like this—and still win.

With one hand braced on the tiles and water cascading over my shoulders, I imagined Nila spread-eagled on the bed, tied to four corners and panting from an orgasm I'd just given her with my tongue.

Her taste filled my mouth as I climbed on top of her and slid deep inside her wet pussy.

Goddammit.

Her moans echoed in my ears as I thrust inside her, giving into her tightness, dropping every restraint and shackle.

I came.

It was the fastest orgasm I'd ever had. Ribbon after ribbon, I spurted over my knuckles.

Jerking beneath the water, I rid my body of the insanity she'd conjured and slowly…interminably slowly…I could breathe again.

"Where are we going?"

Her melodic voice was anything but soothing. After a night of tossing and berating myself for how weak I turned out to be, I wasn't in the mood to deal with her—*especially* with her looking rested and fresh in jeans and an off-the-shoulder jumper with her hair plaited and just begging to be fisted while I took her from behind.

She didn't look nervous or fearful—she looked defiant and ready to battle.

"So, you're ignoring me now?"

"Not ignoring you, just filtering out your useless questions." I didn't turn to face her. Instead, I kept driving. Guiding the four-seater Ferrari FF away from Hawksridge Hall, I looked into the rear-view mirror.

I'd made the mistake of sitting Nila in the front with me. I should've put her in the back with Kestrel.

He caught my gaze, smirking a little as if he knew exactly what I was dealing with but didn't give a toss. Awful thing was he *did* know exactly what I was dealing with and whatever sympathy he'd given me in the past had long since dried up.

It fucking hurt to have my closest ally wash his hands of me.

Nila spun in her seat, the tan leather creaking beneath her. "You tell me, Kes. Why was my morning spent sketching my so-called 'wedding dress' interrupted by a mysterious trip off the estate?" Her voice lowered. "You've only just gotten me back—why am I being given outings when I was told I would never leave again?"

Kes chuckled, his silvering hair longer and slightly shaggy. "That's a lot of questions."

Nila deadpanned. "I have a lot of confusion."

Kes had changed a bit since I'd last seen him—withdrawing from me just like I withdrew from him.

Our fight came back with crystal clarity. It'd been two or three days after Cut had given me the ultimatum: *Drugs and keep Nila for myself. Die and give Nila to Daniel.* Kes had raged at me. He wanted me to give in and trust that together we could find another way. Only, he didn't know the sentence Cut had given. It wasn't his business. It was *my* curse. *My* responsibility to stay alive in order to protect Nila even while being cruel to her. And I had to use the tablets to remain sane enough to do that.

I don't need him anymore—just like I don't need my sister.

Kes laughed harder. The friendship between him and Nila sprang instantly back into place as if she'd never gone. How could they have such a bond when they were practically strangers?

I'd lived all my life with these people and still wasn't comfortable in their company. The numbness from my tablets meant I'd deliberately distanced myself from those I was closest to, so their feelings and thoughts wouldn't sway my conviction. But to have Kes laugh so easily with Nila, when he was stilted and removed with me, hurt in a way I would never admit.

"Perhaps if you practice patience, you'll find out soon enough," I snapped.

Kes scowled, his hands clasped between his legs, his leather jacket and jeans filling up the rear of the car with authority only wealth can bring. "Everything is different now, Jet. You know that. If she asks, we tell her. Cut's orders."

Nila twisted further in her chair, eyes wide. "What does that mean?"

"It means that things have changed and our secrets…well, they're not just ours anymore." He leaned forward, his bulk crowding the centre console. "Try me. Ask anything and I'll answer."

I ground my teeth.

Nila bit her lip. "Okay…answer my first question. Where are we going?"

Kes didn't hesitate. "Diamond Alley."

"Diamond Alley?" Her mouth popped open. "What is that?"

I glanced warningly at Kes in the rear-view mirror. He was right. The rules had changed. But it was still my call what she learned, where she went, who she interacted with. I was both her protector and jailer. Confidant and confessor. Even though I didn't want our connection to hurt me anymore, she was still mine until the end.

Kes scowled at my reflection before giving Nila his full attention. "You want the truth, Nila?"

Her lips thinned. "I've been asking for the truth for months. Of course, I want it."

"The truth is sometimes worse than reality," I murmured under my breath.

She sent me a look, but the question in her eyes assured me she hadn't heard.

Kes settled back in the Ferrari bucket seat. "Okay, here it is. We're taking you to one of our shipping warehouses. Diamond Alley is where most of what we mine enters England. We have a few distribution centres all over Europe, Asia, and America, but this one is closest to home and where we run the others overseas."

And just like that Nila became an honouree Hawk.

I hope you're ready for this ride, Nila, because once you know, you can never forget.

Nila absorbed that for a second, discounting hundreds of questions fleeting in her eyes. Taking a deep breath, she nodded. "Alright…and what does this have to do with me?"

I answered before Kes could. "What you're about to see is the truth. You will know where the stones come from. What they look like. How much we earn. Who works for us. Where the rocks end up. How we pay off the police. How we run fucking England. There will be no more secrets on who we are or what we expect of you. Answers will be given on every topic."

I glared at her. "You'll know *everything*. Every scrap of history, hope, dream, and disaster of our family and yours."

Nila's eyes glowed. "And what did I do to deserve such trust?"

My fists tightened around the steering wheel.

Because you're special.

Kes smiled sadly. "Because you proved yourself."

She tensed. "How exactly?"

"You spoke to the reporter. You dug your own grave," I murmured. "And no matter how much you want to, you won't be leaving Hawksridge again. Cut has made sure of that. Bonnie has made sure of that. You have nowhere else to go."

Nila's face went white, finally realising what she'd done. Kes and I stayed silent, waiting for her to verbalize her fate.

Her voice shook. "You no longer need to hide anything from me, because I won't be around much longer to share it."

Bingo.

I groaned quietly as a despairing cloud filled the car. The unhappiness, regret, and anger resonating from Nila was too much. Flicking the button on the steering wheel, I wound down the windows, blasting cold autumn air into the car.

I inhaled greedily, trying to dispel the lacerations of her anguish.

Nila shivered, hugging herself with white fingers.

Kes said, "You see…the truth is a bitch, but you've earned the right to know everything. Any question you want answered…we'll tell you. Every facet of our enterprise and brotherhood, you'll know."

Placing his hand on hers, he smiled softly. "You're one of us now, Nila. Forever and always. The world knows it. Your father and brother know it. There is nothing else to say on the matter."

She twisted in her seat, looking to the left where the moor and the graves of her ancestors rested. A chill scattered down my spine.

"So I'll be buried on your land to hide all the secrets I'll be privy to. Just like them." Her head fell forward. "I'm so *unbelievably* stupid. About everything."

I opened my mouth to agree—to dig the blade of unhappiness a little deeper. But…I couldn't.

No amount of drugs could make me kick her when she was already bleeding. I wouldn't be able to withstand the backlash, not to mention the rapidly building agony in my heart.

I thought the tablets would save me. Nila wasn't the only one who'd been stupid.

We're both fucked, and it's up to me to hide my issues so Cut leaves her alone.

I couldn't stand the stagnant sadness in the car. Unable to stop myself, I whispered, "You'll like what we have to show you, Nila. You'll see. You're one of us now, and it's time you understand what my family has been fighting to protect for generations."

Diamond Alley.

Nicknamed centuries ago by an ancestor who no doubt graced Hawksridge walls in some depressing painting. It'd gotten its name due to the four huge warehouses facing each other, creating a narrow road between them.

Driving here took a couple of hours, but it was worth it to have our very own port—unwatched and unmolested—yet another example of being above the laws governing the masses.

No light entered, only shadows. Electric fences, keycards, and passwords fortified the entrance. Located on the coast between sleepy seaside towns where the police force was entirely owned by us, we guarded our domain carefully. Greased pockets and yearly bonuses, we paid the coppers handsomely but we required strict loyalty.

I'd bloodied my hands a few times over the years teaching one or two traitors who didn't follow the rules a lesson.

Slowing to enter a key code at the front gate, conversation remained scarce as I drove through the compound and parked the Ferrari. The only cars and motorbikes here were those of trusted employees. No sightseers or holidaymakers. No one had any reason to visit, and it wasn't on any map. The two long fingers of warehouses looked derelict on the outside, but top-of-the-line security equipment, heat sensors, and bulletproof glass guarded their contents.

We protected our investment.

Pity the Weavers didn't do a good job protecting theirs.

The moment the car was stationary, Kes tapped Nila's shoulder. "Shall we?"

She unbuckled her belt and scooted out of the bucket seat without a backward glance. Kes climbed out and slammed the door.

I was left all alone.

Thank fuck for that.

I stretched my arms in front of me, rolling my neck and exhaling the magnitude of emotions I'd absorbed in the journey here. We hadn't spoken since leaving Hawksridge, but Nila's thoughts bombarded me mile after fucking mile.

Nila and Kes drifted away, heading toward the warehouse. With shaking hands, I fumbled for my pills and took another before climbing from the vehicle and locking it.

I had a horrible thought that I'd need a tranquiliser in order to make it through the journey home. It made me contemplate turning to alcohol and nicotine for other escapes—finding respite in chemicals and false highs.

Running my hands over my face, I trailed after my brother and little Weaver. Today was a simple transaction of overseeing a new arrival. Normally, Daniel would take care of it, but there was something else lined up. Something I'd agreed to unbeknownst to Cut and entirely on my own head if it didn't work out.

My Black Diamond jacket kept the sea breeze away, and the watery sun did its best to warm up the cool day. Stringy grey clouds shadowed the bland concrete beneath my shoes. It didn't matter that it was gloomy and bland outside—inside Diamond Alley, we didn't need sunshine.

We made our own.

A few metres away, Kes held out his arm for Nila to take. I waited for her to accept. I waited to see what I would feel. But she shook her head and kept her distance, preferring to glance at the gentle lapping ocean to our right and inhale the seaweed stench of kelp-covered rocks.

We made our way toward the entrance of Diamond Alley. The shadows of the huge buildings swallowed us as we traded open space for cramped alleyway.

My dress shoes clipped regally against the concrete while Kes's biker boots crunched and stomped. Nila made no noise at all, drifting forward in her flat ballet shoes, so young and innocent.

For a month, I'd lived without her. I'd visited the Weaver quarters often and fingered the half-finished designs she'd been working on.

The place had been empty, howling with injustice. I couldn't stay in there long, too attuned to her smell and lingering presence. I'd told myself it was to desensitise myself for when she returned, but in reality, I was looking into the future—trying to see how I'd feel when she'd be gone for good.

Her room would be even emptier.

Her soul vanished forever.

Kes stopped halfway down the alley at a door. He knocked three times in a systemic code, and looked above the bombproof veneer to a camera.

A screen lit up with the face of one of our trusted guards. He glanced at us, nodded, then switched the screen to a keypad that scanned fingerprints as well as demanded a nine-digit passkey.

Nila remained silent as Kes entered everything he needed and the large mechanism unlocked, permitting entry.

Together we moved forward, leaving behind cramped laneways for the most dazzling sunlight imaginable.

"Wow," Nila breathed, squinting against the brilliant light.

It was blazing.

Far, far too bright.

Kes and I came prepared.

He chuckled, placing Ray-bans on his nose. "Rather cool, huh?"

Sliding my sunglasses from my front pocket, I placed the aviators over my eyes. Snapping my fingers, I held out my hand for the guard to give me a spare pair.

Instantly, a girlish retro pair was pressed into my palm, which I passed to

Nila. "The lights are necessary."

Nila took the glasses, fumbling to put them on. "I've never been somewhere so bright."

"You'll see why it's like this."

"I'll get going," Kes said. "I'll come find you when I'm done." Patting his pocket, he moved away. "Got my phone if you need me. Have fun, Nila." With a wave, he prowled down the centre corridor of the huge open plan warehouse and disappeared.

Nila looked left and right. We stood in the centre of the four-story building where track lighting and halogen spotlights dangled like false suns. Not only had we traded a dreary autumn outside, but we'd also traded the cold for muggy heat.

Sweat already prickled my lower back beneath my leather jacket. I used to hate wearing this thing. I was a businessman, not a thug in a gang, but Cut wanted me to take over not just our Hawk legacy but the Black Diamonds, too.

And what Cut wanted, I was determined to deliver.

"Stop standing and staring, let's walk." Placing a hand on her lower back, I guided her forward.

She instantly sucked in a breath at the contact.

I waited for my fingers to burn and my heart to jolt…but I felt nothing.

The extra dose finally did what they should.

Nila drifted forward, her eyes taking in the rows upon rows of tables. They faced each other like little cubicles, some manned with staff, others empty. But all of them had numerous trays, tweezers, magnifying glasses, loupes, and black velvet covering the table-tops.

"Why is it so bright in here?" she asked, keeping pace with me.

"You're in a diamond warehouse. Light is the one tool to highlight flaws from perfections, clarity from cloud."

Despite the size of our operation, only thirty full-time staff worked for us in Diamond Alley. They'd been vetted, tested, and knew when they'd started working for us that it wasn't a simple position. Once they signed on the bottom line, there was no quitting or second-guessing their profession. They were ours for life.

To ensure we had no mutiny or unrest, we increased their salary every year, gave them room for promotion, and even compensated their families.

We'd never had an unhappy staff member. But then again, if they were caught stealing, pilfering, or tampering with the merchandise…well, a human life wasn't worth as much as a diamond.

Nila edged closer. "They're all in their underwear."

I eyed the staff members who didn't bother glancing up—too engrossed in their task and eager to hit their bonus for the day by clearing a certain amount of stones. Various skin colour, contrasting sizes, different sexes—but all one similarity—they all wore black underwear provided by the company.

I nodded. "A condition of employment."

"Why?"

"I thought it would be obvious? Fewer hiding places. Not to mention, they don't need clothing with the amount of heat generated from the lights."

Sweat moistened my brow as we reached the end of the warehouse and climbed the metal steps to the office above. Our footfalls clanged with every climb, shuddering the framework.

"And you sit up there and play God, I suppose," Nila muttered as we ascended toward the glass-fronted office with its bird's eye-view down the length of the building.

"It's a shared office for managers, but in a way we do. After all, we provide a livelihood to the people below us. We treat them well as long as they behave."

"A bit like me then." She darted ahead, opening the door and slinking into the office.

Following her, my eyes drank in the glistening sweat on her upper lip and tendrils of hair from her plait sticking to her nape. "You look warm, Ms. Weaver. You could always strip, you know. You are, after all, technically a Hawk employee."

She bit her lip, the air flaring between us with static electricity.

Shit, why did I say that?

She lowered her gaze, not hiding the way she ogled me. "Perhaps I should."

Instantly, my cock twitched.

"But only if you strip, too."

I slammed the door and brushed past her. "Not going to happen."

Never again. I couldn't afford to sleep with her. Not if I wanted to stay in my drugged-bubble.

The office was sparse. Bare metal floors, filing cabinets bolted to the walls, a cowhide couch, and a desk in the centre.

Nila stalked me, moving toward the desk I placed between us. "Do you want me to strip because you don't trust me around the stones or because you want me naked?" Her hands tugged at the jumper cascading off her shoulder. Pulling it further down, the swell of her breast and the tantalizing hint of black lace appeared. "Get naked with me, Jethro. Or don't you trust yourself around me anymore?"

I gritted my teeth, forcing myself not to react. My cock completely ignored me, thickening to a steel fucking rod in my pants. Doing my utmost to seem unaffected, I switched on the desk lamp and picked up one of the many Post-it notes and memos stuck to the walnut desk. "Don't flatter yourself. I told you before, I'm not interested anymore."

Nila came closer, her fingertips dragging over the table-top. "Not interested...or not allowed?"

My head snapped up. "Be careful."

"No."

"*What* did you just say?"

She narrowed her eyes. "I'm tired of being careful. Being careful only brought me heartache. All my life I've been careful, and you know what? I'm *sick* of it."

With an erotic twist, she grabbed the hem of her jumper and tugged it over her head. Her plait draped down her back and the tiny white camisole she wore didn't hide the lacy bra beneath.

Fuck.

It also didn't hide her pebbled nipples.

"Does this count as being careful, *Kite*?" Nila dropped the jumper onto the desk, cupping her breasts. "Does this count as acceptable to you?"

I couldn't breathe.

Everything I'd been running from made my head pound, my cock beg, and the drugs in my system to fucking disintegrate.

What was it about her? Why did she have this control over me? And why was I utterly, ridiculously helpless around her?

God fucking help me.

Didn't she know the more she antagonised me and made me slip, the more likely Cut would give her to Daniel and slaughter me in my sleep? I wanted to strike her—hammer the precariousness of our situation home.

"Why did you bring me here?" she murmured, skirting the desk.

I couldn't tear my eyes away from the hard pinpricks on her chest. She couldn't be cold—not in this furnace. That meant she was turned on.

My mind instantly went to one question. *Is she wet?*

"Kes told you. Our secrets are now yours."

"I don't think that's the only reason." Closing the distance, she licked her bottom lip. "I think you wanted me off the estate, so you could have me without anyone seeing." Her voice layered with sex and invitation. "You wanted me away from the cameras, so you could drop the act and show me the truth."

Fuck.

I cleared my throat. "What truth?"

"That all of this is a lie. That you're still the man I fell for—playing the same game you said you were sick of before I left."

Shaking my head, I tried to clear my thoughts. "You're once again delusional." Swallowing hard, I ordered, "Go down to the sorting floor. I have a meeting to take care of—"

"No," she breathed. "I'm not going anywhere until you stop being an arsehole and show me the real you." Closing the final distance, she stood beside me, crackling with mischief and lust.

Locking eyes, she undid the button and zipper of her jeans. "Don't hide from me, Jethro. I can't stay strong if you cut me out."

My legs bunched to push the swivel chair backward. One heave and I could launch myself free and run from her web. But somehow, I couldn't. I remained tethered in place; breathing fast, fear swamping my lungs.

She grabbed my wrist. "Don't fight it. You can't fight the inevitable." Without a word, she pressed my hand into her trousers.

Holy shit.

My heart catapulted through my ribcage; my jaw locked as the scratch of her lacy underwear rubbed my knuckles.

Our eyes never looked away as she guided my fingers lower. I tugged half-heartedly, trying to remember why this was wrong when it felt so fucking right.

"Don't…" She rocked her hips, twisting my wrist so my hand cupped her wetness.

She moaned, her head falling back. Her breasts were proud, jutting out, begging for my teeth and tongue. "That's what you were wondering, wasn't it?" She bent over me, licking the rim of my ear. "If I was wet for you?"

I groaned as she deliberately rubbed herself on my fingertips.

My eyes snapped shut as she eased her underwear aside, guiding my finger inside her.

I stopped breathing. I stopped worrying. I couldn't do anything but give in.

My cock punched against my belt. Pain existed everywhere. It took everything I had not to grab her and fuck her over my desk.

Her plait dangled as she breathed in my ear, "Take me, Kite. Fill me like you did in the spring. I'm yours and you belong inside me. Nobody can change that." She rocked again, moaning softly. "I want you."

"Nila…"

I want you, too. I want to tell you everything. I want to fucking run away and never look back…

"Well, this is an interesting sight."

Nila shot upright. "Oh, my God."

Yanking my hand from her jeans, I shoved her behind my chair. "I told you I had a fucking meeting," I growled.

She fumbled with nerves, struggling to do up her trousers. Her eyes narrowed at our guest, anxiety waking off her in droves.

For once, I didn't mind. I rather enjoyed her flustered need. Her unsettled confusion.

Spinning my chair around, so the man in the doorway wouldn't see, I raised the finger that'd been inside her and ever so slowly, sucked it clean. Her taste exploded on my tongue. I could've come right there if we didn't have an audience.

Nila stumbled, her hands crossing over her chest to hide the sheer camisole and bra.

"I have a feeling I interrupted something. However, I'm not going to be the gentleman and say sorry. I'm just going to stand right here and wait." The man laughed quietly. "By all means, continue if you must. I'm a patient guy."

Nila looked over my head, swallowing desire and frustration. "Not at all. I was just leaving."

Moving fast, I latched my damp fingers around her wrist and tugged to whisper in her ear. "Whatever you just started…it's not over."

Her eyes widened as I let her go.

I spun back to face my guest. "Hello, Killian."

Nila sneaked forward to snag her jumper. I chuckled under my breath. How could she be so sensually confident one moment and so flummoxed the next? "Nila Weaver, seeing as you delayed me, please say hello to my business meeting."

The man in the doorway nodded, filling the frame with his large bulk and brown leather jacket. The stitching of his MC glittered with the words 'Prez' and 'Pure Corruption.'

Nila blushed, slipping into her top. "Pleasure to meet you…"

"Kill," the man said, stalking into the room and holding out his hand. A smirk spread his lips, remembering what he'd interrupted. "On second thought, perhaps I won't give you my hand. I don't know what you'll do with it."

Nila turned a deeper pink. Her eyes hit the floor.

I laughed.

Serves her right for unsettling me.

Standing, I crossed the room and shook hands with the president of Pure Corruption. Standing taller than me with muscles bigger than Kestrel and black hair brushing his jaw, Killian screamed violence and influence. He wasn't someone you messed with.

His huge grip clasped mine. "Nice to see you again, Hawk."

Nila sized him up, interest glowing beneath her shyness.

It pissed me off, but I wasn't worried. It was well-known that Arthur Killian of the Florida Pures didn't go after women. He wasn't gay, but for some reason he avoided the opposite sex.

Kill dropped my hand, crossing his arms with a creak of leather. "Now that the intros are out of the way…shall we begin?"

I COULDN'T TAKE my eyes off the new intruder.

I wanted to back away to become as invisible as possible.

The entire atmosphere of the room changed the moment he'd stepped inside. Jethro was sleek and cool—as flawless as ice and as deadly as poison, but Arthur Killian was like a tank. A weapon reeking of biker oil, sunshine, and fearlessness. My body completely belonged to Jethro, but I couldn't deny Killian's massive arms, untamed hair, and glowing emerald eyes didn't flutter my stomach.

Coming toward me, his clothing rustled as he held out his hand. "No matter how much I fear for my hand's safety, I can't ignore such a stunning woman." The air hummed with fierce intensity.

My gaze flickered to Jethro as I looped my fingers with his. Jethro stiffened but didn't retaliate. My cheeks burned as Killian's grip wrapped tightly around mine.

He was so *warm.*

An oven compared to Jethro. And his eyes. Oh, my God, I'd never seen such green, green eyes.

"It's not *your* hand that should be worried."

Only yours, Kite. I shot the silent message to Jethro.

Killian laughed. It sounded like a rumbling earthquake. He shook his head almost sadly, glancing over his shoulder at Jethro before looking back at me. "In that case, I don't know if I should be jealous of Hawk's hand or regretful for my own." His deep voice was rhythmic—an accented drawl different to Jethro's crisp English loquacity.

"You're American?"

Kill took a step back, running a hand through his jaw-length dark hair. He looked wild, ferocious, but with a brokenness about him speaking of unpredictability.

What hurt him? Or *who?*

The vulnerability hiding beneath his rough exterior called to the nurturing side of me. I wanted to protect him from something. But what? There was nothing in the world that could hurt this mountain of a man.

Kill nodded. "Yes, ma'am. Born and bred in Florida."

"What are you doing so far from home?"

His large boots clopped across the metal floor as he sat on the cow-print couch by the door. Bright spotlights shone behind him, casting him in a fuzzy silhouette. His eyes narrowed, tone turning dark. "Business, mainly. And new connections."

The way he said it didn't sound just about business.

I'd been around dangerous men enough to recognise one with a vendetta. "And Jethro is going to help you with that?"

"Nila...don't pry." Jethro appeared by my side, wrapping a chilly arm around my shoulders. His strength suffocated me, tightening like a boa constrictor instead of a simple embrace.

My eyes shot to his. In the presence of a man who wore his vitality and emotions in full view, Jethro seemed even more remote. A damn island surrounded by shark-infested waters with ice for waterfalls and snow for sand.

Stepping out of his hold, I crossed my arms. "Does Killian know what you've done to me? What your family has done to mine?" It was a ridiculous move and one I would never normally do. But Killian made me bold.

Jethro froze.

His eyes turned deadly. "Enough." Pointing at the door, he growled, "Time for you to leave."

Kill laughed. "She your old lady?"

Jethro turned his temper on the burly man commandeering the entire couch with his bulk. "We don't have misses or old ladies in our MC. We're more of a business enterprise rather than a brotherhood."

Kill shook his head. "Doesn't matter. I run the Pures as a business, too. But we're still family."

I jumped in. "The Black Diamonds aren't family. They're employees."

Kill cocked his head, pinning his vibrant emerald eyes on me. "And you...are *you* an employee?" His gaze drifted down my front, drinking me in.

My heart beat faster, subjected to his scrutiny. His interest was visceral, but it wasn't sexual.

I stood taller, balling my hands. "No, I'm—" *His Weaver Whore. The woman destined to die for ludicrous debts.*

"She's not an employee," Jethro snapped. "She's a pain in my ass and needs to leave." He herded me toward the door. "You've pushed and pushed me today." Lowering his voice, he added, "Wait till we get home. You'll pay the price."

I spun in his hold, causing his hand to go from my lower back to my belly. I gasped as his long fingers brushed my bare midriff below my jumper.

"That threat doesn't scare me."

"Oh, no? It should."

I inched closer, cursing the wetness building between my legs. "It doesn't because I'm brave enough to give myself over to you. You're terrified of me and all I need to say is 'Kiss me, Jethro Hawk' and we'll see who wins again."

He sucked in a harsh breath. "You'll pay—"

"Watch me." Tearing my eyes from his, I looked at Kill again. "To answer your question, I'm not his employee. I'm so much more than that." My heart broke a little for a dream I would never have. "I could be his everything, but he's too stupid to see what I'm offering."

Killian's face seemed to shatter, his own heartbreak slamming into mine. I felt a kinship with him. A mirroring echo to our hidden desires. He'd been hurt by someone just like Jethro was hurting me.

Fists and kicks and bullets might maim and destroy, but love…love tears out your insides and leaves you hollow, leaving you destined to live an empty existence until death. Lucky for me, I wouldn't have to live long knowing Jethro could never love me.

Jethro pinched the bridge of his nose, fumbling for something in his pocket. "Goddammit, woman. Get out."

Kill perched on the edge of the couch, a black shadow shading his face. "Wait, you love him?"

My heart lurched. I couldn't look at Jethro as I confessed, "I do. And believe me, if I knew of a way to stop it, I would."

Jethro turned into a vibrating ice sculpture. He tipped something into his palm—something small and white.

Kill glared at Jethro, his temper eddying around the room. "Did you know she loved you?"

Jethro sucked in a breath. "What the fuck sort of question is that?" Throwing the pill into his mouth, he swallowed.

What the hell is he taking?

Kill crossed his arms. "A simple one."

I looked at Jethro, waiting for his answer, begging him to snap out of whatever his father had done and *admit it*. What was the harm? Why couldn't he put me out of my misery and profess he felt what I did?

"Kite…" I whispered. "Answer it."

Jethro's eyes latched with mine. He trembled.

Please…stop pushing me away.

Stop being so cruel.

"There is no simple answer." Jethro's voice was strained, full of rocks.

Kill stood up, a huge wrecking ball about to decimate us. Ignoring Jethro, he brushed past and cupped my cheek so tenderly, it broke something that'd been festering inside me for months. "Love is something that strikes without warning to the most unsuspecting. It's a fucking gift and so goddamn priceless, but only the worthy realise what they have. Only the ones truly deserving fight every fucking day to treasure it. And those who don't…they end up alone."

Dropping his hand, he glowered at Jethro. "I pity people who can't be true to their hearts. But I'm done prying into your private lives." He stormed back to the couch. "Leave, Nila. Hawk and I have business, and I want to get it over with."

Jethro glared. His voice skittered into my ear. "Thanks a lot. Good fucking work."

He shoved me out the door. "Go play with diamonds, Ms. Weaver, and leave me to worry about what repercussions your little stunt has caused."

Before I could say a word, he slammed the door and yanked down the inner shutters. He left me stranded and alone, drenched in spotlights, dancing in rainbows from precious stones.

An hour passed.

A full hour of waltzing down rows upon rows of diamonds while wearing sunglasses indoors. I'd never seen so much wealth in one place and in so many varieties.

There were cloudy, uncut rocks that looked like any old stone. There were brilliantly faceted marquise, cushion, and princess.

Each and every one sent my heart throbbing, because each and every one symbolised just how much wealth the Hawks had and the lengths they would go to protect it.

I snorted. *They value rocks more than human life.*

My mind skipped back to Jethro and the tablets he'd taken. Were they the reason for his dramatic change? And if so…what could I do to detox him and make him mine again?

The staff smiled as I made my way through the middle of the warehouse. I walked strictly down the centre, not wanting to get too close to the desks and black velvet just in case I was accused of stealing.

I would never do such a thing, but for now, I had no clue what went on inside Jethro's head. Cut might be biding his time for me to screw up to hurt me. This might be some crazy test.

I dawdled as long as I could, before turning and making my way back toward the office. Looking into the heights of the building, I frowned. The shutters were still in place, no hint of life.

How much longer is he going to be?

"You can touch, you know."

My attention whipped to the side. A man with a beer gut and goatee motioned me closer. "They're not poisonous."

I shook my head, keeping my hands behind my back. "It's okay. I'm more of a looker than a toucher."

The man grinned, showing a gold-capped tooth and lines around his mouth. With stubby fingers, he chose a stone from the tray in front of him and placed it on his palm. The brilliant lights highlighted the dull quartz, and despite myself, I drifted closer.

"Give me your hand."

"No, really—"

"Look, you came with the owner. You wear millions of their diamonds around your neck. I think they'll let you hold a boring rock like this."

My hand shot to the collar. The diamonds were warm beneath my touch, humming with vitality—almost as if they recognised their kin.

"When you put it that way." Taking my sunglasses off, I pushed them on top of my head and hesitantly held out my hand.

"There you go." He plopped the rock into my palm. I tried to ignore how strange it was to be talking to a half-naked man in a sweltering diamond factory.

When I just stood there, fearing that any moment Kes would arrive with a gun or Cut would chuckle and hurt me, the man shook his head. "Nothing to be scared of." He pointed at the stone. "Roll it between your fingers, feel the smoothness even though it hasn't been cut yet."

I obeyed, stroking the cloudy diamond and feeling the same strange warmth emitting as my necklace. "It feels alive."

The man nodded. "The heat from the lamps keep them temperate, but it also comes from the diamond itself. There's an old tale that true diamonds could heat the world. That they hold enough life and love in each stone that we would never be cold again."

Sadness fell over me. Jethro worked with heat-giving diamonds, yet I'd never known anyone so cold. "If that's true, I should be forever hot."

The man chuckled, reaching to stroke my collar. His chair squeaked as his belly dug into the table. "That you should." His head cocked, eyes feasting on the Weaver Wailer. "I've seen those stones before. They're old…very old." He frowned, then his face shocked white as he stole the rock from my hand.

My heart raced. "When…when did you see them?"

He pursed his lips, keeping his eyes downcast. "Never mind. Forget I said anything. Go on, carry on looking…there are much prettier rocks a few trays away."

I touched his knuckles, sickness and dread swimming in my veins. "You saw her, didn't you?"

He froze. "Saw who?"

I sighed heavily as my mother appeared in my mind. She'd been here. She'd lived through everything I had—a carbon copy of myself. "A woman with shoulder-length black hair, dark eyes, and high cheekbones." My voice trailed to a whisper. "I've been told we look similar…you don't need to deny it. You saw my mother."

The man swallowed. "I don't think I'm allowed to talk about the past, Miss." His eyes shot upward to the office. "Shit."

His curse was out of character. I looked up.

My heart fell into my toes.

Jethro.

He stood on the metal staircase, halfway down. One hand on the banister, the other in his trouser pocket. His requisite diamond pin glinted on his lapel looking small compared to the size of some of the stones surrounding us. The lights dazzled, causing his golden eyes to sparkle like the champagne diamonds on the tray before me—just as unique and perfectly cold. Unlike the diamond I'd held, there was nothing flawed about this man.

Apart from his mind, of course.

The more time I spent with him, the more confident I was that Jethro and I were the same in that respect.

I had a physical imbalance. My body hadn't mastered the art of equilibrium and occasionally malfunctioned. Jethro, on the other hand, had a mental imbalance but in what I hadn't figured out.

You have a sneaking suspicion, though.

Ever since speaking to Vaughn when we watched one line instead of two appear on the pregnancy test, I'd wondered. Could it be that obvious? Or that surprising?

I need to see Jasmine again.

I hadn't forgotten the way she'd sobbed as I left—not for me, but her brother. She knew everything, and it was time she shared that knowledge.

Jethro descended the stairs, his eyes never leaving mine.

"Best move along," the man whispered.

I didn't want to get him in trouble, but I couldn't move.

Jethro glided toward us, his gaze narrowed against the glare of the lights.

"Are you enjoying your time inspecting the merchandise, Ms. Weaver?" Jethro smiled curtly at the man beside me. "Christopher, I hope you are indulging my guest's every whim."

Christopher swallowed, a droplet of sweat running down his naked chest. "Um, yes, sir." He shot me a glance, awkwardness all over his face.

I felt sorry for him but furious for my mother. Grabbing Jethro's arm, I pulled him away from Christopher's table. Anger bubbled in my veins. "He was kind and helpful and under no circumstances will you discipline him, but he told me something interesting." Looping my fingers beneath my choker, I growled, "He said he'd seen my collar before."

Jethro stopped breathing.

"I'm assuming that meant my mother was brought here."

He didn't reply.

"She was given the same privileges, wasn't she? Because everything she learned was destroyed when Cut took her life."

He balled his hands.

Suddenly, it was all too much. I sighed. "Don't worry. I won't force you to talk. I won't ever attempt to make you do anything again. Can we just leave? I want to go home."

The minute I said it, visions of my quarters at Hawksridge came to mind...not home in London with Vaughn. I groaned under my breath. Even my memories had replaced my past with all things Hawk.

Jethro still didn't say a word, his pale skin growing whiter the longer he stared.

I stared right back.

His body vibrated the longer we stood in silence.

Then, he snapped.

Stealing my wrist, he stormed down the aisle, dragging me with him. "Goddammit, why must everything in my fucking life be so hard?"

"Wait." I tugged on his hold. "Where are we going?"

"Quiet."

I looked back to the office; perhaps that massive Pure Corruption biker could save me? If I told him everything—would I stand a chance at getting free? "Where did Kill go?"

"Gone."

"Back to Florida?"

Would I be safe from you if I flew to America?

"No, to the next warehouse to pick up what we promised."

I stumbled; the pace Jethro set was manic. "What did you promise?"

"Something in return for something else."

"What something else?"

"He's a genius with numbers—hides dirty money in many ways."

"And what does he get?"

Jethro groaned under his breath. "Questions. Always bloody questions with you."

I shrugged. "As Kestrel said, I've dug my own grave. My questions can be answered now."

Including the ones I really want to know. Like who you truly are and why you won't let me in!

Coming to the end of the warehouse, he opened a door and dragged me down an empty corridor. At the end of that, there was a single exit. It looked like a janitor's closet, but the moment he opened it, it revealed a ginormous silver barricade with a keypad and spin dial.

Letting me go to enter in codes and spin the dial, he scowled. "Fine. You want to know? I'll tell you." The mechanism *snicked* open and the air pressure shifted a little. With a grunt, he yanked the thick vault open and motioned me to enter.

Deciding to obey and avoid his biting fingers, I entered the large safe.

Jethro followed, sighing in relief at the temperature change. Inside was bright but cool—the buzz of air-conditioners kept the space chilly compared to the warm warehouse.

I expected to see stacks of cash and precious gems, but all that existed were walls of gunmetal grey safety deposit boxes.

"You asked. I'll tell." Waving at the space, Jethro said, "All of this is to control the world we live in. We're untouchable because of these tiny pieces of rock. We've built an empire on wealth accumulated from a single incident in our past that enabled us to leap over the heads of the Weavers and prove that they might've owned England back then but *we* own it now."

"But how? Surely a mine would dry up after a time?"

"We don't just have one mine, Ms. Weaver. We have dozens all around the world."

Having my questions answered was a novelty—a saving grace. I never wanted to stop. "Where?"

"We mine diamonds in Africa, rubies in India, sapphires in Thailand, emeralds in Pakistan. We have the world's most exclusive catchment of Alexandrite—one of the rarest stones—and we also have this..."

Jethro moved to the back wall and used a key to open a safety deposit box. Pulling it out, the drawer went on for ages—a long grey finger sliding free from a wallpaper of squares.

Another twist of a key and the lid opened.

Without a word, Jethro reached into the shallow box and pulled out a red velvet pouch. Stitched into the plush material was the emblem for the Black Diamonds with his initials on the front.

The JKH was exactly the same as the one on my fingers.

My heart raced as he undid the strings, moving toward me. "Hold out your hand."

I didn't hesitate.

Jethro tipped the velvet pouch, plopping into my palm the blackest, richest, most incredible stone I'd ever seen. It looked like the devil's apple from the Garden of Eden. Large and gleaming and wrong. The weight alone made me grasp it with two hands. "Wow."

"The largest black diamond ever found."

The stone was uncut but still shone as if it were alive—as if it sensed me holding it and had eyes looking back at me. My skin tingled. I wanted to put it down—somehow I knew it didn't like me. "How big is it?"

"Six hundred carats." Jethro came closer, his spicy aftershave clouding around me. "It's the reason why we are what we are."

I blinked. "What do you mean?"

Jethro stole the stone, holding it up to the spotlight in the ceiling. "It was the third diamond my ancestors ever found. They didn't know what it was—we didn't know then that diamonds come in colours—pink, yellow, blue. They thought it was obsidian. But they knew they had something special. When they returned to England, they researched it. They had the top specialist from the Crown Jewels make an assessment."

He twisted the rock, his face pensive. "When they were told it was a black diamond, the name stuck. The men who'd helped my ancestors find it immediately became known by that name." He smiled. "Fancy that…a piece of history and you didn't have to pay a debt to hear it."

Chills scattered down my arms.

Up until that second, I'd revelled in hearing how the Hawks came into power. But he'd ruined it. Just like everything.

"How did your family go from serving my ancestors to mining massive rocks?"

Jethro shook his head. "That piece of information will come with a price."

"What price?"

Jethro pulled me into his body, his hardness instantly igniting my blood. "A debt, naturally."

I winced. "Can we not mention those again? Not when it's just us."

His eyes fell on my lips. "When it's just us, it's even more dangerous to talk…about anything." His head bowed; a lock of tinsel hair kissed his forehead. "I have something I need to ask." He tensed. "Not ask…demand."

"I prefer it if you just asked. You should know by now if you give into me, I'd do anything for you."

He let me go. "I need you to watch what you feel around me."

My mouth parted. "What?"

His eyes darted around the space, searching for help in silent corners. "I can't explain it, but whatever you think of me, whatever you think of the way I've treated you since you came back, keep it to yourself. Don't hate me. Don't love me. Don't fear me. Put up a wall and just stop."

"You're asking me to stop feeling?" I gasped. "That's like asking someone to stop *breathing*, Jethro. It's not possible."

He dragged a hand over his face. "Things changed, Nila, and if you want to remain mine—you have to do this for me."

Ice water replaced my blood. "Remain yours?" Drifting forward, I touched his forearm. "He threatened you, didn't he?" My heart lurched, blooming bright with the love I'd tried to smother. Whatever Jethro was or did, he *did* care for me, and that was why he suffered. "What did he do?"

Jethro backed away, his face twisting. "Nothing. That's one question I won't answer. Just do as I ask and your existence will continue without hardship."

I laughed softly. "You don't get it. Having you distant from me is the worst hardship of all." Taking his hand, I placed it over my heart. "You can't see the scars you're leaving on me but they're there, Jethro. As surely as the scars on my back from your whip."

"I can't keep doing this," he breathed, his shoulders caving.

"Can't keep doing what?"

"I can't keep doing *this*." He pushed me away, holding up the dark stone. "A black diamond is completely different to a white one."

I struggled to switch topics.

Why is he changing the subject?

"They have a different crystalline structure. They don't sparkle because they don't refract light." His eyes glittered. "They absorb it."

Where is he going with this?

"Like you? Absorbing Weaver lives."

He didn't answer, sadness darkening his face. "White diamonds are windows for light to bounce and reflect. Black diamonds are souls—sucking in everything, ingesting their environment and giving nothing in return."

His voice bristled with depth—it wasn't just about the stone. *He's trying to tell me something...*

My hands twitched to grab him. My lips burned to connect with his.

Tell me!

He couldn't look at me. He couldn't even admit what he revealed. However, the diamond was no longer an innate object—but him.

He absorbed and ingested. *He* was a direct product of his surroundings.

"You've absorbed me..." I breathed.

My voice shattered Jethro's confession, snapping him into ice. "Time to go." Slipping the mysterious black diamond back into its home, he locked the safety deposit box and took my hand.

I never mentioned the stone again.

Not during the long drive home with Kes.

Not lying in bed that night.

Jethro had finally admitted the truth.

And I had no idea what it meant.

TWO DAYS PASSED.

Two days where I avoided Nila, took copious amount of drugs, and tried my utmost to swim back into numbing fog.

The meeting at Diamond Alley with Killian and Nila in an enclosed space had been sheer fucking hell.

Both of them were so opinionated and strong willed. When Kill asked Nila if she loved me and Nila had fractured into pieces of grief, I'd almost snapped.

Almost.

She must've guessed what I was by now.

I couldn't seem to keep it a secret.

I was at the point where if she asked me again, I would tell her. I would spill every sordid detail and bullshit diagnosis. I couldn't hide it anymore.

The night after dropping her back at Hawksridge, Kestrel and I had dealt with a dispute with one of our traders on the black market. They wanted more stock for less money. We wanted more money for less stock. The age-old upsets between businesses.

The negotiations hadn't gone smoothly.

The tension between both sides drained me of my rapidly dwindling energy, and by the time we returned home, I wanted nothing to do with people and fled.

I'd hidden until the moon rose and I could escape without consequence. I needed fresh air. And I needed it now.

I revved my bike down the long drive, heading away from Hawksridge. Turning right off the estate, I leaned into a corner, speeding up until inertia became an enemy trying to steal me from my vehicle.

The rumble of the machine soothed me. The cool wind on my cheeks gave me room to breathe. And the power from the engine made me invincible.

But it was lacking.

I miss it.

I gritted my teeth.

You miss nothing.

I refused to admit that I missed my fucking horse.

I hadn't ridden since Nila paid the Second Debt. I doubted I would ride again. Not now I was the perfect son and life stopped playing me for a fool.

Every mile I travelled, the fog I craved wisped behind me until I was clearheaded for the first time in weeks. Out here with only squirrels and owls for company, it didn't matter. I sighed in relief as I reached the outskirts of Buckinghamshire and pulled over onto a verge.

I wasn't far from home, twenty minutes at most. But the rock walls and overhanging trees of the country lanes could've been centuries ago—so far removed from humanity and technology.

Killing the engine, I took off my helmet and fumbled for the pills in my leather jacket. I had no intention of going home without more drugs barricading my system.

"Goddammit," I growled, unable to open the bottle with my gloves on. Biting the middle finger of my glove, I yanked it off with my teeth.

The two tattoos of Nila's initials shone in the moonlight.

They sucker-punched me in the gut.

Fuck.

Everything I'd kept buried rose up unhindered on the desolate side of the road.

You're ruining everything.

I'm ruining nothing.

I was protecting my sister, my brother, myself. I was walking the line I'd been born to walk. I couldn't do any more than that, and if Nila expected more from me, then tough shit. I had nothing left to give.

A rustle and twig snapped in the field behind the mossy rock wall I'd stopped beside. My ears twitched for more; my eyes tried to see through the darkness.

I couldn't see a thing.

Ignoring the noise—putting it down to a badger or fox—I tipped a tablet into my hand and tossed it into my mouth. Already, my head pounded and hands shook. Withdrawal was a bitch.

I went to swallow.

I never had time to swallow.

Something hard and brutal struck the back of my skull. I slammed forward, crunching my nose on the handlebars, gushing with blood.

"Shit!" I didn't know which pain was worse—my nose or the back of my head.

"Travelling on your own, motherfucker?"

I stiffened. This was why we didn't go for midnight excursions alone. This was why I had bodyguards and ran a biker gang.

Thieves and vagrants.

Blinking through the pain, I shoved off my handlebars and glared into the night.

Three bikers from the Cannibal Chainmen MC climbed over the wall and landed on the road surrounding me.

Every muscle tightened.

"You." These arseholes had ambushed our deliveries for years. They knew never to step foot in Buckinghamshire. This was our fucking territory. They belonged in Birmingham—dirty scum.

"Get off our turf," I snarled, drinking blood and wiping the remainder on the back of my hand. Swinging my leg off my bike, I stood in their circle, turning slowly to inspect each one. "You know the consequences."

They were lowly ranked members, patched in, but held no position of authority.

"Oh, we know the consequences, alright." A guy with a shaved head and knuckles wrapped in red tape sneered.

"Messing with the Black Diamonds is a sure way to die." I spat a wad of blood on the ground, wishing the throb in my skull would fade. "I suggest you fuck off. Our turf. Our rules."

The biker laughed. "Ah, but if we take out the Vice President of the Blacks, then doesn't that make it *our* turf?"

That doesn't even make sense. Fucking idiots had to take out Cut for that to become a possibility. And that would never happen.

They continued to circle. Even though I was trapped in the centre, I guided them toward the middle of the road—away from the wall and my bike.

I needed open space to win.

I needed silence and darkness and no interruptions.

My hands curled, stretching knuckles and tendons, preparing to fight. I hadn't been in a battle for months. And…I needed one.

Fuck, I truly did.

I needed something to let off steam. To get rid of everything inside. To finally scream and rage and give into the hatred I never seemed to be free of.

These men had no idea what they'd just walked into.

The intensity I'd lived with all my life remained on a leash, but I slowly let it affect me. Drinking in their violence and bloodlust—I became infected.

In that moment, drenched in moonlight and starshine, I was free.

Free like I was on a polo field. Free like I was when I slid inside Nila.

Fuck, I've been so cruel to her.

Away from the Hall and the pressures of my life, I could see clearly. There was no fucking excuse for what I'd become.

"Made your peace, arsehole?" the bald man said, smiling at his two accomplices with dirty brown hair. They slipped out of their jackets, revealing grimy tank tops and tatted arms.

I cracked my neck, smiling with bloody teeth. "Have *you*?"

They laughed.

I laughed.

I moved first.

A shout fell from the leader's lips as I slammed my shoulder into his chest and bowled him to the asphalt. The moment his back smashed against the road, I punched him.

Over and over and *over*.

Face, nose, temple, throat.

I wasn't one to drag out a fight. Once I made up my mind, I did it. No second chances. No second guesses.

A rain of fists came down on my back and skull. I rolled off the leader, shooting to my feet.

The men threw a worried look at their unconscious comrade. "You'll die for that."

I shook my head. "Wrong."

They attacked together.

I wasn't expecting that. They seemed sloppy and unorganised, but they moved as one. I covered my head as they attacked.

It hurt.

The pain was good.

But their anger and feral temper was better.

It siphoned into my blood, feeding me, charging me.

I let loose.

I did what I'd fought against all my life.

My walls came down.

I drank in their poison.

And I killed those motherfuckers piece by fucking piece.

Nila

"IT'S ME. CAN I come in?"

I knocked again on Jasmine's door.

For the past two nights, I'd sneaked up the stone stairs and knocked. And for the past two nights, she'd ignored me.

I knew she was in there. The light shone beneath the door and the camera blinked above the frame. Occasionally, a shadow would roll past, but she never opened it.

I even tried the door handle to barge in uninvited. It was locked.

"Jasmine. I really need to talk to you." I pressed my forehead against the wood. "Before it's too late."

Time had a horrible way of ticking faster here.

Already, the month I'd spent away from Hawksridge faded into scratchy memories. Vaughn and my father messaged me continuously—neither satisfied with my response that I had to return. That I knew what I was doing.

Why would they believe me? Even *I* didn't believe me.

I had no clue how I would do what was needed.

Jethro avoided me. Cut laughed at me. And Daniel lurked in the background like fungus waiting to consume me. Every night hurtled me quicker toward another debt. The final one would soon be on the horizon, then all my options would be gone.

I couldn't afford to be blasé or slow.

I had to be smart and act fast.

I knocked again. "Please. Let me in."

Nothing.

I couldn't walk back to my room, not again. The past few nights, I'd turned into an insomniac and suffered every morning with a vicious vertigo attack.

I hadn't thrown up since leaving London, but every time my thoughts strayed to the contraceptive shot Jethro administered, my gut churned with sadness and rage.

Not that it mattered, seeing as he'd made no move to kiss me after the magazine picture—let alone sleep with me.

If I didn't win, I would never know the joy of having a child or being held in a man's arms while I grew big with his unborn baby. Vaughn would never have a niece or nephew and my father...I couldn't think about him without suffering awful anguish.

He would never have a grandchild. But I think...I think he'd always known that. He'd kept me away from men all my life, so I would never have the opportunity to fall in love and conceive——like my mother did before the Hawks took her.

She'd found her soul-mate before horror found her.

I'd found mine the day I'd been taken.

"Jasmine, I'm not leaving. Not this time." With a heavy heart, I turned around and slid down her door to the carpet.

I wasn't leaving until she came out.

I'd be there all night if I had to.

"Nila..." Jethro's eyes burned as bright and golden as the sun.

I melted in his arms, raising my lips for a tender, love-filled kiss. His lips were like sherbet——sweet and tingling and delicious. "I love you, Kite."

He squeezed me harder, his tongue entering my mouth to lick and taste.

I trembled. Pushing him backward, the field of daisies and clovers swayed magically in the summer breeze. We were all alone in this idyllic meadow; there was no one to ruin it.

No Hawks. No debts. No Weavers.

Just kisses and love.

Our clothes suddenly disappeared, and I ran the tip of my finger down his breastbone, along his defined stomach, following the small trail of hair to his groin.

Sliding down his body, I hovered my mouth over his erection. "I love bringing you pleasure."

His back shot upright as I guided him into my mouth, swirling my tongue and inhaling his taste.

His strong fingers slinked through my hair, holding me firm. His hips raised to meet my lips, pushing gently, pleading for more.

I didn't deny him.

I let him set the rhythm, growing wetter with every stroke of his cock in my mouth. Then I was moving, gathered in strong arms, and placed on top of his naked body.

He didn't speak as I straddled him, positioning myself over his erection.

We both cried out as I sank down his length.

Down and down. Deep and deep.

Planting my hands on his chest, I rocked on his huge size, shivering as he sheathed himself completely. Only once he'd claimed me did I open my eyes and look down.

The joy on his face.

The adoration in his gaze.

The blistering love in his every thought.

Tears bruised my eyes as he held up his hands and intertwined our fingers together. "I'm your anchor now, Nila. Ride me. Use me. Control me. I've always got you. I'll always catch you if you fall——"

I fell backward, tumbling through a wormhole, falling, falling.

The delicious dream shattered.

My spine collided with soft carpet and my eyes shot wide. Gleaming silver wheels and narrowed bronze eyes welcomed me back to reality.

"What the *hell* are you doing?"

Scrambling to a sitting position, I wiped my eyes and hoped my cheeks weren't flushed. Having an erotic fantasy was one thing. Having an erotic fantasy about the brother of the woman now glaring at me was entirely another.

"Normally, if a person doesn't answer their door, it's because they don't want to be disturbed."

"You ignored me. I had to take drastic action."

Jasmine sighed. Her dark hair was flat on one side, her skin rosy from sleep. Looking past her, I noticed the covers of her bed were turned down and her nightgown of white cotton and forget-me-not blue ribbons covered her from head to toe.

I climbed to my feet. "If you don't want to talk to me, tell me where his room is."

"Where whose room is."

I rolled my eyes. "Come on, don't play that game. You know who. If I knew where to find him in this godforsaken place, I'd go and camp outside his door instead of yours."

She huffed. "Firstly, he's not on this floor. Secondly, I wonder how long that would be permitted until Cut dealt with you." Leaving me on the threshold, she wheeled herself back to bed.

I closed the door and followed. Standing awkwardly at the foot of the mattress, I whispered, "Do you want some help?"

Her head snapped toward me. "Do I *look* like I need help?" She waved around the empty room. "Do I have a maid to help me? Do you think I can't manage even the simplest of tasks by myself?"

I flinched. "No, of course not."

Keeping my fingers together, preventing any chance of reaching out, I stood fixed to the carpet as Jasmine locked the wheels and placed her hands on the bed.

It wasn't high and with a small grunt, she hoisted herself from the chair and into the covers.

With brisk efficiency, she slid against her pillows, reached down to direct her legs from twisted and dangling to laying perfectly straight, then covered herself with the duvet.

"See?" she sneered.

I drifted forward, perching on the side. "You're very proficient at that."

A wry laugh escaped her. "I've had many years to get used to it."

Awkward silence fell; I struggled for another topic. "Were you born this way?"

Her eyes glinted. "No."

My heart banged at her simple but very revealing answer. Deciding I had nothing left to lose, I murmured, "Did someone do this to you?"

Her face shut down. She pointed at the door. "I want you to leave."

"No. Not until you tell me where I can find Jethro." *And explain what happened while I was gone.*

She crossed her arms, pouting like a little child surrounded by yellow-lemon pillows. "You come into my room and demand to know where my brother sleeps. God, you've got some nerve." She cocked her head, her bob slicing her jawline. "What? So you can kill him or fuck him?"

I coughed with surprise. "You sound just like him. He said the exact same thing when he dragged me up here for the Tally Mark."

Jasmine sucked in a breath. "Well…which one is it?"

I sat straighter. Now might be my only chance to get Jasmine on my side.

In order to find the truth, I had to give it. No matter how revealing it would be. "I'm in love with your brother. I hate him most days, but that doesn't stop my idiotic heart from loving him. I love the goodness buried inside. I love the way he wants to be better but can't. I love the way he touches me. And I'm not ashamed to admit I love sleeping with him."

My cheeks flared, but I continued boldly, "He's mine as much as yours. I'm not your enemy, Jasmine. I want to be your friend."

Silence fell, thick and cloying.

She never stopped glaring.

Fear darted down my arms. "What happened the day the police came? Before that, you were...nice to me. You were welcoming. But now...you hate me." Hanging my head, I said, "I didn't leave of my own free will. You know that."

Animosity swirled thicker, webbing us together.

Finally, she sighed. "I know you didn't go freely."

"Then why punish me? My brother meddled in things he doesn't understand. I know it cost Jethro hugely, but it wasn't my fault."

She stared at the ceiling, battling a sudden glisten in her eyes. "But it was. It was both our faults. I pushed him to let you inside him, and you won by making him care. We both made him so vulnerable. Cut..." She looked away, biting her lip.

I inched closer, patting her knee. I didn't know if she could feel it, but I squeezed anyway. "What did he do to him?"

Jasmine plucked the bedspread. "I don't know. Kite won't tell me. I can't get through to him. Not like I used to." Her gaze latched onto mine. "He won't talk to me. He won't even come see me. He's cut Kestrel out, too. He doesn't ride anymore. It's like everything that made him my broken brother has been lost."

My soul cracked at the thought. "It can't be lost. There must be a way to change whatever Cut did."

Jasmine shook her head. "I've never seen him this cold, this remote. He's exactly like our father, and it terrifies me to think I've lost him." A tear rolled down her cheek. "I suppose in a way, I should be grateful. At least he's still breathing."

My world stopped. "What do you mean?"

Jasmine scowled. "Oh, don't look so surprised. You must've guessed what would happen when you walked out of Hawksridge and never looked back."

"He *told* me not to look back," I snapped. "He forced me to obey by using my love against me."

Her face turned frigid with anger. "Yes, but you could've found a way to come back sooner. You must've believed Bonnie when she said you'd earned your freedom at the cost of another."

I didn't want to hear anymore.

Jasmine scoffed. "My father is doing everything in his power to destroy your line because of some stupid ancient vendetta that should've been dismissed centuries ago. If he can do that to innocent people, what does that mean for the ones being groomed to take over his throne?" She suddenly leaned forward, snatching my hand off her knee.

Her French-manicured nails dug into my skin. "Whatever Jethro has done or whatever Cut threatened him with is the last resort. I thought I would never see my brother again. I thought the moment you walked out of Hawksridge Jethro would disappear, too. But he didn't. He's still alive—but God only knows what stipulations Cut placed on him."

She jerked me closer. "Just stay away from him. Don't try to find him. Don't try to love him. Don't try to do anything to upset whatever balance he's been able to find. I miss him, but I'd rather have him unattainable and alive than caring and dead."

She threw my hand away. "Now leave, before I call security."

I stood, moving quickly to her door. I needed to go before I burst into tears at the sheer hatred she had for me. Every word was delivered with fury and dislike. I was no longer a friend but foe.

How could she switch so easily?

How could she give up on Jethro when I knew he was so close to snapping back?

She's protecting him. She thinks there's no hope.

"Oh, and Nila?"

My eyes met Jasmine's. She said in a monotone, "Don't ever come back here. Leave my brother alone. Let this madness end. I'm begging you."

It wasn't until I'd descended the stairs and entered my own quarters that I unravelled the message in her final words.

Let this madness end.

She's asking me to let them win.

She's asking me to die.

SLINGING A TOWEL around my waist, I exited my steamy bathroom and stalked across my bedroom to get the first aid kit.

My knuckles were torn, I could barely see out of my right eye, my lip was split, and countless bruises mottled my torso. But fuck, I felt better than I had in months.

I shook like a damn junkie needing another fix, but I relished the win and adrenaline of playing God over someone else for a change.

Passing the full-length mirror, I cringed at my reflection. It didn't look like I'd been the victor, but I was still here and they weren't.

Suck on that, arseholes.

Grabbing the first aid kit from the 17th century dresser, I returned to my bed to begin repairs.

I didn't need stitches or serious medical care, but I did need antibacterial cream and a few butterfly strips to hold the cut on my forehead together while it healed.

Damn Cannibal cunts—thinking they could kill me when I was alone. Their president would have a nasty surprise tomorrow when the local farmer inspected his potato field and found three new varieties sprouting instead.

I'd left a calling card on each—a single worthless diamond. Courtesy of my family and our power over immortality.

There would be no retaliation. They were on our turf—fair and fucking simple.

My muscles ached, my head pounded, but my mind was blessedly clear. I could think straight—free from emotions and pressure. I hadn't run into anyone since my arrival.

A new prescription for pills rested on my bedside table. As much as I loved this clarity, I couldn't stomach it come morning. I made a note to take one the moment I'd finished patching myself up.

Sitting on the edge of the bed, I popped the lid of the first aid kit and selected a tube of antiseptic.

My door flung wide.

Shit, I forgot to lock the damn thing.

I looked up, expecting to see Kes, my father, or even Daniel popping in for a three a.m. chat. Instead…Nila fucking Weaver stood frozen on the threshold.

I dropped the tube of cream.

She brandished her stolen dirk and a brass candlestick from one of the tables lining the halls. Her hair was untethered—a curtain of midnight—and her black camisole and shorts made my mouth instantly dry up.

Fuck, fuck, fuck.

What the *hell?*

I stood up instantly.

The first aid kit slammed to the floor, spewing its gauze and bandages to all corners of the room.

"What the hell are you doing in here?" I stormed forward, ready to slam the door in her face. She couldn't be here. Not with my appearance or condition.

"Oh, my God. I found you."

I grabbed the doorknob. "Go back to your room, Ms. Weaver."

"No, wait!" She darted inside before I could block her. Dashing to my bed, she ran around the large mattress, placing it between us and brandishing her weapons. "I've been looking for hours. I've tried every room on the ground floor. I almost gave up when I found a secret door in the parlour."

She'd been running around all night? *Alone?* Shit, didn't she know how dangerous that was?

Daniel wouldn't hesitate. My father wouldn't, either.

"You're a reckless, naïve little girl." Slamming the door, I stalked toward her. "Do you have *any* idea what might've happened if you'd been seen?"

Her eyes skittered around my space, taking in the soaring high ceilings, old-fashioned priceless toys and artifacts, and Chinese woven carpets. "I have an idea." She raised her chin. "But it was a risk I was prepared to take. After all, what else could I do?"

Tossing the candlestick onto the bed, she rolled her wrist from the weight. "You avoid me for days after telling me something cryptic about black diamonds and absorbing light. You tell me to stop feeling around you. You shut me out all while swallowing a drug you never took before. All of that brings me to one conclusion, Mr. Hawk."

"Oh? And what conclusion is that?"

So, she did understand my half-assed attempt to make her understand.

Why couldn't I just come out and tell her?

Why did I have to continue to hide?

"A conclusion that needs testing." She sighed softly, "I have a theory, you see. And if I'm right…well, it means things are going to change between you and me."

My heart tap-danced a crazy step.

You have no idea how much I want that.

"That will never happen."

"You don't even know my theory."

"I know enough to ask you to leave."

Before you destroy your own life and get me fucking killed in the process.

Having her here, in my space, with no fog to protect me, I tasted everything she felt like fine wine, expensive truffles, rich desserts. Anger, desire, fear…and most of all, love. Beneath her temper, she glowed with it. Vibrated with it.

It was all I could do to remain standing and not buckle under the waves of unconditional acceptance.

I groaned, "Nila, you have to leave."

"No. Not until I find out what you are."

I shivered, forgetting my bodily aches and pains and suffering emotional ones instead. She was breaking me—smashing the rules Cut had fashioned. If she could be so strong, why couldn't I?

Couldn't I indulge for just one night?

"You don't understand." I moved forward. "You can't be here."

"Tell me, then." Placing the dirk on my bedside table, she dropped her hands. In a single move, she went from warrior to sacrifice, inviting me to take her. "*Make* me understand, Jethro."

My head swam. I needed time to decide if I was stupid enough to put us both in danger. If I was going to give into her, it could only be for one night.

Inching closer, I murmured, "To find my room, you must've gone through my entire quarters."

Her eyes narrowed at my subject change, but she nodded. "I did. Your room is the last one along the corridor." Her body softened. "You have so many spaces. Game grottos, offices, a gym. I must've peeked into a dozen rooms after slipping through that secret door."

A lot of space for a man who needed a lot of distance.

It looked like luxury; in reality, it was a gilded cage.

"And doesn't that tell you something?"

She frowned. "Tell me what?"

"That this part of the Hall is private. I don't want guests. I don't want company. I keep my life removed from my family, even though we live in the same house."

She trembled as I continued to close the distance between us. Each step I took, I fought to be strong enough to send her away. She would remain unhurt as long as I could fake the perfect heir.

The longer she stood in my quarters, the more I struggled to deny her.

Almost as if she followed my thoughts, she whispered, "It doesn't matter. I've found you. Now I know where to come when you disappear and avoid me."

My hands fisted as delectable thoughts filled my head: sneaking her into my quarters, sleeping beside her, fucking her without cameras reporting to Cut just how disobedient I was.

My jaw clenched. "There won't *be* a next time, Nila." Pointing at the door, I growled, "You have to leave."

"Why? Give me one good reason and I might consider it." Abandoning her position by my bed, she came toward me.

I sucked in a breath as her gaze danced over my body. Her fingers twitched as she took in my bleeding forehead and knuckles. "You're hurt."

"I'm fine."

She lingered over my split lip before her eyes drifted down my still-damp torso to the towel around my waist.

An image of us walking back from the springs dressed only in towels came swift and strong.

I'd never been so free. Never been so happy at the thought of telling her everything and finally admitting that Nila was it for me. That I might have a chance.

It was a pipe dream. And one that got us both into this mess.

"Fuck." I couldn't have her in here, and I definitely couldn't have those thoughts.

I tried to grab her, but she darted away. Jumping onto my bed like fleeing prey, her tiny feet disappeared in the feather duvet as she pranced across the mattress. She leapt down, once again placing the bed between us.

A headache throbbed and the bruises on my ribcage smarted as I ran a hand through my wet hair. "I don't want to play any more games."

Never taking her eyes from mine, she placed her palms on my bed. "Neither do I. We've both established that." Her voice lowered. "You're hurt, Jethro. Let me help you."

"No. You need to go."

How many times do I need to tell you?

My eyes flashed to the pills on my bedside. If I took one, the numbness might give me enough reprieve to kick her out.

"Who did this to you?" she murmured, inching closer again, forgetting that her intention was to stay away from me, not comfort me.

Her concern was like a mink blanket, soothingly warm and so, so soft.

I wished she would stay away. Her concern might be a blanket, but her love…. Shit, her love was a blade slicing me into pieces.

She kept coming closer, no longer trying to flee.

I held up my hand. "Stay right there."

"Jethro…don't do this."

"No, *you* don't do this," I snarled. "You don't know what you're risking."

Nila didn't reply, and she didn't stop.

My throat dried up. I was stuck between the wall my father had erected and the chasm she created. *I need help.* My hands shook as I charged toward my bedside and scooped up the bottle of pills.

My body blared from the fight, but it was nothing to the way my mind bled being around her. It was like claws on a blackboard, forcing me to listen— regardless if I wanted to or not.

The tablets offered quietness. Peace.

I needed that.

"No!" Nila sprinted forward, knocking the bottle from my hand. The tablets spewed all over the carpet.

"What the fuck?"

"Whatever they are—don't take any more."

My temper bubbled. "They're painkillers!" I held up my torn knuckles, shoving the evidence in her face. "See."

She scowled. "No, they aren't." Rummaging in the first aid kit, she brought out some anti-inflammatories and paracetamol. "*These* are painkillers." Snatching my hand, she dumped the blister packet into my palm. "Whatever those others are—they're hurting you, not helping you."

Throwing away the pills, I ran a hand over my face. Being this awake after a month of listlessness, my old concerns came back. I missed Jasmine. I missed Kes. And fuck, I missed Nila. So damn much.

I looked at her beneath my brow, unable to fight anymore.

She wanted to talk? Fine. I'd talk.

We'd played cat and mouse too many times. The trap had sprung, and if death was the reward, then I sure as hell would make it worthwhile.

Capturing her hips, I dragged her closer. She gasped as I circled my thumbs on the cool satin of her night-shorts. "You came here for a reason. What was it?"

Nila blinked, lust blazing in her black eyes. "Eh...I came to..."

I tugged her closer, fitting her small frame against mine. "Yes?"

My heartbeat raced. My cock thickened. Giving in was an ultimate aphrodisiac, and the pain dissolved in favour of my intense need to fuck her.

I cocked an eyebrow, dragging my gaze down her body.

She had magic. I didn't deny that. Magic that we hadn't managed to take even though we'd treated her like a witch with the ducking stool.

Swallowing hard, I slinked my fingers into her hair, curling them around her nape. She bit her lip as I pressed my thickening erection on her belly. "You didn't come to talk, did you? You came for this." I rocked again.

Her eyes snapped closed.

"Admit it," I purred. "Admit that all of this is our version of foreplay. We argue. We fight. And then..." My fingers tightened around her neck. "We fuck."

She made a breathy noise that made my heart crack and bleed. "You're right..." Her hand disappeared between us, latching around my cock through the towel.

I bit back a growl as her thumb pressed the crown, shooting electric bolts into my balls.

Her nipples peaked beneath the black satin. The lust she'd conjured in my office at Diamond Alley came back in full force.

"Goddammit, you test me." Fisting her hair, I jerked her backward, supporting her spine as I ducked to suck her nipple.

She cried out, her hand releasing my cock to tug on the knot in the towel. "Yes...Jethro."

"You truly are the worst kind of punishment," I panted, sucking, grazing her with my teeth.

She squirmed. She was as fucked as I was—sex-hazed and drunk. Lust infused the very air—desire became oxygen and hunger became life.

We were both destroyed. And the only cure was to give in.

"I'll give you what you're looking for." I walked her backward to the bed.

She looped her arms over my shoulders, leaping into my embrace. "Give me everything. I beg you."

I caught her, holding her weight as her legs wrapped around my hips. She thrust against me.

"Fuck, Nila."

A few more steps and I'd have her on the bed. If I could fucking walk. My entire body vibrated with need. "Why did you come here?"

Her lips parted. Her black hair shimmered in the lowlights of my bedside lamps. "You want the truth?"

I nodded.

Pressing her breasts against my chest, she whispered in my ear, "I came here to be filled, taken, *ridden*. I came to find you again. I came to remind you of what we have. I came for so many reasons, Jethro, but most of all, I came to save you."

My soul swelled as the mattress hit my knees. I folded her backward, drinking in her flushed skin and sparkling eyes. I couldn't speak. What was there to say to that?

I don't need fucking saving?

I don't want you to come for me?

Of course, I wanted that. Anyone after a lifetime of loneliness would dream of someone accepting them unconditionally.

All I wanted to do was crash to my knees and beg—fucking beg for her to finally understand—to see the only way to exist was to let me be who I was born to be. I had to take her life. I had to stay alive. One of us would die—if not both.

She wanted hope—the belief that this could have a happy ending.

But it can't.

And that was too much to bear.

She scooted toward my pillows, spreading her legs. With sexy boldness, she hooked her fingers into the waistband of her shorts and shimmied out of them.

I swallowed. Hard.

I prowled toward her on hands and knees, unable to tear my eyes away from the dampness between her legs. "You want to be ridden? Let me make your wishes come true."

I reached out to touch her, but she rolled away.

I blinked; the urge to chase her hammered at my skull. "Come here."

She sat up, tugging the hem of her top, wrenching it over her head.

Naked.

Gloriously fucking naked.

I reached for her again, but she scrambled over my sheets.

A fleeting thought came. That quote to *Vanity Fair* about miscarrying. Was it true? *Could* she have been pregnant with my child? My heart fisted. I couldn't unscramble how that made me feel.

"Come here," I growled again.

"Come and get me."

I trembled with the idea of her becoming more than just a woman I'd fallen for but *family*. If she carried my baby, we would be joined forever.

And you know what Cut would do.

My heart shut down.

I focused on sex—trying to separate emotional from physical gratification. I lied to myself, but it was better than asking her what truly happened while she was free.

"You want to play? Fine, I can play."

She'd upset me without even trying. I wanted payback.

With a vicious yank, I untied the towel and hurled myself across the bed. I snagged her waist, slamming her onto her back.

Naked skin against naked skin.

I'd never felt anything so delicious.

She cried out as we bounced and collided, coming to rest on top of the blankets. Instantly, sharp unbridled lust laced around us. She smelled so good. Felt so good.

So warm.

So right.

Her chest rose and fell, teasing her nipples against my skin, twining her legs with mine.

I swooped down and bit her throat below her collar. "See what happens when you run?" Her incredible smell punched me harder than any of the bastards on the side of the road.

"You're crushing me," she breathed, her stomach fluttering against mine. Her fingernails dragged along my naked arse. "It's not enough."

Her talons sent shivers up my spine. I was so close to diving inside her. I snagged her wrists, pinning them above her head.

"Do you enjoy being spread-eagled beneath me?" I nuzzled her neck. "You're my prisoner, yet you keep thinking you can win."

She stiffened. "I think it's time we agree we're on the same side." Her gaze darkened, a mask slipping into place. "I don't want to win or lose anymore." Struggling in my hold, she pressed a kiss on my jaw. "I just want you."

My cock twitched, agreeing wholeheartedly.

I no longer wanted to be on anyone's side but hers. That included my own.

Fuck, what a mess this has become.

When she'd left, I'd been willing to sacrifice my life to save hers. I would've died if it meant the Debt Inheritance had been void. But now—now I had to stay alive to ensure the Final Debt was paid.

I rocked against her pussy. "I agree…" Adjusting my hold on her wrists, I locked both with one hand and trailed the other over the delectable lines of her body. "Same team."

She shuddered beneath my touch. "You mean it?"

I grabbed her breast, pinching her nipple. "I mean it."

Her lips fell wide. A sigh escaped. And I took full advantage.

I kissed her.

She moaned, her mouth submitting to mine. Within a moment, the kiss went from a connection of lips to something deep and ravenous.

A kiss was a disaster.

A kiss was power.

A kiss was love and togetherness and faith.

It was so many, many things.

But this…this was something so much more.

More.

I want more.

I want everything.

She moaned again as her tongue dove into my mouth, taking control of the kiss and rocking her hips, seeking more just like me.

I kissed her deep. I kissed her hard.

Her knees fell wide, welcoming my body to claim hers. We both needed to join. Become one.

My fingers skated down her hip to her inner thigh. She bucked, trying to free her wrists as I dipped further with questing traces.

"Jethro…let me touch you."

"No. *I'm* touching *you.*" With no hesitation, I thrust a finger inside her, mirroring the action with my tongue.

She groaned, her back flying off the bed.

Our lips never unglued, driving each other to galaxies beckoning with freedom and sanctuary.

"Oh, God." She rode my finger, her body wet and wanting. "More. Give me more."

I bit her bottom lip. "Your wish is my command." I inserted another finger, driving deep, stretching wide. She was wet but so damn tight.

I wanted to fuck her so badly, but it wasn't a simple matter of climbing on top. It never was for me. I had to prepare—had to make sure she was ready—even when it drove me to agony.

I wanted her hard and ruthless. This wasn't making love. This wasn't even a battle—this was a ceasefire. An admittance that we couldn't keep fighting, but it didn't mean we were dead.

"Kite...please, fuck me. I need you," Nila begged between kisses.

Shit, she called me Kite again.

Every time she did, goosebumps scattered down my spine. All those nights of messaging her, getting into her head and heart—playing a game I never should've started—all crescendoed.

She'd slept with me as Jethro, but she hadn't slept with me as Kite.

I lost all sense of self as I tore my fingers from her wet heat and shifted my body higher. Our eyes locked as the tip of my cock found her heat. The world stopped spinning.

There was so much to say and no words in which to speak.

Gritting my teeth, I nudged inside her.

The second I entered her, all decorum went out the fucking window.

I let go of her wrists and her hands flew downward, digging her nails into my arse and dragging me forward. Her knees came up, opening wide. "Yes. Oh, God, yes." Her cheeks were rosy red, eyes wild.

Clutching the sheets, I thrust without warning, driving too fast and deep inside her.

She screamed.

"Shit!" I clamped a hand over her mouth, pulling out. "Be quiet."

She vibrated in my arms, eyes glassy and lust-stricken. Dropping my hold, I growled, "No one must know you're here." Finding her wetness again, I climbed inside—slower this time, pushing, pressing, invading.

The tight unforgiving muscles of her body resisted me, but I was too far gone to care.

"Feel that?" I grunted as I slowly conquered her.

She moaned, her breath coming in short pants. Her eyes squeezed tight as I relentlessly filled her. "Yes."

"Does it feel good?"

"Yes...so good."

"You want more?"

"I want everything."

I thrust hard and fast, sliding all the way inside. *I'm home. I'm never fucking leaving again.*

I'd killed three bikers tonight with no second thoughts. I was a killer, defender. So why couldn't I be the same for Nila? Could I become a traitor to my family? Could I kill my father and Daniel in order to save the woman I loved?

I drove again, rocking her body deeper into my mattress.

Do I have a choice?

She threw her head back, hair fanning over my pillow. "You belong inside me, Jethro." Her hand cupped my cheek, transfixing my soul to hers with irremovable super glue. "Never forget that."

I just got my answer.

Pills and debts and empires.

Utterly worthless compared to this creature who'd stolen my heart.

Sighing, I gave up. I surrendered to the inevitable. *I have to kill to protect.* She was mine. It was my duty.

"I ache when you're not inside me," she murmured, dragging my mind back to her.

I smiled sadly, consumed with a gruesome future I didn't want. Her face was in shadow from my body suffocating hers. She looked like she might vanish any second.

Tilting my head, I licked the seam of her lips. She opened, welcoming me inside. She was silk and sugar. Despair and happiness.

How could I be so happy yet so shredded at the same time?

Her hands fell to my hips, pulling me into her with every thrust. Our chests stuck together, our bellies glued. Her legs wrapped around the back of my thighs, using her ankles to push up and meet me thrust for thrust. "Harder, Kite. Harder."

Once again, that tiny voice filled my head. *Would you be so rough with her if she was pregnant? Shouldn't you ask?*

But the fear of the unknown and what it would mean silenced me. I obeyed instead, driving hard.

Her head fell back as I fucked under her command.

"I missed you." Her voice broke. A single tear rolled down her cheek.

And that was it for me. I knew there was no going back.

Never again.

"Nila." My voice was lost.

She opened her eyes, anchoring me to her.

"I need you to know that I feel what you feel. This—" I never broke my rhythm, diving inside her over and over. Loving, fucking, claiming. "—this, it's right. I see that now."

Anger blossomed in her eyes. "How long will you see it? Tomorrow? The day after? Or once tonight is over, you'll cut me back out and leave me stranded all over again?"

My pacing stuttered, my cock twitched. "You're right. To you it must seem as if I'm schizophrenic."

Insane.

Just like everyone said.

She was silent for a moment, before brushing her thumb over my lips. "You seem troubled. That's all." Wrapping her arms around me, she sandwiched our bodies together.

I am troubled. More than you know.

The urge to be close—as close as humanly possible—forced my arms to wrap around her and thrust hard. I rode her like that. Arms locked, bodies merged into one. My balls slapped against her as my cock rubbed against her clit.

Pleasure supernovaed into a raging black hole, waiting to consume us.

I picked up speed, chasing the finale.

"Oh, don't stop," she moaned.

Her body bucked beneath mine, jousting and submitting in equal measure. I felt her pleasure as surely as my own. I drank her bliss like nectar.

"Am I hurting you?" I fisted the pillow behind her, rocking faster.

Her forehead furrowed. She nodded a little. "It's a beautiful pain, though. A belonging sort of pain. Don't stop."

"I can't take you without hurting you," I said into her hair. "In a way, it's only fair."

Her fingernails dug into my lower back. "Why...why is it fair?"

I groaned. I didn't want to answer that.

Because you hurt me when you take me, too. When you give me no choice but to let you inside me.

She rolled her hips, rubbing against me. "I'm angry with you. So damn angry at the way you treated me."

I kissed her, forcing her to drink my words. "I know."

Speaking through our kiss, she groaned, "I can't control myself around you, but it doesn't mean everything is fixed between us."

"I know that, too." I rocked harder, driving us to insanity. "But no matter how angry you are, your feelings won't stop you from coming."

I pinned her delicate frame with mine and let loose.

No more talking. No more thinking or feeling or planning.

Just fucking.

She gave in, moulding her body to mine, sighing heavily as my groan echoed around the room like a serrated blade.

She tormented me. But by God, I fucking loved her.

I didn't understand her. I didn't trust her. But my instincts plaited with hers and we fed off one another.

My balls cramped, desperately needing to come.

"Please, Kite. Give me what you're hiding."

Needing this over, craving silence from her all-consuming emotions, I drove faster.

Nila moaned as I reached between her legs, rubbing her clit while fucking her with no mercy.

It took two seconds for her to detonate.

Her eyes rolled back, she stopped breathing, and every molecule of her body exploded.

"Fuuuuck," I grunted as her pussy contracted hard and strong around my cock.

I didn't stand a chance.

I came.

Bliss and pleasure hurtled me into the stratosphere where no thought existed. Together we unravelled, spiralling deeper into chaos.

I didn't care about anything. We journeyed to fucking utopia in each other's arms.

Our hearts thundered against each other, speaking in Morse code just how precious this was. However, beneath the blistering contentment, I cursed myself to hell.

As my seed splashed inside her, all I could think about was the way I'd stolen her right to be a mother. I'd injected her to save her. But now it felt like a coward's actions.

The Grim Reaper himself danced over my spine as another thought came to me.

If she *had* been pregnant, her child—*my* child—would've been murdered.

And nothing on earth could ever make that okay.

This has to end.

When our orgasms faded, I fisted her hair, forcing her to open her eyes. "Look at me."

She breathed hard, staring into my gaze with melted heaven and sweetest satisfaction. "I'm looking, Jethro. And despite everything you do...I *see* you."

"I know you see; that's why I need you to promise me something."

"Anything."

Familiar ice filled me at the thought of what I had to do. I had to be smart. I had to win. Because there would be no second chance—for either of us.

"Outside of this room, I will continue to be cruel. I will continue to do what is expected of me. You have to trust me."

She stiffened. "You're saying after what just happened, things are going to go back to the way they were?"

I nodded. "They have to. Until I can do what's needed."

Her eyes narrowed. "And what are you going to do?"

I kissed the tip of her nose and hoped to God I'd made the right choice.

Please, give me strength.

"I'm going to do what I should've done a long time ago."

Kill my motherfucking father.

LIFE SETTLED INTO a temporary rhythm.

By day, I either sewed or spent it with the Black Diamond brothers learning all there was about carats and mining techniques. I was told where the mines were located. I memorized the wealth extracted from each location and the brand they laser cut onto every stone. By night, I shoved away infrequent vertigo waves and sketched new designs I might never create.

I learned that every few months, one Hawk brother would travel to Brazil or Africa or Thailand to inspect the mines and assess the managers left in charge. They would go with an entourage from their brotherhood, acting as support, discipline, and protection.

I was wrong when I thought the only brothers in the Black Diamonds were the ones who'd licked me at my welcome luncheon. There were factions all around the world—all controlling the empire that belonged to Bryan 'Cut' Hawk.

And soon Jethro.

After our night together, things had become strange between us. He avoided me as much as possible. He didn't come to my quarters. He didn't seek me out for my morning run. And when we met in the dining room with his family for breakfast, he would find subjects to discuss with his father and be detained far longer than I could wait.

His eyes, once glowing with lust and togetherness, became dead, lifeless. Every few hours, he would swallow a white pill and give me a smile that said a hundred things all at once.

Trust me.

Wait for me.

Don't hate me.

The Black Diamond brothers continued to be kind and generous. If I came upon them in the library, we'd chat like old friends. If I bumped into one of them in the corridors, we'd discuss the weather and any titbit of interesting information.

I never went to visit Jasmine again, and my brother and father never ceased in their rally to get me to reply. I'd never been around so many people—all impacting my life in some small measure.

Whenever I moved around Hawksridge, I took my dirk—jammed in my waistband or hidden in the garter around my leg. I'd seen Daniel once on my own—it'd been around nine p.m. He'd caught me strolling back to my quarters after visiting the kitchen for some orange juice.

I knew then why Jethro was so livid that I'd hunted the house for his wing. The look in Daniel's eyes reeked of rape and lawlessness. His hissed promise when the first tally was made came back in full volume. *"The moment you're alone..."*

He'd come toward me, a sneer on his lips. I didn't think, just reacted. I'd thrown my glass at his face, splashing citrus juice all over irreplaceable carpets and tore back to the kitchen.

And there I'd stayed until Flaw returned from a late night delivery and escorted me back to my chambers.

I didn't tell Jethro what'd happened, but he must've seen it on the cameras, because the next day he found me and whispered that from now on his rooms would be locked. That there was no point in going to him because he wouldn't let me in.

I knew he did it for my protection—to stop me recklessly patrolling the halls—but at the same time, it killed me to think the one chance we could be together had been taken away just like the rest.

The dynamics in Hawksridge Hall had changed. Cut had thawed considerably toward Jethro. I caught them laughing together one afternoon and Cut slapping Jethro on the back the next. The stronger the father and son bond grew, the more Kestrel faded into the background.

Daniel didn't seem to notice or care about the alliance that'd sprung between firstborn and ruler. He carried on as if life was fine and dandy with no cares apart from which club bunny to screw that night.

Kes, on the other hand, stopped being his jovial self. He stopped smiling at me. Stopped smiling period.

And despite not knowing who he truly was, I missed him.

I missed the ease and togetherness I enjoyed when I'd first arrived. I missed having him as a friend—even if that friendship came with conditions and hidden motives.

One day, as I made my way outside for a run, I saw Kes disappear over the front garden dressed in a tweed jacket and woollen trousers with a shotgun cocked over his arm.

Where is he going?

Jogging down the portico steps, I zipped up my fleece and was glad I'd put on leggings as the wind howled in welcome.

Autumn was losing every day to winter. Summer was long since forgotten, and I craved the sunshine and greenery of the first few months that I'd arrived.

Kes looked up as I traversed the gravel.

His eyebrows rose. "Nila. What are you doing out here?" He peered at the sky. "It might rain...or snow, feels fucking cold enough." His skin was white, but the tip of his nose was painted red. He'd had a haircut recently and it was trimmed and neat at the side with an unruly mess on top. He looked younger, sadder.

"I'm going for a run. Want to join me?"

I forced away the memory of running with Jethro and ultimately finding my ancestor's graves. Jethro had wounded me too many times over the past few weeks. I wanted to hate him but couldn't.

The way he'd begged me to trust him the last time we were together. The way he looked so close to crumbling under the weight he carried.

He had a plan. I had no choice but to trust him.

It took a strong conviction to trust someone who rarely talked to me and went out of his way to come across as a drug-induced robot.

I blew on my frostbitten fingers. My chill was partly due to the freezing cold day, but it was mainly thanks to living in a historic tomb. Hawksridge Hall was decadent and majestic, but it was damn cold when moving around cavernous corridors. Only the rooms were heated, and even then, the ceilings were so high it was never toasty.

"No, I don't run." Kes jostled the gun over his arm. "Thought I'd go for a hunt. Shoot a pheasant or two for dinner."

We fell into step together. I wrapped my arms around myself, retaining the small amount of body heat I had. "I couldn't think of anything worse—killing something."

Will Jethro kill someone? Cut, Daniel...me?

Grey clouds and a faint dusting of mist dulled the vibrancy of the estate. It was magical as much as it was depressing.

Kes noticed my shivering. He stopped.

Holding out the gun, he waited until I took it, then shrugged out of his thick tweed.

The weapon was morbidly heavy. I was only too happy to trade it for the soft wool of his blazer. "You don't have to—"

"I know." He slung the tweed over my shoulders, encasing me in his masculine scent of musk and heather. "But I want to."

"I can't take it." I tried to slip it off. "I won't need it when I start running."

"Fine." He narrowed his eyes. "Only trying to be kind." The pain flickering in his gaze made me keep it on and place an icy hand on his forearm.

His head snapped up.

"Kes...are you okay?"

He snorted, shoving aside his melancholy unsuccessfully. "Yes, of course. Why wouldn't I be?"

I looked back at the Hall. It sat ominous and frightening, casting shadows over the hibernating gardens. "You miss him, too. Don't you?"

His nostrils flared. "We shouldn't talk about it."

"Why not? You said all secrets were mine to know." I smiled, despite the awfulness of the circumstances. "I'm not going anywhere, and I have no one to tell. The world believes I'm marrying into your family. My brother's reputation is ruined, and my father is a ghost of the man he used to be. What would be the harm in trusting me?"

"You have a point." For a moment, he looked disgusted. With what? What his family had done to mine? Or that I had the audacity to ask him to trust me?

Finally, he sighed. "I wouldn't say this in front of anyone else, but..." He inched closer, ducking to whisper in my ear, "I'm sorry. For everything that's happened."

For the tiniest moment, my heart fluttered. He was so *uncomplicated* compared to Jethro. He kept things hidden—his true agenda being one—but I felt as if he only had one layer beneath his exterior, not thousands.

I placed my hand over his, squeezing in gratitude. "That means a lot. Thank you."

The moment stretched on for longer than it should; we both jumped away guiltily.

Clearing his throat, Kes asked, "I'm going to get the foxhounds. Want to come to the stables?"

Huddling deeper into his jacket, I nodded. "Why not? Perhaps it's not a day for running, after all."

"Well…if you're not going for a run, I have a much better idea."

Holding out his arm, he waited for me to loop mine with his. His smile was still tainted, but life sparked in his eyes. "Let's go do something fun."

Fun.

I envisioned a drink in a warm *boudoir* or hanging out with friends while playing a board game, or even watching a movie with popcorn.

But apparently, that wasn't what Kes had in mind.

Entering the stables, he placed the shotgun in the tack room and motioned for me to follow. We headed into the long cobblestone-paved building where countless horses rested in cubicles. The floor was scattered with sweet smelling hay and the air temperature was warm and inviting. Scents weaved with the comforting aroma of horse and leather.

My tension dissolved, slipping down my spine and leaving my shoulders free from the choke of worry and deliberation.

Jethro said he would save me.

But Kes saved my mental state by reminding me normalcy still existed. Animals were still there to lick away my sorrows, and the sun still rose on days not so bleak.

I needed reminding of that.

Considering I'd never been around horses growing up, something about them tamed my anxiety, giving me a place to hide and regroup.

Kes smiled, moving between the stalls; horses watched with glossy gazes and pert ears. He stopped halfway down the aisle. A long, grey face and the gentlest black eyes popped over the railing. The horse nuzzled his pockets, nickering softly.

Moth.

I moved faster, still madly in love with the dapple grey that I'd travelled to the polo tournament with.

Kes grinned as Moth switched her attention to me. Her velvet nostrils huffed, seeking oats and other treats as I reached out to stroke her powerful neck. "Hey, girl."

She pawed the ground, the metal of her shoe clinking against cobbles.

"Wait there." Kes disappeared to the end of the stables, then came back holding a rosy apple. "Here you go."

I took it.

Moth followed the fruit with sniper-like attention.

"I just feed it to her?"

Kes nodded. "Put it on your palm and keep your fingers flat. You don't want her to bite you accidentally."

Great.

I eyed Moth hesitantly. Her neck strained over the railing, trying to get at the apple. When I didn't move, Kes chuckled.

"Don't be afraid." He stole my hand, bent my fingers till they were flat, then shoved me forward. "Can't tease the poor girl."

The second I was within biting distance, Moth pinched the apple from my hand. A loud crunching noise filled the stables. Every other horse pricked its ears, alerted to the sound of treats and the fact that they weren't getting any.

Apple juice dripped from her lips, plopping onto the dusty floor.

Kes laughed. "She'll do anything for sweets. She's a nutcase for molasses."

I raised my hand, patting between her eyes. Moth nudged closer, demanding more cuddles, telling me exactly how she wanted it.

"She's lovely," I said softly, imagining owning such a magnificent animal.

"She is, I agree." Kes never took his eyes off me. His words hovered between us, not entirely innocent. Something stronger than friendship emitted from him.

I had the insane urge to wrap my arms around Moth and use her as a crutch in this suddenly precarious position.

"Kestrel…"

He cleared his throat. "Sorry."

We both stood awkwardly. I continued to stroke Moth and the yips of foxhounds in the kennel next door reminded me all over again of the first night I'd spent here and the kindness Squirrel had shown by licking my tears.

There was goodness in all of us. Human, equine…canine. We were all capable of good and bad. We were all redeemable—no matter what we did.

Kes rubbed his jaw. "You know…"

I looked up, waiting for him to continue. "Know what?" I prompted.

His gaze narrowed. He suddenly cleared his throat, shaking his head. "Eh, don't worry about it."

I frowned, scratching Moth around her ear, straining on tiptoes to reach. "Okay…"

A few seconds ticked past before he exploded. "You know what? Fuck it. It's *his* fault he can't bloody cope. I'm done with how he's treated me and sick to fucking death of him reneging on everything we agreed." He punched himself in the chest. "*I* was there for him from the beginning. I kept his bloody secrets. I deserve to know what the fuck is going on, but he's cut me out."

I froze. "What do you mean?"

Kes chuckled darkly. "It means, I'm *done*. That's what. I'm sick of waiting for him to crawl back and apologise. I'm also sick of him threatening me to stay away from you—even though I know he's ignoring you as much as me."

What on earth happened between Kes and Jethro to warrant their relationship turning so sour?

He dragged a hand through his hair. "Jethro approached me after the polo game last month. He asked if I wanted a new horse."

I gasped. "Oh, no! You can't get rid of her." I leaned into her, pressing my face against her neck. "She's perfect. Don't ever say such a thing."

Kes smiled, patting the mare. "I know. She's a great girl. She's only eight years old, so she's not going to the glue factory anytime soon."

I grabbed Moth's ears, squeezing tight. Speaking to the horse, I said, "Pretend you never heard of glue or factory. That will never happen to you. I won't allow it."

Even as I said it, I wanted to burst into insane tears. Moth would outlive me by decades. I was the one on the countdown to be put down, not her.

Unless Jethro figures out his plan.

Kes's finger pressed against the underside of my chin, raising my eyes to his. "I don't know why I'm telling you this, because it just makes him look good all over again, but...he wanted to get me a new horse, so *you* could have Moth."

My heart stopped. *"Me?"*

He nodded. "He was going to give her to you the night after the Second Debt. But of course..." He trailed off, both of us aware what happened the next day.

Kes gritted his jaw. "And if I'm completely honest, I'm glad he didn't have the chance to give her to you." A cloud fell over his face, twisting his features with anger. "She's *my* horse. I should be the one to give her away if I choose."

I stroked his arm, hoping to reassure him that no one was taking his horse. And even if Jethro *had* given me Moth, I couldn't have taken her because she already belonged to Kes. "Don't worry, Kestrel. She's yours. No one—"

"I want you to have her."

The air solidified.

Moth huffed, nudging me as I stood mute.

I spluttered, "I—I can't."

Even as I said it, the thought of owning this incredible beast blistered my heart. To have something of my own, while surrounded by things that could never be—it would be...wonderful.

Kes clamped strong hands on my shoulders, staring deep into my eyes. "She's yours. She responds to you more than she does with me. You're meant to have her, Nila."

Gratefulness and overwhelming amazement filled me. "I—I don't know what to say."

Kes smiled. "Say nothing. It's already done." Squeezing my shoulders, he stepped back. "You're the proud new owner of a dapple grey by the name of Warriors Don't Cry." Patting Moth on the neck, he grinned. "I'll find the pedigree papers later, so you can keep them safe, but for now...let's go for a ride."

My eyes bugged out of my head. "I've never been on a horse before."

Not counting with Jethro when he carted me back on Wings, of course.

Kes ignored me, heading toward the tack room. "Doesn't matter. I'll show you."

An hour later, I sat atop my first ever horse.

I'm freaking.

I'm terrified.

I'm beyond exhilarated.

I couldn't remember the last time something affected me so piercingly.

Even Jethro?

Well, apart from him.

It seemed the older I grew and more jaded by life I became, the more I lost the heightened extremes of newness. No longer enjoying the catapulting happiness or devastating lowness. These days my highs and lows were more hills and valleys rather than mountains and chasms.

But looking down and seeing the ground far below, feeling the unyielding metal stirrups beneath my borrowed boots, and the leather reins in my hands, I'd never been more alive. More joyous.

This was Christmas on crack.

This was birthdays all in one.

I own her.

I own this majestic animal.

I couldn't sit still with excitement. Leaning forward, I patted Moth's beautiful grey neck. From up here, I had full view between her ears at the rolling fields and sweeping dark forest.

Kes led his mount from the stables and swung his leg over an inky black horse. Its coat gleamed in the autumn gloom, its velveteen nostrils flaring with huge gusts of breath.

Before Kes could get his seat, the horse skittered sideways with a clatter of hooves.

"Whoa, you damn animal." He jerked the reins, forcing the horse to submit.

"Who's that?" I asked, clutching my own reins as Moth tossed her head at the fiery beast prancing beside her. Her flanks rippled with indignation.

Kes's face pinched in concentration. He swatted the horse with his whip as it bucked and nickered. The horse's ears flattened, eyes rolling in a mixture of hell-bound fury and eagerness.

"This is Black Plague. He's technically my father's horse, but he's in-between purse races right now. He always gets like this if he isn't trained every day." He stroked the pitch-black pelt. "Don't you, boy?"

"Rather you than me."

"Plague definitely isn't for beginners." Raising his eyebrow, Kes pointed at my helmet. "Check that it's on tight. I'm not a conventional teacher and need to make sure you're protected."

I laughed, forcing a finger beneath the strap below my chin, showing him that if it were any tighter, I'd choke. I also waved at the bracing corset he'd made me wear, along with the borrowed jodhpurs and boots. "Completely protected."

I felt like royalty—an equestrian princess who knew exactly what she was doing.

I don't have a clue what I'm doing.

For the past hour, Kes had taught me how to clean out Moth's hooves, curry her coat, saddle her, tighten a girth, and slip a bit into her mouth.

So much to do before going for a ride and so much more to do once we returned.

But every single thing I adored.

I didn't think I'd ever been so happy than standing in the stall listening to Kes's deep voice as he joked and teased and congratulated me when I copied correctly.

He was patient and kind and we got along easily. Being with him made my heart weep for Vaughn. The ease in which we chatted reminded me of the relationship I'd had with my twin.

My heart also cried for another.

A rolling black cloud shaded me whenever I thought of Jethro.

He should've been the one teaching me.

He should've been the one laughing and joking and kissing me in the hay.

I hadn't seen Jethro today, and the lovesickness I suffered whenever I thought of him became a constant sabre to my chest.

How could I love someone with so many demons?

How could I love someone who didn't share those demons with me?

I don't have a choice.

If I did—I would choose Kestrel. He was kind and sympathetic. He made me feel better about myself, rather than condemned me to fear.

"Who are you, Kestrel?" I asked before I had time to censor myself.

He stilled, his hands tightening around his reins. "What do you mean?"

"Well, you seem to have a gift at hiding whatever you're thinking—just like your older brother. However, unlike him, you don't seem afflicted. Jethro responds to you. He obeys you when there's tension and looks to you for help." I squinted beneath my helmet. "Why is that?"

Kes lost his smile, filling with seriousness. "Do you know what he is yet?"

His question slapped me.

I know about black diamonds and absorbing. I know about feelings and pain.

"I'm beginning to understand." Moth shifted below me. "I don't have a name for his condition, though. Do you?"

"I do, but it's not my place to name it." He laughed softly. "Come back to me when you've figured it out. When Jethro tells you what he is—I'll tell you who I am. Fair?"

No, not fair. I doubt he'll ever tell me.

Tipping his helmet in salute, he added coyly, "However, there really isn't much to tell about me. I'm an open book."

Kicking Black Plague, he moved forward. Moth automatically followed. The *clip-clop* of hooves echoed off the kennel as we left the stables behind.

The rocking of Moth and the sheer power of her muscles sent fear skittering down my spine. What if I had a vertigo attack and fell off? What if I didn't steer properly and we ran into a tree?

"Uh, Kes...perhaps this isn't such a good idea." My legs trembled. "Maybe I should learn to ride on something smaller?"

Kes turned around, planting a hand on Black Plague's rump. Ignoring my concerns, he said, "Remember how I said I'm not a conventional teacher?"

I nodded slowly, nervousness billowing in my chest. "Yes..."

"Well, here is your crash course in riding. Hold your reins tight but not too tight. Don't jerk on her mouth. Pretend you have a twenty-pound note between your arse and the saddle and under no circumstances is it to fly free. Keep your heels down and back straight, and if you fall, roll away and *don't* hold onto the reins."

The more he spoke, the more my heart raced.

"Got it?"

Everything he just said went in one ear and out the other. "No. I don't have it. Not at all."

Kes threw me an evil grin. "Too bad." Raising his whip, he kicked Black Plague and shot away as if this was the Championship Derby. "Hold on, Nila!"

I pulled on my reins as Moth bunched and collected beneath me. "No...you are *not* going to follow him, damn horse. I like my neck being attached to my body."

Moth tossed her head, snatching the reins from my hands.

"No. Stop!"

A moment later, I went from standstill to full-blown gallop.

I became a blur of grey.

I became the girl from my past who believed in unicorns.

I became...free.

THE PAST FEW days, I'd done nothing but conspire on how to end this mess. I played my role, took my pills, and avoided the love of my fucking life.

Every time I thought up a plan, I researched each angle and plotted. But each time there were flaws, hurtling me deeper into despondency. The longer I couldn't solve my problem, the longer I avoided Nila.

I was so fucking close to destroying everything.

I *missed* her. So much.

So far, I'd discounted eleven different ways of murdering my father.

Option four: Invite him to go for a hunt. Shoot him and make it look like an 'unfortunate accident.'

Flaws: *Too risky. Witnesses. He would have a weapon to retaliate with.*

Option seven: Invite him to dinner. Poison the bastard's food with cyanide—just like he'd threatened me all my life.

Flaws: *Dosage might be wrong. Contamination to others.*

Option Nine: Arrange a mercenary to attack mid-shipment, dispatch him and keep my hands free from murder.

Flaws: *Kes might be with him and get hurt in the crossfire.*

Each one seemed plausible enough until deeper inspection. But all of that was shot to shit the afternoon he called me into his office.

Once again, he somehow knew.

How the fuck does he always know?

Was it his uncanny sixth sense? Constant monitoring of my behaviour? *How?!*

What gave me away? The look of disgust I could never quite hide? The sneer of hatred I could never wipe away?

Whatever it was, I was once again fucking screwed.

In his office, with rain pelting on the windows, he'd shown me his prized and protected Final Will and Testament.

It was a tome the size of the Royal Decree. Pages upon pages of notary amendments and appendixes. And buried in the fine print were two highlighted areas.

Primogeniture: the section on myself, my role as firstborn, and what I stood to inherit. That part went on for sheets and sheets.

His death: Most importantly his *untimely* death.

Cut was a businessman. He was also cunning, ruthless, and smart.

The clause stated that any unnatural death, be it from bee stings or drowning, horse riding fall or car accident—even as simple as dying in his sleep—would make his entire Will null and void.

And not just for myself but for *all* of us.

My siblings would be tossed out. Jasmine would be sent to a convalescent home against her wishes. The Black Diamonds disbanded. Kestrel cast away without a penny.

What did it mean?

Simple.

Cut had noted that if he died from anything other than cancer or a medically proven condition, Hawksridge was to be demolished. Any death that could potentially be maliciously faked, our mines would be detonated. Our wealth donated to causes that had no right to receive charity.

It would be the end of our lifestyle.

It was his ultimate sacrifice and safeguard to ensure we stayed loyal.

Unlike him, I didn't care about money or ancient rubble. If it meant I could be free, so be it. But no amount of drugs could stop me from caring about my siblings.

And Cut knew that.

He showed me his trump card.

Along with Jasmine's imprisonment in a disabled rest home—her power of attorney stripped away—and Kes's renouncement, I would become a ward of the crown, placed in a straitjacket, and thrown into a padded room.

He had authentic documents stating my mental wellbeing. A sworn oath bullet-pointing testimonies and histories, proving I was legally unfit to represent myself. All decision-making was to be at the discretion of my enlisted doctors—doctors who'd been bribed and coerced for years and knew my past. I would have no power—no room to argue.

The documents were submitted with a letter to his lawyer, stating if anything unseemly happened to him, to look no further for the smoking gun, because all fingers pointed to me.

I would be thrown in an asylum—one I could never escape.

Needing fresh air, I threw down my pen and crossed my office.

There has to be another way.

"Fuck!" I hissed, stepping onto the Juliette balcony the same way I'd done countless of times before. The cool breeze whistled down my back, and the ache in my chest deepened.

Yet, unlike countless of times before, my heart fucking shattered into a trillion pieces.

Below me, with her hair streaming behind her and the happiest, slightly terrified smile on her face was Nila.

She was a grey comet. A thundering silver-shooting star.

She couldn't have been more majestic or sublime.

Moth's elegant legs chewed up the lawn, heading toward the paddock I'd galloped over many times on my own.

Horse and rider merged in utmost perfection.

Only, she wasn't alone.

The ring of male laughter came over the breeze as Kestrel shot past her on Black Plague, his hand in the air and a grin plastered to his motherfucking face.

The picture they presented tore out my heart, turning it to dust.

All this time, I'd worked my ass off to protect Nila, Kes, and Jaz. All this time, I'd distanced myself and done what was required.

And how was I fucking repaid?

By being *forgotten*.

Nila hunched further over Moth's withers, galloping faster. Together, they tore off into the distance, leaving me stricken...hollow.

No amount of pills could stop me feeling the wave of crashing desolation.

The numbing fog couldn't help me.

This was my breaking point.

My utter grief.

I'd wanted to experience that with her.

I'd wanted to make her smile and laugh and slide inside her in the dark, secretive world of the stables.

I'd wanted to grant her the gift better than any material thing.

But that'd been stolen from me.

By the one man I thought had my back forever.

Betrayer. Stealer. Forsaker.

I turned around and went back into my office.

But I returned empty.

My heart was left tagging along like a kite, its strings tied to Nila as she galloped further away beneath the cloud-filled sky.

Nila

IT WAS FINISHED.

The centrepiece of my Rainbow Diamond collection.

I stepped back to inspect the gown, making sure it hung just right.

The mannequin presented the crinoline dress as if I'd stepped through time and created something my great-great-grandmother would wear.

The hoop in the thick petticoats forced the rich grey dress to flare in an elegant bell-like swish. There were no layers or feathers or tulle—not like the corset highlight of my Fire and Coal show in Milan. This was understated and sleek—like a smoky waterfall shimmering with secrets and mystery.

Around the cuffs, I'd sewn cream lace that I'd found in a rusted-shut cupboard in my quarters. The lace held the W sigil. My ancestors must've painstakingly created it decades ago; it was fitting to adorn a gown such as this.

The bodice gleamed with panels of midnight silk, creating a prismatic effect. Tiny black beads decorated from décolletage to hem in a glittering asymmetrical pattern, just like the black diamond Jethro had shown me at the warehouse.

There were no rainbows on this dress.

Only darkness.

But it filled me with terrible pride, along with immense sadness. *This might be the last headline piece I make before leaving this world.*

Instead of becoming more optimistic as my time continued unmolested, I became less and less sure. Jethro couldn't hide his frustration. Breakfast, he barely talked. Dinner, he barely ate. He watched Cut with a mixture of obedience and feral rage. But beneath it all was helplessness.

I'd bumped into Bonnie twice since being back. Each time she stretched thin red lips into a smile so cold my blood iced over. She hadn't summoned me. She didn't want anything to do with me. However, I had a horrible feeling that would soon change.

Moving away from the mannequin, I stretched my lower back. My hands were pinpricked and sore. My eyes achy and tired.

I'd worked nonstop for four days—ever since Kestrel took me for my first ride.

I still had bruises on my inner thighs from gripping so hard, but I hadn't fallen off. I hadn't had a vertigo attack. And I hadn't thought of Jethro once as I soared over the fields and escaped everything that hounded me.

And that made me absolutely wretched.

I didn't think of him. *Not once.*

Kestrel had given me so much that day, and I'd taken it with no thought as to how it would affect my relationship with Jethro. I was guilty, full of shame.

I felt as if I'd betrayed him.

And the longer he stayed away from me, the worse it became.

The next night, I entered the dining room and bumped into the firmest, most delectable chest in Hawksridge Hall.

The moment I touched him, I melted into his body. The tears and guilt I'd been storing inside sprung up to strangle me.

"Jethro…" My fingers swooped to bunch in his t-shirt. "God, it's been days. Such long, awful days."

I looked into his golden eyes, seeking the love I'd witnessed when I'd sneaked into his chambers. However, I recoiled at the angry agony glowing in them.

My skin prickled.

He swallowed and for an enchanted moment, we stood together. Breathing, touching, *living.* Then his mask slipped into place, the emotions in his eyes vanished, and his hands captured mine, tearing them away from his chest.

"Hello, Ms. Weaver."

Was his coolness because of the low murmur of voices of Black Diamond brothers eating behind him? Or was it the drugs he'd once again befriended?

"Don't." I shook my head. "Don't keep doing—"

He took a step back. "I can imagine you've worked up quite an appetite."

"Excuse me?"

"Then again, I would think now that you have your own horse, you'd be out more often—yet you haven't left your quarters since."

My heart fell through the floor.

Freedom. Laughter. Friendship with Kestrel.

"You saw that?"

He sneered. "You mean did I see you riding the horse *I* wanted to give you? Did I see you laughing the way *I* planned with my brother? And did I see the way you revelled in the freedom *I* wanted to show you—then yes." His eyes narrowed. "I saw all of it."

Before I could say a word, he left.

Needle&Thread: *This was a mistake, I. I don't know what possessed me to come back here without a thought-out plan. I need to think of another.*

I did have a plan: get pregnant with his child and nullify the debt.

And look how that turned out.

Last night, Jethro showed me just how much I'd hurt him by living the best I could within the parameters he'd set. I'd found happiness with Kes. I'd proven I wasn't broken and still found joy in simple things.

I wanted to find happiness with Jethro. I wanted to runaway together. To prove that our love transcended duty and family honour—but Jethro wasn't prepared. How could one person be so committed to finding another way, when the other was stuck in the same warped trap from his childhood?

I was angry, upset. But most of all, stricken for the way I'd made him feel. It wasn't logical, but I felt responsible for his pain.

And until we'd talked and made amends, I couldn't rest.

The moment the Hall retired to slumber, I tiptoed to his chambers and tried to enter. But the private door in the parlour leading to the bachelor wing was locked. And no matter how much I poked and prodded, I was no expert on lock-picking.

I'd returned, mournful and frustrated, to welcome the sunrise of a new day.

All I could think about was the mistakes upon mistakes I'd made. With my brother, father…my lover.

What power did I have if I cut myself off from everybody? What hope of survival could I wish for if I was all alone?

Sitting in the silk upholstered loveseat beside my window, I drowned in dysphoria.

I didn't want to eat or sew or read.

I just wanted to…exist.

To pretend I had a simpler life and one not so tangled in treachery.

My phone remained silent in my hands, the screen glowing with invitation to mend bridges between Threads and Kite.

A text said a thousand things. It allowed the reader privacy and time to absorb. Good news and bad were easier to face. Easier to accept.

Uncurling my legs, I opened a new message.

I had no idea what to write, so I turned off my mental critique and let my fingers decide for me.

Needle&Thread: *Kite…how did everything change? My heart beats for you, my soul craves yours. During the Second Debt we shared everything. We were free. I hate this distance now. Talk to me. Tell me what you're thinking. You give me nothing, but I see everything. Trust me. Come to me tonight. Let me show you I'm yours forever. This doesn't have to be complicated. I love you. Love is simple, kind. Love is forgiveness. Can we forgive each other before it's too late?*

Tears ran silently over my cheeks as I pressed send.

"JETHRO."

I looked up from my phone. My father came into my quarters, fastening a diamond cufflink through his black shirt.

I couldn't stop reading Nila's text. Over and over again. Her words embedded into my soul, and no matter what happened in the future, I couldn't carve them out.

Once again, she'd proven her power over me was undeniable, forcing me to face the conclusion I'd finally admitted to myself yesterday.

Nothing would work.

No one would fix me.

I couldn't continue to be responsible for my brother or sister.

I couldn't continue to live in constant fear of being murdered or cast out.

It was time to take what was mine—regardless of the aftermath, and I couldn't do it on my own.

Last night, I'd swallowed a tablet and visited my sister for the first time in almost two months. She'd been cross and short-tempered, but once I laid out my plan, she'd thawed.

Like the perfect sibling, she'd forgiven me and gave me what I needed to face what must be done.

Then, I'd visited Kestrel. I'd apologised, admitted my douche-bag behaviour, and asked for help. Just like Jasmine, he'd granted absolution and listened to my struggles. I hid nothing, revealed everything. For the first time since we hit adulthood, we were completely in-tune and equal.

Lucky for me, after my bout of honesty, he was only too happy to agree to my ludicrously ambitious plans.

Killing Cut wasn't an option—for now.

We had to be smarter

We had to be shrewd.

The time had come.

Hawks against Hawks.

Cut finished securing his cuffs. "Tonight, Jet. I want it done."

My body seized. *What?*

No way.

Every fucking time.

He'd guessed I was breaking and came at the perfect moment with his proverbial hammer to smash me into pieces.

"Not tonight." I clutched my phone. I had a hair-brained concept, but it was still in its infancy. *It can't happen tonight. I'm not ready.*

"Yes, tonight. I want this whole process sped up." He dropped his hands stiffly by his sides. "Those pills are working. You've impressed me more the past few weeks than you have in your entire life. You've killed to protect our family. You've remained distant from those you don't need, and you've cut that Weaver Whore out of your heart."

He came forward and patted my shoulder, harsh respect glowing in his eyes. "I don't want anything to jeopardise the new connection we've found, son. And she's the cause of it all. Let's get the Debt Inheritance over with. Complete your final test and take your place fully by my side." His voice dropped. "When the time comes, I'll gladly hand over the crown because you've earned it."

Despite my hatred for him, relief slithered around my heart. Relief because I'd *finally* been worthy of the gift I'd been fighting to receive for twenty-nine years.

Pity, it was just empty words.

"I'm proud of you, Kite."

I bowed my head, squeezing my phone until the casing cracked.

I would have to be ready…there was no other way.

"Now, tell the lady's maid to prepare the girl. Tonight, we inch closer to the finish line." His teeth glinted with an evil smile. "Tonight, the Third Debt will be paid."

Nila

I FOUND TEX *in the lounge, nursing a brandy and looking as if he hadn't showered in days. He didn't look up as I perched on the arm of his favourite chair.*

Something had changed between us. We no longer had a close bond—it was taut, strained—full of accusations and denials.

I missed him.

I feared for him.

But I didn't have the strength to bring up what I truly wanted to know. So, I sat there, rubbing his forearm with my tattooed fingertips, hoping he knew that I forgave him. He might be my elder, but he wasn't faultless. He needed to let his guilt go before it killed him.

Without looking into my eyes, he spoke. His voice was cracked and brittle, his brandy glass long since dry.

"She told me to hide you."

I knew instantly he spoke of my mother.

"I had plans. I'd booked flights for all of us. I had a whole new life arranged in America. There was no way I was going to let those bastards have two of my girls. I would've died to protect you, Threads. You have to believe me."

My father's head bowed as the weight of wrong decisions pushed him deeper into his chair.

"The night before we were due to leave, I had a visitor. He showed me…things—" He swallowed hard, squeezing his eyes as if he couldn't bear to remember. "He made me believe that no matter where I took you, no matter how well I hid you, they would find you. And if they did, the debts would be twice the repayment. Twice the pain. He made me a promise that if I let his firstborn take you easily, that you would be given a good life. A life that might go on for years."

A tear rolled down his cheek. He clutched my hand so hard blood ceased to flow. "By God, I believed him, Nila. He had too much…too many things to prove he spoke the truth. I couldn't refuse. I couldn't subject you to that. The things they've done—"

Taking a deep breath, he stuttered, "So I cancelled our new life and remained, knowing that one day you would be taken from me." A horrible sob escaped him. "I'm so sorry, little one. I only did what I hoped was right. I chose the lesser evil, do you see? I chose the one with a longer timeframe so I could get you free."

He looked up, his black eyes watering and bloodshot. "I couldn't save your mother, but I'm going to save you. I will. I swear it."

His confession wrenched silent tears of my own. I kissed the top of his head, granting absolution. "I trust you, Dad."

He collapsed in on himself. I didn't have the strength to ask him what I desperately wanted to know.

Where did he think my mother was buried all this time?

And what did Cut show him to leave his wife in the hands of monsters?

"Miss?"

The dream shattered.

Not that it was a dream, but a memory. The one time Tex spoke honestly while I'd been back home. He'd then wiped it from his history by drinking so much, he didn't remember the next morning.

"You awake, Miss?"

I stretched, wincing at the crick in my spine. "Yes. Yes, I'm awake."

How long did I nap for?

My phone rested on the floor and a damp patch where I'd drooled on the silk loveseat hinted at a while.

I shivered, rubbing my arms to ward off the chill. The archaic central heating in this place was intermittent at best. Scrambling to my feet, I eyed up the marble fireplace. Cold ash and black soot looked back. I'd set it last night, but I sucked at making a decent heat-delivering flame.

Picking up my phone, I checked the inbox.

Nothing.

I'd hoped after my message, Jethro would've replied or at least come to see me. I needed him again. I needed him every damn day. The lust in my blood never ceased.

The maid bustled about, picking up scraps of material and tossing them into the wicker basket where my cut-offs ended up. "You have an hour, Miss. Time to get ready."

"An hour?" I rubbed my eyes, chasing off the cloudiness from my nap. "For what?"

The maid with her brown ponytail and pink lips never stopped tidying. "Wasn't told. I only know you have to get ready."

My heart unfurled. Could it be Jethro's way of asking me to prepare for a long overdue conversation?

Could he be taking me on the date he promised the night of the Second Debt?

I hugged myself at the thought. *Finally.* After weeks apart, we could finally connect and be true. Like we should've done at the start.

He'd admitted we were on the same team, yet he'd avoided me ever since.

Teams have to stick together, Kite.

He'd been raised with siblings but always so alone. However, he wasn't alone any longer.

He has me.

"Tell, Mr. Hawk, I won't need an hour."

Without waiting for her reply, I charged into the bathroom.

Fifty-one minutes later, I stepped from the misty steam back into my bedroom.

I'd never been so diligent in my appearance before. I'd used the expensive soaps and lotions stocked in the bathroom. I'd showered, shaved—ensured my legs were silky smooth, and the hair between my legs manicured into a perfect strip hiding just a little but not a lot.

I wanted to be perfect for him.

I fully intended to seduce him and force Jethro to admit who he was, what it meant, and to finally accept that I wanted him—faceted flaws and all.

To ensure I looked the best I could, I'd straightened my glossy hair and shaded my eyes with a mixture of blacks and pewters. My lips however were left virginally pink with just a swipe of clear lip balm.

I wanted Jethro to drop to his knees the moment he saw me. I wanted him panting and so rock-hard, he forgot to be gentle and slammed me against the wall in his rush to take.

I was already wet imagining everything we'd do.

The maid had disappeared, leaving me free to strut around naked if I wished. Instead, I clutched a towel around me and made my way to the imposing carved wardrobe. Swinging open the doors, I inspected my choices.

I'd made a few dresses while here, but nothing screamed first date with the man I would spend the rest of my life with.

However long that might be.

A tentative knock came.

"Come in." I tightened my knotted towel, deciding on a fuchsia pink wraparound dress that would set off my tanned skin.

"Ah, Miss. You don't need to choose. Your outfit has been arranged."

I spun around. *Jethro picked out a dress for me?*

I tripped a little bit more in love. "Really?"

Keeping her eyes downcast, the maid came toward me holding a large zipped clothing bag. "This is the chosen outfit."

My heart did an excited two-step, dying to see what Jethro had chosen. It was romantic. Sweet, in a way. And also telling of his preferences—a glimpse into his inner desires. I shadowed her as she placed the garment on my bed and unzipped it.

"Once dressed, your presence is required in the gaming hall."

I can't see.

I moved around her, eagerness making me rude. She hadn't pushed aside the bag, still hiding the contents. I reached to move it, but she said, "Did you hear me? You're to go to the gaming hall."

My heartbeat switched to a sombre *thud-thud*. Jethro wanted our first date on Hawksridge land? Surely, there were more enjoyable places than a stuffy cigar-fumigated den?

"Did he say why?"

She shook her head. "No, sorry."

And why would he? Jethro was kind and gentle beneath layers of complexities, but he was still a rich, powerful man, and she was but a lowly servant. Such things wouldn't be shared.

"You're running out of time. I was told to help you dress." Frowning a little, she pushed aside the bag and withdrew a simple cheesecloth shirt and...breeches.

The sombre *thud-thud* turned to a more panicky drum. My eyes swooped up to hers. "He said I had to wear this?"

Is Jethro into weird kink that completely escaped my notice? Whenever we slept together, I got a feeling that missionary and the more conventional methods weren't entirely his taste. He held something back—but *this*?

What on earth is erotic about breaches?

She shook her head. "Nothing, ma'am. All I know is I'm supposed to help you dress and get you there within the hour." She reached for my towel.

I backpedalled. "No...that won't be necessary. I can dress myself."

Please...

A silent beg began in my soul, gathering volume with every breath.

Please...

The beg became a prayer, tiptoeing through awful conclusions.

Please don't let this be what I think it is...

The maid nodded. "Okay. I'll just wait outside." She headed for the door, but turned around. "Oh, I almost forgot. There were two instructions. No bra or knickers and tie your hair up."

Oh, my God.

My heart slammed to a stop.

Please. Please, don't let this be...

My beg was no longer a scared prayer but a raucous in every limb.

"Why?" I choked, suffocating on knowledge.

The maid shrugged. "Again, Miss. I wasn't told. But they do expect your presence quickly so..." She nodded at the items. "Best to hurry."

She stepped from the room, shutting the door behind her.

They.

Not him.

They.

The pain came from nowhere. A crippling ripping *tearing* deep inside. It felt as if my body tried to evict my soul—every cell shredding with agony. A silent scream billowed, succumbing to the horrific knowledge, battering me with violence—almost as if I could commit suicide just from fear.

Run, Nila.

Climb out the window and run.

I folded in half, clutching my heaving midriff.

Vertigo swooped like bats of hell, flapping in my hair and screeching in my ears. I toppled to my knees, not stopping my cantilevered descent until my forehead touched the carpet. I stayed that way—with my arms locked around me in a useless embrace and my head at the foot of some deity who refused to save me.

It might not be what you think.

It might not be the Third Debt.

A sob crawled up my throat.

Lying to another was doable. Lying to myself was impossible.

Trembling, I sat up and grabbed the clothes from the bed. They slid from the sheets, scattering on the floor. The material was scratchy, rudimentary.

The urge to bolt grew ever more incessant.

Don't let them do this.

I vaguely knew where the boundary was now. I could make it. I had a beast with four legs ready to carry me away. But even if I made it to the stables and to Moth—even if I made it to the boundary and galloped all my way to London—no one would believe my tale. Not after the press. The interview. Not after the online websites and gossip columns placing wagers on when our big day would be and how the world had been used in an elaborate hoax between family rivalry and an overprotective brother.

Cut had cleverly strengthened my bars to a worldwide level—locked in by hearsay and propaganda.

Swallowing the sickness from vertigo, I slowly stood. The room still spun. The nausea still battered. But I had no options. Deliver myself willingly and pray I was strong enough to get through it. Or wait for them to claim me and administer a worse punishment.

Tears clawed my lungs as I dropped the towel.

An ant's nest of hatred and helplessness crawled over my skin as I picked up the breaches.

A shudder hijacked my muscles as I pulled the abrasive wool over my feet and up to my hips. Instantly, I itched—rasping claustrophobia within the primitive trousers.

Keep going.

Gritting my teeth, I slipped into the cheesecloth shirt, cursing the see-through fabric and my dark nipples. I might as well be wearing nothing.

I can't go out like this.

The maid suddenly appeared without knocking. Her eyes cast over me. "Great, you're almost ready." Pulling a hair tie from around her wrist, she gave it to me. "You need to tie up your hair, too. They said in a bun."

I couldn't speak.

It took all my power to keep from murdering her and bolting.

Taking the elastic, I gathered my straightened hair and twisted it into a rope before twirling it up on top of my skull and fastening it in place.

"You ready to go?"

Ignoring the maid, I padded over to the full-length mirror, hating the fact my chest was in full view beneath the cheesecloth.

My reflection.

A wild moan keened. I slapped my hands over my mouth.

I look...

I look...

My heart decided it would no longer beat. No longer strum to keep me alive. It turned into coal—no longer flesh or blood or diamond—just dirty, dusty coal splintering into kindling.

All my fears had come true.

I was about to pay the Third Debt.

And I knew who I was paying it for.

The Hawk ancestors had a family. I'd already paid for the husband's trial for stealing by whipping. I'd paid for the sins of Mrs. Weaver by drowning the Hawk daughter for witchcraft. And now I was to pay whatever curse befell the Hawk son.

The little boy who worked so hard only to be rewarded with starvation.

I knew that with utmost certainty.

My reflection told the terrifying truth.

Dressed in breaches and a basic shirt with my hair scraped back, I no longer looked like a woman who wanted to seduce Jethro Hawk.

But a little boy about to be ruined for life.

The maid led me down the corridor, through countless living rooms and dayrooms, before stopping on the threshold of a smoke-hazed billiards den.

She didn't say a word, just nodded at the open door. Pirouetting, she left me standing with my arm over my chest, trying to hide my freezing nipples. I couldn't stop shaking. Couldn't stop fearing.

"God's sake, come in, Nila." Cut snapped his fingers, never glancing away from the cards in his hands. The Hawk men sat around a low poker table in leather-studded chairs. The snooker table with its apple green velvet and low hanging Tiffany chandeliers was utterly ignored in favour of gambling.

Unwillingly, I stepped from corridor to room.

"Shut the door; there's a good girl." Cut glanced up, puffing on a cigar dangling from the corner of his mouth. He looked me up and down, his eyes lingering on my hidden chest. "Well…can't say you look very attractive. Drop your arm; at least let us see some tits, so we know you aren't truly a fucking peasant boy."

My teeth clamped together as I fought every instinct to run. Forcing myself to ignore Cut, I focused on the man I loved—regardless of his mistakes, chilliness, and icy words.

Jethro sat with his family but somehow looked so removed. His eyes locked on mine. His face ashen and tight, cheekbones were blades, slicing through stretched skin. His posture spoke of a bound animal seething with the need to kill, while his jaw held a permanent clench of desolation and regret.

It hurt too much to look at him.

Kes caught my attention.

He gave me a sad smile, hiding everything he felt behind the incredible gift of illusion. He was a magician, deleting anything that might give him away. Even the connection we'd built the day he'd given me Moth didn't let me see his thoughts.

Daniel, on the other hand, snickered, leaning back on two chair legs, chewing the end of his cigar. "Can't say you're pretty dressed like that…" His tone lowered. "But I'd still fuck you."

Jethro tensed.

A gasp fell from my lips.

I stepped back, wishing I could ignore common-sense and run. Bolt down corridors and charge through doors. But there was no *point*. I would be caught. I would be hurt. And I would have to survive the debt regardless.

Jethro and Kes weren't smoking, but they had a large tumbler of amber liquid beside them, glowing in the warm sidelights that cast more shadows than illumination. The room lurked in colour palettes of brown, maroon, and earth. Forest green drapery obscured the windows, while the carpet was a thick motif of a huge chessboard with black and white squares.

It truly was a parlour where games were played—the debts being the ultimate game of all.

"Jet, are you going to say something to our guest?" Cut narrowed his eyes.

Jethro's knuckles turned white around his glass.

I stood motionless on the carpet, waiting…waiting for him to doom me to his heinous family once again.

Jethro tore his eyes from mine, glaring at the table. Kes nudged him subtlety.

Sucking in a heavy breath, he pinched the bridge of his nose. Without looking up, he murmured, "Your job is to serve us while we gamble, Ms.

Weaver." His eyes landed on mine only to dart away a second later. "You are to do as we ask in all instances. Understood?"

I didn't listen to his words but his eyes. They shot their own message—but it was scrambled, hectic, unfathomable.

"Grab a fresh ashtray from the sideboard and replenish the peanuts," Cut commanded.

I couldn't move.

Cut twisted his body to face me. "Why are you still standing there? Did you not hear me?"

Oh, God. Oh, God.

My hands fisted and I tried to obey, but my legs seized with terror.

Kes stood up, scattering a few nutshells. "I'll show—"

Cut slammed his palm on the table, toppling stacks of poker chips. "Sit down, Angus, and fucking behave." Glowering at me, he snarled, "Do as you're told, Ms. Weaver, or this gets a hundred times worse."

Jethro hung his head, dragging a hand over his nape. His eyes infernoed with hatred, blazing at his father.

Cut bellowed, "Now!"

Kes hastily sat back down. I somehow found the strength to move. Silently, I made my way barefoot to the sideboard where staff had left an expensive bottle of cognac, more cigars, crystal ashtrays, and an array of nuts and crisps for the game.

With shaking hands, I grabbed a bag of honey-roasted peanuts and hugged them. Suffering another vertigo tilt-a-whirl, I spun to face the men.

Four Hawks.

One of me.

I baulked.

I didn't want to go anywhere near them. The table had an aura of evil around it, dangerous and foreign, screaming at me to run. Even Jethro was shrouded, neither granting me strength through his love nor soothing me that somehow he would save me.

Cut snapped his fingers, cigar smoke wisping toward the ceiling. "We don't have all fucking night."

The grandfather clock chimed the hour.

The heavy gong reverberated like visible notes, rippling through the air.

Clang.

Clang.

I'll move when it ends.

Clang.

Clang.

Four chimes. I forced courage into my veins, even though I'd used every drop. I couldn't bear to look at the clock to see how many were left.

Clang.

Clang.

"Shit, girl. Get over here now!" Cut yelled.

Clang.

Clang.

Jethro looked up. His golden eyes had been cloaked before with chaos, but now they screamed with everything he wanted to say.

I read your text.

I'm sorry.

Clang.

My heart cracked open as Jethro's lips formed two words. Two words that asked so much of me with no hint of deliverance.

Trust me.

Clang.

The final chime hung in the air like a cymbal crash, giving me nowhere else to hide. Ten p.m. and the night had only just begun.

Dropping my gaze from Jethro's, I steeled my heart and trusted not in *him* but in *me.*

I was strong enough.

I was brave enough.

I trusted I could survive.

Straightening my shoulders, I moved toward the Hawks to serve them.

Jethro

FUCK, SHE WAS beautiful.

I couldn't tear my eyes away from the see-through shirt and awful trousers she wore. Instead of turning her into a scullery boy—an unwanted little heathen—the billowing material transformed her into a pixy. An ethereal creature barely fitting into human clothes.

Please, let this work.

I hadn't had much time. I didn't have the assurances I needed.

But I'd done all I could to protect her.

Trust me, Nila.

I waited for her to raise her eyes, but she kept them downcast as she approached the poker table. It was a proper gaming platform with cup holders, chip placers, and leather cushioning for hiding our winning hand.

'Poker Night' used to be a weekly occurrence. The Black Diamonds, my brothers, and my father would set up multiple tables and play until those tables morphed into one. The stakes of each game were high. Buy-ins were fifty pounds, and it wasn't uncommon for a pot to reach five figures before anyone won.

But now, this was a private affair. Four Hawks and one lone Weaver. Along with the disgusting knowledge of what would happen tonight.

Nila leaned over to restock the bowls, trying her best not to get too close. Her smell wrapped around me, spilling rich, fresh scents entirely too sensual. She looked so good. Her eyes were darker, her lips so fucking kissable.

Damn her for being so pretty. She might've been protected if she wasn't so tempting. Just like my family had damned her to this fate, her own genes ensured it would be worse.

"Thank you, Nila," Kes whispered as she moved around the table.

She flinched, not acknowledging him.

My cock twitched; I gritted my teeth. I couldn't handle my brother talking to her.

I couldn't stomach what would happen next.

The intentions leeching off my father were too hard to ignore. Lewd excitement and salacious greed. A lecherous arsehole who thought of nothing more than stealing money and pleasure from those vulnerable.

Fuck!

Breathing hard, I forced myself to slip back into the drug-riddled fog.

I'd tripled my dose.

Cut made the mistake thinking they kept me clearheaded enough to be controlled. I'd learned that they granted clarity to seek other paths. They gave me enough peace to look past the abominable thoughts existing in this house and become as wily as him.

His Will and Testament sewed up my future as a lunatic in some psych ward if I ever tried to dispatch him. But he didn't have a safeguard if I played politics with politics…

Kes nudged me under the table.

I glanced at him from the corner of my eye, pretending to shuffle the deck. I hoped to fucking God I'd done all I could.

I hadn't had enough time to prepare. What would happen tonight would be improv and sheer fucking luck.

If I didn't pull it off…tonight would be a bloodbath. There would be no way to stop myself from slaughtering my entire bloodline—including myself.

So many things could go wrong.

So many unthought-of issues that could destroy my hard work.

Trust me, Nila.

Because you have no other choice.

Without a word, Nila took the used ashtray and spun to return to the sideboard.

Cut grabbed her around the waist, keeping her locked to his side. "I like this on you, Ms. Weaver. It looks rather…provocative." He raised his hand to cup her breast. The wash of lust springing from him overrode my triple dose.

I shot to my feet, showering the table in fifty-two cards.

Everyone froze.

My chest pumped. My fists clenched. My body howled for fucking murder.

Cut cocked his head, glaring deep into my eyes. In a heated challenge, he twisted Nila's nipple through the gauzy shirt.

Shit, shit. Do. Not. Deviate.

"Something you want to say, Jet?" Cut hissed, imprisoning Nila as she wriggled. Her lips pursed, sickness swimming over her face.

I couldn't look at her without drowning in everything she felt. Horror, hatred, hopelessness. She expected me to be her champion. To save her at the final hour.

I will.

I'm trying.

Daniel cackled, stubbing out his cigar. "If what father says is true, brother, perhaps you should leave. After all, you've already had a taste which was against the rules."

Kes stood up beside me. His hand planted on my shoulder. "He has nothing to say. Do you, Jethro?"

I never looked away from Cut. This was between him and me. No one else. We were the main players; everyone else was collateral in our war. Unlike Cut though, I meant to keep everyone alive in the aftermath.

A headache sprang from nowhere. The standoff vibrated stronger and stronger.

It was Nila who broke the tension. "Sit down, Kite." Her voice was raindrop soft and just as watery. My eyes tore to hers.

I had so much to say and no time to speak.

"She calls you Kite now, huh?" Cut shoved her away. "That's a disappointing development."

My heart seized.

Kes's hand pressed on my shoulder, forcing my knees to buckle and deliver me back to my seat.

Keep it together.

"Not an important development, I can assure you." Swallowing my rage, I methodically scooped up the scattered cards. "I think the table needs another drink, Ms. Weaver."

Cut relaxed a little; Daniel laughed.

Nila bit her lip, tears glossing before turning her back on all of us to collect the cognac.

I sighed, shuddering under the tangled thoughts coming from all three relations. Each emotion fucked me up inside until I couldn't fathom my own conclusions.

It was easier to drink from the poisoned well than reject it. I would have to slip a little in order to win.

What Nila was about to go through would break her.

What I was about to go through would destroy me.

And no amount of pills could save us.

I just had to hope. Had to pray. Had to scheme.

Had to motherfucking implore that tonight I would win over Bryan 'Vulture' Hawk.

Clang.

The final chime struck midnight.

Two hours of torture.

Two hours of gambling.

Only Daniel was out; his chips distributed between Kes, Cut, and myself. My own stack dwindled, calling for drastic measures of going all in with an unbeatable hand. Kes was the winner, keeping Cut chasing as they puffed like chimneys and drank thousands of pounds worth of cognac.

Every few seconds, my attention wandered to Nila. She hovered like a ghost, jumping at my father's commands and pre-empting his requests by stocking crisps and emptying ashtrays.

Her presence distracted the hell out of me, but the fact that she refused to look at me drove me insane. She wouldn't let me silently explain or encourage.

She'd cut me out. In fact, she'd shut down emotionally. The only hint of feeling was dismal resignation.

"Your turn, Jet," Kes prompted, pointing at the flop.

I ran a hand through my hair. My mind wasn't on the game, only the fucking chimes of the clock.

One a.m. was the starting bell.

One more hour to go before the catastrophe began.

"I fold." Throwing the cards face down on the felt, I took another sip of my drink. The liquor formed a decent barrier with the drugs in my system, relaxing me enough to remain myself and not fester on Cut's intentions.

We continued to play.

Nila lingered in the background, and second by second, we all inched into the future. The setting was slightly different to what'd happened that fateful night—we weren't in a local drinking hole and Nila wasn't a tavern wench—but her role as waitress was the same.

Kes dealt the next hand.

He'd stopped smoking and slowed his pace on the cognac. His eyes were clear, hands steady. He'd fortified himself just enough with liquid courage but hadn't slipped into drunk.

I'd been an arsehole to him the past few weeks, yet he'd forgiven me before I'd even apologised. He was a true friend. A steadfast ally.

But will you ever be able to look at him again without killing him after tonight?

That question gnawed at my heart until I was riddled with holes.

I honestly didn't know. In order to save Nila, I might lose my brother.

But it was a chance I had to take.

Another round ensued.

The solid *ticks* of the grandfather clock pierced my eardrums. All I could think about was the time.

I flopped. Kes raised the stakes. Cut won. Daniel continued to guzzle.

New round.

I was the dealer. I handed out cards, waited for bets, did my part, then delivered the river. My hand was shit. The worst all evening, but I couldn't play this fucking farce any longer.

"All in." I shoved my small chip pile into the centre and glanced at the clock.

12:55 a.m.

I sighed.

Shit.

Kes threw me a look, his back tensing. Our knees touched, agreeing that from now on, I was on my own.

Nila sucked in a breath, dragging my attention to her. Her eyes were wide, confusion painting her cheeks from our shared message. She shrank further into the borrowed clothes she wore.

The last few minutes ticked past. We kept playing as if we weren't all exceedingly aware of what was about to happen.

"All in," Kes mumbled, shoving his substantial pile into the centre.

Cut glanced at us, rubbing his chin. "You boys are playing with fire." Backhanding his own chips, he spread them over our tidy towers and slapped his cards face up. "All in. Show me the final card."

Daniel chuckled. "This will be interesting." He leaned forward, pinched the deck, and slammed down the rest of the river.

The moment I saw who won, the clock chimed one.

Clang.

Kestrel.

He'd won.

Of course, he did.

Just like he'd won the girl.

THE SINGLE TOLL of the clock sent mayhem racing through my blood.

One a.m.

Closer to the witching hour than daybreak——curtained by deep darkness where sins and perfidious acts occurred with no repercussion.

Fear.

Endless fear.

It compounded, amalgamated until I couldn't breathe.

Time screeched to a halt as the four Hawks discarded their game and turned their eyes on me.

I backed away, clutching my heart.

No!

My voice became a dried-up riverbed with no words to flow.

Jethro placed his elbows on the table, running his hands through his tinsel hair. His shoulders heaved as he fortified for whatever came next.

Cut slapped him on the back, muttering something beneath his breath.

Kes glanced at me then away. His body stiff and bristling.

He knows.

He knew what was about to happen. He knew and couldn't look at me.

Oh, God.

My fear turned to petrified terror.

Daniel stood up first.

Cut nodded as the little creep moved toward me.

"Come here, Nila Weaver. It's time."

I shook my head, backing up until I bumped into a blood-red wingback. "Don't touch me." My gaze shot to Jethro. He stood bowed like an ancient tree that'd weathered far too many storms. His body was knotted and twisted, eyes tight and strained.

"I said, come *here.*" Daniel lunged, grabbing my arm and jerking me against him. "Oh lookie. I'm touching you."

I bared my teeth, struggling in his foul grip. "Get your filthy——"

"Nila…" Kestrel stood, clearing his throat.

I paused, waiting for him to say something more. If his older brother wouldn't stop this atrocity, perhaps he would. Maybe I should've put my faith in Kes all along.

However, he only shook his head, his face once again hiding everything. Cut reclined in his chair, snapping his fingers. "Proceed, Daniel."

"No, wait!"

Daniel dragged me forward. "Come along, whore." Yanking me to stand in front of him, he snatched my hands and secured them behind me with a silk sash. "Can't have you scratching or running now, can we?" He laughed under his breath.

Jethro trembled.

Please, stop this!

He didn't see my silent message as he tossed back another finger of cognac and warily turned to face me. The binds around my skin were tight, already cutting off blood supply.

Cut watched his son closely, not giving instruction but overseeing his every move.

Planting his legs on the chess piece carpet, Jethro said, "Nila Weaver, tonight is the night you will pay the Third Debt. Do you have anything to say before we begin?"

I fought against my restraints as Daniel hovered behind me. He'd secured them too well—they wouldn't budge. "Please...whatever you're about to do. Don't do it."

Cut laughed softly. "Such a waste of words, Ms. Weaver." Nodding at Daniel, he ordered, "Seeing as she has no respect for speaking. Gag her."

"Wait!" I turned feral. "No!" I darted forward, but Daniel dragged me back. I squirmed in his hold, turning into a snake hoping to slither from his trap.

But it was no use.

Within a moment, his wiry strength caught me, subdued me, and threaded a piece of red cloth through my lips. I bit down on it as he tied the knot behind my head, effectively bridling me like a domesticated pony. The material pressed uncomfortably on my tongue.

"Can't speak now, can you, Weaver?" Daniel tapped my cheek.

Jethro!

Jethro ran a shaky hand over his face.

How could he permit this? Didn't I mean *anything* to him?

"Now you have no option but to listen; it's time for your history lesson." Cut angled his chair, looking like a king on the carpet chessboard about to slaughter a simple pawn with no concern. "Listen carefully, Nila. Understand your sins. Then the night will proceed exactly as it did all those years ago." He looked at Jethro. "Continue, son."

With lethargic steps, Jethro took his place in centre stage. He looked paler than a vampire and just as ridden by death. Daniel's body heat repulsed me; I rode the ragged gallop of my heart, trying to calm down enough to persevere.

Jethro's measured, chilly voice filled the smoky room. "Many years ago, your ancestors loved to gamble. As happenstance would have it, most of the time the gamble paid off. Weaver possessed luck and used that luck in business, pleasure, and monetary gain." His voice thickened but never faltered. "On occasion, the head of the Weaver household would visit the local pub to play two-up, rummy, and poker."

My eyes drifted to the finished game of littered chips and empty glasses, seeing the scene and understanding whatever happened to me would be a direct correlation to that night.

"However one not-so-good year, the Weavers' luck ran out. Not only was his wife accused of witchcraft and the Hawk daughter sacrificed for her sins, but his skill at cheating cards was no longer a talent but a flaw.

"The news got out that he was a conniving thief, and the gentry invited Weaver to a game at the local establishment to trip him up. Weaver went—as he always did. And cheated—as he always did.

"When the game was over, however, Weaver hadn't won. The cards had been switched, and Weaver folded with no money to pay back his losses. His playing companions demanded he pay his debts right there and then.

"Of course, he had no funds. He had a profitable business and textile enterprise. He owned silk shipments and exotic inks worth thousands of pounds, but his pockets were lined with lint and buttons, not paper and coins."

Jethro took a breath, his back straightening the longer he talked. I didn't know if it was anger at what my ancestors had done giving him power or that he somehow had a plan.

"They gave him an ultimatum. Pay the debt or lose his hand like so many other thieves. The police weren't there. It was late. Alcohol had been consumed, and men were at their worst. Lust. Greed. Hunger. They wanted blood and wouldn't settle for less.

"Weaver knew he couldn't pay. He stood to lose an appendage if he didn't provide something worthwhile to make up for his lies. That was when his eyes fell on the servant boy he'd brought with him to help tend to his needs during the game. The underling to the butler, the ragamuffin who worked in the cellars. The Hawk son—last offspring of my ancestors."

If I wasn't gagged, I would've lamented in horror for such a plight.

Poor boy. Poor, hungry existence. Whoever he'd been, he'd suffered an awful upbringing watching his father punished, mother raped, and sister drowned. He'd lived through enough strife to last a hundred lifetimes only to end up sisterless—*hopeless*—all alone and dealing with a mob of intoxicated men.

Jethro growled, "He was only thirteen. And small for his age."

His harsh voice dragged my eyes to his. His fists clenched; anger shadowed his face. "A deal was struck. Weaver offered an alternative: a debt paid in human flesh rather than money. When the men argued they had their own servants and didn't need a sickly, scrawny boy, Weaver sweetened the deal." Coming closer to me, Jethro murmured, "Want to know what the agreement was?"

I shook my head, sucking on the gag as my mouth poured with horror.

Jethro whispered, "Weaver offered up his servant—not for cleaning or fetching or menial tasks—but for one night. Twelve whole hours to be used at their discretion."

My knees gave out.

Daniel held me up, wrenching my shoulders with the sash around my wrists. My back burned, but it was nothing to the way my brain fried listening to such grotesque stories.

"The men pondered such an offering and...after much deliberation...agreed."

My spit turned sour, knotting with a vertigo spell and wobbling the world. My mind swam with sickening thoughts.

Daniel whispered hotly in my ear, "You can guess what that meant, can't you?" He pulled me back, rubbing his erection against my spine. "I've been waiting for this night ever since you arrived."

Tears leaked from my eyes.

I moaned around the gag, begging Jethro to snap out of whatever stupor he existed in and slaughter his family.

Save me. End this.

The second he saw my wordless message, he turned away. His voice fell further and further into a mournful monologue. "A night of buggery for a few hundred pounds of debts. Weaver got off scot-free. He returned to his home safe and sound in his horse and buggy, leaving behind his faithful servant."

Silence hovered, pouring salt on flayed wounds.

Cut said, "The payment began at one a.m., and by one p.m., the boy was returned." He laughed blackly. "Alive. But unable to walk for a week."

My heart shattered. That poor, wretched boy. The humiliation, the pain, the degradation. The soul-destroying catastrophe that wasn't his to bear.

Jethro came forward.

I flinched as he cupped my cheeks with cold hands. His chest rose and fell, but no air seemed to fill his lungs. He looked furious, disgusted, entirely not coping. How could he stand there and say this? How could he contemplate making me pay?

Tears cascaded silently from my eyes, drenching the gag.

"In this debt, you shall be used. You shall be shared. And payment will be taken from your body any way we see fit. There are no rules on where you can be touched and no boundaries that won't be crossed."

He swallowed hard, pressing his nose fleetingly against mine. "As firstborn, I will be the last to partake in this debt. This is my sacrifice for my sins, too. You belong to me, and I must sacrifice you in order to earn my place."

Daniel hissed in my ear, "Time for some fun, little Weaver."

My entire body prickled with heaving fury. I didn't have time for fear anymore—not when the very thought of what would happen threatened to switch me from sane to insane.

Jethro's nostrils flared, torment and misery quarrelling over his face. "Do you repent? Do you take ownership of your family's sins and agree to pay the debt?"

I could barely stand up. I couldn't speak. I couldn't even think properly.

"Don't make him repeat the question, Weaver," Daniel muttered.

Jethro crossed his arms, looking as if he'd throw up any moment. "Say it, Nila." His voice was so quiet but throbbed with such sorrow.

How was I supposed to speak when I was gagged?

Cut smiled. "The sooner you agree, the sooner it's all over." Standing, he came toward me. I'd never been so uncomfortable, sandwiched between Daniel and Cut, knowing that this time they were allowed to touch me. That Jethro couldn't stop them from sharing because he was debt-bound to hand me over on a silver platter.

Cut stroked my cheek, his fingertips branding my skin. "Three places to violate you, my dear. And three men. We'll draw straws to see who will claim your pussy, mouth, and arse."

Vertigo plunged me into a rollercoaster roll, sending me stumbling into Cut.

He chuckled, holding me against his chest. "I never knew you were so eager."

The moment I could see without the whitewash of nausea, I growled and fought to get free.

Cut let me go, smiling as I backed away only to end up in Daniel's arms.
This can't be happening!

A sob escaped through my gag. My heart was supersonic—a dying piece of muscle about to combust at any moment.

"Fuck, Nila. Agree to the damn debt!" Jethro suddenly exploded.

The room froze. More tears torrented. More pain imaginable cleaved me in two.

I narrowed my eyes, funnelling my disgust fully into his gaze. *You want me raped by your fucking family? Fine.*

Raising my chin, I hoped he saw just how badly he'd screwed up. I was prepared to forgive him everything. His ice. His lies. His closed off arctic behaviour.

Everything.

But not this.

Nothing could absolve this.

Ever.

You understand, Jethro Hawk? The love in my heart for you. It dies. Right now. It's over!

Jethro flinched, bumping into Kestrel.

Kes clutched his brother's hand, squeezing it hard. Jethro wiped a hand over his mouth as if he could prevent any more monstrous things from escaping.

Kes's voice was strained and sharp. "Do you consent, Nila Weaver? Answer the question."

I never looked away from Jethro. I was the queen on this carpet chessboard. I was the most powerful player in the entire long-winded game, yet my king had just ended the game with one colossal mistake.

Tearing myself from Daniel's arms, I moved forward to stand in the centre of Hawks. With my shoulders proud and body vibrating, I nodded.

One single nod.

Yes.

Yes, I'll pay your sick and twisted debt, but I will never be the same. I will never be so soft and stupid. I will never let love convince me of goodness in others. I will be hatred personified, and I will fucking slaughter every single one of you when you're done.

"That's it, then." Jethro swayed to the poker table. He moved like a soldier who'd been shot in battle—a warrior about to die. Snatching the lid off the cognac bottle, he angled the liquor and drank. His powerful throat contracted, guzzling fast, before he tore it away, slammed it down, and stormed to the exit.

In a moment, he was gone.

What?!

He wasn't even going to be there to *watch*? To have his heart torn out witnessing the awfulness he'd befallen?

My tears dried up in complete shock.

I shut down.

Everything inside turned to ruins.

Kestrel sighed heavily. Silently, he retrieved the bottle Jethro had slammed

170

on the table and poured three fingers into fresh glasses.

Daniel and Cut drifted forward as Kes held out each goblet. The men ignored me—knowing I would wait. That I couldn't run. That I had nothing left.

With a grim smile, Kes held up a toast. "To paying debts and being worthy."

"To debts," Cut muttered.

"To fucking," Daniel cackled.

All three clinked and slammed the liquor down. However, Kes was the last to drink. It was only a fraction of a second, but he watched Cut and Daniel finish first before tipping the amber liquid down his throat.

Tossing their empties on the poker table, the men once again pinned their attention on me.

I stiffened, fighting uselessly in my binds.

Kes was the first to move.

He came forward. I moved backward. We danced slowly around the large room.

He didn't say a thing.

He didn't have to.

Jethro wasn't in control of this debt. He wasn't even here.

This was Kestrel's time to shine.

"Before you came here tonight, Nila, we had a bet. The opening round of poker was to secure the right for first choice."

I bumped into a padded chair, changing directory to inch around the pool table.

Kes murmured, "Any idea who won that round?"

My heart thundered. I shook my head.

Something flashed in Kes's eyes—too fast and swift to be understood. "It was me. I won. I get to choose."

Charging forward, he caught me effortlessly and wrapped his bulky arms around me. In his embrace, I didn't find friendship or liberation. I found a prison cell where the man who'd laughed and chased me over the paddocks on horseback became my rapist.

Breathing into my ear, he whispered, "I get to choose. And I want to go first."

I COULDN'T FUCKING do it.

I couldn't watch.

I couldn't hear.

I fucking *refused*.

The entire time we'd played poker, Cut had watched me. He knew what this would do to me. He knew how I would struggle and cripple and potentially unmask myself completely.

He'd come to the game with the same gun he'd threatened me with two months ago——hooked into his waistband, glinting off the chandeliers—— nonchalantly promising death if I disobeyed.

It'd been fucking torture waiting for the time to creep closer, but it'd been nothing compared to leaving Nila with my family.

I hated leaving. But I had no choice.

Discussing what would happen was one thing.

Watching it come to pass was entirely fucking another.

My skin itched. My heart burst. My thoughts were a turbid wreck.

I need help.

I couldn't live with myself knowing what would happen to Nila.

You could overdose.

Take a handful of pills and slide into a coma, so I would never have to face the consequences of what this debt would do.

I fisted my hair and kicked the wall.

The small act of violence simmered some of my rage.

I kicked it again.

The pain I used to seek before swallowing tablets flared into being.

I kicked for the third time.

Throbbing agony graced my toes. It calmed me. Helped me focus on the bigger picture, rather than the next few hours.

Finding a certain peace in my fury, I went rogue.

I let down my walls and turned into a beast.

Whirling around, I embraced every inch of my anger—the parts I'd always suffered, the parts I'd barely acknowledged—all of it.

I showed my true insanity.

Nila was right.

I suffered a madness.

And she'd doomed me forever with no cure.

She fucking hates me.

"Shit!" I stalked down the hall and plucked a music box that'd been my great-great aunt's from a side table. Hurling it onto the floor, I felt a sick satisfaction as springs bounced free and twangs of music serenaded with broken notes.

"Shit!" I speared gold-gilded candlesticks at the tapestry-draped walls.

"Shit!" I kicked over a priceless French *caquetorie.*

"Shit, shit, *shit!*"

Throughout my tirade, all I could think about was what Kes would do.

And how Nila would react. Through trying to save her, I'd lost her forever.

She hates me.

She despises me.

She loathes everything about me.

And I didn't fucking blame her.

MY WORLD WENT dark.

The blindfold secured around my head.

Kestrel's fingers were soft and firm as he tied a knot, careful not to catch my hair. Once fastened, he ran his fingers over my diamond collar. "Relax, little Weaver. It will all be over soon."

Cut chuckled. "Yes, soon you can go to sleep and pretend none of this happened."

My ears strained for one other voice. The voice of the man who controlled my heart even if he'd thrown it back in my face. *Please, come back, Jethro.*

But only silence greeted me.

Daniel snickered, licking my cheek. "Time to pay, Weaver." A moment later, he undid the gag from between my lips and massaged my cheeks to encourage the numbness to recede.

Cut clapped. "It's time for the Third Debt. Take her, Kes."

I prepared to spit and bite, but Kestrel suddenly picked me up, scooping my legs out from beneath me and toppling me into his arms as if I were a bride on her wedding night.

I might not be gagged by material anymore, but my terror kept me muted as Kes carried me a short distance and closed a door behind us. Another few strides and he placed me on my feet.

He didn't speak and didn't attempt to remove my blindfold.

The awful anticipation stung my very being. My ears ached for the barest of sounds. My wrists throbbed from the tight sash binding me.

Large hands landed on my shoulders.

I tore away from his touch. "Don't!"

He sucked in a breath, letting me put distance between us. However, he stalked me, stepping in sync, chasing me through the darkness.

Something pressed against the back of my knees.

A bed.

I whimpered, hanging my head.

Kes came closer, his body heat so much warmer than Jethro's. "Don't fight me, Nila. Okay? Let me do this. Then it will be over and life can go on."

Life can go on?

"For you, perhaps. Don't you see this is the worst punishment for a woman? You're not just taking what you want from my body. You're invading my very soul." Injecting a plea, even though I wanted to spit in his face, I murmured, "Please, Kes. Don't do this to me. I know you're a better man than they are. Please, prove me right." A sob strangled my voice. "*Please*, don't do this."

His hands fumbled with the front of my cheesecloth blouse, swiftly undoing the eyelets and tearing the fabric down the front.

"Wait!" I bowed my head, trying to ward him off like a bull with no horns. He kept me trapped by the bed with no vision to run.

"It's *because* I'm a better man that I'm doing this." He dropped before me to yank the coarse wool from around my hips.

I cried out as cool air licked my itchy skin.

I'm naked.

Naked and shaved and bound for the wrong man.

If I didn't hate Jethro enough, it was ten times worse now.

I sniffed back tears as Kes stood up and wrapped his arms around me. My breasts pressed against his chest.

His *naked* chest.

Goosebumps broke out all over.

My nipples are against his skin.

I moaned in despair as he cuddled me like any normal lover. "Don't worry, Nila."

I gasped, drowning all over again. "Please, Kestrel...*please*, don't do this."

Kes ran his hands through my hair, tugging on the elastic holding my bun in place. His touch was gentle but persistent. He managed to free the rope of hair, and, with tender fingers, fluffed out the thickness so it blanketed my shoulders and back.

I shivered, comforted somehow.

Ever since he'd secured the blindfold around my eyes, I'd been borderline catatonic. Every few seconds my heart threw in an extra beat, turning my internal balance into a gyroscope with no direction. But somehow, not seeing him kept my mind distanced.

I was free to float away—to leave my body and slip into the darkness of anonymity.

"Do everything I say and you'll get through this." His lips skated over my jaw. His touch was so different to Jethro's—dominating and soft—but lacking sparkle, connection...*love*.

I arched my chin away from his mouth. "You're asking me to obey you while you rape me?" A morbid laugh escaped.

Kes's breath whispered over my exposed breasts. "Yes. It's the only way."

"Only way for what?"

My heartbeat boomed in my ears as he took my hand, guiding me from the pool of woollen trousers around the edge of the bed.

"Only way to make this work."

I scowled behind my blindfold. Make *what* work?

The debts?

His twisted fantasy?

I hated moving around naked. I hated him seeing me.

My skin pinpricked with nervous sweat; I was lightheaded with panic. And that was just with Kestrel. He didn't scare me nearly as much as Daniel or Cut.

If I couldn't survive this, how would I survive the other two?

Another moan echoed in my chest. This couldn't happen. It was the worst nightmare imaginable. Three men. Three rapes.

And Jethro. Where the hell was he? Why wasn't he here to oversee what his family would do? What would he claim once everything had been taken from me?

My heart?

He lost that the moment he made me consent to this god-awful condemnation.

Kes kissed my cheek, pushing me so I fell onto the bed. The mattress sprung beneath me, cushioned and fresh. I winced as I bounced against my tied wrists.

"I'm going to place you in the centre." His strong arms caught me, manhandling me until I was where he wanted. His every touch caused my skin to crawl. My stomach rolled as I kept my legs pinned together.

I lay in the middle of the mattress like a corpse riddled with rigor mortis.

Kissing my shoulder, Kes climbed beside me. The heat of his naked thigh brushed mine; something heavy and hard nudged my hip.

Oh, God!

"I'm going to place you on your stomach." His voice was soothing; his words were *definitely* not.

I bucked as he tried to flip me over. "No! I can't—not that!"

He stroked my side, his fingers way too close to my breast. "It's okay. Don't worry. Just roll over for me." He pressed me harder.

"No!"

He wants to steal your anal virginity.

Horror possessed me. I kicked and wriggled. I was no longer an atrophied skeleton but a furious unwilling victim. My hands remained tethered behind my back, but it didn't stop me from doing my damnedest to hurt him. "Don't! Don't touch me!"

"Shush." He placed a harsh kiss on my shoulder blade. "Obey me. Do what I say, Nila. I'll make it feel good, I promise."

"I'll never obey you. Never!" I fumbled with the sheets, wishing I could see. I wanted to bite him, knee him in the balls.

"Goddammit." Grabbing my hip, he flipped me over with a burst of power.

I cried out as he jerked the pillow away from my mouth, pressing my cheek against the mattress. My breasts flattened and tears spurted from my eyes. "How can you do this to me?" My mind filled with his kindness teaching me how to tend to Moth. How could he be two totally different people?

"No more questions. Alright?" His voice was short with frustration. "Just—for once—let a man fucking control you."

That was the last straw.

"*What* did you just say?" I arched off the bed. "Let a man *control* me?" Hysteria took hold. "I've been controlled all my life by every man I've ever met! How *dare* you say that? How dare you!" I couldn't stop tears cascading down my face, drenching the bed below.

Kes grunted as I squirmed harder.

I couldn't move beneath his weight. His heat warmed me like an unwanted sun. I *hated* him.

Fisting my hair, he pressed my face into the bed. "Listen to me and pay attention. *Behave*. Don't fight me. Don't make Cut believe I can't control you or it'll encourage him to fucking participate. Don't make this worse for yourself." Letting me breathe, he hissed, "Don't believe in the evil of everyone you meet. You'd be surprised just how wrong you'd be."

I froze.

Silence reigned while we both breathed hard.

Slowly, his grip on my hair loosened. "Now…will you be more reasonable?"

I laughed coldly, sucking in cotton from the sheets. "*Reasonable?* You're asking the trussed-up girl if she'll be more reasonable? You're as insane as your damn brother."

Turned out madness ran in the entire family tree. They all had to die.

"I'll let that slide." His fingers dug into my side. "But I need you to listen to me. Okay?"

Every instinct boycotted the idea but what he said before echoed in my ears. *Don't believe in the evil of everyone.*

Could the man who taught me to ride still save me? Could I trust him enough to wait and see? Did I have the strength to hope?

Do I have a choice?

Haltingly, I relaxed.

The instant he felt me give in, he let me go. "Good girl."

I hated that phrase.

All I could do was take whatever he gave and hope I survived.

I have no other option.

This wasn't a physical debt—although parts of it would hurt and no doubt destroy me for life—it was more mental. The stripping of everything that made me female—of any right over my own body.

Rustling sounded as Kestrel grabbed the bedding and placed it over me. The warm comfort of cotton covered my nakedness.

He's drawn the covers.

Why?

Kes's naked body moulded along my side, his hand resting on the swell of my arse. My skin smarted with revolting dislike. "I've covered us. No one will see what we do. It will be our little secret."

I frowned. Secret? Why would it be a secret? He was doing what he'd been told. The bed dipped a bit as he wrapped his arm around my waist, rolling me from my stomach to side.

I flinched as his warmth nestled behind mine in a loving embrace. His hand stayed on my belly. I was achingly aware of how close his fingers were to my pubic bone.

Questions formed: *What will you do to me? How long am I yours before you hand me over?* But I couldn't voice them. I couldn't ask, because I couldn't stomach the replies.

Kes kissed my cheek, nuzzling his nose into my hair. "You're so beautiful, Nila. So goddamn beautiful." Dragging his fingers along my collar and down my spine, he whispered, "I've wanted you since the moment you arrived. I'd never wished to be firstborn before. I'm happy with my allotment within this family, but seeing you that night and knowing Jethro had full rights to you—well, it was the first time I was jealous of my brother."

I gasped as his touch landed on my arse again. Every muscle clenched. My eyes squeezed and I panted faster, terrified of him invading my body—especially in a place I'd never been touched before.

"Just because you have me now, doesn't mean this is right." I kept my eyes closed behind my blindfold—a double layer of blackness.

"I know." His fingers suddenly latched around my jaw, angling my neck. His lips landed on mine.

All sensation ceased to exist.

The switch inside me flipped. I shut down completely. I didn't feel the heat of his lips or taste the flavour of his mouth.

Everything was chalk and beige and nothingness.

His lips coaxed mine, but I clamped them closed—remaining forbidding and not softening in any way.

Pulling back, he ran gentle fingertips over my chin. "I'm not going to make this worse for you by dragging it on." Kes shifted his weight, rolling me closer. Gathering me against his naked form, I tried to ignore the heat of his erection against the crack of my arse.

"Kes, please..." I begged as his hand disappeared down my front and found my clit. His fingers didn't venture lower—just stayed on the outside of my pussy. I flinched but had nowhere to run.

His hips rocked, pressing himself into me. "My father expects me to hurt you. That sex isn't sex unless you're screaming and bruised." He imprisoned my face again, sealing his lips over mine.

I tried to angle away, but his mouth locked against me with swift finality.

He didn't force me to kiss him back, just kept his mouth on mine and his fingers rubbing my clit. His hips rocked harder and a moan swelled despite my horror.

Tearing himself from my mouth, he nibbled on my earlobe. "I'm supposed to rape you, Nila. Take from you what you don't want to give and break apart your mind piece by piece."

My unwilling moan turned into a sob. "You don't have to. You could just let me go."

He chuckled. "No, I can't. That's the thing. No one can leave. Not you, Jet, myself. We're all locked in this game until the very end." He trailed kisses along my cheek. "There can be no victors if there are no players."

Fury prickled my skin. I snarled, "If that's the case, just do it then! Destroy me—seeing as *Daddy* told you to." My mind wouldn't shut up; my lips wouldn't censor. "What is it with you and Jethro? You are *men*. You know right and wrong. You could end this by stopping him. Why don't you grow some balls and do it!"

Kes stiffened. His cock twitched against my lower back. Instead of anger, he laughed quietly. "So black and white to you." Cupping my throat, he thrust once. "Nothing is ever black and white, Nila. You should know that by now. It's all how you survive the grey."

His fingers fluttered over my clit—reminding me he had me at my most vulnerable. His touch wasn't cruel or hurtful—not the way Cut had commanded. My heart scampered in hope.

"What happens next has to be authentic. Do you understand?" His fingers moved faster, teasing my body, forcing nerve endings to respond despite my mind screaming with loathing.

His breathing turned harsh. "You need to relax and let me do what needs to be done."

"What—" My mouth parted as he strummed my clit harder. "What do you mean?"

With a soft grunt, he buried his face in my hair. "I'm going to make you come—to ensure you play your part. But I won't violate you, and I won't take advantage of you any more than I am right now." He angled my face and kissed me again. "You have my word."

My eyes flew open behind my blindfold. I didn't understand.

What does he mean?

He pressed his cock against my arse, rocking seductively. He whispered, "Pretend I'm hurting you. Cry out. Scream."

What?

"Do it," he hissed.

What the *hell* is going on? My body wound tight, growing wet against my wishes. My eyes were blinded, wrists tied, and my mind a mess with confusion.

"Cry, Nila. Otherwise, I'll have to make you cry for real." He pinched my clit, throbbing the bundle of nerves.

I jerked in his arms. More tears escaped. It wasn't hard to cry. It was a relief to complain—to verbalize how much I wanted this to end.

"Stop!"

If he wanted me to beg like a rape victim, I would. He'd given me permission to fight back, even if it was only vocal.

I'll make your eardrums bleed.

I thrashed, rubbing our bodies together and drawing a ragged groan from him. "Fuck you!"

He grunted as I tried to kick his kneecaps. "Get off me, you arsehole."

"Not anger, goddammit. Pain!" He fisted my hair, yanking my head back. "Be in pain, begging. Forget about fighting."

That was asking the impossible. I could hate and curse and scream. But *plead*? It was blasphemy.

"If you want to get through tonight without being fucked in every hole you own, then do it!"

Images of Cut pounding into me, of Daniel strangling me, and the horrific violation of being a Hawk plaything gave me enough obedience to give up my courage and beseech. *"Please!* No, you're hurting me!"

"Good." He bit my ear, pinning me harder against him. "Again, louder this time."

"Noooo!" I gave into the sobs waiting just beneath my ribcage. "Don't. I'll do whatever you want. Just, don't—*no!*"

He groaned, rocking harder against me. "Shit, that's too good. Now I'm hard as fuck."

He rolled his hips, rubbing his erection, making the bed rock.

"Again." He thrust, groaning theatrically. "More. Pretend I've entered you and it hurts."

I couldn't speak through my tears.

His fingers stroked me faster, making my body twitch and tense. His hips worked harder, bruising my back. His voice licked my ear. "I'm not going to fuck you, Nila. But it needs to look like I am."

Suddenly—it all made sense.

That's why he put the cover over us. That's why he wanted me to move and squirm and scream, so our movements would *look* like he fucked me.

Oh, my God.

The sheer relief made me cry harder. And with relief came the performance of a lifetime. My fingers stretched behind me, rubbing his chiselled belly in acknowledgement. The trust that'd tried to grow in the past sprouted into a beautiful flower. I gave myself over to this second-born Hawk, who was a true ally and friend.

"No!" I bellowed. "God, no!"

I arched my back, deliberately pressing into his cock.

He growled, his hands latching around my hips, half to hold me in place and half to drag me back to meet him thrust for thrust.

We lost ourselves as we became what others would see.

"Fuck, you feel good, little bitch!" he yelled, his volume way louder than required.

Cameras. Microphones. Recording devices that would capture this degrading act. It was all for the people watching.

My heart burned. *Is Jethro watching?*

The anger I felt toward him only spurred me on.

Kes wrapped his hand around my nape, holding me away from him while his other hand found my clit again. "Fuck, yes. Take it. Fuck, you're tight."

He paused, waiting like any good actor for his fellow screen star to read her script.

"Ahh! No more. Please, no more!"

"You'll take it until I say fucking otherwise, bitch."

We both groaned as he thrust so hard the boundary between faking and reality became blurred.

My legs scissored as he rolled me from my side to halfway on my belly. His next thrust slipped, sliding between my legs and pressing against my clit.

We both jolted.

"Fuck me," he hissed. His muscles trembled.

I froze.

We were so close to breaking every rule between loyalty and decency.

He bit my ear. "Don't stop. Pretend, I'm ripping you in two. Scream harder. Just—don't stop making them believe."

My body hummed, growing wetter and heavier. I didn't know if it was the pantomime or relief, but my nipples tingled and sensation came back with full force. "Stop! No. It's too much. Nooooo!"

He pressed his forehead against my skull. "You're driving me insane, Nila." Louder, he growled, "Little bitch. I'll teach you a lesson about your place. I'll show you what tonight is all about."

I let go of dignity and bawled. My cheeks rivered with tears; the blindfold was drenched. I stopped trying to talk in sentences and settled for monosyllables instead. "No!"

Thrust.

"Stop."

Rock.

"I'm begging—"

He groaned, bending my body until I slotted perfectly in his strong embrace.

I couldn't ignore his hardness or the way his muscles vibrated with need. In that moment, he was a saint. A man with a tied-up woman rubbing against his body and not using her. My trust layered with respect. He was good. He was kind. He was true.

We both panted as we turned frantic. There was no rhythm anymore—only debasing fake-fucking, rustling sheets, and creaking springs. As much as I despised what tonight represented, I couldn't help the tiny flutter of desire unfurling thanks to his never-ending coaxing fingers.

Unfounded hurt crept over me.

Jethro hadn't tried to stop this. He'd run.

But Kestrel had stepped up to protect me. He put his own life on the line. *That's more than Jethro's ever done.*

My heart twisted in a resentful agonising braid. I didn't want to sleep with Kes. But in a way…I was almost offended that he had the self-restraint to keep me safe even from him.

I was baffled.

I was endlessly grateful.

He was turned on. He'd admitted he'd wanted me since setting eyes on me…yet he made no move to dip his fingers inside me or try to work his cock anywhere but between my thighs.

The bed rocked with every thrust. My back arched as his fingers turned harder and demanding. For non-sex, it gave the ultimate impression of being ridden and used.

Sickness rolled inside to think of Jethro watching this.

But then anger slapped the nausea away.

He should've been the one to stop this. If only he'd given up trying to fit in and realised that he would never be the man his father wanted. If only he could see the *truth*.

Now, it's too late.

"Scream," Kes whispered.

"Fucking, ride my dick, bitch," he yelled.

"Stop. Oh, my God. Stop!"

My body rocked backward, seeking a release against all rationality. Kes panted in my ear, his cock throbbing and hot between my thighs. I pressed my legs together, giving him friction to rub against.

"Goddammit, don't do that." He pulled away, pressing himself against the small of my back. "You're fucking beautiful." His fingers worked me harder. "Shit, I wish I could climb inside you for real."

His words clenched my core. An orgasm I *never* expected brewed into being.

I moaned as my wrists hurt, being squashed every time Kes thrust.

"I'm losing it," he muttered. "I need this to end before we both get into trouble."

His gruff voice attacked my nervous system, sending me into quakes. My body took over; my toes curled with building pleasure.

Kes grasped my wrists, tugging on the sash, arching my back.

He nipped at my throat, running his warm tongue down the top of my spine. His fingers quickened, along with his hips. My thoughts disintegrated as his touch slipped on my clit and found wetness.

"Fuuuuck." His thrusts turned erratic and savage. His fingers lost uniformity.

I moaned.

I couldn't help it.

It felt *good.*

I wanted to cry.

I wanted to embrace it.

I wanted to die for who I'd become.

The covers shifted and clung, no doubt making it seem as if Kes took me with nothing barred. My mouth opened to breathe faster. Kes surprised me by sealing his lips completely over mine.

I stiffened.

I didn't know what to do.

A kiss was somehow even more intimate than the fake-fucking we indulged in. Then his fingers tickled from my clit to entrance. I moaned. I couldn't decide if it was a beg to stop or permission to keep going.

The fear that any minute he might stop being a gentleman trying to save me and fuck me against my will added the element of danger.

He shuddered as he slipped a fingertip barely inside me.

The taboo. The forbiddenness. The wrongness of what we were doing consumed me.

I couldn't stop the detonating bliss just like I couldn't stop my blood from flowing.

I came.

The second my body exploded around his finger, his tongue entered my mouth and I didn't fight it.

I welcomed it.

For one delicious spiralling moment, I let go of right and wrong. I forgot about Jethro and ignored the messy aftermath.

I gave into pleasure.

Kes pulled me back against him, pleasure and need rumbling in his chest.

My fear completely subsided.

I *trusted* him.

All this time he'd been there guiding me. Looking after me.

His hand clutched my hip, forcing me to rock against his fingers. His cock branded my back as my core contracted again and again, heaven shooting through my system.

He spooned me harder, his legs entwining with mine. "Shit."

I let out a cry of ecstasy as my orgasm took me high, high, *higher* before snipping me free and hurtling me back to earth.

My ears rang. My heartbeat was a noisy jackhammer.

His lips sought mine again and I kissed him back. Our tongues tangled and I catalogued the difference between brothers. Jethro was fierce and controlling. A dominant, mysterious man through and through. Kestrel was eager and ferocious, taking everything with boyish charm. "Fuck, I don't want to come. I promised myself I. Would. Not. Come."

I believed him. I understood his decency and I couldn't thank him enough.

But there was one thing I could do to show him my gratitude.

It was a gift I could give on my own accord.

I forced my hips back, crushing his cock against his stomach. His mouth opened wide; his body jerked as he poured curses down my throat. "Fuck, don't do that. I'm going—"

"It's okay," I breathed. "It's okay."

A guttural grunt tore from his lungs as he lost all reason and rode my back.

His body bucked, his arm wrapped tight around me. The sheets glued to our mutual sweat as heat enveloped us. Remembering the performance, I cried loudly, "Stop. Please stop!"

He grabbed my wrists, locking them at the base of my spine.

For a split second, pain blared in my back.

"Shit, I can't. I can't fucking stop." The bed creaked and his hand rose to cup my breast. He tweaked my nipple, gasping as my body bowed into him. "Fuck, he's gonna *kill* me for this." Then a hot wet spurt stuck us together as his legs twitched around mine.

Every tiny tremor vibrated his body.

His orgasm went on for a while, each jerk of his hips gluing me further to him. Our heartbeats raced, and the outside world ceased to exist. In that second, we cemented a deeper bond. Not of lust or love or even erotic connection—but a trust that would be forever lifelong.

We hadn't had sex, but *something* had happened between us.

Something no one could take away.

He'd gone against his family. He'd saved me in the only way he could.

I owed him.

A lot.

And I would never *ever* forget it.

♥Kestrel

I LOVED MY oldest brother.

A fuck ton.

I'd always believed I'd been brought into the world in order to save him from himself.

I'd never begrudged him or wished our roles were reversed. I knew the tightrope he walked every damn day and was happy to be scot-free and living my own easy life.

But when I'd removed Nila's clothing and she'd stood there bound and blindfolded, I fucking *hated* him.

I hated him for being too much of a pussy.

I hated his fucking condition.

I just wished he wasn't so *damaged*. That I didn't love him as much as I did. That I didn't know every single trial he'd been through and just how deep and strong he was—beneath the bullshit layered on him by Cut.

When I'd grabbed her and put her on the bed, I'd been so hard I could've killed someone with my cock. When I'd removed my clothes and slid in beside her, I could've come from the gentle friction alone. And when I'd slipped and felt her wet heat when I had no right to touch that part of her, I couldn't stop it anymore.

I *had* to come.

I would disintegrate if I didn't.

He'd asked me to do this.

This was *his* plan. Not mine.

When he'd come to me with his scheme, I'd told him. Full disclosure. I hadn't held back. He knew that I found her fucking gorgeous. He knew I found her spirit, sharp tongue, and stubbornness a huge turn-on. His temper had flared. His condition reacted. And he'd looked like he wanted to sucker-punch me then tear my dick off. But he'd come to the same conclusion I had.

There was no other way.

His heart had made the decision, and there was no other alternative.

So, we'd agreed. Against my better judgement, I'd promised. And against his instincts, he'd *trusted* me.

Unfortunately, tonight I'd betrayed that trust.

I wanted to fuck her so badly. I wanted her writhing with pleasure and calling out my name. *My* name. Not his.

Seeing her bare dragged desires from me that I'd kept buried out of respect for Jet. He was my fucking brother. We'd grown up together. There was no other loyalty stronger than that.

But Nila…

Shit.

When I'd undone my belt and stepped from my boxers, I'd wanted to tear off her blindfold and show her who would be taking her. I wanted her to look at *me*. Truly *see* me. I wanted her eyes on my cock and her breath on my skin. I wanted her to look at me the way she looked at my brother.

My dick was harder than it'd been since I'd had a foursome with some club bunnies. I craved Nila with every cell, but I didn't want her for my own.

I wanted to 'borrow' her. Taste her—just once live in my brother's shoes and have what he had. Was that so wrong? Was it so scandalous to want a piece of his inheritance?

I could answer my own question.

Yes, it was wrong. Yes, it was scandalous. And no, I would never go behind my brother's back.

He'd given me permission to do this. He'd *begged* me to do this.

I hadn't asked for payment or demanded anything in return.

Nila was gift enough.

When her tongue had tentatively touched mine, I'd wanted to grab her hair and kiss her with abandon.

Fuck the debts.

Fuck the family.

For once, I wanted what I wanted for *me*—not for any other reason.

But I was too damn honourable. Too well trained in hierarchy and fidelity. I couldn't do it.

She was so pretty. So tiny. Her stomach so flat and her small breasts the perfect handful. She truly was a doll. A woman I could easily fall for if I wasn't a loyal Hawk.

Discipline and primogeniture—it'd all taught me my place from day one. But my love for Jethro…that was the padlock on coveting anything I might want.

Touching her pussy had been the hardest part of all. I'd almost fucked up and lost myself. It would've been so easy to open her arse cheeks and slip inside her—like Cut expected me to.

There was nothing worse than having a naked woman, with expectations to fuck her, when I couldn't. But no matter how hard it was for me, it killed me to think of him watching.

I was doing this for him—but every thrust and moan from Nila would've torn his fucking heart out. Pills or no, he wouldn't get through tonight without some serious problems.

Nila didn't know it—but she'd broken him completely.

And I'd been the conductor for his destruction.

Every sweep of my hands up her sides and every press of my fingers on her clit, I forced myself to remember who I was ultimately doing this for.

It was the only way I could continue.

However, then she'd given me permission. She'd understood my intentions and gave into me.

She let me come.

And I'd never been more fucking grateful.

Ever since she'd arrived, I'd been hypnotised by her dark eyes and the simplistic honesty of her truth.

I'd never seen a more perfect woman.

And when I said perfect woman. I meant for *him*, not for me.

He needed someone pure. Someone transparent and honest. He needed unconditional-no-bullshit-love. No lies. No tricks. Clarity and understanding.

Nila was all those things. Against all odds, he'd found his perfect other. What sort of brother would I be if I didn't support him and ensure both our futures were safe?

Our time was over too quick.

If it were real, I would've spread her legs and licked her. I would've pushed her gently down my body and requested she repay the favour with her tongue.

I would've stolen every ounce of her pleasure. I would've worshipped her tits and wrung every whimper from her soul. She would've hovered in erotic pain and drowned in bliss.

I wanted her on top of me, riding my cock and her kissing me, not *me* kissing *her*.

Ah, fuck.

I would've drained her of everything.

But that wasn't allowed.

It took every willpower I had left, but I was able to rein in my needs and focus.

I'd bucked my hips, driving my aching flesh against her lower spine.

Everything I wanted didn't matter. What did matter was the camera footage and what was to come. Jethro and I would win tonight.

We'd broken every rule and hadn't finished yet.

The Third Debt was ours to control—not Cut's.

But now, as I wiped my cum from Nila's back and grabbed the syringe that I'd hidden beneath the pillow in preparation, I knew I'd done the right thing.

By everyone.

Rubbing her arm, I uncapped the needle and slid it into her flesh without warning.

Nila winced, her head tilting to see, even though the blindfold meant it was an impossibility.

"What did you do?" she breathed, fear lacing her tone.

I kissed her forehead, untangling my body from hers.

I'd borrowed her. I'd tasted her. Now, it was time to give her back to her rightful owner.

"I did the only thing I could. I don't want you to be awake for the next part."

"Wait...please, don't...let...them..." Her body twitched as the anaesthetic quickly stole her.

My heart calmed its erratic rhythm and my cock deflated as she fell into the unnatural sleep of medicine. Once her breath regulated, I undid her blindfold and untied her wrists.

Climbing from the bed, I tucked a sheet over her nakedness.

Standing over her, I murmured, "I want you to think I'm the hero in this, Nila Weaver. I want you to believe I'm the saint and that all of this was my concoction." My eyes rose to the blinking red camera in the top of the room. I saluted it. "But I'm not the one who loves you. And I'm not the one who's playing the game better than I ever thought possible."

Bending over her, I kissed her parted lips and gathered my clothing from the floor. "It was all his idea. The only way he could keep protecting you. The only way he could stay alive to save you another day."

Looking at the camera one last time, I hoped my brother would forgive me. With a heavy sigh, I gathered Nila's unconscious form and carried her away.

Jethro

I WAS DRUNK.

Motherfucking obliterated. Off-my-tree intoxicated.

There. I admitted it.

Drunk as a fucking alcoholic.

I'd been clearheaded all night. But the moment Kestrel took my woman into the bedroom and stripped her, I couldn't do it anymore.

I wanted to delete all knowledge any way possible.

It didn't work.

I winced, opening my eyes.

Where am I?

Instead of darkness and flickering flames from the fireplace, the windows welcomed pink, tentative dawn.

The room swirled, balancing on a stomach full of liquor.

Dawn.

The blank slate of a new day.

Dawn.

The eraser of yesterday's mistakes and the pencil of today's new ones.

I groaned, blocking out the pink light with smarting eyelids. I wished the awakening sun could eliminate the past couple of months. I wished everything could be washed away, granting a fresh start.

What happened last night?

The moment I probed my pounding brain, I wished I hadn't.

Thanks to Kestrel, I'd done what I didn't think I would ever be strong enough to do.

Plans I never thought I could put in place. A future I never thought I could earn.

My mind slipped a few hours into the past.

When I left the billiards room, I followed strict orders on where to go and what to prepare.

And I did—just like the fucking pussy I was.

As the Third Debt depicted, one man would rape, the others would wait their turn. An orgy with witnesses. A night of entertainment for devils and a night of horrors for angels.

I stormed into the security room, turned on the feed between the three cameras dotted around the room where the Third Debt would take place and waited for Cut and Daniel.

Only, I added something else to that to-do list.

Opening the liquor cabinet that the Black Diamonds stocked when on security detail, I poured copious amounts of second-rate bourbon down my throat.

The pills were fucking useless. They blocked emotions from tainting me, but they didn't do anything about taming my own.

When Kestrel appeared with Nila in his arms on screen, I almost smashed the bottle and sliced my wrists open with jagged glass. And when he'd stripped her and climbed into bed, I buckled under heartbreak—my insides cascading with broken blood.

Cut and Daniel arrived.

I drank more disgusting alcohol. Their thoughts and enjoyment splashed around my burning body, cocooning us in a cesspit of nastiness inside the small, windowless room.

The sounds of Kestrel grunting tore at my eardrums. The sights of sheets bunching and bed moving dug daggers into my eyes. Nila's begs echoed like a never-ending reflection in my soul.

It was all...too...fucking...much.

Cut and Daniel laughed. They peered closer for a better view. They whispered and high-fived and muttered what horrific things they would do during their turns.

I kept drinking.

And drinking.

And motherfucking drinking.

Each swallow only stoked my pain, and if it wasn't for my trust in my brother, I would've slaughtered everyone in the bloody room.

It felt like it went on for decades—who knew how long it truly was. But slowly, my attention turned from the fiasco on the TV screen to my brother and father.

Their evil plans became slurred and unfinished. Their eyes hazy and glazed. Cut saw me watching him and stole the bourbon to swig a healthy dose.

He could have the damn bottle—it didn't matter. I was past legal levels of blood intoxication. I saw double. I heard triple. I felt quadruple pain.

Keep it together.

Kes assured me, they'd be out cold in approximately ten minutes.

Not long...

I grimaced when Cut slapped me on the back. I hid my murderous intentions when Daniel sneered as Nila screamed.

Inch by inch, I died inside.

All my life, I'd been in pain. Emotional pain. Physical pain. Psychological pain.

But this...

This pain—especially the moment when Nila realised what Kes intended and gave in to him—was like nothing I'd ever felt before.

It was physical, emotional, and psychological all at once.

A ransacking of my very marrow. An acid on my soul.

I couldn't break. I couldn't cry or scream or yell.

All I could do was crowd around the camera with my condemned family and witness the rape of the woman who held my fucking heart. If Kes and I pulled this off, we stood a chance of ending this. I was done trying to win on my own. Nila was my team. Kes was my team. Together, we would win against wrathful corruption.

Kestrel picked up his pace; the sheets tangled harder around two thrusting bodies.

And that was my limit.

I completely lost my shit.

Daniel cackled. "I'm going to fuck that cunt's mouth."

Cut laughed. "Her arse is all mine." He turned to me. "You haven't ploughed that yet, have you, Jet?"

Yep.

I lost it.

I fucking punched Cut in the jaw.

He fell.

Hard.

Cut smashed against the door, folding to the floor.

"Hey!" Daniel launched himself on me, but he was too slow. I slammed my fist into his face. With a grunt, he crashed against the keyboard, bouncing off the desk.

Two throws. Two men down.

My knuckles throbbed. I waited to deliver more.

But they never woke up.

I liked to think it was my powerful punch, but…it was all thanks to Kes.

Everything was all thanks to fucking Kes.

I groaned, grabbing my head, willing the memories to stop.

The hardness of the floor and coolness of sleeping with no blankets forced me to haul myself to my knees. My lips pressed together against the backwash of stale bourbon. The pills I'd taken at the start of the night had worn off, but the liquor was well and truly still controlling my blood.

I should've headed to bed once it was all over, but I couldn't.

How could I?

Inching higher on my knees, I peered over the edge of the bed. The remaining shadows painted her in a ghostly collage.

My hands fisted on the bedspread as her eyelids twitched and fingers strummed a nonsense beat on her sheets.

The drugs Kes had given her would wear off in another hour—it never lasted long. Already, her body fought it off—legs jiggling and feet battling imaginary beasts.

I wanted to step into her dreams and slay the figments for her.

I wanted to reassure her that nothing had happened.

"Nila, I'm so fucking sorry." I stayed vigil, stroking her arm as she whimpered. Silent tears tracked down her cheeks.

She would wake soon to a different kind of nightmare.

She would be told a lie. It would tear her apart, but in order for this deception to work, she had to *believe*. She had to believe, because my father and Daniel had to believe.

My mind skipped backward again.

I looked up as the door to the security room opened.

My brother stood there fully dressed with a grim line for lips.

The moment I saw him, hatred billowed, and I wanted to kill him with my bare hands. "Did you fuck her?"

His eyes flashed. "What do you think?"

"I think you went above and beyond what we'd discussed."

He shook his head. "I did exactly what you said."

"You did more than what I said, Kes." Rubbing my eyes to stop the fucking tears from prickling, I growled, "You touched her. You made her come. You touched what's fucking mine!"

Kes swallowed, dropping his eyes. "I told you everything. I told you how I felt about her—how hard that would be for me. Yet you made me do it anyway. I didn't fuck her." Holding up his finger and thumb, he pinched air. "I was this *close, Jet. This fucking close to taking what I wanted. But… I didn't. I didn't because I'm on your side and have your back."*

My hatred turned inward, battering and pouring yet more acid on my already flayed wounds. I asked more of him than any brother should. I ought to thank him and never speak of it again. But my lips formed another question, spewing it forth. "Did you come?"

He looked away.

Gratefulness or not, I couldn't stop my possessive rage. "Motherfucker."

I lunged.

I caught him off guard, landing a right hook and a left before he wizened up and punched me in the gut.

"Shit, Kite. Calm the fuck down. I didn't do anything we didn't agree."

"We agreed you wouldn't come!"

"We agreed on other things, too." His eyes narrowed. "Or are you forgetting about those?"

I froze.

He's right.

I hadn't honoured past promises, no matter how hard I'd tried.

Looking past me, his attention switched. "Shit, that was fast. How long did it take to kick in?"

Shaking out the pain in my knuckles from punching three of my family members, I glanced at Daniel and Cut on the floor. "It didn't. I helped them along."

Kes dragged a hand through his silvering hair. "What the fuck did you do? You know they can't wake up in the morning and think it didn't happen. Shit—what was the point in all of this if you couldn't even let it run its course!"

The room tilted and weaved.

I heaved as my stomach tried to revolt against the booze. "Had no choice. Couldn't do it anymore."

Suddenly, I couldn't look at Kes without reliving what he'd done to my woman. It shredded my skin, turned my muscles into quivering agony. "I can't—I can't stay in here with you."

Kes stomped forward and gripped my shoulders. "You have no choice. It's not over yet."

I tensed against his thoughts, preparing myself to flounder in his coital bliss from Nila, but like most times, Kestrel protected me. I picked up on faint frequencies, but he kept the majority hidden behind a calm curtain of nothingness.

I sighed, pushing him away. "Sorry."

He nodded. "I get it." Pointing at comatose Cut and Daniel, he added, "Let's finish up. Then we can call it a night, yeah?"

Swaying on my feet, I moved to lock the door. "You're right."

Together, we faced the archives of previous debts and extractions. I pulled up old footage of Emma Weaver. "It's time to get creative."

With a solidified bond, we each took a keyboard and began.

Goddammit, I was a monster.

Covering my face, I folded over her bed.

I was so tired.

So fucking drained.

It's all so fucking hard.

All I wanted was to give in. To tell her the truth and end the lies I'd always lived.

Pulling the tiny bottle from my pocket, I deliberated taking another. The drugs helped me stay sane—they were the only thing that had a power over me—but as much as I appreciated the silence, the numbness from overwhelming intensity, I hated the severance between Nila and me.

She deserved so much more than what I'd given her.

And now she would hate me for eternity.

Clutching the bottle, I cursed the swirling room.

Nila was safe and untouched.

She would *remain* safe and untouched.

I was done being unhappy and selfish. My sacrifice would keep her safe.

I would trade a lifetime in a straitjacket to give her a long, happy existence.

Those were our futures. And her hating me would only make that separation easier on her.

Sighing, I slid back to the floor and curled up beside her bed.

I would guard her for the rest of my days.

It would be the one good thing I'd done before I died.

Falling to my side, the room spun quicker and quicker.

I closed my eyes and succumbed.

THE WORLD SOLIDIFIED.

I traded treacle-unconsciousness for cumbersome reality. One moment I was off in make-believe land with deformed unicorns and black rainbows, the next, I was awake.

Where am I?

Groggy, heartbroken, stupefied.

I clutched my head, warding off the gentle headache and fuzzy taste on my tongue. I smacked my lips, trying to get rid of the taste. The metallic residue was…familiar.

But where from?

It reminded me of the one and only operation I'd had when I was seventeen to remove my tonsils. I'd been sick for a year with tonsillitis until I'd begged to have them out.

Waking up from the operation had been terrifying. Surrounded by piercing beeps and turned into a pincushion with needles.

Massaging my temples, I forced my brain to work.

What happened last night?

I blinked.

The Weaver quarters pieced together like a storybook—bolts of fabric hanging from the walls, messy table with scissors and chalk, and the grey centrepiece for my collection draped otherworldly on the mannequin.

My eyes flew to the towel discarded on the emerald W embroidered carpet.

Did I get dressed in a hurry?

I followed the trail of fuchsia pink dress draped over the wingback by the fireplace. I frowned at the unwanted lingerie on the foot of the bed.

Then I saw the zipped garment bag.

And *everything* propelled into me with razor blades.

Poker. Cognac. Blindfolds. Daniel. Cut. *Kestrel.*

My hands flew to cover my mouth.

Oh, my God. What have I done?

I cringed, reliving the way I've softened toward Kes, the way I'd found unwanted pleasure in his arms, then I buckled under my hate for Jethro at leaving me there. He just left!

And Kes stayed and helped and—

He drugged you!

My heart catapulted into a thousand beats.

Oh, God. What did they do?

Panic and horror shook my hands as I shoved the duvet away and looked at my body. I didn't know what I expected to find—bruises and cuts and obvious marks of rape—but the stark whiteness of a nightdress hid answers.

I have to know.

I had to see, had to come to terms with what foul, disgusting things might've been done while I was unconscious.

I need a mirror.

Swinging my legs over the edge of the thick mattress, I leapt.

My feet touched something cool and hard, rather than warm and soft. My balance tripped, my ankle twisted, and I tumbled forward to land on all fours.

A masculine curse filled the space. Something shoved me, turning my fall into a somersault. I cried out, coming to a halt on my back.

Jethro.

The instant my eyes landed on him, the betrayal over the past few days choked my lungs. Those damn drugs. His twisted family. A lifetime of conditioning and a soul thoroughly broken from circumstances I could never understand.

My heart bled for him. But at the same time, I no longer cared.

He'd thrown me to the wolves and left.

He didn't deserve my compassion or affection or tenderness.

He deserved *nothing*.

Jethro groaned, but his eyes remained closed. The fumes of alcohol soaked the air around him. His arm flung out, seeking something.

I scrambled out of reach.

He mumbled, his face screwed up and sunken.

What the hell is he doing in here?

I couldn't stop the crashing waves of dislike, distrust, and utter resentment taking hold.

He flinched, grunting as if in pain.

Climbing to my feet, I darted around the bed and snuggled back into warm sheets. I wanted him gone!

Curling my legs up beneath me, I wrapped the covers tight like a fortress. "Get. *Out*." My voice was full of contempt.

Shuffling sounded below, but no reply. A few tense minutes ratcheted my heart rate, before he slowly inclined from lying to sitting. His back rested against my bed as he groaned, grabbing his head. "Fuck."

He didn't look up. His long legs bent, the rest of his body wrung out and weary.

The love I'd had for him wanted to comfort, but the repulsion of him leaving me last night made me hunker deeper into my quilt and glower.

Rubbing both hands over his face, he yawned. Every motion was lethargic and reeking of drunkenness.

So he'd left me at the fate of his family to drink last night?

Arsehole. Complete and utter *arsehole*.

Looking over his shoulder, he froze.

My breathing ceased. My blood curdled. "Leave."

The single syllable hung between us like a deflating balloon falling to the carpet.

Jethro swallowed. Pain and intoxication swam in his eyes. Finally, he nodded. Gone was the refined gentleman who hid so much. Gone were the chiselled cheekbones and radiant golden eyes.

The man before me…the man who'd hurt me, crushed me, and still held my heart in his traitorous hands was a mere shadow of himself—not even a shadow—an extinguished, extinct, broken thing.

We stared for a millennium.

Slowly, his lips tilted into a grimace; he bestowed the saddest, sweetest smile and staggered to his feet. "I'm sorry." With an unsteady wave, he swayed to the door. "Didn't want you to wake…alone. Wanted to keep you…safe."

His voice roped around my heart, forcing it to beat and flurry. His steps were terminally empty, staggering toward the exit.

That was it?

No heartfelt plea or fervent explanation?

Just *I'm sorry?*

"No, you know what?" I threw the duvet away and hurled myself out of bed. Storming after him, I grabbed his forearm and dug my nails into his flesh. "Sorry isn't good enough." Tears exploded into being—a salty river flowing unheeded down my cheeks. "*Sorry* doesn't cover what you've done to me. *Sorry* will never be good enough!"

He stood there like a township sacked by pillaging enemies. He didn't move to shrug me off or argue or explain. He just curled into himself, squeezing his eyes as tight as possible.

I hit him.

"Tell me what they did to me!"

I hit him again.

"Look me in the fucking eye and tell me why you let them do this!"

I hit him again and again and *again*.

"Explain to me why you didn't save me. That you left me to suffer when I know you care for me!"

He jerked away from my barrage, backing toward the door. "I'll leave. I won't put you through any more—"

"No!" I screamed. I'd never been so loud. My voice bounced off the chandelier, disappearing into luxury fabrics waiting to be turned into garments. "You leave now and you will *never* be welcome in my life. You hear me? I hate you for what you made me go through last night." My voice cracked. "Kestrel— he proved to be twice the man you are and I *liked* him touching me. At least he deserved a reward for doing whatever he could to save me."

Jethro stumbled backward, rubbing his forehead. "I don't want to hear about—"

"Tough shit!" I stalked him as he lurched away.

My stomach coiled and spat with pain. What Kestrel did last night stained my entire outlook. Yes, I was grateful to him for trying. Yes, I'd come under his touch. But it made me feel dirty and whorish to speak about Kes to Jethro.

I didn't have feelings toward him other than friendship. And even then, I still didn't trust him. He'd drugged me for heaven's sake!

But I wanted to hurt Jethro so much. I wanted him in pieces like I was. I wanted him fucking bleeding at my feet and begging for forgiveness.

I turned feral. Vibrating with the need to hurt. I'd never been so callous to crave others' pain. But this…I'd never experienced anything like this.

Shoving his chest, I snarled, "Where did you go, huh? Where were you while your brother put his finger inside me and came all over my back?"

He grunted, shaking his head. "Nila—don't—"

"No. *You* don't." I pushed him again. My hands curled into fists, raining on his chest. "Talk to me! Tell me what the fuck you were thinking! I'm done existing this way. I won't let you use my emotions against me anymore."

He swallowed hard, running a shaking hand through his hair. "I get it. You hate me and want me to leave." He stumbled forward, pushing past to reach for the doorknob as if it was centimetres away not metres. "I'm leaving…I'll g—go."

The slurs and hesitation spoke of a tongue still tangled with booze.

"You're drunk." I laughed, letting my pain frolic in the brittle sound. "I can't believe you left me last night and got drunk!"

He shook his head. "Not anymore." His eyes watered. "I wish I was. Fuck, I wish I was drunk. Then this wouldn't hurt so damn much."

"What wouldn't hurt so much?!" I plucked the strange nightgown I wore. Who dressed me after they'd finished raping my unconscious form? Who put me to bed to wake alone and discarded?

But you weren't alone. He slept beside you.

"What wouldn't hurt, Jethro? The fact you're a monster? That you're a horrible human being? That you're a pussy? Oh perhaps, none of the above?" My eyes narrowed. Anger boiled over, stripping body from bone. My temper was corrosive—an acid eating its way like a worm inside my mind. I couldn't go on living like this. I couldn't go on loving a man who refused to love me in return. I couldn't exist in this *hell*. "Maybe you hurt, because you finally see how fucking wrong all of this is!"

"Stop." He covered his mouth, shaking his head. "Just stop—"

"No! I won't stop. Not until you tell me. Tell me what they did to me last night. I need to know. Don't you get it? Not knowing is worse!" I balled my hands, wanting to kick him. "I want you to keep your bloody promise. Tell me what you were going to tell me the day the police came for me."

He froze. "I—I can't. Not now."

"Yes. Now. This instant." I pointed at the door. "You leave, you never come back. I'll never again acknowledge you, look at you…kiss you. Do you understand? *Never*, Jethro. This is your last chance."

I ran hands through my hair, pulling the stands. "I don't even know why I'm giving you that. After what you did last night, you don't *deserve* a chance to explain. You deserve to die a miserable death and leave me the hell alone."

A tortured groan echoed in his chest. "Just let me go, Nila. I can't—"

"No!" I stomped my foot. "You don't get off easily this time. Not again. Spit it out. Tell. Me!"

The air around him withered and wilted. He shrunk, closing himself off from everything.

I stood there like an island as his regret and confusion waked around my ankles. His utter devastation undermined my anger, but I refused to break.

It was his turn to grovel. His turn to show me light in this never-ending blackness.

I'd tried to help him so many times. I'd made excuses for him. Trusted in the stolen touches and bone-deep knowledge that he loved me. I'd begged him to let me in. To love him. To cherish everything he was—even his secrets.

But he'd pushed and shoved and hurt me so damn much. And no matter how badly he treated me, I couldn't tear out the love I had for him. He was a confused, cruel, crippled human being who wasn't good for me.

My anger switched to sadness. If he couldn't even give me this—when I was at my most violent and open—he couldn't give me anything.

Just let him go. End this charade.

I sighed, taking a step backward. "Go. Just leave."

His spine stiffened as he glared at the wall.

Tears ran down my face as I stared at the cold animal I'd given my heart to. The icy fear that I'd been abused by Daniel and Cut filled my mind. Was that why Kestrel had drugged me? So I wouldn't have to live through something so heinous? Had he done it out of concern for my wellbeing?

Would Jethro ever do something so heroic?

He gritted his teeth, finally looking at me. "I'm supposed to tell you that my father raped you and my youngest brother degraded you to the point of ruin. I'm supposed to stand here and fill your vacant memories with pain and evil abuse."

He took a step toward me.

My skin crawled at the thought of him coming closer.

"But, no matter how this will backfire, no matter if my plan fails and everything I've tried to avoid comes into play, I can't—I can't do that to you." His eyes were wild and dilated, thanks to drugs and liquor. "Nila, I swear on my fucking life, no one touched you. Kestrel knocked you out, so we could do what we needed behind the scenes." He punched his chest. "But I give you my word as a Hawk that the only person who touched you was me." His eyes fell on my nightgown. "I dressed you, kissed you, put you to bed. And then I curled up on the floor to ward off any more arseholes. Even though I've proven I'm not worthy, even though you hate me—as you should—I couldn't live with myself if I told you a lie on top of all the others."

A sob wrenched through my chest.

Oh, thank God.

Thank, thank *God*.

They hadn't touched me.

I almost puddled to the floor in relief. But the complications in those sentences—the truth, the distress—forced me to keep pushing, keep talking. How could he take my anger and twist it so inexplicably? How could he warm my hate so it boomeranged back on me and made me crumble?

Wrapping my arms around myself, I took a step closer. My need to hurt him hadn't receded but beneath my violent rage, there was the incessant urge to hug him, touch him—fix both of us.

He shied away. "Don't." His voice was strangled—a sharp warning to keep my distance.

We stood apart. Two figurines in an emerald sea of carpeting. The air was cool, coaxing my temper to simmer. Not being allowed to touch was torture. I couldn't deny myself the need to connect—either to strike him or stroke him, it didn't matter.

Ignoring his beg for space, I closed the gap and touched the back of his arm. My eyes flared at how hot he was—how unnaturally warm for his normal frigid form. "Thank you for finally being honest."

I swallowed. "You can't keep fighting. Whatever it is you're going through. Whatever reason that's making you take drugs and obey the vilest man in history, you have to stop." My voice lowered. "You'll end up killing yourself if you don't get help."

He tumbled backward, his voice raspy and low. "You can't help me. Nobody can."

"Don't be a cliché, Jethro. *Everyone* can be helped."

He snorted, pain layering upon pain.

I hugged myself again, trembling and quaking, struggling with the thick tension in the room. "Tell me and I give you my word I'll listen."

What are you doing?

"If you tell me the truth, I won't judge. I'll stay quiet and withhold judgement until everything makes sense."

You're truly giving him another chance?

I gritted my teeth.

Everybody deserved a second chance if they were willing to admit a lifetime of troubles. My father handed me over, even though he knew what my mother went through—I forgave him. My brother made me a laughing stock of the gossip columns—I forgave him. And Jethro? He made me fall in love with the bad guy and trade innocence for corruption. I fell for him when he was closed off and arctic. If he thawed and let me in, there would be no greater gift. No symbol deeper than two souls screaming to connect.

"I'll be able to forgive you if you tell me," I whispered. "I'm here for you. How many times do I need to tell you that?"

Fury twisted his face, dissolving his disbelief at my confession. "You say you won't judge, yet I feel your hatred toward me, Nila. You say you're there for me, but how far will that willingness go?" He stepped back again, moving to the door.

He can't leave.

"You know nothing. And it's best if you continue knowing—"

"Shut up." I stalked toward him, my toes sinking into carpet. "Shut up and tell me. Tell me what you're hiding." My voice remained level, not rising to anger once again budding inside.

This wasn't a fight. This wasn't an ultimatum.

This was the end.

The breaking point of everything that'd been crushing us deeper and deeper into untruths. The sooner he let himself snap, the better we would be.

Sighing heavily, his shoulders rolled. "I wish I'd never met you. I wish all of this would disappear."

His words sliced a wound deep and true. His voice was a horrible blade; cutting my arteries and making me bleed a river.

"Listen to me, Jethro Kite Hawk," I said through fresh tears. "I'm only going to say this one more time. If you listen and see what I'm offering, all of this could be different. But if you don't; if you choose your family over me again, if you push me away and pretend that what exists between us isn't worth fighting for, then I'm done. Do you get it?"

My voice gathered momentum. "You've hurt me. Everything inside wants to switch off and cut you from my soul. I'm close. So damn close to that—to slicing you free and never talking to you again."

He hunched into himself with every word.

I swallowed back a sob. I kept going. "There's a place inside me that's fading. What I feel for you is dying, and once it's gone, I won't have the strength to get it back. Do you think I enjoyed paying the Third Debt? Do you think I enjoyed having Kes do what he did?" Tears spilled with no authority. "It was absolute torture, Jethro. The worst one I've had to pay because *you* weren't there for me. You weren't there to feel my pain or help me get through it. You *left* me! Do you have any idea how much that killed me? To think we had something, only for you to walk out and deliver me to that horror?"

His teeth locked together, backing away from me, moving toward the door.

I advanced all the while talking, hoping he listened. "But despite all that— the Debt Inheritance, the unforgivable handing me over, the lies and horrible behaviour—none of that matters if you make me understand."

I lowered my gaze, looking at his bare feet. If I wanted ultimate honesty for him, I had to be prepared to do the same. It hurt to look deep inside—to give myself no room to hide and to come face to face with a girl I no longer recognised. But I did it. Because I was strong and brave and ready to give in order to receive. "No matter how screwed up and wrong the past few months have been, they've been the best thing that's ever happened to me."

Jethro sucked in a breath.

"If a guardian angel had told me this would happen. If they'd come to me the night before you stole me and explained the atrocities I would live through, I would *still* have come with you."

A groan cut short as Jethro froze in place.

"I would've waited for you with open arms. I would've gladly said goodbye to my life and let you torment me because it made me a better person—a stronger person—a person worthy of what I feel for you." I stiffened. "So *don't* tell me you wish you'd never met me, Jethro Hawk, because I would live a thousand debts just for the gift of having you love me."

Goosebumps covered my naked arms. "I was wrong when I said you were weak. You're not. You're strong. Loyal. So twisted inside, no one can save you but *you*."

Our breathing laced together as we let the impact of truth tear us apart.

If what he said was true and no one had touched me but Kestrel, then I had both brothers to thank. Somehow, they'd conspired together; I owed them my sanity.

Jethro didn't move—he seemed atrophied with guilt and shame.

I breathed hard, forcing myself to expose the last exquisitely vulnerable honesty. "I can't help you if you don't want me. But this…this is me asking you to love me. I'm begging you to trust me. I'm telling you that you're strong enough to survive whatever it is you struggle. I'm asking you to choose *me*, Jethro. Before it's too late."

Choose me. Love me. Save me.

His fists clenched. His head bowed and the most heart-clenching gasp fell from his lips. "I'm sorry," he whispered. "I'm so fucking sorry."

I choked back a sob, caught between needing to hide and going to hold him. "I know. But I'm not looking for an apology for what's happened. I would've paid a million times over to deserve you."

My tummy fluttered with an aviary of birds. *Please, listen. Please, see me.* "I'm looking for a promise, Jethro." I drifted toward him.

He didn't move as the distance diminished. Hesitantly, with the gentlest touch, I placed a hand over his heart. The same irregular beat hammered back. The same uncertainty and lostness from the springs.

"I'm asking you to make me yours," I murmured. "Take me into your heart. Let me enter your soul. Give in to what we have."

He swallowed a moan and everything crested inside him. His eyes snapped to mine. With savage strength, he grabbed my collar and swung me around to press against the door. His lips landed on my ear, his breath fast and erratic. "That's what I've been doing. Letting you inside me—permitting you to ruin me every fucking day. You already know how I feel about you. You already know that I'm worthless because of it."

My heart raced. "You're not worthless. If you show me the goodness inside you, I can prove you're priceless."

He laughed harshly. He looked dangerously unhinged. "Try telling that to my father." His fingers twitched around my collar. "I've made myself clear. I've been nothing but transparent about what happened. I've done everything that I could."

My eyes popped wide, even as more tears fell. "You think you've been transparent!" Shoving him backward, I slapped him. "You're not transparent! You're so damn obtuse—so tied up in your lies—that you have no idea what you're saying anymore!"

His entire body tensed. "The Debt Inheritance is my cross to bear—not yours. This isn't about what your family did to mine—it's about if I'm worthy enough! Don't you get it? This was never about you! It's always been about me, and I'm fucking everything up. I'm killing myself!"

A half-sob half-laugh erupted from my mouth. "The moment you took my hand in Milan, this ceased to be about you. This isn't about Hawks or Weavers or any other bullshit you can come up with." Shoving him again, I screamed, "It's about us! About what we've found. *Together!*"

"There *is* nothing between us but debts!"

I shook my head, my palm itching to slap him again. "How do you explain what happens when you're inside me then? How do you explain the link we feel when we let ourselves be honest?"

"What happened in the springs was a mistake. It was just fucking—"

I punched his chest, making him stumble. "*Liar.* Such a damned awful liar! You love me—you just can't admit it. You want me over wealth and inheritances and family—you're just too fucking terrified to man up and see the truth!"

I advanced on him. Everything I'd been dying to say spewed forth in a torrent of accusations. "I see the way you look at me. I feel the way you touch me. I hear the hidden messages in your voice. Unlike you, I've been blessed knowing the warmth that comes with love. The way a person's eyes glow and body softens. You love me! And if you can stand there and deny it—when it's so blatantly obvious—then there really is no hope for us. You might as well march me outside and complete the Final Debt, because I'd rather you kill me quickly than live through this endless death!"

I sucked in a breath. My lungs gasped for oxygen as if I hadn't breathed since entering Hawksridge. There was clarity and blazing freedom in chopping up our lies, letting them fall around our feet like confetti.

Looking at the carpet, I rubbed the ache in my chest. "I'm done," I whispered. "If you can't say anything after I just revealed everything, then there truly is no hope and I refuse to waste—"

Jethro's breathing turned heavy. He backed away until his spine slammed against the wall. His chin dropped; his hands clutched at the smoothness behind him.

Our eyes met.

A terrible storm howled inside, twisting him into knots. His hands flew to grip his skull, his chest rising and falling with sporadic agony. "What do you want from me, Nila? You want to know that I fucking love you more than I can stand? That I'm breaking because I know I'm not good enough for you? *What?*"

My world stood still.

"...*I fucking love you...*"

He admitted it.

A tortured groan echoed around the room as his eyes squeezed.

Fighting to keep it together, he sucked in huge gusts of oxygen.

He fought the truth.

He fought the tears.

He fought himself.

But...

Slowly...

Gradually...

He.

Lost.

The.

Battle.

He cracked.

The dam, the barrier he'd always hid behind, came smashing down. He crumpled like a paper building until he was stripped bare.

My heart hollowed as he shattered into pieces.

"Christ," he breathed, his voice completely undone. "What have I become?"

He fell.

His knees gave out.

He slid down the wall like a melting glacier.

The moment he hit the floor, his knees came up caging his body, barricading him from the pain he couldn't handle. His arms wrapped around them, curling into himself, pressing his forehead onto his legs. *Hiding.*

I stood there unable to move.

"...*I fucking love you...*"

Then my world turned inside out as Jethro Hawk—the most confusing, complex, and confounding man I'd ever met—started to cry.

His shoulders bunched.

His chest heaved.

He gave up the fight.

The man I feared, adored, and wanted to steal away from a life of emotional blackmail plummeted from lies, and I could *see* him for the very first time.

His anguished groan ripped out my soul, leaving it bleeding in hell.

His legs moved higher, his arms wrapped tighter, but nothing could hold together what was happening.

Blistering agony clutched me as I witnessed him coming apart. It was if every stitch holding him together ripped open, leaving him gasping and dying.

I wanted to be the needle to sew him back together.

But I couldn't.

Not yet.

He needed to do this.

He needed to get it out.

This was his unthreading.

This was him becoming more than just a Hawk.

"It's okay," I whispered.

I pooled to the floor in a nightgown I didn't remember him dressing me in, and wrapped myself around his quaking body. "It's alright." I rested my forehead on his temple, running my fingers through his hair.

He tried to pull away; he tried to stop his tears, but nothing could stop this.

He was utterly ruined.

Hanging his head, his shoulders quaked as silent tears erupted from his beautiful golden eyes. My stomach twisted as the man I loved came completely undone.

I didn't let him grieve on his own. I willed him to feel how much I cared, how much I was there for him, regardless of how damaged he was.

He stopped fighting my hold and let loose.

He cried.

As his tears fell, my own dried up. We changed roles. His arctic shell finally thawed—shards of ice broke into smithereens, blizzards became snowflakes, and permafrost became liquid. There was no space inside him anymore; it had nowhere else to go but out.

Out his eyes, his soul, his heart.

I hugged the man who'd done so much wrong and let him purge until his body wracked and shook.

He didn't make a sound. Not a single gasp or moan.

Utterly silent.

"What did they do to you?" I murmured. "You have to tell me. You have to let it go."

My hands skated down his back, touching every inch: his face, his throat, his knees. I needed him to know that I brought him to this point, but I wouldn't abandon him.

I would be there. Through thick and thin.

He didn't stop crying.

Every quiver and silent sob exhausted me. I wanted to take back every cruel thing I'd said. I wanted to apologise for hurting him and for saying I would stop loving him.

I could never stop loving him.

Never.

He was inside my every cell.

I would never be able to carve him out—even in death.

"Give me your pain. Share it with me." I wanted to do whatever I could to heal him, to fix him, and make him become the man buried inside.

Jethro suddenly turned in my embrace. Gathering me close, he pushed upward to his feet. I didn't move as his arms clutched me painfully, stumbling across the bedroom.

The moment the mattress was within tumbling distance, we fell together.

Facing each other, Jethro never let me go. He buried his face in my neck, hiding his wet eyes but unable to disguise the steady trickle of moisture down my throat.

God, I'm sorry. So sorry I broke you.

I squeezed him so damn hard.

His breathing hitched. His body shook.

No amount of armour or courage could've prepared me for Jethro coming apart.

Tell me what you're dealing with.

Show me how to save you.

"It's okay, Kite. It's okay." My voice was a steady metronome, granting acceptance in repetition. "I'm not leaving. It's okay, Kite. It's okay."

His arms banded until my bones ached in his embrace.

Without a word, Jethro raised his head. One arm unwrapped, and his hand captured my chin, tilting my mouth to his.

Before I could breathe, his lips crashed over mine.

His touch was violent, harsh—all-consuming.

Need sprang sharp and fragrant. Desire hijacked my mind with such weight and demand, I buckled with it.

We spiralled together.

His fingers bruised and his tongue dived into my mouth, stealing my gasp and conjuring lust so brutal, I came alive and died all at the same time.

Together, we merged tighter. Jethro cushioned my head with his arm as he rolled me onto my back, covering my body with his. His hand drifted down my ribcage, branding me with every inch. His lips continued to dance with mine— our breathing harsh, tongues violent.

I cried out as his fingers captured my breast, pinching my nipple. My back bowed, forcing more of me into his hold.

He groaned, his breath losing its brokenness, becoming rapid with lust.

Desire swirled and demanded, giving us nowhere to hide.

I became instantly wet as he tugged the hem of my nightdress, shoving it over my hips. I wriggled as he fumbled between us, undoing his button and zipper. He grunted as he yanked his jeans and boxer-briefs down, only making it to mid-thigh.

His teeth pinched my bottom lip as he forced my knees to spread. His elbows dug into the covers, positioning himself higher.

We both cried out as his hard cock settled between my legs.

There was no foreplay, no preparation. We didn't need it. We were too far gone—too terrifyingly open and desperate for connection. He angled the head of his cock and thrust.

I groaned into his mouth as his size blazed with tender agony.

He kissed me, slinking his tongue with mine, rocking his hips, using my wetness to spread me wider. He forced my body to yield and melt.

His tears continued to fall, trickling into my mouth and lacing his taste with salty pain. I imprisoned his cheeks, rubbing my thumbs in the dampness, hoping he understood how much I loved him.

That I was there for him.

Forever.

His breathing turned ragged, each exhale releasing soul-burning agony he'd carried all his life. With an arm around my shoulders, he reached down and clutched my hip, holding me firm.

He thrust harder, slipping past the final barrier and filling me completely. We sighed as that heavenly link slotted perfectly into place.

My body quivered around his. There was no warning. No anticipation. The moment he'd filled me, his rocking turned from questing to vicious.

Without his arm around my shoulders, I would've shifted upward with every brutal thrust. But he held me for his pleasure.

He used me.

We used each other.

We used passion to defeat pain. Wielded need to combat despair.

It would either heal us or break us, but there was no stopping the tsunami we rode.

"I'm sorry. So fucking sorry," he mumbled into my hair. His tears had stopped, but his voice remained shaky.

His hips never stopped thrusting, driving us higher.

"I'm sorry," I whispered. "Sorry for making life so hard for you."

He groaned, rocking faster.

Our minds switched from words to releases. We gave ourselves over to pleasure. Somewhere deep inside me, I let go. I floated upward, acknowledging that fate stole me from a life I thought I wanted, but that was never my true destiny.

He was.

Something slotted into place—bigger than a puzzle piece, more poignant than scripture or knowing.

It was the accumulation of fighting for something and finally earning it.

It was *home*.

Jethro pulled back, his jaw locked. His eyes burned as he rocked headfirst into a devouring tempo. I couldn't look away. His body inside my body. His soul inside my soul.

I couldn't contain the magic we sparked. "I need to tell you—how I feel...what this means."

He shook his head, his lips grazing mine. "I know. I feel it, too."

Tears leaked from my eyes as his mouth sealed tight. The wet heat of him and the scorching power of his cock splintered me in two.

There was no break or reprieve. Jethro fucked me, made love to me, and consumed me with no thought to us being watched or catalogued. Long, deep, dominating strokes dragged echoing moans.

Arching my hips, I rubbed my clit on the base of his cock. "More," I begged. "Harder."

He obeyed.

I couldn't breathe, straining for an orgasm that would shatter me. "Faster, deeper."

He grunted, following my every command.

I'd never lived through something so intense.

It broke me.

It fixed me.

It stole. It gifted.

Overwhelming.

Rewarding.

Destroying.

Renewing.

"I'm going to fill you. I need to fill you," Jethro groaned.

His voice whispered through my blood, setting fire to the gunpowder between my legs.

I came.

Spindles and shooting stars and spectacular bliss.

He swallowed my pleasure, his tongue diving in time with his erection.

"God, Nila." Every emotion he'd kept hidden lashed around me like a vow. "I love you."

Wetness spurted inside me as he let go.

He let go of everything.

For a split second, my heart hardened remembering what he'd done. How he'd stolen my right to carry his baby for the foreseeable future, but then I gathered him closer. There was time for that. Time for us to grow together with no more games or traps.

This was us.

This was freedom.

He'd conquered whatever demons had ridden him. He'd given them to me to share the weight.

When his body relaxed and the last wave of his orgasm filled me, he pulled away.

His eyes locked on mine; he traced his thumb over my mouth. "No more winners or losers. No more hiding or pretending or lies.

"I'm ready to tell you. I'm ready to face something new."

I settled back into bed, never taking my eyes off Jethro.

He placed the tray he'd brought from the kitchen between us, tucking his long legs under the sheets, giving me a fearful smile.

For the past hour, he'd prepared himself.

We'd showered silently.

We'd dressed wordlessly.

Then he'd disappeared to the kitchen to grab some freshly made baguettes, pâté, cheese, and grapes. He'd also fetched some painkillers for his hangover but didn't make a move to swallow any of the drugs he'd popped like candy.

All he wore was a pair of black-boxer briefs and a dark grey t-shirt. I'd slipped into an oversized jumper and a pair of white knickers. Together we'd made camp in my bedroom. I never wanted to leave.

His tinsel hair was still damp from the shower and his eyes kept flickering away from mine. He focused on preparing a cracker with smoked cheddar and mushroom pâté before passing it to me.

I took it, brushing my fingers with his.

He winced but smiled softly.

I didn't rush him.

I couldn't. Not after seeing him crack so deeply.

We ate in silence for a time.

Jethro was the one to start—as I'd planned—as he needed to be.

"Remember that text I sent you?" His head tilted, watching me closely.

I swallowed a grape and sat back, ready to talk with no distractions. I knew the one he meant. The one he sent after I saw the graves of my ancestors. "Yes. You said you felt what I felt. That my emotions were your affliction."

He nodded. "Exactly. I told you the truth right there. I'd hoped you'd guess, but I suppose it's hard to understand. There was no trick in those words. No lies. It was God's honest truth."

I waited for him to continue. I had so many questions, but I needed patience. I believed Jethro would answer them when he could.

Jethro sighed. "The reason why I don't like anyone calling me insane or crazy is because I've been told I was throughout my entire childhood. My father never understood me. Kes didn't. Jaz didn't. Shit, even I didn't know what was wrong with me." His eyes glazed over, thinking of the past. "Some days I was fine. Hyper like a boy should be. Happy to play with my siblings. Confident in my place within my family. But other days, I'd cry for hours. I'd claw at myself, trying to rid the overwhelming intensity from my blood. My mind would seize with darkness and sadness and anger—such, such anger.

"I wanted to kill. I craved violence." He smiled wryly. "That doesn't sound so unique, but it was when I was barely eight years old. I had fantasies of tearing men apart. I stressed over money and business—things I had no right to worry about as a kid. It got so bad, I was admitted to a local hospital. I'd stopped eating or drinking; I attacked Jasmine whenever she got too close. I couldn't handle the thoughts inside my head. I fully believed what people said— that I was crazy."

I shifted closer, looping my fingers through his. He didn't pause, almost as if now he'd started, he had to finish as fast as possible.

"The hospital was even worse. There, I worried about dying. I fretted over a child down the hall dying of terminal cancer. I cried all the fucking time, devoured by grief and feeling the keen absence of someone I loved dearly—only thing was, I didn't *know* any of the other patients.

"A nurse found me one night trying to hang myself after watching a movie of a man who couldn't survive life anymore."

His lips twisted into a smile that held both annoyance and appreciation. "If she hadn't have found me, I would've been free. Free from living a life no one could understand. But she did...and she both condemned and saved me."

"How?" I breathed.

"She was a psych major. After a few days of me screaming and self-harming due to a busload of students slowly dying in the ward next to me, she gained permission to check me out and take me to a psychiatric facility instead."

He laughed. "I know this isn't helping my case when I said I wasn't insane."

I shook my head, willing him to continue.

Jethro looked off into the distance, seeing things I wasn't privy to. "Once there, I was even worse. I started having seizures and developed heart arrhythmia. I screamed for no reason, spoke in tongues no one could understand. I self-harmed to the point of disfigurement—all to get the fucking intensity out."

With every glimpse into his past, his present made so much more sense.

"Did—did they diagnose you?"

Jethro nodded. "It took a year of being shuttled between my home and that mental hospital. A year of working with the young nurse who took it upon herself to rescue me from myself."

I held my breath, waiting for a final answer.

But Jethro stayed silent.

I squeezed his fingers. "What was wrong with you?"

He snorted. "Wrong?" Shaking his head, he said condescendingly, "Everything. Everything was wrong."

Untangling his fingers from mine, he traced the blue veins visible beneath my tanned skin. "One day, my father flew in a child psychology specialist. The doctor made me do a lot of tests. After a week of assessment, he was as clueless as the rest of them.

"But there'd been one saving grace. The entire time I'd spent with the doctor, having no contact with others, locked in a cool white room with only puzzles for company, my thoughts became calm, diligent, focused on facts and data. I wasn't emotional or crazed. I found happiness and silence once again. And that's what gave the answer away."

"What answer?"

Jethro huffed. "The one that ensured Cut would never accept me, because there was no cure for what I am. Back then, it seemed like I was making this shit up. That I was rebelling and putting on a show. Nowadays, it's one of the first things a doctor checks for."

I needed a name—something to call what Jethro was. I leaned closer, waiting.

"I'm a VEP, Nila."

I blinked. He'd announced it as if it were a foul, common disease that would make me hate him. I had no idea what it was.

He half-smiled. "Also known as an HSP."

I frowned, racking my brain for any remembrance of such a thing. "What—what is that?"

He smirked. "Exactly. No one knows, even though approximately twenty percent of the population has it. Most people don't understand when I say a touch is a curse or a noise is a fucking bomb. People's misfortune is a damn tragedy to me. Joy is utopia. Love is divine. Failure is ruin. Unhappiness is absolute death."

I shook my head. "I—I still don't understand."

Jethro laughed sadly. "You will. Basically...my senses are heightened. I feel what others do. I *live* their pain. I go insane living too close to people who exist in hate or revenge. It consumes me to the point where I can't breathe without being influenced."

"What does VEP stand for?"

Jethro sighed, pinching the bridge of his nose. "It stands for Very Empathetic Person."

My heart ran faster. "And HSP?"

"Highly Sensitive Person."

"And that means..."

His eyes tore to mine. "Weren't you listening? It means I'm screwed up. It means I'm more attuned to others' personalities and emotions than most. Their moods overshadow mine. Their goals steal mine. Their hate corrupts my happiness. Their fear and rage eclipses everything. I can't control it. Cut's tried.

Jasmine's tried. Hell, I've tried. But every time we think we've found something that works…it fails. Not only am I doomed to always feel what others do, but I'm oversensitive to smell, noise, touch. My brain is too damn perceptive, and I suffer every fucking second of every day."

We sat in silence.

I digested everything he said, slowly piecing together what I knew about him: how he reacted in situations. How cold he was when he first came for me. He was the perfect image of Cut when he collected me—because that was all the influence he had.

Then I came along and made him *feel*. Made him live my fear, my lust, my never-ending fight.

It's true. I did break him.

Jethro muttered, "Whenever I told you to be quiet. Whenever I couldn't handle it and snapped—it wasn't your voice I was trying to hush but your emotions. You're the worst of them, Nila. You project everything you feel. You're like a damn kaleidoscope with the range of emotions you go through. Falling for you, sleeping with you... Fuck, it was all I could do to stay standing and not cripple beneath the weight of it."

Tears shot to my eyes. I hated that I'd hurt him. Unintentional or deliberate. How did I miss the warning signs? How did I not see the changes in him—the anger hiding pain and the commands cloaking calls for help?

I pictured Jethro as a young boy going through so much trauma. Of being poked and prodded and called insane. It physically hurt to think about what he'd gone through—surviving a family such as his.

I touched his hand. "Are you sure the doctors got it right? That they diagnosed it correctly and there's nothing they can do?"

Surely, there must be a cure?

Jethro snorted. "Do you want the hallmark characteristics? Okay, here we go: One, Empaths feel more deeply. Two, we're emotionally reactive and less able to intellectualize feelings. Three, we need down-time away from everyone if we're to survive living with others. Four, it takes us longer to make a decision because we're bombarded with so many scenarios every time we try to decide. Five, I'm more prone to anxiety or depression. Six, I can't for the life of me watch a horror movie. I relate too much to the character about to die. Kes made me watch one when I was ten. I had to be drugged for two nights just to calm me down."

He looked away, laughing darkly. "Seven, we cry more easily—it's the only way we can purge. Eight, we have better manners when we're in control of ourselves. More cordial to fight the chaos we're feeling inside. Nine, every criticism slices through my heart until I feel as if I'll fucking die. Needing my father's approval is more than a stupid boyhood wish but a goal that rides me into an early grave. Ten, we look for ways to hide. We become chameleons by adopting the habits of those strongest emotionally. And finally eleven, we're highly intuitive."

He dwindled off, twisting the sheets. "Does any of that sound familiar?"

Pieces slotted into place, all making perfect sense now I knew.

Jethro was explosive because he felt everything so much more. He rode Wings a lot to outrun the emotional upheaval forced on him by living with men like Cut and Daniel. He kept switching alliances between his father and me, unable to make a decision when faced with two personalities. He turned inward and festered when everything became too much. He shut down when he'd reached his limit and was so damn cold when we first met as it was the only way he could survive.

"The tablets, they were to—"

"Block the over-sensory perception. To numb me." He fisted the duvet. "They worked while you weren't here. In fact, they were the first thing in my life that actually gave me silence." He smirked. "But then you came back with your screaming feelings and battering ram of ideals and tore that apart."

My heart beat faster. "So when we slept together at the polo match...when I asked if you knew what I was feeling..."

He sighed. "I told you the truth. I knew. I felt your need, your sadness, your confusion. You'd fallen for me, but you weren't happy about it. I bore your worry as if it were my own, but I also basked in the love you had."

Leaning forward, he cupped my cheek. "I'd never felt so much emotion from anyone. You selflessly gave me something warm and safe and so fucking delicious to hide in. There were no conditions or commands—you were fully open, letting me inside."

His eyes darkened. "It killed me to think you were still unsure. That you could feel such a way but not want it."

I leaned into his palm. "I'm sorry."

He shook his head. "Don't be. I've had this curse all my life." He gathered me close, nuzzling into me. "I've never let myself give in. But before, when I slid inside you, I stopped fighting. I did what Jasmine told me to do. I let myself drown in what you feel for me. And fuck, it was the best thing I've ever felt."

My heart cast into a never-ceasing knot. "And Jasmine told you to do that?"

He dropped his gaze. "Jaz has been researching my condition ever since I was diagnosed. She read somewhere that Empaths who remain single and cloistered from society don't have long life expectancies. Others slowly chip us away, until one day, it's too much. I swore to her that I would never find love. That the agony I had from loving her as my sister was enough to swear me off ever marrying. But she showed me another article about Empaths who *do* find their perfect others. They live longer than most because they no longer have to fight on their own."

His hand never stopped stroking, his body tense but happy.

I asked, "What does that mean?"

His eyes became hazy, dreamy. "It means we rely on the person we love to love us so much in return that we can forever hide in their adoration and acceptance. Knowing there's a well of immeasurable affection helps heal us if we encounter a mourning mother or psychotic serial killer. We can stay level— or at least better than we would if we're alone."

"So when Jasmine yelled at me for hurting you and cursed herself for destroying you—that's what she meant?"

His forehead furrowed. "When did you see Jasmine?"

Whoops.

"Doesn't matter. Is that what she meant?"

Jethro scowled but nodded. "Exactly. She pushed me into making you fall for me. In fact, just before the polo match, she told me to stop fighting and make you love me. To forget about the debts and inheritances and find something far more precious."

I couldn't speak.

"She told me to find my cure in you, Nila. She saw what I couldn't. She hoped for something I never dared dream of. She taught me that love can be the cruellest force imaginable, but it also heals."

He pressed a kiss reverently on my lips. "I'm done fighting. You're mine and I'm yours, and now you know everything there is to know about me. Now you know I'm broken and can never be cured. Now you know why I am the way I am."

IT WAS DONE.

Out in the open.

My disease verbalized and acknowledged.

And she hadn't run.

She hadn't looked at me with pity or disgust. She'd accepted it and loved me even more.

Her emotions came in crashes, echoing in my soul. By being honest, I'd given her answers. And with answers came freedom to give in and trip from new love into forever love.

I wanted to crush her to me and never let go. I wanted to get on my fucking knees and thank her for the rest of my days for being brave enough to accept me.

Life together hadn't been smooth. Our past was full of debts and degradation. Our future—if we even had a future—would be full of miscommunication and misunderstanding.

I'm not an easy person to love.

I knew that. Kestrel knew that. Jasmine knew that. There were times when I was too much. When their good intentions just weren't enough and I'd have to leave to regroup on my own.

I could never hate them for that—for needing timeout from dealing with a fucked-up brother. But Nila...she would be drained of everything. I would take and take and take until that blistering, joyous love would turn to putrid ash.

Can I do that to her?

Could I suck her dry and hope to God she was strong enough to save us both?

Do I have any right to expect her to?

No. I had no right at all.

I should ship her overseas and kill my father to end this entire fucking mess. But now that I had her...how could I ever let her go?

Nila hadn't moved or spoken, her eyes full of thoughts.

I murmured, "The day Kestrel gave you Moth, I very nearly broke. I came to your room that night. I sat outside for hours, trying to get myself together so you wouldn't see how much it fucking hurt that he'd given her to you."

Nila sucked in a gasp. "He told me it was your idea. That you wanted to give her to me the day after the Second Debt."

I flinched. It sounded like I'd hoped to buy her forgiveness for the ducking stool by gifting her a horse. "It wasn't like that. I only wanted you to have something you'd never had before." I would've stopped normally, censored my thoughts and deleted things that would show the truth, but now...I had more to say. There was so much more, and for the first time, I was able to speak openly.

Pushing the food tray further down the bed, I reclined against the pillows and pulled Nila beside me. We lay down, legs entwined, arms around each other.

For an extraordinary second, I held her and drank in her thoughts. To have no barriers between us—no lies or deceptions—*it's more than words can say.*

"That moment in the horse float, heading to polo, I knew how you felt about her. The softening in your soul, the desire to own another's life, to have something reliant on you—all flowed in a wash of desire." Inhaling the floral scents of her hair, I whispered, "You fell in love with her a lot faster than you fell for me."

Nila snuggled closer, squeezing me tight. "All this time you knew how I was feeling?"

Does that hurt you? To know I felt what you did, heard your panic, lived through your agony? Did that make me a terrible person to be able to withstand, not only doing awful things to her, but receiving the consequences of my actions through her, too?

I nodded. "Every debt. Every argument. I felt you."

She stayed silent; a wave of unfairness flowed from her. I didn't want her feeling as if I used her—that I'd eavesdropped on her emotions.

I said quietly, "That's why Cut hates you. He can see the power you have over me—a power that I've been taught to hide my entire life."

Nila went still. "It's not only Cut who has a power over you. Jasmine does...and Kestrel."

My muscles locked, but I forced myself to relax. I'd committed to being open. I would continue to keep my promise. "Yes, Jasmine has the same condition as me but not nearly as bad. There are different levels of HSP. I'm on the unusual end of the scale where I'm borderline sixth sense—if the doctors believed in that phenomenon, of course. I'm highly empathetic, to the point where I'll grow sick when others are ill. My heart rhythm becomes irregular if the stress of the person I'm with goes past my realm of capabilities."

Nila twisted in my arms. "Oh, my God. The springs." Her mouth popped wide. "Your heart was irregular then. I thought you were ill..." She dropped her eyes. "Actually, I didn't think that. I thought you were..."

"What? Tell me."

Her black gaze swooped upward, capturing me completely. "Lost. I thought your rhythm was lost."

I swallowed hard. "Perhaps you're an HSP yourself. Not many people notice my moods or complexities—unless I get terribly bad. Over the years, I've been able to hide it better. From the ages of nineteen to twenty-six, I was pretty perfect. Apart from a few episodes from my father's temper on a deal gone south or my little brother's arrogant lunacy, I managed to keep their thoughts from creeping too much into mine."

Nila smiled almost smugly. "But not me."

I kissed her, slinking my tongue into her mouth. Taking my time, I tasted her as if this was the first time I'd kissed her. And it was in a way. The first time I'd let myself be so open and honest.

I was a changed man.

A totally different person.

"I couldn't withstand you." I licked her softly.

I couldn't stop touching her. Couldn't stop the need to be close.

Perhaps, I can show her exactly what this means? What I truly need from her?

She broke the kiss. "How does Kes have a power over you?"

My gut churned to think of Kes with Nila last night. But I also couldn't deny it was my idea—my choice. He'd only obeyed and done the best he could. I'd forgive him…in time.

I sighed, thinking how selfless my brother truly was. How helpful and kind he'd been ever since he'd come to bust me out of the mental hospital. It'd been the third I'd visited all before I hit fifteen. He'd only been twelve, but he'd packed a bag and run away from Hawksridge. He hitchhiked across town and sneaked through the compound to get me.

Needless to say, we never managed to get free. The doctors found us and sent him home, but our bond was forged that night and nothing—no anvil, blade, or threat—could sever it.

"Kes is special." I shrugged. "While I was going off the rails crying over things I couldn't control and wanting to murder people for no apparent reason, he learned how to control his inner thoughts around me. He mastered the art of blocking his every whim, desire, and impression until I could hang around him and have my own thoughts for once. I became addicted to his emptiness and silence. The doctors said he acted like a shield for me. That as long as we stayed close, he helped me cope."

Nila never took her gaze from mine, her body taut with understanding. "I always wondered why Kes was able to touch you when you were about to lose it. I expected you to hit him, but you never shrugged him off. You always seemed to…relax."

I nodded. "That's because I *did* relax. Kes manipulates me in a way, but I let him because it's the only reprieve I get."

"And Jasmine?" Her voice lowered. Her eyes dropped from mine, filling with nerves. I knew then what she wanted to ask. It was a question I wasn't ready for. I would never be prepared to speak of what happened to my sister that night.

Pressing a finger over her mouth, I shook my head. "I don't want to talk about Jaz. Not yet."

She frowned. "I can accept that." Clouds formed over our idyllic oasis; I tensed against the next question forming in her thoughts.

I groaned, wishing I didn't have to answer but knowing I had to. "You want to know why I put you through what I did last night, don't you?"

She stiffened. "I don't think I'll ever get used to you knowing what I'm about to say. But yes…I would."

Every second that ticked past, she rebuffed me a little more, remembering the way I'd shut off and abandoned her last night. But I'd never abandoned her. I left her to play a part in an orchestra that hadn't finished playing yet.

"It's complicated."

"Try me."

I stared at the ceiling, holding her tight. "You knew you were being recorded last night." It wasn't a question.

She shifted in my embrace. "Yes. I know Kes wanted me to act hurt and terrified."

My fists curled, recalling what Kes had done against my wishes. I couldn't begrudge either Nila or my brother for finding a small measure of pleasure, but it didn't mean I would ever get over it. It would take time to live with it but forever to forget it.

"There are other recordings, Nila."

She bit her lip, sadness coming thick and heavy. "I know. I guessed you'd have videos of my mother and her payments of the debts."

"I asked Kestrel to do what he did to give the drugs long enough to knock Cut and Daniel out."

"What?"

"You and Kes were the performance, while I created a bigger show." My heart bucked, knowing she'd hate me for what I'd done. She'd have to come to terms with it, because it'd been the only way I could think of to keep Cut's suspicions down, prevent her from being raped, and live to see another day to find another solution.

"Do you trust me?" I murmured.

She tensed. For a moment, her emotions screamed *'no.'* Then she relaxed, letting love replace her resentment. "Yes."

My heart swelled; I ached to kiss her again—to prove her trust would never be squandered or broken. "I know what I'm doing. Just leave it with me."

It took a minute, but she finally melted against me, pressing her mouth against my chest. "Okay…"

Okay…

Such sweet permission. Such ardent concession.

I'd never been so weightless and free. It was a damn novelty to let down my bomb-battered walls and truly give myself over to her. I didn't tense or hide in ice—I permitted myself to feel everything she did. To sense how much she wanted to save me. How much she wanted to keep me. How much she needed to understand me.

I even acknowledged the parts she tried to keep secret—the things she would never say aloud but I knew anyway.

She wanted me to choose her over everyone.

Over Jasmine.

My inheritance.

My world.

She wanted it so fiercely, it throbbed with every beat of her heart.

She was afraid I would cut her out again. Afraid I would ask more heinous things of her. Terrified that I'd once again put up my walls, sink back into snow, and fall under my father's command.

Once upon a time, I would've. I would've reverted to what I knew because I'd been too chicken shit to believe I could be better.

But not this time.

Coming apart before her had changed me irrevocably. I hadn't wanted to break. I'd tried to keep it together. But the moment she told me to leave; the second she said the part of her that loved me was dying—I'd *felt* it.

I'd felt the ember of affection flickering its last breath. She told the truth. I tasted the end. And I shattered to have something so pure taken from me.

I knew what it was like to live alone. I knew what it was like to live with her loving me.

There was no comparison, no choice.

Not now.

And the honest to God truth was, she didn't need to worry. I would *never* hurt her again. I would spend the rest of my life ensuring I protected her like the fucking goddess she was. I would dedicate my days building a fortress, a shrine, an entire world for her, and it would all pale in relation to what she'd given me.

She was my number one.

Over everyone.

Even myself.

There was no turning back from this.

She is my salvation, my reason for existence, my queen.

Nila

"YOU'RE SURE YOU have to go?"

I looked down at my fingers, twisting, turning——never resting. We'd spent a blissful few hours together, but now the sun was at its zenith, and Jethro tensed with anxiety. I hadn't asked why he slipped from sated to stressed, but I could guess.

If Daniel and Cut didn't touch me last night, something had been done to protect me. And it was precarious.

"I don't want to, but I have to." His golden eyes glimmered with openness. After talking, we'd dozed in each other's arms——perfectly content to let silence heal the wounds left behind by honesty.

I shuffled, digging my toes into the carpet. We stood by my door. I'd gone to escort him out, but in reality, I couldn't stomach the thought of being away from him longer than a second. The connection we'd built throbbed with intensity.

I knew he had to leave to fabricate whatever tale Cut had to believe. I knew our very safety was at stake. But it was inconsequential when faced with saying goodbye.

"I'll miss you." My voice was sex-laden and a blatant invitation. *Come back to bed, so I won't have to miss you.*

He sucked in a breath. His eyes flickered down the empty corridor behind him. He'd slipped back into his clothes from last night and the faint scents of cigar smoke and cognac clung to him. "Don't tempt me, Nila…"

My nipples tingled. He was as reluctant to end this as I was. "I don't want you to go."

His lips parted as he leaned into me, planting his hand on the doorframe beside my head. "I don't want to go, either."

Sadness pinched. "Then don't."

He shook his head, looking weary and tired. "I have to. I can't be here when they wake up. And I have to delete the camera footage of what just happened in your room."

My shoulders slumped. "Okay, I understand."

Whatever he'd done to rig the Third Debt was reliant on Cut and Daniel believing a lie. If they saw evidence against that lie, everything that'd been done last night would be for nothing.

It would be a waste.

Jethro groaned. His hand dropped from the doorframe, capturing mine.

The instant he touched me, I sparked from head to toe. I shivered as he stroked my knuckles with his thumb. "Goddammit, I never want you out of my sight again."

I swayed toward him. "Surely, we have a little more time?"

You're playing with fire, Nila.

That was true. My core burned for him. My body blazed for his. I couldn't think of anything but sex. I was reckless, drunk on him.

His forehead scrunched.

I couldn't help myself. I stood on tiptoes and kissed the faint lines around his mouth.

He froze.

"Nila…"

I kissed him again. A butterfly kiss. A goodbye kiss.

Suddenly, he grabbed my chin, slamming his lips on mine.

His touch was delicate but fierce. His tongue teasing but demanding.

With a soft moan, I opened for him and the kiss waltzed straight into forbidden.

Breathing hard, he pulled away. "Come with me." Wrapping his fingers around my wrist, he dragged me my room and down the corridor. His eyes were nothing but lust and urgency.

I trotted beside him in knickers and a t-shirt. "Where are we going?"

"I can't say goodbye. But I can't do what I want in there."

My stomach somersaulted. "What do you want to do?"

He lowered his head, watching me from beneath his brow. "Do you trust me?"

I no longer had to think or doubt or lie. "Yes."

His lips twitched in love and gratefulness, moving quicker through the Hall. "I want to do what I've needed ever since I knew you cared for me. I want to show you what it's like for me." We careened around a corner like two eloping lovers. "Will you let me do that, Nila?" The devoted need in his voice circumnavigated any excuse or negation I might've had.

"I'll let you do whatever you need."

Yanking me to a stop, he kissed me fiercely. His fingers held the back of my skull as if he was afraid I'd float away and leave him. "Thank you. A thousand times thank you."

Dropping his hand, he looped his fingers with mine and together we ducked around corners, scurried beneath paintings, and entered the secret door to his bachelor wing.

He's no longer a bachelor. He's taken. He's mine.

My eyes drank in the maroon painted walls as Jethro prowled the halls of his own quarters. He seemed more at ease here, safe. Ever since finding his chambers, I'd wanted to return. I wanted to explore and see how many secrets his personal space would divulge.

Jethro guided me past gaming rooms, studies, and elaborate dayrooms until he opened the last door and pushed me through.

The moment we were inside, he locked it.

My eyes darted, taking in plasterwork of swooping birds of prey, the deep red carpet, leather-gilded walls, and priceless furniture that out-shadowed any antique my family had back in London. His room was masculine, almost medieval, yet there was a tranquillity about it, too.

I trembled as Jethro came up behind me, wrapping his arms around my front. His lips kissed the diamonds around my throat, drifting to my collarbone. How did he feel about my collar now? Did he have a strange love-hate relationship with the beautiful jewellery like I did?

I swayed backward, pressing myself into him.

His hot breath cascaded over my shoulder. "There aren't any cameras in here."

"Oh..." My heart rate skyrocketed.

Jethro's hand cupped my breast, rolling my nipple between his fingers. "I can do whatever I want to you."

Once upon a time, that would've been a terrifying threat. Now, I knew him. Now, I trusted him.

I moaned as he palmed my other breast. "You can?"

"I can do whatever I need."

"And what do you need?"

His teeth sunk into the flesh between my neck and shoulder, his tongue stealing the sting. "I can be completely myself. I can take everything you have to give."

Words deserted me as he spun me around and captured my lips.

His taste slipped down my throat. His eagerness wrapped around my heart.

We only kissed for a moment.

But it felt as if we kissed forever.

Sliding, licking, tasting.

He swept me away from this dimension, guiding me to a different one—a more spiritual one where our hearts beat to the same rhythm and our desire thickened with every breath.

Walking me backward, his arms swooped down and hoisted me off my feet. I gasped at his power, kissing him harder. Instinctually, I wrapped my legs around his hips. He groaned as my pussy pressed against his straining erection.

Still kissing, he headed forward. Arms bunched, lips slippery, he marched me to the bed.

Then I was falling.

And he was falling with me.

The soft mattress cushioned me, while the hard demand of Jethro landed on top, squashing me with fervent need.

My lungs deflated; a small vertigo wave tried to steal the magic of the moment.

He chuckled. "I've gone dizzy from switching from vertical to horizontal."

In that second, I loved him so much I might burst. "Now you know how I feel most days."

He pulled back, brushing hair from my face. "Is it terrible? To have your brain work against you all the time?"

His question was so much deeper than just enquiring about my imbalance deficiency. It was a probe into how I coped—a mutual understanding of what it was like to have a condition rule your life. "I manage."

"You manage better than me."

I cupped his cheek. "Everyone has complications. Some harder than others."

He smiled softly, pressing another kiss on my mouth. "Yes, but some of us are stronger than others." His lips trailed to my ear. "And you're the strongest person I've ever met."

His hand disappeared down my side, tugging at my t-shirt. I wriggled, helping him slip it over my head. I lay in just my knickers in the arms of the man who'd been given a task that would never come to pass.

Jethro would never kill me.

I knew that with utmost certainty.

He couldn't because it would kill him, too.

His jaw locked, eyes devouring my naked chest. "You're so fucking beautiful."

A prickle of sensitivity darted over my skin, centring in my core.

He ran his fingertip around my nipple, causing it to pebble. "I've never felt this way about anyone. Ever. Never let myself open to the pain it can cause." His finger drifted down my sternum, moving toward my bellybutton. "I need you to know." His finger coasted lower, dipping into the manicured curls between my legs. "I need you to know that I adore you. I worship you. I don't just love you, Nila Weaver. I treasure you. I've never had anything so goddamn precious as you."

My mouth fell open as he pressed a single finger inside me. Words flew from my mind as every part of me focused on his touch.

"I'm going to show you what it's like in my world. Will you let me?" His finger slipped deeper, pressing against my inner walls.

I bit my lip, nodding. My eyes were heavy, body begging.

I was warm, content, and truly happy for the first time in my life.

I didn't want to move or talk or do anything to burst this magical bubble.

Another finger entered me, stretching, coaxing, dragging me from needful to insane with desire.

"I'll never be able to repay you for last night. I'll never be worthy of what you've given me. But I'll make it my life to repent and prove how fucking sorry I am for what I put you through."

I opened my eyes. My heart clenched at the sublime beauty of the *true* Jethro. He blazed brightly in the softly lit room. His every thought and desire, his every fear and insecurity—it was all there for me to witness and wonder.

Never looking away, he withdrew his fingers and used the glistening digits to pull his t-shirt over his head. Shadows danced over his muscles, highlighting ropes of power in his forearms, chiselled planes of his stomach, and faint bruises on his ribcage.

His injuries from whatever fight he'd been in the night I found his room had healed and faded.

Sliding off the bed, he unbuckled his belt and eased the denim down his legs. Stepping free of the material, he didn't hesitate pulling his boxer-briefs to the floor.

My mouth dried up at his naked perfection.

His cock hung heavy and hard between his legs. His hands opened and closed by his side self-consciously.

I couldn't tear my eyes away from his incredible body. He was mine now. This insane specimen of a man was *mine*.

Lifting my hips, I shimmied free from my knickers, tossing them over the edge of the mattress. His eyes zeroed in on my exposed core. The smell of sex and musk filled my nose.

He smirked, slipping from intense to playful. "What we did before was the entrée to what I truly need. Taking you so quickly didn't satisfy either of us. And I mean to satisfy you *extremely* well."

I quirked an eyebrow. "Oh? What does 'extremely satisfied' entail?" I dropped my voice as a delicious thrill ran through my belly. "What are you going to do to me?"

He bent over and grabbed my ankles. "You'll see." His signature scent of woods and leather seemed stronger, more intoxicating as he pulled me down the bed. "Stay there."

Moving toward his private bathroom, he returned with several long sashes from a bathrobe. Without a word, he tied it around the post at the bottom of the bed. Never looking away, he imprisoned my ankle and ever so gently wrapped the terry-cloth sash around me.

My heart splattered with a mix of erotic excitement and spellbinding fear.

Jethro paused, his eyes tight. "I feel what you're thinking, Nila." He stroked my calf, calming me. "You're intrigued what I'm about to do to you, but afraid of being tied up again. Am I right?"

I blinked. *I will never get used to that.* "Yes."

Every time he'd tied me up, he'd done something awful.

His jaw clenched. "It's understandable. Every time I've tied you up, I've done something unforgivable."

I jolted at how eerily close his conclusions were to my own. I nodded slowly. "You're right—"

Jethro scowled. "And why wouldn't you despise me for what I've done? The First Debt I tied and whipped you. The Second Debt I bound and drowned you. The Third Debt—"

"I know what happened, Jethro. You don't have to torture me or yourself by reminding us."

There was no telling how I would react to being tied while he pleasured me. It could cancel out the bad he'd caused but also ruin whatever good he attempted. If I was honest, I didn't want to be trussed up. I didn't want to be helpless to his whims. But at the same time…wasn't that what trust was? To have faith in someone that they wouldn't go too far?

His fingers stroked my ankle. "I promise on my soul I will never hurt you again."

My body screamed yes. My mind screamed no. I struggled to choose.

"This is pleasure," Jethro murmured. "I give you my word; I'll release you the second you ask." His eyes glowed with need, begging me to grant one more sacrifice.

Slowly, I nodded.

He exhaled heavily, moving his attention to my other ankle. "Thank you."

He wrapped a similar sash around me, spreading my legs apart. The vulnerability and almost degrading way my legs were held open made me squirm with nervousness and need.

Jethro ran a hand over his face, drinking in my body. "Fuck, you're stunning." He grabbed his cock, working himself. "I've never been so attracted to anyone as I am to you. Never wanted to worship anyone. Never been so fucking besotted."

My nervousness popped like champagne bubbles, leaving me tipsy on lust.

"What I want to do to you isn't degrading or demanding, Nila. It's so much more than that."

Breathing shallowly, I didn't move as Jethro climbed onto the bed, crawling over me to place my hands above my head. "It's not about control; it's about showing you my world." Climbing higher, he fastened my wrists above my head with another sash.

His cock nudged my chin as he bent forward, reaching over me.

Without thinking, I opened my mouth and sucked him. The tang of his desire coated my tongue as I swirled around his crown.

He froze.

A groan wrenched from his lungs. "Christ, Nila."

His hips twitched, feeding a little more of his length into my mouth. He trembled as my head bobbed, sucking him as much as I was able to while imprisoned below him. I looked up.

His eyes scorched mine, melting with love. "You're so perfect."

With a grimace, he withdrew. "I'm too fucking close as it is. This is for you. My pleasure can wait."

I licked my lips, missing the small burst of power I'd had over him. I wriggled, completely constrained but not helpless.

"This isn't about dominant or submissive, Nila. This is about showing you how I feel. How earning your ultimate trust is better than any drug, better than any promise. This is about making you understand."

"I don't need to understand. All I know is my heart belongs to you."

Jethro placed his fingertips over my mouth, shaking his head softly. "That isn't enough—I owe you so much more than that. I want to show you the level of intensity I live with. I want you to know first-hand the sensory overload I suffer now that I've fallen in love with you."

Fallen in love with you.

No words would ever compare.

I trembled as he stood up, gazing at my spread body. He stepped back; the bedside lights illuminated his spattering of chest hair and gleaming cock. His eyes hooded, filling with salaciously carnal intentions.

Even though I was the one tied up, he was the one bound—locked in a life that demanded so much from him. The longing on his face clenched my core, making me wet.

"You look incredible like that," Jethro whispered. "Knowing you can't run. Can't hide. That you're all mine." He prowled to the side of the bed, dragging his fingertip over my knee, my thigh, between my legs, my belly, my breast, my chin, my mouth.

With a gentle press, he pushed his tattooed index past my lips. The thought of my initials stamping ownership on him reminded me we hadn't done the tally for the Third Debt. I shouldn't want something so ridiculous on my flesh, but I wanted him to sign and approve every inch of me. I wanted to be his completely and forever.

My tongue swirled around his finger.

He pulled his digit free. "Wait here. I have to get a few supplies from next door."

Supplies? What supplies?

Ignoring my racing heartbeat, I laughed. "Where exactly can I go?"

He grinned—such a light-hearted sight. "Precisely. And that's what makes this such fun." He kissed the tip of my nose. "Wait for me."

Then he was gone.

The moment he disappeared, doubt filled my mind. Did I want this to happen? What would he do?

Testing the bindings, I squirmed. Fear lurked on the outskirts of my brain, but my body only grew wetter. No matter what rational thinking told me I should want, I couldn't deny I'd never been so turned on.

Jethro appeared again, locking the door behind him. He kept his hands behind his back, obscuring what he'd collected. "Remember you said you trusted me."

Stopping at the base of the bed, he slowly brought forth the hunting whip he'd used the day he chased me through the forest. I recognised the diamond glinting on the handle. I'd seen it while hiding naked in the tree, begging for a chance to escape.

I flinched. "Hell, no…"

He can't be serious.

He shook his head, his eyes flashing with pain. "It's not what you think." He stalked around the mattress, trailing the tip of the crop along my skin. Every touch sent my nipples pebbling, core dampening. I didn't want this—yet my body only grew more sensitive.

A stroke was no longer a stroke but a tease.

A smile was no longer a smile but a promise. A deliciously dark, *dangerous* promise.

"You trust me?"

I breathed faster. How could I say I trusted him then doubt him the moment that trust was tested?

Locking eyes, I nodded.

Jethro relaxed a little, then his wrist flicked and he brought the whip down across the top of my thigh. Not hard, but hard enough that heat flared.

I jerked, panting at the scrambled messages my nervous system gave. Was it hot or cold? Did it feel good or bad? Did I want to run or stay?

I don't know!

Jethro swallowed hard.

Can he sense my confusion?

His voice was thick as he demanded, "Tell me how it feels."

I shook my head, drowning under another influx of sensation. There was no way to describe it.

"Try, Nila. I want to know."

I scrunched up my face. "Um…it's warm…tingling."

Jethro chuckled. "No, I don't want to know physically. I don't care about physically." He sat on the edge of the bed, stroking my cheek with tenderness. "I know how it feels on your body." His stroking dropped to my breast, not touching flesh but something so much deeper. "I care about what you feel in *here*." His fingers pressed firmer as if he could carve out my heart and protect it forever. "I want to know how your heart feels, your mind, your thoughts, your soul. I want everything. I want the truth."

I gasped as his hand drifted from breast to pussy.

His mouth tightened as he pressed a finger inside me. "Tell me how this makes you feel."

My hips arched, wanting him to push deeper, give me more. "I'm wet…"

He withdrew his fingers. "No." Drawing my wetness up my belly and back to my heart, he murmured, "In here. Tell me. Go deeper than physical. Ignore mental. Tell me your deepest, darkest sensation."

I trembled as his hand returned between my legs; his long, delicious finger pressed inside me.

I moaned. My head fell back as I clenched around his touch. He made me feel idolized and wanted, dropping all his barriers, driving me upward to a familiar goal.

My mind was a mess. I couldn't understand the threads of racing thoughts. But he needed this from me, I would do my best.

Jethro crooked his finger, rocking. "Tell me or I'll stop."

Don't stop!

"I—I feel heavy. As if I'm too full and filling more and more the longer you touch me."

"Good. Go on."

"Um…I feel weightless as if I'm exactly where I need to be. I'm confused and crazy and needy and hazy. But through it all, I'm excited."

He grunted. "Fuck, that's a turn-on." Bending over, he kissed me hard. "Having access to your body isn't what I crave. It's access to your mind. Your feelings I can sense, but your thoughts I can't. It's the one part of you I need to own—in order to give in completely."

I quivered as he removed his finger and raised the whip again, torturing me slowly with it licking over my skin. "Do you understand what I need?"

"Yes, I think so." I bit my lip as he circled the bed, never stopping his incessant stroking with the supple whip. With every stroke, I forced myself to focus on how I felt *inside* rather than how I reacted outside.

The physical was so much easier. My pulse thundered. My skin prickled. My blood raced. My core clenched. My body needed him desperately. And my libido scaled a mountain that terrified me.

But emotionally…I wasn't prepared to go so deep. It was foreign territory to look so far inside. How could I truly understand who I was—not just as a woman or Weaver but as a human—a creature of breath and bone…of animalistic desires?

Were my thoughts normal? Were they acceptable? Was I weak or strong or broken? I didn't know.

And Jethro wants to know…

On his second circuit, Jethro flicked the whip, striking my clit with a short, sharp burst.

"Oh, my God!" The intensity swooped hard, jerking my shoulders as a blistering wave of need spread from my core. The sweetest strangest buzz travelled through me. I became weightless all while heavy with colliding thoughts.

"Tell me how you feel," Jethro purred.

I had no clear-cut answer, but I'd promised. *I have to try.* Closing my eyes, I focused inward. "There are too many thoughts to articulate. They're all racing too fast." Pulling on the restraints, I begged, "Jethro…"

"Quiet." He dragged the whip up the centre of my body.

Every muscle bunched, preparing for the next strike.

He didn't disappoint.

He struck me short and sharp on my bellybutton.

I convulsed, soaking up the decadent bite. One moment, my thoughts were tamed, untangling themselves from the twisting mass of nonsensical nonsense, the next, they were a jumble of madness.

"And now," Jethro said. "Now, how do you feel?"

"Now...I'm quiet. I'm tense. I can feel something inside me unlocking, opening."

That's the truth. I don't know what's unlocking but keep going—I want to find out.

Jethro sucked in a breath. Our eyes connected.

The unlocking inside flung wide open like a rusted gate. It was the weirdest thing. To feel your own soul unfurling. I'd never taken the time to truly *feel* myself. To know who I was. To rifle through my history, experiences, and fears.

"I'm—I'm letting you in."

Jethro flicked the whip again. "More." The leather kissed my ribcage.

I cried out at the sweet, burning sting.

"That's what I want. That's what I need." He circled the bed again, flicking me in different spots: my hip, my bellybutton, my nipple.

Oh, my God, my nipple!

Fire flamed through my blood. A trickle of wetness slipped between spread thighs.

My body sang. My soul rejoiced. I'd never been so free...so unencumbered even while bound in place.

The crop licked my throat, slapping quickly on my diamond collar. The sound of chastisement and the swift burn of intoxicating pain throbbed my nipples. Jethro rained gentle punishment down my sternum toward my pussy.

My head tossed back as I writhed, wanting him to strike faster. To fuck me. Love me. Claim me.

"Does it feel good?"

"Yes," I whimpered. "Better than good. It feels..." My eyes closed as I threw myself into a maze of complexities. My body had brought me to this place, but my thoughts took over. They made this more than sex. More than love. They made this *transcendent*.

Jethro struck me quicker—like tiny breaths—working his way all over my body.

"Please." I thrashed. "Take me. I need you inside me."

"Why? Why do you need me inside you?"

Why?

There were so many reasons why. One fell from my lips before I could think. "Because I can't handle the intensity anymore!"

Jethro sighed heavily, wrenching my eyes open. "Now you know...now you know how it feels to live with my curse." He struck me particularly hard. "There is no stopping for me. No reprieve. It's one piercing thing after another."

The agony in his voice sent me higher; I strained for a release. "That's awful. So awful." I couldn't handle the poignant need to explode another second. "But please, Jethro. I need you."

"Quiet." He struck my clit again. "I love feeling what you feel. I love having no barrier between us."

Shit!

I almost came. My core clenched; sparks detonated in my blood. I never expected something like this could unravel me so quickly.

I was lost.

Drifting on an ocean of everything.

"God, you're wet." Jethro dragged the tip of the whip through my folds.

I moaned.

He consumed me. His body was supple and noble—every muscle proudly ridged. Something had melted inside him. He was no longer ice but magma. No longer snow but sunshine.

I wanted to grab him. Hug him. Fuck him.

My thoughts became a froth of temper. "Take me, Jethro. Fuck me, Kite. I can't do this any longer."

I didn't think he'd obey, but without a word, he threw the whip across the room and climbed on the bed. Straddling me, he fisted his cock and bent to kiss me. "You want me to end your misery. If I do, can you end mine?"

He didn't give me a chance to reply. His mouth crashed on mine, and we turned savage. Biting, licking, tasting. His hand clutched my hair, pulling hard, forcing my mouth to open and take whatever he gave.

His hot thighs imprisoned my hips, twitching as he worked his cock.

The kiss ended. He collapsed on top of me.

I moaned at the comfort of having him touch me after so many teasing strikes.

"God, Nila, you're incredible." His lips covered mine again, feeding me his voice. "I want to make you come. I want to come inside you over and fucking over again."

His hips slotted between mine. His fingers dove inside me, testing my wetness. Then I screamed as he filled me with one wicked impale.

There was no pain. No bruising. Only the most majestic completion imaginable.

I couldn't hold on. I wanted to grip his strong shoulders for balance. I wanted to wrap my legs around him for connection.

He thrust deeper, slipping through my wet heat. In some mystical way, this felt like an ending to everything he'd been and the beginning of everything we'd become.

A beginning he was finally strong enough to face.

It's exquisite.

It's raw.

It's debasing

and

mind-blowing

and

real.

I gritted my teeth, riding the tsunami of pleasure. Jethro took hostage of every thought and dream I'd ever had, making it his.

My body hummed with possession. Every part of me was ravaged, disconnected, unable to concentrate on anything but the way he thrust and took.

I cried out, biting his shoulder as every cell tightened, quickened.

"Come. I need you to come," Jethro panted in my ear.

I'd never been commanded to do something outside of my control. I never believed I could do something as miraculous as come with only a few words. But his cock stretched and filled. His lower belly rubbed and stroked my clit and every part of me combusted.

My body obeyed him utterly. I let go, spindling into the sharpest, quickest orgasm I'd ever had.

"Fuck, Nila." Jethro pinned me to the mattress, taking me faster. His guttural groan wrapped around my body, replacing it with unlimited pleasure. "Goddammit, you feel good." His face buried in my hair; his heart beat a war drum against mine.

I wanted to cradle him—give him safe harbour to come undone and find himself in this new world we'd conjured.

Thrust after thrust. We were stripped totally bare.

Jethro never stopped. His arms curled around the top of my head, keeping me in place. The ropes around my ankles jerked with every rock, bruising me.

I dissolved into his embrace. I was exhausted and spent. Aftershocks of my orgasm continued to squeeze my pussy.

Jethro suddenly reached toward his bedside and pulled a knife from the drawer. I tensed as he sliced the binds around my wrists and pulled my torso up with him. He sat on his knees, still inside me. Twisting around, he sawed the sash around my ankles, freeing me.

Throwing the blade to the carpet, he cushioned me in his lap. "Wrap your legs around me. I've got you." His arms cradled my spine, creating a basket of muscle. I melted into him, bouncing with every thrust.

His large hand captured my nape, pressing me firmly, keeping my body pinned close and his cock deep inside.

With a savage rock, he groaned, "I'm going to ride you. And then I'm going to come."

I nodded, every part of me drained. I'd never been so used, so abused, so *sleepy*.

His lips found mine, pouring energy down my throat as he drove deeper and deeper. Straddling his lap gave him complete control. His cock hit the top of me again and again.

His kiss turned demanding. His hands roved up my back and around my sides to palm my breasts. His dextrous fingers tweaked my nipples, tugging in time with his thrusts.

I moaned, biting his throat as I fell into him.

"You have the most incredible body." His hands swooped to my back again, moulding me tight against him. "You're so damn wet. I fit inside you. You take me completely." Wonder dripped in his voice, sheer joy at finding me and me finding him.

"Hold onto me. I need to take you hard and fast." He grabbed my hips, hoisting me higher on his lap. He looked at me.

I gasped at the molten love evident in his gaze. Tears prickled my eyes. *He loves me.*

He'd said it. Whispered it. Cursed it. But now he'd shown me: he unequivocally loved me.

He smiled softly. "You sense what I'm feeling, don't you?"

I shook my head. "I don't sense, I know. It's not a feeling but the truth in your eyes."

His fingers dug into my hips, pressing me down, giving me nowhere to hide. "You should know you're it for me, Nila. There's no turning back from this. I'm on your side until the end." He surged upright, filling me endlessly deep. His hand disappeared into my hair, wrapping the long black strands around his wrist, holding me firm. "I love you."

The burn in my scalp scorched my body.

To be so adored but controlled.

To be so loved but dominated.

The combination was the best aphrodisiac in the world.

He slammed into me, bouncing me in his embrace. My arms wrapped around him as we glued ourselves together, holding on and riding each other fast.

My muscles burned, my legs wobbled, and my scalp yelped in pain, and through it all, another orgasm brewed.

Shit, I can't come again.

I'd collapse.

I'd never come twice so quickly. I wouldn't survive—I knew it as surely as I knew my heart was one beat away from exploding.

Jethro kept riding, kept fucking. And my body kept responding, gathering tighter and stronger, wanting to release and snap me into paradise.

"I'm yours, Nila. All fucking yours." Jethro's lips skated over my jaw.

I became nothing but lust and spirals and mindless passion. The ache in my womb increased, throbbing with the familiar agonising urge to let go.

His harsh breathing filled my ears.

My body detonated again.

I cried out as I clenched with delirium.

I didn't think I had the power to combust so spectacularly. I feared I'd splinter into teeny, tiny pieces and flutter away in the breeze.

"Christ, yes. Take me." He thrust hard and deep, following me. His teeth latched onto my shoulder as we rode waves of bliss. Spurt after spurt, he filled me, coming apart in my arms.

Minutes passed where all I could think about was liquid. Liquid and wetness and heat. We clung to each other until my muscles started to seize and cramp, and a chill turned my sweat into goosebumps.

I never wanted to let him go.

Jethro slowly pulled out, laying me gently on the bed. Our ragged breathing matched as he pulled me into him, spooning me, protecting me.

If I could move, I'd cuddle him back but I had nothing left. I was drained beyond all comprehension.

"Thank you." Jethro kissed my hair. "Thank you for letting me in." His arms squeezed tighter, giving me gratitude in both actions and words.

I yawned, snuggling into him.

"Was it hard?" he asked quietly. "Was it painful to look inside yourself?"

I shook my head, unable to keep my eyes from closing. "No. To be honest, it was scarily easy."

"It's not hard to let go when you trust the person you're with."

I nodded. "You made it right, Jethro. You made it perfect."

A few minutes passed. Sleep settled heavier on the outskirts of my thoughts.

Jethro sighed. "I want to do more with you. Fall deeper into you. Would you let me do that?"

The moment hovered. I could pretend to be asleep. I didn't have to answer. The thought of stripping myself even further scared but also excited.

"Yes," I whispered. "Yes, I would." My voice was soft and full of love.

He hugged me hard. "I love you, Nila." Pressing a kiss on my cheek, he said, "I've only just started. I have so many ways to show you the depth of my feelings."

My eyes flared. Did he want more *today*? There was no way I had the stamina or strength. I was utterly spent.

"You can do whatever you want with me. But first, I have to sleep." With his body heat and legs tangled in mine, I'd never felt so safe.

Jethro chuckled. "I want more—so much more. More than you can possibly imagine. But I'm patient. I've waited this long for you. I can wait another hour or two." Kissing me again, he murmured, "Sleep, Ms. Weaver. Dream of me. And then I'll steal you away."

He gathered me closer.

Together, we drifted from this world into dreams.

LIFE WAS PERFECT.

The most perfect it'd ever been.

I couldn't remember the last time I'd been this happy or this uncaring about my fate.

Nila was mine. I'd found my one true place.

I should've known a man like me would never be worthy of such a gift. I should've known that death was around the corner. I should've seen the devil rubbing his hands together, waiting.

I didn't deserve peace or togetherness or a future I wanted more than fucking anything.

There was nothing good left for me.

Only death.

No matter that I'd lived my entire life beneath death's shadow, no matter that I'd expected it around every trial, and feared it every time I closed my eyes to sleep, I still wasn't prepared for when it finally came for me.

It was quick.

It was painful.

It was over.

I'M SO LUCKY.

I looked over the balcony. Below me, bright lights and camera flashes immortalized my newest collection. The grey dress I'd made before paying the Third Debt caused a standing ovation among critics and fashionistas alike.

"You did so well, wife."

I swayed into my husband's arms. Jethro's hair caught the lights, making him seem like some fantasy knight come to life. We'd eloped two weeks ago. We'd barely left the bedroom since.

My pussy clenched just thinking about what we would do when we returned home after the show.

Something cold and sticky splashed against my silver ball gown. Time turned to slow motion as I looked down in horror.

Blood.

Gallons upon gallons of blood.

It stained my bodice, train, hands...everything.

The audience below no longer watched the show but looked up at us. At me specifically. "What?" I screeched. "What did I ever do to you?"

Then, I heard the most dreadful sound in the world. The symphony of dying. The excruciating noise of ending life.

"Get up, you filthy fucking whore!"

My eyes wrenched open. My heart lurched into my mouth. Warmth and cocooned-safety was traded for biting fingers and hard floor as Cut wrenched me out of bed and threw me across the room.

"Wh—no!" I landed on my wrist, screaming in agony.

"What the—" Jethro's sleepy voice rang out but was sliced short by a punch to his face.

"You motherfucking backstabbing son of a fucking bitch." Cut rammed his fist into Jethro's jaw again, drawing blood, crunching cheekbones. "Get up." He tore off the sheets, jerking him from his bed.

Jethro groaned, falling into a pile of limbs at his father's feet.

"No, wait!" I crawled forward, flinching at my wrist.

Daniel appeared, blocking me with his hands on his hips. "Ah, ah, ah, little Weaver. You can no longer interfere with family matters."

Through the barricade of his legs, I watched Cut kick Jethro repeatedly in the stomach, screaming obscenities, puce with fury. "Did I not give you every fucking chance? Did I not respect you and trust in you as my fucking son!" He kicked him again. "Goddammit, you leave me no choice!"

This can't be real.

It had to be a dream…a nightmare.

Please, don't let this be real.

Cut turned his back on Jethro, storming toward me with throbbing anger. "And you! You're done meddling with my fucking family, girl. You're through. *Both* of you!"

Grabbing my hair, he jerked me to my feet.

He strength was insane—no residue of the drugs Jethro had used. No hint that he'd been unnaturally asleep for hours. He was a demon.

I screamed, dangling in his enraged hold. My bare legs showed the faint whip marks from Jethro's attentions, and his t-shirt I'd slipped on when I went to the bathroom barely covered my knickers. "Let me go!"

"You and him—you've fucked me over for the last time." Cut breathed hard, his face gleaming with sweat. "Did he think I wouldn't notice? That I would let you get away with this shit!"

I fought his hold, willing tears to hide. "I don't know what you're talking about! Stop hurting me. Let me go!"

Daniel cackled. "You know *exactly* what we're talking about, bitch." He marched over to his brother, scooping the bloody body of Jethro into his arms. Jethro moaned, his eyes squeezed and blood rivering from his mouth. He tried to fight Daniel off, but the vicious attack before left him half dead.

"I don't! Leave him alone."

"Yes, you fucking do," Cut snarled. "I just witnessed the so-called video of you paying the Third Debt. Kestrel thought I'd buy his bullshit doctored video?!" His eyes turned deathly cold. "Two of my sons. Both of them betraying me. But it's the last time. The last fucking time they make a mockery out of me."

Dragging me from Jethro's room, he didn't stop or care that I crawled and stumbled beside him. His fingers noosed in my hair, leaving me no choice but to fumble in agony.

I couldn't see Jethro, but Daniel's footfalls vibrated the carpet behind me.

"Please!" I scratched Cut's hands over and over, but he didn't flinch. Too amped on fury to feel a thing. "Please, let us go!"

"Oh, I'll let you go alright. I'll fucking let you go to Hades."

Hawksridge Hall covered acres of land with twining halls and cavernous rooms, but it seemed like a postage stamp with how fast we left the bachelor wing and burst into the day parlour with its swan-silk loveseats and ornamental music boxes.

The moment we exploded through the doors, Cut threw me forward. I fell with vertigo and inertia, slamming to the floor. I crawled away as fast as I could. Daniel mimicked his father, tossing Jethro to his knees, kicking him violently in the gut.

Jethro coughed loudly, air refusing to filter into his lungs. He fell to his side, gasping, bleeding.

I scrambled toward him, but Daniel stepped in front of me. "Look behind you, whore."

I glowered. I wanted heaven to smite him into stone. "Leave him alone!"

He chuckled. "You sure about that?" Leaning over me, he yanked me to my feet, twisting my head to look behind me. "You sure you choose him?"

I fought in his hold. I worked up saliva to spit in his face. But then I set eyes upon my undoing.

The past twenty-four hours, disappeared.

The love I'd found, vanished.

The promises I'd made, disintegrated.

Gone.

Dust.

Ash.

No. *No, no, no.*

I keened in awful horror.

This can't be true!

"Threads," Vaughn mumbled through bleeding lips. His eyes were puffy and half-shut, his body as mangled and bruised as Jethro's. He sat on the floor between two Black Diamond brothers who I didn't recognise. His entire demeanour weary and beaten. He was no longer Robin Hood sent to rescue me but a thief about to be killed.

Terror fed my heart—it raced out of my chest straight toward my twin.

"No!" I tore myself from Daniel's grip and crawled toward V. Tears waterfalled down my cheeks. Guilt and self-hatred layered. I'd done this. *I'd* cause this. V was hurt all because I made a Hawk choose me over everyone.

"V!"

Vaughn shook off his handler's hold, throwing himself toward me. We crashed together, hands clutching, arms hugging, hearts thundering. "What happened? Are you okay?"

V hugged me hard. "I'm okay, Threads. I'm so sorry."

Daniel stood over us, arms crossed; his lips twisted in a sadistic laugh. "Fucking cocksucker deserved it."

Jethro let out an agonising cry. My attention split from my twin to my soul-mate. Cut kicked him, his fists clenched and ready to rain. "I saw the fucking video, Kite." Cut's voice was death and eyes evil incarnate. "Kes might know computers, but did you honestly think I wouldn't notice!"

Everything happened too fast. Way, way too fast.

What is going on?!

"Stop!" Jethro shouted, bracing himself for another kick. "Let me explain."

"Explain?" Cut laughed coldly. "Explain the fact that you drugged Daniel and me, then proceeded to splice a fucking video of Emma Weaver. You had the fucking nerve to trick me into believing we'd had a turn with Nila?"

Vaughn choked, his face turning ghostly. "What—what are they talking about, Threads?"

As much as I feared for my brother, my loyalties were to Jethro first. He was my family as much as V was. I staggered to my feet, balling my hands. "Don't take it out on him. It was my idea."

Cut paused, his eyes spinning with hatred. "Your idea?" He stalked forward. "*Your* idea. So you were the stupid one to believe I didn't imprint every moment of that night. I remember everything about Emma. I have fucking dreams of using her. Do you think I wouldn't fucking notice!"

My heart split with a thousand swords, thinking of my mother being hurt by Cut. But that was the past. She was gone. I couldn't save her anymore. But I could save Jethro and V. They were mine to protect—mine to rescue.

"I'm sorry! Just forget it. Leave my brother alone and don't hurt Jethro anymore."

Cut dragged hands through his hair, shaking his head with abhorrent disbelief. "You think I'll listen to you? Why should I, bitch? What will you give me in return?"

Jethro stumbled to his knees, wrapping an arm around his side. Every breath rattled in his lungs like broken china. "Don't, Nila. It was my idea. My mistake." Speaking to Cut, he glared. "Do whatever you want with me, but leave her the fuck out of it. Kill me. End the Debt Inheritance. Let this all be over!"

Cut whirled on his firstborn. "This isn't over until *I* say it's over." Pointing a livid finger at me, Cut snarled, "She didn't pay. The Third Debt was never completed."

Daniel stepped in front of me, slapping me hard on the cheek. My head whipped, and a vertigo wave made me trip sideways. "You fucking drugged us. That's against the rules."

"Leave her alone, you bastard!" V shouted, trying unsuccessfully to climb to his feet.

Vertigo attacked harder. I swallowed, doing my best not to vomit. My cheek ached but it was nothing compared to the pressuring terror building inside.

I cried, "Just let him go!"

Please, end this. Someone save this disaster, before it's too late.

"Don't touch him!" I shouted again. "Please, leave him alone."

Daniel snickered. "Leave who alone, princess? Your pussy brother or my brother who you're fucking?"

Vaughn threw himself at Daniel's legs. With a yelp, Daniel punched him but fell sideways, landing on the carpet. The fight didn't last long. Vaughn was strong and stayed fit with regular gym visits, but it was nothing compared to Daniel's manic insanity.

Rolling away, Daniel kicked him right in the jaw.

V crumpled.

My heart shattered. "No!"

"What on *earth* is the kerfuffle in here?" a prim, papery voice said.

All eyes turned on the recent addition to the parlour.

Bonnie Hawk.

Her attention surveyed her son, grandsons, and me before smiling coldly. Leaning heavily on a brand new walking stick, she snapped her fingers. "Jasmine. Kestrel. Would you come and join us, please?"

The sudden madness seemed to cease—her appearance granted a strange kind of peace to the battleground. She acted as if we'd all popped by for tea and cakes, completely ignoring or not caring that blood stained the pristine carpet and my brother was unconscious at her feet.

My heart stuck in tar as Jasmine rolled sedately into the room. Her bronze eyes hid her terror, but her face couldn't hide her dislike. She didn't look away from Jethro.

Jethro looked back at his sister, hanging his head in shame.

Kestrel came into the room, his hands tied behind his back, his face a mismatch of purple, black, and blue.

He gave me a sad smile, flicking his attention between Jethro, V, and his father.

"Glad you could join us," Cut snarled, glaring at his offspring.

Jasmine sat taller in her chair, her pink angora jumper matching the deep rose of the blanket thrown over her legs. "Father, don't do this. Think about what this will—"

"He knows the consequences, child," Bonnie interrupted. "And he's accepted the payment as a necessary sacrifice." Her matching skirt and blazer were black, as if she were already in mourning. A string of pearls graced her throat, bobbing with every swallow. Her eyes landed on Cut. "It's your decision, son."

Cut nodded, getting his temper under control, slipping back into a ruthless, terrifying man with far too much power.

I trembled, trying to work out the dynamics in the room.

What is going on?

No answers came, and in a seamless move, Cut reached behind him and pulled free a pistol.

My heart stopped.

I stood transfixed in the centre, stuck between Jethro and Vaughn. I couldn't move. Couldn't decide who was the most at risk of a madman waving a gun.

"Help him up, will you, Daniel?" Cut pointed the muzzle at Jethro.

I blinked back another vertigo spell as I darted forward. "No!"

Cut trained the gun on me. "Do not move, Ms. Weaver."

Daniel obeyed, grabbing Jethro under his arms, yanking him upright. The moment he was on his feet, Jethro bent forward, looking like he would throw up or pass out. Sweat darkened his hair, his naked thighs bunched with effort to remain standing. He looked so defenceless in a t-shirt and boxer-briefs—clear evidence that we'd broken every rule and slept together.

Cut cocked the weapon, glaring at his son. "I'm going to give you one last choice, Jethro."

Jethro shook his head, smacking his lips. "No more choices. Just kill me and let the Weavers go." His eyes flickered to my unconscious brother. "*Both* of them."

Daniel snickered—completely in his element. Bonnie just watched while Jasmine and Kes remained mute with nerves.

No one spoke. No one wanted to bring attention to themselves while Cut wielded a gun.

"One more choice," Cut repeated. "You better choose wisely." Planting his stance in the thick carpet, he raised the weapon.

Jasmine whimpered as the muzzle pointed at Kes. "Father, please...don't do this. We love you. We're your children!"

"Silence," Bonnie commanded. "You will do as I say, child. No more talking without permission."

Jasmine seemed to wilt, but her shoulders remained defiant.

Kestrel puffed out his chest, facing death with the decorum of any worthy fighter. "You'll never live with yourself if you do this," he muttered. "I'm your son."

Cut bared his teeth. "You ceased being my son the moment you uploaded the atrocity of a video and thought I was so fucking stupid to buy it." His head whipped to Jethro. "Choose, Jet!"

"I don't know what you want me to do!" Jethro yelled. "You expect me to name a sibling for you to murder? Why would I when it was all my fault? They had nothing to do with this. Nothing!"

Cut stiffened, closing his eye to aim.

I ran forward—to do what? Who knew. But I was too late.

"Wrong choice." His finger squeezed the trigger.

The gunpowder ignited.

The room ricocheted with noise.

A bullet leapt from the gun, tearing faster than sight to lodge into a Hawk offspring.

"No!" Jethro bellowed, charging forward.

A flare of red appeared on Kestrel's chest the second before he collapsed to his knees. His face went blank with shock, lips round with disbelief.

"You never had a choice," Cut murmured, aiming at his daughter.

Jethro moved the second Cut pulled the trigger.

I saw it all.

I felt it all.

One moment, Jethro was alive. His heart beating. His soul linked with mine.

The next, he threw himself in front of his wheelchair-bound sister, accepting the bullet into his own body.

I didn't react for the longest moment.

I couldn't believe the story before me.

He couldn't be dead.

He can't be dead.

He's not dead!

I staggered forward, my hands clamping over my mouth.

He cannot be dead!

Jasmine screamed as her brother fell over her, his torso slamming against her atrophied legs, his knees crashing to the carpet.

And then he rolled.

He rolled off his beloved sister, lying face down on the carpet.

"Nooooooooo!" I threw myself beside him, shaking him, begging him. "Jethro. Please, open your eyes!"

Daniel laughed. Bonnie stared. Jasmine screamed.

And through it all, Cut said nothing.

I could barely stay in one piece. My body wanted to dissolve into a billion fractals and float away in despair. I trembled so badly, it took two attempts to roll Jethro onto his back.

His eyes were closed, lips slack, blood blooming from his chest like a morbid rose—petals upon petals spreading with glowing crimson.

"Jethro…" Tears gushed down my face. Breaths were non-existent as I gagged and choked on sobs. "Please, don't leave me. Not now."

Then I was plucked up and away, dragged further and further from my lover.

I lost awareness of my body.

I shut down.

In my mind, I still knelt beside Jethro feeling him grow colder by the second—leaving me.

Cut appeared in my vision, his face tight and strained. I hung lifeless in

Daniel's arms, unable to comprehend what just happened.

I was numb.

I was lifeless.

I was gone.

"Listen to me, Ms. Weaver. I'm only going to say this once." Turning me in Daniel's arms, Cut pointed at Vaughn. My brother lay splayed on the carpet just like Jethro and Kestrel, but unlike them, he was still with me. Still alive. Still in danger.

"Your brother is a recent addition to our family. He's what you'd call collateral." He stroked the sulphur-smoking muzzle of his gun. "I'm sick of you not obeying and I'm sick to fucking death of pinning hopes on a son who isn't trustworthy. There's been a change of plans."

Daniel held me closer. "A *good* change of plans."

Cut pointed at V. "If you're good, he lives. If you're bad, he dies." He shrugged. "It couldn't be any simpler than that."

V moaned, rousing.

I wanted to feel something, but I'd switched off. Unable to cope.

I was a brittle leaf about to turn to dust in the wind.

Cut whispered, "Jethro and Kestrel are no longer your concern. They've paid for their lies and stupidity. I only hope you're smarter than they were."

Daniel sneered. "Only the worms will be interested in them now."

No...it can't be true.

Bending over me, Cut cast both Daniel and me in his monstrous shadow. "You should keep that in mind. I won't hesitate to hurt you, Ms. Weaver. Think how easily I dispatched my sinning sons." His face shadowed. "I would be afraid if I were you. Afraid and *highly* obedient."

Cupping my chin, he pressed a dry kiss on my mouth.

My innards shrunk and died.

Jasmine's sobs were background noise. V's curses nothing more than a hum.

I'd just lost everything in a few short minutes.

He's just lying there.

Get up, Jethro. Please, get up.

Cut ran his gun over my jaw. "Say hello to my new heir, Nila."

No, he can't mean...

Daniel jiggled me in his arms, never letting me go. He cupped my breasts with harsh fingers. "Be polite, whore. Say hello."

I clamped my lips together.

I kept staring at Jethro, begging for this to be some terrible mistake.

"Along with inheriting my power, my fortune, and my title, Daniel has acquired the Debt Inheritance's responsibility." Cut placed himself in front of me, blocking Jethro's bleeding body.

Every word made me crave a bullet. I wanted to end it. I wanted to chase Jethro to the underworld and leave everything behind.

There's nothing left. Not anymore.

Bonnie shuffled forward, her cane sinking into the carpet. "We've all agreed to nominate a new master. If Daniel carries out the remainder of the tasks, he will take over my son's position before his thirtieth."

She came closer, bringing the stench of death with her. Her hazel eyes flashed, red lips spread in a victory grin. "When you left two months ago, I knew something special would have to be done upon your return. No one makes a mockery of my house like your family has done without paying a serious price. Consider this the beginning of a bigger debt. You owe us for the inconvenience your brother caused."

Cut laughed, pressing cold fingers beneath my chin, angling my face to his. "Understand, Ms. Weaver, Daniel will carry out the Final Debt. And if he does, as I trust he will, everything goes to him. And unlike my previous sons, he will *not* disappoint me." Placing another dry kiss on my lips, he murmured, "Congratulations Ms. Weaver. You now belong to Daniel 'Buzzard' Hawk…

…

And he's going to make your life a living fucking hell."

Information on HSP & VEP taken from http://healing.about.com/od/empathic/a/HSP_hallowes.htm.

***Jethro's comment about his condition was taken from: Pearl S. Buck, (1892-1973), recipient of the Pulitzer Prize in 1932 and of the Nobel Prize in Literature in 1938, said the following about Highly Sensitive People:

"The truly creative mind in any field is no more than this:

A human creature born abnormally, inhumanly sensitive.

To him… a touch is a blow,
a sound is a noise,
a misfortune is a tragedy,
a joy is an ecstasy,
a friend is a lover,
a lover is a god,
and failure is death.

Continues in FOURTH DEBT

"We'd won. We'd cut through the lies and treachery and promised an alliance that would free us both. But even as we won, we lost. We didn't see what was coming. We didn't know we had to plan a resurrection."

Nila Weaver fell in love. She gifted her entire soul to a man she believed was worthy. And in the process, she destroyed herself. Three debts paid, the fourth only days away. The Debt Inheritance has almost claimed another victim.

Jethro Hawk fell in love. He let down his walls to a woman he believed was his cure. For a moment, he was free. But then he paid the ultimate price.

There is no more love. Only war. Hope is dead. Now, there is only death all around them.

THE ENTIRE SERIES IN THE INDEBTED SERIES ARE OUT NOW!

Playlist

Bet my life by Imagine Dragons
Shots by Imagine Dragons
Gold by Imagine Dragons
I Know You by Skylar Grey
The Fall by Imagine Dragons
Coming Back by Dean Ray
Let it Go Tonight by Foxes
Yours by Ella Henderson
Echo by Foxes
Battlefield by Jordin Sparks
Hurts by Only You
Bleeding Out by Imagine Dragons
Tainted Love by Marilyn Manson

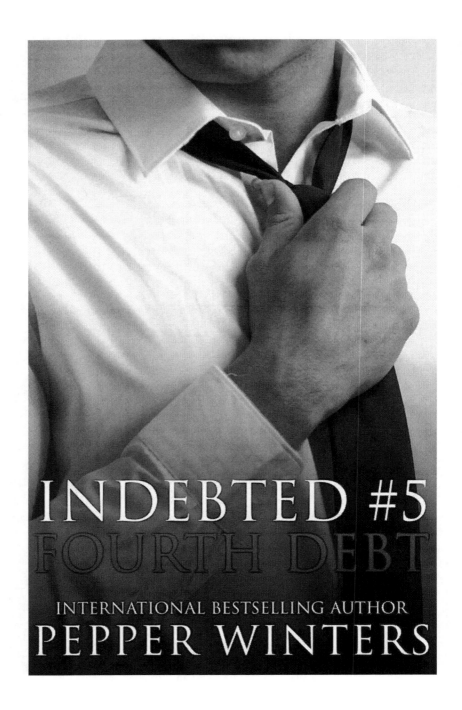

INDEBTED #5
FOURTH DEBT

INTERNATIONAL BESTSELLING AUTHOR
PEPPER WINTERS

FUNNY HOW LIFE plays practical jokes.

The past few days—that had to be a fucking joke, right?

No logical answer would make sense of what I'd seen, heard, and lived the past seventy-two hours.

My sister.

My best friend and twin.

This was what she'd been living with? This was how she'd been treated? This was what she wanted to *return* to?

Motherfucking *why*? Why would she ever want to return to this insanity?

We'd been raised in a broken home, chained to an empire that absorbed us right from birth. But we were kept safe, warm, and loved. We grew up together. We shared everything.

But now…I had no fucking clue who my sister was.

But then *she* came to me.

A woman I never knew existed.

The most stunning creature I'd ever seen.

Only she didn't come to me on feet or wings of an angel. She rolled into my life and demanded my help.

And for better or for worse…

I helped her.

Nila

"LET ME GO!"

Daniel cackled like a mad hyena, his fingers stabbing into my bicep. Without breaking his stride, he stole me further away from the parlour and into the bowels of the house.

I didn't want to go. I didn't want to go *anywhere* with him.

"Take me back!"

He can't be dead!

Just because he lay unmoving and bloody didn't mean he was gone.

That's exactly what it means.

I shook my head, dislodging those awful thoughts. *He's alive.* He had to be.

I couldn't tolerate any other answer. I refused to live in a world where evil triumphed over good. That wasn't right——life couldn't be that cruel.

It's always been that way.

My mind filled with images of my mother. My father's desolation. My broken childhood. Evil had puppeteered us from day one. Why should now be any different?

He's not dead!

I swallowed a sob.

Please don't be dead…

I fought harder. "Let me see him. You can't do this!"

Daniel cackled louder. "Keep begging, Weaver. Won't do you any good."

He's not dead!

I locked my knees, fighting him every step. "Stop!" Looking back the way we'd come, the door to the parlour seemed so far away—a bright beacon at the end of a festering corridor. "They were your brothers, you insane psychopath. Don't you feel anything?!"

Please let me go to him. He has to be alive…

Please let my twin stay alive…

Let all of this be a nightmare!

I couldn't cope with Jethro murdered; I'd go clinically insane if they killed V, too.

"I feel relief. I no longer have to put up with their simpering bullshit." He flashed his teeth. "Cut did us all a favour."

Cut will die.

He was evil incarnate. He deserved to die in excruciatingly painful ways.

I refuse to believe they're dead.

"I said *stop*!" I wriggled harder, only succeeding in Daniel's fingers tearing into my flesh. Goosebumps covered my skin while ice steadily froze my veins. Every second was endless torture. I couldn't live without Jethro.

It can't end like this!

"You won't win, Weaver." Daniel tugged harder. "Accept what's fucking happened and *obey* me."

The vacantness I'd endured when Jethro and Kes collapsed hadn't lasted long. The moment Cut had given me over to Daniel—the exact *second* he'd delivered my life into his sick son's control—I'd lost that blanket of numbness.

Agony I'd never experienced cracked my heart into tiny irreplaceable pieces. My every thought bled with murder and death. My wails had mixed with Jasmine's. Vaughn's curses and shouts drowned out by grief.

It was a never-ending loop.

He's dead.

He's dead.

He's left me.

He's dead.

He's dead.

He's gone.

God, I wanted it to stop. I wanted this to end—for the curtain on this madhouse production to fall and for the director to shout 'cut.' For it all to be make-believe.

But what if it's true?

He's dead.

He's dead.

He's abandoned me.

I sagged in Daniel's hold, bombarded with incapacitating sadness. If it was the truth, what else mattered? Why did I care what my future entailed when I no longer had anyone to fight for?

Vaughn…fight for him.

Tex…fight for him.

My lungs crushed. I could fight for them—but ultimately, they didn't need me. Not like Jethro had needed me. He'd finally opened up to me—finally let me in and given me a new home in his love. But now I'd been cast out all over again; I couldn't stomach the empty wasteland without him.

He's dead.

He's dead.

He's lost…

I tripped, succumbing to the weight of the boulder on my back, the rock of eternal grief. I didn't bother trying to stabilise. I wanted to curl up into a ball and never move again.

He's…dead…

"For fuck's sake." Daniel hoisted me on to my feet. "Get a grip! Walk. Do what I say or—"

"*No!*" My voice ripped down the corridor, frigid with fear. Somehow, my mourning lashed into a violent whip, lacerating my insides with fury. "I'll *never* do what you say. You might as well end it now because I *refuse* to listen to scum like you!" I scratched his hand holding my arm, but just like Cut when he'd dragged me from Jethro's bedroom, he didn't twitch or respond. "Never! Do you hear me? I'm *done*."

Desperation tore raging holes inside my mind. I wanted to collapse by Jethro's side and scoop up his blood and feed it back to him—to force him to come back to life. I wanted to hold my twin and tell him it would be all right—to wash away his panic. And I wanted to say goodbye to Kestrel—to send him to the ether knowing how grateful I was for what he'd done.

But I couldn't do any of those things.

Daniel's pincer grip caged me, leaving me to rot in his deluded embrace. Bastard.

Sick and twisted *bastard*.

My temper screeched out of control, and for the first time in my life, I gave in to it. I opened my arms to the tornado of loathing and screamed at the top of my lungs. "Fuck you, Daniel. Fuck you! Fuck you and fuck Cut and fuck *all* of you!"

The world stopped.

Daniel froze.

I trembled.

Then, he slapped me.

My head snapped sideways. His handprint decorated my cheek with blazing fire, and everything spun out of control.

"You little cunt." He yanked me forward. His inertia gave me no choice but to stumble into him. "Have your little tantrum. Go on, scream and make a spectacle of yourself. But it won't change facts." Trailing his fingertips over my flaming cheek, he murmured, "You just contradicted yourself. First you said you wouldn't obey me, but then you said you'd fuck me…" He chuckled. "I'm taking the 'fuck you' part literally." Digging his fingers into the sides of my cheeks, he kissed me. "You don't have to listen for me to fuck you. You don't even have to obey me. Whatever power you had over my brothers is over, Weaver. You'll see."

Jethro…

Letting my face go, he grabbed my arm and tugged me down the corridor.

Further and further from Jethro, Kestrel, and Vaughn.

Further and further into hell.

He's dead.

He's dead.

He's nothing…

Everything inside shrieked with disbelief. He couldn't be dead. He just *couldn't*. I needed to see him again. How could I go on when I didn't believe what had happened? How could I hope to breathe and exist when all I wanted was to give up like he had?

I swallowed another tsunami of tears. My soul didn't believe. But my circumstances said otherwise. This was my life now—this endless misery.

"You won't get away with this."

Daniel snickered, looking over his shoulder. "Get away with what?"

Murdering my future.

Murdering any chance of happiness I ever had.

"Everything."

Only thing is…they've gotten away with it for centuries.

Every step I died a little more, leaving my beating heart beside Jethro as his body grew cold. The further apart we became, the less human I felt. It was as if the tether binding us would snap at any moment, leaving me smarting, empty, and alone.

He's dead.

He's...dead...

It's...truly...over...

Cold tears stained my cheeks, putting out the fire from Daniel's slap.

Thick lethargy hijacked my limbs. Sleep...it beckoned me. All I wanted was to fall into its fluffy cradle and disappear.

Daniel dragged me deeper into the house, past foyers and alcoves, and into a wing I'd never entered.

Every step pained me; every breath a blade. My eyes never rose from the monogrammed carpet. I wanted to give up, but an incessant need to fight never left. I forced myself to stand up to him, no matter that it was pointless. "Your father just killed two of your family members. Aren't you afraid he'll do it to you? Too many people know, Daniel. The media, online—"

"You think a few fucking tweeters and social media posts can stop us?" He propelled me into his arms with a vicious yank. "I thought you'd stopped being delusional." His lips turned into a sneer. "Then again, you willingly came back. That makes you a dumb bitch who deserves what's coming to her."

I came for him.

But now he's gone.

I recoiled in his arms. The last liveliness in my heart vanished. I'd witnessed the love of my life die in front of my eyes. I'd been audience to two murders and too many ruined lives. I couldn't...I couldn't cope any more.

I sank...

I gave in.

I evaporated inside.

I'm in shock.

Daniel chuckled, continuing to tug me down corridors I didn't recognise. I stopped paying attention, following like a good sheep, stumbling over a threshold I'd never crossed before.

He shoved me forward. "Welcome to your new home, bitch."

I tripped forward, arms whirling, mind fighting against vertigo.

A loud slam ricocheted from behind me. A door. A prison gate.

I spun around, breathing hard. I didn't have any words or energy left. I was sick, terrified, heartbroken. But through it all, I was numb.

I'd accepted my fate, acknowledged the truth, and finally seen what it all meant.

He's truly, truly dead.

Daniel stalked toward me.

Automatically, my feet shuffled back—not from conscious instruction but some primal need for self-preservation. In reality, I no longer cared what happened. It was as if I watched myself from the safety of the ceiling, peering down at the poor unfortunate Weaver, no longer caring what happened to blood and bone when I no longer inhabited it.

He's dead.

He's dead.

I want to die, too.

Daniel never stopped corralling me around the space. Through blurry eyes, I took in the rich emerald brocade on his four-poster bed, the priceless antiques, and moss-coloured walls. The shades of green looked like we'd traded indoors for some woodland glen.

He was the hunter, raising his shotgun to shoot the dismal deer.

I'm that deer.

His hands outstretched; face alight with manic lust. "You're all mine now, Weaver. Locked in my room, bound to my rules, at my mercy. Fuck, this is gonna be good."

My ears rang with his voice. My eyes smarted with his appearance. I wanted to leave—to chase Jethro into the stars. Suicide didn't compute. Taking my own life didn't register. It wasn't a matter of life and death, killing or surviving, but about transcending from one world to another.

He's not dead.

He's just…evolved.

And I didn't want him to leave without me.

We were a pair. A duo.

I'm done with this existence.

My mind was gone—unfocused and slow. But my body still wanted to survive. My feet tripped backward for every one of Daniel's, but there was no finesse. I moved like a robot with no one at the controls.

From my sanctuary in the ceiling, I pitied the delusional girl below. Why was I backpedalling? Why prolong the inevitable? The sooner Daniel caught me, the sooner he would hurt me and ultimately send me to Jethro.

Let go.

Let it happen.

The numbness inside would block external pain, surely.

It was best to stop everything. To stop thinking, stop breathing, stop surviving.

My knees locked. I stood steadfast.

Daniel quirked an eyebrow. He stalled when I didn't continue our morbid dance. Cocking his head, he searched for a trap. "Giving up so easily, whore?"

I didn't respond. Not a whisper of a shrug or a flicker of an eye. I stared right through him—at a new dimension that promised a fresh beginning with Jethro and an end to hardship.

Daniel growled under his breath. "You're seriously just giving up?" Stomping forward, he grabbed my hair, fisting it in his sweaty hands. "You're not going to fight me like you did my brother?"

I was right.

No pain registered. No agony or discomfort.

My senses were meaningless decoration.

"Fight back! Where's the fucking sport if you just give in?"

He tugged my hair, raising my eyes to his. If I focused, I would've brought his putrid face into vision. I would've cringed at the sharp bone structure, small black goatee, and swept back dark hair. If I still had my sense of smell, I would've inhaled his musky excitement, unable to be hidden beneath thick notes of aftershave. And if I had sense of touch, I would've felt his body heat infecting mine, seeping into me like a disease.

But I had none of that, so I noticed none.

All I saw, heard, felt was a void: nothing but silent wind across my face and emptiness before me.

His mouth twisted with rage. "Fuck you, Weaver. You're mine now. What do you have to say for yourself?"

The burn in my scalp chased away the icy tears on my cheeks. My heart had given up the moment a bullet slammed into the love of my life. If he wanted a reaction, he wouldn't get it.

Not this time, you bastard.

Nothing.

I have nothing.

"My brothers are dead. How does that make you feel?"

Nothing.

I feel nothing.

"Answer me, cunt! Tell me how much you don't want me to touch you. How much you're afraid of me!"

Nothing.

I care about nothing.

Jethro was gone. I'd never seen anyone die before. Never been to a funeral or witnessed a pet succumb—even my own mother just vanished rather than died. My first participation in death and it'd been two men who'd captured my affection, turning me into a completely different person.

The old Nila died the day she entered Hawksridge. But this new Nila was a fading photograph, vanishing piece by piece while her lover bled out on priceless carpet.

Daniel threw me away from him. "Snap out of it!"

Vertigo caught me in its sickening embrace. For once, I didn't fight it. I tumbled to the carpet, letting a whirligig of rollercoasters and nausea take me, thanks to my broken brain. Normally, it was the worst kind of punishment, but now it was better than facing reality.

Vibrations in the carpet alerted me to Daniel's closeness. He towered over me, rage painting his face. "Pay attention to me, Weaver!" His boot shot like a black meteor, connecting with my belly.

Air exploded from my lungs.

Pain crept over my senses—pain I didn't want to feel because it reminded me I wasn't dead...wasn't free. I was still here—in this pointless game of madness and deception.

He's dead.

He's dead.

I'm all alone.

Daniel kicked me again.

His boot crunched against my belly, sending white-hot agony up my chest.

Agony.

And with agony came life.

You're not alone.

Vaughn. My father. I still had family who mattered. People I couldn't abandon.

I'm not dead.

I don't have the luxury of giving up.

Jethro and Kes had been murdered by men who'd polluted the world for long enough. I'd made a promise to my ancestors to end this. I now made a promise to them.

I will kill your family.

I will end this once and for all.

My eyes shot wide. Energy zapped into my limbs. Agony made me reckless, granting false courage. I was stronger than this. Hadn't I proven as much with what I'd lived through? Each debt I'd endured, I'd evolved from naïve little girl into a woman.

I'm braver than this.

Scrambling backward, I put as much distance between Daniel's next kick and myself as I could.

He placed his hands on his hips, laughing coldly. "Finally decided to play, huh? Took you long enough."

Coughing, I held my bruised belly and forced myself to stand.

He didn't approach me, giving me time to regroup. He enjoyed me fighting—he wanted me alive and screaming.

Bastard.

"I'll kill you," I whispered, wincing with every breath.

He chuckled, moving toward me. "What did you say?"

Standing taller, I locked eyes with him. My ribs bellowed from his kick, but steel entered my tone. "I said *I'll kill you.*"

He ran a hand through his dark hair, smiling. The evil tainting his soul suffocated him—he wasn't attractive even though outwardly he had good bones and sex appeal. To me, he was a troll, a stinking pile of excrement.

"I'd like to see you try." He closed the distance between us one boot at a time.

I parried backward. "You won't see it coming."

"You won't be able to get close enough to do it." He winked smugly. "You're nothing compared to me."

I bared my teeth. "It'll happen when you least expect it."

"It will never happen." He flexed his muscles. "I'm invincible."

"You're human."

And that makes you killable.

Every word filled me with power. Conviction and confidence shoved aside my numbness and grief.

Jethro and Kes were dead. But it wasn't the end for me. I had a purpose. I would *complete* that purpose.

"Want to know why I came back? Why I didn't run or hide?" The snow in my veins made its way into my heart. "I came back to ruin you." Spit pooled in my mouth. If I'd been braver, I would've spat it all over his face. "I came back for *him*, but that's over now."

I'll avenge him, so help me, God. Kestrel, too. And myself. And my brother. And my mother and grandmother and generations of Weaver women.

This was the beginning of the end.

The Debt Inheritance was null and void—Cut had seen to that. It was time to slaughter the Hawks and extinguish a dynasty of torture. Every second made me stronger, filling me with a strange acceptance. Happiness wasn't my life path—but destruction was. I would be that instrument of destruction.

Daniel shook his head, positively glowing with insanity. "You came back to watch him die? How thoughtful."

"Wrong. I came back to end this." Darkness settled around my soul, blotting out any remaining light.

He's dead.

He's dead.

But I'll keep my promise.

I hadn't been able to save Jethro, but I wouldn't abandon him. "I made an oath to myself." I narrowed my eyes, glad that they'd stopped watering—that I could look at him with strength rather than terror. "Want to know what that oath was?"

He stiffened. "Don't want to know anything about you, Weaver." He licked his lips. "Scratch that. I want to know three things and three things only."

I shivered in disgust. "My oath was to destroy you. To end your father. To end you. No matter what you do—"

He shot forward and slapped a hand over my mouth. His palm silenced me, sending my heart chugging with hatred. "Ah, that's fucking rude. You were meant to ask what three things *I* want to know, not spout ridiculous bullshit." His golden eyes—so similar to Jethro's and Kestrel's—glittered. "Go on...ask me."

His fingers pulsed on my cheeks as I shook my head. I couldn't speak, but it didn't stop me from screaming with every molecule.

Never!

His temper eddied around us. "Fine. Don't need you to ask, 'cause I'll tell you anyway." He crowded me, pressing his body against mine. "Three things, bitch. I want to know how your screams will sound in my ears." His fingers dropped from my mouth, tracing my lips with his salty touch.

"I want to know how your tiny hands will feel fighting me off." His palm drifted down my throat, over my diamond collar, to my breasts.

I closed my eyes as he kept going, lower and lower and *lower.*

My teeth clamped on my bottom lip as he cupped my core with rancid fingers. The thin knickers and t-shirt I wore from sharing Jethro's bed left me vulnerable. "And I want to know how your pussy will taste on my tongue." Without any warning, he plucked me from the carpet and threw me against a wall.

My shoulder slammed against a portrait of waxy fruit. I slithered to my knees. Pain flared, fear swelled, and vertigo did its best to steal me away.

He's dead.

He's dead.

Don't you dare give in.

"I'll show you that I get what I want. I'll teach you to fucking respect me." He towered over me, fists clenched. "Isn't that what you think of me? That I'm some spoiled brat who was the *'mistake'*? That I was never good enough for this family or to have my own Weaver to torment?" His voice deepened with rage. "Saw the tampered video, Nila."

I struggled to stand, never taking my eyes off his boots.

He stood poised, ready to kick. "Always knew Kes was a pillock, but I never took him for a fucking dreamer. Anyone could tell that wasn't you with Cut. And it was a fucking mockery to believe I'd buy the badly spliced images of me with some whore. He couldn't even overlay your face onto her body right. Not to mention the fact I remember the night I disfigured that bitch and Jethro tried to save her."

His hand lashed out, grabbing my hair. "She could've survived if he'd tried. He killed her—said it was what she wanted. That it was the only way she could live with what I'd done. I call fucking bullshit."

He shook his head, eyes wild. "He's always been a pussy, and Kes was always a fucking sap. Jet drugged and lied to us—but fool on him. Cut will make you repay the Third Debt. Kes screwed up with that shoddy film—it could've been the best-edited video in all of bloody Hollywood, and I wouldn't have bought it." Slowly pulling me to my feet, he hissed, "Know why?"

Kes had been a true friend. Jethro had been a true lover.

They're dead.

They're dead.

Two friends gone.

My heart cracked all over again, but instead of sinking into depths of despair, something happened. My temper warmed, growing brighter and stronger, nudging aside grief.

Something was changing…building, *evolving.*

"Answer me!" Daniel shook me. "Tell me why I would never have bought that fucked-up video."

Temper turned to rage, which turned to fury, creating a bubbling concoction of revenge.

I stood before him proud and undefeated. "I know why. Because you're a sick, deranged pervert who remembers things like rape and torture."

He barked with laughter. "Well, fuck me, you do understand."

Breath by breath, I sold my soul to the churning anger inside. I gave up my innocence. I traded all resemblance of peace and purity, letting the blackness consume me.

Jethro had confused me—making me believe the debts were liveable. That, in the end, we'd win because we deserved to. His kindness outshone his cruelty, mixing the messages he sent.

But Daniel.

There was no more confusion.

I knew as surely as the sun would rise, Daniel would rape, maim, and kill me. There was no compassion or affection inside him.

That fantasy was done.

But with that knowledge came clear-headedness. I no longer wanted to fight hate with love or pain with tenderness.

I meant to meet Daniel in the abyss and kill him before he killed me.

"I know enough to destroy you, Daniel Hawk."

My heart beat for the last time, frosting over—protecting itself for what I would do. I'd never planned on becoming a villain. But I'd never planned on losing my soul-mate, either.

Daniel snarled, "You're a dead woman." He squeezed my throat below my diamond collar, wedging me against the wall. "I mean to fill your final days on Earth with suffering. You'll see. You'll *beg* me to kill you before I'm finished."

I gasped. Every instinct urged to scramble at his tight fingers. But I didn't beg or plead. The numbness turned to coldness, and I understood my predicament better than ever before.

I'm a killer.

I just needed a weapon to fulfil it.

"Buzzard!"

Daniel froze, turning to face the door. His hand never let go of my throat, anger filtering through his grip.

I couldn't turn my head, but in my periphery stood my second target. The man I would kill after dispatching his youngest son.

Bryan Hawk.

"Let her go for a moment. There's a good boy." Cut tapped a key against his chin—the key which no doubt unlocked the entrance to Daniel's bedroom. Inching over the threshold, he came further into sight.

Daniel gathered me close, spinning me around so I squashed against his front. His breath wafted in my ear as his hand fisted my breast like I was a trophy to be touted.

I didn't care. My body was as numb as my soul.

My eyes widened as a red-faced, tear-stained Jasmine rolled in behind her father. If I hadn't locked away my pain, I would've burst into tears and shared her grief.

Why was she here? How could she stand to be around her father after what he'd done?

Two of her brothers, gone.

Half of her family obliterated by the man who should've protected them from everything.

He'd tried to kill her, yet she willingly breathed the same air as him.

Why?

"What are you doing?" Daniel grunted, kneading my breast. "You said—"

"I know what I said." Cut prowled closer, his gaze taking in my dry eyes and balled hands. His jaw ticked, but that was the only sign of emotion. "Something has come to light."

Jasmine looked at me. Something didn't seem right. Her cheekbones sliced through pale skin, her normally sleek bob messy and tangled. But she had an edge about her speaking of unpredictability and almost…deranged mania.

He's dead.

He's dead.

Of course, she wouldn't cope.

"Get out!" Daniel took a step back, hauling me with him. Our legs entwined, but I didn't fight. I had the power to kill him, but we had to be alone. That was the only way.

Cut tucked the key into his pocket. "Buzzard, listen—"

"No, listen to *me.*" Jasmine shoved the rims of her wheelchair, barging past Cut and coasting at supersonic speed toward us. "Let her fucking go, Dan!"

Daniel flinched.

Jasmine cursing was wrong—as if she'd never sworn in her life. She looked too perfect to stoop so low. However, the unhinged glint in her bronze eyes and whitewashed face held no hint of weakness from watching two brothers die.

She looked livid rather than heartbroken.

What is going on?

Daniel's gaze swooped to Cut. "What the fu—"

"Do as she says," Cut ordered.

I swallowed as Daniel tweaked my nipple. "Like shit I will. She's mine. We've all decided."

"Listen to your father, child." Bonnie appeared, entering the room and resting two hands on her walking stick.

Shit, they're all here.

My hackles rose.

In my melancholy and newly budding fury, I'd forgotten about Bonnie. I'd counted only two victims. Two men who would suffocate in dirty graves, eaten by worms.

I have three targets.

Three lives to steal to avenge so many others.

Daniel stepped back, dragging me with him. "No chance. Get out. The lot of you. The door was locked for a motherfucking reason."

Bonnie growled, sounding like a grizzly bear about to teach her cubs a lesson. "Drop her. Don't make me say it again."

Drop her? Like I'm some dog's chew toy.

The bubbling darkness inside wanted to strike and rip out her voice box. I wanted her bleeding at my feet.

Just like him.

Jethro's blood stained this house.

Hers will, too.

"This is bullshit," Daniel spat, shoving me away from him. The moment I was free, Jasmine rolled toward me and captured my wrist with cold fingers.

My stomach churned.

I didn't like this turn of events. I didn't want any more confusion. Daniel was black and white. *I* was black and white. Death or life—those were my two choices. This scuffle was a grey area and if I let myself lose my cut-throat mentality, I wouldn't be able to continue.

He's dead.

He's dead.

He's not coming back.

The grief threatened to wash me away again.

"She's mine. I'm the oldest." Jasmine spun her chair, dragging me to face Bonnie and Cut. "You agreed. Tell him."

I looked over my shoulder at Daniel, hating the fact he was behind me. I didn't want to take my eyes off the little creep.

You're a dead man walking, Buzzard.

My mind raced with images of my pilfered dirk sliding between his ribs. Of slashing his throat. Of cutting off his balls.

"You have a valid argument, Jasmine." Bonnie nodded. "And we'll discuss it further when the mess of today is over with."

I swallowed a gasp. The *mess* of today? She talked about the murder of her two grandsons as if it was an inconvenient *mishap*.

Who are these people?

"No, I want to hear that she's mine. Right now." Her fingernails dug into my flesh, breaking my skin, imprinting crescent moon cuts.

I didn't flinch.

Jaz's eyes met mine. They were just as lifeless and cold as me. A switch had triggered in both of us, leaving us lost in this new world.

"You belong to me, Nila Weaver. You're the reason my two brothers are dead." Yanking me down to her height, she hissed, "You'll pay. I'll make you pay so damn much for what you've done."

What?

A cloud worse than numbness consumed me.

She'd lost everything back in the parlour. She'd even lost herself.

Who *was* this woman? Sure, Jasmine had never been ultra-friendly with me. In fact, she'd asked me to die the last time I'd visited her to save her brother. But I'd never seen someone so remote and vastly changed.

Then again, what did I expect? Why would she soften toward me now that the worst had happened?

Cut jumped in. "We'll discuss it at greater length. But I do agree; Daniel doesn't get full rights to her. You are my daughter and the successor matriarch. You know our empire inside out, whereas Daniel is yet to be trained. It's only fair that you have joint ownership of the final debts, and the pain she is required to pay."

I bit my lip, unable to tear my eyes away from Jasmine.

What did this mean? Would I have to dig four graves instead of three? I never wanted to kill Jasmine. But I would if she gave me a reason.

It was me versus them now. I wouldn't back down again.

I'm done being tortured.

It was their turn.

Daniel stomped forward, throwing his hands up in a bad boy tantrum. "But, you fucking promised."

Cut sniffed. "I promised nothing. You will still inherit, but as I'm tearing up all the rules lately, there might be a dual inheritance. Primogeniture is over. I'm looking at all bases now."

"But that's not fair! There are rules, contracts!"

"Yes, and if I'd followed those rules, you wouldn't have her either, you fucking ingrate," Cut snapped. "I need a few days to unscramble this shit-storm. Then we can proceed correctly once the documents have been amended."

Wait. Documents? What amendments?

Daniel laughed, slipping beside me and wrapping his hand in my hair. The long strands tangled around his wrist, providing a perfect rope to jerk me away from Jasmine.

Only, she didn't let go. Her nails dug deeper into my wrist, keeping me pinned between the two fighting siblings.

"Let her go. She's mine!" Jaz slammed on her brakes.

"You can have her when I've taken what I want." Daniel yanked me toward him.

I cried out, tripping and swaying, two parts of me caught by two Hawks.

Oh, my God.

I was a piñata in the middle of a feuding family—tugged and devoured and ultimately beaten until I'd split open and die.

I laughed out loud at the insanity stinking up the room.

Jasmine was as bonkers as the rest of her bloodline. She would have to go, too.

He's dead.

He's dead.

He was good where they're all bad.

"Quit it!" Cut roared at the same time as Bonnie screeched, "Behave yourselves!"

The Hawk siblings quit squabbling like brats. We looked at Cut and Bonnie, panting hard, trapped in a cycle of idiocy.

"For fuck's sake." Cut dragged a hand over his face. "You're acting like two-year olds. I have a good mind to take the strap to both of you." His gaze fell on his children, searing and intense. "She'll be locked up until we have a family meeting. Then we can decide who has her first and what punishments shall be divided."

Jasmine sneered, "See, Dan. Let her go."

"You let go first."

"God, you're such a moron." Jasmine relinquished her hold. Instantly, blood seeped from the slices she'd given, trickling down my wrist.

"You're just an invalid who's never been laid." Daniel threw me away. "You always had it so easy, sister. Ever since your 'accident.'"

My ears pricked. The aura of mystery surrounding Jasmine only grew thicker. I wanted to know everything about her before I ended her. Just like I wanted to know everything about Bonnie, Cut, and Daniel. I would wear their history like a talisman. I would be the last person to know their tales before they faded into obscurity.

Jasmine sniffed. "You're pissed that your worthless *invalid* sister has won. I'm the eldest now; therefore, my word is law."

"Don't get ahead of yourself, Jaz," Cut said.

Daniel ignored him. "That's not it at all." Slamming his hands on the handrails of Jasmine's chair, he hemmed her in. "Now I have two women on my shit list instead of one." He dragged a finger across his throat. "I'd watch out if I were you."

Pushing off, he deliberately shouldered Cut out of the way, scowled at Bonnie, and stalked from the room.

The moment he disappeared, my muscles quivered. Somehow, I'd avoided whatever would've happened. I'd slipped into shock and come out ready to murder. And I'd been given to yet another Hawk who hated me.

Cut shook his head, looking at his mother. "They never fucking learn."

Bonnie laughed. "Neither did you, dear. Not for a long time."

He wrapped an arm around her brittle shoulders. "I can't imagine ever being so terrible."

My fingernails dug into my palm as I witnessed a seemingly normal bond. How could evil have so many layers? How could it be so obvious one moment, then hidden by family ties and hierarchy the next?

Bonnie tapped her cane against Cut's foot. "You're not forgetting what you did, are you? Because I have news for you—you were worse. A lot worse." Moving forward, she dislodged his hold. "But I straightened out the mess you made. I put things right. I have every faith you will, too."

Cut nodded. "Damn right, I will." His eyes strained but apart from a few cracks in his smooth veneer, I would never have guessed he'd pulled the trigger on two of his children.

He's dead.

He's dead.

All because of me.

Inching closer to Jasmine, I whispered so only she would hear. "He tried to shoot you, but Jethro saved you. Do you have no shame?"

Her eyes zeroed in on mine. Thoughts and emotions flickered over her face but she didn't reply.

Her betrayal hurt. Jethro and Kes had loved her. They'd *died* for her. Who could claim to love them in return yet continue to be in the same house as the man who'd shot them?

My stomach twisted. "You make me sick."

Her hands tightened around the rims of her wheels. Shutters slammed over her eyes, but still no response.

Tears stung but I had nothing else to say. Only one promise that she might as well hear, so she'd know who truly loved her brother. "I'll kill you for this. Just like I'll kill them."

She sat taller. Locking eyes with me, she said icily, "I guess we'll see, won't we?" Raising her voice, she pointed at the door. "Your fate will be discussed and decreed. Go to your room. Leave us."

I rubbed my wrist, smearing the blood she'd conjured. When I didn't move, she herded me with silver wheels toward the exit.

"I said leave." She didn't stop, pushing me between Cut and Bonnie.

My skin crawled as Cut reached out, gathering me to him. He brushed aside black hair that'd stuck to my clammy cheeks. His golden eyes shone with power. "I'm afraid our timeframe has accelerated since you've arrived. Emma was in my control for a delightful length of time. I'd hoped Jethro could manage the same. But...I raised lacklustre sons and have to hope my daughter can do better."

Jasmine nudged against the back of my thighs. "Let her go, Father. She has to be trained in obedience." Her legs remained covered with a rose-coloured blanket, but temper flared her cheeks. "That was her issue with Jet. She never listened. I'll teach her otherwise."

How did I judge someone so wrong? All this time, I thought Jasmine was half-way sane—a crutch for her brother and stronger than all of them combined. But she was just as diabolical.

"If anyone can do it, it's you, Jasmine." Cut released me. "I have no doubt."

Bonnie smiled, leaning on her stick. "Jasmine is an exemplary student. She'll rise to the challenge."

"You never have to doubt, Father." Jasmine's frosty voice sent goosebumps over my skin. "I'm ten times the man my brothers were."

Who *was* this person? This cold-hearted harpy who didn't care. How could she sit there and speak to the man who'd killed her brothers, let alone agree to torture me.

He's dead.

He's dead.

He's free from this insanity.

I couldn't control the frothing animosity any longer. My lips pulled back. "You're all monsters. Every single one of you. You'll all pay."

Cut sighed, "You were told to leave, Ms. Weaver. I suggest you listen."

Bonnie swatted the back of my calves with her stick. "Move, you little guttersnipe."

"Wait, Grandmamma." Jasmine wheeled herself in front of me with a few expert manoeuvres. "I have something else I want to say."

The room sucked in a breath, all of us waiting.

Her gaze fell on mine, dead and empty. "You, Nila Weaver, are the reason my best friend is dead. You are the reason I am now sister to only one brother. And you are the reason my family is falling apart." Her face darkened, manicured eyebrows shadowing angry eyes. "I asked you once to let the debts take place. I asked you to give your life for him—like it has always been. But you didn't listen."

Rolling away, she waved at the door. "Go to your room and think about that. Because this time, I'm not giving you a choice.

"This time, I'll make you pay."

Nila

I WOULD NEVER sleep again.

Not while Daniel roamed the corridors and Cut held my life in his hands. I would never relax while they breathed. I would never drop my guard while they plotted my demise.

But while they plotted, *I* plotted.

Together, we would meet in hell, and I was past caring who would win. As long as I exterminated them, I would happily trade my life for justice.

Twelve hours passed.

Twelve hours where my heart bled for Jethro and every minute erased his imprint on this world.

Twelve hours where I'd been alone.

I hadn't seen anyone but Flaw. He'd knocked on my door around 9:00 p.m., bringing venison stew and crusty baguettes. He'd looked as bad as I did—his piercing eyes fogged with stress, his dark hair a turbulent mess. He was a direct mirror of grey disbelief and desolation. I'd wanted him to stay—to protect me if Daniel decided to pay a nocturnal visit, but the moment he'd delivered my dinner, he left.

Food was ash inside my mouth, but I forced small bites, painstakingly swallowing and providing energy to the only weapon I could rely on. Once I'd eaten every morsel, I'd sat cross-legged in the centre of my bed and tightened my grip around the ruby-encrusted dirk.

I couldn't lie down because Jethro's smell laced my sheets.

I couldn't close my eyes because his handsome face and blazing love haunted me.

And I couldn't relax because I needed to be ready to attack if any Hawk came for me.

Only, they never came.

Daybreak brought a smidgen of peace, illuminating Hawksridge—yet again, hiding the filthy evil that seemed so obvious at night.

My cheeks itched from the salt of my sadness, and my head ached from dehydration.

For one heart-ripping moment, I permitted myself to fall face first on the bedding where Jethro had told me everything. I allowed grief to grab me with thick arms and smother me in terrible tears.

I relived his touch and kisses. I punished myself with memories of him slipping inside me, of him saying he loved me for the first time. I came completely undone as I hugged my knife and inhaled the last reminders I would ever have of him.

I had no photographs, no love letters.

Only a few texts and recollections.

They weren't worth any monetary value, but in a blink, they became my most prized possessions.

Once I'd shed a final tear and drugged myself on his subtle flavour of woods and leather, I hauled myself out of bed and into the shower. Stepping into the hot spray felt like a betrayal to Jethro—as if I washed away the past, moving into a future without him.

I thought I'd cried my final tear, but beneath the waterfall, I purged again, letting my tears swirl down the drain.

I will kill them.

And I will dance on their graves when I do.

Dawn morphed to morning, one hour blending into another, drifting me further from Jethro's memory.

I tried to leave. My body was weak, needing fuel, mimicking my aching heart with emptiness. But the doorknob refused to spin.

They'd locked me inside.

Could I break it down? Destroy it? But why should I waste my fury on an innocent door when Cut and Daniel deserved to be torn into smithereens?

So, I did the only thing I could. I sat on my chaise and gripped my cell-phone with chilly fingers, begging for a miracle to happen.

Text me, Jethro.

Prove it's all a big mistake.

Over and over, I repeated my prayer, only for the stubborn phone never to answer. It remained blank and unfeeling, the battery slowly dwindling. The battle to keep going drained me to the point of exhaustion.

I could call for help. I could ring the police chief who'd taken me back after the Second Debt. But they'd wiped my file when I did the *Vanity Fair* interview. I'd cried wolf and they wouldn't believe me—especially as most of them were bought by Cut.

Plus, I can't leave Vaughn. I couldn't risk giving them ammunition to hurt him.

Indulging in the past, rather than dwelling on a desolate future, I opened every text he'd sent, reliving the rush and sexual frustration of forbidden whispers.

Kite007: *Me and my wandering hand missed you.*

The intoxicating innocence when I didn't know it was him.

Kite007: *If I said I wanted one night of blatant honesty, no douche-baggery, no bullshit of any kind, what would you say?*

The first crack in his cool exterior, revealing just how deep he ran.

Kite007: *I feel what you feel. Whether it be a kiss or a kick or a killing blow. I wished I didn't, but you're mine. Therefore, you are my affliction.*

The first taste of truth when he told me his condition in riddles.

Kite007: *Don't go into the dark alone, little Weaver. Monsters roam the shadows, and your time is officially up.*

The last darkness inside him that'd vanished entirely the night we revealed everything.

All of it.

Every letter and comma were still tangible, while the author had now vanished. I would've given anything for him to reappear—to magically reverse tragedy and come back to me.

Jethro…

Hunching over my phone, I let go again.

Wracking sobs, heaving ribs, and a dying soul screaming that nothing would ever be the same.

He's dead.

He's…

dead.

At lunchtime, Flaw appeared.

My only visitor and I didn't know if he was friend or foe.

For the past while, I'd stared into space, picturing gruesome ways to end it.

I couldn't cry anymore.

I couldn't read Kite's texts anymore.

All I could do was exist in a room where scents of love mixed with smells of war, settling deeper into hate.

Flaw didn't speak, only delivered a meal of salad and cured ham. With sad eyes, he retreated from my room and locked the door.

It'd taken over an hour before I had the energy to move from my crumpled, soggy ball. Along with the agony of grief, I'd surpassed the craving of hunger, leaving me blissfully blank of basic necessities.

I shivered, but I wasn't cold.

My stomach growled, but I wasn't hungry.

My heart kept beating, but I was no longer alive.

I wasn't human. I was a killer waiting for first blood.

Blood.

The thought of extracting hot, sticky red from Cut and Daniel kick-started my energy. My hand curled around my blade as I crawled across the carpet and poked the food.

Eat.

Stay strong.

Kill.

The ham settled like salty concrete on my tongue. Every mouthful wasn't about nutrition or satisfaction—it was about building power so I was ready for war.

Minute by minute, my anger solidified. The Hawks had been untouchable for long enough. They believed no amount of treason or rebellion could dethrone them.

They were wrong.

Their reign was over. It was time for a new ruler. One who stood for justice rather than debts. One who would avenge those she'd lost.

They've underestimated me.

And they would die because of it.

Dusk crept silently across my carpet.

The tentative darkness sucked the light from glittering sequins, sinking into rich velvet from the fabric bolts on the walls. Every minute its gloomy fingers made their way stealthily from window to bed, reminding me that my world might've ended yesterday, but the rest of the globe didn't care.

The sun still rose.

The moon still set.

And my heart still beat regardless.

My ears pricked as the harsh scrape of a key echoed from the opposite side of the room. I sat up in bed, rubbing my eyes, grabbing my dirk from the covers.

The door swung open.

I shifted to my knees, wielding the knife. After my shower last night, I'd dressed in black leggings and an oversized cream cardigan. But no matter how many layers or quilts I snuggled beneath, I couldn't eradicate the chill of loneliness.

My ears still echoed with gunshots.

My mind replayed the moment when Kes collapsed with blood blooming on his shirt, and Jethro dove to protect his sister.

The sister who didn't deserve to be saved.

My jaw clenched.

Jasmine.

She was in equal running for my dislike with Daniel. In fact, she was worse. Always coming across as gentle and removed from her mad family—when, in actual fact, she'd been the instigator and in cahoots with Bonnie.

Flaw appeared.

Peering around the door, he wore his typical outfit of jeans, black t-shirt, and Black Diamonds jacket. His gaze drifted to the knife in my hands, raising an eyebrow. "If you don't want that confiscated, I'd hide it if I were you."

My hands shook. "Why are you here?" I didn't see any trays of food. A social call was out of the question. Shuffling higher, I narrowed my eyes. "Why do you care if they take my knife or not?"

He ran a hand through his hair, opening the door wider. "Don't like this situation any more than you do."

His voice sounded loud and obtrusive, spilling secrets. It was the first time I'd spoken to someone since I'd been locked up; I'd forgotten how to do it.

My heart ached. "You miss them, too?"

Jethro...

Kes...

The only ones not tainted by Hawk insanity.

He nodded. "Kes has been a close friend for years. Didn't have much to do with Jethro until recently, but he proved he was a good bloke. Almost as good as his brother."

His comment hurt irrationally. To me, Jethro was better than anyone. Then again, my heart was biased. Kestrel was a genuine, caring friend who'd sacrificed far too much for people who didn't deserve him.

Myself included.

I hugged my knife, stroking it with the thought of spilling Cut's blood. "He was the best. His death won't go unpunished."

Flaw came closer, his boots silent on the emerald W carpet. "Words like that can get you into trouble."

I ran my thumb along the sharp blade. "I don't care. All I want is for them to die."

He cleared his throat. "Can't say I don't understand or feel your pain, but it's best to stop saying such things." Inching closer to the bed, he held out his hand. "I was told to bring you."

My head snapped up. "What?"

The last time someone had come to take me somewhere, the maid made me dress in breaches and cheesecloth, then delivered me to the worst poker night in history.

I tightened my grip on the dirk. "I'm not going anywhere with you."

He scowled. "Don't make this harder than it already is."

I moved away from him, inching to the other side of the bed. "Tell me why."

"Why?"

My heart cantered faster—almost as fast as Moth, the day Kes took me for a ride. I should've been nice to him. Kinder. Less suspicious.

I bared my teeth. "If this is to re-do the Third Debt, I'm not going. I'll kill you first." My threat wasn't empty. I boiled with the urge to do it—to prove I was done being weak.

Flaw jammed his hands in his back pockets. The action made him appear personable and less threatening.

I didn't buy it.

He'd been there that first night when Jethro stole me from Milan. He'd witnessed what they'd done to me in the months I'd been there.

"I haven't been told anything. I guess you'll just have to come and find out for yourself."

"Tell Cut he can come for me himself."

My eyes darted around the room. I had weapons here: needles, scissors, scalpels for sculpturing lace. If I could entice Cut into my nest, I could ambush him with tools I knew how to wield.

He wouldn't stand a chance.

"Look—" He shrugged. "I was told not to tell you, but fuck it. They're in the library. And they have guests. I doubt they'll do anything of a…family matter…in front of an audience."

No, but they keep such blatant evidence.

Their audacity at keeping mementos of my ancestors' pain infuriated me. Once I'd killed them, I'd gather up every video and document and burn them. I'd demolish every evidence and set my ancestors' souls free.

Why not turn it into the police?

I shuddered. The thought of men in suits—men who the Hawks might've paid to turn a blind eye for so long—watching video-tapes of my mother's agony almost made me black out with a vicious vertigo wave.

Gripping the sheets, I let the dizziness subside before blinking my vision clear.

Flaw hadn't moved; a relaxed employee who knew I'd have to obey eventually.

"Why should I trust you? What's to stop you from lying?" He might've been Kes's friend, but he was still a Black Diamond. And they weren't to be trusted.

"Because I might be the last remaining friend you have in this godforsaken place." His face tightened for a moment, filling with thoughts he refused to share. "You need more? Fine. I happen to know the guests are lawyers." Holding out his hand, he said, "Happy? Now, let's go."

"Lawyers?" I shook my head. "Why?"

What on earth are lawyers doing here?

Flaw gave half a smile. "Instead of all the questions, how about you just get it over with?"

I didn't want to move but I couldn't deny he had logic on his side.

With one last glower, I swung my legs off the bed and padded toward him. The room wobbled from getting up so fast, but other than that, my bloodlust for Cut's life kept me focused on an anchor.

Jethro is no longer my anchor.

I was once again a shipwrecked boat, drifting on an ocean of misfortune.

Flaw's gaze fell to my knife. "You planning on taking that?"

"Do you have a problem with that?"

I waited for him to snatch it from me. To confiscate it. Instead, he pursed his lips. "I'm not the one on your shit list."

"Not at the moment, you aren't."

He sucked in a breath.

Rebellion and power siphoned through my blood. I didn't trust Flaw, but he wasn't my enemy. Holding eye contact, I hitched up the hem of my slouchy cardigan, tucked the dirk in my waistband, and concealed it.

He didn't say a word.

I was playing with fire. He was on their side. He could tell them I had it and leave me defenceless, but at the same time, I had to push and search for allies. Flaw had been kind to me whenever we'd crossed paths. He'd escorted me to my room late at night if Daniel caught me sneaking to the kitchens. He'd been there whenever I'd popped in to see Kestrel, laughing and seeming normal and carefree.

Anyone who was friends with Kes couldn't be too bad—Kes wouldn't tolerate it.

And I learned that the hard way.

He's dead.

Just like his brother.

My heart panged. No matter how strong I forced myself to be, I couldn't stop the lacerations of grief. It was like a rogue wave, lapping at my soul, tugging me under with its rip.

Flaw crossed his arms, challenge sparking in his eyes. "You know the knife won't be enough."

"I know."

He cocked his head. "Then why bother?"

Running my hands through my hair, I twisted the black length to drape over my shoulder. "Because they won't expect it. And the element of surprise can make a tiny knife become a sword."

He chuckled. "Deep. Sounds like Confucius or some other metaphorical bullshit."

I shrugged. "Doesn't matter. I know what I mean. I know what I'll do." My tone slid to ice. "And I suggest you stay out of my way and keep your mouth shut."

He laughed quietly. "Hey. As long as you stay away from me, I don't have a problem. Always knew things would change. Ever since Kes told me what Jethro planned to do on his thirtieth, I knew my lifestyle was up."

I froze.

He'll never age another day.

Jethro's corpse would forever remain twenty-nine—immortal and unchanging.

"What? What was he planning?"

"He didn't tell you?" He crossed his arms. "I thought you were deep as fucking thieves. That was the reason all of this grew out of control."

Breathing hard, I swallowed sadness. "No, he didn't tell me."

Flaw softened. "Sorry."

I swiped at my face, dispelling any sign of tears. "So, what was he planning?"

He's dead. But he's still here...holding me...guiding me.

Learning more about Jethro, even though he was gone, was awfully bittersweet.

Flaw looked behind him at the open door. His face shadowed, and for a moment, I thought he'd refuse to say, but then he lowered his voice. "Once everything was his, he planned on ripping up the contracts. Ending it."

My eyes grew wide. "Forever?"

"Yup."

"He would have that power?"

Flaw turned rigid, his thoughts obviously on topics he didn't enjoy. "Of course. He was a Hawk. They made the contract. They had the power to absolve it. Jethro planned to split up the estate equally between his brothers and sister and ban Cut and Bonnie from the grounds." He rubbed his chin. "I only know that because Kes told me in a couple of years they might not require the Club to transport shipments because the shipments would stop altogether."

"He didn't want to smuggle anymore, either?" *Wow.* All this time I'd grown close to Jethro, yet we'd never shared our future together. Never lain in bed and murmured about what we wanted or dreamed.

Because our future was bleak.

Death for me. Heartache for him. Why focus on a fantasy when the reality threatened to destroy us?

Flaw moved toward the door. "Would you continue doing something illegal when you had more money than you could ever spend in hundreds of lifetimes?" His eyes darkened with nostalgia for his friends. "With the estate broken up, everyone could've gone their separate ways. Kes planned to take a few years off and spend it in Africa injecting some of the money taken from its soil back to its people." He sighed. "Like I said, a good man."

Placing his hand on the doorknob, he tilted his head. "Enough talking. They'll be waiting. Better get you there before they suspect something."

The cold steel of the blade wedged against my back. It gave me courage but couldn't stop my sudden tremble. "Will you give me your word you're not taking me somewhere for those psychopaths to hurt me?"

His jaw clenched. "I just told you insider information that could get me killed if you said anything. Doesn't that deserve a little trust?"

"It does if it was said out of understanding rather than manipulation. I've fallen for the kind act far more times than I'm comfortable with."

Flaw frowned. "Would it help to know I give you full permission to gut the next bastard who tries to hurt you?"

My heart stuttered. "Permission? You think I need your *permission*?" Moving toward him, I stood close enough to smell his spicy aftershave and leather from his jacket. "Give me something better than your permission, Flaw."

He straightened. "Like what?"

"Like freedom." I waved at the window. "I could've run. I could've somehow found my way to the boundary and vanished, but they have my brother. Bring V to me and we'll go. I'll take my family and disappear."

And then I'll come back and murder them in their sleep.

His eyes burned into mine. "You know I can't do that."

"So, all your talk of a better future and good men…that was what? Empty words?"

He scowled. "There are things going on that you don't know about."

I threw my hands up. "Oh, really? Funny, I've never heard that before."

Once again, thoughts flickered over his face, secrets shadowing his eyes.

"If that's true, tell me. What's going on?"

He looked away. "I can't answer that."

I laughed morbidly. "No, of course, you can't."

"That's not fair."

My temper frayed, entirely unleashed. "That's not *fair*?" I poked him in the chest. "What's *fair* about me being subjected to more Hawk insanity? What's fair about having the love of my life shot in front of me? What's fair about waiting to die?!"

His hands fisted.

"You know what; I'm done." Shaking my head, I brushed past him into the corridor. "Just take me to them like a good minion and get out of my sight."

He growled under his breath. "Don't judge me. Don't judge my actions based on what you can't see." Stomping in front of me, he said over his shoulder, "I know who I am, and I know what I do is right."

Animosity flared between us.

I stayed silent, following him down the corridor toward the wing where I'd spent most time with Kestrel. We passed the room where he'd given me the Weaver Journal and headed into the hall where the library was located. My mind flickered back to the afternoon he'd found me, asking if Jethro had been to see me since completing the First Debt.

At the time, his question wasn't too unusual. But now it took on a whole new meaning. He wasn't asking about me. He'd been asking about his brother—keen to know how absorbing my pain had affected his empathetic sibling.

God, how bad had Jethro felt? How much did my thoughts destroy him?

"In there." Flaw stopped outside the library.

So many memories were already stored in this place. So many breakthroughs and breakdowns as I grew from girl to woman.

Not making eye contact, he muttered, "They're waiting for you. Better get inside." Without a goodbye, he turned on his heel and left.

His retreating back upset me all over again. He was the last connection I had to Kestrel's kindness and to Jethro's ultimate plans.

Come back.

My soul scrunched tight as the ghosts of Jethro and Kes haunted the walls of their home. In twenty-four hours, I'd gone through the cycles of bereavement: disbelief, shock, despair, rage…I doubted I'd ever get through acceptance, but I embraced my anger, building a barrier that only clearheaded, cold-hearted fury could enter.

I didn't want any other emotion when facing Cut and Daniel.

Touching the dagger hilt, I straightened my shoulders and pushed open the library doors.

My eyes widened as I stepped into the old world charm of book-bindings and scripted letters. The large beanbags where Kes had found me dozing still scattered. The window seats waited for morning sunshine and a bookworm to absorb themselves in fairy-tale pages.

This place was a church of stories and imagination. But then my gaze fell on the antichrist, polluting the sanctity of peace.

"Nice of you to join us, Nila." Cut waved at the one and only empty chair at the large oak table.

My teeth clamped together. I didn't reply.

"Come." He snapped his fingers. "Sit. We've waited long enough."

You can do this.

Obey until an opportunity presents itself.

Then…

kill

him.

I drifted forward, drawn by the multiple pairs of eyes watching me.

Bonnie, Daniel, Jasmine, Cut, and four men I didn't recognise waited for me to join them. The four men wore sombre black suits and aubergine ties—a uniform painting them with the same brush.

I drew closer to the table.

Daniel stood up, wrapping a vile arm around my waist. "Missed you, Weaver." Planting a kiss on my cheek, he whispered, "Whatever happens here tonight doesn't mean shit, you hear me? I'm coming for you, and I don't fucking care what they say."

I shuddered with disgust.

Withdrawing the hate from his voice, Daniel transformed into a cordial smile. "Sit." With a gallant act, he pulled out the empty seat. "Take a load off. This is going to be a long meeting."

I wanted to touch his pulse, count his heartbeat, relish in knowing they were numbered.

Soon, Daniel…soon…

Locking my jaw, so I didn't say anything I might regret, I sat down.

The men in matching suits never looked away. They ranged in age from sixties with greying hair to mid-thirties with blond buzz cut.

Daniel kicked my chair forward so my stomach kissed the lip of the table. I sucked in a breath, straightening my spine uncomfortably in order to tolerate the tight arrangement.

His golden eyes met mine, smug and vainglorious.

I'll cut that look right off your face.

My fingers twitched for my knife.

Daniel sat beside me, while the person on my other side hissed, "No speaking unless spoken to. Got it?"

My eyes shot to Jasmine. Her hands rested on the table, a cute gold ring circling her middle finger, while her seat perched on a small ramp, bringing the wheels in line with the chairs of the other guests. She looked like a capable heiress, dressed in a black smock with a black ribbon around her throat. She was the epitome of a mourning sister.

I don't buy it.

I'd misjudged her—thought she was decent and caring. She'd fooled me the most.

Tearing my gaze from her, I glanced at the remaining Hawks. Just like Jasmine, they all wore black. Bonnie looked as if she'd jumped into a jungle of black lace and fastened it with glittering diamond broaches. Cut wore an immaculate suit with black shirt and tie. Even Daniel looked fit for the opera in a glossy onyx ensemble and satin waistcoat.

I'd never seen so much darkness—both on the outside and inside. They'd discarded their leather jackets in favour of mourning attire.

All for what?

To garner sympathy from outsiders? To play the part of grieving family, even though they were the cause of murder?

I hate you.

I hate all of you.

My hands balled on the table. I wanted to say so many things. I wanted to launch onto the table and stab them with my knife. But I heeded Jasmine's warning and stayed put. There was no other way.

Cut cleared his throat. "Now that we're all here, you may begin, Marshall." His gaze pinned the oldest stranger. "I appreciate you coming after work hours, but this matter has to be dealt with quickly."

Bonnie reclined in her chair, a faint smile on her lips.

Every time I looked at the old bat, I got the feeling she was the meddler in all of this. She was the reason Cut was the way he was. She was the reason why Jasmine was disabled and Jethro and Kes were dead. I guessed she was also the reason why Jethro never mentioned his mother.

I'd been in their lives for months, yet no one had uttered a thing about Mrs. Cut Hawk.

Unless it was a miracle conception and Cut carved his children from his bones like some evil sorcerer, she had to have existed and stuck around long enough to give Cut four babies.

Where is she now?

Images of Jethro and Kes reuniting with their mother in heaven gave me equal measure of despair and comfort.

If she's even dead.

She could be trapped in the house, on a floor I didn't know, in a room hidden from view. She might be alive and not know that her husband killed two of her sons.

God, what a tragic—

The stranger coughed, stealing my attention. "Thank you, Bryan." Meticulously, he aligned a wayward fountain pen beside his tan ledger before looking at his colleagues. "I'll start, gentlemen."

His grey eyes locked on me, gluing me into my chair. "You must be Ms. Weaver. We haven't had the pleasure of meeting up till now."

My back bristled.

Any man who'd studied the law and permitted the Hawks to continue to get away with what they did wasn't someone I wanted to speak with.

Daniel nudged me. "Say hello, Nila."

I clamped my lips together.

"You don't want to be rude." He snickered. "These guys have met all the Weavers. Isn't that right, Marshall?"

My heart stopped.

What does that mean?

Marshall nodded. "That is correct, Mr. Daniel. I, personally, am lucky enough to have met your mother, Ms. Weaver. She was a fine young woman who loved you very much."

I thought the pain of Jethro's death had broken me past any other emotional agony.

I was wrong.

The mention of my mother *crippled* me. A sob wrapped wet tentacles around my lungs.

Don't cry. Do not cry.

I would never cry again. Not as long as these people lived.

I'll slaughter you all!

Jasmine arched her neck condescendingly. "Instead of torturing an already tortured girl, let's get on with it, shall we?" Her eyes gleamed. "Leave the emotional battery to me once the legalities are straightened out."

Cut chuckled, eyeing his daughter with newfound awe. "Jasmine, I must say, I never knew you were so capable."

Bonnie preened like some proud mother hen. "That's because I told you to leave her to me." White tendrils of hair escaped her chignon, wisping in the low-lit room. "She's stronger than Jet, Kes, and Dan combined. And it's all thanks to me."

I wanted to vomit. Or slash her to pieces. Either would work.

How could someone of that age, who should be tender and kind, be so heartlessly cruel?

Jasmine merely nodded like a princess accepting a compliment and turned her attention back to the life-stealing, blood-sucking, soul-leaching lawyer. "You may continue, Mr. Marshall."

Marshall stretched his wrinkly face into a smile. "As you wish, Ms. Jasmine." Waving at his partners, he said, "Ms. Weaver, before we begin, we must honour the common niceties. I am principal director of the firm Marshall, Backham, and Cole. We have provided legal counsel and been sole conservator of the Hawk family for generations. My father was proud to be of service and his father and his father before him. There is nothing about the Hawk legacy that we are not a part of." His eyes narrowed. "Do you know what I'm saying?"

I stopped breathing.

A part of everything?

So outsiders were aware of what went on inside these walls? Lawyers knew what the Debt Inheritance entailed and yet they were *okay* with it?

My body throbbed with another flush of fury.

I didn't just want to steal three lives but theirs, too. The corridors of Hawksridge Hall would flow with blood by the time I eradicated the amount of people in on this ancient serial killing spree. Their innards would drape the walls, and their bones would rot the foundations with their malicious ideals.

That's all they are.

Rich, eloquent, intelligent murderers hiding behind false pretences of contracts and signatures.

Would they sign a new contract giving me the right to slash their throats and tear out their hearts in payment for atrocities committed?

It doesn't matter.

I didn't need their permission.

I focused on the table, on the swirls of wood grain, rather than his face. If I looked up, I wouldn't have the strength to stay in my chair. "You're saying you presided over my ancestors' executions? That you helped bribe away the truth and protect these sick bastards?"

Cut shot to his feet. "Nila!"

I ignored him, my fingernails digging into my palms. "You're saying you helped change the law and enabled one family to destroy another? You're saying you had my ancestors *killed?*"

I slammed my chair back, my voice reaching a glass-shattering octave. "You're saying that you can sit there, talk to me, tell me whatever bullshit you're about to do, all the while *knowing* they mean to chop off my head, and you don't have a *problem* with that?"

Jasmine snatched my wrist. "God's sake, sit your arse down."

"Let go of—" I cried out as Daniel grabbed my hair and shoved me forward. I lost my footing; my face smashed against the table. Instantly, blood spurted from my nose, pain resonating in my skull.

Sickness drenched my senses with agony.

"Drop her, Daniel!" Cut yelled.

Daniel's fingers were suddenly torn from my hair, letting me slouch backward, landing in my chair. Jasmine fought off her brother, slapping him away. "Don't fucking touch her. What did I say? *I'm* in charge. *I'm* the oldest."

My eyes watered as more blood gushed from my nose. I didn't think it was broken, but the room spun with an induced vertigo wave.

God, what was I thinking?

The plan was to remain cool and invisible, looking for the perfect chance. Now I couldn't think straight with pain.

"You're not in fucking charge, Jaz. She's mine." Daniel pointed at Marshall. "Tell her. Amend it, so my sister can shut the fuck up about the rules."

Marshall looked awkwardly at Cut. "Sir?"

Cut ran a hand over his face, slowly sitting back down. "No, the conversation we had yesterday still stands." His lips turned up at the rapidly building stain from my nosebleed. Every red drip redecorated the table and the front of my cardigan. "Someone get her a damn napkin."

Jasmine shuffled in her wheelchair, pulling out a white handkerchief. "Here." Shoving it into my hand, her eyes flickered with compassion.

It only made me hate her more.

Scrunching up the material, I held it to my nose, getting sick joy from destroying the white perfection. The stuffiness made me breathless, and my eyes drifted to the corner where initials had been embroidered.

JKH

I dropped it.

Oh, my God.

My hand splayed open, tinged with crimson and sticky but unable to hide the two tattoos on my fingertips. JKH.

Jasmine kept her brother's handkerchief.

Why? To rub salt in already hollowed wounds or to laugh over fooling him just like she'd fooled me.

I locked eyes with her, pouring all my rage into my stare. "You'll pay for what you've done." Glancing at Bonnie and Cut, I added, "You'll *all* pay."

Marshall cleared his throat loudly. "I think the little interlude has come to an end. Shall we continue?"

"Yes, let's," Bonnie sniffed. "Never seen something so unruly in all my life." Sniffing in my direction, she tilted her chin. "Another word out of you, Weaver, and you won't like the consequences."

Daniel moaned, "But Grandmamma—"

"Buzzard, zip it," Cut growled. "Sit down or leave. But don't fucking talk again."

Daniel muttered under his breath but plonked back into his chair.

Jasmine grabbed the red-sodden material and shoved it under my nose. "Hold this, shut up, and don't get into any more trouble."

The skirmish ended; no one moved.

Silence hovered thick over the table.

The only sound was the heavy ticking of a grandfather clock by the gold ladder leading to the limited editions above. Side lamps had been switched on, filling the large space with warm illumination, while curtains blocked any remaining light that dared trespass on priceless books or fade cherished words.

Finally, Marshall sucked in a breath. He rearranged his fountain pen again. "Now that we're all on the same page, I'll carry on." Looking at me, he said, "For the rest of this meeting, you may address me as Marshall, or by my first name, which is Colin. These are my colleagues."

Pointing to the man closest to him: a potbellied, watery-eyed bald guy, he continued, "This is Hartwell Backham, followed by Samuel Cole, and my son Matthew Marshall."

My nose ached but the bleeding had stopped, leaving me stuffed up. I glowered at the men. There wasn't an ounce of mercy in their gazes.

They were here to do the job they'd been entrusted. Their loyalties were steadfast. Their intentions unchangeable.

I doubted they saw me as human—just a clause in a contract and nothing more.

Daniel poked me under the table. "After your little stunt, the least you can do is be nice." His voice deepened. "Say hello."

Yet another way to make me obey. He didn't care about pleasantries— only about making me submit to his every childish whim.

I sat straighter.

I'll do nothing of the sort.

Jasmine nudged me. "If you won't listen to him, listen to me. Do it."

I glared at her. "Why should I?"

"Because you belong to her, you little cow." Grabbing her cane, Bonnie struck her chair leg as if the furniture would turn into a horse and gallop her away from there. "Start. Now."

Marshall launched into action. "Of course, Madame Hawk. My apologies." Slapping open the file in front of him, his partners copied. Ledgers flung open and pens uncapped.

"Let me assure you that we're honoured to once again provide service to your impeccable family," Marshall twittered like a buffoon.

Cut groaned, steepling his fingers. "Lose the arse kissing. Did you bring the file or not?"

Paper scattered the wooden tabletop like fallen snowflakes, reminding me all over again of the icy way Jethro protected himself—the arctic coolness and thawing as I slowly made him want me.

The pain in my nose shot to my heart.

He's dead.

He's dead.

Don't think about him.

Marshall selected a certain page. "I did." Looking at his son—the blond buzz cut douchebag—he pointed at a box by the exit. "Grab that will you, Matthew?"

Matthew shot to his feet. "Sure." In a whisper of cashmere suit, he went to retrieve the large white box.

Curiosity rose to know what was in it. But at the same time, I was past caring.

More bullshit. More games.

None of it mattered because I was playing a different game. One they wouldn't understand until it was too late.

Jasmine scooted her wheelchair back a little, giving Matthew access to the table.

He smiled in thanks, placing the heavy box before his father. Marshall stood up and opened the lid while his son sat back down.

I sniffed, trying hard to clear my nostrils of blood. The pounding headache made everything fuzzy—a struggle to completely follow. I wanted to be coherent for whatever was about to happen.

No one spoke as Marshall removed reams and reams of paper and stacked them in neat piles on the table. The more he withdrew, the more aged the paper became. The first pile was pristinely white, neat edges, and uniformed lettering from a computer and printer.

The next stack was thin and cream-coloured, smudged edges, and the fuzzy blocks of a typewriter ribbon.

What is going on?

The third was yellowed and crinkled, shabby with torn edges, and the spidery scrawl of human penmanship.

And the final stack was moth-eaten, the colour of coffee, and swirling calligraphy of an art lost long ago.

That colour...

Its coffee bean shade was similar to the Debt Inheritance scraps Cut had given me at my welcome luncheon.

Could it be...

My attention zeroed in on Cut.

"Do you hazard a guess as to what that is, Nila?"

I shivered at the fatherly way he said my name, as if this was a family lesson. Something to be proud of and honoured to be an exclusive member.

I don't need to guess.

I cocked my chin. "No, I don't."

He chuckled. "Come now. You already know. I can see it in your eyes."

"I don't know what you're talking about."

Jasmine huffed. "Just be honest. For once in your life." Her voice dropped to a harsh curse. "Don't make this any worse, for God's sake."

Whoa...

After everything she'd done. After cuddling up to her father after he shot Jethro and Kes and promising me a world of hurt for being responsible for such a tragedy, she had the *audacity* to make it seem as if I were unappreciative and uncooperative.

Not going to fly anymore.

Screw being meek and quiet.

I'd tried that.

Now, I snapped.

Turning to face her, my hackles rose. The claws I'd grown when I'd first arrived unsheathed, and I wanted nothing more than to drag them across her face. "I'd watch what you say to me...*bitch*."

The room sucked into a dark hole, hovering in space, glacial and deadly.

The curse hovered between us, not fading—if possible, only growing louder the more the silence deafened.

I never swore. Ever. I never called people names or stooped to such a crass level. But since Jethro had died, I'd sunk steadily into profanity, and the power of that simple word bolstered my courage a thousand times.

I *loved* the righteous power it gave me.

I loved the shock factor it delivered.

Jaz gaped. "What did you just call me?"

I smiled as if I had a mouthful of sugar. "Bitch. I called you a bitch. A motherfucking bitch, and I think you'll find the name suits you."

Bonnie slapped her cane onto the table, cracking the palpable tension. "Watch your tongue, hussy. I'll have it ripped out before you can—"

Jaz held up her hand. "Grandmamma, let me handle this." Her eyes narrowed to bronze blades. "Let me get this straight. *I'm* the bitch? I'm the bitch for loving my brothers so much that I now want to avenge their deaths by killing the person who took theirs? I'm the bitch because I gave everything to Jethro, including the use of my legs, and don't deserve to honour his memory by making you suffer?"

Her face turned red. "Excuse me if you don't think I'm worth that, Ms. High and Fucking Mighty. Perhaps, we should kill your brother and see what sort of person *you'd* turn into."

My heart exploded at the mention of harming Vaughn. "Don't you *dare* touch him."

"Address me properly and we'll see." Jasmine shoved her face close to mine. "Behave yourself and your twin will walk away when you die. Don't, and his head will be in the basket beside yours."

Oh, my God.

I couldn't breathe.

I couldn't even speak through the horrors of what she'd said.

"If you so much as touch him—"

"You'll what? Kill me? Yeah, right." Jaz rolled her eyes. "Like anyone believes you're capable of that, little Weaver. Even Jethro knew you could never hurt him and that's why he—"

I slapped my hands over my ears. "Stop it!"

Daniel broke out into loud guffaws. "Well, fuck me, sis. You're kinda badass."

Jaz looked at her younger brother. The harsh glint in her eyes increased with maliciousness. "You have no idea, baby brother."

Cut clapped his hands. "Marshall continue. My mother must rest, and we have a lot to cover. Ignore any further outbursts and get on with it."

Marshall nodded. "Yes, sir. Of course."

Jasmine twisted away from me, facing the lawyers. She breathed steadily with no adverse reactions to our verbal war.

The lawyers shuffled and stacked their files. No one was fussed that Jaz had just announced every sordid detail. That she'd admitted to holding me and my twin hostage or that they callously planned a double homicide.

And why would they?

They belonged body, heart, and soul to the devil born Hawks.

Marshall pointed at the piles of paperwork. "Mr. Hawk has advised me that you were shown the original document labelled the Debt Inheritance. Is that correct, Ms. Weaver?"

My muscles quaked with the need to bolt or fight. Both would be preferable. Sitting sandwiched between Jaz and Daniel only wound me tighter.

My mind ran with profanity.

Fuck you.

"Answer him, Nila," Cut said.

"You already know that that's correct."

Marshall warmed to his task, finally having one of his questions answered without Armageddon breaking out.

God, I wish you were here, Jethro. Sitting beside me, granting me strength.

I was all alone.

"Fantastic. Well, that document is just the first of many that you're about to become acquainted with." Laying his hand on the oldest looking stack, he lowered his voice. "These documents are the originals, passed down through our firm and our connection with the Hawks to keep safe and protected. In here exists every note, amendment, and requested clause update. It has been lodged in accordance with the times and royals in power, drifting through kings, queens, and ultimately, prime ministers and diplomats."

My headache came back at the nonsense he spouted. "You're telling me people in power kept signing these...when they knew all along what it was?"

Hartwell Backham answered, his voice rich as burnished copper. "Don't underestimate the power of a family crest or the name of the oldest law firm in England. We have garnered centuries of goodwill, and our clients sign what we suggest. They trust our judgement and don't have time for consuming activities such as reading every document that crosses their tables."

There was so much wrong with that sentence, it astounded me.

"You're saying that—"

Marshall interrupted me, doing what Cut had told him and powering through my retaliation. "Over the years, the Debt Inheritance has had to...how shall I say? Adapt."

I couldn't argue. I couldn't win.

All I could do was sit and silently seethe.

"All contracts are amended at some point or another, and this is no different." Marshall uncapped his fountain pen. "I hope that's self-explanatory, so I can skip to the next topic."

"No, it isn't self-explanatory." I snarled, "What you're saying is all this talk of being set in stone and law-abiding is actually not—it's revised to suit your benefits with no input from my family?"

My stomach roiled at the unfairness. How could they change the rules and tote it over our heads like gospel? How could they notarise something without both parties agreeing?

Who were these corrupt, money-grubbing lawyers?

Cut tutted under his breath. "Don't force me to gag you, Ms. Weaver." His eyes blackened as if I'd offended his moral code.

What moral code?

He was scum.

"Everything we do is within the parameters set by our current law. We've made sure nothing is carried out until it's first written, signed, and witnessed."

"Even rape and murder?"

Bonnie leaned forward. "Watch your tongue."

Cut clasped his fingers. "I'll allow that one last question. Perhaps, if you finally understand that all of this is meticulously recorded, then you might stop thinking you've been indisposed and suffering an injustice."

Sitting taller in his chair, he buffed his fingernails on his cuff. "Things outside the realm of understanding can become approved if it's drafted and agreed to. What do you think war is, Nila? It's a contract between two countries that men in their comfy offices sign. With one signature, they deliver countless resources and sign the death warrant of so many lives. That's murder. And it's all done with no comeuppance because they had a *contract* stating they had the full use of enlisted men's lives all for greed, money, and power."

I hated that he made sense; hated that I agreed with my archenemy. The world had always been twisted in that respect. Sending men off to war, only to die the moment they landed on enemy soil...then to send yet more men to the exact same battlefield, knowing the outcome would be death.

That was homicide on a negligent global scale, and those in power never paid for their crimes.

I sat silent.

Cut smiled, knowing he'd gotten through to me in some way. "When I say everything was done by the law, I do mean *everything*." He nodded at the stacks of paper. "In there, you'll find every deviation from the Debt Inheritance along with a Hawk signature and a Weaver's."

My heart skipped painfully. "You're saying my family *signed* this?" I snorted. "I don't believe that. Did you force them under duress?"

Marshall huffed. "At no point would my firm accept such a thing. We have iron-clad records that protect our client's reputation. We have proof to show there was no hardship signing the amendments."

Like I believed him. He let murderers get away with it for six hundred years.

Plucking a piece of paper from the fourth pile, he handed it to me. "See for yourself."

Part of me wanted to crumple it up and throw it in his face, but I restrained.

Calmly, I accepted the page and scanned it.

The scraps Cut had given me in return for serving them lunch had been taken from this document. The Debt Inheritance was there in its entirety.

My eyes highlighted certain lines, remembering the ridiculous contract.

For actions committed by Percy Weaver, he stands judged and wanting.

Even I agreed with that after he'd sent an innocent girl to her death by ducking stool and a boy to be raped for twelve hours.

Bennett Hawk requires a public apology, monetary gain, and most of all, bodily retribution.

How much money did Weaver pay? Was it enough for the Hawks to somehow leave England, find their diamonds, and became untouchable through wealth?

In accordance with the law, both parties have agreed that the paperwork is binding, unbreakable, and incontestable from now and forever.

That part I didn't believe, but it wasn't arguable. In the minds and pockets of the Hawks, Weavers had to pay continuously toward the bottomless debt.

But Jethro would've ended it.

We could've been the last generation to ever have to deal with this brutal nonsense.

Percy Weaver hereby solemnly swears to present his firstborn girl-child, Sonya Weaver, to the son of Bennett Hawk, known as William Hawk. This will nullify all unrest and unpleasantries until such a time as a new generation comes to pass.

So the boy who'd been raped for Weaver's gambling debts was the one who'd carried out the first Debt Inheritance? Had he taken great joy in hurting the daughter of his enemy, or had he hated it as much as Jethro?

This debt will not only bind the current occupancies of the year of our Lord 1472 but every year thereafter.

How something had lasted for so long was a testament to feuds and grudges of wealthy madmen.

Once I'd reached the bottom, Marshall handed me another page. "This was the last amendment to the contract before today's meeting."

Doing a switch, I scanned the new document. The page was white and modern—only a few years old rather than decades.

In the case of the last surviving line of Alfred 'Eagle' Hawk and Melanie 'Bonnie' Warren, the succession of the Debt Inheritance will go to Bryan 'Vulture' Hawk over his recently deceased brother, Peter 'Osprey' Hawk.

I frowned, absorbing the legal jargon.

What did it mean?

I looked at the very bottom, sucking in a breath as I double-checked the feminine sweep.

No.

My mother's signature.

"What—"

I read it again. No matter how much I wished it wasn't true, it was. My mother's signature inked the paper, prim and proper, just as I remembered her writing style to be.

Right beside hers was Cut's masculine scrawl.

My brain scrambled; I glared at Cut. "You weren't firstborn."

Cut smiled slyly. "Never said I was."

Bonnie's red lips spread into a sneer. "Sad day for all involved." She tapped her fingers on the table. "I'd groomed my firstborn to be a worthy heir. Peter would've been a good leader but circumstances I didn't foresee came to light." Her gaze narrowed at Cut, full of reproof and history.

Cut shrugged. "A little mishap. That's all."

Bonnie coughed. "Call it what you want. I still haven't forgiven you."

Cut only laughed.

What on earth happened in that generation? What about the ages of the men? How was Cut allowed to claim my mother? Was that why she'd had children? Hearing that the firstborn Hawk had died, had she believed she was unbound to the debts?

If that was the case, how did she know what the future entailed when I hadn't been told until Jethro appeared in Milan? *Tex kept it from me. Emma might've been forewarned.*

So many questions. So many scenarios.

When did Peter Hawk die?

If he died when my mother was young, maybe that was why she fell so hard for my father. Drunk on the thought of freedom, she'd started a family far younger than she might've done thinking we were all…safe.

What a horrible, terrible joke.

Questions danced on my tongue. I chose the most random but most poignant. "What happens when you run out of Weavers to torture? I won't have children. Vaughn won't. What then?"

Daniel laughed. "Remember that sister I joked about?"

Oh, my God. It's true?

Cut interrupted. "You have no other siblings, Nila. I would've told you if you did. Merely a farce."

Daniel scowled. "Thanks for fucking ruining my fun. Had her believing that for months."

I hadn't believed it…but I'd wondered.

"So, it was all nonsense?"

Cut shook his head. "Not quite. You have a cousin. A few times removed but still bearing the Weaver name. We would look at all avenues if the future required it."

Poor cousin.

I overflowed with rage. "Do you ever listen to yourself? You're talking about people, for God's sake."

If Cut went after my unknown cousin, that didn't explain the previous generations that'd had no children or were killed off before carrying on the bloodline. How did it continue for so long when having a child was never a guarantee?

I knew how. They'd amended it. Tweaked the so-called unbreakable contract to fit with the Hawks' demented ideals.

Marshall plucked the paper from my hands. "I believe we're getting off topic, Ms. Weaver." Waving the parchment, he said, "Let's focus on today's subjects. Happy now you've seen the evidence with your own eyes?"

"Happy isn't a word I know anymore." I bared my teeth. "She wouldn't have signed that without being threatened. I don't care what you say."

That fleeting afternoon when my mother returned home, adorned with the diamond collar and hugging me so tightly, came to mind. She'd been terrified but resigned. Broken but strong. I hadn't understood back then, but now I did.

She'd reached the same stage I had. The stage where nothing else mattered but getting even, claiming justice.

There's a point to this meeting.

My heart froze solid, finally understanding. "I won't sign anything. I can assure you of that. You might as well pack up and piss off because I'll tear apart anything you put in front of me."

Jasmine growled; Cut merely chuckled. "I'm sure if you did that, you'd make Daniel a very happy man."

Daniel draped an arm over me. "Oh, please, Weaver. Do it for me. You have my full permission to refuse the amendment and cut Jaz out of the updated terms."

"Like hell she will." Jasmine looped her fingers together in aggression. "You'll sign, Nila. You'll see."

I didn't reply, glaring at the table instead.

Marshall shuffled the paper. "All right, let's carry on." Pinching the top sheet from the newest looking tower, he pushed it toward me. "This is the latest amendment and requires your signature."

My blood charged through overheated veins. "I told you—"

"Shut it." Jasmine snatched the paper and stabbed the bottom where an empty box waited for my life to spill upon it. "Do it. It's your only choice."

Our eyes locked. Not only did I hate her for what she'd done and how much she'd tricked me, but I hated that she looked so much like him.

Jethro.

The shape of her nose. The curve of her cheekbones. She was the closest in appearance to him, and it hurt to hate someone who looked so much like the man I loved.

"I told you. I'm not signing anything."

Jaz's cheeks flushed. I wouldn't put it past her to slap me. In fact, I wanted her to because then I'd have an excuse to fight with a girl in a wheelchair.

Could I kill her? Could I slide my blade into her heart all while knowing Jethro had cared for her?

He was tricked…same as me.

I would honour his memory by destroying yet another person who'd betrayed him.

Hartwell shifted in his chair. "You don't know the terms yet. Listen before being hasty."

Jasmine tore her eyes away from mine, glaring at the lawyer. "The terms being that I have full right to both Weavers, Nila and Vaughn. In return, Daniel can have the estate and all monetary wealth that comes from being heir."

I flinched, shivering in the sudden arctic hatred she projected.

"That has been discussed, Ms. Jasmine. I feel you'll be satisfied with the arrangements."

Jasmine sniffed haughtily. "Discussions aren't conclusions. There is no negotiation on the matter. I want to extract the Fourth and Final Debt. That right is mine."

"Jasmine, calm down. I'm sure you'll be satisfied with the new arrangement." Cut held out his hand. "Give me the contract, Hartwell. Let me see everything has been noted before we make it official."

Marshall stole the paper from me and slid it up the table.

Cut caught it; he took his time reading, his eyes darting over fine print.

I breathed hard, suffering a crushing weight of grief and revulsion.

He's dead.

But they're not.

Why couldn't Cut and Bonnie be dead instead of Jethro and Kestrel?

Because life is never fair and it's up to me to carve out justice.

Jasmine remained rigid until Cut finally raised his eyes and shot the contract over the satin wood toward us. "I'm happy with that. The Fourth Debt will be repaid slightly differently to the rest, but that will be another discussion." His eyes met his children's. "In this case, three signatures will be required— Nila, Dan, and Jaz."

He made it sound like a school permission slip for us all to go play happily together.

I snorted, rolling my eyes.

Cut gave me a stern look.

Samuel Cole, who hadn't made a sound since I'd arrived, spoke up. "In that case, it is my duty to advise all of you that this new clause will be forever known as amendment 1-345-132."

My eyes widened. How many amendments had there been to warrant such a crazy number?

Judging by the stacks of paperwork…a lot. Far too many. Was there anything left of the original contract?

Mr. Cole continued, "Due to the unfortunate deaths of the firstborn, Jethro Hawk…"

Pain slammed into me.

Agony tore out my heart.

Misery crumbled me into dust.

Jethro.

God, I wish you hadn't left me.

I couldn't sit up straight; howling winds of grief ripped me apart. I hunched into myself, holding my ribcage to keep from sobbing.

I managed to remain silent.

But Jasmine didn't.

Her lip wobbled, tears streaking her cheeks. She cracked, but it didn't last long. Sucking in a breath, she reached into the small satchel attached to her wheelchair and pulled out another handkerchief.

Bowing her head, she dabbed at her eyes.

My lips twisted in disgust. "I don't buy your crocodile tears. Don't bother putting on a show when I know you were part of this murder from the start."

Her head shot upright. Our souls duelled, violence sparking between us.

Cole cleared his throat. "In natures of the firstborn perishing, the following may occur: The Debt Inheritance can be called null and void, leaving Ms. Weaver to propagate and provide a new heir for the payment at a later date, or, if both parties agree, a new heir instated. In the case of Jethro 'Kite' Hawk's demise, the second in line, Angus 'Kestrel' Hawk also suffered an untimely end."

God, how much longer can this nightmare continue?

I huddled further into my chair, a silent tear escaping. More swelled, wanting to river, but I refused to show my pain.

Jasmine blew her nose, her cheeks glittering with moisture.

I wanted to snatch each fake droplet and ram them down her lying throat.

Daniel smirked, showing no other emotion. "Guess that leaves me in a lucky place."

Cole ignored him. "In this case, we've been asked to draft the following arrangement to protect both interests and move forward." Placing a pair of silver-rimmed glasses on his nose, he picked up an identical copy of the contract. "On this day, the Debt Inheritance will be carried out by the remaining bloodlines of the Hawk family against the crimes committed by the Weavers. Jasmine Diamond Hawk will have sole custody and responsibility for Nila Weaver's wellbeing until such a time as the Final Debt is claimed."

Daniel squirmed in his chair. "What the fuck? But—"

"Let him finish," Bonnie ordered.

"Upon his thirtieth birthday, Daniel 'Buzzard' Hawk will gain the wealth and many estates associated with the Hawk empire and become the next undisputed heir to both the estate and future Debt Inheritance. It will be his responsibility to provide a firstborn son or the next generation will be exempt."

I sagged, finding a smidgen of silver lining.

At least there would be no more Weavers from my bloodline to claim the debts from—and Daniel would be dead. I pitied my cousin's family tree if the Hawks had another heir in mind, but I would never have children and Vaughn wouldn't be stupid enough. He'd never let another one of our family go through what we had. The Hawks were screwed. They'd burned those bridges completely.

Cole carried on in his smooth voice. "The final note to be observed is the matter of who will carry out the Fourth Debt."

The room tensed.

"Jasmine will oversee the Final Debt, but Bryan Hawk has overridden the request for the right of Fourth Debt and granted it to Mr. Daniel."

Tension ricocheted out in a burst of savagery. "No way!" Jasmine glared at Cut. "Father, we agreed. You said she was *mine*. I've proven myself time and time again. Give her to me."

Cut steepled his fingers, unruffled by her disorder. "There's a method to why you won't carry out the Fourth Debt, Jasmine." His attention fell on Marshall. "Finish, please, then we can carry on to the next point on the agenda."

The next point?

My God, what else could they discuss?

I'd just learned I was the property of Jasmine with loopholes for Daniel to hurt me.

Didn't I have a say in any of this?

Daniel snickered, capturing my hand and tugging it into his lap. "Guess we have a date, after all, little Weaver." Raising my hand to his mouth, he kissed the back of my knuckles. "Including the matter of finishing the Third Debt."

I convulsed.

Cut chuckled. "Oh, yes. Unfinished business." His eyes narrowed. "Don't think we've forgotten about that, Nila. You don't wear the tally mark yet because it wasn't completed. We'll get to that a bit later, though. Give you some time to adjust."

My fingertip wearing Jethro's initials itched. His mark still existed in this world while he didn't. Would I continue to be marked in his name for debts extracted or would I wear DBH instead?

Steeling my heart, I scoffed. "Gee, thanks. So thoughtful of you."

Daniel squeezed my hand. "Watch it."

Every molecule wanted to extract myself from his slimy, grip.

Cole shuffled in his chair, barrelling through the air of hostility with a contemptuous look. "May I continue?"

Cut nodded. "By all means."

Bonnie scoffed under her breath, the diamonds of her broaches gleaming like death rays.

Cole looked back at the contract. "The first part of the Fourth Debt will be explained at Cut's discretion."

First part?

"And the second part, hereby known as the Fifth Debt, will be carried out by Daniel Hawk due to the nature and requirements of the debt."

Was there always a Fifth Debt or was that new?

I trembled to think of more pain but I was glad in a bizarre way. *It means I have more time to kill them before they kill me.*

"An able-bodied person must extract payment and..." His eyes fell on Jasmine, pity glowing. "...requires a journey not fit for someone in Ms. Hawk's condition."

My back stiffened at the look he gave her—the look I'd seen so many people give others less fortunate than them.

What was I talking about?

Less *fortunate?* Jasmine had more wealth than she could ever spend. She came from a lineage that banded together and protected their own no matter the cost. Not having use of her legs was a downside, but it didn't handicap her, nor did it make her a nicer person for her struggles.

Jasmine fisted her hands on the table. I didn't know if it was from the misplaced condolences or anger at being denied.

Either way, I laughed under my breath, unable to stop my derisive frustration. "Don't pity her."

Cole glanced away guiltily.

Jaz flicked me a cold look. "Don't you dare speak on my behalf."

I turned to face her, war ready to break out between us. I thought I'd find the courage to fight by sparring with Daniel or Cut. Not Jasmine. I'd hoped, woman to woman, we would rally together. I'd hoped she'd be on my side.

Stupid hope. Stupid, stupid dreams.

Marshall sent a fountain pen skittering toward me, breaking the strained standoff. "If you would be so kind to sign and initial the amendment, I'll ensure it's kept safe and on record."

They hadn't listened to a word I'd said. Once again, treating me as a clause to fix, an amendment to be filed.

For a split second, I was glad Jethro and Kes were dead.

They were free from this. Free from suffering more insanity.

My heart imploded on itself as Jethro took over my mind. His tinsel hair, golden eyes, and unbearable complexities.

He's dead.

There was nothing else for me but to play their game until there was a winner and a loser.

I'll be the winner.

I picked up the pen. With steady hands, I uncapped it and had a sudden daydream of breaking it in half and splashing ink all over the so-called contract.

My mind raced with thoughts of my mother. Had she sat in this exact chair and signed the previous amendment? Why had Cut become heir and what'd happened to his brother?

Did he kill that family member, too?

I glared at him.

Cut glared right back.

I wanted answers, but how would I get them?

The Weaver Journal?

Could the diary actually have anything worthwhile inside and not just brainwashing drivel that Cut wanted me to believe? I hadn't bothered with it because every time I touched its pages, a sense of evil had warned me away.

Lies and misfortune and fraudulent deceit.

I'd suspected Kes gave it to me to keep me in line by reading about the adversity of my ancestors—striving to be better to avoid such things—but what if he gave it to me for another reason? What if he'd been trying to help me from day one?

Why didn't I study the damn thing?

Because I'd been so wrapped up in Jethro. Falling in love, attending polo matches, and accepting horses as gifts.

God, I'm so stupid.

"Ms. Weaver." Marshall slapped the table, wrenching me from my thoughts. "If you would be so kind…"

Jaz stiffened in her chair. "We don't have all day, you know." Ripping the page away from me, she snatched the fountain pen, and signed the bottom where her name and date waited.

Pushing me out of the way, she scooted the contract and pen to Daniel. "See, Nila? Wasn't so hard."

Daniel smirked. "Watch again how easy it is." He signed with an unintelligible scrawl. "Signing your life away, literally. Kinda fun, isn't it?" He placed the two items back in front of me. "Your turn."

"I'm surprised you don't expect me to sign in blood."

Bonnie gave up being the silent matriarch and slid into a caustic temper. "For shit's sake, you stupid girl. Be reasonable!"

The table froze.

My heart sprinted with hostility. She wanted to fight? I'd give her a damn fight. "I *am* being reasonable. You expect me to die for you. It would make sense to make me sign in blood—I'm sure you'd get a kick out of that, you witch."

I smiled, glowing in resentment. In the course of one meeting, I'd called Jasmine a bitch and her grandmother a witch. Not bad considering my past of being shy and scared of confrontation. Even vertigo gave me a reprieve, keeping me levelheaded and strong.

Bonnie shot pink with fury. "Why you little—"

Marshall jumped in, waving his hands in a ceasefire. "We don't expect it in blood. Ink will more than suffice."

"And if I don't?"

"If you don't what?" Cole frowned.

"If I don't sign it—like I've been saying since I got here. Then what?"

Marshall flicked a glance at Cut. His jaw worked as their eyes shot messages above my comprehension. Finally, he bowed his head. "Then a certain type of persuasion would be used."

I laughed loudly. "Persuasion? Torture, you mean. I thought you had integrity to uphold. Didn't you just say you had evidence that all documents were signed without—as you put it—*persuasion?*"

Marshall hunched. "Well…eh…in some cases—"

"Sign the bloody paperwork, you ingrate!" Bonnie stood up stiffly, her cane in hand.

"Nila, fucking—" Cut growled.

"Shut up! All of you." Jaz suddenly wrapped her fingers around mine, pinching the pen into position. Dragging my hand over the paperwork, she muttered, "The things I fucking do."

"Wait, what are you doing?" I struggled, but found out that she might not have use of her legs, but she had strength in her arms that I couldn't fight.

"I'm putting an end to this. I've wasted too much time dealing with this as it is." She forced the nib onto the paper.

"No, wait!"

Digging her fingernails into my hand, she directed the pen and printed a rudimentary name.

My name.

Signed and witnessed on the Debt Inheritance amendment.

"What the hell have you done?"

She released me. "I did what I had to."

My chair screeched backward as I towered over her. "What the fuck is wrong with you?"

She wheeled away from the table, wobbling a little on the ramp. "What the fuck is wrong with *you?*" She stabbed me in the belly with her finger. "You're the one dragging this out when you know there's no way out." Tears gleamed in her eyes. "He's *dead.* They're both dead. The sooner you are too, the better."

My heart plummeted to the floor. Jethro's voice and touch and smell and kisses all slammed into me.

He's dead.

He's dead.

God, it hurts.

"I wish it were you!" I screamed. "You never deserved him. You should've died instead of him. He leapt in front of you to save you and this is what you do to repay him! I hope the devil—"

"Enough!" Cut soared upright, eyes shooting golden sparks. "Jasmine, calm down. Nila, shut up immediately." He splayed his arms like a messiah seeking peace. "It's done. It's unfortunate that this had to happen, but—"

"My brothers' deaths are a *misfortune,* Father?" Jaz's cheeks glowed red. "I'll tell you what's a misfortune—having to deal with this bullshit!" Her hands latched around chrome wheel rims. "I'm sick of this. I want her gone. Now! I want this finished!"

The lawyers scrambled to their feet. "I think it's time we departed." The towers of paperwork quickly disappeared back into their boxes.

The men bowed. "Pleasure being of service once again. We'll be back in touch once the, eh…once the final part of the inheritance has taken place."

The final part?

The *final part*?

That was my final part—the last straw on my willpower.

I cracked. I was a girl, but now I was a monster.

I've had enough.

Enough!

Darting around the table, I planted myself in Colin Marshall's path. His eyes flared. My palm twitched. And I slapped the bastard full on the cheek.

My hand blazed with fire, but I loved it.

I embraced the pain.

I gave myself over to fury.

His mouth popped open. "What on earth? Ms. Weaver!"

Chairs screeched as Hawks leapt to their feet. I ignored them.

"Listen to me." I stalked Marshall as he backpedalled. "That final part you just so loosely mentioned is my *death*. The day they cut off my head and steal back their necklace from my decapitated throat." I looped my fingers through the diamond collar. "How can you stand there discussing my life like a simple business transaction? How can you delete the lives of two men—two men who would've put an end to this insanity—and think you're upholding something legal? How can any of you breathe the same air as me and not be struck down for the devils you are?"

My arms were suddenly wrenched back, pinned on my lower spine. Daniel's fingers squeezed hard. "That's not the way we deal with lawyers, Nila." Stomping backward, he gave me no room but to trip with him. "You'll pay for that, and I'll have a lot of fun teaching you some manners."

I was too far gone to care.

Marshall rubbed his cheek. Bowing one last time at Cut, he continued with his holier-than-thou arrogance. "Like I said, we'll be in touch." Touching his hairline, he smiled at Bonnie. "Lovely seeing you again, Madame Hawk."

Bonnie's red-painted lips thinned. "I won't say likewise."

Daniel didn't let me go as the four men gathered briefcases and boxes and left the room in a sea of black suits and purple ties.

The moment they'd disappeared, Jasmine slid down the ramp and glared at her brother. "Let her go. She isn't yours to play with." Without another word, she spun her wheels and disappeared after the lawyers.

My heart stopped beating. I prepared myself for pain. My outburst filled the room with echoing bloodshed, but…incredibly, Daniel let me go.

Cut ran a hand over his face, looking at his mother. "Well, that wasn't peaceful, was it?"

Bonnie never stopped glaring at me. "No. It wasn't."

Daniel laughed, slinging an arm over my shoulders. "You're free to go, little Weaver. But don't go too far." He kissed my cheek like any lover or sweetheart. "Don't forget what I said about our private meeting."

A shudder worked through my body.

The private meeting would turn into war.

I'd slipped into murderous; there was no going back from that.

Without another look, I turned on my heel, and positively flew out the door.

I needed space to think and fortify. I needed time to prepare and commit. *Daniel will be the first to die.*

Darting from the library, I careened around a corner and slammed to a halt.

My chest rose and fell as I plastered myself against the wall, spying on the scene up ahead.

I remained hidden as Jaz ran fingers under her eyes, swiping away tears.

Only, she wasn't alone.

A man crouched before her, his hand on her knee, talking quick and low. She nodded, looping her fingers through his. Their heads bowed together; she grabbed the lapel of the man's Black Diamond jacket.

Her pinched, ghostly face animated with hissed whispers.

They didn't notice me as Jaz pulled the man closer and spoke into his ear. I slipped deeper into shadows as the man nodded.

He said something that made her convulse and a fresh wash of tears flow. Then my heart stopped beating as the man gathered her into a hug.

The man...

It was Flaw.

DIARY ENTRY, EMMA Weaver.

I found out what happened to Bryan's brother today. I don't think he meant to tell me, but I've learned how to manipulate him so occasionally he slips. I wouldn't normally write that, but tomorrow…it's all over. I've seen where they'll do it. Bonnie took great pleasure in having me weave the basket that will catch me. I'm beyond thinking about how sick everything is. I tried my best. I pretended to care for Cut. I made him believe I was in love with him. I willingly shared his bed and portrayed the besotted woman around his family. But it was all a lie. You hear that, you evil son of a bitch? If you're reading this, then good riddance. At least you can't touch me anymore. You told me things I doubted you would've if you knew that every time you touched me, I wanted to slaughter you with my bare hands. You wouldn't have let me into that frosted heart of yours if you knew that every time you slipped inside me, I gave myself over to the devil, all for him to fulfil one promise.

You won. But one day, you won't. One day, your sins will catch up with you and it will all be over. My daughter is already twice the woman I am, and she's still so young. If you go after her, it will be the last thing you ever do. I swear it on every religion, every sanctified God. You will die, Bryan. Mark my words, you will die—

A noise sounded outside my room.

My head wrenched up. My breath came hard and fast. I ached with the pain my mother had transcribed in the Weaver Journal. Somehow, she hadn't used ink—she'd used her desperation and frustration. Her emotion throbbed from the pages, fisting around my heart. It made me angry, so damn angry that I wasn't there to save her.

She'd done what I had.

She'd made Cut fall for her—just like I'd gone after Jethro—to control him.

Only, unlike Jethro, Cut hadn't been so easily broken.

He'd still carried out the Final Debt. He'd killed the woman he was in love with.

And all for what?

The noise came again.

My pulse skyrocketed. With shaking hands, I closed the journal and slid it beneath the covers.

After the lawyers' visit, I'd headed to the kitchens and stockpiled food. I didn't know how often I'd be locked in my room in this new world without Jethro.

He's dead.

He's dead.

He's...not coming back.

I balled my hands, forcing the grief to stay away.

No matter how often I thought about him, I always thought of him as alive and only a corridor away.

My brain played tricks on me. Whenever the old Hall creaked, I heard my name whispered in the walls. Whenever the wind whistled and twitched my curtains, I heard him beg for me to find him.

I was slowly going mad.

I can't. Not yet. I have a job to do first.

I focused on the door to my room, ears straining for the noise. After my raid on the kitchens, I'd hauled my stash back to my quarters. The cook had given me a canvas bag to cart canned fruit, cured meat, packaged biscuits, and cereal. I'd hidden the food in the cupboard where I stored my needles, thread, and ribbon.

If they meant to trap me, at least I wouldn't starve to death. I could stay strong and wait to strike them down.

Once I'd prepared myself for war, I'd deliberated if I should message my father. I'd wanted to tell him how much I loved him. How fortunate we were that this might be over soon.

If Vaughn and I died ...there would be no more Weavers. No more children to torment.

The debt would end for our lineage—some other poor Weaver blood would pay.

Not the way I would've chosen, but it was a conclusion I had to live with, a legacy I had to leave.

Jethro.

My heart fisted, but my eyes remained dry.

The noise came again.

It was slight but there.

A scratching, scurrying sound.

Rats, perhaps?

Or one rat in particular.

My heart clanged.

Daniel.

Had he come to honour his promise of raping me tonight? Our private meeting away from the view of Jasmine and Cut?

I looked at the windows. Pitch-black reflected my room in perfect symmetry, distorting colourful fabric, swirling them into some kaleidoscopic artwork.

After the meeting, a thunderstorm had crashed over the estate, drenching everything in damp darkness. I'd had my lights on ever since, reading and engrossed in the Weaver Journal.

Only select generations had added to the large tome. My mother hadn't been diligent, and other snippets weren't signed. It made me wonder if the Hawks gave them an outlet for truth, rather than used it against them. It wasn't a requirement to write—but a *choice*.

My eyes darted to the clock above the turquoise fish tank.

11:00 p.m.

Shit!

Scrambling out of bed, I darted across the room. My bare feet padded over thick carpet, and the leggings and cardigan I'd worn all day were rumpled. My back and quads ached from the exercise I'd endured after returning to my room.

I hadn't been for a run, but I had used every muscle in my body.

How? By protecting myself.

My door suddenly swung open, slamming against the dresser I'd painstakingly emptied and pushed in the smallest increments across the carpet. The ancient wood weighed a ton, but I'd spent hours shoving it across the room—just in case.

I jumped a mile as the door smashed against the dresser again, an aggravated sigh exploding.

He might have a key to lock me inside, but I had a better barricade. He would only touch me when I was ready. And then, it would be the last thing he ever did.

I supposed I should thank him for his prior warning. Allowing me to prepare for a midnight visitor.

Not only had I manhandled the dresser across the door, I'd also fashioned pieces of fabric with sharp needles embedded to make a simple knuckleduster. I'd counted how many scissors I had, how many tools I could use to defend myself, and what would cause the most damage.

I'd hidden my arsenal around the room. Some I stashed in my bedside table, some beneath my workstation, and even tucked in pockets sewn into my duvet. My clothing had also undergone an upgrade with knitting needles and scalpels carefully sewn into cuffs and hems.

Once I'd moved the dresser, I'd replaced the drawers and heavy fabric bolts that'd rested inside its carcass. There was no earthly way someone could move it. Not unless they had ten Black Diamonds outside my door.

Which I wouldn't discount as a possibility.

Jethro was gone. But it didn't mean I would go quietly.

I'm ready, you asshole.

Just try me.

Almost on cue, the door slammed open again, smashing against the dresser with a resounding crack. A curse fell in the silence; they jiggled the knob, followed by another smash.

I stood vibrating on the other side, pulling my dirk free from my waistband.

Daniel would need a bomb to move the dresser, but it didn't mean I was safe. Who knew if he had secret passages into this room? Ancient houses such as Hawksridge had rabbit warrens of unseen pathways and secret compartments.

The door slammed again, banging louder with frustration.

I huddled into a battle stance, preparing to stab Daniel's hand through the crack. My mouth watered with the urge to hurl profanity and curses. To threaten and thwart.

"Nila, open the damn door."

I froze.

It wasn't Daniel.

Time ticked past, stretching uncomfortably.

"Nila…it's me."

Me?

The voice was feminine. Sweet and soft but hushed and worried.

Not a man with rape on his mind but a sister with grief.

A sister I couldn't stand.

I laughed coldly. "So forcing me to sign myself over to you this afternoon wasn't enough, huh?" My hand curled tight around my blade. "Come to cause more damage just like your fucked-up family?"

Jasmine sucked in a breath.

I inched closer to the door, nervousness popping in my blood.

"Just open the door. Now."

"What? So I can welcome you inside for a sleep-over and we can paint each other's nails?" I snorted. "I don't think so, Jasmine. You're a traitor to your brothers—a snake just like your grandmother." Filling my voice with venom, I spat, "You're just like them, and I want nothing to do with you."

"You have no choice. Let me in the damn room."

He's dead because of you. He's dead because he loved you.

My teeth clamped together. God, if she were in front of me, I'd stab her through her heartless chest.

"Piss off."

"Let me in."

"No chance. The next time we see each other, it's not going to end well. I suggest you get out of my sight."

Jasmine punched the door or rammed it with her chair—the noise signalled rapidly fraying anger. "Ah, fuck, what did he ever see in you?!" She bumped against the door again, lowering her voice. "We need to talk."

"I don't talk with betrayers."

"You want me to get someone to help? 'Cause I will. And you won't like the consequences."

My hand rose, the light from my side lamps kissing the blade with promise. "Do whatever you want, but I assure you it'll be you who doesn't like the—"

"Fine!"

Silence fell.

Animosity throbbed, slowly settling the longer we remained quiet.

Finally, a small whisper met my ears. "Just give me two minutes. Just listen. Can you do that? Or is that asking too much?"

I paused.

Two minutes was nothing in a lifetime. But two minutes to me was too high a cost. I existed on borrowed time.

"Why should I?" I drifted closer to the door despite myself.

"Because…it's important."

The genuine honesty in her voice dragged me forward. She sounded more real and true in that one microsecond than she had all afternoon.

Leaning around the dresser, I looked through the crack.

Not much was visible, but Jasmine's face glowed in the dark corridor. Red-rimmed eyes, sad-bitten lips, and sorrow-dusted cheeks—she didn't look well.

In fact, she looked ten years older than when I'd seen her at the meeting. Almost as if the past few hours had drained her of everything.

I wanted to slap myself.

Don't believe it!

It was all an act. The perfect con-artist making me trust her because she looked so undone.

"It won't work, you know." I scowled. "I'm not buying into your sad sister act. Not after what you've done."

Jasmine looked up, her face haggard. "I know you hate me. I feel it. But you have to put that aside and listen to me."

If the door didn't separate us, I'd wring her neck and throttle whatever conniving words she wanted to spout. "I don't have to do anything."

She reached through the door.

I stepped backward, raising my knife. "Don't, unless you're happy with four fingers instead of five."

"God, why don't you listen?!"

"Because I don't believe a word you say!"

"No, not with your ears, you silly cow."

I laughed. "Great way to get me to listen. Call me a cow again and we'll see—"

"Didn't Jethro teach you anything?"

I froze.

Livid rage cascaded down my back, into my legs, my arms, my mind. "Don't you ever—"

"Talk about him? He's *my* brother. He's been mine a lot longer than he's been yours."

My ears bled. "*Was*, don't you mean. He *was* yours. But he's gone. He doesn't belong to either of us, and that's all your fault!"

She sighed, rubbing her face with her hands. "Why are you so damn stubborn?"

"Why are you so damn confusing?" My eyes dropped to her attire.

I paused, forehead furrowing.

A black blanket covered her legs, along with a black hoodie and black gloves. She'd either taken mourning to a new extreme and fashioned her pyjamas in darkness too, or...

"What are you up to, Jaz?"

Her eyes wrenched up. "Finally! You finally ask a decent question." She looked over her shoulder. "Let me in. I'll tell you."

I shook my head. "Nope. Not going to happen."

"I don't have all freaking night, Nila. Let me inside before it's too late."

My heart skipped a beat. "What—what do you mean? Too late?"

"I'll tell you if you open the door."

"Tell me *before* I open the door."

I wasn't naïve anymore. I wouldn't fall for any more Hawk traps.

She had her motives and secrets—same as everyone else. Only, what she'd said about listening...what did she mean? With my instincts? With my heart? What could she possibly have to tell me that I didn't already know?

She was a heartless bitch who should've died and not her brother.

She scowled, her sleek black bob pinned back from her face. The more I looked at her, the more my heart raced. Something was off—something was wrong.

She looked like a ninja about to go on a robbery spree.

She looked as if she knew something I didn't.

She looked as if everything she'd lived through the past few hours was a lie. And this was the truth.

This was real.

I lowered my knife. "What—what's going on?"

She smiled tightly, fresh tears streaming down her cheeks. "Will you believe me? Are you finally listening?"

Goosebumps scattered over my arms.

I swallowed. I nodded.

She sagged as if she could finally share the burden she carried.

"In that case…" She sucked in a breath. "I need your help."

It took an eternity for me to find courage.

I knew the moment I spoke, my world would change all over again.

Finally, I murmured, "Why?"

Reaching through the door, she grasped my hand.

Her eyes glossed.

Her lips trembled.

Her voice split me in two.

"I need your help…because…" She squeezed my fingers, joy exploding on her face. "Nila, he's alive."

DEATH WAS WORSE than I ever imagined.

I'd hoped when the day came that it would be gentle—a tender snip when I was old and grey—a simple transition from one world to the next. It didn't matter that I never believed I would reach old age...it was what I'd fantasised.

However, if I had known how excruciating it would be, if I'd guessed how prolonged and agonising actual dying was—I would've put myself out of my misery years ago.

Because this? There was nothing survivable about this.

This wasn't heaven. Shit, it wasn't even hell.

It was damnation on Earth and still I clung—no matter how fucking painful.

"You still—" I coughed, unable to continue. My lungs were heavy, my body on fire. I existed on the brink. The brink of slipping far, far away and never coming back.

I wasn't dehydrated or starved.

I wasn't cold or unprotected.

But none of those simple human requirements could save me. I'd run out of time, and it was now a simple matter of gambling on which malady would kill me.

The steady bleeding?

The spreading fever?

The bullet hole?

I'd given up trying to choose. I thought I'd faded hours ago, finally giving in to the pain.

But no.

I still clung, dangling off the proverbial cliff, too weak to let go and too weak not to.

God, please let it end!

I flinched as I sucked in a deeper breath.

Breathing...funny how I hated and loved the action.

Hated because another breath meant I'd survive another few minutes. Loved because another breath meant I still existed for Nila.

Nila...

My heart tried to hurry, conjuring the dark-haired seamstress who'd captured my heart. But all it managed was a pathetic patter.

Groaning with the weight of a thousand daggers, I looked at the cot across the dungeon from mine.

How we arrived down here, I had no fucking clue.

Why we had drips in our hands, blankets bundled around us, and crudely administered medicine was an utter mystery.

Who did this?

How long had we been here?

How much time had passed?

Was this perhaps purgatory? A place of in-between, a deplorable existence where only the worst went to pay penance?

We couldn't possibly be alive. *Could we?*

A flickering light in the corner kept the vampires of the crypt at bay, but it offered no warmth—no reprieve from the ancient ice seeping into my bones from the godforsaken catacombs.

I stared fuzzily at the shape of a man cocooned in blankets. Only, he hadn't moved, moaned, or made a sound in hours. My gift—no, my curse—no longer worked.

There was someone else down here with me. Yet, there were no thoughts, no fears, no pleas.

I didn't want to admit it, but my brother…he was no longer alive. However, I had to try to bring him back from the dead. I had to remind him I was there for him—for him not to give up, even though slipping off the cliff became more enticing every minute. "You—you still a—alive, K—Kes?"

I never heard his reply.

The moment I finished, I fell into a stupor that lasted God knew how long. My energy flat-lined and I drifted into dreams, nightmares, and fantasies.

One moment, I flew through the forest on Wings.

The next, I was back in that hated room hurting Jasmine to fix myself.

One second, I made love to Nila, sliding inside her heat.

The next, I was shivering with ice running away from Hawksridge when I was fourteen.

Each hour, I grew weaker. Each hour, I slipped a little more.

If it weren't for the terror at leaving Nila in the heinous world I'd helped create, I would just let go and disappear.

I want so fucking much to disappear.

I wanted freedom from pain.

Sanctuary from agony.

I wasn't strong enough to live with such soul-crushing torment.

But no matter how hot and flaming my pain became. No matter how delirious and wracked with trembles I was, I couldn't die.

I *refused* to fucking die.

I can't. Not while they're alive.

It was my duty to end them. To end the madness of my heritage that'd gotten away with murder for centuries.

Only once I'd balanced the scales of right and wrong could I relax and let go.

Only once I'd saved the one who'd saved me could I say goodbye and slip into the void.

My heart occasionally stuttered, out of sync, out of power—almost as if it recognised death and wanted to give in. I forced it to do the bare essentials, keeping me from a grave. I was in the coffin ready to be buried, but I wasn't a corpse just yet.

I squinted in the lacklustre light, following the contours of my brother's body.

He still hadn't moved.

Time had an odd context down here. It could've been decades since I'd asked if he was alive, or only seconds.

I could turn to face him, expecting to see a blood-flushed body, only to come face-to-face with a dusty skeleton instead.

Anything was possible on the cusp of death.

My dying lungs did their best at working through ash and mildew to speak again. "K—Kes…"

A minute ticked past or maybe it was an hour——but, finally, my brother shifted. His grunt of agony echoed around the walls.

I wasn't alone.

Not yet.

More time passed.

I had no way to measure it.

I raised my head off the scratchy pillow, staring at the iron bars.

Our coffin was the same catacombs that housed my ancestor's bones. The same cell where Daniel beat me on Cut's command. The same dungeon where I'd started the course of drugs to numb me.

Those memories had been sharp and recent. But now they were muddy and distant.

Same as all my memories.

Nila's voice faded from my heart. Jasmine's promises disappeared from my ears. My life deleted itself as if I wasn't allowed to carry any memento from this world to the next.

I didn't want to forget.

I don't want to forget!

I willed my dried-up, malnourished brain to remember: how we arrived here. How a night of intimacy and love had transformed into my murder.

But try as I might, I couldn't.

There was nothing but splatters of mismatched images.

Blazing hot pain.

Jasmine's screams.

Bonnie's barks.

Nila's sobs.

Then more pain shoving me deeper and deeper down the drain of consciousness.

My blood was weak, diluted with agony. My soul broken but refusing to abandon a body that was hours away from succumbing to the black shroud of everlasting sleep.

Help us…

The bars were locked. There was no way out.

However, they could've been wide open and there wouldn't have been a hope in fucking hell of moving.

We were dead.

The fact we were holding on was merely a formality.

More time passed and I stopped trying to catalogue it. I was drifting, twisting, fading…

Not long now.

A sudden burst of strength let me say something I should've said many times in the past. Something I always took for granted. "I—I lo—ove y—you, Kes."

A cough wracked my body, clutching my pain, increasing it tenfold.

As the fever bathed my skin and my lungs rattled with sickness, I sighed and gave up. I'd said goodbye. I'd done everything I needed.

My senses slipped across the room to my dying brother and I held on. Hopefully, we'd find each other again. Hopefully, I'd find Nila again when I deserved her and paid for my sins.

Hopefully, all would be better in a different world.

I'm sorry, Nila. For everything.

Brother to brother. Soul to soul.

There was nothing else here for me.

I closed my eyes.

I let go.

I CHASED HER.

He's alive!

Vertigo tried to trip me as I jogged in the wake of her wheels. Disbelief and suspicion did their best to kill my intoxicating high.

He's alive.

He's alive.

It's a miracle.

I'd never had such words affect me. Never had a voice slammed into my heart, tore it out, restarted it, and dumped me into a hope so cruel, I didn't want to breathe in case I unbalanced this perilous new world and found out Jethro wasn't alive after all.

I wanted to cry. To scream. To laugh.

He's alive!

I ran faster as Jasmine shot forward.

I'd never been friends with someone with a disability. I liked to think I was open-minded and treated everyone the same way—but society still had a stigma about equality.

Jasmine shattered every misconception I had.

I thought I'd have to dawdle beside her. Wrong—I had to jog to keep up.

I thought I'd have to open doors and offer assistance around tight corners. Nope—Jaz manoeuvred her chair, doorway, and lock faster than I ever could.

She was fierce and strong, and even though she sat below my eye level, her personality consumed mine.

I was in her shadow.

He's alive.

But how?

She hadn't given me answers. The moment she'd told me Jethro hadn't died, I'd emptied the dresser, shoved it out of the way, and followed her with no other encouragement.

Was it a trap? A cruel joke?

Entirely possible, but I couldn't ignore the chance of saving Jethro. I had to break this heartache before it broke me.

Finally listening to Jasmine gave me new comprehension. I stopped listening with my ears and trusted with my heart. I noticed things that'd been so obvious, but I'd been so blinded. She adored her brothers. She was shattered with their pain. Yet, instead of hating me…she was…*she's trying to save me.*

Could that be possible?

Could everything that'd happened—the fighting for ownership and contract amendments all be for him?

Had he asked her to do that?

To protect me.

"You weren't going to hurt me…were you?" I whispered, darting down yet another labyrinth of corridors. No lights lit our way, and the security cameras above didn't blink. No red beacon hinted that our midnight run was recorded and ready to tattle.

I didn't know how she turned them off. I didn't know how she knew Jethro was alive. I didn't know anything.

I'm blind.

"About bloody time," she muttered, wheeling forward like a tank. "Thought you were supposed to be intelligent."

Tapestries hung silent and repressive. Paintings of dead monarchs sniffed with disdain as we scurried silently like tiny mice. The awful feeling of being swept away with no control fisted around my heart. I wanted to ask so many questions, but something held me back.

He's alive.

And I wanted him to stay that way.

"How was I supposed to know? You were so—"

"Believable?" She looked over her shoulder, her arms propelling her forward. "I've learned from the best."

Awkward silence fell. We headed deeper into shadow.

Jasmine broke the brittle tension. "What made you doubt now?"

I paused. I'd asked myself that same question. The only conclusion I could come up with was: *because I'm finally listening to the truth rather than what I hear.*

I didn't reply. Instead, I answered her question with another. "Everything that happened in the meeting…that wasn't real?"

Her lips twisted into a mysterious smirk. "You already know the answer to that."

"I don't know anything anymore."

She laughed under her breath. "That's a testament to my planning skills."

We ducked under another camera. "Aren't you afraid they'll catch us?"

She gave me a hard smile. "Nope."

"But won't Cut see the recordings?"

She smiled wider. "Nope."

I didn't bother asking again. She'd done something. And I guessed I'd never know.

My fitness level wasn't useful as we ducked and weaved through the ancient Hall. Jasmine kept up a wicked pace, and every heartbeat crushed me with the same unbelievable message.

He's alive.

He's alive.

Get to him faster.

Chasing Jasmine in her all-black attire and swiftness, my mind filled with other questions. Where did she spend her days? How did she get around? How had she kept this a secret? "How do you move from upstairs to the ground floor?"

Her eyes widened at my seemingly random question. "I have a private elevator in the centre of the house. It leads to a few floors."

"There are more?"

She snorted. "Seriously? Haven't you seen the size of this place? There's probably hundreds of rooms you still haven't seen.

Prisons and bedrooms and secret vaults full of treasures.

Could Jethro's mum be hidden in one? Could there be countless hidden mysteries just waiting to bring the Hawks down?

A chill ran down my spine. "Tell me what's happening. Where's Jethro?"

She shook her head. "You'll just have to trust me."

"I've already proven that I do." Removing the dresser and following Jasmine had shown two things: one, that I was willing to put my life in her hands, and two, that I was willing to do anything in order to save her brother.

He's alive.

He's alive.

It's not over.

"All you need to know is he's holding on, and I need your help."

"Anything. I'll do whatever you need."

Her eyes softened. "I was hoping you'd say that." The mask of collected woman slipped, showing her terror over her brother's life.

My heart tripped into a knot. "Kes. Is he alive, too?"

My spine locked, bracing for bad news. It seemed too much to have Jethro back from the dead, let alone another.

Jasmine sucked in a breath. "He is. For now."

My hands fisted. I wanted to sprint faster. "What does that mean?"

She glared ahead, stress lining her mouth. "They were moved before Cut could dispose of them. We've done what we could, but it isn't good enough." She swallowed hard. "We're running out of time."

We...

Her and Flaw?

"Where did you put them?"

"The only place not monitored."

"And where is that?"

She lowered her voice. "It doesn't matter. You're not coming with me."

My stomach flipped. I had to see him. Had to hug him and kiss him and tell him I never stopped loving him. "You came for my help. I'm coming with you."

Jasmine pursed her lips. "It has to be this way. It has to be tonight. And it has to be now. The longer you argue, the less time we have and the worse it will be for all of us. Got it?"

I wanted to argue—to slap her and let go of the helpless anger inside. Instead, I curbed my temper. "Fine."

But the minute he's safe and well, I'm claiming him. He's mine, not yours.

Flying around a corner, Jaz whispered, "Now, hush. Answers will come later."

This part of the house hinted at its age.

We were no longer in the manicured wealth of parlours, dayrooms, and libraries.

This part had an aura of forbidden.

An abandoned aura.

An aura of death and warning.

Portraits didn't hang, showing pockmarked faded walls. The threadbare carpets misted with dust as our footsteps disturbed ancient dirt, and my cardigan and leggings weren't enough to combat the icy chill emitting from the walls.

Hawksridge Hall lived and breathed as surely as its inhabitants, but down here...here was forgotten, only fit for cretins and rodents.

I blew on my fingers, gritting my teeth against a shiver.

"Here." Jaz suddenly stopped. "This is the room."

I skidded to a halt, staring at the imposing door with a brass locking plate engraved with weasels and stoats. "What is this place?"

"It used to be the servant's quarters, but an old water pipe burst a century ago and destroyed everything. My grandfather never got around to fixing it. This wing has been ignored ever since."

Sounded about right. The Hawks only seemed to value those worth something valuable to their needs and wants. The moment they outlived their purpose, they were either dispatched or cast aside.

A tiny shadow scurried past my line of sight. I inched closer to Jasmine's chair. I wouldn't be against leaping into her lap to get off the floor if rats came to visit. "And what are we doing here?"

He's alive.

He's alive.

Surely, she didn't keep him here.

Her bronze gaze glowed in the gloom. "Using one life to save another."

A shiver that had nothing to do with the cold shot down my back. "What does that mean?"

I'm asking that question a lot lately.

She looked away, fumbling in the black blanket over her legs. "You'll see." Pulling free an old-fashioned key, she inserted it into the lock.

With a loud groan of protest, the rusty mechanism sprang open, cracking open the large moisture-logged door.

A noise sounded inside—fleeting—like a small gasp of dismay.

"Come on." Jasmine pushed her rims, coasting from corridor to room. The moment we were inside, she closed the door. "Get the light, will you? The switch is to your left."

I spread my fingers out in the dark, tracing the chilly wall and finding an ancient nub, which I assumed was illumination.

I pressed it.

Light spilled from a single cobwebbed chandelier above. The room came into view. Out of every place I'd visited in Hawksridge Hall, this was the worst room by far. Faded, chipped mint-green paint covered the walls. Beige carpet stretched across floorboards, moth-eaten and musty.

And the cold.

I hugged myself from the bitter bite of winter.

An entirely different season lived in this place. No central heating, no fire to ward off frost and snow.

Had Jethro ever been here? Was this where he learned how to embrace the coldness, so he could hide his condition?

He's alive...

"Who—who's there?"

No! Oh, my God.

My stomach clenched; vertigo stole my vision in a blip of blackness.

I didn't have to see to know.

I'd know that voice anywhere.

"It's me!" My legs unlocked, hurling me across the large room to the single cot pushed against the wall. Condensation dripped like frigid tears down the cold surface, and the only window didn't perform its job of keeping the outside elements from entering. The stunning stained glass depiction of summer flowers had turned into a dartboard of holes. Intricate violets had been smashed, leaving a whistling draft to funnel around daisies and dandelions, slipping into the space unwanted.

Falling to my knees by the bed, I reached for my beloved twin's face. "It's me, V."

"Threads?" He rolled onto his back, revealing swollen cheekbones, bruised jaw, and cut lip. His hands were tied, resting on his belly, and a black blindfold covered half his face, flapping over his nose every time he breathed.

"God, I'll rip off their balls for this." I fumbled behind his head. "Lean forward; let me get this off you."

He did as I asked, groaning as he arched his head off the rank pillow.

Scrambling at the knot, I shoved it away the moment it loosened.

His eyes opened, blinking a few times. His mottled face turned to me. My heart cracked all over again, drinking in the signs of the horrendous beating he'd endured at the hands of Cut and Daniel.

In one afternoon, Cut had almost killed my brother and shot his sons. Yet, he hadn't hurt any of them enough to end them.

Perhaps, there is hope after all.

Good had triumphed over evil.

Good would *win* over evil.

Just wait and see.

His eyes focused, face twisting in rage. "Threads. Oh, fuck, I'm so glad to see you." He tried to sit up but cried out with pain. His fingers weren't a healthy pink but blue-white from being trapped in such an arctic cell.

"Relax." I pushed his shoulder. "Let me untie you." Moving from my knees to the edge of the bed, I pulled at the twine around his wrists. Tears sprang to my eyes as dried blood and scabs reopened. Fresh crimson seeped, making the knot too slippery to undo.

"Goddammit," I hissed.

"Here, try this." A box-cutter appeared in front of my nose. I jumped. In the rush of seeing my brother, I'd forgotten about Jasmine.

"Who the hell are you?" V snapped, his eyes drinking in Jaz.

I accepted the knife. "Thank you." My own dirk rested down my waistband, cursing me for not using it.

Jasmine glanced at my black and blue twin. Her eyes remained cool and standoffish, but her voice was warm enough. "You'll find out soon." Rolling backward, she graciously gave me some privacy as I slit the rope around V's wrists and freed him.

The instant he could move, he hitched himself up and threw his arms around me. His muscular bulk wasn't warm like normal—the ice from the room leeched everything from him, making it seem like I hugged marble.

He clutched me harder. "Fuck, Threads. What the hell is going on?"

I fell into him.

Vaughn was alive.

Jethro was alive.

Even Kes was alive.

A trifecta of happiness, yet all I wanted to do was burst into tears.

"It's a long story." I breathed in his familiar aftershave.

His body shuddered, his chin pressing on the top of my head. He didn't let me go; if anything, he hugged me tighter. "God, I thought they'd killed you, too." He shook his head. "Those gunshots. That fucking maniac. What the hell?"

I untangled myself. "Like I said, long story."

Anger curled off him. "Where are the fucking cops in all of this! They came to get you. They brought you home. Yet, you touted that bullshit for that magazine and ruined everything. You cried wolf, Threads, and now we're really fucked—"

"Stop it, alright? I know I've done a few things that don't make sense. I know I made our family a laughingstock by denying everything you said and the police want nothing to do with us, but none of that matters." Giving him a watery smile, I rubbed my eyes, doing my best to stay calm. "The main thing is you're still alive. I'm still alive, and we're going to fight back."

His jaw worked. "Damn fucking right we're going to fight back. I want every single Hawk dead."

"Not every Hawk deserves to die." Jasmine's voice carried on a puff of frozen breath.

I turned to face her, sharing a kindred smile. "Only the rotten ones."

He's alive.

He's alive.

Both our brothers are still in this world.

Vaughn growled. "They're all rotten. Every last one of them."

Jasmine scowled.

We didn't have time to fight.

"We'll talk about that later. For now, tell me if you're alright. No broken bones or anything?"

V sighed, hugging me again. His strength hinted that apart from a few bruises, he wasn't too damaged. "I'm stronger than I look, little sister." He couldn't stop touching me—tucking my hair behind my ears, tracing my cheeks and arms. It was tender, but it wasn't because of love or the need to connect.

Ever since our mum became Hawk property, Vaughn had always patched me up. He'd find me sprawled at the bottom of the stairs from tripping with vertigo and plaster the scrapes on my hands. He'd somehow be there first if I fell and cut myself—always armed with bandages and painkillers for his delinquent sister.

He was so used to me hurting myself, he had a system. A process.

Words could lie about a fall—brush it off as if it were nothing. But touch couldn't hide the truth. Touch could feel the heat of a new bruise or the bump of a broken bone.

Even hurt himself, he was still trying to fix and protect me.

I pushed him away. "I'm okay, V. Honest."

"We need to get you out of here." He swung his legs off the bed. "Now. Tonight."

"You're not going anywhere."

Both our heads whipped up to face Jasmine. She'd rolled closer, sitting with her hands in her lap. I didn't trust for a second she was as meek as she seemed. She probably had hundreds of weapons hidden in her blanket.

"I've given you time to say hello. I've given you time that I didn't have to give. But now you have to come with me."

Vaughn stiffened. "I don't have to do anything." Grabbing my hand, he squeezed. "I'm taking my sister, and we're leaving."

"No, you aren't." Jasmine's face darkened. "You'll do what I say."

I froze. Once again, my loyalties split. I used to belong to Vaughn entirely. He was blood. He was the exact replica of me in every way. But my heart had replaced him with my chosen one.

The one I thought was dead.

We would never be as close because we would never need each other as much as we once had.

It was both sad and freeing at the same time.

"She's right, V. We can't leave. Not yet."

Vaughn's eyes popped wide. "What the fuck does that mean?" Raising a finger, he pointed at Jasmine. "Wait a minute...who are you?" His voice slipped into a hiss. "Are you one of them? Because if you are, so fucking help me I'll wring your neck—girl or not."

Jasmine didn't back down. She didn't even flinch. "If you're asking if I'm a Hawk, the answer is yes. If you're asking if I love my brothers as much as you love your sister, then the answer is yes. And if you're asking if I'm on your side, the answer isn't so simple."

Vaughn let me go, pushing off the bed to tower over her. He stumbled a little, but it didn't stop him from sucking in a breath and whipping the room with temper. "If what you say is true, then you know what I feel and I'll do anything to protect my twin. I won't put your needs before hers. *Ever.*"

Jasmine gritted her teeth. Her eyes flashed with frustration for Jethro and Kes. The longer we argued, the less time we had.

They need us. Now. Before it's too late.

"Vaughn, listen to me—"

"No, Nila, *you* listen to *me*. I don't know how she brainwashed you, but it's over. They're all noxious; therefore, they'll all die." He took a step closer to Jaz. "And if you don't move out of my fucking way, you'll be the first to go."

Her eyes pinned him in place; her elegant throat poised with defiance. "I'll tell you something you don't know, Mr. Weaver. And then we'll see if you'll do what you're told."

V snorted but Jaz ignored him.

"Your sister has survived my family for almost six months. She's the one who stood up to us. She's the one who helped my brother all because she believed in him. She had the power to destroy him, but she didn't. And if anyone deserves to kill those who deserve to die, it's her." She swallowed hard, forcing herself to continue. "Seeing you together is hard. You both look so similar. Twins in every sense. My brothers and I might not be the same age, but we share something in common. We share a desire for freedom. And I won't let you take that away from us."

Her eyes fell on me. "Have you told him, Nila? Have you told him who Jethro is to you? Or did you continue to let him slander his name in social media when you left us?"

I flinched.

She's right.

While trapped at Hawksridge, I lived in truth far more than I ever did in London. I hadn't had the guts to look my father or twin in their eyes and tell them that I was in love with a Hawk. That I belonged to him and him to me. That I was a traitor to my family name.

"What is she talking about, Threads?" Anger glazed V's eyes along with a faint hint of fear. "Tell me."

"V, I—"

How could I tell him that I loved Jethro as much as I loved him? How could I tell him that it was no longer simple between us?

"She took him from me, Vaughn," Jaz said quietly. "She fell in love with my brother, and overnight, I became second in his life." She gave me a twisted smile—half-accepting, half-unwilling. "He doesn't belong to me anymore, just like she doesn't belong to you."

Vaughn shifted, running a hand through his dark hair. The beard he'd sported in London had been shorn, but a few day's growth shadowed his jaw. "I don't—I don't understand."

"One day, you'll end up belonging to someone you love. But for now, you belong to me. *I'm* the one who's come to rescue you. *I'm* the one who holds your life in my hands. And I'm the one who says you'll do what I ask."

My shoulders hunched. "Probably not the best way to make him help you."

She glared at me.

I shrugged.

I'd been on the receiving end of Jasmine's willpower—her perfect deception. She could spin any tale—give life to any lie. She'd completely fooled me at the meeting, and I'd never underestimate her again. I still couldn't shake the hatred I'd felt. But she didn't know my brother or how pig-headed he could be when *told* to do something.

V turned to me. "Threads...is that true? You fell in love with that bastard?" His face fell. "Is that why you slept with him?"

Jaz sucked in a breath, watching us like some soap opera.

I moved to stand in front of my brother. "What she says is true. I love him, V. And he doesn't have much time. Jasmine needs your help." Laying a hand on his chest, I murmured, "I *want* you to help her. For me. Please..."

His heart thundered under my touch; his eyes dove into mine. "This is for real? You love the bastard who's going to kill you?" His face contorted. "Could you be any more stupid?"

"He would never have been able to do it." Jasmine rolled forward. "He fell for her before she fell for him. I knew even when he didn't."

She locked her brakes, staring up at V. "If you won't help me because I'm telling you to, help me because I'm asking. Don't let him die. Don't destroy your sister or condemn my brother when he's the only one who can stop all of this for good."

For the longest moment, we all held our breaths, waiting for V to accept defeat and agree to help. But then his shoulders stiffened, and he shook his head. "I don't believe either of you. I think you're both fucked in the head, and we need to get the hell out of this shithole."

Snatching my wrist, he jerked me toward the door.

For someone who'd been in a fight and locked in a chiller, he moved quickly.

"V! Let me go." I stumbled after him, vertigo teasing with the outskirts of my vision.

"Vaughn, listen to her." Jaz spun around, her knuckles white on her wheels. "You can't leave."

V ignored her and reached for the door. "Oh, really? Funny, this is me leaving."

I breathed hard. "Vaughn, I'm not going anywhere with you. If you won't help us, fine. But I'm not going to leave him—"

"Yes, you are. Because I'm doing something he never did." His nose almost brushed mine as he yanked me close. "Saving your arse."

"You don't understand!"

"No, Threads. *You* don't understand. They've kept you here, treating you fucking awful for months. They've twisted your thoughts and made you suffer that Stockholm shit. Well, it's over. We're going home."

His hand landed on the doorknob, wrenching it side to side.

Locked.

He whirled on Jaz, carting me back like a prisoner. Shoving his hand beneath her nose, he growled, "Key. Now."

Her chin rose. "No. Not until you agree to help me."

"Never. Give me the key." He bent down, crazed with rage. "I won't ask again."

"And I won't ask for your help again. I'll just make you."

Vaughn raised his hand.

"Wait!" I jumped forward, barricading him from slapping her. "Don't!"

V's mouth popped wide. "You're seriously defending her, Threads? After every-fucking-thing her family has done to you?"

I couldn't believe it, either. If V had been there after the meeting with the lawyers, I would've willingly given him a gun and loaded the bullet myself. But that was before I started listening—*truly* listening. Jaz was on our side.

He's alive.

But for how much longer?

Waving my arms, I whisper-shouted, "Enough! Yes, I'm defending her. Yes, I'm in love with Jethro. And no, I won't go anywhere with you until he's safe." Trembling, I looked over my shoulder at Jasmine.

She sat unruffled, her hand curled around a black gun that'd appeared from under her blanket.

I knew it! I knew she'd have an arsenal hidden in there.

Our eyes met.

I could make a big deal out of the weapon or I could focus on the task at hand.

Jethro and Kes...

Ignoring the pistol, I asked, "What's your plan? Why do you need my brother to help?"

"Mr. Weaver here is going to carry me where I need to go and do everything I tell him."

"Like fuck I am." Vaughn paced in front of us.

"V!" I scowled. "Just...listen, okay?"

A small glisten of emotion showed before Jaz added, "I can't do this on my own and, Nila, you have to go back to your room."

I shook my head. "I'll come with you. I don't want to go back—"

"It's not a matter of what you want. It's a matter of necessity. We'll be gone a while. I need you to lie for me if it comes to that."

"Lie for you?"

"You need to take my chair and tell them that I spent the night with you." She eyed up V as he paced like a feral animal. "While he'll be my legs and strength, you'll be my safeguard. I need you to come up with any tale you need to in order to keep the truth about my brothers' lives a secret. I don't care what you say. Just keep it hidden."

My mind swam. I had no idea how I would achieve that if Daniel or Cut came knocking.

"And why do you need me, exactly?" Vaughn asked, his voice laced with animosity. "Why should I put my life on the line?"

Jaz took in his bruised face and blood-stained t-shirt. "Do you want children, Mr. Weaver?"

V's eyebrows disappeared into his hairline. "What? What the fuck does that—"

"Answer the question. Yes or no."

My heart raced, waiting for him to reply. I'd grown up with V, but we'd never talked about what we wanted in the future. Never discussed the idea of raising our own families—too caught up in designing and promoting and working tirelessly for a company that was more parent than we'd ever needed.

V breathed out heavily. "I don't know...before, I might've entertained the idea, but now never. Not after what they did to Nila." His eyes fell on me. "Or our mum."

"Exactly. My family has cast a shadow over yours for far too long. You should have the right to have children if you want, knowing they are safe to grow old." She inched closer, her voice filling with passion and truth. "I need your help to make that a reality."

I tensed, waiting for another argument, for more curses.

But V's black eyes met mine, mirroring my unspoken begging for his help. He had the power to save, not only the man I loved, but both our futures, too.

Finally, he slouched. "If I help you, you'll keep my sister safe? You'll make sure this ends?"

Jaz held a fist over her heart. "You have my ultimate word. Keep my brothers alive and I swear to you this will all be in the past."

Vaughn closed the distance between them, his eyes lingering on Jasmine's chair. With slight hesitation, he held out his hand. "In that case. We have a deal."

Jaz blinked back tears as she dropped the gun and placed her hand in his. "Thank you. A thousand times, thank you."

I didn't want to interrupt the sudden tender moment, but my heartbeat was a clock, striking the passing minutes with terror.

He's alive.

He's alive.

It's time to go.

"What next?" I whispered.

Jaz smiled softly. "Vaughn and I have a date in the crypt."

V looked at her blankly.

Jaz held up the key, rolling herself toward the door. "This is our last chance."

"What is?" I ghosted forward, drawn by the anticipation of hope and righteousness.

She slipped the key into the lock. "Our last chance to rescue Kestrel and Jethro and get them to the hospital before they die."

Jethro

"NO. NOT LIKE that, dammit."

"Hush it, woman. I think I know how to work a cutting torch."

"No, you obviously don't. You don't have the valve open for the acetylene."

A curse, a scrape, then a loud hiss.

Images of writhing snakes and striking cobras filled my cloud-riddled mind. *What the fuck?* Had I finally left Earth and plummeted to hell where reptiles and dragons waited for my demise?

Something bright and fierce sliced through the darkness.

I flinched.

Yep, definitely hell.

They're waiting for me.

Heat from their fire-breathing mouths battled away the penetrating cold.

"Now you have too much. Mix it with the oxygen, you moron."

"Moron? Keep name-calling to a minimum. Otherwise, you'll have to find another donkey to help."

"Just—let me." Shuffling sounded, followed by another gust of heat and light.

The voices echoed as if they drifted through chasms of water and rubble. Female and male—husk and lilt.

Since when do dragons talk?

"How the fuck did you get this thing down here, anyway?" The hissing grew louder, sparks lighting up the dimness behind my eyes.

"A friend put it here. The only thing we had on the estate that would open the lock."

"Never heard of a fucking key?"

More light. More hissing.

"He made a mistake. He closed the door to keep them safe, not realising there was only one key."

"And you didn't feel like using it? Too easy? Wanted to go the James Bond route?"

A curse followed by a rain of sparks brighter than any firework.

"Shut it. For your information, it wasn't possible to get it."

"Why? Dear ole dad has it?"

A squeaking, followed by another blast of heat. The girl growled, "Yes."

"I've never known anyone so under the thumb of their old man."

A pause followed by a loud curse. "That's what you get for talking about things you don't understand. Now, shut up. Get the mixture right. And get my brothers out of there before I hit you again."

"Anyone ever tell you that you're evil?"

"All the time. Now do what I say."

Their talking ceased, replaced with the lullaby of fire and burning.

I lost track of reality and life. I wasn't human anymore. I wasn't pain or death.

I was just... *time.*

No sensation or memories. No hardships or heartaches. Only time ticking past unwanted and unseen.

I was nothing, no one... gone.

"God's sake. Pick me up again. I'll freaking do it."

"I'm doing it, woman! How many fucking times do I need to tell you that?"

"You're not going fast enough."

The yellow light turned white with power, beckoning me forward, promising a better existence than the one I endured.

I wanted to reach for it, squinting in my mind as the light grew larger, brighter, inhaling me into its orb.

I'd never seen something so pure—as if I stared at the nucleus of the sun or the entrance to heaven.

Am I worthy of paradise, after all?

"Hurry. We need to leave."

"Woman, give me a damn moment, okay?"

The light supernovaed. Hissing increased in decibels until it echoed in my teeth. Electricity sparked in my muscles, slowly bringing me back to life. I tried to move, to see what beast hissed so loudly, but my body was no longer mine to command. It was weak and broken and past listening to such requests.

My foggy mind wouldn't focus; wisps of thoughts and flickers of images all faded with every failing heartbeat.

I didn't know why I continued to cling to whatever semblance of life I had.

This was no life.

This was just damnation.

"Shit, it's not cutting."

"I know it's not freaking cutting. You've got the ratio wrong!"

"If you're such a fucking know-it-all, you fix it."

My ears rang with bickering.

I didn't know the man, but the girl reminded me of my sister. A little girl who I'd loved since childhood but also drove me nuts. She'd constantly pinch my favourite toys and hide them where I could never find them.

She ran circles around Kes and me. Driving us mad, proving that love wasn't enough to protect an infuriating sister from retaliation—usually in the form of frogs in her bed or beetles on her cereal.

I attempted a smile, thinking of happier times.

The light went out, followed by a scraping noise.

"Now, turn that gauge to the left and that to the right. See those two lines... that's the ideal ratio."

"Fine. Done. Now what?"

"Now, I want to work the wand."

"What? No way."

Something clanged off the earthen walls. My ears twitched, reminding me they still worked, even when other parts of me didn't. I'd long since stopped feeling the soft splash of internment droplets on my forehead or tensing when a fresh wash of agony bathed my skin with fever.

"Pick me up and then give me the wand. Got it?"

"God, you're such an arse."

"Kind of you to notice. Now...pick me up."

"But it should be me who—"

"Why? Because you're male and playing with power tools is a man's job?"

A heavy sigh. "No...because it's—"

"Look, the original plan was for me to use the torch. If you hadn't gone all *He-man* on me, they'd be free and halfway to London by now."

Silence again.

For a while, minutes swept me away, granting that odd sensation of no time passing but hours slipping anyway.

"They're probably already dead. They haven't moved since we started this."

A livid curse littered the rank air. "If they don't make it, our bargain is over. I promised Nila would be safe if you helped me rescue my brothers. If they die...why should I honour that?"

Nila...

The name...

Like an angel.

Nila...

My heart suddenly woke up. Shedding death, sending lethargic blood through my veins.

Nila.

Mine.

The woman I want but failed.

"Threads is walking out of here—regardless if they don't."

"Guess the only way to know for sure is to bust my brothers out of here before it's too late."

I sucked in a useless breath—it was like breathing cremated ash.

Before, the void I existed in had no emotion, no feeling to suck me dry. But these two people? Fuck. They had so much to say and no correct words in which to say it. The woman wept with helplessness and despair, hiding it beneath bluster and rage. The man...he was just as helpless and lost; only he wrapped his in confusion and disbelief.

"Alright, alright, I get your point." Boots thudded on the dirt floor. "How should I do it again?"

A derisive laugh trilled, chasing back ghouls and monsters. "I told you how. Arms under my knees and around my shoulders. You can't break me."

"No, but I've heard about people like you—"

"People like *me*?"

"Shit, I just meant people with your—"

"My disability—is that what you were going to say? People like 'me' who can't feel anything below their waist?"

An awkward cough. "I just meant, I know you can bruise easily and it's not so simple to heal like a normal—"

"Wow, this just gets better and better. You're saying I'm not normal?!"

"Whoa, fucking chill—"

"You know what? I don't have time for this. Pick me up, give me the damn torch, and shut the hell up. When they're safe in the hospital *then* we can discuss the politically appropriate ways to discuss my condition. Got it?"

A deep sigh. "Fine."

I couldn't make sense of anything.

What the hell did this mean?

Was my brain playing tricks? Giving me an angst-loaded argument, all for what? To keep me strained enough to stay lucid? Or were there truly two people trying to save me?

"There. You okay?"

"I'll be okay once we get them out of here. Right, hand me the wand."

A pause.

"Good. Take me closer."

A few seconds later, the hissing began. I wanted to raise my head and see. But all I could do was bask in the meagre happiness the sound gave and slip again.

The brightness suddenly flared, cutting past my eyelids, imprinting on my retinas. No talking, no bickering, only the licking of flames against whatever enemy it destroyed.

Time skipped again—like a faulty record, jumping ahead, screeching backward, never playing the track in order.

"You're almost there," the man said.

Almost on cue, a snapping sounded, followed by a skeletonish groan.

"Ah, see. How little you trust me."

More shuffling. "I take it back. You're a girl, and you know how to use power tools."

"Damn right, I do."

Silence fell except for the occasional footfall and clang of metal on metal.

I sighed as the tempers eddying around me faded as companionship and victory stole their frustration. Inner peace settled, and I gave up trying to hold on.

The excitement disappeared, giving me a body that was cold, hungry, and riddled with pain.

I'm ready to go now. I'm ready to leave.

But then another sense came back to life.

The sense of touch.

"Kite...can you hear me?"

The softest warmth flittered over my cheek and forehead.

I wanted to moan with sheer pleasure. To answer their question and prove I hadn't given up, no matter how much I craved sanctuary.

"You're okay. You'll be fine." Warmth darted over my chest, my arm.

Then the sweetest voice whispered in my ear. "I've got you, Jet. You're safe now. Just hang on."

Nila

"SHE'S IN THE bath."

"She's not feeling well and can't come to the door."

"I have her chair—see? Of course, she's in here with me."

"She's in bed. We had a sleepover and can't get up."

I groaned, wiping both hands over my face.

"Nothing will work."

The empty room swallowed my words, keeping my fibs from reaching Hawk ears.

Ever since leaving Jasmine and Vaughn in the corridor leading toward the kitchens, I'd practiced a believable lie. Only thing was, there was nothing believable. After the visible hatred between Jaz and me at the meeting with the lawyers, no one would buy the excuse of a sleepover or girl chat or time willingly spent together.

It's hopeless.

The best I could hope for was no visitors and for V and Jaz to get back as soon as possible.

My mind skipped back to last night.

My spine had tingled with foreboding as V bent down in the dark and hesitantly plucked Jasmine from her chair. I'd never seen her legs in full view without baggy pyjamas or a blanket hiding the emaciated muscles but seeing them dangle over V's arms hit me hard.

Once upon a time, she could run and ride horses and chase her brothers.

Now, she had to rely on the brother of her enemy to be her transport.

A brutal price to pay for a payment I didn't know.

The look in V's eyes as he'd turned his back on me and left me in the empty corridor with an empty wheelchair squeezed my heart until I couldn't breathe. Helping a Hawk went against everything he believed in. In his mind, he betrayed his stance on blackmailing with social media, slandering the Hawk name, and standing up for our mother and me.

Yet, here he was, abandoning his sister in order to help another save her brothers.

It wasn't easy, but he showed me more loyalty and strength than I'd ever seen. Gone was the cocky joker who summoned women with one smirk. Gone was the slight player who'd worked hard but somehow managed to indulge in life with a silver spoon.

As he disappeared with a black-dressed Jaz in his arms, he grew from boy to man, and I'd wanted to run after him and thank him for saving Jethro—for once again putting my happiness above his own and doing what I bade.

It'd taken all my control not to follow. To clutch the handles of Jasmine's chair and wheel it in the opposite direction.

They're coming for you, Jethro.

They'll save you.

It killed me that I wouldn't be there. That I wouldn't be the one coaxing him to liveliness, rescuing him from pain. But, at the same time, that right belonged to Jaz. Jethro had sacrificed his life to save hers—it was only fair she did the same.

Then again, she'd dragged my brother into her plotting. There was no telling her plans—whatever they were—would be executed without a hitch. No saying they would be safe.

If Cut found out, Jaz would be punished, Jethro and Kes killed for real, and Vaughn repeatedly beaten. I had no doubt they would destroy him until he begged for death.

And all for what? For the unfortunate curse of being my blood.

Stop thinking about it.

I glared at the wheelchair, lurking in the shadows by the door. It looked so sad, so empty without its owner. The metal machine grieved for its occupant, no longer wanting to provide a purpose without her.

Dawn lurked on the horizon.

Pink swirls and purple splashes slowly pushed aside midnight black.

For the fiftieth time, I looked at the clock.

6:37 a.m.

I'd returned to my room at ten past twelve. Over six hours ago.

Where were they?

What had they been doing?

Are you still alive, Jethro?

Are you safe?

I hadn't slept. I hadn't relaxed. How could I when they were out there, sneaking beneath sleeping cameras and saving men who in Cut's mind were dead?

The dresser was back across the door, firmly wedged and protective. But that didn't stop my growing panic as each hour traded night for day and the chance of getting caught increased.

"What do you mean Jasmine's missing? No, she isn't. She's here…in the bathroom. And no, you cannot see her."

I groaned, pacing at the end of my bed. That would fail. If she were in the bathroom, she'd need her chair to move around.

"She's taking a nap; I don't want to disturb her."

All Cut would have to do was bang on the door and 'wake her up' to realize there was no nap to disturb.

"God, this isn't going to work."

Please, hurry!

The last of moonlight turned to sunlight, glinting off the silver rims of Jasmine's chair. I had the strangest feeling of not being alone. As if the inanimate object was somehow alive, as if it had a presence in the room—the ghost of Jaz, leaving her impression with me even while she ran escapades with my brother.

What are you doing?

Has it gone to plan?

How much longer will you be?

I couldn't stop thinking about it. I hated being left behind, left to worry and fret and create insane theories on what'd happened without me.

I would've given anything to be with them.

He's not dead.

He's alive!

Joy effervesced.

I held a hand against my chest, forcing the happy bubbles to disperse. It was too soon to celebrate. Too soon to believe he was safe. In some awful way, I didn't want to jinx it by believing in the best when the worst might still happen.

Time continued onward, turning my fear into depression.

What if Jasmine underestimated her plan to save them? What if they'd waited too long? What if? What if? *What if?*

Looking at the clock, I bit my lip as the hour hand struck 7:00 a.m. No one in Hawksridge was an early riser, but Jasmine was playing with fire. She had to get back and *soon*. She had to return my brother.

I paced the thick carpet. Every creak of the ancient house warming in the early winter sunshine made me jump. Every crank and glug of old plumbing sent my heart racing.

She has to have made it.

She has to have saved him.

A tapping sounded. Faint and fleeting.

I slammed to a halt, eyes flying to the ceiling, the walls, the window, the door.

It came again.

The softest rap and the quietest voice. "Threads, open up."

After pacing tens of kilometres and biting off my nails in concern, they were back.

I flew.

With super-human strength, I shoved aside the dresser and opened the door.

"Let us in. Quickly." Vaughn's voice was raspy and tired, but alive.

Thank God.

I stepped aside. The dark corridor hid my secretive visitors until they traded the gloom and darted inside. Vaughn prowled forward with Jasmine locked in his arms, moving through puddles of sunlight, as he headed straight for her chair.

Immediately, I closed the door again, deliberating whether to put the dresser back or not.

Jaz's arm was slung over his shoulders, her body relaxed in his embrace. Something was different.

When he'd picked her up and disappeared seven hours ago, they'd been awkward and stiff. Now, they shared an experience, a mission I hadn't been privileged to participate in.

Vaughn's back bunched beneath a new t-shirt as he placed Jasmine gently into the wheeled contraption. I eyed him. *He wasn't wearing that last night.* The previous wardrobe had been a bloodied dark blue shirt. This was a dark grey tee with a sports brand tagged on the front—not at all what my brother would wear.

My heart thudded with mysteries. What had they seen and done together? What rapport had they built? And why couldn't I have been a part of it?

My jaw clenched as Jasmine smiled at V.

He tucked her useless legs onto the stirrups and took a step back. "You good?"

She nodded. "Thanks."

I moved forward, feeling left out, lost, and entirely too close to tears.

She was on our side. She'd done what she could to save the men we both loved, but at the same time, I couldn't forget how nasty she'd been. The ruse of making me hate her caused my feelings to split. I wanted to like her, but some part of me was still wary, still on edge.

She asked me to die for her brother.

But…wouldn't I do the same if it were V?

Swallowing my hurt, I crossed my arms. "How did it go?"

Please tell me it was a success.

The rest of it: the sadness at not sharing their adventure and the grief at not being able to see Jethro would diminish the moment I knew he was in the hands of those who could heal him and Kes.

Jasmine adjusted herself in the chair as Vaughn took a step back.

Her eyes met mine. "We got them to the hospital."

"Oh, thank God." My heart tried to leap from my chest. "Did the doctors say anything?"

"Lots to tell you, Threads." Vaughn came closer. His arms banded around me, squeezing tight.

Tears pricked my eyes.

I hadn't realised how lonely I'd been, so afraid and on tenterhooks all night.

I accepted his embrace but quickly wriggled out. I couldn't handle his hug when every part of me was jealous that I hadn't been the one to help. I couldn't find comfort in his arms, otherwise I'd burst into waterworks. "Tell me. Tell me everything."

V let me go. "We stayed as long as we could. We got them there, filled in the paperwork, and waved goodbye as they took them to surgery, but we couldn't wait any longer to find out the prognosis."

His stomach growled loudly, shredding the taut atmosphere.

"But they'll make it?"

His tummy grumbled again. Finally given a task I could perform, I headed to my secret stash in the fabric cupboard.

Vaughn looked at Jaz.

Her face was pinched. Her black hoodie and leggings painted her like a thief in the night. If anyone saw her dressed like that, she'd have a lot of explaining to do. "They were when we left them. But they're with the experts now. All we can do is hope."

Unwilling to fall into another pit of despair, I forced my mind to focus on one scenario.

They'll make it.

Wrenching open the cupboard, I pulled out a box of muesli bars.

Glancing at Jaz, I asked, "How did you keep them alive for so long? And where?" Ripping the box open, I tossed a bar to V and one to Jaz. They both caught them.

Jasmine smiled in thanks, tucking hers into the satchel of her wheelchair. V, on the other hand, tore off the wrapper with his teeth and devoured it in a few mouthfuls. "Fuck, I haven't eaten in forever."

Hadn't they fed him? My heart hardened. More daggers of hatred grew toward Cut and Bonnie. I wanted to murder them slowly, *painfully*—to do to them what they'd done to innocent men and women.

Jasmine replied, "It wasn't just me. I had help."

"Damn right you did." V winked. "Me."

She smiled, a scowl plaiting with genuine amusement. "No, hotshot." Her eyes met mine again. "Flaw."

I froze. *I was right.*

My mind skipped to our conversation. Something about me not judging him, and how he was a good person. "He helped? How?"

Yesterday in the corridor.

They'd huddled together...discussing Jethro.

Jasmine sighed, "I was a freaking mess when Cut shot them. I'd wanted to walk again ever since I lost the ability, but in that second I'd wanted to *fly*. To soar across the room and tear out his motherfucking heart."

My hands curled around the box of muesli bars. "I know that feeling."

"Afterward, Bonnie took me upstairs and tried to calm me down. The rest I'm not entirely sure about, but Flaw was given the task of cleaning up." She swallowed, eyes turning dark. "He noticed they...weren't dead."

"They had drips and shit...medical paraphernalia down there." Vaughn jumped in. "Who did that?"

"Flaw again. He dropped out of medical school after he discovered diamonds were a lot more lucrative than sewing up flesh. We had the equipment, but he didn't tell anyone. He moved their bodies, set up what they needed, then came to me the minute I was alone. Everything went according to plan, apart from the mishap of shutting the cell door."

That was happening all while she came to save me from Daniel.

How had she come up with a plan so fast? And why did Cut listen to her demands as oldest child?

My mind raced. "So...Flaw kept them alive?"

She nodded. "If it hadn't been for him, they would've drained out on the carpet."

I shook my head. "But there was so much blood. They were unconscious."

Jaz rolled closer. "He performed a miracle, Nila. I'll be forever grateful for that. But there's no guarantee they'll pull through. The doctors tried to be optimistic when we arrived, but..."

Vaughn picked up where she trailed off. "The docs' faces, Threads. You could tell they didn't have much hope."

The joy of knowing Jethro and Kestrel were rescued punctured, deflating like a hot air balloon, crashing faster toward Earth. "So...they might still..." I couldn't finish.

Jaz smiled tightly, her eyes glittering with unshed tears. "Let's focus on the positive. They're away from Hawksridge with people who know what they're doing. That's all we have."

Terrible silence fell, like a curtain already stealing Jethro and Kes from us.

Vaughn finally muttered, "Why keep them down there? It was a fucking dungeon."

His train of thought gave me something to focus on.

Jasmine jumped to answer, as if unable to handle the quietness when we couldn't stop our minds from picking at 'what if'.

What if they don't make it?

What if we were too late?

"It's the only place in Hawksridge that has no cameras. All rooms, bathrooms, cellars—they're all monitored. We couldn't run the risk of Cut seeing them."

I straightened. "What about the cameras last night?"

Her hands dived into her hair. Unpinning the clip, she let her sleek bob fall into place around her chin. "A few months ago, Kes taught me how to upload a virus that put the cameras into hibernation for a few hours. After a time, they reboot as if nothing happened. If anyone attempts to fix them while they're down, the virus hijacks the hard drive and ruins two months' worth of data." She shrugged. "Either no one noticed and will think the lack of recording was a technical fault, or someone did and will put it down to a damaged hard drive."

"Interesting." Vaughn rubbed his face. "You'll have to show me that handy trick." His stomach growled again, even louder than before.

I couldn't help Jethro or improve his prognosis, but I could help another man I loved. Turning back to the cupboard, I grabbed an armful of apples, biscuits, and another box of muesli bars. I shoved them at my brother. "Here. Have these." Dashing to my wardrobe, I pulled free a few extra-large jumpers that I liked to wear off the shoulder with a belt and gave those to him, too. "And these. To keep you warm."

Jaz wheeled forward. "That's a good idea. That room is freezing." Her shoulders rolled. "V, it hasn't exactly been easy dealing with you tonight, but you've been amazing. Helping move Jet and Kes, driving the van, filling out the paperwork at the hospital. Don't think I'm not grateful because I am. But..."

Vaughn had his mouth full with a crisp green apple. "But you have to take me back."

Jaz nodded.

"No, surely you can just let him go—" I moved between them.

Vaughn swallowed his breakfast. "No chance of a warmer room? Something without a broken window?"

She smiled sadly. "Sorry. We have to make it seem like nothing happened. Cut can't know Jet and Kes are alive. Any escapes or room changes will make him suspicious. However, I'll do what I can and move you in a few days."

I stood in front of V, cutting Jaz off. "I won't let them keep him in that place." Putting my hands on my hips, I glared. "Why can't you just let him go? You were off the estate tonight. Just take him back to London and let him hide until this is all over. Cut can just blame me if he gets suspicious."

Vaughn grabbed my shoulders. "You think I'd do that? Run away and leave you here?"

I shrugged him off. "If you're not here, they have nothing to control me with. I'll be free to do what needs to be done."

Vaughn's eyes flashed. "Don't be so stupid, Threads. I'm not going anywhere without you. End of fucking story."

Jaz stiffened. "You do realise saying 'when this is all over' is accepting your death, right?"

I groaned. *Great.* Perfect thing to say in front of an overprotective twin.

"What?" Vaughn demanded. "What the fuck does that mean?"

I rolled my eyes. "I'm not accepting death. I have my own plan to end this. Either way, I need you gone, V. I can't have people I love here."

Jaz suddenly shot forward and grabbed my hand. "Don't do anything reckless, Nila. I made an oath to Jethro to look after you. I can't break that promise."

My eyes widened. "When did you make that?"

Her face softened. "There are a lot of conversations and stolen moments in this house that you don't see or hear. The day the police came for you after the Second Debt, I knew you'd changed him. He refused to speak to me. He pushed me out of his life completely, but he didn't need to tell me for me to understand."

"There is so much shit I don't know about," Vaughn grumbled. "I need some education. Someone needs to fill me in on what I missed. Second Debt?"

Jaz and I ignored him.

My heart galloped, drunk on the thought of Jethro. Imagining him alive and happy. The fact he'd talked about me…that his sister knew how he felt about me—it made our love so real. Even if it was forbidden.

My voice dropped to a whisper. "You're like him…aren't you?"

"Like who?" V asked around a mouthful of hobnob biscuits.

Jaz lowered her gaze. "He told you?"

Her tone was both awed and slightly miffed.

"Does that offend you?" The residual dislike for her tainted my voice.

She shook her head. "Offend? No. Surprise? Yes. But…I knew he'd fallen in love with you. I could feel it in him."

"Feel it?" V wiped crumbs off his t-shirt. "That's a strange thing to say."

I turned to face him. "She's a VEP." After Jethro's lesson the other day, I felt cocky to know the term. To know the technical name for a condition so common in people that it'd become a regular flaw, according to society.

V scrunched up his nose. "What the hell is that?"

Jaz chuckled. "No. And Nila has it wrong. I'm empathic to the point of emotional sensory but nowhere near as bad as Jethro. I don't call myself anything different. Just attuned to my brother—same as you're tuned to each other." She waved at V and me. "You're twins. There are differences between you, but overall, you share enough genetic make-up to sense each other on a deeper level."

Vaughn nodded. "That's twins for you."

Jaz smiled. "Twins and Empaths."

A loud noise slammed a few rooms down.

We all froze.

The inhabitants of Hawksridge were waking up.

I hated that answers had to come later, but I would hate it even more if we were caught. "As much as I want to continue talking, I think…it's time to hide."

Jaz nodded, rolling toward the door. "You're right." Without looking over her shoulder, she said, "V, I'll take you back to your room."

My heart twitched at the casual way she called my twin by his nickname. I wanted to tell her she had no right. But, then again, I *had* stolen her brother. I'd forced myself into his life and replaced her with myself.

Suddenly, I understood Jaz a whole lot more. She liked me because I was good for her sibling. But at the same time, she despised me taking him away from her.

Rushing forward, I opened the door a crack but put my foot out to prevent her from disappearing. Bending down, I whispered, "I just want to thank you. You have my word I won't hurt him—ever again. I'm in this for life, and I hope you know that I would never take him away completely." I smiled. "I'm very good at sharing."

"Sharing what?" V asked, coming to place his hands on Jaz's shoulders.

The unthinking action after a night of escapades and contact spoke more than words ever could. They were relaxed around each other. Whatever had happened had formed a trust far quicker than Jethro and I had built.

I'm...I'm jealous.

But also, strangely happy.

"Nothing." I backed up, smiling at V.

Jaz understood, though.

She shrugged, dislodging V's touch. "I think there's hope for you and me, yet, Nila Weaver." Patting my hand, she wheeled into the corridor.

V followed, pausing to kiss me on the cheek. He'd draped the two jumpers I'd given him over his shoulder and hugged his pilfered food. "I'll see you when I see you, I guess."

Sooner, rather than later.

I squeezed him hard. "Everything will be okay. You'll see."

Jaz sucked in a breath. "I hope so. If Kes and Jet make it, there will be hope for all of us." Her eyes captured mine, dark thoughts lurking in the depths. "One thing's for sure. It's no longer Hawk versus Weaver. We're the new generation. We've inherited the sins of our forebears.

"But we'll be the ones who will change history."

Jethro

NILA LAUGHED.

I looked up from my report on the latest smuggling shipment and covered my eyes from the overwhelming sunshine behind her.

She stood haloed in golden warmth—like the goddess I worshipped daily. She was ethereal, magical…mine.

"What's so funny?"

She skipped to my side and took my hand. The instant her skin touched mine, my heart tripped over. Even after all this time together, even after entwining our lives completely, I was still hopelessly smitten. She was my queen——the custodian of my soul——just like I'd promised when I'd given in to her the night I told her everything.

With a tender smile, she placed my hand on her growing belly.

My jaw clenched with a mixture of all-consuming love, pride, and protectiveness.

She's carrying my child.

We made this unborn creature together.

Half her, half me. It would be a Weaver and Hawk. Seamstress and diamond smuggler.

Ours.

"He kicked."

"Really?" I pressed my hand harder.

The firmness of her belly didn't move.

Nila's face fell. "He's stopped."

I gathered her close, pressing a kiss on her cotton-covered bump. "You keep saying he. We haven't found out the sex yet. It could just as easily be a girl."

She shook her head, her long black hair soaking up the sun as if she somehow harnessed its power. I loved her hair. I loved how free it made her.

"It's a boy."

Tugging her onto my lap, I kissed her lips. This woman utterly beguiled me. "What if I don't want a boy? What if I want a little girl who is as perfect as you?"

"He's coming to."

"Move aside, please."

Loud beeps filled my ears. Pain swamped. Heaviness shackled. Agony battered from all directions.

Fuck, make it stop.

I didn't like it here. I wanted to go back. Return to where the sunshine glowed and my wife carried my child.

More pain crescendoed. I gave up fighting.

Fuck, make it stop…make it stop!

My heart accelerated, shoving me head-first into my wish.

With a sigh, I let go of my body, ignored the summons trying to drag me back to life, and fell.

"You want a girl?"

I nodded. "More than anything."

"And what if I want a son?"

"You'll just have to wait."

Nila giggled. "Wait?"

I pulled her close, inhaling her soft scent of wild-flowers and summer. "Until we have another one."

"Mr. Ambrose. Come on."

The warm illusion shattered again.

I tensed, preparing for pain to welcome me back. There was no pain. Only a fog. A metallic blanket blocked the fever and excruciating agony. For the first time in forever, I could think without being handicapped by suffering.

With the discomfort gone, it opened the gates for everything else to become known.

My body was *tired*. Beyond tired. Bone weary and sluggish.

I don't want to be here.

I missed my dream world where everything was sunshine and smiles, away from whatever memories snarled on the outskirts of comprehension.

I want to forget…just for a little longer.

Sleep gripped my mind, tugging me backward, slipping me under the surface and delivering me back to Nila.

"Another one?" She swatted my chest, laughing in the bright afternoon. "Getting a bit greedy, don't you think?"

I nuzzled her neck. "Greedy? I wouldn't call it greedy."

Her lips parted as I trailed kisses up her throat, skirting her chin, hovering over her mouth. Her breath cracked and shortened, waiting in anticipation of a kiss. "Oh? What would you call it?"

I paused over her lips. I wanted so badly to kiss her. To drink her taste and pour my love down her throat. I wanted so desperately to heal her. To forget about the past and remind both of us that it was over. That we were free.

"I call it building a better future."

Nila's head tipped back. I captured her nape, keeping her locked in my control. My mouth watered, still millimetres from kissing her.

"How many?" she whispered as my lips finally touched hers.

My tongue slipped into her mouth, tangoing with hers, dancing the same dance we knew by heart. I would recognise Nila even if all my senses were stolen. I would know her if I was blind, deaf, and mute. I would always know her because I could feel her. Her love had a certain flavour—a sparkling liquor that intoxicated me whenever I let down my walls and felt what she felt, lived what she lived.

I murmured, "As many as we can."

"Mr. Ambrose, you have to open your eyes."

That damn voice again. And that name…it was wrong. That wasn't my name.

Once again, I tried to ignore the tugging, wanting to fall backward into sleep, but this time the gates were shut. I couldn't slip.

I hovered there—in an in-between world where darkness steadily became lighter and the world slowly solidified.

The pain was still blanketed, the tiredness not as consuming, but there was strangeness everywhere.

Strange smells.

Strange noises.

Strange people.

Where am I?

"That's it, wake up. We won't bite."

I cringed against the false, upbeat tone. I didn't tolerate insincerity and whoever encouraged me hid his true thoughts.

My condition was the first sense to return with full force, feeding off the man beside me—the man who cared, worried, and clinically assessed me. In his mind, I belonged to him. My progress, my recovery—it was all testament to his skills as my…

Doctor.

The unfamiliar place and unfamiliar smells suddenly made a lot more sense.

Bright lights were brighter and the blanket hiding me from pain lived deep in my veins.

Drugs.

I couldn't move. I couldn't speak. I could barely breathe.

But I was alive.

And mistakenly being called Mr. Ambrose.

The beeping sound flurried faster as I slipped back into all facets of my body. Fingers to fingers. Toes to toes. It was like dressing in expensive cashmere after weeks of wearing scratchy wool. It was *home.*

"He's coming to."

"That's it. We're here. No need to fear. You're safe."

The doctor's voice reached into the remaining darkness in my brain, plucking me to the surface. My eyes were heavy drapes, musty and full of moths, refusing to open.

A wash of frustration came from nowhere—tugging me faster from my haze, slamming me into a body I no longer wanted.

My eyes opened.

"Great. Awesome job, Mr. Ambrose."

I promptly closed them again. The room was too bright, too much to see.

"Give it a moment and the discomfort will pass." Someone patted me on the shoulder. The drumbeat resonated through my body, awakening everything else.

I tried again, squinting this time to limit the amount of light.

The scene before me crystallised from a sea of wishy-washy watercolours to shapes I recognised.

I knew this world. *Yet I don't know these people.*

I was back in a broken body, battered within an inch of my life. I was cold and feeling nauseous, and interminably tired. I preferred my dream world where Nila was safe, we were happy, and there was no mad evil threatening to tear us apart.

The doctor clasped my hand—the one free of an IV needle.

I tried to tug away but my brain failed to send the message, leaving me in his grasp. "You gave us quite a scare, Mr. Ambrose."

I swallowed, forcing my emaciated throat to lubricate. "Th—that isn't m—my—" I cut myself off before I could finish.

My name...what was my name...?

It only took a fraction.

I'm Jethro Hawk. Heir to Hawksridge, firstborn, and recently murdered by his own father. Everything of my past, my trials, and my love for Nila slotted into perfect place, leaving me clearheaded and aware.

As far as my father knew, I'd died when the bullet meant for Jasmine tore into my body. Whoever had delivered me to the hospital was on my side. And the name was a mask keeping me safe.

A flash of agony made its way through whatever painkillers they'd given me, kick-starting me onto another subject. "W—who are y—you?"

The doctor studied me. His brown handlebar moustache and shock of unruly hair didn't match the somber light green scrubs he wore or the softness of his hand around mine. He looked like an eccentric farmer, someone more at home hugging a chicken, than nursing a patient back to life.

"My name is Jack Louille. I was the surgeon who operated on you." His eyes cast down to my stomach, covered in starchy white sheets. "It was touch and go for a bit, but you responded well to treatment."

"W—what treat—treatment?"

He beamed, a rush of pride emitting from him, his emotions of a job well done and workplace satisfaction buffeting me. "I don't know how much you remember, but you were shot."

I nodded. "My m—memory is fully in—intact." The more I spoke, the more my throat found it easier to talk.

"Ah, that's great news. As you are aware then, a bullet sliced through your side." He leaned over me. "I don't need to tell you how close it came to being a fatal wound. An abdominal injury can rupture intestines, liver, spleen, and kidneys. There are also major vessels that can be nicked—all of which equal a lower possibility of survival—especially in your case, since you were unable to seek treatment straight away."

Why was that?

I couldn't recall.

Memories of time skipping and fire hissing tried to make sense. Kestrel had been beside me...

Kes!

I lashed out, grabbing the doctor's wrist. My body flared with agony, but I ignored it. "The other m—man. Is he here, t—too?" I didn't dare say his name. I doubted he would be under it anyway—same as me.

Doctor Louille paused, his happiness at my recovery fading as helplessness smothered his thoughts. "Your brother is still with us, but...we don't know for how long. His injuries were more extensive, less straightforward to operate." He cleared his throat. "I'll tell you about him soon. First, let me explain your condition and then you need to rest. There is time for everything else later."

No, there is no time.

If Kes wasn't doing well, I wanted to see him before it was too late.

I need my brother. My friend.

"You're what I call an extraordinary luckster." Louille smiled. "I once had a patient who slipped in the bath and shattered a window. The glass sliced his neck but missed the jugular and carotid artery. Do you know how nearly impossible that is? But he was lucky. I've had many patients that, by right, should be dead but somehow tricked death into leaving them alone." He patted my shoulder. "You're the latest luckster. The bullet sliced through the high side of your abdomen, passing through the muscles surrounding core vitals, and never entering the abdominal cavity. You would've passed out from the overload of adrenaline and pain, and it would've been horrendously messy and bloody, but here we are."

My head pounded.

Here I was.

I've been given a second chance.

I wasn't so rotten that I deserved to die; wasn't so evil to merit a one-way ticket to hell.

I'm not going to waste it.

I would use this new life to fix all my wrongs and ensure I deserved the luck I'd been given.

"H—how l—long?"

Doctor Louille ran a hand over his moustache. "You were in surgery for three hours and asleep for three days in intensive care. Your vitals were finally strong enough to wean you off the sedative and let nature take its course."

Three days?

Three fucking days!

Shit, what about Nila?

My heart clanged out of control. An exorbitant amount of adrenaline swamped me. Hurling myself upward, I lurched for the edge of the bed. Pain be damned. Motherfucking bullet wound be damned.

Three days!

"I—I have to g—go."

Louille slammed his hands on my shoulders, pushing me back against the mattress. "What the hell are you doing? I just told you you were lucky. You trying to ruin that luck?"

I struggled, seeing a clock ticking closer to Nila's death everywhere I looked.

Nila!

Three days!

What had they done to her in that time?

"Let—let me g—go!"

"No chance in hell, buddy. You're my patient. You'll follow my rules." Louille's fingers dug into my biceps, holding me in place. "Calm down or I'll restrain you. You want that?"

I froze, breath wheezing in and out. My stomach gnashed with agonising pain.

Three days...

My energy disappeared. A wash of sickness almost made me vomit. *Oh, fuck.* The room turned upside down.

Louille sympathised, letting me go. "The nausea will pass. It's the morphine. Just lie still and you'll be okay."

All I could think about was Nila and the fact I'd abandoned her.

Fuck!

"Molly, perhaps increase Mr. Ambrose's dose and arrange a sedative."

"No!" I'd already lost so much time. No way in hell would I lose anymore. I needed every minute awake to heal and run back to my woman.

My eyes fell on a girl in the background. A nurse with blonde hair in a bun and a clipboard in her hand. Her emotions were shuttered, barely registering on my condition. Either she guarded herself well or the nausea kept my sensitivity to a minimum.

Forcing myself to remain sane—at least until the doctor left so I could plan my escape—I asked, "H—how long will I h—have to s—stay here?"

"Why? You got some skiing trip to attend in Switzerland?" Doctor Louille laughed. When he noticed I was dead serious, he cleared his throat. "I estimate three weeks to be fully fixed. Two weeks for the wound to heal and another week for the internal bruising to recede. Twenty-one days, Mr. Ambrose, then I'll sign the discharge papers and send you on your merry way."

Three weeks?

Fuck, I couldn't wait that long.

Even three days drove me insane.

I shook my head. "I can't be a—away for that l—length of ti—time."

Don't give up on me, Nila.

I had to be there to keep her safe. She couldn't be subjected to more horror—especially at the hands of my bastard father and brother.

Fuck, fuck, fuck!

My heart squeezed like a fucking lemon, cauterizing my insides with citric acid at the thought of her being so vulnerable and alone.

"I'm sorry, Mr. Ambrose, but you're not fit to leave. And you're under my care until I say you are." Turning his attention to the nurse, he waved her closer. "Give me that phone number. We best let the family know he's awake."

My heart burst through my ribs. "Wh—what family?"

Don't tell my bastard father.

I'd be poisoned or slaughtered before the day was done.

Doctor Louille reached for the phone on the white bedside table. Everything in the room was either white, glass, or light blue. A flat-screen TV hung on the wall, while a small table and chairs squashed in the corner.

"The woman who dropped you here, of course." He gnawed on his bottom lip as he dialled a number and put the phone to his ear. He waited for it to connect. "Yes, hello, Ms. Ambrose? Yes, it's Doctor Jack Louille calling."

A pause.

"I have some good news. He's just woken up. I'll put him on."

Covering the mouthpiece, he passed the phone to me. My mind whirled, trying to keep up. I shook my head. What if this was a trap? What if it was Bonnie?

The doctor didn't take my hesitation as any sign to stop his persistence. "It's your sister. She's called every hour for the past few days. Get her off my back and let her know you're okay." Nudging the phone into my hands, he said, "Talk to her. Rest. I'll be back later to answer any more questions and assess your pain levels. And keep your arse in bed, or else."

My fingers curled around the phone.

No promises.

I was running as soon as I could breathe without wanting to throw up.

I trembled, battling tiredness and the thought of talking to someone still at

Hawksridge, someone I loved, someone I'd failed as much as I'd failed Nila.

Waiting until the doctor and nurse had left, I held the phone to my mouth. "H—hello?"

The longest pause crackled in my ear.

"H—hello? You there?"

A sniff came down the line. "About bloody time, you bloody arse."

My heart beat stronger.

I might have failed Nila.

I might have been dead for a few days.

But Jasmine had achieved the impossible. If she'd kept me alive, I had to trust she'd done the same for Nila.

"You al—always had a gr—great way with your t—temper, Jaz."

"God, it's truly you…" Her voice broke then she burst into noisy tears.

I found out later what she'd done for us. How she'd saved us. How Flaw had kept Kes and me alive long enough to smuggle us from the estate unseen. How he'd hidden us in the crypt, providing medicine, leaving us to slowly fossilize and turn into skeletons beneath the house I'd lived in all my life—working against the clock to get us somewhere safe.

I owed Flaw a huge debt. I would pay him handsomely. But I would also never underestimate my sister or take her for granted ever again. I couldn't believe she'd willingly left Hawksridge.

After a lifetime of chaining herself to the Hall, she'd commandeered one of the many vehicles in our garage and somehow delivered Kes and me to the hospital. From the way the doctors spoke, it sounded as if she'd only just made it. Another hour or two and Kestrel would've been dead and me not long after.

How she managed to do that, I had no idea. The phone call had been brief, hushed—a quick catch-up so Bonnie wouldn't overhear. Her relief had been genuine, but she'd also kept something from me.

Something I meant to find out.

After I hung up, the nurse had slipped back in and against my wishes fed more sedative into my drip.

I couldn't try to run. I couldn't assess how weak I was. All I could do was slip into empty dreams like some drugged arsehole. Nila didn't come visit me and I awoke pissed and hurting a few hours later.

Kestrel stole my thoughts for the billionth time since I'd woken. My heart splintered for my brother.

According to Louille, he still hadn't woken up. He was in intensive care and an induced coma. The bullet I'd saved Jaz from had been a clean shot. By Louille's own admission, I was a 'luckster', a fluke of nature, a fucking miracle. No bones shattered, no organs ruptured. A single entry and exit wound leaving me bleeding and infected but otherwise intact.

But if I was a miracle, then that came with certain obligations and privileges.

Privileges I would call on in order to end the man who'd killed me.

Obligations I meant to uphold now I was free.

I'd returned from the dead.

And I'd bring the wrath of hell toward my enemies.

DIARY ENTRY, EMMA Weaver.

He told me tonight. Lying in my arms, believing he was safe, he told me what he did to his brother. Part of me can understand it—to spend a lifetime being told you're second best, only to snap when something you want more than anything torments you. But another part of me could never understand because I could never be that selfish, self-centred, or cruel. One thing is for sure—his children are damned. Even the ones not infected with his madness are ruined because of what their father did to their mother and uncle.

A shrill ringing pierced my concentration.

No!

I had to find out what Cut did. Why were Jethro and his siblings damned? What the hell happened all those years ago?

Three days had passed. Three nights where I slept in sheets fading with Jethro's scent. Three mornings where I'd paced and fretted and begged. Daniel had been offsite, leaving me to boredom rather than torture. I hadn't seen Vaughn or Cut, and I'd been kept isolated, locked inside my room like a true prisoner.

Wasting three days in limbo was sacrilege. I wanted *vengeance*. However, my mind couldn't stop swimming with worry. Jethro, Jethro, *Jethro*. Nothing else mattered. Nothing else was important.

The discordant ringing persisted; I wrenched my eyes from the remaining blank page. There was no more. My mother had left the mystery unsolved.

The Weaver Journal was the only thing with the power to steal me away from repeating thoughts of Jethro. However, reading the journal's pages gave me the strangest sensation—as if I'd lifted up the veil of time and looked at Hawksridge in a capsule of *then* and *now*. Hearing about Jethro when he was young, about Bryan loving my mother, and even Bonnie thanking Emma for making her dresses—it was surreal.

Wrong.

Ring. Ring. Ring!

Tossing away the journal, I scrambled out of bed. Dashing across the room, I peered at yards of apricot fleece, searching for the origin of the ringing. Pushing aside fabric and opening a small cubby inside the storage cupboard, I found the source.

What on earth? Why have I never seen this before?

Plucking the phone off its tarnished cradle, I held it to my ear. "Hello?"

Instantly, a female voice said, "He's awake."

My knees gave out.

Slamming against the dresser, I clutched the edge. Adrenaline drenched my system like a tropical rainstorm. No matter how much I'd prayed and hoped he'd stay alive, I hadn't truly believed it.

"Are—are you sure?" My voice was quiet as a mouse. "How can you be sure?"

Don't give me false hope. I won't be able to stand it.

"I'm sure." Jaz sniffed happily. "I spoke to him myself."

My heart leapt over mountains of joy. Bending forward, I placed my forehead on trembling hands. "Thank heavens."

Jaz didn't speak for a moment.

I stayed silent, too.

Both of us breathed loudly, living in happiness bought with hard-earned fortune.

Things would be better now.

Letting the knowledge settle, I focused on the other man in my heart. "V…did you move him?"

"Yes. He's in a different room. Warm with regular food." She paused. "I'll keep an eye on him. I promise."

I squeezed my eyes. "Thank you."

An awkward silence fell, amplifying our unspoken need to talk about Jethro.

Jethro is still heir. He'll end this. I know he will.

"Jasmine? How—how long—?"

How long will he be gone?

I was greedy. He'd been awake for only minutes, yet I wanted him now. I wanted to touch him, kiss him, hold him—cradle the truth in my hands. But that wasn't my only reason. The real reason sat like a sinister splodge on my joy. *How long will I have to endure Cut's whims?*

I'd been lucky these past three days. I had no illusion that luck would last.

Jasmine read between the lines. "How long is irrelevant. You're mine. I'll do what I promised, Nila."

Fresh tears sparked into being. "I know."

You'll do your best, but ultimately, I'm alone.

Just like I'd been alone when Jethro controlled my fate. I guess nothing had changed. It was still up to me to slice out their loathsome hearts.

"And Ke—" I cut myself off. *Stay in riddles and code.* Who knew what lines were tapped and which walls had ears. "The other one…is he awake?"

Jasmine sighed heavily. "No."

The single word throbbed with sadness, giving no room for questions.

A loud rustle, then a quick, "I've got to go." A second later, the dial tone rang loud and empty.

Pushing away from the cupboard, I placed the phone back onto its cradle. Her phone call left me jumpy with hope and desolate with sorrow. I wanted them both to make it—hearing only Jethro was awake was bittersweet.

He's awake!

I hugged myself.

He hasn't left me.

Slowly, I padded toward the bed where I'd set down the Weaver Journal.

At the last second, I changed my mind. I couldn't handle reading about ancient conspiracies and pain. I needed to cleanse my thoughts with something I had utter control over.

Switching direction to the chaise lounge, I upended the basket where I'd stuffed a damask panel and Georgian lace.

He's awake.

Those two words were now my favourite in the entire English language. I smoothed out the damask and pulled a needle free from a pincushion.

He's awake.

Better than alive.

He's awake.

Fate had finally been kind—the tables had finally turned.

Everything will be different now.

Cut, Daniel, and Bonnie would take Jethro and Kestrel's place in the ground. The balance of good and evil would right itself. And Vaughn and I would continue with whatever dreams we had with no guillotine hanging over our future.

Switching on another side lamp, I bent to my task of repairing the lace with painstaking needlework. It wasn't late, but the sun had set a few hours ago and Hawksridge creaked around me, depositing its residents into the night. The growls of motorbikes shattered the wintery air, Black Diamonds disappearing to run another smuggling delivery.

I lost myself in the exquisite craftsmanship, giving myself over to scattered thoughts. Jaz and Vaughn's rescue mission had gone unnoticed. Flaw had done the impossible. Jethro had cheated death.

We won.

Could Cut tell? Could he feel that his sons weren't dead?

It didn't matter.

His arrogance was his undoing.

Tick tock. Tick tock.

His time is running out.

"She wants you, Nila."

My head snapped up.

My room was no longer empty. It had invited a visitor while I napped on the chaise. The lace I'd been working on littered the carpet and the needle harpooned my denim skirt, sticking upward like a tiny lance.

Flaw headed toward me, hands in his pockets. "Did you hear me?"

I blinked.

By day, I left the dresser pushed away from the doorway in case legitimate requests meant I had to open it quickly. But by night, I shoved the heavy armoire across, allowing a false sense of safety.

How long have I been asleep?

Sunshine sparkled on the horizon, turning my side lamp mute with fresh daylight.

Oh, my God, I slept all night?

I didn't feel rested. I felt tired and foggy.

Jethro...

He'd been in my thoughts all day. All night. All my life.

He's awake!

I missed him so much—missed his golden eyes, his hesitant smile. I missed the epiphany when he finally broke and let me put him back together again.

I miss you...

"Nila...you awake or sleep walking?" Flaw clicked his fingers in front of my face.

I flinched. "I'm awake. Sorry, just a bit fuzzy."

"When was the last time you slept properly?"

I shrugged, plucking the needle from my skirt and stabbing it into the pincushion. "Can't remember." My eyes burned from tiredness; wooziness existed in my brain.

He scowled. "You do realise they're safe. You can relax a bit without grief ruining your sleep."

Standing, my body creaked in protest from sleeping on the chaise. I stumbled forward with vertigo and my cell-phone thudded to the carpet by my feet.

Huh. *I don't remember retrieving it from my bedside.*

Flaw stayed silent as I blinked away my illness and collected it from the floor. I must've grabbed it while dreaming, hoping for a text.

Did he message?

I swiped it on.

Nothing.

No messages. No calls. No emails.

I've been completely forgotten.

Some part of me hoped that now Jethro was awake, he'd text me. That for the first time in months, we'd talk like we had before this mess started. Kite to Threads. Inbox to inbox.

"Has he been in touch?" Flaw glanced at my phone.

My lungs deflated; I shook my head. "No." Brushing stray hair from my eyes, I said, "I heard that he's awake, though. You?"

A slight smile tilted his lips. "Yes. She told me."

I smiled back. I'd entered Hawksridge believing everyone was my enemy. Turned out, only a few people were worthy of that title. Most of them were kind and honourable, wrapped up in their own issues, but ultimately generous and just like any stranger—frightening and mysterious until the boundary of no acquaintance distorted into friendship.

Kes had proven that. Then Jasmine. And now Flaw.

I knew all along I could win Jethro.

In a way, I think I'd known he was mine ever since I was young.

Once this was all over, I wanted to find out how many times we'd met. How many instances we'd spoken in our childhood—being groomed for our roles.

"Anyway." Flaw swayed on his heels. "I'm not here for a social call. Been instructed to bring you to her majesty."

My eyes widened. "What?"

"Not the Queen of England." He smirked. "The Queen of Hawksridge." Jamming his hands deeper into his pockets, his eyes darkened. "She wants a word."

"A word or a beating?" I clutched my phone. "A conversation with the old bat, *alone*, isn't high on my list of priorities."

If you're alone, though, you could kill her.

The thought welded me to the carpet.

"I wouldn't recommend calling her 'old bat' in person, if I were you."

My mind ran away, forgetting Flaw existed. The only way I could kill those who needed to die was to be strategic. I couldn't do it around others. I couldn't do it in plain sight. I had to be sneaky and wily and smart.

Every night, I stared into the darkness, using the black emptiness as a chalkboard for my plotting. I wished I had a treadmill in my room. Running always helped me problem solve. But even though my body remained stationary, it didn't mean my mind did.

I'd never been so enamoured with death before or so hyped on hypothetical murder.

I knew from television to expect copious amounts of blood and a struggle if I stabbed my victims to death. I also knew that strength would mean nothing against Cut and Daniel, so I had to have the element of surprise.

A gun would've solved my problems, but the noise and lack of experience in aiming could potentially be my downfall.

All opportunities led to one conclusion…I had to be quick and quiet. I had to be *ruthless*. And it had to look like an accident or remain hidden long enough to steal three lives before I was slaughtered in retribution.

I can't kill Bonnie.

Not yet. It had to be Daniel or Cut first…then her.

She'll be my last.

"You better go. I doubt she'll make allowances for lateness even if you haven't written her on your social calendar." Flaw's voice dripped with sarcasm. "New day. New psychological plague to administer."

I narrowed my gaze. "Ha-ha. Not funny."

Taking a deep breath, I placed my cell-phone on the end of the bed. "I guess I have no choice." Spinning to face him, I gathered my long hair and secured it in a messy ponytail with an elastic band from my wrist. "Did she say why at least?"

"Do I look like I have tea and crumpets with the fucking woman?" Flaw rolled his eyes. "All I was told was to get you." He held up his hands. "And no, I don't have insider knowledge like I did with the lawyers. This time, you're on your own."

His eyes skated down my white jumper with a filigree seahorse and denim skirt. "I, eh…don't have to tell you what happened a few days ago has to remain secret…no matter what she, eh…does?"

My heart spiralled into a tailspin. "What are you saying? She'll torture me?"

I was no stranger to pain but deliberate extraction of information through agony? *How long can I endure something like that?*

He stiffened. "If she knew you had something you weren't telling…I wouldn't put it past her." Coming closer, the strain around his mouth and eyes was prevalent.

I'm not the only one not sleeping.

"I don't need to tell you how——"

"How important it is that those who shall not be named remain dead?

Yes, I understand." I placed my hand on his arm. "I won't tattle. What you did to help them has firmly earned my loyalty. My lips are sealed."

The air in the room turned heavy with seriousness. "I'd understand if she did something to make you tell."

I blanched. "You think I'll crack? I'm in love with him. There's no way in hell I would jeopardise their lives."

His shoulders slumped. "Okay. Sorry for pushing. My neck's on the line, too."

I dropped my touch. "I know. You've gone above and beyond...only..."

My forehead furrowed. Details were often the crux of impending ruin. Flaw and Jaz had freed them, but now Jethro and Kes were in the hands of doctors, nurses, and people who would talk.

"Only what?" Flaw prompted.

"How did you do it?"

He pursed his lips. "Do what?"

I lowered my voice to a whisper. "Get them to the basement. How—"

"Easy." He ran a hand through his hair, wincing at memories. "Don't suppose you know how many secrets live on the estate. How many animals exist—all bred for different purposes."

"What do you mean?"

"Well, you've seen the pheasants for shooting, horses for riding, dogs for hunting. But I doubt you'll have seen the pigs."

I took a step back. *"Pigs?"*

"Pigs are an excellent way to dispose of things you never want found again."

My mouth hung open. "Excuse me?" In the months I'd lived in Hawksridge, I hadn't seen a single pig. "Where?"

"They're hidden over the chase. Having a few pigs and not a pig farm can be suspicious these days, thanks to the recent mobster movies, serving shall we say 'alternative food.'"

I wrung my hands. "You're saying Cut feeds his enemies as food to his pigs?" My gullet churned, wanting to evict all knowledge of this conversation. "Shit, he's barbaric."

Worse than that—he has sewage for a soul.

Flaw raised an eyebrow, neither confirming nor denying it. "Whatever you think, it's smart business." His voice lowered to a sepulchral whisper. "Anyway, Cut asked me to get rid of their bodies. Only, Kes and Jethro had already come to me first. They knew something like this might happen. After all, they've been playing with their lives for months. We'd all agreed that I would remain in Cut's good graces and do what I could to give them a second chance."

I kept my voice quiet—hidden from microphones trying to record our treason. "But how did he not notice they were still alive?"

He frowned. "What do you mean?"

Pacing away, I scowled. "Didn't he ask if they were dead? Didn't he get on his knees and see for himself if he'd killed his sons?" Even asking those questions turned my saliva into a sickly paste. How could a father not even stand over his children and say a prayer or goodbye? How could he just pass off their remains to a servant without a backward glance?

A monster, that's who.

Flaw grinned, a calculating glint in his eyes. "Aren't you glad he didn't? If he had, the outcome of this would've been entirely different."

Ice ran through my blood. *He's right.*

In a way, Cut's cold-heartedness had destroyed Kes and Jethro but saved them, too.

"Once I'd removed them from the lounge, it was a simple matter to take them where I needed. Cut didn't question me. In fact, I happen to know Jasmine kept him and Bonnie plenty entertained with her screaming about wanting revenge on you." His eyes warmed. "That girl thinks fast on her feet. It was a good diversion."

Yes and kept me safe from the full Debt Inheritance.

I ought to be nicer to Jasmine. The risk she'd played would've silenced any lesser woman. She truly was Jethro's sister—strong, formidable, and slightly scary with her temper.

"After I returned from hiding them and setting up the medical equipment, I reported to Cut that it was done." He rubbed the back of his neck. "All he cared about was if the carpet was cleaned."

My heart shattered under an anvil of hostility.

Cut was more worried about an object than his sons' souls.

Utter bastard. Sick, twisted freak.

And who taught him those qualities? His dear old mother.

Bonnie—the female version of the devil.

My hands balled. "I've heard enough."

Bonnie had summoned me. She'd scared and intimidated me but she was no match for my sheer hatred. I wanted to throw her in a cauldron and watch her bones bleach white. I wanted to behead her and witness her body twitch with death throes.

That'll come true before this is over.

"Take me to her. It's time we had a little chat."

"About bloody time." Bonnie sniffed as Flaw beckoned me over the threshold.

The second my sock-covered feet padded onto the pale pink carpet of Bonnie's domain, he cocked his chin in goodbye and abandoned me behind the closed door.

All alone.

An opportunity or a disadvantage?

She couldn't hurt me. Names and slurs weren't enough to subdue me anymore.

Screw surprise and secrecy.

If I have an opportunity, I'm taking it.

"What do you have to say for yourself, girl? Tardiness is a dirty sin and must be abolished." Bonnie tapped her cane like a cat flicked its tail.

No matter how much time I spent in the Hall, I doubted I would ever explore all the rooms and levels it offered. Bonnie's quarters were yet another surprise. Flaw had guided me up the stone staircase where Jasmine and Cut's study rested, only to pace down a different corridor and up another set of stairs made of winding red carpet and unicorn spindles.

Straightening my shoulders, I looked down my nose at the shrivelled old woman. "I have nothing to say for myself. I was in the middle of something important. I couldn't let a simple summoning derail me."

She made a strange wheeze—like wind through wheat or ghosts over a graveyard. "You insolent little—"

"Guttersnipe. Yes, I've heard it before." Moving forward, I didn't ask permission as I inspected her domain. Every part of me shook. I was angry, afraid, livid, *terrified*. Lying in the dark, bolstering my courage and fermenting in hatred hadn't prepared me for face-to-face duelling. This was new—putting my thoughts into action.

Now that I knew Jethro was alive, I had something to risk.

A future.

Jethro's alive.

I'm alive.

We can be alive together—far away from here.

If I became too impertinent, I could ruin my plans and destroy my future. But if I didn't stand up to them, I might not see the next debt coming—just like I didn't see the Third Debt until it was too late.

I had to be strong but aware, vengeful but intelligent—it was an exhausting place to be.

Bonnie's room wasn't what I expected. The peach coloured walls, white fireplace, and rose fleurs on the ceiling plasterwork all spoke of a law-abiding, cookie-baking grandmother.

How can a room fulfil the stereotype of elderly nana when the woman is anything but?

The wainscoting gleamed with gold wallpaper, while cross-stitch framed artwork graced every inch of wall space depicting bumblebees, dragonflies, and multihued butterflies.

I expected torture equipment and the blood of her many victims on the wall.

Not this…

I hated this room because it made me doubt. Had she been nice once upon a time? Had she become this hard-hearted dinosaur thanks to situations in her past? What had Cut done to his brother in order to turn his mother into such a beast?

Because it had to be his doing. Whatever happened with his brother reeked of sedition and backstabbing lies.

It doesn't matter.

She is what she is.

And she'd pay for what she'd done.

Bonnie didn't say a word, watching me with the signature Hawk attentiveness. The room throbbed with power; subjugation coming from her and rebellion from me. If our wills could battle, the tension would suffocate with unseen clashes.

I paused over a particular stitched oval, trying to make out if it was a praying mantis or a stick insect.

"Jasmine did them for me." Bonnie's voice was sweet venom. "Such a wonderful, obedient granddaughter. It was part of her etiquette and decorum training."

My eyes widened. "She did all of them?"

Bonnie nodded. "You're not the only one good with a needle and thread, girl." Snapping her fingers, reminding me so clearly of her grandson who rested in some hospital, she said, "Come closer. I refuse to scream. And you need to pay strict attention."

My socks ghosted over the pale pink flooring, sinking into a few sheepskin rugs before stopping beside Bonnie Hawk. My nose wrinkled at the familiar smell of rose water and overly sweet confectionary. I didn't need to know her diet to guess she loved desserts.

She was rotten—just like her teeth from consuming too much sugar.

In my head, I cursed and hexed her, but outwardly, I stood calm and silent.

Do your worst, witch. It won't be good enough.

She narrowed her eyes, inspecting me from head to toe. I let her, glancing out the window instead. Her chair rested beside a long table pressed up against the lead light glass overlooking the south gardens of Hawksridge. A water fountain splashed merrily, depicting two fawns playing a pipe. The colourful pansies and other flowers that'd run rampant when I first arrived had long since gone dormant, replaced by skeleton shrubs and the dull brown of winter.

"Do you have any skills in this arena?" Bonnie pointed at the hobby scattered over the table. The array of dried and freshly cut flowers painted the table in a rainbow of stamens and petals. Roses, tulips, lilies, orchids. The perfume from dying flora helped counteract the sickly stench of Bonnie.

"No. I've never arranged flowers, if that's what you're asking."

She pursed her lips. "Hardly a lady fit for society. What skills apart from sewing do you have then? Enlighten me." Reaching for a crystal vase, she snapped off a piece of green foam and shoved it into the bottom. "Well...go on then, girl. Don't make me ask twice."

What the hell is going on here?

The past few days had a strange consistency, as if I was stuck in quicksand. If I moved, it sucked me further into its clutches, but if I stayed still, it treated me as a friend—keeping me buoyant in its greedy granules.

What's her point?

My back stiffened, but I forced myself to stay cordial. "I run my own fashion line. I can sew any item of clothing. My attention to detail—"

"Shut up. That is all one skill. One lonely talent. A frivolous career for a trollop such as yourself."

Don't retaliate. Do not stoop to her bait.

If her aim was to make me snap so she could punish me, then she'd lose. I'd learned from them how to fight.

My hand rubbed my lower back, checking my dirk was in place and ready to be used.

Wouldn't now be the perfect time to dispatch her?

We were alone. Behind closed doors. Regardless of my past conclusion to kill Cut and Daniel first, I couldn't waste an opportunity.

My arm tensed, agreeing.

Do it.

Almost as if she sensed my thoughts, Bonnie cooed, "Oh, Marquise? Can you come in here, please?"

Immediately, a door I didn't see, camouflaged with matching wallpaper, opened. Marquise, a Black Diamond brother with shoulders like a submarine and long greasy hair pulled into a ponytail, appeared. "Yes, Madame."

Shit.

Bonnie's eyes glinted. "Could you keep us company, dear? Just sit quietly and don't interrupt. There's a good chap."

"No problem." He flicked a glance at me.

I hid my scowl as Marquise did as bade and perched his colossal bulk on a dainty carved chair. I was surprised the tiny legs didn't snap under his weight.

"Now, what were we saying?" Bonnie patted her lips with a fresh rose.

I didn't know how she'd read my body language so perfectly, but it put me on the back foot. I swallowed, letting go of my dirk. Grabbing a lily, I twirled it in my fingers. "Nothing of importance."

Bonnie glared. "Ah, that's where you're wrong. It was *very* important." Snipping the end of the rose with sharp shears, she jabbed the stem into the green foam at the bottom of the vase.

She caught me looking. "It's called an oasis. It's flower arranging basics. If you'd applied yourself at all, you would know that."

My skin prickled. Hemmed between Bonnie and Marquise, my hands were tied, my mouth effectively gagged.

Damn you, witch.

"Applied myself? I was working until 10:00 p.m. most nights before I'd even turned twelve. I sewed my way through high school and college—I had no free time to indulge in useless hobbies."

Bonnie swivelled in her chair. Her eyes shadowed, cheeks powered white. "Watch your tongue. I won't put up with such contumelious talk."

I sucked in a breath, doing my best to be quiet even though I wanted to stab her repeatedly. My eyes skittered to Marquise.

Damn him, too.

Grabbing a sprig of leaves, she wedged the plume into the oasis. "Know why I summoned you?"

My fingers tightened around the lily. I wanted to crush the white petals and scatter them over Bonnie's coffin.

A coffin I'll put her in.

"I've long since given up trying to understand you." I narrowed my eyes, unable to hide my livid hatred. "Any sane person could never guess what madness will do or not do."

Bonnie scowled.

Her tiny stature sat proud and stiff; arthritic fingers tossed aside a newly snipped tulip and wrapped around her walking stick. Never breaking eye contact, she stood from her chair and inched forward.

I stood my ground even though every part of me vibrated with the urge to smash the crystal vase over her head.

We didn't speak as the distance closed between us. For an old woman, she wasn't bowed or creaky. She moved slowly but with purpose. Hazel eyes sharp and cruel and her signature red lipstick smeared thin lips. "That mouth of yours will be taught a lesson now that you're in my youngest grandson's care."

Not if I kill him first.

I balled my hands, keeping my chin high as Bonnie circled around me like a decrepit raptor. Stopping behind me, she tugged my long hair. "Cut this. It's far too long."

Locking my knees, I forced myself to remain tall. She'd lost the power to make me cower. "It's my hair, *my* body. I can do whatever the hell I want with it."

She yanked on the strands. "Think again, Weaver." Letting me go, she continued her perusal, coming to a stop in front of me. Her eyes came to my chin. The height difference helped me in some small margin to look down on her—both physically and metaphorically.

This woman was as twisted as the boughs of an ancient tree, but unlike a tree, her heart had blackened and withered. She'd lived long enough. It was time she left the world, letting bygones be bygones.

Her breath rattled in antique lungs, sounding rusty and ill-used.

Minutes screeched past, both of us waiting to see what the other would do. I broke first, but only because my patience where Bonnie was concerned was non-existent.

Jethro's alive.

The sooner I evicted Bonnie from my presence, the sooner I could think about him again.

"Spit it out."

She froze. "Spit what out?"

My spine curved toward her, bringing our faces closer. The waft of sugar and flowers wrapped around my gag reflex. "What do you want from me?"

Her gaze tightened. "I want a great deal from you, child. And your impatience won't make me deliver it any faster." Snatching my wrist, she grabbed a thorny rose from the table and punctured my palm with the devilish bloom.

I bit my lip as blood welled.

She chuckled. "That's for not knowing how to flower arrange."

She let me go. Instead of dropping the rose, I curled my hand around it, digging the thorn deeper into my flesh. If I couldn't withstand the discomfort of a small prick, how did I hope to withstand more?

This is my weapon.

Conditioning myself to pain so it no longer controlled me.

Blood puddled, warm and sticky, in my closed fist. Taking a breath, I reached around Bonnie and elegantly placed the rose into the oasis, opening my palm and raining droplets of blood all over virgin petals and tablecloth. "Oops."

Bonnie's face blackened as I wiped the remaining crimson on a fancy piece of ribbon. "Anyone can arrange flowers, but it takes a seamstress to turn blood into a design." My voice lowered, recalling how many nights I'd sliced myself with scissors or pricked myself with needles. I was used to getting hurt in the process of creation.

This was no different.

I would be hurt in the process of something far more noble—*fighting for my life.*

"You can't scare me anymore." I held up my palm, shoving it in her face. "Blood doesn't scare me. Threats don't scare me. I know what you are and you're just a weak, old woman who hides behind insanity like it's some mystical power."

Marquise stood from his chair by the wall. "Madame?"

I glanced at him, throwing a condescending smile. "Don't interrupt two women talking. If she can't handle a silly little Weaver, then she has no right to pretend otherwise."

"Sit down, Marquise." Bonnie breathed hard, glaring at me. "I've never met someone so unrefined and uncouth."

"You obviously never paid close attention to your granddaughter then."

She's rough as sandpaper and tough as steel.

Jasmine could lie like the best of them, but beneath that silk and satin façade, she outweighed me in strength of temper ten to one.

Why tell Bonnie that then? Shut up.

Bonnie shoved her finger in my face. "Don't talk about her. Jasmine is a woman of eloquence. She knows how to speak three languages, play the piano, stitch, sing, and run a time-worn estate. She outranks you in every conceivable way."

She has you fooled as wonderfully as she did me.

My respect for Jasmine increased a hundred-fold.

If any of us were playing the game best—it was her. *She* was the true chameleon, pulling the wool over not just her grandmother's eyes but her father's and brother's, too.

She's a powerful ally to have.

I couldn't stop pride and annoyance from blurting: "Shame you're delusional as well as decrepit."

Bonnie's papery hand struck my cheek. Her palm didn't make a sound on my flesh, merely a swat with no sting. She might have the power of speech and ferocity, but when it came to physical threats—she was brittle and weak.

"My family eclipses yours in every way. It's a shame you didn't have such an upbringing. Perhaps you would be more pleasing company if you—"

I couldn't listen to her cackling drone anymore.

"You're right. It *is* a shame I didn't have someone there to teach me how to do my makeup or bake cakes or learn an instrument. I'm sure I would've been happier and more rounded if I grew up with a mother. But she was taken from me by *you*. Don't twist my past and make it seem like I'm some underprivileged girl who's here by the grace of your family because I'm not. I'm your *prisoner,* and I hate you." I backed away from the table. "I hate you, and you *will* pay for what you've done."

Her face twisted with rage. "You ungrateful little—"

"I agree. I *have* been ungrateful. I've been ungrateful for falling in love with a good man only for it to be too late. I've been ungrateful for a brother I adore and a father who's been lost since his wife was taken. But I'm not ungrateful for this. I've found a fucking backbone, and I mean to use it."

Marquise stomped forward. "Madame. Just give the word."

I threw a caustic look at both of them. "You're proving Bonnie's too weak to discipline me herself."

"Enough!" Bonnie brought her walking stick down onto the table with a resounding *thwack.* "Don't you dare use my name without my permission!"

"Tell me what you want then, so I don't have to look at you. I don't want to be here another minute."

Don't go too far.

Bonnie convulsed. Her face turned puce, and for a second, I hoped she'd die—just keel over from exploding blood pressure or ruptured ego.

Don't get yourself killed over pettiness.

I had a lot more to achieve before that day.

Swallowing hard, Bonnie clasped both hands on her cane. Her thick skirts rustled as her ancient carcass bristled. "Fine. I'll take great pleasure in doing so."

God, I feel sick. I don't want to know.

"Just let me leave. I've had enough." Storming to the door, I tried the handle, only to find it locked. The air turned thick, the heating too hot. I'd drenched my system in too much adrenaline and now paid the price.

Pacing in a circle, I ran my hands through my hair. "You hear me? You make me sick, and unless you let me out, I'll just vomit all over your precious study."

Vertigo swooped in, throwing me to the side.

Jethro's alive.

He's alive.

I need to stay that way, too.

I gulped, needing fresh air. I'd never been claustrophobic, but the walls loomed closer, triggering another vertigo wave, forcing me to bend forward to keep the room steady.

Bonnie limped closer. "You're not going anywhere. You want to know why I summoned you? Time to find out."

Every cell urged me to back away, but I held my ground. I refused to be intimidated. Swallowing back nausea and dizziness, I gritted my teeth.

Bonnie pointed at the wall behind me with her walking stick. "Go on. Look over there. You want me to get on with my point? The answers are there."

Suspicion and rancour ran rampant in my blood, but I found the courage to turn my back on her and face the wall. My skin crawled to have her behind me—like some viper about to strike, but then my eyes fell on a few grainy sepia-toned photographs. The pictures' time-weathered quality hinted that they were old. Older than Bonnie, by far.

Drifting closer, I inspected the image. In browns and sienna, the fuzzy photograph depicted a man in a fur coat with a pipe furling with smoke. Snow banks hid parts of Hawksridge, making it seem like some fantastical castle.

There's something about him.

I peered harder at the man's face and froze.

Oh, my God.

Jethro?

It couldn't be. The picture was ancient. There was no way it could be him.

Bonnie sidled up beside me, dabbing her nose with a handkerchief. "Notice the resemblance?"

I hated that she'd intrigued me when I wanted nothing more than to act uninterested and aloof. My lips pinched together, refusing to ask what she was obviously dying to say.

"That's Jethro's great, great grandfather. They look similar. Don't you think?"

Similar?

They looked like the same person.

Thick tinsel hair swept back off sculptured cheekbones and highbrows. Lips sensual but masculine, body regal and powerful, even the man's hands looked like Jethro's, wrapped around his pipe tenderly as if it were a woman's breast.

My breast.

My cheeks warmed, thinking what good hands Jethro had. What a good lover he was. How cruel he could be but so utterly tender, too.

My heart raced, falling in love all over again as memories bombarded me.

Jethro, I miss you.

Having a likeness of him only made our separation that much more painful. My fingertips itched to trace the photograph, wanting to transmit a hug to him—let him know I hadn't forgotten him. That I was fighting for him, fighting for a future together.

Bonnie coughed wetly. "Answer me, child."

"Yes, they look similar. Eerily so." My eyes trailed to the following photographs, hidden between cross-stitches. One picture had the entire household staff standing in ranking order on the front steps of Hawksridge. Butlers and housekeepers, maids and footmen. All sombre and fierce, staring into the camera.

"These are the few remaining images after an unfortunate fire a few decades ago." Bonnie inched with me as I moved from picture to picture. I didn't know why I cared. This wasn't my heritage. But something told me I was about to learn something invaluable.

I was right.

Two more photographs before I discovered what Bonnie alluded to.

My eyes fell on a woman surrounded by dark fabric as if she swam in an ocean of it. Her tied-up hair cascaded from the top of her head thanks to a piece of white ribbon, and her eyes were alight with her craft. Her hands held a needle and thread, lace scattered like snow around her.

It was like staring into a mirror.

No...

My heart bucked, rejecting the image, unable to make sense of how it was possible. Unable to stop myself, one hand went to the photo, tracing the brow and lips of the mystery woman, while my other sketched my own forehead and mouth.

I was the perfect replica of this stranger. A mirror image.

She's me...I'm her...it doesn't make any sense.

"Know who that is?" Bonnie asked smugly.

I shook my head. There was no date or name. Only a woman caught in her element, sewing peacefully.

"That was your great, great grandmother, Elisa." Bonnie stroked the photo with swollen fingers. I wanted to snatch her hand away. She was my family, not hers.

Don't touch her.

Why didn't our family albums contain images of Elisa? Why had we kept no records or comprehensive history of what happened to our ancestors? Were we so weak a lineage that we preferred to bury our heads in the sand rather than learn from past mistakes and fight?

Who are we?

Dropping my hands, I breathed deeply. "What is her image doing on your wall?"

"To remind me that history isn't in the past."

I turned to face her. "What do you mean?"

Bonnie's hazel gaze was sharp and cruel. "I mean history repeats itself. You only have to look through generations of photographs to see the same person over and over again. It skips a few bloodlines; cheekbones are different, eye colours change, bodies evolve. But then along comes an offspring who defies logic. Neither looking like their current parents, or taking on the traits of evolution. Oh, no. Out pops an exact imposter of someone who lived over a century ago."

She looked me up and down, her nose wrinkling. "I don't believe in reincarnation, but I do believe in anomalies, and you, my child are the exact image of Elisa, and I fear the exact temperament, too."

A chill darted down my spine. "You say it like it's a bad thing." My eyes returned to the image. She looked fierce but content—resigned but strong.

She chuckled. "It is if you know the history."

Wrapping her seized fingers around my elbow, she pushed me onward, following a timeline of photos of Elisa and Jethro's great, great grandfather.

Seeing Jethro's doppelganger in images side by side with Elisa sent goosebumps scattering over my skin. "What was his name?"

"Owen." She paused by a particular one of Elisa and Owen staring sternly into the camera, spring buds on rose bushes and apple blossoms in the orchard behind them. They both looked distraught, trapped, *afraid*. "Owen 'Harrier' Hawk."

Did you have the same condition Jethro has, Owen? Were you the first to hate your family? Why didn't you do anything to change your future?

Bonnie let me go. "I could rattle off tales and incidents of what befell those two, but I'll let the images speak for themselves. After all, what is the common phrase? A picture tells a thousand words?" She laughed softly as I repelled away from her, drinking in image after image.

The copper and coffee tones led me from one end of the room to the other, following a wretched timeline of truth.

Bonnie was right. A picture did say a thousand words, and seeing it captured forever, imprisoned and immortalized, sank my heart further into despair.

Elisa slowly changed in each one.

I gasped as I stumbled onto the First Debt. An ochre image where blood wasn't red but burnt bronze, trickling from lash marks on Elisa's creamy back.

It was as if time played a horrible joke, slapping me with the knowledge that my life was on repeat—my very existence following in the footsteps of another, no matter how unique I felt.

Just like when Jethro came to collect me.

That night in Milan when I'd found out my life was never mine. That Jethro was just as indebted as me. That we were both prisoners of a tangled predetermined fate.

My limbs quaked as I moved to the next.

The tarnished image showed Owen, standing with the First Debt whip in his hand, a tortured expression on his face. He was more than just Jethro's ancestor—he could've been his identical twin. Seeing another man look so conflicted brought tears to my eyes. He tried to hide it, but regret and connection blazed through the grainy picture.

We weren't the only ones to fall in love.

Owen and Elisa had defied the Weaver-Hawk boundary and fallen hard.

Photo after photo.

Trial after trial.

Their love deepened and blossomed, only to be slowly hacked away as time went on.

The Second Debt and the ducking stool. Elisa dangled on the same chair I'd been strapped to, the black lake glittering below her.

The Third Debt in the gaming den. Owen fisted crumpled playing cards, his mouth tight and unyielding, eyes begging for a reprieve.

Amongst the extracted debts were personal images. Photos of Elisa sewing, sitting in the gardens, trailing her fingers in the fountain, looking up at the cloud congested sky as if she could fly away. There were also secret images taken of Owen watching her, his fists in his pockets, his face transmitting apology, sorrow, *anguish*.

We're living their history.

An exact replica of two people's lifetimes that'd taken place decades ago.

Yet another example that I was no different from my ancestors. That I had no hope of changing my fate.

I jumped as Bonnie brushed aside my hair, her swollen knuckles hot against my throat. "See, child. You think you're different. You think you'd won by claiming the heart of my grandson, but I had forewarning." She waved at the timeline boldly placed on her walls like jewels. "I saw what happened with my ancestors before you even arrived. The day I saw the resemblance between Jethro and Owen, I studied the records. I armed myself years before you came to us. I knew you wouldn't behave. I knew this generation wouldn't be straightforward and I planned accordingly." Her smile was priggish. "There is no winning, Nila. Both of our families are cursed to bear such a trial, and only the worthy are permitted to inherit."

I couldn't reply.

Taking my wrist, she guided me toward the last seven images all framed in one intricate gilded frame. "Study this well, child. This is what happened to Elisa once Owen was dealt with for his infractions. And this is what will happen to you."

I clapped a hand over my mouth.

Owen was dealt with? He was killed, too?

My eyes burned as the sepia photos engraved themselves on my brain.

Torture after torture.

Misery after misery.

Methods I never knew existed.

Barbarous items I couldn't even name.

Elisa faded in each image from a fierce, heartbroken woman into a ghost already departing the world.

She suffered horrendously, subjected to methods of persecution no one could endure for long.

My soul wept for her. My temper broiled for her.

Poor woman. Poor girl.

Was this my fate? Would I become her?

Will I break eventually?

Bonnie stabbed the bottom picture where the only visible part of Elisa was her head. A large barrel with spikes driven through the sides encased her body. "Each of those is…what shall we call it…an extra toll you must pay. Disobedience is never tolerated—from a Weaver or a Hawk. Elisa watched Owen die and tried to return the favour by killing his father." She tapped my nose. "Just like I suspect you think you'll do, too."

I choked.

No…how could they…

"Are you planning on killing my remaining family, Nila?" Bonnie's voice dropped to a hiss. "Because let me tell you, you'll never achieve that. Not over my dead body."

My pulse exploded into supersonic beats, gushing blood, preparing to bolt.

Run!

I needed to be far away. Far, far away where they could never touch me again.

Slapping my cheek, her strike brought heat and clarity. "Look at me when I'm talking to you, child." Standing to her full height, she glared into my eyes. "I have news for you. Whatever plans you think you have, whatever backbone you think you've grown, and whatever revenge you think you'll deliver—forget all of it. You're done, you hear me? Jethro is dead. Kestrel is dead. There is no one here who will save you—including yourself. Starting tomorrow, you will pay for your sins. You will repent so your soul is pure enough to pay the Final Debt. You will lose, Ms. Weaver. Just like Elisa lost all those years ago.

"You're already a corpse, and there is nothing, absolutely *nothing*, you can do about it."

FOUR DAYS.

A full ninety-six hours since I'd awoken from surgery.

An eternity of staring at the powder blue ceiling with a cheerful puppy poster going out of my fucking mind with worry for Nila.

What were they doing to her?

How was she coping?

Jasmine had said she'd do everything in her power to keep her safe, but as much as I trusted and loved my sister, I knew what my brother and father were capable of.

She's not safe there.

I have to get her out.

I also knew what Bonnie was capable of and that scared me to fucking death.

Sighing heavily in the stagnant room, I gritted my teeth and pushed upright. I was sick of lying horizontally. I was pissed at being told what I could and couldn't do. And I'd had enough of trading one imprisonment for another.

Louille had threatened me on a daily basis with restraining me. Especially, when he'd found me on the floor the day after my surgery, bleeding from launching myself out of bed, believing I was cured enough to fight.

I was stupid to try—but I *had* to. I had no choice.

I couldn't just lie there. That wasn't an option. Nila needed me. And I wouldn't let her down again.

It's time to do things my fucking way. Otherwise, it will be too late.

The first three days, Louille had been a damn Nazi on my attempts to walk. I got that he was responsible for my welfare. That he'd done his job and patched me up to ensure I lived another day. But what he didn't get was I didn't *want* to live another fucking day if Nila wasn't there with me.

It's my responsibility, goddammit.

I wouldn't fail her. Ever again.

Yesterday, I'd won one battle. I positively despised my demotion to a lump of decomposing meat, lying in bed with drains in my side and a catheter in my fucking cock.

I'd shown just how healthy I was with a shouting match, ensuring the removal of the catheter and the drains. Time was an enemy but also a friend. Every *tick* left Nila out of my protection, but every *tock* healed me so I could finally set right my wrongs.

I just wished I had a magical device that paused time at Hawksridge and sped up my existence so I could be strong once again.

Wait for me, Nila.

Stay alive for me, Nila.

Swinging my legs over the side of the bed, I looked at the sterilized linoleum floor. At least I felt more like a man rather than a healing vegetable. The past few days had been awful, but I was getting better—no matter how weak I was.

I hated being so fucking feeble. Too feeble to be of any use.

But no matter my frustration, I couldn't battle through the tiredness or soreness of my body knitting back together. It healed as fast as it could. I just had to learn patience.

I snorted. *Yeah, right. Patience when my deranged family has my woman.* Like that would ever fucking happen.

You have no choice.

If only I could heal faster.

Taking a deep breath, I pushed off the bed. My bare feet slapped against cool flooring. The room swam, reminding me all too much of Nila and her imbalance. *We're perfect for each other.* Both slightly broken. Both slightly flawed. But perfectly whole once we let our hearts become one.

My toes dug into the smooth linoleum, keeping me upright. The back of my hand twinged as the drip line tugged. I groaned, wiping away sweat already beading on my brow.

I'd learned the hard way when I first attempted a bathroom visit that I had to roll the contraption feeding my drip with me; otherwise, the needle in my hand jerked me back.

That'd hurt. But not nearly as much as my heart did whenever I thought of Kes still holding onto this world. He hadn't died; no matter how adamant Doctor Louille had been that he might never wake up.

Don't think about him.

I had too much to worry about. Being in a high-traffic public place meant my emotions were scrubbed raw. Luckily, I had a private room, but it didn't stop emotions from soaking through the walls.

Snippets of grief and misplaced hope trickled under my door from family members visiting loved ones. Horrible pain and the craving for death drifted like scent waves from patients healing from trauma.

I fucking *hated* hospitals.

I have to leave—if not for Nila's sake, then my own.

I would be able to heal a lot faster away from people who drained the life right out of me.

Gritting my teeth, I shuffled forward. The large bandage around my middle gave my broken rib some support but agony radiated anyway. Doctor Louille had cut down my painkillers at my request. I needed to know the truth—to monitor my healing and be able to cope with the discomfort on my own terms.

Because three weeks was far too fucking long.

I'm not waiting that long.

The minute I could get to the bathroom without it taking fifteen bloody minutes, I was checking out, and I didn't care what anyone said.

Every step fed energy to atrophied muscles.

Every shuffle forced my body to revive.

And every stumble ensured I could leave that much sooner.

Eleven minutes.

An improvement from sixteen minutes yesterday.

Not the best achievement to go from bed to bathroom, but I'd whittled off five minutes in just under twenty-four hours. I was healing faster—bolstered by my unrelenting pressure.

Wobbling back toward the despised mattress, I paused in the centre of the room. The thought of getting back into the starched sheets and staring yet again at the powder blue ceiling with no fucking purpose other than to torture myself with images of Nila didn't inspire me.

I was no good to her yet. I had to be sensible and heal before saving her, but I couldn't lie there another moment without talking to her. Without telling her how much I loved her, cared for her, missed her, *craved* her. I needed her. I needed her smile, her laugh, her touch, her body.

I need you, Nila, so fucking much.

After talking to Jasmine the first day, we'd agreed to keep communication few and far between. It was hard not to know what happened at Hawksridge, but Cut didn't know we'd made it out alive. For all my dear doting father knew, Kes's and my bones were now pig shit at the back of the estate.

And I want to keep it that way.

Jaz had done all she could to hide our reincarnation from everyone. The doctors and nurses called me Mr. James Ambrose. No one knew my true identity. She'd even taken us to a hospital we'd never been to before—boycotting our usual medical team in favour of strangers who would keep us unknown.

It didn't mean I trusted anyone, though.

I risked anonymity by contacting Nila, but I couldn't deny myself anymore. Just thinking of messaging her like we did before I claimed her made my heart beat stronger and blood pump faster.

She was my cure—not drugs or doctors. I was stupid to avoid contacting her for so long when all I wanted to do was drag her into my embrace and keep her safe forever.

Wrapping my arm around my waist, adding pressure to the throbbing wound, I inched barefoot out of my room, dragging the drip on its little wheels behind me.

I'm a fucking invalid.

The hospital was quiet.

No emergencies. No visitors.

It was a nice reprieve from daylight hours when I had to focus entirely on the itching of my stitches and ache from my rib to negate the overpowering overshare of emotions from such a busy place.

I didn't know the time, but the bright neons were dimmed, giving the illusion of peace and sleepiness. However, the morbid silence of death interrupted the false serenity, lurking in the darkness, waiting to pick off its latest victim.

Move along, death. You're not taking me, my brother, or Nila.
Not this time.

My mind jumped back to the images that Bonnie had shown me a month or so ago. Her study had always been a festival of flowers and needlepoint, but when she'd invited me to tea, she had a new acquisition.

Photographs.

Images of a Weaver, who looked exactly like Nila and my great, great grandfather.

I'd always known I looked like Owen Hawk. Cut had told me a few times as I grew up. But that'd been the first time I'd heard how similar Owen and Elisa's tale was to my own life.

It was meant to scare me. To keep me in line and show me what would happen if I followed that path.

It hadn't stopped me.

I snorted under my breath.

And it came true.

Owen was murdered, just like I'd been. But that was where the similarities ended. Owen had died and left Elisa to suffer.

I'm still alive and I will *save her.*

My forehead dripped with sweat, and I gulped agonizing breaths by the time I finally shuffled down the corridor toward the front desk of the recovery wing. A nurse I'd seen once or twice looked up from her keyboard.

Plaited dark hair crowned her head while no makeup painted her face. Mid-fifties, matronly, and no-nonsense dress-code, she suited the role of caring for others rather than herself. But despite her lack of jewellery and personal adornment, her eyes were caring. In one glance, she gave me more motherly affection than I'd ever had in my youth.

For the first time in a long time, my mother made an appearance in my thoughts.

My heart thudded hard at the intrusion. I never liked thinking about her because I couldn't stomach the memories that came with it. She'd been such a good person just stuck in a bad place. She'd done her best and given birth to four children before her strength deserted her, leaving her only legacy to fend without her.

For a while, I hated her for being so weak.

But now I understood her.

I *pitied* her.

The nurse shot from her chair as I stumbled forward, grabbing the desk for balance. "Mr. Ambrose, you really shouldn't be out of bed." Darting around the partition, she wrapped an arm around my waist, flaring my injury.

Dressed in a backless gown, and already feeding off her caring impulses and frustration at having an unruly patient out of bed, I waved her away. "Just give me a moment. I'm fine."

"You're not fine."

I narrowed my eyes, blocking off her thoughts and focusing on my own. "Truly. I promise I won't keel over and die on your shift."

She huffed but moved away, staying within grabbing distance. I just hoped my arse wasn't hanging out of the god-awful gown.

Wedging my back against the desk so she wouldn't get an eyeful, I smiled grimly. "I needed some fresh air and a change of scenery."

That's not all I need.

She nodded as if it made perfect sense. "I get that a lot. Well, the media room is just down there." She pointed further down the corridor. "I can get a wheelchair and settle you if you like? Lots of DVDs to keep a night owl entertained."

I cocked my head, pretending to contemplate the idea. "Sounds tempting. But you know what I'd really like to do?"

She pursed her lips. "What?"

"Is there a convenience store in the building? Somewhere I can buy a phone? Something that can connect to the internet as well as basic calling?"

She frowned. "There's a small shop on the bottom floor by the café, but I can't let you go down there, Mr. Ambrose. It's four floors and late. Besides, I doubt it will be open at this time of night."

My heart squeezed with dejection.

Nila.

I have to speak to her.

I couldn't wait any longer. Grabbing the nurse's hand, I flicked a glance at her nametag. Injecting as much charm into my voice as possible, I murmured, "Edith, I *really* need that phone. Any way you can help me out?"

She tugged in my hold, blinking. "Um, it's against hospital policy to assist with patient requests outside of medical requirement."

I chuckled, wincing as my muscles heralded another wash of agony. "I'm not asking you to grab me a burger or something bad for my health."

She laughed softly.

"Surely, popping downstairs and grabbing me a phone would be okay?" I ducked to look deeper into her gaze. "I'd be forever in your debt."

Debt...

Shit, I hated that word.

Nila would never be in debt again for as long as she lived. I would eradicate that word for motherfucking eternity the minute this was all over. No rhyme or reason existed for why my family did what they did to the Weavers. What'd started as vengeance swiftly became entertainment.

Boredom.

That was the cause. It had to be.

My ancestors were never equipped to deal with vast wealth having nothing better to do than pluck the wings from innocent butterflies and hurt those less fortunate.

There was such a thing as too much time and decadence, turning someone into a heartless monster.

Edith bit the inside of her cheek. "I don't know." Looking down the corridor toward my room, she said, "I'll tell you what, head back to bed. You can discuss it with the morning manager and see what they can do."

My stomach clenched.

It has to be tonight.

"No. I can't run that risk. You're here now. One request, then I'll leave you alone. What do you say?"

Fuck this backless gown and lack of worldly possessions.

I was so used to towering over people in rich linen and tailored cotton, pulling out a wallet bursting with money. Money always got what you wanted. Cash always enticed someone to say yes.

It truly was a double-edged sword.

"If you go now, I'll pay you triple what the phone is worth."

Her entire body stiffened.

Shit, shouldn't have said that.

"I don't accept bribes, Mr. Ambrose."

Pain shot through my system, drenching me in sweat again. I couldn't be vertical much longer. My shoulders rolled in defeat. "Please, Edith. I wouldn't ask if it wasn't very important." Going against all instinct, I let down my walls and begged, "Please. I need to speak with someone. They think—they think I died. I can't let them continue worrying about me. It isn't fair." Hissing through my teeth as a hot wave of discomfort took me hostage, I muttered, "You wouldn't do that to a loved one, would you? Let them sit at home and fear the worst?"

Her face fell. "No, I guess you're right."

Thank God.

Suddenly, she moved back around the desk and grabbed a purple handbag. Rummaging inside, she passed me an older model cell-phone. "Here. Text them now. My shift is almost over. I'll get you the phone tomorrow when I come back into work."

It wasn't ideal, but beggars couldn't be choosers.

My hand shook as I reached for it. "I can't thank you enough."

She waved it away. "Don't mention it."

The moment I held the phone, I wanted to sprint back to my room. To hear Nila's voice. To beg for her forgiveness. To know she was okay.

I shoved away pain, holding the gift and the knowledge that I could finally reach out to her.

Hating that I couldn't steal Edith's phone and find some privacy, I shuffled away a little and swiped on the old device.

The time blinked on the home screen.

2:00 a.m.

Where are you, Nila?

Are you in bed? Sneaking out to ride Moth to find some peace like I used to do? Is your phone even charged?

Questions and worries exploded in my heart.

Cut had said her life would continue unmolested, but that was before he shot us. Who knew what new rules and madness he'd put in place now we were gone.

If he's touched her, I'll make him fucking pay.

My shakes turned savage as I opened a new message. My memory was rusty as I input her number. I hoped to God I got it right. I'd sent hundreds of messages to her but never took the time to imprint her number on my soul.

Please, please let it be right.

Using the keypad, I typed:

From one indebted to another, you're not forgotten. I love you. I miss you. I only think of you.

I pressed send before I could go overboard. Already, that gave away too much, especially if Cut had confiscated her phone.

Then again, the number was from a stranger. It would look like any other reporter digging for a story or publicity stunt. Even with our *Vanity Fair* interview, the dregs of magazines looked to revive a has-been tale by piecing together fabricated facts.

That was another issue of recuperating in a hospital with nothing to do. Daytime television was enough to rot anyone's brain—demented or otherwise.

I didn't leave my name. I didn't send another.

But she would know.

She would understand.

She would know that I was coming for her.

The next night, Edith fulfilled her promise.

Her shift started at 10:00 p.m. and by half past, she appeared in my room bearing a gift in the form of a brand new phone.

I couldn't speak as I took the box, digging my fingers into the cellophane. Motherfucking tears actually sprang to my eyes at the thought of finally having a way of contacting Nila while we were apart.

Fuck, I need to hear her voice.

Edith's emotions washed over me. Pride for helping a broken man. Compassion for my predicament. And attraction mixed with guilt over our age difference.

Sniffing back my overwhelming relief, I smiled. In one action, Edith had given me the strength to sit up taller, knit together faster.

I'm leaving soon. I'm ending this soon.

Taking her hand, I squeezed. "You have no idea what this means to me."

She blushed. "I think I have an idea." Tugging free, she looked away. "She's a lucky young lady."

And I'm a lucky fucking bastard.

I remained silent.

Awkwardness wafted off her, mirroring my own. No matter how much I appreciated Edith's help, I wanted to be alone. Now.

A thought snapped into my brain. "Oh, did you receive a reply?"

Edith tilted her head. "Excuse me?"

"From the message I sent on your phone last night?"

"Oh…uhh." Her emotions stuttered, shadowing with grief that she didn't have better news.

Goddammit.

I didn't need her to vocalize what my condition told me. Nila hadn't replied.

Why not?

Is she okay?

Edith shook her head. "No, I'm sorry."

I sighed heavily.

What does that mean?

Nila didn't see the message?

She's hurt and imprisoned and suffering?

Fuck!

My heart bucked against my ribs, feeding anxiety to an already strained nervous system. Jaz said she'd keep her safe. *Please, Jaz, keep your word.*

My attention left Edith, unable to wait any longer. Ripping into the plastic, I unwrapped the box like a spoiled brat at Christmas and grabbed the phone.

With trembling fingers, I tore open the SIM package and battery and inserted both into the device.

I pressed the power button, waiting for it to come alive.

"Oh, almost forgot." Edith passed me a receipt with a recharge pin. "That will get you on the internet and unlimited calls for a month."

Shit, I'd forgotten that part of prepay. My old phone had been on an account, deducted and sorted by our personal accountant, along with other menial bill payments.

"Thanks." I took the docket, anxiously entering the code once the phone illuminated. "I'll bring the money to you tonight."

I had no idea how I would do that seeing as I had no identification, bankcards, or way of leaving the hospital, but I would pay her a small fortune for such kindness.

She waved it away. "Just when you can. No rush." Smiling one last time, she made her way to the exit.

My mind immediately discounted her as I focused entirely on the phone. A text pinged saying the voucher code was accepted and the number was ready for use.

The wave of indecision from Edith and small creak of the door wrenched my head up. "Anything else?"

Edith blanched, her eyebrows knitting together. "I was going to ask something, but it's not my place."

It killed me to pause when I was so close to contacting Nila, but I grinned softly. "You've earned the right to ask me anything."

She bit her lip. "Do you know?" Her eyes darted to the floor. "You were shot. There's secrecy about how it happened and only one number on your next of kin."

I waited, but she didn't go on. Only the gentle pulse of curiosity from her inquisition.

"What's your question?"

She patted her plaited hair. "Like I said, not my place. But I wanted to know…if…you knew the person who did it?"

I froze. What sort of answer should I give? Pretend amnesia and hide yet another aspect of my life?

I'm sick of hiding.

All my bloody life I'd hid from my condition, my obligation, my future.

I was done pretending.

"Yes, I know who did it."

Her hand curled around the door handle. A wave of injustice for my situation washed from her.

I grinned, letting myself indulge in my condition without repercussion. "In answer to your next question, yes, I will make them pay."

Her eyes popped wide. "How did you know I was going to ask that?"

Her surprise reminded me of Nila's shock when we spent the night together, when I truly let down my guard and felt her tangled thoughts.

Someone like me had the ability to seem as if we read the future. The perfect mystic able to decipher palms and speak with the dead—all the information you ever needed to know about a person was right there ready to be felt if more attention and empathy was used. Pity the human race was so wrapped up in themselves that they forgot to think about others.

"Just a knack I have."

Edith blushed again. "You're quite the interesting patient."

I managed to keep it together while she vibrated with more embarrassment.

"Anyway, I have to start my rounds." Giving me one last look, she slinked around the door and disappeared.

I breathed a sigh of relief as the room quietened and the door shut me away from the outside world. The instant I didn't have an audience, my heart crumpled. I gritted my jaw to stop the overwhelming pain from eating me alive.

Only this pain wasn't from the bullet but the terrifying fear that Nila had been hurt.

She didn't respond to my previous text.

She had to have known it was me.

I swallowed against more agony. I wished I could sense her from this far away—tune into her thoughts and find out if she was safe like Jasmine promised or needed my help before I was any use to her.

My muscles quivered as I fumbled with the phone's menu, inputting her number and opening a new message. I didn't want to be reckless, but I also couldn't lie there another moment fearing for her safety.

The debts she'd lived through were nothing to what was ahead. I had to kill my father before that happened. Before he took her away from me. Nila hadn't been told how many debts she had to pay and to be honest, I'd read paperwork where more were added and less were taken, depending on how bored or cruel my ancestors were.

The Fourth Debt was coming. But the Fifth Debt...

I shuddered.

That won't happen. I *would* never let it happen.

Sighing, I forced happier thoughts and typed a message.

Unknown Number: *Answer me. Tell me you're okay. I'm okay. We're both okay. I need to hear from you. I need to know you're still mine.*

I pressed send.

I STOPPED COUNTING time by hours.

One day.

Two days.

Three days.

Four.

Nothing had meaning anymore.

I thought the Hawks couldn't hurt me once I'd sunk to their level and played their games. I thought I'd be safe to plot my revenge and hold on until Jethro came for me.

I was such a stupid, *stupid* girl.

Bonnie proved that over and over again. Breaking me into pieces, scattering my courage, burning my hatred until there was nothing left but dust. Dust and cinders and hopelessness.

Five days or was it six...

I no longer knew how long I'd existed in this hell.

It no longer mattered as they slowly broke my will, ruining my conviction that I could win. However, Jethro never left me. His voice lived in my ears, my heart, my soul. Forcing me to stay strong, even when I couldn't see an end.

If it wasn't for the passing of autumn into winter, I might've thought time stood still. The ticking of clocks was only punctured by pain. The passing of night and day only pierced by Bonnie's whims and wishes.

I'm dying.

On my lowest moments, I thought I was dead. On my highest moments, I still fantasised about killing them. It was the only thing that got me through the hellish week they subjected me to.

My hate evolved into a living, breathing thing. There was nothing left but loathing.

What else was there to feel when I lived with monsters?

My mind often tortured me with thoughts of happier times...Vaughn and me laughing, of my father being so proud, of the sweet satisfaction I got from sewing.

I wanted this to be over. I wanted to go home.

Every time my thoughts turned to Jethro, I shut down. The pain was insurmountable. Every day, I stopped believing he'd survive and worried about the worst instead. In my rapidly unthreading mind, he was dead and I believed a lie.

Jasmine tried her best to keep me from the worst.

The Rack she'd denied.

The Judas Cradle she'd flat-out refused.

But there were others she couldn't reject—she couldn't disobey her grandmother, no matter that her eyes screamed apologies and our unspoken bond knitted tighter.

Jethro was no longer there. But Jasmine was.

And I learned to love and hate her for helping me.

Her help wasn't love and kisses and tender stolen moments. No. Her help was selecting the punishment I was strong enough to survive, carving my soul out dream by dream, keeping me alive as long as possible to find some way out of lunacy.

The worst part of my punishment was Vaughn saw it all.

He witnessed what the Hawks did.

He knew now what I was subjected to.

His screams were what undid me; not Bonnie's laughter or Cut's smug chuckles—not even Daniel's demented cackles.

Love was what ruined me the most.

Love was the ultimate destroyer.

But no matter how much I tried to let go…I couldn't.

"Do you repent, Nila? Do you agree to pay the Final Debt?"

I squirmed in my bindings, choking on terror as Daniel marched me toward the guillotine. All around me stood ethereal figments of my exterminated family, their detached heads hovering above their corpses.

A wail howled over the moor. Was it death? Was it hope?

I would soon find out.

"No, I do not repent!"

Cut came toward me. His face was covered by an executioner's black mask. In his hands rested a heavy gleaming axe, polished and sharpened and waiting to sever my neck.

Bending toward me, he kissed my cheek. "Too late. You're already dead."

"No!"

"Oh, yes." Daniel chuckled. Shoving me forward, the guillotine grew from simple bascule and basket into something horrendous. "Kneel."

I crashed to my knees, sobs suffocating me. "Don't. Please, don't. Don't!"

No one listened.

Bonnie pressed my shoulders, forcing me to lean over the lunette and stare at the woven basket below. The same basket into which my head would roll.

"No! No! Stop! Don't do this!"

"Goodbye, Nila Weaver."

The axe swung up. The sun kissed its blade.

It came slicing down.

A bell woke me.

A tiny tinkle in the heavy swaddling of darkness. My heartbeat clashed with cymbals, and my hands swept up my throat. "No…" The diamonds still imprisoned me. My neck was still intact.

"Oh, thank God."

I'm still alive.

Only a dream...

Or was it a premonition?

I coughed, chasing that question away.

My fever had brought many hallucinations over the past day or two: images of Jethro walking into my room. Laughter from Kestrel as he taught me how to jump on Moth. Impossible things. Desperately wanted things.

And also dread and dismay. The torturing didn't stop when Cut had had his fun...my mind continued to crucify me when I was alone.

The bell came again.

I know that sound...but from where.

I was tired and sore. I didn't want to move ever again but deep inside, I managed to find the strength to uncurl from my nest of bedding and reach under my pillow.

Could it be?

My fingers latched around my phone, my heart trading cymbals for drums. The rhythm clanged uncertainly, drenched in malady and doing its best to keep me alive. My nose was stuffy, eyes watery, body achy.

I was sick.

Along with my hope, my body had given in, catching dreaded germs and shackling me to yet another weakness.

I'd come down with the flu four days ago. A day after Bonnie told me what would happen. Twenty-four hours after I'd seen what'd happened to Elisa in those feared photographs. But none of that mattered if the bell signalled what I so fiercely needed.

For days, I'd hoped to hear from him. But every day, I was disappointed. I drained my battery so many times, trancing myself with the soft blue glow, willing a message to appear.

I squinted in the dark, malnourished and fading from what I'd endured. Luckily, the fever had crested this morning. I'd managed a warm shower, and changed the bedding. I was weak and wobbly but still clinging to Jethro's promise.

I'm waiting for you. I'm still here.

The screen lit up. My heart sprouted new life, and I smiled for the first time in an eternity.

Unknown Number: *Answer me. Tell me you're okay. I'm okay. We're both okay. I need to hear from you. I need to know you're still mine.*

I dropped the phone.

And burst into tears.

For so long, the world outside Hawksridge had been dark. No messages from my father. No emails from my assistants. I'd been dead already—not worthy of vibrations or chimes of correspondence.

But I *wasn't* dead.

Not yet.

No matter how many times I died in my awful nightmares, I was still here. Jethro had found a way to text me.

Sniffing and swiping at tears with the back of my hand, it took a few minutes before I could corral my fingers into replying.

Needle&Thread: *I'm okay. More than okay now I know you're okay.*

I pressed send.

My sickness and fever no longer mattered. If I ignored it, it would go away. I didn't have time to be sick now Jethro had given me an incentive to get better.

Is he coming for me?

Could it all be over?

I wanted to say so much, but suddenly, I had nothing to share. I couldn't tell him about the past few days. I would never share because I didn't want to hurt him any more than he already was.

My mind skipped backward, forcing me to relive the horror ever since Bonnie showed me Owen and Elisa's fate.

My door opened.

Jasmine sat with one hand on the doorknob and the other around her wheel rim. "Nila..."

The moment I saw her, I knew something awful was about to happen. My spine locked and the beaded fabric I'd been working on fell from my hands. "No. Whatever it is, I won't do it."

She dropped her eyes. "You have no choice."

I shot to my feet. "I do have a choice. A choice of free will. Whatever that witch thinks she can do to me, she can't!"

Jasmine huddled in her chair—an odd mix of apologetic frustration. "She can and she will." Her bronze gaze met mine. "I've kept you out of Daniel's hands but I can't keep you out of Bonnie's. I've given you all the time I could." She looked away, her voice filling with foreboding. "It's going to get worse, Nila. I've never been told the exact details of the debts— I'm not a man, and therefore, Bonnie insisted I be protected from such violence—but I do know Cut is planning something big. I need to find a way to save you before..."

I didn't want to listen but her anguish gave me strength. "You need me to stall by giving in..."

"Yes." She sighed heavily. "Forgive me, but I have no choice—just like you. No matter what you think."

I had no reply. But my body did. A last ditch attempt at fleeing.

My feet moved on their own accord, backing away until I stood against the wall. I wanted to scream and fight. I wanted to shove her out the door and lock it forever.

But there was nowhere to hide. No one to save me. Only time could do that. Time that neither Jasmine, Jethro, Vaughn, nor myself had.

"Have you heard from him?" My hands fisted against my denim-clad legs. The large grey jumper I wore couldn't thaw the ice around my heart. My mind kept splicing images of Jethro and Owen. Elisa and myself.

Their demise had been terrible—especially hers.

Bonnie told me my punishment would begin immediately. She hadn't lied.

"No." She rolled further over the threshold. "We agreed to minimum contact. It's for the best."

That made sense, even though it was the hardest thing in the world.

If only I could talk to him. It would make me so much braver.

"Nila, come with me. Don't let her see your fear any more than you have to. It will hurt but it won't harm you. I give you my word. You've withstood worse."

"I've endured worse because I knew it hurt Jethro to hurt me. It gave me strength in a way."

She smiled sadly. "I know he's not here to share your pain, but I am. I won't leave you." Swivelling her chair to face the door, she held out her hand. "I'll take his place. We'll get through it together."

My shoulders sagged.

What other choice did I have?

I'd made a promise to remain alive, waiting for Jethro to return. His sister was on my side. I had to trust her.

Silently, I followed Jasmine away from the Weaver quarters toward the dining room. We entered without a word.

Jasmine's wheels tracked into the thick carpet as we made our way around the large table. Unlike at meal times, the red lacquered room was empty of food and men. The portraits of Hawks stared with beady oil eyes as Jasmine guided me to the top of the large space where Cut and Bonnie stood.

They smiled coldly, knowing they'd won yet again.

Between them rested a chair.

Bonnie had said the first punishments would be easier.

Once again, I'd been stupid and naïve.

The chair before me had been used for centuries to extract information and confessions. A torturous implement for anyone—innocent or guilty. It was a common device but absolutely lethal depending on its use.

Did Bonnie suspect I was hiding something?

But what?

Was this her attempt at ripping out my secrets?

She'll never have them.

My heart thundered faster. My blood thickened in my veins.

The chair wasn't smooth or well-padded with velour or satin. It didn't welcome a comfortable reprieve. In fact, the design mocked the very idea of luxury.

Every inch was covered in tiny spikes and nails, hammered through the wood. Seat, backrest, armrest, leg rest. Each point glittered in the late afternoon sunshine. Every needle wickedly sharp, just waiting to puncture flesh.

I swallowed hard, forcing myself to hide my terror. Jasmine was right. Their satisfaction came from my reactions. I was stronger than this—than them.

I won't let you get pleasure from my pain.

"Do you know why you're paying this toll, Nila?"

My eyes flew to Cut. He stood with his hands by his sides, his leather jacket soaking up the dwindling sun.

I shook my head. The power of voice deserted me.

All my courage at killing them vanished like a traitor.

"It's because you must be stripped of your nasty plots and wishes to harm us. It's because you caused the death of two Hawk men." Bonnie shuffled closer, rapping her cane against the horrific chair. "Along with the repayment of the Third Debt, you must endure a few extras—to ensure you are properly aware of your place within our home."

I flinched as Bonnie closed the gap and stroked her swollen fingers along my diamond collar. "You've lived in our hospitality for six months. The least you can do is show a bit of gratitude." Grabbing a chunk of my long hair, she shoved me toward the barbaric contraption. "Now sit and be thankful."

Jasmine positioned herself beside me, holding out a hand to help me lower onto the spikes. I thanked my foresight for wearing jeans. The thick denim would protect me to a degree.

Trembling a little, I turned around to sit.

Unfortunately, Cut must've read my mind. "Ah, ah, Nila. Not so fast." Gripping my elbow, he hoisted me back up. "That would be far too easy."

My heart stopped.

Laughing, he tugged at my waistband. "Clothing off."

Jasmine said, "Father, the spikes will hurt enough—"

"Not nearly enough." His glare was enough to incinerate her.

Sighing, Jaz faced me. "Take them off." Holding out her arm like a temporary hanger, she narrowed her eyes. "Quickly."

Gritting my teeth, I fumbled with the hem of my jumper. I should be comfortable being naked around these people—it'd happened often enough—but being asked to strip brought furious, degrading tears to my eyes.

Breathing hard, I yanked my jumper off and undid my jeans. Shimmying them down my legs, I shivered at the biting air. The dining room had a fire roaring in the imposing fireplace, but the flames hadn't extinguished the wintery chill.

A resounding thud landed behind me.

Oh, no!

Cut's eyes dropped to the ruby encrusted dirk lying in full view.

I wanted to curl up and die. I'd become so used to it wedged against my back, I forgot the knife was there.

Cut gave me a sly smile, bending to pick it up.

Quick!

Squatting, I scooped up the blade before he had chance. His eyes widened as I brandished it in his face. "Don't touch me."

He chuckled. "I wouldn't do that if I were you, Nila."

My mouth watered at the thought of somehow stabbing everyone in the heart all at once.

Jabbing the air between Cut and me, I snarled, "I should've done this months ago. I should've murdered you the moment I met you."

His body stiffened. "Just try it." His eyes flickered behind me. "You have two choices. Try and attack me and pay. Or hand over the knife and pay."

"I'd rather kill you and win."

"Yes, well, that will never happen." Snapping his fingers, he ordered, "Colour, take the knife."

I whirled around but was too late. Colour, a Black Diamond brother who I'd seen once or twice, yanked the dirk from my hand like a rattle from a baby. My fingers throbbed with emptiness as Colour handed the blade to Cut.

My fight evaporated.

I'd tried.

My one rebellion was over, and what was my reward?

Pain and humiliation.

"Thank you, Colour."

Colour nodded, retreating back to his hidey-hole by the fireplace. The large rococo style fire-surround hid most of him from view, giving the illusion of privacy.

Cut waved the blade in my face. "Rather interesting piece of equipment to have down your jeans, Nila." Running the sharp edge over my collar, his face darkened. "Not only are you a troublemaker, but you're also a thief."

Placing the dirk down his own waistband, he smiled evilly. "I'll remember that for future payments."

Standing in a black bra and knickers, I squeezed my eyes. Nothing was going as I'd planned. Where was my courage—the belief that I would plunge that blade into his heart the moment I had the chance?

My chance was gone.

"Get rid of the bra," Cut said. "Unless you want me to use the knife to help you."

My hands flew between my shoulder blades, grabbing the clasp.

Bonnie coughed. "No, I think not. Keep your undergarments on."

My eyes soared open.

"What?" Cut scowled.

She wrinkled her nose. "Seeing a naked gutter rat will ruin my appetite."

Cut chuckled. "You have the strangest ideals, mother."

She sniffed. "Excuse me if I prefer to enjoy my meal without being repulsed." Swatting her cane at the chair again, she added, "Sit down. Shut up. And reflect on what you've done."

Jasmine nudged me forward, playing the perfect role of enemy.

The cold tightened my skin, flurried my heart, and pinpricked my toes as I bent my knees and sat. I bit back a cry as thousands of nails kissed my butt and thighs.

My legs shook as I lowered myself slowly, doing my best to stay aloft and hovering over the sharp, stabbing needles.

"Stop fighting the inevitable, Nila." Cut stepped behind the chair.

I tensed.

Then I screeched as he pushed on my shoulders, pressing me cruelly onto the nails. Pulling me back toward him, he wrapped an arm around my chest, hugging me from behind.

His breath wafted hot in my ear. "Hurts, doesn't it? Feeling thousands of pins slowly sinking into your skin?"

I couldn't concentrate on anything but the millions of tiny fires slowly worming their way through my flesh.

Bonnie stole my wrists, yanking my arms forward and pushing them against the spiked armrests. The entire chair bristled with armament and agony.

"Stop!" I fought her, but Jasmine took her grandmother's place, forcing my arm against the nails and wrapping the leather cuffs around me.

She couldn't make eye contact, fumbling with the buckle. "This isn't to kill you, so the binds won't be tight. It's merely to keep you in place."

Tears ran unbidden down my cheeks as every inch throbbed with pain and tension. I couldn't relax—I kept every muscle locked, so I didn't sink further onto the spikes.

"Don't fight it, Nila." Jasmine tested the cuffs before rolling away. "It'll get easier."

Easier?

Every inch of my skin smarted. My sense of touch went haywire, flicking from my back to forearms to calves to arse. It couldn't distinguish which part hurt the most. I couldn't tell if certain areas bled or pierced or if the nails were blunt with age and only tenderising instead of stabbing.

Either way, it was awful. As far as torture equipment went, I wanted off the chair immediately. I would take the First Debt again because at least the pain came in waves and was over quickly—this…it would strip my mind, throb by throb, until I was a quivering mess of agony.

Panting, I breathed through my nose. My scattered mind bounced like a wayward squash ball, not letting me tame my anxiety.

Cut chuckled as he dropped to his haunches before me. "The beginning is the easy part." Rising, he pecked my cheek with a gentle kiss. "Just wait and see what'll happen as the clocks tick onward."

He looked at Bonnie. "How long did we say, mother?"

Bonnie checked a dainty gold watch around her wrist. "Elisa suffered two hours during dinner."

Cut grinned. "Perfect. Make it three."

I slammed back to the present, coughing with a rattling explosion. My fingers rubbed the healing scabs dotted like constellations down the back of my thighs, back, and arms. The sores had switched from blazing to itchy as my body healed, but the remnants of the nails had marked me far more than superficially.

Even now, days later, I still felt the numerous stings.

I fell asleep with phantom nails stabbing me and woke up hyperventilating, dreaming of being trapped in a coffin lanced with millions of needles.

Three hours in that chair had been the worst three hours of my life.

I supposed I should be honoured that they went out of their way to destroy me. I'd proven to be an anomaly, a challenge they hadn't anticipated. I'd screwed up their grand plans and set in motion things that no one should have to endure.

And that was just the start.

That night, after the Iron Chair, I succumbed to a rattling flu.

I had no reserves. Barely eaten. Lacked sunlight and love.

Living with such evil and negativity stripped my immune system, shooting me straight into chills and body aches.

And there was no one to nurse me better.

Vaughn was banished from my sight. Jasmine was missing.

The rest became a blur as I'd huddled in a sweat-riddled bed and shivered.

My room never rose above a chill. I had no energy to start a fire, and even if I did, I'd been given no fresh wood to start one.

I was cold and hungry and desperately wanted to leave. I tried to remember what life was like before Hawksridge, before Jethro left, before my mother died. But I came up empty. All those happy memories were blank.

Unknown Number: *Fuck, I miss you. Knowing you're okay…I can't tell you how thankful I am. Is that the truth? Is she keeping you safe?*

My heart fell off its pedestal, splattering on the floor. I was okay. I was stronger than I looked, but I wasn't as brave as I believed.

I coughed again, wracked with sick shivers.

Jethro, I want to tell you everything.

Tell you what you mean to me.

Tell you what they've done to me.

I wanted to cry on his shoulder and share my burdens—to eradicate what I'd lived through, so I could let go and forget. Instead, I bottled it up and kept my secrets.

Needle&Thread: *Yes, I'm safe. She's been wonderful. They haven't touched me. Don't worry about me. Just get better.*

Keeping the truth from Jethro was the least I could do for him. I shuddered, unable to stop the memories of what'd happened once I'd been strapped to the Iron Chair.

The Black Diamond brothers entered an hour into my torture. They watched me with sympathy but didn't go against Cut's command to leave me be. Apart from Flaw, I hadn't spoken to any of the brothers since the shooting. They'd been ordered to keep their distance, cutting me off from any ally I might've found.

Dinner was served and I squirmed as my body weight pushed me slowly onto the spikes. The burn of each spread into one blanket of painful horror.

Blood smeared the arms of the chair and I didn't dare look at the floor to see if I dripped over the carpet. I was hot and cold, covered in sweat and goosebumps. My muscles seized; every twitch sent wildfire through my system.

And then Vaughn arrived.

His eyes met mine.

"Threads!" He almost collapsed in rage. "Fuck! Let her go!" Charging up the room, V moved so swiftly and furiously, he managed to sucker punch Cut in the jaw before anyone reacted.

"V, don't!" Part of me loved that he'd landed one on Cut. The other was horrified. "I'm okay. Don't get yourself—"

"Stop hurting her, you fucking bastard!" V swung again but missed as Cut ducked and snapped his fingers for the Black Diamonds to grab V.

"Leave him alone!"

My screaming didn't do any good.

Commotion shot to mayhem. Men shoved back chairs. Fists swung. Grunts echoed.

"Stop! Please stop!"

They didn't stop.

Not only did millions of tiny nails trap my body, but I was forced to watch my twin beaten and kicked and left gasping by my feet.

It'd only taken a few minutes.

But the punishment was severe.

I groaned, slapping my forehead.

Stop thinking about it.

After the Iron Chair, I'd been locked in my room with no bandages or medical salve. I wasn't allowed to see Vaughn, and I'd tended to my injuries in a lukewarm bath that I lacked the strength to climb out of.

I was exhausted.

They'd found a recipe that could well and truly break me forever.

Unknown Number: *I'll be back as soon as I can. Every day I'm getting stronger. Just a little longer, then this will all be over. I promise.*

I sighed, curling around the phone. My fever came back, dousing my insides with frigid unwellness. I had every intention of fighting back. I would make them hurt. *I will make them pay.*

Somehow, I would keep my oath.

But a little longer? It made time sound like it was nothing—such a flippant phrase, a small segment of moments—but to me, it was a never-ending eternity.

I don't have much longer, Jethro.

Not judging by Bonnie's antics. Every day she had something worse.

I truly was Elisa, fading hour by hour, wasting away beneath torment.

Swallowing more tears, coughing with wet lungs, I typed:

Needle&Thread: *I'll be here waiting for you. Every night I dream of you. Dream of happier times—times we haven't been lucky enough to enjoy yet. But we will.*

As if fate wanted to banish those dreams, to prove to me that I should've given up months ago, it brought forth the memory of what'd happened the day after the Iron Chair.

I'd been summoned to the kitchen, believing Flaw had some good news for me or Vaughn had been given free rein. It'd taken my last remaining strength to shuffle to the kitchen. Perhaps, the cook would give me some warm chicken soup and some medicine for my flu.

Instead, Bonnie found me. "Seeing as you refused to confess your sins on the Iron Chair, you will pay the opposite price."

"Confess my sins?" I coughed. "There's nothing to confess. You're doing this for your own sick pleasure."

She chuckled. "It is *rather pleasurable, I must admit.*" *Coming forward, she wrapped her fingers around my arm and dragged me through the kitchen to a small alcove where herbs and small plants grew.*

My fever turned everything hazy. My blocked nose and stuffed sinuses granted everything a nightmare-like quality.

Cut stepped around the corner, dangling something in his hands. "Good morning, Nila."

I stiffened, yanking my arm from Bonnie's hold. Looking at them, I tried to understand what this would entail. Whatever swung in Cut's hands glinted with wicked silver and barbarism.

My skin still oozed from the Iron Chair. I could barely stand. "I'm sick. For once, have mercy and let me go back to bed." *I coughed to prove my point.* "I'm no good if I die before you want me to."

Cut chuckled. "Your physical health is no longer my primary concern." *He held up the shiny mask, waving it from side to side. His golden eyes gleamed with haughty smugness.* "Know what this is?"

Nerves careened down my back. Their role playing and games slowly conditioned me to cower even when standing fierce before them. Jasmine wasn't here. Daniel wasn't here. It seemed that the older generation had taken control.

"Stop wasting time." *I coughed again, looking for a way out of the herb alcove.* "I don't care for guessing games—" *An explosive sneeze interrupted me.* "I just want to be left alone."

Bonnie swatted the back of my thighs. "None of that backtalk, trollop."

My heart quivered in fright even as my stomach turned to stone. Standing up to them came with its own kind of torture—a fleeting aphrodisiac of rebellion followed swiftly by suffocating regret.

No matter that I would do everything in my power to kill them, I couldn't stop their power over me.

They took my knife.

I hated *being defenceless.*

I hated *being so weak by my body's own design.*

Damn this sickness!

Cut came closer. "This, Nila, seeing as you refuse to play along, is known as a Scold's Bridle." *He held it up, blinding me as a ray of light caught the silver, turning everything white.* "It's given to harlots and gossipers for spreading lies. They're gagged and their ability to speak is taken away until they've learned their lesson."

Every instinct bellowed to run.

Who was I kidding? I couldn't run with my lungs drowning in mucous.

Cut moved behind me, bending around to hold the silver mask in front of my face. "Let me explain how it works."

I staggered sideways trying to dislodge his embrace. How had he trapped me so effortlessly?

The flu turned everything gluggy and thick—slowing time down, using it against me.

My eyes devoured the mask, already understanding. The textbook Vaughn had shown me when we were young had a similar instrument. Unlike the medieval item in the book, this was rather sleek and refined.

It wouldn't make it any more pleasant.

Two holes for eyes, a hole for the nose, but the rest was solid silver. Where the mouth hole should've been there was a silver spike, fairly wide and sharp, waiting to wedge on my tongue to force silence or wretched gagging. The back was curved to cradle its victim's skull, trapping their entire head in its nasty hug.

Cut rocked against my back, inhaling my hair. "You already know how it works, don't you?" Bringing the mask closer, he chuckled. "Good. That dispenses unnecessary conversation."

"Lock her in, Bryan." Bonnie shuffled forward.

My heart galloped as the silver came closer. "No wait! I won't be able to breathe! My nose is blocked."

"Yes, you will. Open wide." Cut tightened his arms as I tried to run. "Do it. Otherwise, I'll just hurt you until you do."

My lungs gurgled as Cut wrangled me into position. I thrashed and moaned, but it didn't help. "Stop, please!"

The world went dark as the icy metal settled over my face.

"No!" I clamped my lips together, preventing the spike from entering my mouth.

But Bonnie ruined that by swatting my shins with her cane.

"Ahh!" The pain forced my lips wide, welcoming the silver wedge.

I gagged and yanked away, only succeeding in slamming backward into Cut's arms. The cool metal on my tongue sent spasms through my body. Water sprang to my eyes as I choked.

His elbows landed on my shoulders, keeping me pinned. "Don't struggle, Nila. No point in struggling."

I fought.

But he was right.

There was no point.

All I could do was ignore my body's begging to gag and do my best to breathe.

Bonnie brought the back piece of the mask behind my head, securing it with a tiny padlock by my ear.

The instant it was locked, the worst claustrophobia I'd ever suffered swallowed me whole. Vertigo entered the darkness, spinning my brain, throwing me to the floor. I gagged again.

It terrified. It degraded. I was trapped.

My nose blocked worse.

My head pounded.

My ears rang.

My fear consumed me.

I

Lost

Control.

I screamed.

And screamed.

And screamed.

Cut let me go.

I no longer saw, heard, or paid attention.

My cries echoed loudly in my ears. I gurgled and coughed and lamented for help. My blocked nose stopped oxygen from entering; I inhaled and exhaled around the silver tongue press, recycling my screams in a rush of poisoned air.

I suffocated.

I panicked.

I spiralled into craziness.

My world reduced to blackness. Hawksridge Hall, with its sweeping porticos and acres of land, condensed into one tiny silver mask. Condensation rapidly formed from my breath. I gagged again and again.

I lost everything that made me human.

My screams turned to whimpers.

I'm going to die.

Each breath was worse than the one before. I fell to my side as vertigo got worse.

Nausea crawled up my gullet.

Do not throw up.

If I did, I'd drown. There was no way out, no mouth piece. Only two tiny nose holes that didn't provide enough oxygen.

Images of the ducking stool came back.

This was just as bad. Just as heinous.

Claustrophobia gathered thicker, heavier, chewing holes in my soul.

I can't stand it.

"Let me out!" The words were clear in my head, but the paddle pressing on my tongue made it garbled and broken.

The faint sounds of laughter overrode the hiss and gallop of my frantic breathing.

My hands shot to the fastenings, fighting, tugging. I ripped hair and scratched the side of my neck, doing my best to get free. I broke a nail, scrambling at the padlock. Screams and moans and animal caterwauls continued to escape.

I couldn't form words, but it didn't stop me from vocalizing my terror.

Bonnie kicked me, laughing harder. "I think an hour or two in the Scold's Bridle will do you a world of good. Now be a good girl, and endure your punishment."

The tiny bell saved me.

My heart asphyxiated all over again, remembering the dense heat, the overwhelming panic of the bridle. I never wanted to relive that again. *Ever.*

You're free. It's over.

I didn't think it was possible, but the bridle was worse than the chair. Even remembering it caused the walls to warp, squeezing me uncomfortably tight.

I had a new affliction: claustrophobia.

Unknown Number: *I sense you're not telling me something. Remember what I used to call you? My naughty nun? God, I was such an arse. I fell for you even then. I think I was in love with you even before I set eyes on you.*

All residual fear and ailments from the past week vanished. Fear was a strong emotion, but it had nothing on love.

Fresh tears cascaded over my cheeks.

You have no idea how much I wish to return to such innocence.

To only suffer worries of fashion lines and unpaid custom orders or whether Vaughn had ordered enough taupe buttons. Such frivolous problems—such easily solved concerns.

Not like what I deal with now.

My heart broke all over again. The punishment of abuse slowly turned my mind and body into rubble, fit only for sleep or death.

Needle&Thread: *I love you so much.*

Unknown Number: *I love you more. I love you with every breath I take and every heartbeat I live. I love you more every day.*

Tingles shot from my scalp to my toes.

Needle&Thread: *I wish you were here. I'd kiss you and touch you and fall asleep in your arms.*

Unknown Number: *If you fell asleep in my arms, I'd hold you all night and keep you safe. I'd trespass on your dreams and make sure you know you belong to me and give you a future you deserve.*

Needle&Thread: *What do I deserve? What sort of future do you envision?*

Unknown Number: *You deserve everything that I am and more. You deserve happiness on top of happiness. You deserve protection and adoration and the knowledge that we will never be apart. You deserve so fucking much, and I mean to give you all of it.*

I sighed, feeling the warmest, softest blanket covering me. Jethro might not be here physically, but spiritually he was. His unwhispered words were hugs, and his concern the sweetest of kisses.

Needle&Thread: *Just tell me we'll get through this. Tell me that we'll be together and grow old together and build a life that no one can take from us ever again.*

His reply took a moment, but when my phone chimed, he somehow gave me everything his family had stripped from me. He deleted the appalling events and gave me hope.

Unknown Number: *Not only do I plan on having you by my side forever, but I want you as my wife. I want you as the mother of my children. I want you as my lover and best friend. We'll get through this. It will all be over soon. And when it is, things will change for the better. I'm going to spend the rest of my life making it up to you, Nila, and proving that you took a coward and made him want to be a hero. Your hero.*

My lips wobbled with happy tears. I whispered, "I love you, Kite."

Staring at my phone, I read and reread his messages. As much as I wanted to print them off and sleep wrapped up in his words, I had to delete them.

I couldn't run the risk of Cut finding them.

I had no choice.

Die or kill.

Fight or defeat.

It killed me to drag the entire conversation to the trash and remove it.

Come save me soon.

Come end this before it's too late.

My happiness suddenly squashed as the walls squeezed in on all sides. My mind ricocheted backward, probing old memories.

I couldn't move from the floor in the alcove. I didn't know which way was up. I couldn't breathe. I couldn't speak. All I could do was hold onto the slate tiles and ride wave after wave of vertigo and claustrophobia.

My racing heart deleted years off my lifespan with undiluted panic.

I passed out.

It was a blessing.

By the time Bonnie returned to undo the padlock, I was no longer coherent.

Shaking my head, I rubbed my face.

How many tortures had Elisa suffered before she'd been 'purified'?

Unknown Number: *Goddammit, Nila. I need you so much. I need to show you how much I love you. How much I miss you.*

My heart was in pieces without him.

Needle&Thread: *I need you, too. So much. Too much. When we're together again, I'm going to—*

A noise wrenched my head up.

No!

My eyes fell on the unprotected door.

Please no!

The one awful thing about being so sick was I'd had no strength to push aside the dresser to keep me safe.

The phone came alive in my hands, claiming my attention.

Incoming call from Unknown Number. Answer?

The device vibrated urgently, begging me to accept its challenge.

Jethro...

My soul wept. I wanted so, so, *so* much to answer.

But I can't.

Locking the phone screen, I shoved it under my pillow.

You didn't delete the last message.

The door swung open.

Too late.

Daniel appeared, gloating and cocky. "It's time for another game, Nila. And we can't be late."

Jethro

I LEANED OVER my brother.

The tubes and heart monitor made him look like some Frankenstein monster—pieced together with scraps from the man I once called friend, held together by sorcery and sheer luck.

His skin held a slightly yellow hue; his lips cracked and dry, parted to allow the tube down his throat.

The doctors had done all they could—patched him up and kept his heart pumping. It was up to him now.

A week and a half had passed. Ten excruciatingly long days. If it wasn't for regular messages with Nila, I would've gone out of my mind with worry.

Her texts kept me sane.

Every hour, I grew stronger. I pushed myself until pain bellowed and my endurance improved. Every minute, I plotted my game plan, and every second, I thought of Nila.

She replied at night. Both of us under the same sky, writing by starlight, sending forbidden messages. She was in the world I used to inhabit; I was in a grave sent there by my father.

Yet nothing could keep us apart.

Soon, we'd both be free.

However, her messages weren't like before. When Nila was still at home with her father and brother, she'd been timid and easily embarrassed. She'd been sweet and so damn tempting in her innocence. But now her texts were shaded with what she *didn't* say. She kept so much back, only telling me what I wanted to hear.

It was fucking frustrating.

Why don't you answer my calls, Nila?

Every time I'd dialled in-between our messages, she'd always ignored me and disappeared. Almost as if lying to me by innate characters was all she was capable of.

I needed to talk to her. I needed to find out the truth.

What I really need is to get out of this fucking place.

My side twinged, reminding me that I might be going out of my mind with impatience but I still wasn't fight worthy.

Goddammit.

Kes's heart rate monitor never stopped its incessant monotone beeping. I willed it to spike, to show some sign of him waking up.

Clasping his hand, I squeezed. "I'm here, man. Don't give up."

My other hand drifted to my torso, prodding the tender rib. Louille said I was lucky the bullet had passed so cleanly. He couldn't explain the trajectory to miss such vital organs, but I could. Flying through the air, twisting into position to save my sister had kept me alive.

The bullet hadn't found a perfect target.

Tracing the puckered skin through the thin cotton of a t-shirt I'd been given, I gritted my teeth. This morning, they'd removed my stitches. They'd discontinued my antibiotics and announced the good news.

I was healing quickly.

I'd agreed that was good news. I'd demanded to leave early.

But Louille just laughed as if I should be moved to the psych ward rather than recovery. His emotions shouted he was pleased with my irritation—it proved he'd excelled in his profession as healer—but his mouth said it wouldn't kill me to wait another few days.

What he didn't know was his words were too close to the truth.

Kestrel, on the other hand...

I squeezed his fingers again. He hadn't woken up. He'd been in an induced coma for almost two weeks, giving his body time to heal. The bullet had entered his chest, rupturing his left lung, shattering a few ribs. Bone fragments had punctured other delicate tissues, ensuring his body had a lot more mending to do than mine.

His left lung had taken the full impact, deflating and drowning with blood. He'd been on the ventilator since arriving. Louille said if he caught pneumonia due to his system being so weak, there wouldn't be much they could do.

I couldn't think about that 'what if.'

For now, he breathed. He lived.

You'll get through this, brother. I have complete faith.

He'd always been the stronger one.

Louille also said Kes was alive thanks to the small calibre bullet Cut used and the rib that'd taken a lot of the original impact. He said it was surprisingly hard to kill someone with a gun—despite the tales—and proceeded to tell me a bedtime story—completely unsolicited—about a gang war in south London. A sixteen-year old had five bullets fired into him—one lodged in his skull, the other damaged his heart—yet he stayed alive and healed.

Kes would, too. I had to keep that hope alive.

The gentle whooshing of air being forced into my brother's broken body soothed my nerves. Even though he wasn't awake, I offered company and acceptance.

Hovering by his side wasn't just about companionship.

I had a purpose.

My senses fanned out, waiting to see if any of his thoughts or emotions tugged on my condition. Day after day, I hoped he'd wake up. My sensory output stretched, seeking any pain or suffering—if I could sense him, then he was awake enough to emanate his feelings.

However, just like yesterday, I sensed nothing but blankness.

Sighing, I smoothed back his unruly hair. "You'll get better. You'll see. You're not going anywhere, Kes. I won't allow it."

DANIEL'S LITTLE GAME turned out to be tic-tac-toe.

Only there was no winning, under any circumstance.

At the beginning, I'd refused to play, but he'd soon taught me that that wasn't an option. Jasmine couldn't do a thing about it. She was a spectator while I was the pawn for entertainment.

Family night, Bonnie called it.

An evening spent huddled in the gaming room where the Third Debt had been attempted. With no care or comeuppance, they played Scrabble, Monopoly, and cards.

Cut smiled smugly whenever I shuddered with memories of that night, peering at the walls and chess chequered carpet.

Kestrel had been so kind and honourable. Jethro had been so conflicted and hurt.

Jasmine did her best to keep me in one unbloodied piece, but Daniel was given free control that night. His rules: play the game he wished or submit to a kiss instead.

And not just any kiss. A sloppy wet slurp with his tongue diving past my gag reflex and hands pawing my breasts.

After the second kiss, I gave up rebelling and played.

Cut merely laughed.

Bonnie nodded as if she was a lioness teaching her cub how to play with its food.

Something had fissured deep inside. My soul folded into pieces, trying to protect my final strength and endurance.

My memories, my happiness, my passion…all slowly dried up the more I drank their poison.

It was happening. They were winning. I was so close to giving up.

They wanted me to submit by playing a stupid game? Fine.

They won.

Unknown Number: *Are you around? I want to speak to you.*

The seventh time he'd asked since we'd started messaging last week.

How many days had passed since then? Four? Five? *I've lost track.*

Every morning was a new challenge to break me. Two days ago, Cut had given me a bucket of icy water and told me to scrub the stoop of Hawksridge while snowflakes decorated the air. Yesterday, Bonnie summoned me to her quarters, forcing me to take her measurements and create her a new gown.

I preferred scrubbing the stoop to making that witch a dress with the same skills she'd belittled.

They've done other things.

My heart filled with fury and rage—welcomed after so much weakness and grief.

No! Don't think about it.

I refused to sully my mind with them when I finally had a moment's peace on my own. I wouldn't tarnish this precious time with Jethro with memories of his demonic family.

Clenching my jaw, I replied:

Needle&Thread: *It's not safe. Anyone can hear me. Just message…it's easier.*

I sighed as the message sent.

Easier to lie to you, to keep you from knowing how bad things have become.

Unknown Number: *That's bullshit. I'm calling you right now. If you don't pick up, I'll have Jasmine drag a phone to you so you can't hide from me anymore.*

Shit!

Sitting stiffly against my pillows, I jumped as the phone buzzed with an incoming call.

Shit. Shit. Shit.

How could I talk to him? How could I pretend I was still the same woman, when I'd faded into someone I didn't recognise? How could I keep my voice steady and lie through my teeth?

I've always been a terrible liar.

The phone jumped and danced in my grip. It's vibration repeating what I knew: *Li-ar. Li-ar.*

You have no choice.

Running a hand through my tangled hair, I pressed 'accept.' Taking a deep breath, I held the phone to my ear. "Hello?"

"Fuck." The curse whispered its way into my heart, warming me, kick-starting happiness that I'd forgotten how to feel. "Nila…thank God, you picked up."

Him.

My friend. My soul-mate.

Why was I scared of talking to him? Why had I waited so long?

Curling into a ball, I breathed, "Jethro…"

"Fuck, I miss you."

My eyes closed, fighting a wash of sorrow. "I miss you, too." *So unbelievably much.*

"Are you okay? Tell me the truth. I know you're keeping things from me."

Don't do this to me, Kite….

I attempted diversion, deflecting the conversation to him. My heart flip-flopped with tragedy. "I'm fine. How are you? Have the doctors been good to you?"

"Don't change the subject. Tell me, Nila. Don't make me beg." He sucked in a shaky breath. "Hearing you, knowing you're there and I'm not—it's fucking killing me. The least you can do is reassure me with the truth."

Reassure him with the truth? I almost laughed. There would be no reassurance—only lies would do that. Lies and blatant dishonesty.

"Kite…honestly, I'm fine. Jasmine has done an amazing job. She made Cut amend the Debt Inheritance so she has full control."

Liar.

Half control. And not over the debts.

I'd been lucky the past couple of weeks. Yes, I'd been hurt and tormented, but there'd been no mention of a debt. No extraction of the Third or hint of the Fourth.

Long may it last.

"What have they done to you?"

Everything.

"Nothing. Honestly, I'm alive and waiting for you. I'm just so happy you're safe."

"Nila…you're lying."

I swiped at a renegade tear. "What about Kes?" I kept my voice to a murmur. "Has he improved yet?" I asked daily in my messages, but there was never any change.

Jethro sighed. "Goddammit, you infuriate me." He paused. "No, he's still unconscious."

"I'm sorry."

"You can make it up to me by telling me how you truly are."

I glared across the room at the tropical fish tank with its finned creatures swimming unmolested in their perfect environment. They were free to be happy. I wasn't. And I refused to make someone else unhappy when there was nothing they could do. "Don't badger me, Jethro."

Don't be like them.

I hung my head. "I'm alive. That's the truth. I'm not happy. That's another truth. But what good is it to tell you what they've done when you can't do anything to fix it?" My voice hardened. "Just accept that I'm okay and move on, alright?"

Silence.

My heart thundered against my ribs.

"Jethro?"

A hitch sounded in my ear. "I'm sorry. So fucking sorry."

I melted. "I know. But it's not your fault."

"I'll make them pay."

"I know. We'll do it together."

"I wish I could hold you. Kiss you. My arms are empty without you."

I felt that same emptiness—a terrible void ripping me into ribbons with its aching vastness. "I would give anything to be with you."

Both of us fell quiet. What was there to say when we couldn't talk about what we needed? What words could offer solace when only pain awaited?

"How long?" I finally whispered. "How much longer before I can kiss you again?"

"Too long." Jethro sighed. "They said three weeks, but I'm almost ready. I'm not waiting that long. It's already been too much. I refuse to leave you there another hour more than necessary."

His passion soothed me even though I didn't believe him.

He thought he'd be here in time.

I wished with every fibre of my being that he was right.

But there was something monstrous inside me...slurping me deeper, telling me that my time was running out. I didn't know where the countdown beast had come from, but it was snarling louder and louder.

Jasmine was right. Cut had planned something big. Daniel knew it. Bonnie knew it. *I* knew it.

My life was quickly running out.

Hurry, Jethro.

Hurry...

Before it's too late...

NINETEEN HOURS SINCE I'd spoken to Nila.

I'd waited until nightfall to message her again; I'd almost torn myself apart with impatience. The only thing that'd kept me inside the hospital and prevented me from hijacking a motorbike and hurtling toward Hawksridge was the lingering throb in my side.

I was better, but I wasn't one hundred percent.

Not that I needed to be completely whole to destroy my father but I wouldn't be stupid this time.

I wouldn't ruin my surprise.

Finally, after my nightly check-up and disgusting hospital dinner, it was safe to message Nila without fear of her being caught.

Unknown Number: *I need to speak to you again. I want to touch you——even if it means I can't do it physically. Call me.*

Hearing her delicious voice last night had turned me on, angered me, and set my nerves on edge. It felt as if I was the one with a guillotine blade over my head—punished by the desire to protect and love her.

My cock hadn't softened all night but I'd refused to satisfy myself.

I wanted to wait for Nila.

We can offer each other a small measure of comfort.

I'd never had phone sex before, but if it granted a smidgen of contentment in our separation, I'd give it a shot.

My heart fisted.

Nila's messages were so selfless. So concerned about Kes and me. She barely spoke of herself, no matter how many times I begged. Last night, when I'd talked to her, only confirmed my suspicions. She'd deflected a lot of her replies. And I fucking hated it.

She's hiding things from me.

After ten minutes of only receiving blankness, I tried again.

Unknown Number: *Call me. I need you.*

No reply.

No notification.

Nothing.

My heart hollowed out, bleeding with every tick of the frustrating clock.

Unknown Number: *Answer me. Are you okay?*

Still no reply.

Snow flurried on my soul, dragging me quicker toward a horrible conclusion.

Nila…what's happened?

The landline beside my bed jarred the silence.

The ringing imitated an awful alarm, ripping my eardrums.

Wrenching the receiver off the cradle, I tossed my cell-phone onto the sheets. "Yes?"

"Jet…are you safe to talk?"

Instantly, my body stiffened. *Fuck.* Sitting up too fast, my rib throbbed. "Jaz…what's happened?"

She paused for too long.

Something's gone wrong.

Nila!

That was it. I couldn't heal any longer. My body had rested long enough. I was done with this fucking place.

Swinging my legs over the bed, I leapt to my feet. I didn't give in to the gushing pain. I didn't let my body rule me.

I'm done. I'm ending this.

"Spit it out, Jaz. Right fucking now."

I needed to leave. I was strong enough to kill Cut and steal Nila away.

Jasmine sniffed loudly.

"Talk to me!"

Tears immediately sprung into her voice. "I—I tried, Jet. I did my best."

My blood turned to sleet. "What did they do to her?"

Not the Third Debt. Fuck, if they touched her—!

Jaz's voice was water and grief. "They lied to me. They told me I would be present at every punishment. I found out today that wasn't true."

"What punishments, Jaz?" The room closed in. My heart rate exploded. "What have they done?"

"Bonnie had the elevator blocked for maintenance. I couldn't get downstairs, Jet. I—" A loud sob escaped her.

Fuck this.

"What did they *do*?! Is she alive? For fuck's sake, talk to me!"

"They've been tormenting her, Kite. I'm so sorry! So sorry."

I had no winter clothing. Nothing to change from the sweatpants and t-shirt I'd been given. I didn't care.

I'd run buck-fucking-naked to Hawksridge if I had to.

"Get Flaw here, now. Have him bring clothing and supplies. I want him here in an hour. Do you hear me?"

She sucked back a sob. "I'll—I'll tell him. Kite…they've been using the old equipment. They used it on Elisa in those pictures. You know?"

I froze to the linoleum. "What the fuck did they use?"

Jaz went quiet.

"What did they use, Jasmine?!"

"The Iron Chair, the Scold's Bridle, the Scavenger's Daughter." She cried again. "I'm so sorry, Jethro. I was there for most of them. I did my best to comfort and support her. But I couldn't say no. I couldn't run the risk of them knowing you're—" More tears.

Conflicted emotions ran through me. I hated that she couldn't save Nila. But I understood at the same time. It was too much to ask from my crippled sister. Too much for anyone living in that insane asylum.

My soul sank further. "What else, Jaz?"

Her voice shook. "Tonight...they hurt her. I tried to stop it, but I couldn't. I didn't even know until it was too late."

My heart shattered. "Tonight. Fuck, Jaz. What happened tonight?"

She sniffed loudly. "They used the Heretic's Fork. She...slipped."

"Shit!"

The fork was lethal. One trip and it was death. My mind swam with images of the neck brace padlocked around the accused's throat, forcing them to hold their head high for days. The deadly sharp prongs wedged against sternum and throat, just waiting for tiredness or a fall to jerk their head down and stab them through the heart and jaw.

"That—that's not the worst of it," she stammered.

My body turned to lava and hate. "Goddammit! What else could they do?!"

"Part of the Fourth Debt. They—they—" She couldn't finish.

No.

No.

Fucking no!

I tore off the hospital wristband and traded patient for wrathful avenger.

They wouldn't get away with this.

Not anymore.

They're motherfucking dead.

"Get Flaw here. I'm coming home."

A Few Hours Earlier…

"NICE OF YOU to join us, Nila."

Cut clasped his hands in front of his black jeans. His salt and pepper hair glistened from the sconces around the room.

Daniel shoved me forward. I tripped on the blood-red rug in the centre of the space. A cough escaped as my eyes danced around yet another never before entered part of the Hall.

Amber drapes and bronze accents. War memorabilia along with a few glass cabinets displaying Luger pistols and bloodied ribbons from some battle long ago. Dust motes hovered in the air, swirling a little from the heat escaping the fireplace. The low ceiling and dark orange walls made the space den-like and cosy, full of history and artifacts.

"It's time we moved forward with the next stage…don't you think?" Cut sipped his goblet of cognac. "You've had time to repay a few of the smaller sins, but my schedule is running behind, and I can't delay my upcoming surprise any longer."

Vertigo tried to tackle me, but I did my best to stand tall. Furious tears froze in my eyes, glinting like daggers but not daring to fall.

I will not cry.

Not for them.

Not for anyone.

"You're gonna enjoy the surprise, Weaver." Daniel laughed, circling me like a vulture. "Gonna go on a little trip soon."

A trip?

Where?

Why?

Bonnie shifted in her chair beside the fire. A woollen blanket covered her knobbly knees. "Don't ruin the surprise, Buzzard. She'll find out soon enough."

Sour mistrust and hate filled my mouth. "Whatever you're planning, I hope you've arranged your own funerals."

Cut coughed on his liquor; Daniel burst out laughing. Slinging an arm over my shoulders, he whispered, "You're becoming so much fun. I like this side of you."

"What side? The side that doesn't give a shit about you anymore?"

My illness had left me weak but Jethro had made me strong. His messages and assurances that we would have a future allowed me to stand up and be heard, even if it fell on deaf ears.

Dragging his foul tongue along my chin, Daniel cocked his head. "No, the side that pretends she doesn't care but she does." His spicy aftershave polluted the air.

It was late and I'd believed I'd avoided yet another night in this nest of vipers. When he'd come to collect me, I'd been plotting how to end it. Sitting on my bed, dressed for sleep, I wasn't thinking empty thoughts anymore. Hidden in my fabric chest was a large piece of black cotton with chalk scribbles on how to kill each Hawk.

Poison.

Shooting.

Bludgeoning.

I'd explored every avenue, and Jasmine even offered me the use of her personal gun. She'd told me that if Cut died from unnatural causes, the estate and his children's futures died with him. She told me that his Last Will and Testament pretty much screwed everyone. However, she had faith I could come up with a way to revoke the fine print and somehow save them.

Our relationship had changed into a mutual liaison. She leaned on me. I leaned on her.

"Know why we've summoned you here, Nila?" Suits of armour watched me as Cut smiled. "Care to guess what you'll pay tonight?"

No...

Jethro...

"Before we begin, we're going to have a little 'show and tell.'" Daniel left me on the rug, heading toward a small table covered with black cloth. "I'm sure once you've seen what's under here, you'll thank your fucking stars that you have the power to stop us from using them."

My heart charged, pumping blood through my veins.

"What power?"

"Obey and do what we say and they remain purely ornamental." Removing the cloth, Daniel grabbed something and held it behind his back. "Know what this is, Nila?"

I hated that question.

Every time I'd heard it, it delivered yet more torment.

I wanted to dismantle the sentence, burn the vowels, tear apart the consonants. I never wanted to hear that jumble of words again in my *life*.

Keeping my head high, I didn't look at him.

"You'd be best to answer me, Nila." Daniel came closer, stopping in front of me. His voice hammered nails into my coffin.

I looked into his demonic eyes, nostrils flaring with anger. My hands opened and closed for a weapon. "No, I don't know what that is and I don't care. You're like a bloody child looking for your parent's approval."

Bonnie chuckled. "Oh, tonight will teach that tongue of yours a lesson."

"Take me back to my room. I'm done playing."

Daniel laughed, catching my wrist and holding me steadfast. "Not so fast, Weaver." Stroking my nipple through my white nightgown, he murmured, "Did you forget who called it quits the other night? You were tired. I could tell. The Scavenger's Daughter would've driven you mad if I hadn't stepped in." He pinched me. "I was the one who unbuckled the iron and let you go."

He's right.

His concern for my wellbeing could've come across as kind and caring—if he hadn't also been the one who'd swatted me with willow reed while I was bowed and imprisoned by the awful Scavenger's Daughter.

He'd been tasked with teaching me manners after I'd refused to eat with them. He'd been told to make me bleed.

Surprisingly, he hadn't.

He'd been happy just drawing my tears.

However, according to Cut, I was a spoil-sport.

The Daughter had been used to crush its victims. Bowing with my head on my knees, the iron bars had been excruciating, slowly tightening with a winch, folding me into fatal origami.

"What do you want from me? Appreciation? An award for mercy? What?"

Daniel narrowed his gaze, holding out the item. "What I *want*, Nila, is for you to play along."

I snorted, unable to hide my disgust. "Play along while you torture me? Sure, why didn't I think of that?" My eyes fell on the object. For once, I had no clue what it was. I didn't recall seeing it in the torture book that V owned, and I couldn't piece it together.

Bracing my spine, I said, "I told you. I have no idea what it is. Hurry up and get it out of my face."

He ignored my command, smiling like a Cheshire cat. "Good. Gives me the chance to teach you something for a change."

You've taught me a lot, Buzzard.

How to hate.

How to crave death.

How to plot your demise.

Daniel laughed, stroking the roundish brass device with a corkscrew in the middle and petals lodged together with a small circular handle. It was pretty in an old-fashioned, barbaric way.

"This is a Pear of Anguish." He shoved it beneath my nose. "Ever seen one before?"

"I just told you I didn't know what it was."

He beamed. "Allow me to show you how it works." I recoiled as he held the pear and twisted the small lever at the bottom. Slowly the petals expanded outward, forming a morbid four-leaf flower. "This ingenious device has three uses."

I swallowed hard as he kept spreading the petals.

"Use number one was for liars and instigators. The pear was forced into their throat and slowly opened until their jaw cracked."

I shuddered.

"Use number two was for gay men or priests who broke their faith. It was shoved up their arse and cranked wide until their arsehole ripped." He laughed, flaring out the pear to full expansion. "The third was for women. Adulterers and nuns who'd lied about being virgins for their God or faithful spouses. It was shoved up their twats, and only once they'd been stretched were they deemed repentant enough to deserve the Judas Cradle or Brazen Bull."

I closed my eyes. I didn't want to imagine the rest of the torture devices. There was too much joy in creating so much pain. I couldn't stomach it. I'd seen photos of the Brazen Bull—of stuffing a poor person inside a bronze statue and lighting a fire beneath. The victim roasted alive, while the smoke of their charred remains escaped through the nostrils of the bull.

I shivered.

His fingers caressed my cheek. "Don't worry. I won't use it tonight. Only show and tell, remember?" Snickering, he placed the Pear of Anguish on a side table and picked up a wicked pincher device.

Cut said, "You'd do well to behave, Nila. One misstep and they become part of the toys used. Got it?"

I glowered, not stooping to his level with a response.

Jethro...

Keep my thoughts on him.

Whatever they planned to do tonight would be bearable as long as my mind found a way to be free.

Daniel waved the next piece in my face. "Any clue?"

I shook my head, hating him more every passing second.

"It's called a Breast Slicer." Daniel opened the pinchers which were formed into two wicked spikes. "This would be stabbed into the outer edges of a woman's tits, impaling her."

My nipples twinged as blood raced faster.

"Then they'd be ripped out as fast and as hard as possible." He demonstrated with a quick jerk. "No more tits." Fondling the awful item, he laughed. "Women had it pretty hard in medieval England. Wouldn't you agree?"

That one I did agree with.

I nodded.

I expected more tormenting, but Daniel grew bored.

Tossing the Breast Slicer to clang against the Pear of Anguish, he looked at Cut. "Can I start, or do you want me to do something else first?"

What's going to happen?

Whatever it was, he'd given me fair warning. It would be only fair to use that knowledge for my benefit. My mind charged ahead with gruesome plans. If I remained untethered, I might be able to use the Breast Slicer on him and then ram the Pear of Anguish down Bonnie's throat. Cut would have to wait—or I could skewer him with a poker from the black marble fireplace.

Cut steepled his fingers. "You can start, Buzzard."

Daniel clapped his hands. "Hear that, Nila? Permission. Fucking sister has done a good job at keeping you out of bounds, but tonight she's not invited." He grinned. "She's also not invited to the secret surprise we have for you. That will just be you, me, and Cut. Jasmine thinks she's won. But she won't be coming with us." His golden eyes darkened. "And that means there won't be anyone to stop me."

Loathsome repugnance ran through my body.

He's talking about the Third Debt.

"Get on with it, Dan," Bonnie muttered.

Daniel prowled around me. "Don't rush me, Grandmamma. I'm enjoying myself." He gathered my long hair, playing with it.

I couldn't unglue myself from the rug.

"You're very pretty, Nila. I can see why Jethro thought with his cock rather than his brain." Braiding my hair, he inhaled me. "But unlike my broken brother, I can keep a level head around you." His entire body reeked of greed and gluttony—not on food or money—but power over another's life.

My life.

His hands dropped from my hair, ensnaring my wrists. "Because of that, I don't trust you. And tonight, it's all about obedience."

I gasped as he yanked my hands behind me, binding them with a rope I hadn't seen. I squirmed in his hold, wanting to escape whatever would come next. *So much for my plan of killing them.*

"Don't do this." My voice was heavy with fury. *Don't take me away from Jethro when he's only just come back to me.* To have such love and hope granted and then stripped away was the height of cruelty. I loathed my fate. I despised my karma.

Daniel laughed loudly, his baritone bouncing off the den walls. "Don't worry. You have full control over tonight."

"You keep saying that. What does it mean?"

Spinning me in his hold, he stroked my cheek. "I mean that you'll have a choice of what happens."

"If I have a choice, then I choose for this to end. Right now."

He chuckled. "Not that simple, Weaver."

My wrists fought against the twine. I forced myself to ignore the discomfort and rapidly building fear. My unhappiness didn't matter to Daniel. He only saw what he wanted—a girl to torture and daddy's approval to do it.

It's all over.

Jethro had come back from the dead. But it was too late.

Cut placed his goblet on a side table, standing upright. "Are you ready to begin, Nila? Ready to pay the Fourth Debt?"

What answer could I give? I reverted to illiteracy. I forgot how to talk because speech never saved me. Only actions would, but I couldn't do that, either. My arms were fastened tightly.

Daniel pushed me forward. Cut caught me but I refused to look him in the eye. Instead, I looked over his shoulder—back ramrod straight, chin tilted with defiance.

Cut's golden gaze glowed. "I'll take that as a yes." Chuckling, he stroked my diamond collar. He bent closer, his breath echoing in my ear. "It's a new era, Nila. And I can't wait to share my secrets with you when we get to where we're going. Tonight you'll pay the easier part of the Fourth Debt. And later…you'll pay the rest."

I shivered. The depths of depression I'd crawled from tried to tug me back. I had to look strong, even if I didn't feel it.

"Where are we going?"

"You'll find out when we get there. But I'll give you a name…*Almasi Kipanga.*"

My nose wrinkled. It didn't give any hint. "What the hell is that?"

He smiled. "You'll see."

Bonnie stood. The rap of her cane was a third footstep as she inched toward her family and victim. Her hazel eyes met mine.

Without the black blanket covering her legs, her outfit was visible: a maroon skirt and dark brown jacket. Cynical thoughts ran riot in my head. *She's wearing colours that won't show blood.*

My heart unhinged, racing erratically.

What the hell will they do?

Bonnie smiled, showing yellowing teeth and far too much smug exhilaration. "Let's begin, shall we?"

Daniel wrapped his fist in my hair, yanking me against him. The long strands licked around his wrist, binding us together. "I'm up for that."

Horror consumed my reflexes, nulling me from intelligence.

Think.

There must be something—

There is something.

I could call for Jasmine. I could scream as loud as I could for Bonnie's protégé and hope to God she could save me.

But then I'd ruin her life, too.

How many more people had to die before this was over? Kestrel was dying. Jethro was healing. Jasmine had already paid more than I knew.

Bonnie snapped her fingers. The door behind me opened and shuffling feet announced we had visitors. I held my breath as the guests made their way to stand by the fireplace.

"No..." My heart layered in tar as Vaughn marched to a stop, courtesy of the mountain of malice, Marquise. His black eyes met mine and in twin language we held an entire conversation. Possibly our last conversation forever.

I'm so sorry, Threads.

I'm so sorry, V.

I love you.

I love you, too.

"Mr. Weaver here is going to help us extract the first part of the Fourth Debt," Bonnie said, limping closer. "You've paid the First, Second, and Third— well, not quite, but we'll get to that—you've paid debts for our ancestor, his daughter, and son. But you're yet to pay for his wife."

"Whatever this is about, just leave her alone." Vaughn struggled in his identical bindings. Hands behind his back, wrists locked together—I felt a kinship with him that I hadn't had in the other debts.

All of those, I'd been on my own. Jethro had been beside me, but he wasn't family.

This one was personal.

My brother would see just what I'd been dealing with.

I hated that but was grateful, too.

His presence would force me to be stronger than I might have been.

Jethro...I'm sorry I lied to you.

Cut cleared his throat. "Daniel will inform you of your history lesson, and then we shall begin. You *will* consent to this debt being claimed, Nila. Just like you'll consent to the rest."

"Stop. Wait! Leave her alone." Vaughn struggled against Marquise, his eyes frantic. "Whatever you're about to do. Fucking stop it. She's suffered enough, goddammit!"

Bonnie sighed. "Marquise."

The big man quirked an eyebrow, holding on to my brother as if he were a fly on a string. "Yes, Madame?"

"Gag him."

"Of course." Marquise let V go with one hand and dug into his back pocket. With inhuman strength, he slammed my brother against his mountainous chest and forced the black bandana through his lips.

"Wait!" I launched forward, only to be jerked back by Daniel. "This is between us. Let him go."

Bonnie sneered, "Oh, he'll be let go, alright."

My heart slipped from tar to fossil. "What do you mean?"

Please don't mean death. Please!

"I mean if you play this game correctly, Vaughn can go home tonight."

My heart exploded with hope. "Truly?"

Do I dare believe them?

Disbelief shook its head, but the cruel spark of optimism begged it to be true.

Bonnie smiled. "Play correctly, and he goes home, untouched. He returns to his family because of your sacrifice out of love."

Vaughn mumbled something unintelligible behind the gag.

"However, if you play incorrectly, he'll stay here. He'll suffer right along with you and we'll end his journey the same moment we end yours."

He'll die with me.

That could never happen. I couldn't be responsible for my brother's death.

"You have my word, I'll play. Send him home now. You don't need him to make me behave." I couldn't look at Vaughn while I traded my life for his. He'd be full of guilt and rage at not being able to stop me.

Cut rubbed a hand over his mouth. "If you are a good girl, Nila, and he goes home, don't think he's untouchable. Don't think this is mercy or that we've overlooked his ability to bring havoc to our world again. This is another checkmate in a game you're too stupid to understand."

A question burned in my chest. I needed to know the answer, but at the same time, it led to such confusion. "Why?"

Cut paused. "Why? I just told you why—if you don't obey—"

"No, not that." *I can't believe I'm doing this.* "*Why* let him go? I thought you were keeping him until I paid…"

My voice trailed off.

I know why…

Cut chuckled. "Answered your own question, didn't you?"

My head turned into a bowling ball, sagging on my shoulders.

Vaughn was going home because *I* wouldn't be. Whatever Cut's surprise was…it was the Final Debt. Somehow, he believed he could keep the police at bay. That my brother wouldn't bring down their empire. That he was safe to continue with his murdering schemes.

Imbecile.

He's truly slipped from malicious to insane.

Vaughn exploded in Marquise's grip. He kicked and wriggled, yelling at the top of his voice, nonsense curses spilling from his gagged mouth.

"Shut him up," Bonnie snapped.

Marquise clamped a hand over Vaughn's nose and mouth, slowly suffocating him.

"Stop!" I wriggled in Daniel's arms.

"Don't make me hurt you before we've begun, Weaver."

I couldn't tear my gaze away from my brother as his face turned pink and eyes bugged for breath.

Cut checked his gold Rolex. "Right, let's begin. I have somewhere else to be tonight."

Daniel let me go, and Marquise dropped his hand. Vaughn sucked in wheezing breaths as Daniel planted himself in the middle of me and Vaughn. "Grandmamma, the dice?"

Bonnie inched forward, her arthritis turning her stiff. Pulling a dice free from her jacket pocket, she handed it to her grandson. With eyes ordering obedience and no room for error, she stepped back.

Daniel puffed out his chest. "As you know, Nila, you've paid the debts for the original Hawk family, but you haven't paid for the glue that held the family together. The mother was the reason we outstripped your family in wealth, power, and rank. However, before you learn what she did to make such a thing happen, you must learn the daily struggle she went through to keep her family alive."

Cut nodded proudly, giving Daniel the limelight.

In a sick way, the history lesson was a reprieve. Storytelling by a monster before he ate me for dinner.

"You're not a mother, so I doubt you'll understand completely, but this little game will prove how far she'd go to save her children."

Daniel held up the dice. "For every roll, I'll give you two scenarios. Option one, you have the ability to save yourself. Option two, you'll have the ability to save your brother. You will learn the depth of my ancestor's compassion. She wasn't a martyr—she was a fucking *saint*. Putting everyone she cared about first."

Daniel rolled the dice in his fingers. "If there was food, she'd feed her family and starve herself. If there was shelter, she'd make sure her children were warm while she would freeze. If there was pain, she'd put her loved ones first and accept the punishment. She truly was an exemplary woman."

His voice deepened. "And your fucking ancestors took advantage of her kind-hearted spirit. They tortured her by holding the lives of her children over her. They went above and beyond to make her suffer. Weaver used a dice, similar to this one, whenever he wanted her to do something. Fuck him or sleep in the pigsty. Crawl on her knees or go hungry. She was the strongest member of our lineage because, not only did she never break, but she also singlehandedly destroyed the Weaver's stature, became friends with the sovereign, and ensured the Hawk name became one of the most feared and wealthiest overnight."

He laughed. "Strong fucking woman, huh?" His eyes darkened. "Bet you wish you were half as strong as her."

He wasn't wrong. My emotional sadness and bodily weakness from the past few weeks haunted me. I'd let them get to me. I'd cracked, if not broken completely.

I'm weak.

Knowing I came from such an awful bloodline made me guilty for our wealth and success. Our prosperity was built on the destitution of others, but just like the crown and church terrorized its people, the gentry picked on lower class. It didn't make it right, but that was the world back then. Corrupted by power and free to torture.

It wasn't my responsibility to pay for their sins. It wasn't anyone's. It was evolution from barbarism to better behaviour.

Daniel smirked. "What are the most basic instincts of a mother? What is the fundamental requirement for having children?"

I pursed my lips. My eyes remained locked on Vaughn.

To defend against people who mean them harm. Just like I'll defend V from you.

Daniel continued, "We all know it's a mother's job to sacrifice herself for her children. Let's see if you can be that strong for your sibling." He shoved the dice under my nose. "This isn't an ordinary dice. No numbers. See?"

I flinched.

"Only two colours. Red and black. Want to know what those colours mean?"

God, please let this end.

"Red is for blood—a physical toll you'll have to submit to, in order for your brother to avoid the punishment for you." He chuckled. "And black is for psychological—those hard to swallow decisions where there's no right answer but only two shades of fucked-up."

"Wrap it up, Dan," Cut said. "Let's get on with it."

Daniel nodded. "Fine." He tossed the dice from palm to palm. "What should your first trial be, Weaver? Something easy or hard?"

Vaughn fought in Marquise's hold.

I ignored him. This wasn't about him. This was about me *protecting* him. The Hawks already knew I'd accept every task, no matter what it was. It wasn't a choice, but a necessity. Bearing pain myself was doable, watching my twin go through it…unthinkable.

Rubbing his chin, Daniel murmured, "I think my first roll will be…" Shaking the dice, he released it. The plastic bounced against the thick carpet, coming to a stop on black.

Black…psychological.

I stiffened as an idea lit his face. Leering at Vaughn, he said, "You have two choices, Nila. First, stay where you are and watch your brother suffer two blows to his gut, courtesy of Marquise. Or…"

I stood taller. "Or what?"

"Or…do what my ancestor had to do every night. She had to fuck her employer."

My stomach bubbled with disgust. My tongue desiccated with horror. "I—I—no."

Daniel grabbed his cock. "Gonna fuck me for the Third Debt. Might as well get used to it, bitch."

I wanted to throw up.

Vaughn wriggled and groaned in his binds.

Visions of willingly submitting to Daniel in front of my brother caused tears to swell. I couldn't…could I?

Incredibly, Bonnie came to my rescue. "I'm not watching a rutting. Kiss him, Ms. Weaver. Save the rest for a room without my presence."

My heart scurried like a terrified rabbit.

Daniel bared his teeth. "Don't override me. I'll get her to do whatever the fuck I want."

Cut crossed his arms. "Not tonight. You'll have her. And it's going to be a far sight better than a quick fuck on the floor." Coming toward me, his eyes lit up with secrets. "We'll be somewhere no one can touch you. And you'll do whatever we say."

Vaughn struggled as Cut pressed a fleeting kiss on my mouth. "Now, go kiss my son to avoid your brother being punched, and then we can move on."

Daniel grumbled, "Fine, kiss me, whore. But not just any kiss; something that will make me *believe* you mean it."

V jerked in Marquise's hold, the groan in his chest a resounding plea for him to take the punishment. Didn't he see? I couldn't live with myself if I had a way of sparing him more pain.

A kiss is nothing. A kiss I can do.

A small price to pay for my brother's wellbeing.

Linking my hands together, I lashed myself tighter than the twine. Holding my chin high, I turned to Daniel.

His eyebrow rose, intrigued and eager. His eyes slowly filled with lust as I crossed the small space and stood on my tiptoes before him. His chin came down, lips parted, but he didn't cross the final distance.

He waited for me.

He waited to accept a kiss I swore I'd never give him—no matter how much they tried to break me.

Incredulously, I felt as if I cheated on Jethro.

I'm sorry.

Holding my breath, taming my roiling stomach, I pressed my mouth against his. He was warm and tasted slightly salty, but he didn't force me to deepen or stick his tongue down my throat.

It all hinged on me.

I have to make him believe.

Otherwise, it would've been for nothing.

Repulsion worked my gag reflex. I wanted to pull away. But I pressed my mouth harder against his, squeezing my eyes to annul the truth of who I kissed.

I'm stronger than this.

Finding my last remaining strength, I licked Daniel's bottom lip.

He groaned as I slipped my tongue into his mouth. I wasn't tentative or hesitant. I'd learned how to kiss thanks to Jethro's majesty at drawing desire from me.

If Daniel wanted me to make him believe, I'd make him bloody believe.

His chest rose and fell, brushing my nipples, reminding me of what Jethro had done to me. The anger inside him seemed to pause, lulled by whatever magic I held over him.

My throat closed; I ran out of breath.

I reached my limit.

Pulling away, I spat on the rug by his feet. "You believed me. You can't deny it."

Breath was hard to catch as I stared triumphantly at his trousers. "There's evidence that you can't hide, Buzzard." I cocked my head at the tented material. "You can't touch him. I did what you asked."

The softness of him taking what I gave vanished. Lashing out, he grabbed my hair. He shook me, rage darkening his face. "Just wait till we make you repay the Third Debt, whore. You'll regret that."

Vaughn grunted again, but no one paid him any attention.

Bonnie remained quiet, letting her youngest grandson do what he wanted.

Letting me go, Daniel plucked the dice from the floor. Shaking it, he tossed it down again.

Red.

Pain.

I swallowed hard, doing my best not to show fear.

Vaughn didn't do such a good job. He fought and squirmed, earning a punch to his gut—even after I'd kissed Daniel to prevent it.

"Don't! I paid the damn requirement!"

Cut clucked his tongue. "Marquise. She's right. Don't hurt him unless she refuses."

Vaughn doubled over, his legs buckling in Marquise's hold.

Daniel pointed at the dice. "Pain, Nila." Tapping his chin, he pretended to think. "What can I make you do?"

Cut murmured, "Hang on, I'm calling rights on this one."

I tensed.

He tilted his head in my direction. "Nila will pay that one for me with no complaints but she'll do it when we get to where we're going. Isn't that right, Nila?"

My eyes flickered to V.

Cut's voice licked around me. "You'll know what it is when I ask, and you'll permit it. Because if you don't, I'll just kill your brother and be fucking done with it."

V growled. I stayed quiet. I'd played this game longer than he had, and I knew how to deal with Cut now.

Narrowing my eyes, I asked, "Why drag it on? Why not just kill me here?"

Cut clenched his jaw. "If you have to ask that, you haven't been paying attention." He stalked forward. "Agree to what I just asked and you'll learn before the end."

There was no other answer I could give. I glowered. "Fine."

He smirked. "Good girl."

Daniel pouted but shook off his disappointment by collecting the dice. "Oh, well, my turn again." Shaking the dice, he snickered, "Ready for another?" He rubbed his lips in lewd reminder. "Maybe I can have you blow me next."

Acid drenched my insides.

Daniel rolled the dice. The horrible thing bounced off the rug, coming to a stop on red.

Shit.

I sucked in a heavy breath.

You can do it. Do it for V.

Daniel grinned. "Red, huh? Pain..." His eyes drifted to the table where the Pear of Anguish sat.

God, no!

Marching over, he picked up an awful looking contraption peeking out from under the black cloth. "This will do."

I stiffened as he came back, dangling the torture equipment just like Cut had with the Scold's Bridle.

"This ought to be painful enough."

My eyes drank in the leather collar and long metal bar on the front. Each end was carved into two sharp prongs.

"Know what this is?"

That damn question again.

Unfortunately, I knew the answer this time. "It's a Heretic's Fork."

Was this a manor house of the fucking Tower of London? Where did they keep these barbaric devices?

"Smart girl." Daniel grinned. "And you know how it works?"

I made the mistake of looking over at Vaughn. Saliva dripped down his chin from the gag, his eyes blazing with sorrow.

I looked away. "It's strapped to the accused neck and the fork forces the person to keep their head high to avoid the prongs from entering their chest and throat."

Bonnie smiled. "You've finally shown some aptitude, Ms. Weaver." Cocking her head, she ordered, "Strap it on her, Daniel."

"Be my pleasure." The thread of insanity that infected Cut glowed in Daniel's eyes as he moved behind me. His cold hands brushed aside my hair as he brought the horrible thing beneath my chin. "Put your head up."

Tears prickled my eyes as I raised my chin, staring at the ceiling. The square wooden panels kept me company as the fork buckled around my throat and diamond collar.

My neck arched, keeping the delicate skin safe from being stabbed. My teeth hurt from clenching, and my head pounded with a rapidly spreading headache.

You're failing again. Don't give in.

I blinked back tears, straightening my spine as if that would bolster my courage.

You're breaking. They're winning.

I wished I could tear out my brain from tormenting me. The Hawks did that enough without my mind disabling me, too.

Once the buckle was firmly fastened, Daniel inspected his handiwork. "You look rather regal like that. Guess I can't make you blow me this round; otherwise, you'd kill yourself with every suck." He cackled at his tasteless joke.

Vaughn groaned in the corner but I didn't look over.

I let my vision unfocus, granting a small reprieve from everything.

Please, let this end soon.

Slapping my arse, Daniel commanded, "Walk a few laps. Show me how well you can move with your head high and your wrists bound."

My heart chugged hard as my worst enemy swooped into being.

No, not now!

The room swirled with vertigo. Sickness fogged my head, and I lost all sense of balance.

Don't fall!

I'd kill myself.

Moaning, I did my best to equalize.

It didn't help.

The room shot black; I stumbled forward, falling, *falling.*

Someone yelled, "Catch her!"

Arms wrapped around my body as I plummeted. I jerked to a stop, hanging in some horrible embrace as the world dipped and swelled. Slowly, I traded oppressive blackness for the orange den.

Swallowing hard, I shoved away the remaining episode. "I'm—I'm fine."

Daniel planted me on my feet. "Got a fucking death wish, Weaver?"

I wanted to shake away the cobwebs left in my head, but I didn't dare. I trembled in place, itching with claustrophobia. My neck strained beyond comfort, aching already.

"You gonna faint on me again?"

I calmed my breathing. "I didn't faint. It's vertigo, you arsehole."

"She's had it since she arrived," Cut said. "Three laps, Ms. Weaver. Get through that without killing yourself and we'll remove the fork."

Three laps. Three lifetimes.

"Can you untie my hands?"

"Nope." Daniel pushed me forward. "Go on, be a good prancing pony and show us what you can do."

My knees wobbled, but I shuffled forward. I didn't know the room enough to avoid ottomans and small coffee tables. My eyes couldn't look where my feet went. I was basically blind.

Their gaze burned into me as I made my way to the perimeter of the room and followed the wall as best I could. Couches forced me to go around; I bashed my knee on a magazine rack and stubbed my toe on a desk.

I felt like a prized pony on a race-track—keeping my head high, my knees higher, prancing for my life, only to fail and be shot for my efforts.

It took a long time to navigate and vertigo kept playing with my balance. I had to stop a couple of times, swaying uncomfortably. By the time I made my way past V for the third time, silent tears spilled from my eyes and I was on the precipice of breaking.

I wanted it over with. I wanted to be free. I wanted to *run*.

Run. Run. Run.

Vertigo grappled me again, hurling me headfirst into a vicious attack, scrambling me like whisked cream.

Shit!

I fell, tripping over something and colliding with air. There was nothing to catch me, nothing to stop me soaring from standing to dying.

Time slowed as I tumbled forward. My hands fought against the rope, and my mind screeched instructions.

Keep your head up! Keep your chin high!

My hands were tied. I couldn't stop my trajectory. All I could do was pray I survived.

The thick carpet cushioned my knees as I slammed to the ground. My shoulders crumpled, and I cried out in agony as the prongs bit into my jaw and chest, biting their way into my flesh.

Am I dead?

I couldn't tell.

Pain smarted from everywhere.

A shadow fell over me as Cut ducked to my level. "Whoops." His lips spread into a horrific smile. "Sorry, my foot got in the way."

And that was it.

That final tiny straw that made it almost impossible for me to keep going.

I withdrew into myself. I felt myself disappearing. My hate fizzled. My hope died. I had nothing else to give. Nothing else to feel. The throbbing of the wound no longer bothered me because my senses shut down.

There came a point when the body ceased feeling pain. The receptors were tired of transmitting an important message—only to have that message ignored.

I'd neglected my body for far too long and now it'd abandoned me.

Cut paused mid-chuckle, understanding I'd reached rock-bottom. Without a word, he unbuckled the fork and left me alone on the carpet.

Silence reigned heavily in the den. No one moved.

I didn't care if I never moved again.

You won.

I don't care what you do anymore.

They'd taken my innocence. My vengeance. My love. My life.

I had nothing to go back to. Nothing to move toward.

Stagnant. Locked in a present I could no longer survive or endure.

"Get up, Weaver." Daniel stood over me.

I stood.

"Come here." He snapped his fingers.

I went.

"Let's roll again, shall we?"

I nodded.

Monochromatic and hell-bound thoughts. That was all that remained of me.

I didn't notice as Daniel tossed the dice.

I didn't look as it rolled to a stop by my foot. I didn't care when it didn't flop to one side, staying poised on its edge—neither black nor red, both physical and psychological pain.

As far as the debts went, as far as their fun continued, I'd checked out and left.

I had no future. What did I care about my present?

Daniel ducked to collect the dice. "It's as if the ghost of our ancestor controlled it."

Bonnie nodded. "It *is* rather serendipitous."

Cut came forward, pulling free a large pair of shears from his back pocket. "Here you go, son." His eyes met mine, but he faded once again to the side-lines. Deep in his light-brown eyes was the smallest level of concern. He sensed I'd given up. His enjoyment had been taken away from him.

Daniel held up the scissors. "Know what these are for?"

I remained mute.

"Know what I'm going to use them on?"

I rejected his every taunt.

"These are to take something from you. Something they took from my ancestor." Wrapping his arm around my shoulder, he pointed the scissors in Vaughn's direction. "The Hawk woman did anything she needed in order to feed her family. She sold her every asset until she had one last remaining. Know what that was?"

V's red-rimmed eyes howled with sadness.

I tried to care, but couldn't.

V would move on.

I'd stay here.

Locked in this world with dice and Hawks.

Daniel squeezed me, trying to cultivate a response. "It was her hair. She cut off her hair in order to keep her family alive for a few more days." His voice turned to gravel. "Now it's your turn to sacrifice. Your choice is simple. Allow me to cut off your hair—suffer a psychological toll—all in order to save your brother from a painful handicap."

I continued to stare blankly.

Take what you want.

I no longer cared.

"Marquise, hold up his hand," Bonnie ordered.

Marquise spun V around to face away and splayed his fingers. I glanced at the swollen blue digits from being tied so tightly. My own fingers felt the same—numb and dying from lack of blood.

"Hair or his finger, Nila. That's the deal."

His voice sliced like a sickle through my blankness. But I didn't move.

Daniel vibrated with anger. "Hair or finger, bitch." He gnashed the shears together. "One or the other. You have ten seconds to decide."

I didn't need ten seconds.

I already knew my decision.

I wasn't vain enough or alive enough to care.

"Hair. Take my hair."

Daniel scowled. "Where's your fight gone? You're being a fucking wet fish."

I found a magic in ignoring him.

He couldn't torment me anymore.

None of them could.

I didn't think about Jethro or Jasmine or home. I didn't think at all. About anything.

Prowling behind me, he gathered my hair in his fist. "You have such beautiful hair. Last chance to change your mind, Weaver."

My voice held no fear or objection. If my tone were a colour, it would be colourless. "Do whatever you want."

I'd never cut my hair.

Ever.

It was a stupid reason but one I'd done for my mother. She'd loved to play with it. To plait it, thread it with flowers and ribbon—show me off as her little princess.

That was my last remaining memory of her, and Daniel had stolen that, too.

"Gonna slice every strand off your head," Daniel promised. His touch tugged on my hair, twining it into a rope. "Ready to say goodbye?"

My heart didn't hurry. My eyes didn't burn.

"Don't fucking answer me. See if I care." Daniel's fingers yanked harder and the rusty yawn of the scissors bled through my ears.

My eyes closed as the first snip turned me into a stranger.

Physically, I couldn't feel pain, but spiritually, I *howled* in anguish. It hurt. It hurt so *so* much to have such a poignant piece of me stolen without fighting, without screaming, without protecting what made me *me*.

The second snip broke me.

It hurts, it hurts, it hurts.

The third snip destroyed me.

Stop, stop, stop...

The fourth snip completely annihilated me.

I have nothing left.

"Can't tell you how satisfying this is." Daniel laughed, cutting with no finesse, hacking through the thick black strands.

I was alone in this.

Alone and shorn like some animal for slaughter.

All I could do was mourn silently.

Snip, snip, *snip.*

My curtain of ebony hair disappeared with every scissor-slice. Cascades of thick blackness puddled, devastated and dead, on the blood-red rug. I'd given up the last part of me—the final toll for my brother's freedom.

I'm doing it for him, for love, for family, for hope.

I said goodbye.

To my youth.

To my childhood.

Snip, snip, *snip...*

This was the end.

Snip, snip, snip...

It was over.

I BECAME SOMEONE I never knew I was capable of.
A monster.
An avenger.
The hero I needed to be.
Nobody would touch her again.
Not me.
Not my family.
Not even pain itself.
I stepped onto Hawksridge land. *My* land. *My* legacy.
I'm here for you, Nila.
I'll fix this.
I just hoped I wasn't too late.

SLEEP.

It was the only peace I got these days.

Peace from my fracturing soul. Peace from breaking.

They'd won.

They'd finally broken me. Finally proven that no one had unlimited resources to remain strong. That we all break eventually.

I wasn't proud of myself.

I hated that I'd lost.

But at least Vaughn was safe. At least I'd done right by him.

I had no weapons to defend myself. No energy to push aside the dresser and protect myself. My belief that I could ruin them disappeared into dust.

Nothing mattered anymore.

I was theirs to do with what they wanted. And my heart was officially empty.

My reflection in the bathroom mirror showed a terrifying transformation. Hollows existed in my cheeks, shadows ringed my eyes, and the blood on my chest glowed with crimson fire.

But it was my missing hair that hurt the most.

Ragged and shorn, my glossy black strands were now in tatters. They hung over my ears, all different lengths, hacked into dysfunction by Daniel's sheers. I no longer looked like Nila Weaver, daughter of Tex, sister to Vaughn, empress to a company worth millions. I looked like a runaway, a slave, a girl who'd seen death and no longer existed with the living.

I look ready to pay the Final Debt.

I feel ready to pay the final price.

There was no power left inside me.

Staring into my black eyes, I shivered at my listlessness.

They didn't even let me say goodbye.

The moment the last strand hit the floor, Marquise had marched Vaughn from the room without a backward glance. I'd never seen V so wild or so helpless.

In two seconds, he'd disappeared.

I'd wanted to cry, to sob, to snap.

But I'd just stood there until Cut gave me permission to leave.

I was in a billion pieces.

How can I ever find my way back when I have no more glue to fix myself?

Bowing my head, I hated the unfamiliarity, the frigid breeze whistling around the back of my neck. My head was light as air and heavy with thunderclouds.

I'd lost everything. My backbone. My faith. They'd stolen more from me than just vanity—they'd stolen my right to myself.

I didn't look away as I washed and tended. I couldn't stop staring at my new face.

I didn't have kind words to bolster my courage. I didn't have hope to patch up my weeping heart. All I had was emptiness and the bone-deep desire to go to sleep and forget.

Using a torn piece of calico, I washed my wound as best as I could. Water whisked away the blood, but nothing could wash away the filth existing inside me.

I'd given up.

I'd vanished just as surely as Cut had won.

I was done.

Stumbling from the bathroom, I left behind the last remaining part of me. I said goodbye to the woman I once knew and fell face first into bed.

No thoughts.

No wishes.

Just emptiness.

I let sleep consume me.

Jethro smiled, holding me close.

His body heat, normally negligible with his cold temperature, roared with love and healing.

"I've got you now, Nila. It's okay. I'll make it all go away."

Having someone look after me after so long, undammed my tears, and I fell into his embrace. "I've missed you so much. I tried to be strong. I tried." I cried harder. "I tried to be so strong but it's not enough. Nothing will ever be enough. I'm empty. I'm lost. I don't know how to get back."

Jethro's lips kissed my forehead. "You're so strong. You'll heal. Hush. I've got you. You'll be alright. Hush." He rocked me, soothing my hair, never letting me go.

"I can't do this anymore, Jethro. I can't." I curled into his arms, wanting to fade away and stop everything. "There's nothing left. I have nothing...nothing!"

He kissed my hair—my beautiful, long hair. A low growl built in his throat. "You won't have to. I'm ending it. I'm going to save you. It will all be over soon."

The dream unwound from my thoughts as a tap against glass roused me.

The vacant despair inside me throbbed, but sleep had patched me together infinitesimally—letting me hold on just a little longer. Jethro's dream embrace stitched the vanishing pieces together just enough that I didn't burst into tears.

Whatever the Hawks did to me, no matter what affliction I suffered, no matter how desolate my mind became, I still existed—still survived.

I'm not done until I'm dead. And even then, I'm immortal.

Remember that and be strong.

The rapping came again, guiding my eyes to the dark window.

The heavy emerald drapes puddled velvet from ceiling to floor. They blocked the night sky and any hint of the mysterious noise.

Tap. Tap-tap.

Could a tree have fallen? Could Flaw be throwing stones at my window to get my attention?

Curiosity overrode my stiffness, forcing me from the warmth of slumber. Shuffling from the covers, the room swirled with vertigo. The imbalance was worse because I'd given in. I couldn't fight it anymore. I let the black wave take me, gripping the mattress until it faded. The cut on my chest burned as I breathed hard and slow.

The tapping came faster, louder.

Climbing unsteadily to my feet, I padded across the room and wrenched the curtains aside.

My eyes dropped to the sill, searching for answers.

I tripped backward.

What—

Something feathered and flighty hopped away, only to soar back and tap against the glass. I'd expected to see a wayward branch or even some flotsam that'd lodged against the frame.

I hadn't expected this.

Had some messenger from God come to slap me for being so lost? Was it some mystery of Mother Nature saying she believed in me?

I'm not alone...

My heart swelled as lost hope unfurled.

The people I lived with might not care about me...but others did. I couldn't stop fighting because I *was* loved. Out there, somewhere, I was loved by people who mattered.

My heart twisted as I bent closer to inspect.

The bird of prey rapped its beak on the window, hopping on the sill outside. Its beady black eyes tore through me, as if in one glance it knew what I'd dealt with and how close I was to the end.

You understand me, little bird. Are you my saviour?

Backing away from the window, I balled my hands.

You don't need a saviour...if you only believed in yourself again...

So what, your hair is gone? So what, your brother is gone? So what, Jethro is gone?

You're not gone.

So fight!

The bird charged the pane, rapping its beak with fury.

I froze.

Winter ice had chased away autumn far too fast. The spidery lace of frost decorated corners of the glass. The radiating cold cut through my cotton nightgown like knives.

Poor thing.

I hated to think of the poor creature in the cold. No animal should be without shelter.

I moved forward and opened the wrought iron catch. Cracking the window open, the bird immediately hopped inside.

No fear. No hesitation.

Where the hell had this bird come from?

I froze as the raptor spread its wings, ran across the interior window, and hopped onto my hand.

"Ah!" I snatched my hand back. Its talons were sharp and its beak deadly. I'd had enough pain at the hands of human hawks to let a feathered one hurt me, too.

The bird puffed out its chest. Its beak glinted wickedly while it cocked its head and stared at me with intelligent eyes.

It saw right through me.

It saw how broken I was. How tired. How desolate.

It made me drown in guilt for being so feeble.

Unwanted tears crept into my eyes.

"I don't have anything for you. I doubt cereal will impress a carnivore like you."

The bird chirped.

The noise whipped through the room, sending my eyes darting to the door. I didn't want to give any reason for Daniel to visit me. He'd done enough. He'd done too much.

Backing away, I shooed it. "Go on...get out of here."

Instead of flying away, it hopped closer, once again targeting my hand.

"No, wait—"

It didn't listen. With a single flap, it hopped off the sill and landed on the back of my knuckles. Its wings soared open for balance, its talons digging into my flesh for purchase.

My bicep clenched beneath its weight and I steeled myself against its uninvited presence. Its scaly legs shuffled, doing its best to remain in one place. Taking pity on it, I curled my fingers, creating a rudimentary perch. It chirped, wrapping its sharp talons around my skin. Its weight was surprisingly heavy, its plumage dense with feathers of coppers and brass. "Hi."

It tilted its head sideways, chirping again.

A draft whistled through the gap in the open window. I moved to close it, but the bird nipped at my knuckle.

"Ouch." I went to shake him off, but my eyes fell on its leg.

The hawk or kestrel flapped its wings, dispelling a rogue feather to flutter to the carpet. It somehow knew I'd seen its message.

My heart stopped beating as I looked through the window, squinting into the darkness. Who'd sent it? Were they still out there?

No shadows moved outside; no hint of midnight visitors.

"Who sent you?" I murmured as I glanced at the white parchment wrapped around its leg. Reaching for the red bow, I tugged it loose.

The bird screeched, bouncing up and down with impatience. Its sudden agitation forced me to yank harder. The roll of paper fell away, dropping to the sill.

With the heavy bird on one hand, I did my best to unroll the scroll and read.

However, the raptor didn't wait. It had done its duty—it had delivered its message. Without a backward glance, it soared off my hand and slipped like a winged demon through the window crack and into the sky. Instantly, the camouflage of its feathers vanished against twinkling stars.

My heart steadily increased its tempo; my breathing turned erratic. Pinching the note, I smoothed it out until the finest, tantalizing, most *miraculous* sentence I'd ever seen imprinted on my brain.

Come to the stables.
My knees wobbled.
My heart grew wings.
Jethro.
He's here.
He's come back for me.
I am not forgotten.

MY LIFE WASN'T mine anymore.

It was hers.

Hers.

Hers.

I'd told her that, but I didn't think she believed me. But now I was back. I was alive and ready and motherfucking angry. She was mine to protect and adore, and up till now, I'd failed her.

I should never have brought her here. I should've had a fucking backbone and ended this when Cut killed Emma. I should've found help for my condition the night I hurt Jasmine. I should've ended their evil the day my mother couldn't cope.

So much history, so many lessons and decisions. At the time, I'd played the game—I'd waited and learned and prayed.

But I'd been stupid to think there was any other conclusion.

It'd taken Nila to slap me awake, electrocute my heart with her courage, and show me that I was a good person inside. That the thoughts I suffered—of torture and ruin—weren't mine. That the horrors I'd committed in the name of family values didn't make me the monster I'd been groomed to be.

I'm my own person.

And it was time to show Nila just what a transformation I'd undergone.

The moment she appeared on the ridge, I struggled to breathe.

Nila…

The moonlight cast her in silver as she padded down the small hill, her white legs flashing beneath the white hem of her nightgown. A long black coat swamped her body, while a hood covered her head, fluttering around her face. She didn't run. She glided over the frost-glittering grass.

I wanted her to soar to me. To *fly*.

But something was wrong. She moved too slowly. Like a woman who'd lost her fire.

My heart shattered as she slowly closed the distance. She looked magical and mystical and far too precious to tame.

But I *had* tamed her. And she'd tamed me.

Come faster, Nila.

Hurry.

My hands curled as she didn't increase her pace. I stayed where I was, lurking in shadows, waiting.

My body vibrated, wanting so fucking much to charge toward her. To tackle her on the soft grass and kiss her senseless beneath the stars. I couldn't stand another second without her in my arms.

I took a step onto the cobblestone courtyard.

Don't.

Common-sense forced me back into the shade. I couldn't leave the safety of the stables—couldn't risk anyone seeing me from the Hall.

Wait.

Every second was fucking torture.

She moved as straight and true as the kestrel I'd sent her.

Kes.

His name and memory was a stain upon my joy.

My brother had to survive because he deserved to see the new future. He and Jasmine were owed a happier life than the one we'd been dealt.

I wanted them by my side when I introduced Nila to Hawksridge and showed her that this place had not been kind to her, but once it was mine, it would be our private haven.

Come. Faster. Run.

My heart thundered with erratic syncopation.

Nila skidded down the small incline, the flash of glittery ballet flats catching moonshine.

Every step brought her closer. I sighed heavily. The throb from my rib faded; the twinge from my newly removed stitches disappeared. For the first time since waking up in the hospital, I felt truly healed. My body had mended, but without her, my soul would've been torn forever.

Trading grass for cobblestones, Nila's shoes slapped quietly, closing the distance between us. Her breathing wheezed—as if she'd been sick but healing—and her hood hid her stunning long hair.

My skin sparked as she sprinted around the mounting block and sailed through the double doors of the stables.

Finally.

I grabbed her.

She screamed as my arms snaked around her, trapping her vibrating form, saying hello with echoing heartbeats. Spinning her in my hold, I planted both hands on her hips and walked her backward to the wall.

I never stopped moving.

Pushing, shoving, coming fucking apart at having her in my arms.

Her eyes met mine. Her fright disappeared, consuming me under an avalanche of love. "Oh, my God...it's true...you're here."

I smiled, opening myself completely. I fed off her happiness, loving how deeply she cared for me. I couldn't stand it. I didn't deserve such unconditional acceptance. But something shadowed her. She felt...different...quieter. She didn't have her usual spark or vibrant will.

My soul growled at the thought of her fading from me.

I'd bring her back.

I will.

Her back hit the brick wall, my hands soared from her hips to her cheeks, and nothing else fucking mattered. "Christ, I've missed you." Ducking my head,

I captured her mouth in a brutal kiss.

Live for me. Breathe for me. Come back to life for me.

My lips bruised with how hard I kissed her. I hadn't meant to be so rough, but Nila exploded. The passion and ferocity missing inside her suddenly detonated into being.

I groaned as her hands disappeared into my hair, grabbing fistfuls, yanking me closer. She melted and fought; her tongue shooting into my mouth.

She whimpered as my kiss turned violent, driven by the need to affirm that this was real. That she was truly in my arms and still fighting, still surviving.

Our heads tilted, changing the kiss's direction. Her fingers tugged harder on my hair. I kissed her deeper.

"You're here." I poured words with kisses, not knowing if I spoke or yelled it from my soul. "Fuck…you're truly here."

Her tongue swirled with mine, her chest pressing hard as she sucked in rapid breaths. My side ached but nothing would stop me from kissing her until we passed out from pleasure.

She'd returned to me, but she was still quiet inside, still hesitant and unsure.

"I'm here." She kissed faster. "You're alive." Her fingers dug firmer. "God, Jethro…you're okay." Her voice broke, and the world ceased to exist.

It was just taste and love and heat.

The dam of her emotions drowned me, and I cried out as she reincarnated in my arms. Fuck, I'd missed her. Fuck, I'd worried about her.

But she was alive.

She was still mine.

Her hands swept up my back, touching fiercely. She winced as I sucked in a breath when she skated over my healing rib.

She gasped. "I'm sorr—"

I yanked her head back with a fistful of her hood, forcing her to look at me. Her lips were swollen, glistening in the darkness. "You can't break me, Nila."

I kissed her again, unable to stand the overwhelming emotion in her eyes. She opened for me, welcoming me to take whatever I wanted. Within seconds, I was drunk. Entirely intoxicated on her taste—all my forward thinking, my plans to put into action—they could all wait.

Because this goddess couldn't.

I couldn't.

I couldn't get enough of her. I would *never* get enough of her.

We stumbled sideways, my mind awash with need, my body and hands completely uncontrolled. My shoulder slammed into a stall as Nila lost her balance, falling against me. I spun her around, pressing her against the new obstruction, kissing her harder.

She moaned and we staggered again, clashing and fighting but always kissing.

Never stopping.

"I can't believe you're alive." Her hands tangled deeper in my hair, keeping my face locked with hers. "Every night I prayed you weren't gone."

I ducked to capture her throat, kissing my way along her jawline, glowering at the glittering diamonds lacing her neck.

No matter what happened and the freedom we earned, Nila would forever wear that collar. I hated it, but I would prefer to see her wear it every day for the next eighty years, than see it sitting back on its pedestal in the vault just waiting for its next victim.

I bit her neck, sucking her taste, inhaling every part of her.

I wanted those images out of my head. Forever.

She groaned as I captured her breast, squeezing the unrestrained flesh through her nightgown.

"Jethro—"

My cock fucking pounded with desire, my heart permanently located in the rock-hard flesh. I had to be inside her. Only then would this insane need to devour her cease.

Not yet.

Things had to be discussed.

It took all my strength, but I pushed away, dragging a hand over my face.

Nila stayed locked against the stall, her chest rising and falling; her coat opened, showing nipples pinched with lust. The damn hood kept me from seeing any further than her mouth and eyes.

Her gaze met mine in the gloom, tears sparkling on her eyelashes. "Why— why did you stop?"

I couldn't tear my gaze away from her lips. So plump and red and wet.

I'd done that. I'd practically eaten her alive.

The urge to do it again drove me fucking insane.

"We have to talk." My voice was hay and dust, cracked and dry.

"Oh." She looked down, her fingers pulling at her coat. The damn hood kept her face in shadow. She hurt as much as I did. Hurt with passion. Lacerated by lust.

Shit.

I squeezed my eyes, cutting off my vision but feeding more perception to my other senses. My skin begged to connect with hers. My heart growled to thump against hers. And my cock fucking punished me for not being inside her.

"Fuck it."

I gave in.

Falling on her again, she gasped as I shoved her hard against the stall.

"Fuck talking." I kissed her lips, her chin, her cheeks. "I need you, Nila. I need every inch of you."

"Take me." She cried out as my hand gathered her gown, bunching it over her hip. "Please—please don't stop."

"I've never wanted someone as much as I want you," I groaned as she opened her legs. "Never loved anyone as much as I love you."

She gasped as I grabbed the back of her knee, hooking it over my hip. Something ripped—her hem or coat—I didn't care. Her heel dug into my arse as she ground against my cock.

I shuddered. My hand slapped against the stall to prevent my body from crushing her.

"Don't stop." Wrapping her arms around my neck, she dragged me back to her.

My side twinged and my forehead pricked with pain, but I didn't care. My cock ruled me now and it wanted to be inside her that fucking instant.

Fumbling with one hand, I wrenched aside my belt and jerked down my jeans and boxer-briefs. The clothing had come courtesy of Flaw, along with a lift back to Hawksridge, sworn silence, and a note to deliver to Jasmine.

My cock leapt from my trousers, rippling with need and sticky with pre-cum. Fisting the base, I rocked against her, desperately trying to find her entrance.

Her fingers clawed my shoulders, tugging me closer but holding me away at the same time. "Wait—wait—"

"I can't wait."

"But you were shot…you probably shouldn't—" Her hands dropped, stroking my naked hips, digging her nails into my flesh. "Are you okay to do this?"

I kissed her again. "I'm going to show you how okay I am by making love to you." I thrust against her.

She shook her head. "Wait!" Her attention shot to my torso, seeking wounds. I had no intention of taking my t-shirt off and showing her the bandage hiding the stitched area or mentioning my broken rib.

Didn't she get it? None of that fucking mattered as she was the best painkiller around.

I'd never felt so good having her in my arms, trumping death, defeating the impossible.

"You argue with me again, and I'll make you come apart over and over until you believe me."

"But—"

"Stop it." Pressing a finger over her lips, I silenced her. "Quiet." The tip of my cock found her tight heat. "If you stop me from taking you, I'll die. I'll literally have a heart attack."

Her head fell backward as I teased, hovering so close but not taking her. Pushing up the tiniest bit, we trembled with pleasure. My head bowed, pressing against the stall behind her as I did my best to stay in control. My thighs bunched as every instinct bellowed to drive inside her. "I need you so much I can scarcely breathe."

Her emotions ran crazy, battering me from all directions.

Lust.

Fear.

Questions.

Love.

"Quit thinking so hard; you're distracting me." Looking into her eyes, I traced her cheek, soothing her rioting thoughts. "All I want to feel from you, Nila, is desire. All the other stuff…we can talk about it later." I kissed her softly. "Now, be quiet, stop thinking, and let me fuck you."

She shivered and obeyed.

Her emotions switched to one thought: wanting me to take her.

It would be my pleasure to comply.

Bending my legs, I drove upward.

Her back arched as I slid inside her liquid heat. Higher and higher, stretching her.

"God, Jethro—yes!"

I gathered her close, holding her tightly as I climbed deeper. Only once she fully encased me did I thrust.

Our lips glued together, and we rode each other.

It wasn't rhythmic or sensual.

It was purely animalistic and primal.

"I won't last—I can't last."

"I don't care." Her pussy tightened as I drove faster. "Just prove to me you're alive."

"That I can do."

It didn't take long.

My body had no endurance and time spent apart meant everything about Nila bewitched me into exploding far too fast.

With each thrust, the pleasure turned catastrophic; my balls tightened.

"Oh, fuck…" Lightning shards shot up my cock, spurting inside her. "Hell, yes." Waves of release crippled me as I splashed inside the woman I wanted forever. I bit my lip as my legs seized, my cock impaling her over and over again.

The last spurt left me lightheaded, but it'd been the shortest, sharpest, and most rewarding orgasm I'd ever had.

"Goddammit, it's good to see you."

Having her in my arms, coming inside her, knowing we were together again, helped wipe away my worries and just *be*.

"Where's Moth and Wings?"

Nila's voice wrapped around my satisfaction, dragging me back to her. The chill of the stables faded thanks to the heat lamps I'd turned on above.

I rolled over to face her; my unbuckled belt and jeans clinked.

Somehow, after I'd orgasmed, we'd stumbled down the corridor of the stables and collapsed on top of one of the hay bales in a spare stall. Nila had lost her shoes, and her black jacket was rumpled and dusty from rubbing against the wall but she'd never looked more beautiful. She still hadn't removed her hood though, and strange emotions trickled from her—hidden and quiet—scaring me more as minutes ticked past.

I was exceedingly aware of her every thought and also intimately mindful that Nila hadn't come.

I mean to rectify that.

Her mind raced, sending flickers of ideas and questions in every direction. I let them wash over me, not wanting to focus on reality just yet.

This might be the only time we get to steal perfection like this before it's over.

I meant to indulge as long as I could.

"They're in the paddock behind the chase. If they're not needed for regular riding, they're turned out."

She relaxed. "Oh, that's good. I had a horrible thought that they might've hurt Wings—because you're de—well…" She smiled. "…you *were* dead."

Gathering her close, the sweet smell of clean hay threaded around us. "I still *am* dead according to my father. Kes, too."

My forehead furrowed thinking of my brother. *He has to wake up.* Being away from the hospital went against my desire to watch over him, but I had to trust that Doctor Louille knew what he was doing. That eventually, once Cut was dead and things had been dealt with, Kes would wake up and I could rib him for sleeping through all the hard work.

Wake up, brother. Don't leave me when we're so close.

"How is he?"

I glanced at Nila. The simplistic beauty of her onyx eyes and sexy lips twitched my cock again. "He's still alive." My voice hung in the stagnant quiet. No horses were hobbled tonight—the dogs slept across the yard, and the witching hour gave us our own seclusion from reality, hiding us from nightmares.

Nila plucked at the plaid blanket that I'd placed over the hay bale. "Will he remain that way?"

My heart clenched. *I hope so.* "He will if he knows what's good for him."

She smiled but didn't laugh, too full of melancholy to lighten the mood. There *was* no lightening the mood—not when a brother and friend was dying.

Changing the subject, I looped my fingers with hers. "Can I ask you something?"

She nodded slowly. "Of course."

"Can you take off the hood? I want to see you. You're in too much shadow."

Instantly, her emotions scrambled. Fear drenched, followed by despair. Sitting up, she shook her head. "I'd prefer to keep it on. I'm cold." To add value to her lie, she gathered her coat tightly and hugged herself.

I soared upright. "Bullshit. I know when you're lying. Just like I knew you were lying in most of the texts you sent."

Her shoulders hunched. Her hands went to either side of her hood, keeping it tight around her face.

Moving in front of her, I tugged on the black material. "Nila…take off the hood."

"No."

"Nila…" My voice dropped to a growl. "What are you hiding from me?"

Tears glassed her eyes.

My heart splintered. "Nila, please. I can't stand it when you don't tell me the truth." My hands pulled again, fighting against her hold.

A single tear slipped down her face. "Please…don't make me."

My heart stopped beating.

"What happened to you? When I first saw you, you were almost dead inside. I feel you coming back to life, but something's changed." My voice turned heavy. "Please, Nila. Let me fix this. Whatever happened; let me try to help."

More tears ran silently down her face. She looked away. "I—I was weak. I gave in. I didn't think I had anything left inside me." Her breath caught. "But then I saw you, and I remembered why I was fighting. You gave me purpose again. You reminded me that I'm still cared for and it's my duty. Not to stay alive for myself, but for *you*. You've already helped, more than you know."

"Fuck…Nila…" My chest seized as her sadness crested over me. "What can I do to make this right?"

She smiled weakly. "You've already done it. I'm piecing myself back together. I'm better now. I've remembered who I am." Her fingers tightened. "Just…please, don't ask me to take off the hood."

I couldn't stand it. My temper thickened. "Take it off. I have to know."

She shook her head.

"Don't make me tear it off you. You have to show me. We're in this together, remember? That means sharing our pain and telling the truth."

Her shoulders hunched. She hesitated for too long. Finally, her head bowed. "Please...please don't find me ugly."

"What?" My air exploded. "Why would you ever ask such a thing?"

Sucking in a shaky breath, she let go of the hood.

My condition soaked up her thoughts—despair, pain, confliction, anger. But most of all, paralyzing hopelessness. My soul pulverised as I slowly slipped off the shadowy material and saw what she'd tried to hide.

I couldn't speak.

I couldn't think.

All I could do was stare and fill with such fury, such motherfucking *hate*, that tears sprang to my eyes.

She couldn't look at me, her shoulders hunched dejectedly. "I—I—" She gave up, hiding her face in her hands and letting go of her sadness.

Her stunning hair had been replaced with multiple different lengths and shapes. The bedraggled strands cascaded over her hands.

They would pay. *They will fucking pay for this.*

Trembling with rage, I gathered her to me, crushing her in my arms. "Those fucking bastards."

She turned in my embrace, wrapping her arms around me, crying silently into my neck. I stroked her back, her neck, the scruffy locks of hair. It felt so different, so strange.

That was what was so wrong. Why she felt so peculiar.

Her courage had been stripped, just like her beautiful hair.

I have to fix this.

I had no idea how, but I couldn't let her suffer.

Letting her go, I stalked to the end of the stable and grabbed a pair of scissors from the tack room. Stalking back, I sat behind her on the hay bale and without a word, brushed out the tatty strands with my fingers and kissed her neck.

With silence heavy between us, I snipped the mismatched ends.

I poured my love and commitment into her with every cut, sacrificing myself for every strand I snipped.

My heart raced as her hair fell to the hay, entwining gold with black. She shivered and hiccupped with teary breaths, but she didn't stop me. If anything, her shoulders relaxed and she let me fix the agony my family had caused.

I took my time.

I stroked her like I would any broken filly, reminding her that I cared and adored and would never hurt her. The soft thickness of her hair slipped through my fingers, slicing into uniformity the more I tended.

Not only did I fix her hair, but I fixed her soul, too. I sensed her reforming, gluing her scattered pieces, slipping back into the Nila I knew and worshipped.

I fell in love with her even more at the strength it took to come back from the brink of losing herself.

And she did it for me.

Under my touch, she came alive.

Under my willpower, she breathed freely and with a smidgen of happiness.

It didn't take long, working my way around her jaw, I combed the ebony strands. With a final snip, I sat back, drinking her in, reacquainting myself with this new woman who held my heart as surely as the one I'd left behind.

Cupping her face, I brushed aside the jaw-length hair and kissed her softly. "You're somehow even more beautiful, Needle."

She gasped.

The nickname I'd used in our texts slipped off my tongue effortlessly. The word symbolised everything I loved about her. Everything I'd grown to adore.

Her lips parted, welcoming me to kiss her deeper.

I groaned as I slinked my tongue into her mouth, licking her sadness and doing my best for her to see the truth.

I would never be free of her. Ever.

Silently, we lay on the hay, face-to-face, kissing gently. My fingers slipped into her hair, massaging her scalp, keeping her there in my arms instead of in her head with torment.

Time passed, and still, we kissed and existed. Silent and safe, falling in love all over again. We gave each other a sense of normalcy we'd never had before— pretending this was our world where nothing could ever touch us.

Finally, I pulled back, stroking her cheek with my knuckles. "I take it Bones delivered my message."

"Bones?"

"The kestrel."

Nila's face lit up for the first time since I'd seen her. The pain of her shorn hair faded a little. "Yes. I had no idea birds of prey could be trained to do that."

I flopped onto my back, hiding the wince of agony. Fucking Nila standing up hadn't exactly been recommended for a healing patient. "They can do all manner of things." My lips twitched, remembering what we'd done to Jasmine when we were younger. I over animated to keep Nila entertained, doing my best to forget about her hair and enjoy our peace together. "For example, Kes once trained a hawk to fly into Jasmine's room and deliver dead voles every evening just to piss her off. She'd screech and chase the bird all the way back to the mews."

"Mews?"

"Aviary." I waved my hand in the direction of the kennels. "Last count, I think we had six raptors on the estate. They live in the converted loft of the kennels. The bird I sent you will have returned home after delivering its message."

Nila played with a piece of hay, still quieter than normal. "First, I find out there are pigs hiding here and now birds. The longer I live at Hawksridge the more I realise how little I know."

And do you want to know more?

As much as I hated my father's hierarchy, I loved this estate. The Hall had no hold on me—it could be rubble for all I cared, but I loved the land. The acres of freedom and sanctuary and wildlife.

Eventually, when evil was eradicated, I hoped Nila would adopt this place as hers and make it as pure as she was.

Those are thoughts for after this is all over.

I frowned as I concentrated on the other part of her sentence. "Pigs?"

Her face tightened. "Forget it."

I went to argue, but she arched her chin, dragging my eyes down her throat to the small stain on her nightgown. A few crimson droplets soaked through the white cotton. "What the hell is that?" I shot upright. My own pain couldn't stop myself from feeling hers. I let my condition strengthen, searching for her secrets, trying to learn how she'd become injured.

I know how.

My fists clenched.

Nila immediately placed a hand over the cut on her breastbone. "It's nothing."

"Like fuck, it's nothing." Knocking her hand away, I glowered. "Who did that to you?" Cold rage settled over my soul. Her tension and secrets waked around me. "Who did it, Nila? Answer me."

Her face contorted; she looked away. "Like I said, it doesn't matter. You saw my hair…this was nothing compared to that."

Catching her chin, I brought her eyes to mine. "It fucking matters to me. I need to know." All I wanted to do was storm into Hawksridge and repeatedly stab my father in the motherfucking heart. I wanted him to feel the pain of dying. I wanted him to suffer forever. "Cut?"

She squeezed her eyes. More emotion washed from her—fear, sickness, weakness, guilt. What the fuck did she have to be guilty about?

Glancing at the two deep cuts marring her perfection, I knew Jasmine was right. The marks could've only been caused by one apparatus.

"That fucking cocksucker. He used the Heretic's Fork."

She flinched. "How did you—"

"What else have they done to you, Nila? Your hair, your skin." I rubbed my face, unable to shed the self-loathing for leaving her in the hands of my father and brother. "You should've texted me, told me what they were doing."

She sat up. "How did you guess about the Heretic's Fork?"

I scowled. "At least one person tells me the truth rather than trying to hide it to make me feel better."

She looked away, anger lighting her eyes. "Jasmine."

"Yes, Jasmine." Grabbing her wrist, I forced her to look at me. "The sister who I tasked to keep you safe. The woman you were supposed to trust and tell if you needed help or protection." I wanted to shake her. "Yet you didn't. You endured and lied to me that everything was fine—"

She snatched her hand out of my grip. "What was I supposed to do, Kite? I thought you were dead. I became someone I didn't recognise. And then I heard you were alive and I made a promise to stay that way so we could end this together."

Her eyes lowered, cutting me off. "Besides, I've lived through worse. I just had a weak moment before coming here tonight, that's all."

"That isn't all and you know it." I swallowed hard as her emotions shouted the obvious while her mouth refused to speak. "You're on the edge, Nila. I sense it." Grabbing her shoulders, I shook her. "Goddammit, you're stronger than they are. Don't let them win. *Promise* me."

She'd lived through worse at my hands.

The ducking stool. The whipping.

But I'd hurt her the most by not being there for her.

"God, Nila." I brought my knees up, caging myself in. This position had been preferred when I was a kid. Knees up, arms braced, head down—a little fortress from the overwhelming intensity I couldn't switch off. "I'll never forgive myself for what I've done."

My eyes pricked with fury at who I'd let myself become. For being so fucking *weak*.

Nila darted to her knees, snuggling against me. "Stop. You don't need forgiveness. We've moved past that."

"I'll never move past that. Not as long as I live." Looking into her black gaze, I vowed, "I'll never stop making it up to you."

She smiled sadly. "There's nothing to make up." Cupping my cheek, she ran her thumb over my bottom lip. "After what you just did for me—cutting my hair, giving me back what I'd lost—we're even. You came back from the dead for me, Kite. You've proven yourself far more than words ever could."

Lashing out, I wrapped an arm around her, hugging her fierce. "I can never again feel your pain. It fucking crippled me before, but it would murder me now."

She shook her head. "The only pain I'll ever feel from you, Jethro, is if you die again." She snorted quietly, doing her best to lighten the mood. "So, promise you won't do that and the rest will be fine."

"The only pain I ever want to endure is pain endured protecting and deserving you."

She stiffened. "What does that mean?"

It means I have a plan to end this but war has casualties on both sides.

"Nothing." Brushing away her short hair, I nuzzled into her neck. "I don't want to talk about this anymore."

Silence fell between us. She wanted to ask more questions, the barbs of curiosity stuck into my skin like thorns, but she swallowed them back.

"You haven't asked me how I escaped to come see you." Wriggling out of my embrace, she lay on her back, patting the blanket beside her. "They keep my door locked now, so I couldn't run through the Hall."

Reclining again, I inconspicuously held my healing side, granting some pressure from the building discomfort. "How did you get out then?"

Her teeth flashed in the darkness. "I scaled the downpipe outside my bathroom and used the grass lattice on the turret to shimmy to the ground."

I groaned. "Shit, Nila." Hawksridge had evolved over the centuries—indoor plumbing being a new addition with unsightly pipes ruining the prettiness of the façade. My ancestors had done their best to hide them with lattice grass, growing the patchwork up the building. It would've been an easy climb, but not for someone with the inconvenience of vertigo. "That was stupid."

If I had known she'd had to sneak and risk breaking her neck, I wouldn't have summoned her.

Who are you kidding?

I would've gone after her if she hadn't gotten my note. Being on the estate—being so close but so far—I couldn't stand it. "You could've fallen." I traced her pretty neck beneath the wreath of diamonds. "You could've hurt yourself for nothing."

"Nothing? You're hardly nothing." She shivered under my touch. "I would've flown here with broken bones just to be with you."

The air switched from stagnant to electric.

"You make me a better person." Gathering her close, we lay nose to nose. "I mean to deserve you more every fucking day."

Her lips parted, her gaze latching onto my mouth. Her thoughts turned from conversation to sex, dragging me deeper into her spell.

I'd lived through years of horror.

I'd gone through so many stages of denial.

And I'd done my best to remember who I was beneath the influx of commands from Cut. But in one look, Nila shredded me into pieces and shone light upon the man I'd forgotten existed. A man who'd found happiness in animals rather than humans. A man who'd tried so hard to please but only became broken. And a boy who'd met a girl in his past, who'd been raised to hate her, told he would torture and kill her, only to find the courage to love her instead.

"I want you." I bent to kiss her. "I want you forever." Our lips touched; shockwaves danced down my spine. My cock thickened and Nila once again took me hostage.

Her breathing caught, rattling in her lungs.

I pulled back. She'd been sick with no one to help her. How many other fucking secrets had she kept from me? "You were ill?"

She flushed. "It's nothing. Just a cold. I'm fine."

It wasn't just a cold and it wasn't fine. I'd let her down again. But as much as I hated her lying to me, I loved her all the more for being so selfless.

I don't deserve this woman.

Nila's lips whispered over mine again. "Besides, none of that matters now. You're back. We can run."

I froze.

Run?

There was no more running.

She pulled away, her face slowly sinking into despair. "Wait…you *are* here for me, aren't you?" Her voice babbled. "We're leaving this place. We're running tonight. We'll get you better so we can end this when you're strong enough. You *have* to take me away, Jethro. I can't go back. I *can't.*"

My heart fisted. I wanted to carve out my soul to make her understand. "I'm here for you, Nila. A thousand times here for you."

She shuffled backward, but I trapped her wrist.

Tears shone in her eyes. "But you're not going to save me tonight?"

I'm going to save more than you. Don't you see?

So many lives rested on my shoulders—just like I'd carried all my life.

"We can't run. I refuse to run again."

She wiped away a tear, refusing to look at me.

I groaned, tracing the translucent skin of her wrist. "Running isn't an option anymore. If I run and lick my wounds, he wins again. We have the element of surprise now. They think I'm dead. It gives me the perfect opportunity to end this. To be free. But it has to be *now.*"

"But you're not well enough."

Grabbing her hand, I placed it directly on my side. Gritting my teeth against the flare of pain, I growled, "I proved to you I'm alive by fucking you. I'm here to save you; you have my ultimate word. But there are others I need to save, too."

She deflated, knowing I spoke the truth but not ready to accept it. Her emotions turned selfish, wanting to keep me for herself. She already agreed we couldn't run—her thoughts blared it—but it didn't stop her from indulging in one make-believe moment.

"But if we ran, we'd be free." She looked up, speaking words she didn't mean. "You have money. I have money. We could disappear." Her conviction and selfishness faded the second she finished.

She sighed, her heartbeat slowing with resolution.

I tucked short strands behind her ear, my soul cursing the death of her gorgeous hair all over again. "You already know what I'm going to say and you agree with me, but I'll say it anyway. Running isn't an option. Vaughn is still here. Tex. Your family's company. You're saying you'd leave it all behind when just a few more days it could be over for good? Why should we be the ones to run when it's our lives that we're fighting for? Our future is here. Our families are here. I'm not going anywhere and neither are you."

She pursed her lips. "They let Vaughn go. He'll be back with my father and hopefully be smart enough to hide. We could run." Her emotions overwhelmed with suffering. "I *need* to leave, Jethro. I can't go back. I can't. I'll break. I'm so close to breaking. I'm not strong enough. I *can't*—"

I grabbed her, holding her shaking form. "Calm down. I'm not asking you to go back for long." As much as it killed me, I added, "And do you truly believe they set Vaughn free? They haven't done anything decent yet; why would they start now?"

She froze.

"The only thing we can do to ensure your family's safety is to *fight*. You're the bravest person I know, Nila. You've proven I'm strong enough to do what needs to be done. And I *will* do what needs to be done. But in order to do that I need you by my side. I need you with me which means we aren't running. We're staying here and fighting."

She shook her head, even though her emotions agreed with me wholeheartedly.

I kissed her head. "You're so incredible, Needle. So beautiful and strong. I'll end this, okay? You just have to believe in me a little longer."

She cried quietly, snuggling into my embrace. She couldn't verbalize it, but she gave me permission. And I fucking loved her for it. For being strong enough to agree. For being with me even when I asked so much.

I dropped my voice to a whisper. "Nila...I love you. I'm never going to hurt you again. Unequivocally, deeply, totally—you have my heart and soul. I *will* make this right, I promise." Taking her hand, I kissed her knuckles. "You trust me still, don't you?"

A flicker of a seductive smile crossed her lips even as tears spilled from her eyes.

Memories of asking her if she trusted me when I'd shared my secrets came back. At the start she'd said yes, even as her heart screamed no. But, by the time I'd shown her intensity with my crop and made love to her, she'd trusted me completely.

Her skin was the palest cream in the dark. My lips ached to kiss her again. My cock throbbed to be inside her.

Her eyes tore past my humanness and into the part of me that was eternal. "I trust you."

I couldn't stop myself.

I pushed her onto her back and climbed on top of her. Her short hair fanned out like a black halo, tangling with hay. She didn't stop me as I pressed my weight over her. Her legs opened, her hands gathered the material of the nightgown, and she welcomed me to wedge between her delectable thighs.

I groaned as her body melted. My cock punched against my boxer-briefs wanting to fill her all over again.

As much as I needed to be inside her, I didn't want to rush it. My fingers threaded through her hair, keeping her pinned. Nila wriggled, softening beneath me.

Biting her bottom lip, her fingers moved to my waistband. "If you're strong enough to fight now, even after being shot, then prove it again." Her fingers dipped into my briefs, wrapping around my cock. "Prove that I can trust you."

My erection leapt in her hand. Her diamond collar sparkled as I kissed the swell of her breast. "You drive me insane."

"Good." Her breathing quickened. "I want you insane. Mad about me. Completely consumed by me."

I thrust into her palm. "I already am."

A shadow crossed her face, bringing with it a flicker of thought I didn't catch. Propping myself up on my elbows, I stared at her. What had she been thinking? Did she not trust me? Did she not believe me when I said I'd never let anything happen to her again?

"What is it?" I asked, my heart thumping out of control. "Tell me what you're not saying."

She sucked in a breath, looking at the ceiling. "Nothing. Everything's perfect." Her fingers tightened around my cock. "I want you, Kite."

Her voice echoed with love, but I didn't let her derail me. Not this time.

"Tell me. Do you hate me? Do you secretly loathe me for what I've done?"

I won't be able to live if you do.

"How can I make it up to you?" My voice turned ragged. "How can I prove I mean what I say? That I'm so fucking sorry. That nothing else will ever—"

She hushed me, pressing a finger over my mouth. "There's nothing else you can do. I believe you."

Her voice said one thing, her thoughts another.

I hated when people lied. It tangled me into fucking knots trying to figure out their true meaning. That'd been the problem from childhood. Cut would order me to do one thing, but his cold-hearted cruelty guided me to do another. Kestrel learned from a very young age never to lie to me. I needed utmost honesty to survive living in a household with so many conflicting ideals and hierarchies.

"You can't lie to me, Nila." My blood thickened with impending doom. What wasn't she saying? Would it destroy me if she did? I pressed my forehead against hers. "You can't keep things from me. I know there's something you're not saying and until you clear the air that emotion will overcast everything until it drives me mad."

Her face tightened. "Your condition can be a real pain, you know that?"

I laughed wryly. "You've only just noticed?" The derisive humour didn't shred the tension between us. "Spit it out. Now."

A single tear escaped.

Fuck.

"Nila...don't." Ever so gently, I licked the salty drop, taking her sadness and vowing to turn it into endless happiness. She deserved so much happiness.

Eternal happiness.

And I would be the one to give it to her.

My chest cracked open. "I'm so sorry, Nila." Burying my face in her hair, I clutched her hard. "So sorry for everything—for what I am, for what I demand of you, for the things I can't fix."

Her arms wrapped around me. "You don't need fixing, Jethro. You're bombarded every day with stimuli. You're so strong to have endured a childhood living here. You put mechanisms in place to protect yourself. Only…"

"Only?" I traced her cheek with a fingertip. "Go on…"

She tensed, hesitation and reluctance seeping from her. Sucking in a deep breath, she rushed, "I know I love you. I've never known anything so clear, but I can't help wondering if you love me."

I reared back. *"What?"*

She couldn't have hurt me more if she'd tried.

"How can you even *think* something like that? What have I just been saying? You think I've been *lying* to you?" I rolled off her, trembling with rage. "What does that fucking *mean?*"

She sat up, twisting her fingers together. "I just mean…you feel what others feel. Could you be reflecting what I feel for you? How do you know what's real and what's not? It makes me wonder if I forced you to love me. That any woman who cared for you after a lifetime of living with Cut and Bonnie would've made you fall—not fall, but mirror her affection." Her eyes glossed with unfallen tears. "How can I trust that you know what you feel isn't just me putting those thoughts into your head?"

I shoved off the hay bale, unable to keep still. "I can't fucking believe this."

How could she be so clueless? So heartless to say I was so lost to not know my own wants and dreams. How could she even ask that after I cut her hair and almost fucking cried at her pain? "I'm a human being, Nila. I have the same thoughts and feelings as the rest of the population."

She hung her head, dark hair curtaining her face. "You do, but you also have so much more. Your condition, Jethro…I mean, I had one goal when you took me to Hawksridge: to make you love me so I could use you to free me." She swallowed, her eyes tight with confession. "What if I succeeded?"

Of course, you succeeded.

But I'd fallen for her of my own free will.

I should be appalled, but really—I'd known all along. I'd felt her conspiring, pushing me to let her in. Thing was…she didn't need to make me love her. I'd already fallen—long before she started her games. Even before she forced me to kiss her, I'd given her my heart without knowing it.

"You have no idea what you're saying."

"Don't I? Ever since you told me what you were, I've wondered. When you died, it killed me to think I'd never know the truth. Never know if you felt the depth that I feel for you—or the pain I felt when you were taken from me."

Dragging both hands through my hair, my side burned with pain. Her words whipped me like a thousand bullets. As an empath I was subjected to hundreds of emotional pulls and tugs every day. I was whittled down within an inch of sanity every second.

But that didn't mean I copied the strongest thoughts. It didn't mean I was weak and couldn't think for myself. If anything, my condition made me stronger. Not only did I cross-examine every opinion and sentiment but I also learned how to barricade my own conclusions from being tainted by others.

My true thoughts were in a fortress, untouched and pure and I knew *exactly* what I felt toward her—regardless that she'd lied to me.

She doesn't trust me.

I stopped pacing, turning to face her. "Is that what you've thought all along? That I'm not truly in love with you?"

Goosebumps covered her skin; she looked away. "Honestly, I didn't want to think. I wanted to believe in the fantasy, rather than pick our relationship apart. This past month has been hell; I won't deny that. Those first few days when I thought you were dead, I really wanted to be, too. But having you back ...it all seems too good to be true. How can I trust that you're here for me? That you'll save me? End this?"

Her eyes narrowed on mine. "Do you want to do that for *me* or for *yourself*? Because if it's for me, then how can you pick your family over a girl who made you love her? How can you even consider killing your father—no matter how horrid he's been to you—when you can't be sure I didn't manipulate you the same way Cut did all those years."

I backed away.

She successfully sliced my soul into ribbons, making me doubt that her emotions for me were genuine. Had they all been an act to get me on her side?

You don't believe that.

She confused me—tore apart the only thing that'd been true in my life, and made me doubt.

Damn her. Damn all of this.

Deliberately, I dropped my guard and let my condition reach for her, tasting her cocktail of lust and panic.

I did my utmost to find a thread of lies. To see if her affection for me was bullshit. But unlike my father and his rare moments of comradery and respect, there was no sulking undertones or passive-aggressive control.

She was honest and true. She *loved* me. She might not have set out to love me, but it happened anyway.

Sighing, I dropped to my knees in front of her. "You have it backward, Nila."

She shook her head. "I don't see—"

"You don't see because you don't fully understand." I looked at the yellow stalks of hay, wishing we were somewhere safe and bright. This conversation had brought shadows between us that had no right to be there. "Yes, I'm more influenced by others' emotions but I'm still my own person. I still have the right of choice and reflection. I've been around women. I've been around friends and enemies. I've lived a normal life like any man and could've found happiness if I chose it."

She flinched. Her fingers fiddled with her nightgown.

Stopping her fidgeting fingers with mine, I smiled. "But, Nila, I'm still governed by my heart. Did I let you influence me? No. I let you in because I saw how strong and brave you were. I let you in because I remembered the girl I met and the way I used to feel around her. I let you in because I saw someone lost and just as controlled as I was when I first messaged you."

She gasped, trembling in my hold.

I wasn't done.

"I was envious that a girl destined to die for the sins of her ancestors was more courageous than I could ever be. I fell in love with your tenacity. Your fearlessness. Your flaws. I fell for you because you taught me to trust myself—to trust that I had the power to be better." Rising off my knees, I cupped her face, my voice throbbing with truth. "You made me a better person by *showing* me rather than forcing me. I fell in love with you because you're the one for me. Not because you were a woman in my home and in my bed."

I sat beside her. "How low must you think of me, to think I could ever stoop to such a level?"

My heart stopped beating. Would we ever find happiness, or would we always second-guess and be clouded with conditions and pasts?

She thinks I'm powerless.

That I didn't fight as hard for her as she did for me.

And she's right.

I'd locked away my true wants in favour of obeying my father. I let him control my life when I should've taken responsibility for my actions. But I knew that now. I was strong enough now.

Because of *her*.

Gently, I pushed her onto her back, climbing on top of her again, slipping between her thighs. "Do you believe me now?" I kissed her once. "Do you believe that my thoughts are my own? That my heart knows it's yours through *my* decision—not your manipulation?" I kissed her again. "I'll make this right between us. You'll see. I'll prove to you that what I feel for you isn't a by-product of my condition or something I couldn't control. I'll show you that I willingly gave you my soul before you even knew me."

Her eyes hooded. "Thank you."

"What are you thanking me for?"

"For showing me how stupid I've been."

I chuckled, growing hard for her again, wanting her so much. "Just *trust* me."

She moaned, her mouth seeking mine. "I do trust you. I *will* trust you."

The instant our lips connected, we lost ourselves.

We fell into each other, desperate to reaffirm our spoken truth with bodily affection. There were too many misconstrued conclusions between us. I needed to show her I meant every word. And then reality would have to intrude. I'd have to tell her my plans and prepare her for what would happen next.

"Can I?" I slinked my hand up her nightgown, pushing aside cotton.

Her thighs quivered beneath my touch. She sucked in a gasp as my fingertips brushed her core. "Yes…"

Her permission sent my cock jerking with need. I gritted my teeth as I dragged my finger through her folds. "Now we've cleared the air, I want to know something very important."

She arched as my tattooed NTW fingertip drifted up to press against her clit. "Oh? And what's that?"

I nipped her bottom lip. "Did you miss me?" I slipped one finger slowly inside her.

She opened her mouth, sweeping her tongue into mine. "So much."

"How much?"

Her fingers slinked into my hair, holding me tight. She kissed me with every ferocious strength she possessed. My breathing accelerated until my side burned.

Letting me go, she grinned coyly. "That much."

I never took my eyes off her as I thrust my finger, stretching her inner muscles, claiming her. "Good answer."

She twitched as I pushed a second finger inside. "I can't wait to fill you. To prove that what I feel is real." She was so tight, her body fighting my invasion.

My thumb stroked her clit. She shivered in pleasure, her hands catching my t-shirt. "More..."

My mouth watered to taste her. To drink and worship her. We didn't have time. I should get her back to safety and wait until this was over, but I couldn't stop myself.

"I'll give you more." Sliding down her body, I shoved her nightgown up over her waist, revealing her glistening pussy.

Her eyes popped wide as I imprisoned her thighs in my hands and bowed my head over her dark curls.

"Kite..."

My heart leapt. I grinned. "Have I ever told you how much I love it when you call me that?"

Before she could reply, I sucked her clit into my mouth.

"Oh, God!" Her legs spasmed, latching around my ears.

I rimmed her entrance, driving both of us mad. She writhed on the blanket, trying to get free from my questing tongue.

I didn't let her go.

"Kite, oh...I need you."

I smiled. "That can be arranged." I sank my tongue desperately inside her.

"Oh, shit!"

I growled, "You didn't specify which part of me you needed, so I'll take liberties if you don't mind." I plunged my tongue again, licking her, drinking her—just like I wanted.

My cock throbbed, twitching inside my briefs.

"I want you—all of you!"

I chuckled, dragging my tongue upward, swirling around her clit before thrusting back inside her. "You already have all of me."

She grasped the hay, her legs locking tight as I licked her harder.

Her taste drugged me. I had to have more. My pace increased, swirling, fucking, showing her I was alive and here and I would *never* hurt her again.

My teeth ached to bite.

My hips rocked needing to drive inside her, but I wouldn't stop pleasuring her—not yet. Not until she came undone and accepted my gift. The gift of everything that I was.

Her fingernails jerked into my hair. "Enough. I need your cock."

I shook my head, sucking harder. "Not yet." Teasing her entrance again, I breathed, "Every night apart was fucking torture. Every time I closed my eyes, I dreamt of you." My finger replaced my tongue while I flicked her clit, driving her skyward. "Do you want to know what fantasies I had while I healed?"

She moaned.

"I'll take that as a yes." Thrusting two digits into her pussy, I purred, "I didn't picture you as you might think. Yes, I grew hard for you, picturing you bound to my bed and accepting everything I gave you. Yes, I tortured myself with images of your hard nipples and flushed skin."

She moaned as I rocked faster.

"But it wasn't those images that undid me." I kissed her inner thigh. "Want to know what did?"

She looked down, locking eyes with me.

She nodded.

I smiled, once again bowing to my task of worshipping this woman. "It was a dream that gave me hope. A dream where we do ordinary things. Talk about ordinary life. Become friends as well as lovers. I want to know you inside out, Nila. I want to know everything about you."

Her legs trembled around my shoulders. Her onyx gaze matched the darkness of the stables. "I want that, too."

She whimpered as I bit her. With a wicked wet lick, I forced her leg over my shoulder, giving me greater access and depth.

Her skin scorched, blazing with lust. Part of me wanted to drive her to a climax. I wanted her to come on my tongue and lap up every drop. But the other part wanted her snuggled in my arms, her legs wrapped around mine, our two bodies giving, taking, driving, *craving*.

"I want you forever."

"Forever." Her hips arched involuntarily, seeking more.

I splayed my hand on her lower belly, holding her down as she bucked into my mouth.

"Jethro...please."

"What do you want?"

"You. I want you. All of you. Every part of you. Just you."

My mouth went dry. I couldn't deny her.

Her eyes were wild as I withdrew my fingers and prowled up her body. Without looking away, I licked her dampness from my digits and bent to kiss her mouth.

"Taste yourself on me. Know that I fully belong to you."

She moaned, seducing me with her trust. "I want you inside me. I want to feel you deep, driving me insane."

She was my ultimate fantasy come true. Dark hair, lithe body, vicious strength, and undeniable power. I'd licked her but instead of feeling like I'd given her a part of me, I felt as if she'd given me more. So, so much more.

Grabbing her wrists, I pinned them above her head. Hay crackled beneath the blanket, stabbing my knees, itching unprotected skin. But it was the best goddamn bed in the world because it was just us. No cameras. No locks. No fear.

"God, I want you." My voice was rough, obsessed with her.

Her lips were red and swollen, matching the colour of her nipples through the white cotton. I'd never seen her look so sexy. "I want you whimpering—I need those incredible sounds you make when I slide inside you."

Her lips parted. "I'll do whatever you want if you stop talking and fuck me."

I laughed. "Your wish is my command."

Settling over her, I shoved my jeans and boxer-briefs to my knees and wedged my elbows on either side of her head. I should've supported more of my weight, but I needed to feel her beneath me. For her to know that she was blanketed by my body and soul—that I'd protect her forever. That she was *mine*.

"Let me inside you," I whispered, nudging her pussy with the broad crown of my cock.

She bucked in my arms as I pushed upward, sliding through her slick arousal, taking her as surely as she'd taken me. My arms wobbled as she grabbed my arse, dragging me forward.

I couldn't stand it. It was too good. Too intense. Too fucking much.

I groaned, burying my face in her throat. Without warning, I surged upward, impaling my thick length completely inside her.

Her wetness offered no hindrance, accepting every inch.

"Christ, Nila." I grinded my hips against her as she whimpered.

"More. More!" The desperation in her voice took me hostage. I'd done that. I'd broken her by being shot and making her doubt my affection.

I was hers for eternity. I'd spend the rest of my life making her believe it.

Her hot wetness fisting around me drove me out of my fucking mind. I thrust harder.

We quickly turned from making love to fucking—straining to steal more from each other, driven by the need to hurt but also please.

Her lips landed on my chin.

Instantly, I brought my mouth to hers, slinking together, mimicking the action of our hips. Breaking apart, I groaned, "When I saw you coming to the stables...I fell even more in love with you." I thrust faster. "When you let me take what I wanted while licking you, I gave the last shred of my heart to you."

She threw her head back, sweat glittering in the hollow of her throat.

I licked it, avoiding the iciness of the diamonds around her neck. "So beautiful. So perfect." My stomach clenched. I tightened my fingers around her wrists, loving the rapid thump of her pulse. "I'm never letting you go."

Her eyes clouded with lust. "I don't know who I am anymore without you." She arched up, kissing me, moaning with my thrusts. "I believe in you."

I wanted to shower her with kisses. "I'll never get used to you wanting me."

"Wanting you?" Her eyes flared. "Jethro, I *am* you. I'm not a whole person anymore without you."

I winced as her words squeezed my heart. "Fuck, Nila." Hugging her closer, I plunged harder.

She moaned, inner muscles rippling.

"Shit, that feels so good." She closed her eyes, pressing her breasts against me; reminding me we were still clothed, still barricaded from being completely free. "You're so deep."

"I can go deeper." She groaned as I fucked her faster. My side hurt with every thrust, but an orgasm spiralled into existence. My balls sparked and the delicious gathering pressure at the base of my spine gritted my jaw. "I want to come so fucking bad."

"Then come."

"I want to come all over you, inside your pussy, your mouth. I want you every way imaginable. I want everything from you."

"I want that, too."

"I need you on your back, your knees, your stomach, against the wall, everywhere. I could fuck you for the rest of my life and still not get enough of you."

I kissed her, sucking her tongue, turning every whisper and touch supercharged with erotic passion.

"God, I'm close." She returned my kiss, wet and passionate—her lips dancing, stealing my soul all over again. Her thighs squeezed my hips, imprisoning me as I drove into her again and again. "I'm coming...God, I'm coming."

I pumped harder, giving into bliss and stars. "Come. Fuck, I want you to come."

"Come with me."

"It would be my fucking pleasure."

Nothing else mattered. Nothing but bliss and togetherness.

We gave in.

Our motions turned rabid, seeking one goal, devouring each other in a fit of sin.

"Fuck me. Oh, Kite. Love me. Fuck me. Ride me."

I couldn't hold on anymore. Digging my knees into the hay, I gave her what she wanted. I lived in her begs and drove faster until red pain flashed through my system.

I plunged into her, our groans and moans drowning out the sounds of our fucking.

Her core tightened.

I rocked harder, rubbing myself against her clit. My balls smacked against the curve of her arse and the hay prickled like tiny needles. Our bodies battled each other—a perfect avenue of violent emotions.

I thrust again and again and again. "Fuck, I'm going to come."

Her back locked, her core clenched, giving me nowhere else to go.

Her legs locked tight around my waist. I cried out as her knee caught my injury.

"Yes!" She came hard and furious, fisting around me, dragging painful pleasure from every inch.

My orgasm unravelled without warning, exploding like a thunderstorm through every muscle. Lightning and rain drops, I spurted my very fucking soul into her.

One thing was for sure, I didn't just come. I came *undone*.

And only Nila had the power to stitch me back together.

TIME WAS MY worst enemy.

Nothing good ever came from time.

It passed too quickly—good moments and happy memories gone in a blink. Or it passed too slowly—bad experiences and unhappy circumstances dragging for an eternity.

And now, when all I wanted to do was fall asleep in the warm stable with Jethro wrapped around me and the sweet scent of hay in my nose, all I could focus on was...*time is limited.*

We'd carved out all we could, and now it was over.

I looked at Jethro. My freshly cut hair whispered along my jaw. My heart suffocated with love for him and what he'd done.

He'd single-handedly brought me back from the brink, giving me back my self-worth, fixing me enough to stay strong—for a little longer.

He pulled up his jeans and buckled them. Without a word, he slipped off the hay bale and helped me stand. We hadn't talked about what would happen now, but I already knew. He meant to send me back.

He's leaving me again.

Sadness and fear tingled my spine.

I can't go back.

But I had no choice.

I'll break.

But I had to remain strong.

I couldn't look at him as he smoothed down my nightgown, readjusted my coat, and plucked wayward strands of straw from my hair.

Say it. Tell me we're about to go our separate ways after everything that's happened.

Jethro stiffened, obviously sensing my frustration and terror.

Time would come between us again. I would hate it all the more.

"Nila...stop." Gathering me in a hug, he kissed my cheek. "You already know what I'm about to say. I feel it."

I snuggled into him, despite wanting to shove him away. All that talk of keeping me safe, yet he expected me to return to the monster's den without him.

Please, don't do it...take me with you.

"What are you going to do?" I inhaled his skin, flinching against the strange scent of antiseptic and musk. He normally smelled so delicious but now he reminded me of death and toil. "Whatever you're planning, don't. We could still leave. Tonight."

Time doesn't need us apart again. It's had its fun.

I wanted to create my own time where we became immortal and lived a safe, happy existence forever.

But you know he's right.

No matter how much I wanted to, I couldn't leave Vaughn and he couldn't leave Jasmine. And if Kestrel ever woke up, Jethro owed him a safe home to return to. As much as I wanted to scream and beg, I forced down my weakness. I was on his side—I would do what he asked of me, even if it was the hardest thing I'd ever do.

Damn obligations and common-sense. Hadn't I deserved some fantastical ideology where we could run off into the sunset and exist happily ever after?

Why couldn't life be like storybooks?

Jethro sighed, hugging me hard. His muscles vibrated; his heart thundered. He was alive, in my arms, and his orgasm was drying on my inner thigh.

He's alive.

I had to trust he'd stay that way to carry out whatever he had planned.

"I need to end this, Nila." Jethro pulled away, looking into my eyes. "You know as well as I do that we can't be free until it's dealt with."

The cuts on my breastbone flared, agreeing with him. We'd suffered enough—it was their turn.

My eyes fell to his waist. It hadn't escaped my notice that he refused to take his t-shirt off. However, he couldn't hide the small pinprick of blood coming through the light grey material.

I reached for it.

He jolted back, clamping an arm around himself—glaring at me, daring me to question his conviction that he was strong enough to do this. "One day, two at the most. I'll have everything in place and we can finally be happy."

I shook my head. "Something will happen. It always does." Tears rose. I hated that I was weak but I couldn't deny it—the thought of going back to Hawksridge alone petrified me. "I can't go back, Kite. Please, don't make me."

So much for not begging.

"They've hurt me. They almost won. I know you believe in me but I honestly don't believe in *myself* anymore. Please...*please* don't make me go back."

I couldn't stop shaking. I didn't have the power to walk back there.

Jethro kissed the top of my head. "You've been so damn strong— stronger than me by far. I sent a note to Jasmine telling her what I'm planning. I asked her to make up an excuse to keep you in her room. She'll watch over you. She'll say you're teaching her how to sew or something." His voice dropped with love. "She'll make sure you're safe and out of their hands for two days."

I didn't have the heart to tell him that Jasmine's power was minimal, slipping further on a daily basis. Bonnie had her ways to restrict Jasmine. I wouldn't put it past the old witch to poison her for going against dear ole' granny.

If Bonnie ever finds out Jasmine's working against her...

"What are you going to do? Two days is too much time."

Time again.

The enemy to us all.

The sands of hell.

"I'm going to call for help." Jethro's jaw twitched as if the thought of admitting he needed others frustrated him.

"Who?"

He frowned. "Just leave it to me. Don't worry about it."

"Tell me. I want to know."

"You need to get back before they find you're missing." His eyes narrowed. "Don't climb up the drainpipe. Go through the front door and ask Jasmine for a key. She'll wipe the camera footage in the morning."

I took a step backward, needing to distance myself so I could walk out of there without kneeling and begging to go with him. "You're changing the subject. Tell me what you're planning."

He exited the stall, forcing me to follow him down the aisle. "What do you want to know?"

Why couldn't he see that by asking me to trust him and willingly return to the Hall, he owed me everything?

It's taking everything that I am not to show you how terrified I am. How lonely. How defeated. You have to give me something to cling to. Something that will keep me strong.

"I want to know what you mean to do."

He looked over his shoulder, holding his side.

Was it just me or was his skin whiter than before? A fever kissing his brow?

I wanted to strap him to a bed and nurse him back to full health. He still had a long way to go—no matter how adamant he was.

His golden eyes flashed in the darkness. "Fine, I'm going to call Kill. The guy you met at Diamond Alley. I'm going to enlist his help."

"And he'll give it?"

"Let's just say, we have an agreement. He'll come."

"But he's in the States. It'll take him two days just to get here."

Jethro spun around, coming to plant his hands on my hips. "I also plan to contact someone else. Someone who's been doing a great deal of conspiring over the past month. Someone who has had enough like me."

My heart skipped. *Vaughn?* "Who?"

Jethro kissed my cheek, brushing aside my hair with gentle fingers. "Your father."

I froze. "Tex?"

He nodded. "Arch has been busy the past few weeks. While I've been healing, I've kept an eye on him. He's gathering an army, Nila—not just media this time, but a proper bought team. He's ready to hunt and I'll give him the perfect target."

"How—how do you know that?"

His teeth gleamed with anger and commitment. "I looked into his background. Pulled a few favours to find out if there's been inconsistent spending in his accounts."

"Wow—"

"Eh, Jet?" A figure appeared from the blackness.

I jumped. However, instead of cowering behind Jethro like I would've a few months ago, seeking protection and others to save me, I unthinkingly placed myself in front of him. My arms up, fists curled, teeth bared in defiance.

I might be almost broken, but I protected those I loved.

The hunchback came closer, skulking from the shadows. "Impressive stance, Nila. But if you mean to follow through with a punch, make sure your thumb is on the *outside* of your fingers. Otherwise, you'll break it."

I narrowed my eyes as the figure dumped two duffels from his shoulders to cobblestones. The dense fabric slapped loudly in the night silence.

"Flaw?"

A low chuckle reached my ears as he stepped from the darkness. "Hi, Nila." His eyes skated over me, widening with understanding of what Jethro and I had gotten up to.

Jethro hugged me from behind, planting a kiss on my cheek. "I didn't think I could love you any more than I do. You just proved me wrong. Thank you for protecting me."

My heart burst.

Letting me go, he skirted in front of me and held out his hand. "Once again, you've earned my thanks."

Flaw nodded, shaking Jethro's grip. "Jasmine's been told. I've got what you asked, and nobody is the wiser." His eyes fell on me. "I can take you back to the estate, Nila. Give you an alibi if anyone's up at this ungodly hour." Fishing in his pocket, he held up a key. "I have the key to your room."

Jethro rubbed his chin. "That might not be a bad idea. Just think up a decent excuse." He narrowed his gaze in my direction. "You've been sick with the flu—you can't deny it—I can still hear it in your lungs. Use that as a reason for midnight wanderings. You needed medicine." His face darkened. "Which I doubt you asked for while you suffered."

I looked away. "What I do when you're not around is my business. Just like you getting shot and making us all believe you were dead is yours."

Hear what I'm saying? That I'm not a victim anymore—I'll stand up for myself regardless if you're there to help me or not.

Jethro clenched his jaw.

Flaw laughed. "Tension in paradise, huh?"

Growling under his breath, Jethro changed the subject. "Did you manage to catch him okay?"

Flaw grinned, his strong jaw shaded in dark stubble. "Bit of a bugger to start with but nothing a handful of oats couldn't overcome." Pointing at the bags, he added, "Medical supplies in that one. Along with water and food enough for a week. Clothing, tent, and survival stuff in that one. I doubt you'll want to make a fire in case they see the plume, so I brought a gas heater to cook on and to keep you warm, along with an electric blanket that's solar-powered."

My eyes widened. "Wait, why does he need all that?"

Jethro turned to me. "Because you might be going back into the Hall alone, but I made a promise that I'd never leave you again." He took my hand, guiding me away from Flaw and outside where the moon drenched the forecourt. Before it'd been empty and silent. Now Wings stood patiently, saddled and bridled, his back hoof cocked with boredom.

Seeing the black beast caused hope to explode all over again.

I whirled in Jethro's arms. "You're staying close by?"

"Staying on the grounds. Yes." Pulling out a silver phone, his eyes darkened. "I'll send you messages. I sent you a couple yesterday that you didn't reply to. Did they take your phone away?"

No, I was just trapped in the Heretic's Fork and tormented.

I shook my head. "I haven't checked it. I keep it hidden—just in case."

"You have to stay in constant contact now," he growled. I need to know where you are, that you're okay. Otherwise, I'll lose my fucking mind."

My heart reacted like a love-struck teenager. "I must admit, I'm very impressed you remembered my number."

Jethro smirked, the first lighthearted reaction since he'd returned. "I haven't forgotten anything about you."

I rolled my eyes. "I suppose that's only fair seeing as I remember your number, too. I used to repeat it over and over again as I fell asleep." The seemingly normal part of dating, of secret messaging, and the delicious joy of finding that the person you were in love with felt the same way glowed inside.

He truly does love me.

It wasn't a projection of my love. Not a mirror or mirage.

It's true.

I'd never been more thankful.

He stepped closer, eyes hooded. "I can recite everything about you. If someone asked me how you tasted, I'd have the perfect description. If someone ordered me to list every freckle, I'd have the exact number. And if anyone wanted to know how brilliantly perfect you are—or hear about any of your accomplishments—I'd be able to regale them for hours." He wrapped his arms around me. "I'll never forget anything because it's the little things that make you real."

Flaw chuckled. "Good God, man, you have no shame."

I wanted him to bugger off. My heart disintegrated and my core clenched to have Jethro inside me again. I was wet, wanting.

Jethro laughed. "I'm not embarrassed to be honest for the first time in my life. This woman is mine. I love her, and I don't fucking care who knows it."

I blushed. My soul ached at the thought of him leaving. He couldn't leave me. Not now. Not now we'd been honest and finally talked outside of debts and pain. "Don't go…we can work out something else. Stay…please."

Jethro's smile fell, sadness cloaking him. "I have to. Another day or so and then we'll be safe to do whatever we want, go wherever we please." Taking my hands, he squeezed tightly. "Go now, Nila. I need you to return." Looking over his shoulder, he held out his hand.

Flaw came forward and dropped the key into his palm.

Jethro gave it to me. "On second thought, it might be best if you go on your own. Tell them Jasmine gave you the key because she often has tasks for you outside the realm of Cut's requirements." His voice cracked with frustration. "I wish to God I didn't have to make you do this. But I promise it will all be over soon."

Flaw muttered, "Cut's been pretty fucking happy the past couple of weeks. Been a lot more lenient with the Black Diamond brothers. Doubt he'll cause any trouble for the next two days."

Jethro sneered, "I guess killing his troublemaking sons makes everything hunky-fucking-dory in his world." Kissing me one last time, he urged me toward the Hall. "Go now. I'll message you when everything is in place and tell you where to go."

I opened my mouth to argue—to demand he keep me with him. Wherever he was going, I deserved to be by his side. "Jethro—"

I don't think I can do this…

He groaned, yanking me back to him. "God, I'll miss you." His mouth slammed on mine, kissing me roughly. As sudden as he claimed me, he relinquished me. "Leave. I love you."

As much as I wanted to argue, the desperation in his gaze forced me to obey.

I had no other option.

I'm strong enough to do this.

He would keep me safe.

I trust him.

To prove that I did, I turned my back on him and returned alone to Hawksridge Hall.

I didn't look back.

I should've looked back.

I did as he asked.

I shouldn't have done what he asked.

I climbed the small hill and turned to hell.

Dawn did its best to push aside the moon; the ground glittered with blades of frost. My heart was a lump of snow by the time I ascended the front entrance.

It was the hardest thing to ask of me—to willingly go back.

I didn't know if I'd ever be able to forgive him if he betrayed my trust.

If something happens...

I shook my head.

Nothing will happen.

Two days...it's nothing.

Pausing on the stoop of the Hall, I glanced fleetingly behind me.

There, on the horizon, was the faint outline of a black horse and its rider disappearing into the woods.

Jethro was gone.

I should never have let him go.

I should've run in the opposite direction.

I obeyed because I trusted him.

I should never have trusted him.

Unfortunately, I was right.

Two days was too long.

In two days, my world would end.

MY NEW HOME.

For the next thirty or so hours.

I surveyed my camp. Wings stood tethered to a tree and my tent stood sentry in the small glen. It'd taken an hour or so to set up—it would've been less if my body wasn't low on fuel and the pain from my wound hadn't decided to make itself known.

Payback for ignoring the warning signs while proving to Nila that I was strong and capable and deserving of her trust.

Louille would have a fucking fit if he knew what I'd done only hours after checking myself out from the hospital.

I swore under my breath, prodding the fresh blood stain on my side. The stitches had done their job and knitted me together, but at the very edge the skin had torn slightly. A throb resonated from rib to lung.

Oh, well. It was a good test to judge what I'm able to do.

Not to mention, I would do it all over again even if my side burst open mid-thrust. Nila consumed my every thought, my every sense. I'd only been away from her for sixty minutes, yet I missed her as if it'd been sixty years.

Opening the front zipper on the duffel, I pulled out some extra strength painkillers. Popping a few, I swallowed them dry and returned to securing the last peg of the tent.

I didn't know why I bothered. I wouldn't sleep. I could never rest knowing Nila was in the Hall being mentally and physically tortured.

How fucking dare they use the Heretic's Fork and cut off her hair? How dare they fucking think they had that right?

Insane, the lot of them.

If I was stronger and had better odds, I would've stormed Hawksridge tonight and slaughtered my father in his bed. But he had the Black Diamonds on his side. He had an army where I did not.

I wouldn't kill myself by being stupid.

I'd been stupid for long enough already.

I was home.

This was my empire, and I'd had enough of my family's madness.

Throwing the smaller duffel inside the tent, I crawled in after it. This campsite wasn't a stranger to me. I'd spent many nights huddled in the glen away from the Hall—away from screaming tempers, guilt-infested excuses, and anger-laden requirements.

When Cut tossed me out to make it to the boundary in the dead of winter, I wouldn't have survived if I hadn't already self-taught how to build shelter, hunt, and navigate. I liked my little sanctuary. If I'd had the strength to climb, I could've forgone the flimsy tent and scaled the boughs of an ancient oak tree where I'd built a tree fort in my youth.

I used to take Kes and Jaz there before we were old enough to know our duties.

Before life ruined us.

It was barely sunrise, but by tomorrow morning, I hoped to change the future of Hawksridge. I wouldn't just have the glen for peace and safety; I'd have the entire estate.

I'd finally have what was mine.

No waiting for my thirtieth. No obeying a psychopath.

Not anymore.

Twenty-four hours to put into place the rest of my life.

Another few hours to implement it.

I'd told Nila two days. I would stick to that promise.

Taking a deep breath, I hoisted myself onto the fold-out stretcher. Flaw had truly come through for me. He'd even packed a small generator so I could charge my phone and keep a light against the slowly creeping dawn.

Goosebumps covered my body, hidden below the thick parka Flaw had given me at the hospital. Winter had well and truly taken hold, determined to remind me that once upon a time I'd *welcomed* the frost. I'd mimicked winter by absorbing its ice and doing my best to freeze out other emotions.

It was like an old friend, a new enemy, a family member I no longer needed for help.

Grabbing the small electric heater stuffed into the bottom of the duffel, I plugged it into the generator and placed it by my feet. My body didn't have the reserves it needed to keep warm—not while most of my cells focused on healing my side.

My thoughts drifted to Nila.

Had she arrived at her quarters safely? Was she warm in bed, thinking of me—reliving my fingers inside her, my tongue sweeping hers?

"Shit." Shaking my head, I did my best to force those thoughts away. My cock was far too eager to attempt a third time.

It didn't work.

Nila's moans echoed in my mind. Her voice vibrated in my ears as she admitted she loved me.

How am I supposed to concentrate?

Nila was replaced with images of Kestrel—slowly dying alone in a strange hospital. Then my father leapt into my head, laughing, tormenting.

He'd never grown out of the spoiled brat syndrome—just like Daniel.

I didn't know the full story of how my father became heir, but my mother had dropped hints. Emma, too—when she was alive. Cut was many things, but he'd told some of his darkest secrets to Emma, knowing they'd die with her with no repercussions.

Livid rage heated my veins, better than any heater.

Now, he'll pay.

And I knew exactly how I'd do it.

Pulling out my phone, I sent a message to Nila.

Unknown Number: *I love you with every breath and heartbeat. Stay true to yourself. Trust me. You're strong enough; you're brave enough. You're my inspiration to end this. Don't give up on me, Nila. Two days and it's over.*

I didn't wait for a reply. Waiting would drive me crazy and horrid conclusions would consume me. I had to trust that Jasmine would keep Nila safe and allow me to do what was needed.

Reaching into the duffel, I pulled out the little black address book I'd kept hidden in my room. I'd given Flaw directions on where to retrieve it when he collected me. An address book was archaic nowadays with phones and computers, but I'd never been more thankful for old-fashioned practices.

I had no clue where my old phone was. This was my last record.

Flicking through the dog-eared pages, I sighed with relief, grateful for contacts I could rely on. Men I'd met and were loyal to me, not my father. Men who were ruthless in their own right. Men who could help me win against Cut and his legalities.

My eyes skipped over numbers for acquaintances I'd met on smuggling routes. Outlaws and pioneers, tanker captains and bribed coastguards.

I might have a need for them in the future, but not for this.

I had one man in mind.

There it is.

Arthur 'Kill' Killian, Pure Corruption MC.

I doubted many heirs to an English estate would have the personal contact of a president of an American motorcycle club.

But, thank fuck, I did.

Inputting the number, I pressed call on the phone and held it to my ear.

The line crackled, lacking a proper signal in the woods—struggling to connect Buckinghamshire to Florida.

The ringing stopped, followed by a loud screech. "You've reached Kill."

My hand tightened around the phone. "Hawk calling."

A pause, followed by some shuffling. "Hang on. Let me get somewhere private."

"Sure."

I waited for faint voices to fade; Killian came back on the line. "What's up?"

"I need your help. Do you have trusted brothers in the UK?"

"I might. Why?"

"I need your help overthrowing someone. Give me some men, don't ask questions, and our alliance will be cemented for whatever you need in the future. Diamonds, smuggling—you name it. It's yours."

Now wasn't the time to mention that when I was in power, I planned on ceasing that side of the business. Diamonds to me were covered in blood and death. I wanted no part in it.

Silence for a moment.

Kill growled, "Give me a few hours. I'll see what I can do."

He hung up.

Phase one complete.

The next part of my strategy would be tricky, but I had no alternative. I didn't spread myself over Plan A or Plan B. This first attempt was my only attempt.

It will work.

Refreshing the screen, I dialled another number—one I'd never called before—but knew by heart because of our association.

It rang and rang.

A dawn phone call wouldn't be acceptable to anyone, but if he knew what was good for him, he'd answer it.

Finally, a sleepy, almost drunk, voice answered, "Hello?"

My heart squeezed to think my family had browbeaten this proud business owner into the spineless grieving father he'd become. We'd won over his family—more times than I could count. "Tex Weaver?"

He sucked in a breath. Rustling sounded; his voice lost its haziness. "*You.* You have the fucking nerve to call me after what you've done." He coughed, his temper howling down the line. "I'll fucking kill you with my bare hands. Where's my son? My daughter?"

"That's what I wanted to talk to you about."

Tex raged, "The time for talking is *done*. I'm sick of it. Sick of all your threats and promises. You took my Emma but I won't let you take our kids." Breathing hard, he snarled, "I've put things in place, Hawk. I'm ending this. Once and for all."

I plucked an oak leaf from the tent floor. "I know what you've been doing, Tex."

"Doesn't matter. Won't stop me. Not this time. You can't scare me away like you did with Emma. I'll die before I let you hurt my children anymore."

"I was hoping you'd say that."

He paused. "What—what do you mean?"

Leaning forward, I stared through the tent gap at the woodland around me. This was my office, my headquarters, and it was time to arrange a battalion for battle. "I'm on your side. I want to help you."

"I don't believe you."

"You don't have to believe me. It's the truth."

"What have you done with my children? If you've hurt Nila—"

"Sir, she's the one who has hurt me."

Tex sucked in a breath. "Good for her. I hope she tears out your motherfucking heart."

I chuckled. "I'm in love with your daughter, Mr. Weaver. I have no intention of letting her tear out my heart."

Tex's temper soared into my ear. "Yet you'll happily behead her just like her mother! What sort of sick fuck are you?"

"You're not listening to what I'm telling you."

"I'm listening perfectly fine, you son of a bitch, but you can't scare me with these twisted phone calls anymore. Your father played the same game. Calling to tell me Emma was too sweet, too pure to die—that he'd find a way to end it. Only to call me on the eve of her death to tell me it was all a lie! He destroyed me, and now you're destroying the dregs that are left." Something crashed in the background. "I'll tell you right now—I'm not listening. I'm coming for you, Hawk, and I'm going to make you fucking pay."

My anger boiled over, meeting his. "Christ's sake. *Listen* to me. I'm in love with Nila. I'm putting an end to this feud. You don't have to believe me. Just listen. I'm offering you everything you want. Your son, your daughter…grandchildren who won't be taken for some ludicrous vendetta. Do you want that? Will you risk talking to me so we can work together to end this?"

Silence.

More silence.

What did I expect? Our families had been raised to hate each other. Archibald lost his wife to my father—of course, he'd hate me.

I can do it without him.

Maybe then he'd believe me when I said Nila was now mine and I would do everything in my power to keep her safe.

I sighed, "Look—"

Tex interrupted. "What do you expect from me, Hawk?"

My shoulders slumped with relief.

I had him.

"I expect you to help me save the woman we love."

Nila

TAPESTRIES WATCHED ME as if I were already dead.

The very air prickled my skin with foreboding.

Hawksridge Hall embraced me, sucking me back into its morbid evil. Every step, I wanted to cry. Every breath, I wanted to sprint out the door and never return.

I can't do this again…

I can't…

The strength I'd found in Jethro's company rapidly dissolved, and the cracks and fissures from what they'd done to me ruined my determination.

My courage bled out, trailing like a bloody stain the deeper I travelled through the Hall.

There was no more happiness, only torment and despair. I didn't know how I'd survive another hour, let alone two days.

You can do it.

Can I?

I wasn't so sure.

Following the corridor, I swallowed a gasp as Daniel charged around the corner.

"No!"

His hair was wet and combed back. His little goatee gone, his face baby-smooth, and eyes bright with excitement rather than hazy with sleep.

It's not yet dawn.

How could he be up? What sick joke had fate played?

No. This can't be happening. Haven't I given enough?!

Daniel slammed to a stop, surprise painting his face.

I froze, wanting to miraculously turn invisible.

His chest puffed with glee; he grinned. "Well, well, well." He took a step toward me, then another.

I couldn't move.

Time spilled faster through its hated hourglass, sucking me into its sand.

"Where the fuck have you been sneaking off to?" He kept prowling toward me, tiny steps, baby steps, giving the illusion that I could run before he caught me.

Run!

The message shot to my legs and I bolted.

But I was too late.

Daniel's feet thundered on the carpet, scooping me up in his arms before I even ran a few strides.

"Let me go!"

He chuckled, holding me tight against his front. His erection dug into my lower back and his breath echoed in my ear. "No chance. Never letting you go again, little Weaver."

He wrenched open my fingers, revealing the key tight in my fist. "Where the fuck did you get that from?" Plucking it from my grip, he palmed it. "Not that it matters."

I squirmed in his hold, doing my best to ram his nose with my skull. "Let me go!"

You won't break me. Not again.

He laughed loudly. "Oh, I'm going to fucking enjoy this." Slamming me back onto my feet, he struck my cheek with the hand holding the brass key.

The thick metal crunched against my cheekbone, spurting hot tears from my eyes.

I clutched my face, sucking in heavy breaths. Short hair whipped around, stinging my cheeks.

Don't cry. Don't show weakness.

Daniel wrapped his fist around my throat, yanking me into him. "Know what, Weaver, I don't even care that you're out of your room uninvited. I don't care what shitty shenanigans you've been up to or how you got the key. None of that matters anymore."

Throwing my head back, I screeched as loud as I could. "Jasmine!"

"Oh, no you fucking don't." Slapping a hand over my mouth, he whispered, "You don't belong to Jasmine for this next part, whore." His tongue traced the heated imprint of the key on my cheek. "You belong to me. Remember what Cut said last night? About a surprise...well, surprise! Get ready to pay for all your sins in one."

I fought harder, screaming behind his palm.

Dragging me down the corridor, he laughed as cold as the depths of Hades. "No one can save you now, Nila. Know why?"

I screamed again, kicking anything I could.

"In a few minutes, you're going on a little trip, and there you'll learn everything there is to know about us. You'll finally understand how we triumphed over your family. How we won and you lost. How all of this will fucking end."

Daniel stroked my cheek. "Our first vacation together. Won't it be fun?" His voice turned gruff. "And the first thing I'll make you do when we arrive is repay the Third Debt."

Throwing me against the wall, he grabbed my hand and placed it on his thick erection. "I'm going to fuck you. My father's going to fuck you. And then...you'll pay the debt we've kept secret. The one that will tie all of this together. The Fifth Debt. You'll finally understand."

Fury fired through my blood. I struggled in his hold. "I don't want to understand! Just let me go!"

He grinned. "You'll never be free again. And you'll see why. It will all make sense. You'll be fucked, but at least you'll finally know how we won."

Kissing me hard, his putrid tongue tore past my lips.

I gagged.

In a flash of defiance, I bit him.

Rearing back, he slapped me hard.

My ears rang, and bright lights exploded behind my eyes. Pain registered but all I could think about was Jethro.

Come back!

Come claim me!

Come save me!

Shaking me, Daniel snarled, "You have six days, bitch. Six days to pay your remaining debts. And fuck, will I have fun extracting them."

I spat in his face. "Go to hell, Buzzard. You'll die before I do."

He sighed indulgently, his temper simmering with cockiness. "Nila, Nila, Nila, so delusional. You're not paying attention to what I'm telling you. No one can save you. No one will hear you scream. Six days. That's how long you have to live. We're leaving for *Almasi Kipanga* right now—this very fucking second."

His teeth glinted in the dark. "Do you get it? Do you understand what this means? We're taking you to South Africa, to our diamond mines, to where it all began. You'll see the last things you'll ever see. You'll hear the last things you'll ever hear. And you'll live your final moments on foreign soil."

My heart shrivelled.

No, no. God, no.

Daniel morphed from man to monster, shadowing my future, my soul, my hope.

I didn't have two days.

I didn't even have two hours.

Jethro!

They were taking me away.

They were stealing everything!

Daniel marched me from life to death, laughing with every step. "Oh, and another thing I should mention. This little trip…it'll be your last as you won't be coming back alive."

"No!"

After everything we'd been through. After everything we'd promised and planned.

It was all for nothing.

Time had fucked us once again…

. . .

Jethro

was

too

late.

Continues in FINAL DEBT

"I'm in love with her, but it might not be enough to stop her from becoming the latest victim of the Debt Inheritance. I know who I am now. I know what I must do. We will be together—I just hope it's on Earth rather than in heaven."

It all comes down to this.
Love versus life.
Debts versus death.
Who will win?

THE ENTIRE SERIES IN THE INDEBTED SERIES ARE OUT NOW!

Playlist

The Handler by Muse
Love Me Like You Do by Ellie Goulding
Crystal by Monsters And Men
Ghost Town by Madonna
Only Love can Hurt like This by Paloma Faith
With or Without You by U2
Skyfall by Adele
Do You Remember by Jarryd James
Holding You by Stan Walker
Diamonds by Rhianna
1965 by Zella Day
Stand by Me by Imagine Dragons
Best of Me by Sum 41
Give You What You Like by Avril Lavigne
Hurt by Johnny Cash
Love me Again by John Newman
Unconditional by Katy Perry
Beggin for Thread by Banks

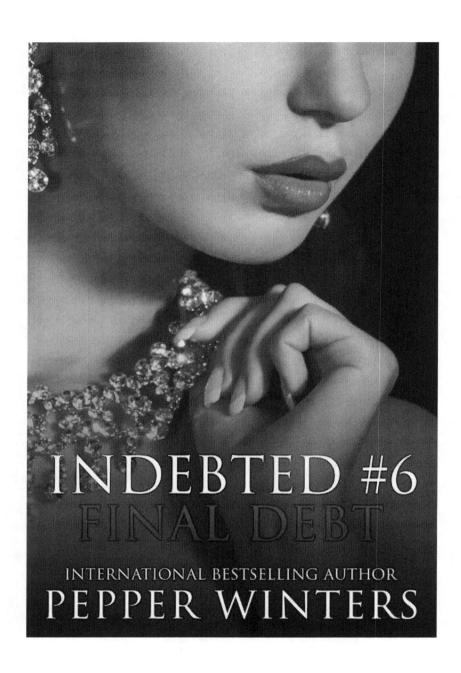

INDEBTED #6
FINAL DEBT

INTERNATIONAL BESTSELLING AUTHOR
PEPPER WINTERS

"READY TO DIE, Nila?"

Cut's voice physically hurt me as he forced me to my knees. The ballroom splendour mocked me as I bowed unwillingly at the feet of my executioner.

Velvet and hand-stitched crewel on the walls glittered like the diamonds the Hawks smuggled——a direct contrast to the roughly sawn wood and crude craftsmanship of the guillotine dais. No finesse. No pride. Just a raised podium, framework cushioning a large tarnished blade, and a rope dangling to the side.

"Don't do this. Cut…think about what you've become. You can stop this." My voice mimicked a beg but I'd vowed *not* to beg. I'd seen things, understood things, and suffered things I never thought I would be able to endure. I refused to cry or grovel. I wouldn't give him that satisfaction.

"In five minutes, this will all be over, Weaver." Cut bent to the side and collected a wicker basket.

The wicker basket.

I didn't want to think about what its contents would be.

He placed it on the other side of the wooden block.

My lungs demanded more oxygen. My brain demanded more time. And my heart…it demanded more hope, more life, more love.

I'm not ready.

Not like this.

"Cut——"

"No. No more talking. Not after everything you've done." Ripping a black hood from his pocket, he didn't hesitate. No fanfare. No second guesses.

I cried out as the scratchy blackness engulfed my face, tightening by a cord around my throat.

The Weaver Wailer chilled me. The diamond collar that'd seen what I'd seen and whispered with phantoms of my slain family prepared to revoke its claim and detach from around my neck.

This was it.

The Final Debt.

Cut pushed my shoulders forward.

A heavy yoke settled over the top of my spine.

I closed my eyes.

I said goodbye.

. . .

I waited to die.

One Week Earlier

"NO!"

I pushed back, gripping the handrails of the private jet, throwing my weight against Daniel's incessant pushing. "Stop!"

"Get up the fucking stairs, Weaver." Daniel jabbed his elbow into my spine.

I stumbled, bashing my knee against the high tread. "You can't do this!" How had this happened? How had mere hours turned the entire universe against me? *Again.*

I wanted to smash every clock. Tear out the cog from every watch.

Time had once again stolen my life.

Jethro!

Daniel cackled. "I think you'll find we can." He shoved me higher.

My heart hurt—as if every mile between us and Hawksridge was a blade slicing me further from Jethro's protection—a disharmony in an already discorded symphony.

One moment, I'd been love-bruised and adored, tiptoeing back into the Hall; the next, I was trapped, forced to dress in jeans and a hoodie, and obey Daniel as he lurked in my doorway, barking orders to pack a few meagre belongings.

He hadn't left me alone.

His eyes followed my every move. I couldn't grab the gun I'd hidden thanks to Jasmine. I couldn't text Jethro to tell him I'd been caught. All I could do was run around my room with my lover's release still damp on my inner thighs and submit to my nemesis.

The only saving grace was beneath Daniel's hateful stare, I'd managed to pack the clothing I'd altered a few weeks ago. The cuffs full of needles and hems armoured with tools of my seamstress trade. Those garments were my only hope. There was no loophole. No way to refuse.

I had to trust Jasmine would get word to Jethro. That he would come for me...

Before it's too late.

The desolation I'd suffered when Daniel first caught me faded to

---

indignant anger. I'd been so close to being free. I'd been in Jethro's arms. I'd been away from his psychotic family. My heart hardened a little toward Jethro for making me go back.

Why? Why did you send me back?

I didn't know if I'd have the courage to forgive him.

You know why. And you will. Of course, you will.

I couldn't hate him because I wasn't selfish. He'd sent me back to protect *all* of us. Those precious few who'd accepted him and he'd accepted in return. Love was the worst enemy, winding its commitment, ensuring no freedom when it came to clearheaded thinking of adversity.

Jethro loved too much. Felt too much. Suffered too much. And his siblings would be our downfall. Kestrel and Jasmine relied on him—just like I did. The responsibility of settling his family's wrongs was a terrible burden to bear.

But he's not alone.

I might've been stolen. Jethro's plans to save me might be ruined. But I was still alive. Still breathing. I wasn't the naïve girl who'd first arrived at Hawksridge. I was a woman in love with a Hawk. A Weaver who would draw Hawk blood.

It's not over…

Pain exploded in my spine as Daniel stabbed me with his fist. "Get in the fucking airplane."

"No!" I threw myself backward, looking frantically at the private hangar. We weren't at Heathrow, but a small, private airfield called Turweston. "I won't!"

No strangers I could call for help.

No police or air marshals.

When Daniel had stalked me from my room and shoved me outside, Cut had been waiting. With a victorious smile, he'd stuffed me in the back of a limousine.

With a purring engine, we'd pulled away from Hawksridge, tyres crunching on gravel as we followed the long driveway off the estate.

My eyes had scoured the trees, their silhouettes growing stronger as the sun tinted the sky with pink blushes. Daniel and Cut sat opposite me, toasting each other with a chilled bottle of champagne. However, I hadn't been alone on my side of the limo—I had a guard.

Marquise, Bonnie's damn henchman, sat beside me; a mountain of muscle, unyielding and impenetrable.

"Come along." A strange voice raised my gaze.

A man in a captain's uniform smiled from the top of the aircraft steps. The private plane's fuselage glinted in graphite grey. Sparkling diamonds, inlaid in the shape of a windswept ribbon, decorated the tail.

"I don't want to leave England."

Daniel laughed behind me. "Like you have a choice."

"I always have a choice, *Buzzard*." I glowered over my shoulder. "Just like this choice of yours will not end well for you."

If I don't kill you, Jethro will.

As far as Daniel knew, his slain brother was supposedly rotting in some unmarked grave. Jethro was right. The element of surprise trumped any of Cut and Daniel's grand delusions.

He snarled, "Watch it, bitch. Everything you say to me here will be paid in full when we're there."

"Now, now. No need for threats." The captain climbed down a rung, holding out his hand. "She'll get on board. Won't you, my dear? No need to be afraid of flying. I have an exemplary record." White hair tufted from either side of his pristine flying cap. In his mid-fifties, he looked fit and toned and impatient to take off.

"I can't leave."

I can't be so far from Jethro.

The captain smiled, waving at his vessel. "Of course, you can. Plus, I bet you've never travelled in such style."

"It's nothing against your mode of transport. It's the destination I disagree to. I'm staying *here*." I dug my heels into the metal grate, fighting against Daniel's perpetual pushing. "I don't have my passport, visa… I can't travel across borders, so you might as well let me return home."

Home.

Had Hawksridge Hall become my home?

No, don't be absurd.

But Jethro had. It didn't matter where we ended up. What we did for work. How our lives panned out. As long as I was alive with Jethro by my side…I would be home.

"Don't fuss about that." The captain waved his hand in invitation. "Travel is good for the soul."

Not my soul.

Travel meant my soul would become untethered from my body, thanks to Cut and the Final Debt.

The sun barely peeked over the horizon, hidden by soupy fog and reluctant night. The world refused to warm, unable to shed the morning frost or dislodge the claws of winter. England didn't want to say goodbye as much as I did, its reluctant dawn wanting me to stay.

"If you don't get on the motherfucking plane in two seconds, Weaver, you'll live to regret it," Daniel growled.

I glared at the youngest Hawk. "Haven't you learned by now your threats don't scare me?"

Forcing myself to stand taller, I hid the quaking in my bones, the quivering in muscles, the rampant terror scurrying in my blood. "I know where you want to take me, and I refuse."

Daniel pinched the bridge of his nose. A second later, he cuffed me on the back of the head. "Behave!"

I gritted my teeth against the wash of agony.

"*Almasi Kipanga* is a fucking treat for the likes of you, Weaver. Get on your knees and show some goddamn appreciation. Otherwise, I'll rip out your fucking tongue and ensure peace for the rest of the trip."

"Ah, as I said, there's no need for violence." The captain took another step, prying my hand off the railing and tugging me upward. "Come along, my dear. Let's get you inside. And don't you worry about visas and things. Leave it to me. Airport control won't be an issue."

Vertigo cast the world in monochromatic greys as I swayed toward the captain. "But—"

Cut barrelled past Daniel—reaching the end of his patience. Grabbing my arse, he shoved me upward, forcing me like unwilling livestock up the final steps. "I have your passport, Nila. Get on the plane." His breath skated over the back of my neck. "And don't think about refusing again. Got it?"

Gripping the fuselage, I looked over my shoulder. "My passport? How did you—"

He waved a black binder in my face. "Everything is in here. You have no more excuses, and I won't ask again. Get on the fucking plane or I'll knock you out and you can wake up when we get there."

Daniel laughed as one last shove sprawled me up the final step and into the captain's arms.

Shit.

"Ah, there you go." The pilot steadied me, holding my shoulders as I stumbled with another swoop of imbalance. The sickness stole my eyesight before dumping me back into hell.

Find an anchor, hold on tight. Do that and you'll be alright.

Vaughn.

His little poem for me.

My heart cried for my brother and father. Would I ever see them again?

The captain led me further inside the immaculate plane. He puffed proudly. "See how nice it is? All your concerns are over nothing. We'll take great care of you." Patting my hand, he let me go. "Take any seat you like. Don't forget your seatbelt."

My eyes widened. He spoke as if this was an innocuous vacation between father and adopted daughter. Did he not see the animosity? Not hear the pre-designed fate?

I opened my mouth to tell him. But what was the point?

He was owned by Cut. Just like diplomats, lawyers, and royals.

He didn't care.

The remnants of the flu, the vertigo attack, and the fact I hadn't slept all night caught up with me. Dropping my eyes, I padded to a black leather chair and sat. Trying to clear my thoughts, I hung my head in my hands.

How the hell do I get out of this?

Backing toward the cockpit to free up the gangway for Cut, Daniel, and Marquise, the pilot said, "Pleasure to fly you again, Mr. Hawk."

"Nice to be back." Cut nodded, choosing a seat beside the one I'd slumped into. Placing the folder on the small table bolted to the floor, he asked, "All flight plans logged?"

I glanced up, familiarizing myself with the black and chrome interior. Everywhere I looked, the Black Diamond logo embossed everything. From leather seats to plush carpet to window shutters and napkins.

The plane had three zones: two black couches faced each other at the end, a large boardroom table took up the middle section with bolted swivel seats, and eight single chairs took up the front part, looking like any first class on a normal airline.

Not that I've ever flown first class.

My heart stuttered. The last time I'd been on a plane, Jethro had drugged me and stolen me from Milan to England on a red-eye. He'd allowed me to text Kite in the bar; all the while hiding it was him.

This far exceeded that flight in luxury, but it was just another glorified cage. And the one person I'd grown to love didn't even know I'd disappeared.

The captain nodded. "Yes, all logged and ready to go. We'll have to refuel in Chad as normal, but it should be smooth sailing down to Botswana."

I froze, gripping the soft leather armrests. "Botswana?"

Africa.

I'd be unprotected and unprepared in the middle of a lion and hyena-infested countryside, captured by men who were worse than the wildlife.

Daniel had told me in the corridor, but I hadn't calculated the ramifications. Now I was on a plane about to take off—about to leave *England*. My motherland. My safe zone.

Oh, my God. How will Jethro get to me in time?

He wasn't fully healed. He needed to put whatever plan he'd organised into action. Even if Jasmine got word to him, he would still be too late to help.

I'm on my own.

My fingers fiddled with the pocket of the hoodie I'd slipped on before Daniel stole me from my quarters. A long knitting needle rested unseen. The needle wasn't flimsy or weak. Single pointed, metal construction, approximately thirty-five centimetres long. If my hoodie hadn't had a big front pocket, I wouldn't have been able to conceal it.

I wasn't much of a knitter—preferring to sew rather than deal with yarn and wool, but on this occasion, it'd become my most favourite implement.

Please, let it be enough.

I didn't have bullets or blades, but I did have my namesake. Hadn't I promised I would become a needle rather than thread? That I would be sharp, ruthless? Able to puncture and defeat?

The bubbling anger and capable fight returned, settling into my soul. I might be on my own, but I'd achieved a lot. I'd learned how to fight monsters and win.

So what I wouldn't be in England?

I would make Africa my personal battleground.

Cut looked at me, a vicious smile on his lips. "Not just to Botswana, Nila. To the diamond mecca. To our mine."

His words echoed Daniel's from before.

Stroking the hidden needle, I narrowed my eyes. "Why?"

Cut laughed quietly, accepting a flute of champagne from a blonde-haired stewardess. "Why do you think?"

The captain cleared his throat. "If you don't need me, sir, I'll leave you to it." With a quick salute, he disappeared into the cockpit, leaving Daniel to slink down the aisle and choose the seat behind me. Marquise kept going, not saying a word, just throbbing with sheer muscle.

The plane became a sardine can, imprisoning me with three men I despised.

"You want to tell her or shall I?" Cut glanced at Daniel.

Daniel leaned forward, fisting my newly cut hair. Every time I thought of the recently sliced strands, I froze with sadness then warmed with contentedness. Jethro had righted his brother's wrongs. Fixing his family's brutality with gentle soothing.

The new style only solidified my will to win. I would avenge. And my hair would grow back while they decomposed in their tombs.

I sat dead straight, vibrating with hatred as Daniel murmured, "I told you already, Weaver. It's time for a few catch-ups. You still owe us for the Third

Debt. You still owe us for the Fourth Debt. And once your debts are paid, there's the matter of the Final Debt to call it even." He laughed, running his monstrous fingers over my scalp. "It's extremely convenient that the rest of the Fourth Debt takes place away from the estate. Not just for the change of scenery but so my fucking sister stops meddling."

Pain burned where he held my hair.

Cut stroked the back of my hand. "Yes, Jasmine proved she's strong and got her way with the new laws for the inheritance, but my dear daughter and her high and mighty morals won't be welcome where we're going."

My voice reigned with righteousness. "She'll never forgive you for what you've done."

Cut cocked his head. "What makes you think she has a choice? We're family. All sins are forgivable by those who share the same blood."

I choked on a laugh. "Seriously? You truly think that?"

"I don't *think* that. I *know* that. Families stick together. That's why our business has done so well. Why we rose above you and ensured centuries of retribution." His touch on my hand flew up to tap against my diamond collar. "Ever wondered about the story behind the Weaver Wailer? Ever stopped to think how it was created?"

I pursed my lips, not giving him the satisfaction of a reply. Of course, I'd wondered. But I wouldn't weaken myself by enquiring—not when Cut seemed to think the knowledge would hurt me.

"This collar, the one I will soon take from your corpse, was fashioned by the grandson of the woman Mr. Weaver raped every night. She sketched something so beautiful it could only be hideous in its intent and William Hawk ensured his grandmother's final wish was created once she'd died."

Confusion clogged comprehension.

I didn't understand how they were linked. "Why?"

Cut scowled. "Why?"

Breaking his hold on my collar, I turned to face him. "Why only hurt the Weaver women? Why not the men? It was Mr. Weaver who harmed the Hawks. Take your vengeance out on the men. Pick on your own sex."

"We still would have won, Nila, because like it or not, the Weavers are weak." Cut laughed, his teeth flashing with mirth. "And besides, taking their women hurts them more than physical wounds ever could."

I didn't need to ask why. I knew.

Stripping the men of their loved ones highlighted not only their failure to protect but their weakness at saving them. They would live forever haunted by those they failed—troubled and plagued by their downfalls, turning into twisted, broken men—just like my father.

I sighed, looking out the window at my final glimpse of the country I'd been born, raised, and indebted.

Cut placed his palm on my thigh, squeezing. "You'll learn everything soon enough. Every secret. Every tale. It's all yours from here on out, Nila. Ask questions. Pry and interrogate. You might as well as your time is tick, ticking away."

Closing his eyes, he settled into his chair. "I'd get some sleep if I were you. Once we land, you'll have some debts to pay."

We touched down in darkness.

How long had it taken to trade homeland for foreign soil?

Ten hours? Twelve?

I'd lost track.

However, it could've been bright sunshine and it wouldn't have made a difference. With the Hawks imprisoning me, it was perpetual darkness in my world.

I twisted in my seat, catching glimpses of runway lights and buildings as the captain taxied to a private hangar. The moment the plane slipped inside, Cut yanked me from my seat and shoved me to disembark.

I didn't speak.

Cotton wool and candyfloss replaced my brain. My back ached, my energy dwindled, and my eyelids scratched like cat claws. All I wanted was rest and safety. I needed to regroup and prepare.

But I had to stay alert and ready.

The cool night replaced the stuffy heat of the cabin as Cut herded me from the plane. The chilly air tore through my hoodie and jeans. I gulped in large breaths to wake me.

Daniel grabbed my arm, escorting me to the armed vehicle waiting in the middle of the hangar. Pieces of airplane bric-a-brac littered the walls and counters lining the aviation perimeter.

Cut's logo stamped his ownership on everything—from cars to wheelable scaffolding and hydraulic tools. Everywhere I looked, I couldn't ignore whose territory I existed in and who ultimately controlled me.

The Jeep wasn't like a typical one in the U.K. This had armoured panels, large bumper guards, and tinted windows. Pockmarks of bullets and splattered mud added a story of violence.

This isn't England.

I wasn't blind or deaf. I'd watched reports on how dangerous Africa could be. How ruthless the people. How fatal the landscape. How deadly the animals.

I'd become protected by the same devils who would hurt me. Reliant on the Hawks to save my life, only so they could take it when suitable to their timeline.

"Get in." Daniel pushed me into the Jeep and climbed in after me.

Cut followed but didn't enter. His arm slung over the roof, leaning his bulk against the door. His leather jacket creaked and his crumpled shirt showed evidence of a long flight, but his eyes gleamed bright and shrewd. "Put your seatbelt on, Nila. Can never be too careful."

If I hadn't agreed with him, I would've spat in his face.

My hand shook a little from hunger as I pulled the belt over my chest and buckled in. Now, if only Daniel didn't put his on and we had a car accident—flying through the windscreen and splattering like a gnat on the road.

My stomach twisted as the images switched to Jethro. Thousands of miles now separated us. Oceans and valleys, continents and mountains. My fingers itched to text him. My hands empty of the one possession that'd allowed me communication for the past several months. My phone had become more than an outlet of transmission; it'd become a lifeline.

But I hadn't had time to grab it. The device sat abandoned in my quarters at the Hall.

I couldn't tell Jethro—couldn't advice plans or activities.

I'm on my own.

I'm all alone.

My hidden knitting needle grew warm, humming with a war beat.

It doesn't matter.

I'm ready.

"Remember what I said, Nila. The next few days are of mutual benefit. Treat it as such." Looking at Daniel, Cut rubbed a hand over his brow. "I'll meet you there. Have a few errands to run on the way."

Daniel nodded. "Fine."

"You'll sort everything out?"

"Don't worry about us." Daniel smiled, squeezing my thigh with biting fingers. "We'll have a fantastic time on our own, won't we, Nila?"

I flinched. My mind raced with scenarios on how to stop my future from unfolding. I didn't know how long the drive would be, but the minute we arrived at our destination, I was ruined.

There was no one to tell him no.

No one to interrupt if he tried to rape me again.

And he will try again.

My left hand disappeared into my hoodie pocket, fisting around the needle.

I have to be ready to do whatever is necessary.

If that meant becoming a killer with a tool of my trade, then so be it. Cut wouldn't be there. Perhaps this was the perfect opportunity to slaughter Daniel and put one demon into his grave.

Cut leaned into the Jeep, grabbing Daniel by the scruff of his neck. The symbolism wasn't lost on me. He held his son like an animal would hold its troublesome young.

"You are not to touch her, understand? Put her to bed and guard her. Let her rest. And by rest, I mean prepare for what's in store."

Letting Daniel go, Cut wiped his hands on the front of his jeans. "You touch her, Buzzard, and you won't be in fit shape to claim the Third Debt. Got it?"

My heart galloped.

Cut was the one person I wanted to die a gruesome death, but he'd just saved me from his vile offspring. Was it jealousy at not getting first dibs? Or some sick chauvinistic protection?

Daniel scowled. "No fair. You said—"

"I said we'd make her pay the Third Debt when we arrived. However, that means we *share*." Cut's eyes glittered. "I find out you didn't share, Hawksridge gets locked in a trust and goes to Jasmine's heir."

"Fuck!" Daniel glared into the night, seething.

I'd never known a stricter, more delusional parent. Cut had shot his two sons. He willingly did whatever he had done to his own brother to inherit my mother. He had his ludicrous laws and absolutely no scruples.

Yet, he controlled Daniel so effortlessly.

Daniel puffed in retaliation then softened in respect. "Okay, Pop. You got it."

"Good." Slamming the top of the Jeep, Cut ordered, "Move out."
Shutting the door, he stepped back.

The vehicle instantly became stifling. Daniel breathed hard, his temper
curling around me like rancid smoke.

"Fucking arsehole. Rules. Always bloody rules with him."

"Yes, and you'd do well to remember those rules."

His eyes shot to mine. "Fuck you, Weaver."

An African man slid into the driver's seat while an accomplice took the
passenger beside him. The clank of metal from his rifle struck the top of the car.

A gun?

Why the hell did he need a gun?

The guard in the passenger seat swivelled around, his black skin turning
him almost invisible in the dark interior. The perfect assassin. "We'll get you
there, Mr. Hawk. Not too much unrest this month. Should be safe."

My eyes flew wide.

Danger.

From all corners.

If I somehow survived the Hawks, I'd have to beg for a miracle to return
to England. I was stranded in a foreign country with my archenemy clutching
tightly to my passport.

Daniel inched his hand further up my thigh. "Good to hear. I want to get
to camp and put my darling Weaver to bed, so she's fully rested for her busy
itinerary."

In a swipe, I shoved Daniel's grip off me. "Don't touch me."

Daniel cursed under his breath.

The African man glanced in my direction, eyeing me once before turning
back around. "Right you are, boss."

The driver turned on the ignition, sending silence screaming with the
rumbling engine.

Daniel inched closer, deleting the negative space between us with threats.
"If I want to touch you; I will fucking touch you."

I squeezed my eyes as Daniel slapped a possessive hold on my leg, sliding
quickly up, up, up until he cupped my pussy. The memory of him doing
something similar when Jethro first took me to Hawksridge had bile rising in my
throat.

Daniel breathed hot in my ear. "You're all mine now, cunt. Away from my
sister. No brothers to interfere. Just me and dear ole' dad."

His fingers pressed on the seam of my jeans, right over my clit.

I shuddered in revulsion. "Pity for you, dear ole' dad just cut off your
balls." Fire blazed in my heart. "You were told not to touch me. You're nothing
more than a glorified messenger boy. Do you honestly think Cut cares about
you?" My laugh echoed with ice. "Really, Daniel? He loved Jethro and Kestrel
more than he loves you and he shot them in cold blood. If I were you, that
would make me think twice about my worth."

His fingers dug harder. "Jet and Kes were nothing compared to me.
Always weak. Always running off to play together while I watched and learned."

"Did you ever think they would've accepted you if you'd been a little
nicer? Been a *brother* to them rather than a lunatic?"

Daniel snorted. "You know nothing. Jet was always a pussy, and Kes thought he could save him. We're Hawks. We're meant to be indestructible not need to be fucking fixed. Why would I want to be friends with rejects like that?"

My heart cracked as Kes and his warmth and kindness filled my mind. "Maybe if you had, you'd be redeemable and not so one-dimensional."

Daniel chuckled, his teeth white in the dark. "Who are you calling one-dimensional? I've got lots of tricks up my sleeve, bitch. Just wait till we get to the mine." Letting me go, he sniffed his fingers obnoxiously loud. "Can't wait to taste you. Can't wait to claim you. I'll obey my father, for now. But you keep pushing me and you'll see who's fucking sorry."

The Jeep lurched forward.

And for the first time in my life, I prayed.

Jethro

MY PHONE RANG.

A few birds took flight, their feathers rustling in the leaves of leering trees. My empathetic illness throbbed in my blood, fanning out, searching for signs that Nila wasn't far from me. That I had time to do what I needed. That all of this would be over.

Shutting the top of the laptop, ceasing the email chain of instructions I'd been sharing with Kill, the Pure Corruption president in Florida, I swiped on my phone and pressed answer.

The number signalled the caller was at Hawksridge.

Nila?

My heart thundered. *Please, be okay.* "Jet speaking."

"Kite, it's me." Jasmine's worried voice came down the line, scattering fear in an instant.

Shit.

I loved my sister, but her call wasn't good news. Even though she wasn't close by, and our only connection was the phone, I sensed her panic and horror. My condition amplified her terror, injecting it directly into my bloodstream.

My hands curled tighter around the device. "What happened? Where's Nila?"

My heart raced as Jaz swallowed a sob. "They took her!"

What?

My legs shot me upright. "Who took her?" I winced, gripping my healing side as agony flared. *Stupid fucking question.* Not waiting for an answer, I growled, "*Where* did they take her? Where, Jasmine?"

Tears tainted her voice. "Bonnie was secretive all morning, not letting me leave my room, saying we had important things to go over. She wouldn't let me go downstairs. She wouldn't let me go to Nila's quarters."

My fingers clutched the phone like a mortal enemy. "Get to the point. Spit it out, Jaz! Where did they take her?"

Jasmine cried louder, wrapped up in her own grief. "I can't believe I did it, Kite. I grabbed a pair of her flower cutting scissors and demanded the truth." Disbelief and horror lurked in her tone. "I wheeled up to our grandmother and threatened to kill her if she didn't tell me. I've become as bad as they have. I'm the same as Cut!" Her sobs came louder. "I've become *them.*"

Shit, I don't have time for this.

445

Rage at her timewasting battled with my need to calm her. All her life, that'd been her ultimate fear: turning into Cut. Forgetting her humanity and being swept up in the evil romanticism of debts and death and blood.

Lowering my voice, I forced myself to remain calm. This was my sister. My blood. My fear for Nila was equal measure to my loyalty to Jasmine. "You're not the same."

Dashing into the tent, I grabbed the backpack with already packed essentials. "You did what we both should've done years ago. So what you threatened her? We should've killed her for the things she's done. She's the catalyst in all of this, Jaz. Not me, not you, not Kes. Not anyone. *Her.*"

Breathing hard, I stuffed last-minute necessities into my jean's pocket and plotted a new plan. "We're putting things right. If we have to kill to do that, we will."

Jaz hiccupped, tears still clogging the line. "I just—I've let you down. She knows I'm on your side now. The way she looked at me, Jet. All this time she let me get away with things I know you would never have been permitted to. She indulged me as I'm the only girl. But she knows now. She knows what I truly think of her. I've ruined the trust you told me to gain."

Her voice broke. "You asked me to keep Nila safe. You gave me a task. And because I'm stuck in this fucking chair, I let you down."

I slammed to a halt.

My stomach twisted; it took everything inside to keep my voice level and not wobble with guilt. "Jaz...you're in that chair because of me. It was selfish of me to put so much on you. You *did* keep her safe. You dealt with Bonnie all these years. You got Cut to change the Debt Inheritance. That's fucking huge. The rest is on me."

"No, no it's not."

Sudden wrath hijacked my hand—I pummelled a fist into a sapling. "Yes, it is. I had her in my arms a few hours ago. I thought I knew best. I stupidly thought I had time. I'm a fucking idiot. *I'm* to blame. Not you. Never you. Understand?"

Jasmine didn't reply.

My time had run out. My voice lowered to a soothing whisper. "I can't comfort you. Not yet. It fucking kills me that you're dealing with this on your own but, Jasmine, I *need* you to spit it out. Where did they take her?"

Diamond Alley?

The integration house in Devon?

Where?

Jaz sniffed loudly, shoving aside her grief. "They've taken her to *Almasi Kipanga.*"

"Fuck!"

My mind swam with images of our mine. The cavernous caves and labyrinth of chiselled pathways. Our fortune had come from there. Our name. Our titles. Everything we had came from the dirt.

Almasi Kipanga.

Swahili for Diamond Hawk.

"When? How?"

"I don't know. But they took her. They left hours ago. I checked with air traffic control. The plane left on route to Chad then to Botswana. You'll never make it in time."

Everything inside went ice, ice cold. "In time for what, Jaz? What else do you know?"

I paced in the clearing, going out of my fucking mind.

"Bonnie took great pride in telling me Cut will make her pay the Third Debt the moment they get there. And the Fourth Debt the day after...Jethro...they plan on carrying out the Final Debt by the end of the week."

Motherfucking shit.

My mind ran wild, calculating time zones and travel distance.

Even if I left now and there was a charter leaving immediately, I would still be hours behind. I would be too late to prevent the Third Debt.

My heart crumbled to ash.

How could I do this to her? After everything she'd already lived through. How had I failed her so fucking spectacularly?

Christ!

Shrugging into the backpack, I vowed I wouldn't let Nila suffer anymore. Fuck the plan. Fuck timing.

I won't give up.

"I'll take care of it." My voice was a tombstone. Even as I swore I'd save Nila, I knew the truth. The awful, disgusting truth.

Kes had done what I couldn't and saved her from the Third Debt. He'd held her. Comforted her. Been there for her while he protected her from being raped.

All of that had been in vain.

He'd been shot because of me.

He might never wake up because of *me*.

I wanted to slaughter my father with my bare hands. I wanted to tear out my heart because no matter what I did, I would fail Nila.

She would pay the Third Debt.

And she would hate me forever.

My knees wobbled as I gasped in agony. I'd condemned her. I was the one she would blame. How would she recover from that? Why would she ever want me again after I left her alone?

She would never be mine again, but I would *never* let my father execute her.

Six days.

My father wanted to kill the love of my life in six fucking days.

My plan had just escalated.

I will stop this.

Even if it meant dying alone and unwanted because of it.

"How! How will you take care of it?" Jasmine screeched. "They're in fucking Botswana, Kite!"

My jaw locked, and I stormed toward Wings. He stood obediently, hidden in the tree line. Neither tethered nor saddled, he looked up when I got closer. His black eyes gleamed with ancient knowledge, so smart, so empathetic. He sensed my turmoil. He knew what I was about to ask him and he didn't hesitate.

Moving toward me, the giant animal placed himself sideways for me to mount. No rope or bridle, just a bond between man and beast.

"I don't care if they're at the ends of the earth. I'm going after them."

Grabbing a fistful of Wing's mane, I tucked the phone under my chin. In a practiced move I'd done countless times, I leapt upright and swung my leg over Wing's back.

My side bellowed, but I ignored my discomfort, focusing on the pain I'd caused Nila by making her return to the Hall without me.

Stupid. So fucking stupid.

Wing's silky coat offered no friction against my jeans. I'd been raised riding bareback. I'd spent many nights building a relationship with my horse. He would obey and fly wherever I needed.

The minute I was seated, he burst into a gallop. I bent low, gripping with my thighs.

Run.

Faster.

My rucksack slapped against my back as Wings flew toward the Hall. Wind stole Jasmine's voice, but I caught enough. "Jethro, what are you going to do?"

The noonday sun drenched Hawksridge, mocking my choices and who I'd become. I vowed this would be over soon. That Nila would be in my arms. That my brother would wake from his coma. That my sister might finally find peace.

So much to fix.

So much unhappiness to erase.

Wings gathered more power, shooting faster than any bullet across the paddock. My legs tightened, my heart pounded, and my fury crescendoed into a breathable entity.

Cut had made his last mistake.

I'm coming for you.

"I'm going after her, Jaz. And this time, I'm going to fucking end it."

Nila

IF DIAMOND ALLEY was the place where diamonds were sorted, raining eternal sunshine from giant spotlights, then *Almasi Kipanga* was the scar in the earth that'd created them.

The entire journey from the airport, Daniel kept his hand latched around my knee. I'd stewed in annoyance and repulsion but hadn't argued or struck up conversation.

I had so much to say.

But each word would only herald more punishment.

Besides, Daniel didn't deserve conversation. He was a lost, little boy, unable to see he was already dead. He might be a Hawk about to hurt me, but I was a viper in his nest just waiting to bite and poison him.

I had time.

I had stealth.

I'll wait.

The driver escorted us through the silent night without a syllable spoken. His passenger-guard never rested, glaring out the window, his reflexes flinching and finger soaring to the gun trigger more than once. Especially when we stopped at red lights and drove down dirt roads.

When we traded human busyness for sparseness, he unsheathed a machete, placing it reverently across his knees. Starlight bounced through the windscreen, kissing the tarnished blade.

Hoots and howls replaced sounds of suburbia, scuttling premonition down my spine.

Inside the Jeep, we were safe…but out there…out there feasted animals far more equipped at killing than we were. Out there, they hunted; their yellow eyes flashing in the headlights.

My fatigue evaporated the deeper into Africa we drove. The driver and passenger granted me copious amounts of adrenaline as I fed off their alertness. They lived here yet they didn't relax. They stayed on edge the entire journey.

What had they seen that I hadn't?

What had they lived that I never would?

I didn't want to know.

The four of us travelled together but apart——each wrapped in their own thoughts and journeys.

By the time we left barely sealed roads and clunked onto gravel trails, my muscles cramped from anxiety.

Every bump, I flinched. Every cackle from hyenas and every growl from lions, I squeezed my eyes with fear. The weapons our guides carried weren't to subdue me; they were to prevent whatever was out there from consuming us.

Civilisation was no more. We'd entered the heart of nature where survival superseded wealth and common-sense triumphed over stupidity.

As we pulled into the horrendous hell of Hawk territory, more and more animal eyes gleamed in the darkness as the high beams illuminated wilderness. My heart banged against my ribs as a flash of predator and the squeal of prey echoed in the night. Some poor creature died only metres from me.

I'm next.

If I didn't kill first.

Daniel chuckled, licking his lips at the thought of some poor animal becoming dinner.

I curled my fingers in disgust, looking out the opposite window. There, I could vaguely make out knobbly trees and sun-beaten terrain. The silver cast of moonlight forgave Africa's sins but couldn't hide its danger.

After crossing a dried-up riverbed and navigating the death plains, we finally pulled into a permanent camp.

The driver slowed, slipping through gates that sent a shiver down my spine. For all my strength and committed confidence at killing before being killed, I couldn't swallow the lie any longer.

I finally understood that this place was more than just a mine. More than just Hawk property. More than just their ticket to wealth.

This was my grave.

"Welcome to our office." Daniel opened the door once the Jeep wrenched to a halt. His fingers pressed on my seatbelt, freeing me, then wrapped around my wrist and yanked me from the seat. I slid out the door, stumbling a little as my legs woke up after being useless from sitting so long.

"Where are we?" I stretched, working out the kinks in my spine while my eyes danced over the camp. A congregation of shipping containers had been converted into offices, wooden shacks with thatched roofs decorated the outskirts, and trodden muddy paths spoke of hardship and toil. The moon offered some illumination, competing against the watery lights strung in bushes and the brighter warmth of electricity spilling from dwellings.

If I didn't know who this place belonged to, it might've welcomed. I might've relished the thought of being in Africa for the first time. Going on a safari and witnessing the creatures I was afraid of, all from the safety of an organised tour.

Instead, all I wanted to do was run—to scale the fence barricading us and take my chances with the sharp-toothed lions prowling the boundaries.

At least I knew what they would do to me.

"Are you deaf or just fucking dumb?" Daniel wafted at the site as if it held every answer. "This is ground zero. The place where the first diamond was found. The place where your family's future became shadowed by mine." Tightening his cruel fingers around my wrist, he marched me through the encampment.

I guessed about thirty to forty shacks and canvas tents decorated the space while seven or so containers oversaw whatever work they undertook. The surrounding fence was patched like an old quilt—wood recently replaced and other wood that needed to be. Everything was sun-scorched and dust-sprinkled.

But it held a wild vibe. A homey vibe.

Somehow, the people who lived here had made the most of what they had and transformed it into more than just a mine but a sanctuary.

Out the corner of my eye, I saw something I didn't think I would ever witness.

Daniel seemed to…relax.

His shoulders smoothed out. The feral desire to be seen and noticed calmed. The insanity inside him muted by the freedom he found here. Perhaps, he wasn't just a psychopath, after all. Perhaps, I'd misjudged when I called him one-dimensional.

Just like I'd broken Jethro by using his lust for me and Kes's kindness to become my ally, I tried to do the same with Daniel. "You like it here."

His eyes snapped to mine. "Shut up, Weaver."

"No. I want to know. You've got me all to yourself, Daniel. Cut said I could ask anything I want. Alright then, my first question is about you."

His mouth hung open as if he couldn't believe I'd just willingly entered into a conversation with him.

That's right.

See me.

Hear me.

Feel me.

Then perhaps you won't try and hurt me.

It was wishful thinking, but maybe, just maybe, it might payoff.

Just like it did with your brother.

"Is this some sort of trick?"

I shook my head. "No trick." Pulling on his hold, I forced him to stop in the centre of the camp. A large fire pit charred the dirt while hacked up logs acted as seating. "You like it here. Why?"

His eyes darkened, but he answered. "Because it's away from Hawksridge."

"You don't like that place?"

"I never fucking said that." His temper smouldered.

I backtracked, trying to read between the lines. "You prefer this place over Hawksridge though…why?" Sudden understanding dawned. "Because you think of this place as yours and Hawksridge as Jethro's."

His hand lashed out, wrapping around my collar. "Wrong, bitch. Hawksridge is mine. Jethro is dead. Remember? Shot. Cold and buried."

I kept my secret while my heart warmed, rolling around in the truth.

He's alive.

Looping my fingers over his wrist, I held on while he imprisoned my throat. "It's yours now—if you behave and follow what Cut tells you, of course. But something makes me think you've always been happier here." I cocked my head. "Why is that? Because it's away from Bonnie, perhaps? It can't be because Jasmine doesn't come here. I don't see you interact, but she's harmless."

As if.

Jasmine terrified me.

He didn't answer, shoving me back and wiping his hands.

I tried again. "Jethro was hurt because of his condition. Jasmine was disabled for something I don't understand. Kes was tolerated because he kept the peace. But you…you…" I gasped. "I know. You were the mistake. The third son—the unneeded backup to an inheritance that already had two heirs."

Daniel suddenly exploded. His palm struck my cheek. "Shut the fuck up. I'm. Not. A. Mistake."

I gasped against the pain, fighting an ocean of heat.

He could hit me. But he couldn't deny it. The way he argued throbbed with past history and conviction. How many times had he been called that? How many times had it undermined his place in the family and turned him into this evil creature?

Holding my cheek, I muttered, "I didn't say *I* thought you were a mistake. I asked if that was why you prefer it here." I rubbed my flaming skin. "You're his child. Same as all his children. It wasn't right to make you feel any less than them."

"Stop with the fucking psychoanalyzing. You don't know what the fuck you're talking about." Imprisoning my wrist again, he hauled me toward a large canvas tent.

I went with him—what choice did I have? But I did have a deeper understanding of my nemesis now. His childlike hatred. His out of control temperament. He might not have a soul to implore but once upon a time…he did. He was just a kid. An unwanted kid who did everything he could to be accepted.

The similarities with Jethro didn't escape my notice. The only difference was Jethro allowed himself to finally change, improve…see his own self-worth.

"It wasn't Cut who told you first, was it?" I couldn't stop my runaway mouth. But this might be my only chance at understanding Daniel enough to defeat him.

He didn't turn to look; his footsteps moved faster. "Shut up. Before I make you."

"It was Bonnie, wasn't it? She's the one who told you you were a mistake."

What are you doing?

Our pace increased and my eyes sought out escape paths. Climbing the few steps onto the wraparound deck, the fabric tent wasn't a temporary abode. It'd been swallowed by the ground and had become part of the landscape with outdoor chairs, a veranda, internal reception room, bedroom, and bathroom.

Breathing hard, Daniel ducked and dragged me from mud to carpet, moving forward into a large bedroom with alcoves. Immediately, my gaze dropped to the bed.

I swallowed my heart.

Daniel chuckled. "If you want to ask questions, get your fucking facts straight first. Yes, I always knew I would get shit having two brothers in front of me. Yes, I wasn't planned and Cut had great pleasure in telling me that my life is a fucking gift and to be thankful. But that isn't the reason why he's such a bastard."

Wishing I could put some distance between us, I whispered, "Why?"

Daniel stepped closer, pressing his chest against mine. "Because she didn't love him. She never loved him—no matter what he did. And that fucking screwed him up."

"Who didn't love him?"

"Rose."

"Who's Rose?"

"Peter's wife."

"Peter?" My mind raced, grasping at half-remembered recollections.

Daniel growled, "Fuck, you are stupid. Cut's brother. That's why Bonnie never liked us. We weren't supposed to exist. Get it? Cut stole Peter's wife behind his back. He got her pregnant."

My mouth hung open. "Is that why Cut killed him? To not only claim the inheritance but the heirs, too?"

Daniel shook his head. "No, he killed him because Bonnie told him to. She pretends like Cut betrayed her, but once she knew Rose was pregnant, she changed the game. She's always fucking changing the game."

My mind swam. "So—"

"No more fucking questions." Grabbing my chin, he forced me to look at the bed. His dark laugh sounded forced but evil. "Gonna put that to use very soon." He shoved me, chuckling as I bashed my knee against a coffee table with metal cups and a water jug. The jug wobbled, spilling cold liquid down the shins of my jeans and puddling on the floor.

"For fuck's sake, Weaver." Marching forward, he grabbed the back of my nape, forcing me to bend over the mess. "See what you just did?"

He treated me like a dog that'd pissed on the rug.

All conversation and questions disappeared. His actions concealed any weakness he might've shown, cleverly reminding me that everyone had issues, everyone had skeletons and secrets, but it didn't matter. What mattered was the person you became *despite* your past. And Daniel had no intention of changing.

"Clean that shit up."

Marquise entered, not caring Daniel held me so roughly. He nodded as if it were perfectly acceptable and placed my suitcase beside the bed. Without a word, he left again.

Fisting my short hair, Daniel hoisted me up and planted a foul kiss on my mouth.

What the—

I wanted to vomit.

Once he let me go, I swiped at my tongue, backing away. "Just because—"

"I've had enough. One more word, Weaver. One more fucking word." His hand shook as he pointed at the puddle on the floor. "Clean that up and have a shower. You stink. I expect you and this bedroom to be clean for our little get together when my father gets back."

I bared my teeth. "You think you're so untouchable, Daniel Hawk, but let me tell you. You aren't. I understand you a little better, but it doesn't mean I'm going to let you rape me. It might be tonight, or tomorrow, or the day after, but I will hurt you. I'll—"

He laughed loudly, cutting me off. "Such stupid promises from such a stupid Weaver. Know what I believe? Tonight, I'll be fucking you. Tomorrow, I'll be hurting you. And the day after, I'll inherit one of the wealthiest estates in the world because you'll be dead. I'm no longer the *mistake*. I'm the chosen one. So fucking shut up and get ready for me." He kissed me again, his putrid tongue trying to gain entry into my mouth.

My stomach revolted and in a flash of lunacy, I opened my lips and permitted him to lick.

Then, I bit.

Hard.

So, so hard.

Coppery blood tinged my taste buds, triumphantly splashing the first blood drawn. And it hadn't been mine.

"Fuck." He yanked me back. Pain exploded on my scalp as his fingers tore at my hair. "You do that again and you won't wake up."

"We'll see."

Grinding against me, he inhaled me like a beast. "You want me to disobey my father? You want me to fuck you right here, right now?" His nose dragged shivers over my skin. "Say one more word and you're on your fucking knees."

I gagged on horrible images but somehow found the courage to retaliate. I couldn't show fear. I wouldn't show fear ever again.

I laughed in his demonic face.

Daniel's eyes met mine, hooded and manic. "Want my cock, Weaver? I'll gladly give it to you if you piss me off again." He waited, focusing on my lips. His erection jammed against my lower belly.

Stomping on my terror, I glared. "You touch me, you die. Cut won't like you disobeying him. You'll be back to being the mistake. The unwanted. The unneeded."

Jethro.

Kestrel.

Would Cut kill Daniel, too?

From three heirs to none.

Daniel trembled with lustful rage. "You fucking—"

"Go ahead and fuck me but you'll be the third son your father shoots."

He froze.

For the longest second, we glowered. The sound of wilderness and our shallow breathing was our serenade.

Finally, he threw me away and stormed toward the exit. "I'm not that crazy. And you're not worth a bullet. I'll wait."

I couldn't stop my muscles trembling.

Thank God.

I'd pushed too far. I'd been idiotic in taunting him. It would've been my fault if he'd raped me. But I'd gotten under his skin and unsettled his equilibrium. I'd shown him I wasn't a wallflower he could pluck the petals off and stomp beneath his shoe. I had thorns...needles...pain to deliver.

His fist grabbed the tent flap, shaking with vehemence. Turning, he smiled coldly. "You're being so patient, little Weaver. I know all those questions were to make me snap. I know how much you want my cock—you're practically begging for it." His eyes narrowed. "How do you think that would make Jet feel? Knowing his corpse is barely cold and you want to fuck his younger brother?"

Clucking his tongue, he blew me a kiss. "I'll make sure to reward you for being so patient. Expect a lot of *persuasion* to scream later."

Before I could hurl obscenities, he was gone.

I stood there forever, hugging myself. My knees shook, threatening to dump me to the floor.

What have I done?

I knew what I'd just done.

I'd made whatever my future held worse.

Why? Why did I antagonise him?

Because this was it. The end. There would be no going back from here. No second chances. They would take from me. Tear apart everything I had to give. And I hoped to God I would take from them before it was over.

With numb fingers, I stroked my knitting needle hidden in my hoodie pocket.

Stay strong. Don't stop fighting.

Daniel's silhouette graced the outside of the tent as he snapped his fingers at Marquise. His lumbering form marched closer, waiting for orders.

"Stand here. Arm your weapon. If she tries to run, shoot her."

Tears tried to crest but I shoved them down. This wasn't Hawksridge. Daniel wasn't Jethro. And this was no longer a game. The stark truth couldn't hide: I was in deep shit.

Marquise nodded. "Right-o."

Sticking his head back into the tent, Daniel grinned. "Just so you're aware, if you try to run, you'll know what Jethro and Kes felt when they died by bullet. How's that for a bedtime story?"

His boots crunched on the deck as he leapt to the dusty ground and left. Marquise popped his head inside, only to give me a cold smile before zipping up the mosquito screen across the door.

Cocking his gun, he turned his back on me.

Alone.

Finally.

I didn't waste any time.

I didn't know how long Cut would be, but it wouldn't be long enough. I needed to switch off any sentiments or remaining hints of the girl I'd been and prepare to become a ruthless killer.

Snatching my suitcase, I hauled it to the bed and unzipped it. Every garment and item were in disarray. When Daniel ordered me to pack, folding wasn't a top priority.

Tossing clothes that didn't have weapons sewn inside to the floor, I hurriedly selected the fleece jacket with a scalpel hidden in the collar and the leggings with a pair of delicate scissors smuggled in the waistband.

Daniel wanted me to have a shower?

Fine. I would shower.

I would prepare.

And I would go to war when he returned.

ECONOMY CLASS.

Public airline.

The *worst* possible environment for a man like me.

I huddled in my seat, gritting my jaw; doing my best to remember the exercises I'd been taught.

Focus on my own thoughts.

Concentrate on inner pain. Pinch, slice, do whatever it takes to put that barrier up.

Fixate on mundane influences: reading, looking at nature.

I swallowed a groan.

None of it worked.

Glancing around the plane, my condition picked up on homesickness, regret, excitement, loss, and fear. Every person had their own thoughts and those thoughts flew kamikaze in the small space.

Squeezing my eyes, I focused on my ice. Cut had done one thing right raising me. He'd taught me how to focus on hatred and selfishness, shutting everyone out—even their pain.

The lesson hadn't been easy. If I slipped or didn't succeed, Jasmine bore the brunt. Cut understood that the pain of those I loved affected me triply hard. In a way, forcing me to listen to his emotions of discipline and control, while blocking out my sister's agony and unhappiness, gave me the strength to combat the influx of paralyzing emotions from others.

Even while she was hurt right in front of me.

I could stomach my own pain, but when it came to hers…

Just like I can't stand Nila's now I love her.

Forcing those memories away, I did my best to relapse into the capsule of snow, but even as the tendrils of ice made their way around my heart, one person centred in my thoughts.

Jasmine.

Because of me, she would never walk again. And that was another reason why I couldn't abandon her when Nila begged me to leave last night in the stables. Why I owed Kes and Jaz everything because, without them, I would've died years ago.

Maybe I *should've* died years ago.

Maybe Nila would've remained safe, and Kes wouldn't be fighting for his life.

Kes would've been next in line. If Cut followed the Debt Inheritance rules—without turning into the power hungry bastard he'd become—with the firstborn dead, the contract couldn't be fulfilled and both Kes and Nila would've been free. Nila would've married someone far away from the Hawks and would've given birth to a daughter as beautiful as her.

Only to be ruined a generation later.

The ice I tried to cultivate thawed, leaving me wretched.

It wasn't the thought of future debts, but the thought of Nila married and happy with another that flayed me alive.

She was mine. I was hers. We were meant to fall in love and finish this. Just like Owen, my doomed ancestor, and his love, Elisa, never could.

Fuck, Nila.

What had she lived through in the hours we'd been apart? What had they done to her since I'd failed her?

"Juice?"

I opened my eyes, glaring at the stewardess. Her emotions bounced between job satisfaction and claustrophobia. She loved to travel but hated to wait on passengers. If I listened harder, I would've learned most of her secrets and guessed a lot about her life.

"No." I looked out the window. "Thank you."

The darkness of the sky illuminated every few seconds with a red flash from the wing tip, keeping time with my ragged heartbeat.

I hadn't calmed since Jasmine's phone call.

After galloping to the garage, I'd left Wings to find his way back to the stables and traded him for a different kind of horse-power. My Harley snarled in the afternoon sun, hurling me down our driveway and to the airport.

I didn't think to seek out Flaw. I didn't have time to tell my sister my plan. All I focused on was getting to the airport and a charter.

However, I should've used my brain rather than my fearful heart. There were no charters or private planes available that late in the day. No pilots on call. No one to bribe to fly.

I had no choice but to hurtle to Heathrow and board the next available flight to South Africa. Getting to the airport, buying a ticket, and arguing over the fastest service had all cost valuable time.

Time I didn't have.

No quick routes. No private planes.

My only option had been a cramped, overbooked flight with three stops before reaching my destination. Even if I'd waited for twenty-four hours and hired a private jet, the long haul commercial flight would've been faster.

So I bought a ticket.

I sent Nila a text:

Kite007: *I'm coming. Hang on. Do whatever it takes to stay alive. I love you so fucking much.*

She hadn't replied. If she had been able to take her cell phone, she wouldn't have reception in the sky. And if Cut had stolen it from her, I would have no way to warn her of my arrival.

Yet another problem in my problem-riddled future.

Flying while fearing for the life of a loved one was bad enough. But flying with an empathetic condition and a healing gunshot wound was a hundred times fucking worse.

Every takeoff and landing, every airport and taxi, I lost more of my humanity and focused on bloodlust, plotting what I would do to Cut and Daniel when I arrived.

The promise of wide open spaces and empty African plains helped me remain sane in the tinderbox of airplane madness.

I'd always avoided public spaces for long periods. Flying with Nila from Milan had been the first time I'd suffered in years. For all intents, before Nila came into my life, I was a recluse. Hawksridge my sanctuary and Diamond Alley my office. I had no need to mingle with strangers.

Another whirlpool of conflicting passenger emotions bottled up in a tiny fuselage with no outlet. I did my best to ignore them. Did my best to cultivate my hate and let the single-minded determination give me peace.

Grabbing the napkin from the cognac I'd ordered an hour ago, I shredded it as my heart worked double time. My side bellowed and a fever dotted my brow. Timelines and countdown clocks swarmed my mind as I worked out how far ahead Nila was.

At best, eight to nine hours.

At worse, ten to twelve.

Nila might've been spared pain and rape.

She might still have time.

But three-quarters of the way over the Atlantic Ocean, I knew I'd run out of minutes.

They'd arrived at *Almasi Kipanga.*

She was on her own.

Nila

I STOOD ON the lip of a colossal mine.

The teeth of the earth yawned wide, its tongue and tonsils butchered by spades and diggers, its innards exposed to the night sky in the hunt for diamonds and wealth.

Staring into the pit hurt something deep inside. It wasn't for the broken trees left to rot unwanted, or the ebony-skinned workers toiling in the muck. It wasn't the stagnant air of degradation and robbery. It was the sadness that something as precious and rare as diamonds—that the earth had created over millennia—had been so callously stolen with no grace or thanks.

"Impressive. Isn't it?" Cut slung his arm over my shoulders.

I flinched but didn't move away.

Not that I could.

A coarse rope bit into my wrists, wound tightly by Cut when he'd come for me.

I'd expected the Third Debt to be carried out the moment Cut returned from whatever errands he ran. I'd sat on the bed, pricking the tips of my fingers with the hidden knitting needle, never taking my eyes off the entrance to my tent.

My stomach grumbled. Energy depleted. But I'd refused to fall asleep. I would face my nightmare while awake.

It was the only way.

The cool African night had gnawed on my skin; goosebumps prickled as the *humph humph* of lions echoed through the fabric house.

They sounded so close. So hungry.

Then, all at once, it seemed as if an orchestra conductor arranged a quartet of laughing hyenas, bays of zebras, and hoots of owls.

The animal song raised my stress levels until I'd shivered with terror.

"Are you listening to me?" Cut's voice sliced through my thoughts. I hadn't rested or slept in forever; my reactions were sluggish.

I blinked. "You were saying something about quantity and how much—"

"No!" He jerked the rope around my wrists. "I was telling you how deep *Almasi Kipanga* goes. In centuries of mining, we've found seams and seams of stones. We continue to expand and the mine is currently half a kilometre below earth. Can you comprehend that?"

I shook my head. All I could think about was how dark and

claustrophobic it would be. A tomb just waiting to fall like countless dominos, smothering anyone inside it.

Daniel smiled. "That's years of digging. Millions upon millions of diamonds carved out of the dirt. If a seam dries up, a new route is planned." His teeth flashed. "One lucky worker is given the job of setting explosives to disrupt any loose landslides or cave-ins."

"What happens if the explosives set off a disaster and he gets crushed?" My eyes widened at such a dangerous occupation.

Daniel shrugged. "That's why we only send one. If he doesn't make it, then tough shit. We don't evacuate, we just seal."

I swallowed my disgust. "You kill men in so many ways."

"Thanks for the compliment."

My eyes narrowed. "It wasn't."

"I don't care." Daniel smirked. "I'm taking it as one."

I wanted to wipe that idiotic greed and insanity and entitlement right off his heinous face. "I wouldn't be so bloody cocky if I were you. You act as if killing an employee is a sport—that they're as disposable as broken tools." Tilting my chin at Cut, I snarled, "But your father doesn't just stop there. What makes you think you're safe, Daniel? When all signs point to you being the reject and least desirable?"

"Why you—" Daniel fisted my hair, jerking me from his father's grip. His free hand shot to his belt where a dirty rag was stuffed in his pocket. "Gonna shut you up once and for—"

Cut yanked me back, tucking me under his arm once again. "I don't know what happened between you two while I was gone, but stop squabbling like spoiled brats."

Squeezing me, he murmured, "Now, Nila. Behave, be silent unless spoken to, and you'll get to visit something not many people get to see."

Cut glared at his son. "Calm the fuck down and be a man, Buzzard. Nila's right. At this point, you're less than desirable. And if you keep it up, I'll be the one extracting the Third Debt without you. I don't share with ingrates."

I shuddered with loathing.

The thought of Cut touching me any more than he was now shrivelled up my insides until they turned to ash.

Daniel burned red with fury but swallowed his retorts.

Cut let me go. "Come. Let's take a closer look." He raised my bound hands, kissing my knuckles as if this was a perfectly normal night on a perfectly normal vacation. After his outburst, he looked positively carefree. Happy…

How can you be happy, you bastard?

I vowed on every fallen tree and hacked up dirt that I would wipe the smug smile off his goddamn face.

"Come along." Cut strode ahead, jerking me behind him.

My ballet flats skidded on pebbles as I struggled to match his pace. Greyness danced on the outskirts of my vision, but I refused to give in to vertigo.

I was already in a perilous situation. I wouldn't let my body subject me to more.

My mouth dried up as we moved forward on the tiny path. The deeper we headed, the more claustrophobia clawed. The track had been carved from the mountain, steadily curving with bare earth on one side, damp and musty, and a steep drop on the other, giving no second chances if you tripped.

One wrong step…

If I could guarantee Cut's demise, I'd throw myself over the edge and take him with me.

African men and women bowed as we traded the narrow path for a wider road, exchanging foot power for an electric golf cart.

The simple cart was nothing like the armoured Jeep we'd driven in.

Once Cut had returned from his errands, he'd bundled me into another car and driven Daniel, Marquise, and me to the mine. I didn't have a watch and my phone—which I missed like a lost limb—remained in the U.K. But I guessed the trip took about twenty minutes before arriving at the wound of *Almasi Kipanga.*

I'd held my breath as a wall the size of China loomed in the distance. Gates soared high; the perimeter fortified with electricity, barbed wire, and countless notices in Swahili and English warning of mutilation and death if they were caught stealing.

"Get in, Nila." Cut's rough hand pushed me into the backseat of the mud-splattered golf cart. Daniel sat beside me, while Marquise, silent as always, took the front beside Cut.

The deeper into the chasm we drove, the more Cut's pride shone. He looked upon this place like it existed because of him. Like he was the creator, founder, and architect.

But it wasn't him. He couldn't take credit for something that'd been here since the dinosaurs roamed. Nor take pride in something the earth had created. He'd done *nothing*. If anything, he'd tainted the preciousness of diamonds and smeared them with the blood of his workers.

The battery whir of the cart could barely be heard over the squelching of mud as we descended down the serpentine road into purgatory.

Workers milled everywhere. Some with buckets on a yoke, others driving diggers and dump trucks full of earth. Armed guards stood sentry every few metres, their hands ready to shoot for any infraction. The air reeked of malnourished slavery.

Daniel caught me staring at one man as he dumped a pick-axe and bucket beside a growing tower of tools. "You'd be surprised where people will stuff a diamond, Weaver. The imagination can make a human body quite the suitcase."

I bit my tongue. I wouldn't speak. Not because Cut told me not to, but because I was done trying to figure him out. Jethro had redeemed himself, Kes never had anything to redeem, but Daniel…he was a lost cause.

The questions Cut gave me permission to ask had lost their shiny appeal. I didn't care. I truly didn't bloody care.

"Like what you see?" Cut asked as we neared the looming entrance to the belly of hell. Driving into the open-aired entrance was bad enough. The thought of entering the pitch-black crypt sucked all my courage away.

Apart from the obvious destitution of the workers, Cut's treasure trove looked like any other mine—no diamonds strewn on the ground or sparkling in large barrels in the African night. If anything, the pit was dusty, dirty…utterly underwhelming.

I faced him with an incredulous look. "Like what I see? What exactly? Your love of hurting people or the fact that you murder whenever it benefits you?"

"Careful." His golden eyes glowed with threats. "Half a kilometre below ground gives many places to dispose of a body and never be found."

I looked away, wishing I had use of my hands so I could wring his neck. *Perhaps, I'll dispose of you down there.*

My hoodie didn't offer much warmth against the cool sky, but knowing my knitting needle rested in easy reach mollified me.

If I wasn't tied up, of course.

My fingers turned numb from the tight rope around my wrists.

The lack of sleep and overall situation made my nerves disappear. "Threats. Always threats with you. There comes a time, *Bryan*, that threats no longer scare, they just make you look stupid."

Cut sucked in a breath. I didn't know if it was my use of his given name or my retaliation, but his gaze darkened with lust. "Was I threatening when I killed Jethro or Kestrel? That was decisive action—cutting out the tumour before it infected the host."

"No, I call that insanity growing more and more rampant."

His throat constricted as he swallowed. He didn't say a word as he guided the golf cart to a stop beside a sheer rock wall. The air temperature dropped even more as shadows danced around the mouth of the mine. In front of us, a large opening beckoned. There were no welcome mats or happy wreaths on the door, just rough timber frames, well-tracked mud, and the occasional light disappearing into the belly of this monstrous beast.

Cut launched from his seat and plucked me from mine. "You'll learn that I don't believe in threatening, Nila. I believe in action. And tonight, once we return to camp, you'll find that you'll *crave* action, too."

The way he stressed the word 'crave' made my heart rate spike. What did he mean by that?

"No time to waste." Stepping back, Cut stole my roped hands, guiding me toward the crudely made entrance. Daniel followed, content to listen and watch rather than interrupt.

The second we traded starlight for thick, thick dirt above us, my urge to run accelerated. The timber framework gave way to jutting wooden poles, holding up a tin structure, keeping droplets at bay from the dripping earthen roof.

Exposed light bulbs dangled from the ceiling, casting us in stencils and shadows as we followed the corridor down, down, down then branched off to a large cave-like space.

I blinked, drinking in the array of clothes pegs and large bins labelled with what their contents entailed: dungarees, boots, hammers, chisels, and axes.

I shivered as the cold dampness ate through my clothing.

Daniel moved forward and grabbed a waterproof jacket. His cheeks dimpled cruelly as he sneered, "If only you'd been nice. I might've given you a jacket. It gets cold down here." Grabbing a torch from another barrel, he shrugged. "Oh well, guess you'll freeze and I'll have to work extra hard to warm you back up when we return."

Cut let me go, grabbing his own jacket and slinging it over his shoulders. He merely smiled and didn't override his youngest's decision not to give me extra warmth.

So be it.

I gritted my jaw, locking my muscles to hide my shivering.

Daniel patted my arse as he stalked past. "Let's go to the tally room then we'll go below."

Below?

Further...down into the ground?

I...I...

I swallowed, forcing away my panic as I focused on the other word I dreaded.

Tally.

Tally room?

Like the marks on my fingertips?

I looked down at my twined wrists. Smudges and grime covered my index but beneath it, Jethro's marks still rested.

My heart twinged, remembering Jethro bent over and carefully inscribing my skin with his initials. The ink wouldn't last forever; it'd already faded from washing my hands, but I loved having his mark there—in a way, it made him immortal. Even when I thought he was dead, his signature remained on my skin.

He'll come for me.

I knew that. But I also knew he wouldn't be in time.

I sucked in a heavy breath. If I never saw him again, at least we had the night in the stables. At least I got to see him one last time.

"Good plan." Cut took my hand, dragging me deeper into the mine. More carts and trolleys, even an old Jeep littered the underground pathway. I hadn't expected such a huge size. The mine had the air of an unseen city, complete with transportation, inhabitants, and daily commuters heading to their offices.

The lights did their best to push back the gloom, but between the strung bulbs, a cloying blackness permeated my skin and clothes. The stench of damp earth couldn't be dispelled, nor could the underlying fear that any moment the world could collapse and I'd be buried forever.

Goosebumps scattered over my arms as we entered another small cave where numerous tables had been set with scales, plastic containers, and ziplock bags. This room was brightly lit, pretending it had its own sun and not banished to the underworld.

"This is where every worker must drop his haul at the end of the shift." Cut waved at the room. "The diamonds are washed, weighed, measured, and lasered with the fair trading IPL code before being sorted into equal distribution for shipment."

My eyes widened at the willingly given information. I knew Cut had no intention of letting me spill what I'd learned to others, but I couldn't get used to how open he was.

I supposed from here on out, every secret I'd be privy to, every hidden action shown.

I frowned, remembering what he'd made me promise at the dice game at Hawksridge. He'd demanded I save him a debt in return for whatever he would share.

What did he expect me to do? And what made him so sure I'd obey, now Vaughn wasn't here to torture?

Shoving those thoughts away, I focused on the already processed ziplock bags. If he wanted to share in-depth details of his family's enterprise, who was I to stop him?

Knowledge was power.

In a few questions, I'd learned more about Daniel than I had in six months.

I could do the same with Cut.

My voice boomeranged around the cave. "How do you get the stones out of the country?"

Daniel stroked a bag gently. "Oh, we have multiple ways."

Cut prowled to a table and plucked a dull stone from a pile of dirt. "We use private planes and bribe air traffic control. We use shipping containers and smuggle contraband in the captain's quarters. Other times we use trucks and pay off officials at the borders. Sometimes, we bribe a trusted few in the Red Cross who disguise the stones in medical supplies. There is no end to transport if you start looking at avenues available. Each tactic helps us export blood diamonds to borders where ludicrous taxes and regulations don't exist."

My lips curled at the mention of Red Cross. How could he use something that was supposed to benefit those in need by turning them into mules for something that hurt to procure? "That's immoral."

Cut laughed. "You think that's bad? Silly girl, you should hear what my ancestors used to do." Coming closer, he traced my arm with his dusty fingertips. "Before your time is up in Africa, you'll learn of one such method." His eyes glowed with demons. "And then you can decide which is immoral."

I shivered, wrenching away from his touch. "You can keep your methods. I don't want to know."

Daniel gathered me close from behind, pressing his hips into my arse. "You'll get your history lesson, same as always, Weaver. Once you've repaid the Third Debt tonight, you'll be told what's in store for you tomorrow."

Tomorrow.

Tomorrow.

Jethro...

How far away are you?

A question flew into my head. I wanted to ignore it. It probably wasn't wise to ask. But I was past censoring. "Why drag this out? Why not get it over with?"

Cut grinned. "Eager for a raping, my dear?"

I balled my hands. "Stop with the torment. I get it. You're rich. You have power. I've lived with you for months. I know that already."

Cut's fingers tucked short hair behind my ear, fingering the strands he'd allowed Daniel to hack. "It's a method of torture, Nila. Just like the history lessons inform you of your demise, the delay adds weight to what will happen." Dropping his fingers from my hair, he clutched my hipbones, dragging me from Daniel's clutches into his own.

Like father, like son.

I hated that both their erections pressed against me in a matter of seconds.

My heart lurched with sickness. I'd slept with Jethro willingly. I'd made Kestrel come as a thank-you gift for being so decent, and if I didn't find a way to stop my future, I would become intimately acquainted with Daniel and Cut, too.

Four men.

Four Hawks.

One Weaver.

My stomach recoiled, threatening to evict the nothingness inside me.

"Let me go—"

"No." Cut grabbed my nape.

Before I could squirm away, his mouth landed on mine.

Stop!

He'd kissed me before. Licked me. Touched me. But this was the first time he let down his guard and fully gave me a part of himself. His tongue fluttered over my tightly pressed lips. His goatee bristled my tender chin. His rough skin hinted at his age. And his impatience at getting me to respond unravelled his decorum.

His nostrils blew scalding air on my cheeks as he forced me to kiss him back.

I stood there unmoving. I didn't open. I didn't budge. He might be able to drag out my persecution, but he didn't have the power to make me fear it.

His kiss suddenly switched from savage to sweet, peppering soft kisses on my lips.

For one tiny second, he wasn't a monster. He projected a fantasy that he truly cared for me. That somewhere, deep inside his rotting chest, beat a heart that wasn't pure evil.

But that was a lie. A terrible, *terrible* lie.

The worst one yet.

Yanking my mouth away from his, I spat at his feet. "Don't *ever* do that again."

He chuckled. "Oh, I'll do more than that, Nila." Slinking his arm around my waist, he smiled. "You taste just like your mother."

"You're a pig."

"That's your misconception. I'll have great pleasure showing you otherwise." His whisper tangled in my hair. "Tonight, you'll want me just as much as she did. I give you my word on that."

"No way in hell will I ever want you, you bastard."

Chuckling again, he let me go. "We'll see." Snapping his fingers, he stalked to the exit. "Come, I want you to see what your mother saw on the eve of her final task. I want you to know how insignificant a human life, especially a Weaver life, is compared to all that we have."

Daniel grabbed my elbow, guiding me from the tally room. "I suggest you enjoy your tour, Nila, because once it's over, there's a certain protocol that has to be followed here. Certain superstitions to be entertained, local spirits to appease."

I ducked beneath a mildew covered beam. "What do you mean?"

Cut said, "He means that you're more than just our bed companion tonight. You're our sacrifice."

I gasped.

What?

Tucking my hand into the crook of his arm, Daniel guided me toward the gaping black hole and the unknown world beyond. "Now, let's go explore, shall we? Time to see below the earth…time to see where diamonds are born."

Drumbeats.

Heartbeats.

Wingbeats.

It all melted into one as Cut guided me from the Jeep and back to the camp. My bones ached from the dampness of the mine. My clothes hung with icy humidity. And my mind couldn't shed the tunnel of blackness where expensive stones were found.

How long had we been underground? Two hours? Three?

Either way, I'd seen enough of the birthplace of diamonds and never wanted to return. I couldn't stop shivering, even as I thawed beneath the open skies. Fresh air fed my lungs, doing its best to eradicate the earthen soup found below the ground.

Cut had taken great pleasure in showing me catacombs where the first seam was found then scars where workers had pinched diamonds from the soil. He'd taken me in a wire-cage elevator to the furthest point in the mine. He'd shown me underground rivers, white-washed crosses on walls where cave-ins had claimed lives, and even skeletons of rats and vermin that'd stupidly decided to dig beside the workers.

The entire experience had ensured I loved my vocation even more. Material couldn't kill me. Velour and calico couldn't suffocate me.

I never wanted to go near a mine again.

However, I couldn't stop fingering my collar, counting how many stones had been torn from their home. I'd expected the weight of the diamonds to grow heavier the longer I was in *Almasi Kipanga*. If anything, the necklace grew lighter. Almost as if the diamonds were of mixed decision. Half of them wanting to return to their beds of dust, and others happy to be in sunlight rather than perpetual darkness—regardless of the bloodshed they'd witnessed.

Cut smiled. "Time for the next part of the tour."

The cacophony of drumbeats tore me from my thoughts. Cut shoved me through the camp, barred behind fences, ensconced in a human habitat rather than diamond tomb.

Drumming and singing guided us toward the central fire pit.

"What the—" My mouth fell open as we rounded the path, entering a different dimension. I felt as if I'd time travelled—shot backward a few decades where African tribes still owned the land, and their life was about music rather than gemstones.

The pounding of fists on animal-hide drums echoed through my body, drowning out my nerves of what was to come. The air shimmered with guttural tunes and barbaric voices.

I'd never seen such a cultural fiesta. Never been enticed to travel to somewhere so ruthless and dangerous. But witnessing the liveliness and magic of the group of ebony-skinned dancers made tears spring to my eyes.

There was so much I hadn't seen. So much I hadn't done or experienced or indulged.

I was too young to die. Too fresh to leave a world that offered so much diversity.

This.

I want more of this.

Living...

"Your mother liked this, too," Cut murmured, his face dancing with flame-ghosts from the bonfire. Topless women weaved around the crackling orange, their skirts of threaded flax and feathers creating stencils on the tents and buildings. Men wore loin clothes, pounding an intoxicating beat on animal drums of zebra and impala.

"This is what you meant when you said superstitions being appeased?"

Cut nodded. "Every time we return to *Almasi Kipanga*, our workers welcome us home."

"Why? They must hate working for monsters like you. You treat them like the rats living in the mine."

Cut grinned, softened by the tribal spectacle. "To them, we are their masters. Their gods. We feed them, clothe them, keep them safe from wildlife and elements. Their families have grown up with my family. As much as you hate me, Nila, without our industry, these people would be homeless."

I didn't believe that. People found a way. They would've found a better life rather than slaving for a man who didn't deserve it.

Daniel patted his father on the back. "Gonna get something to drink. Make the rest of the night extra special." Winking at me, he faded into the mingling workers and guards.

I ought to be relieved he'd left. I only had to focus on Cut. But somehow, Cut's promises of *craving* action and enjoying what he would do to me layered my lungs with terror.

Cut pressed on my lower spine. "Come along. Time for your part in tonight's festivities."

My heels dug into soil. "My part?"

"I told you." His gaze glowed. "You're the sacrifice."

"No. I'm nothing of the sort."

I'd been my father's sacrifice. Tex had given me up to Jethro that night in Milan with no fuss. I was done being forfeited for the greater good.

"You don't have a choice, Nila." Cut dragged me closer to the fire, despite my unwillingness.

Nervousness exploded in time to the tribal drum as he led me through the dancing throng and pushed me onto a grass mat at the head of the bonfire. My wrists burned in their twine, sore and achy.

The entire time we'd been in the mine, he hadn't released me. What did he think I'd do? Grab a pick-axe and hack away at his head? Run and dig myself to safety?

The texture of the woven mat beneath my toes told me this tribe were weavers, too. It took great skill to create items from plant life and not cloth or silk.

Cut sat beside me on a raised platform decorated with ostrich feather and lion skin. He didn't look at me, just wrapped the rope tethering me in his fist and smiled as the women danced harder, faster, wilder.

I didn't want to be distracted. I didn't want to fall under the spell of magical music and sensual swaying, but the longer we sat there, the more enthralled I became. I'd only seen this culture on documentaries and television. I'd travelled to Asia with V and Tex to gather diamantes and fabrics, but I'd never been on this continent.

My horizons were so small compared to what the world had to offer.

Sitting there at the feet of my murderer, watching his employees dance and welcome, highlighted just how much my life lacked. I'd let work dictate and rob me of living.

If only Jethro was here.

His handsome face popped into my mind. I wanted to run my fingers over his five o' clock shadow. I wanted to kiss his thick, black eyelashes. I wanted to kiss him, forgive him; pretend the world was a better place.

The more the music trickled into me, the more my body reacted. Sensual need replaced the damp panic of the mine, making my nipples ache at the thought of Jethro touching me.

My body grew twisty and excited, cursing the distance between us and the circumstances I was in.

My eyes smarted as smoke from the fire cast us in sooty clouds. The rhythmical footsteps and infectious freedom of the melody slowly replaced my blood.

There was something erotic about the dance. Something slinked nonverbally, speaking of connection and lust and love and forever togetherness. Bodily communication superseded that of spoken languages.

My heart throbbed with lovesickness. I missed him. I wanted him. I needed to see him one last time and tell him how much he meant to me.

I love you, Jethro…Kite.

Cut hadn't lied when he said superstitions had to be acknowledged. Over the course of three songs, the local tribe welcomed their boss with handmade gifts of beads and pottery, delivered food of roasted meat and fruits, and danced numerous numbers.

At one point in the ceremony, a woman with bare breasts and white paint smeared on her throat and chest reverently placed a flower headband on Cut's head.

He nodded with airs and graces, smiling indulgently as the woman merged back with her tribesman.

My skin prickled, a sixth sense saying I was watched.

Squinting past the brightness and sting of the fire, I searched for the owner's gaze.

Buzzard.

Daniel lurked on the outskirts of the fire, his eyes not on the half-naked women but on me. His lips parted, gaze undressing me, raping me from afar. In his hand rested a crudely made cup, no doubt holding liquor.

One song turned into a mecca of soulful salvation. A young girl broke away from the dancing women, moving forward with a small bowl and a blade.

I sucked in a breath as she looked at Cut and pointed at me with the knife. A knife?

Why the hell does she have a knife?

Cut nodded, tugging my leash. I tried to fight it, but it was no use. Effortlessly, he forced me to present my tied hands.

My lungs seized as the girl bowed at my feet, placing the bowl on the dirt. Unfurling my palms, she kissed each finger, murmuring a chant that sent spiders scurrying down my spine.

I tried to tug away, but Cut held me firm.

"Wait—"

The girl flashed her blade.

I gritted my teeth. "No—"

Before I could stop her, she sliced the flesh of my palm and held the bleeding cut over the bowl.

Ow!

Pain instantly lashed over the wound, stinging and raw. Blood welled, dripping thickly into the girl's collection.

"Why did you do that?" My voice bordered on rage and curiosity. My hand begged to curl over the wound and protect it.

The girl didn't reply; she merely waited until a small crimson puddle rested in the bowl before letting me go.

The music turned to a fever, the men pounding their drums, the women kicking their heels. The little girl returned with her bloody prize, dancing and howling at the moon as voices rose in an ancient euphony.

My entire body was on fire.

My blood flowing fast.

My skin flushing bright.

My fear twisted into intoxication.

I wanted to join them. To become *wild*.

My wound was forgotten. My predicament and future peril ignored.

The moment the girl took my blood, I'd become more than just an outcast in this foreign land, I'd become *one* of them.

Cut sucked in a breath, something odd and not entirely unwelcome throbbing between us. He tore his gaze from mine as the girl finished her pirouette and with a squeal the bowl landed in the fire, shattering against hot coals, hissing with burning blood. A potent smell laced the air as the dance turned crazed, choreographed by gravity-defying shamans.

To be somewhere where life wasn't about TV or work-stress or mundane normalness—to see people having fun and partying—intoxicated me better than any experience.

The night came alive with singing and stomping feet and the unravelling power inside billowed faster. I wanted to get up. I wanted to dance. I wanted to forget who I was and let go.

This was an experience of a lifetime and my lifetime was almost over. My mother was here. My grandmother was here. Every ancestor had somehow come to life and existed in the flames of the enchanted fire.

We all lived the same path…and failed. I was supposed to be the last Weaver taken but time no longer held sway on my plans. It charged forward, dragging me with hardship, hurtling me toward a conclusion I didn't know how to stop.

A woman appeared in front of me. Coconut beads and crocodile teeth decorated her neck, draping between naked breasts. "You. Drink." Shoving a crudely made bowl beneath my chin, she tipped the milky substance toward my lips.

I reared back, shaking my head. "No, thank you."

Cut tugged on the rope, his face alive with power. "Drink."

I pursed my lips.

"You must." The woman tried again.

I turned my face away. The liquid smelled rank and rotten.

"You will drink, Nila." Lashing out, Cut fisted my hair, keeping my head in place as the woman once again held the bowl to my mouth.

I scrunched my face, protesting. The silty liquid splashed against my lips.

I didn't know what it was, but it was powerful—the otherworldly smell warned me I wouldn't be the same if I ingested it. I wouldn't like the results if I gave in.

Stop! Please, stop.

The woman tried again, bruising my mouth with the rim of the bowl. Crushed up leaves and smashed up roots lingered on the bottom, splashing with her attempts. The woman cursed in Swahili, looking at Cut for help. "She won't."

"She will." Still holding my hair, he reached with his free hand and captured my bleeding palm. "Open." With ferocity, he dug his fingernail into the fresh wound. I did my best to prevent drinking, but his hold was agonising.

The heat and pain wrenched my mouth open, and a gulp of disgusting liquid shot down my throat.

My eyes watered.

My stomach retched.

I spluttered.

The woman nodded with satisfaction. "Good." She stood, slipping back to her fellow dancers.

Alone, Cut hugged me, kissing my cheek. "Good girl." His tongue slipped out, licking a droplet off my lower lip like a lover would his bride. "Let it transform you. Let it own you."

I shuddered, fighting his embrace. "Let go of me."

Cut chuckled, kissing the corner of my mouth. "Don't fight it. You *can't* fight it."

"I'll fight whatever you do to me." Our eyes clashed. My heart roared with hatred.

But then...

Something mellowed.

Something simmered.

Tiptoeing through my blood, stealing rationality and sanity and coherence.

"What...what did yo—you give m—me?" My ability to speak in correct dialect fumbled as the drink merged faster with my thoughts.

Cut beamed wide; his face rollicked as my vision washed in and out. "Give it another moment. You'll see how useless fighting is." His lips caressed mine again. Softly, teasingly, coaxing me to react.

And this time...I couldn't hate it.

My loathing turned to liking. My hatred to harrowing welcome.

My heartbeat left the epicentre of my chest, cannonballing into every extremity. My toes felt it. My ears felt it. Even the strands of my hair *thump-thumped* in time.

I'm hot.

I'm cold.

I was sick.

I was cured.

What's happening?

A gust, a gale, a monsoon ripped through my body. Whatever the woman had given me tore up my denials and aversion, switching them into the sudden overwhelming desire to kiss him back.

God, a kiss. Such a delicacy. A tongue, such a gift.

Kiss him.

I tore myself away, spitting on the flax mat. "No!"

Cut turned into a rippling watermark, decorated with flames and starlight. "I don't believe you." His fingers traced my skin, drawing hungry blood to the surface. My mouth said no but my body said *yes*.

No...this can't...

I moaned, struggling against the ropes as I fell deeper and deeper into whatever spell he'd fed me.

I didn't know what lacquered my mouth.

I didn't know what made its fiery way into my belly.

But I did know it was aggressive and possessive and persuasive.

Vicious.

Far, far stronger than anything I'd ever had before.

I can't fight it.

My tongue went numb, followed by my throat and skin. My pussy throbbed for release. My mind howled for connection. I'd never been so disappointed in myself nor so annoyed at preventing such delicious need from billowing.

I split in two.

I became something I wasn't.

I became a creature with no morals or humanity, just an animal wanting to fuck.

Shivers hijacked me as I fought against the overwhelming sensation to let go. To give in to the magic. To be swept away by the river of sin.

"Do it, Nila. Let it take you." Cut's fingers were tiny birds upon my spine, feathering into my hair.

I moaned, trembling and wanting.

"Let it win and tonight won't be rape. Tonight will be the best fucking sex of your life."

No.

Yes.

No!

Oh, my God.

His words were invitations to my destruction, beckoning closer with every word.

My heartbeat thundered harder, feeding the drug into every part of me.

"That's it. Let go. Forget about the past and future. Think about how good my cock would feel. How delicious it would be for me to fuck you right here."

Fuck.

Sex.

Mate.

God...

I squeezed my eyes, swirling down a rabbit hole of fanaticism.

His fingers licked through my hair, blazing with lust and horror. "You want me, Nila. Admit it."

My soul turned wild, snarling at the power of the drug.

The fire burned brighter.

The stars twinkled faster.

The dancers twirled harder.

The world twisted and turned, rushing quickly then slowing down as the hallucinogenic played havoc with my senses.

I lost track of time.

I lost track of myself.

My mind swam with images of the dark dripping walls of the mine. My hands locked and squeezed, smearing my blood over Jethro's initials, wanting nothing more than to touch myself and orgasm.

I need to come.

I need to fuck and love and consummate.

I was a black and white painting, an enigma, a shivering contradiction.

I was numb.

I was alive.

I was dead.

I was reborn.

What's happening to me?

I shook my head, fighting the intensity, refusing to become hypnotised by sex and want and music.

But then hands were grabbing mine, tugging me to my feet.

Cut's laughter laced around me. Commands to dance consumed me.

I tried to dart away, but the ground rolled like a funhouse. Vertigo latched me in its horrendous arms.

I fell forward. I was caught.

I swayed to the side. I was propped up.

Daniel's eyes. Cut's eyes. Laughter. Dangerous promises. Lust and greed and pain.

I couldn't.

I couldn't fight it anymore.

My vertigo balanced. My veins sang with drunkenness and I lost everything.

In a circle of sweaty ebony women, I shed my worries, my fears, my hopes. I ceased to be Nila. I stopped being a victim.

The diamonds on my throat increased in weight and warmth, squeezing me tight and drenching me in rainbows from the fire.

I stopped pining for Jethro.

I stopped fearing my future.

I stepped into the magic and danced.

Jethro

AFRICA.

The witching hour stole the continent as I ran through customs and exploded through the arrival gates. Sir Seretse Khama Airport welcomed me back before spewing me out into the chilly night of Gaborone. I hadn't been in Botswana for two years, yet it felt as if I'd never left.

I avoided coming here. I couldn't handle the emotional currents from our workers. I hated feeling their toil and trouble. I hated seeing secrets and shimmers of how unhappy they were.

The last time I'd come, I'd talked to Kes about doing something about it.

He became our official mediator. Behind Cut's back, he travelled often and built a rapport with the men who'd been in our employment for centuries. In his quintessential style of helping and generosity, he improved the living conditions, gave them higher salaries, safer workplace, and secret bonuses for their plight.

He ensured Cut's slaves turned into willing employees with health benefits and satisfaction.

Cut didn't know.

There was so much he didn't know.

But then again, what Cut didn't know didn't hurt him. And it meant our enterprise ran smoother because no ill will and destitution could undermine it.

"Goddammit, where are the fucking drivers?" I jogged toward the vehicle stand, searching for any sign of hailing a lift.

Taxis were few and lingering opportunists rare at this time of night.

I hadn't slept in days. My wound had ruptured and my fever grew steadily worse. But I didn't have time to care. My senses were shredded from the flight and it was all I could do to remain standing.

But Nila was with my father.

Nila was running out of time.

I'm coming.

A single shadow appeared up ahead. Turning my jog into a sprint, I clenched my jaw and approached the scruffy African man. His long hair was braided and his jeans torn in places.

I pointed at his muddy car. "Is that your four-wheel drive?"

The guy glowered, crossing his arms. His black eyes looked me up and down, his muscles priming for a fight.

In Africa, you didn't approach strangers unless you had a weapon and were prepared to battle. Humanity wasn't as civilized here, mainly because so much strife kept the country salivating for war.

"What's it to you, white boy?" His Afrikaans accent heralded memories of playing in the dirt at our mine as a child. Of digging beside workers and chipping unwilling diamonds from ancient rock.

"I'll pay you two thousand pounds if you'll drive me where I need to go."

His territorial anger faded a little, slipping into suspicious hope. "What about I just steal the money and leave you dead on the side of the road?"

I stood to my full height, even though it hurt my side. "You won't do that."

The man uncrossed his arms, his fists curling. "Oh, no? Why not?"

"Because in order to be paid you have to take me. I don't have the money on me."

"This a scam?"

"No scam."

The guy leaned forward, his eyes narrowing for battle. "Tell me who you are."

I smiled.

My name carried weight in England, just like it carried weight here.

However, here I was more than an heir to a billion dollar company. I was more than a lord, and master polo player, and vice president to Black Diamonds.

Here, I was life.

I was death.

I was blood and power and royalty.

"I'm a Hawk."

And that was all it took.

The man lost his indignation, slipping into utmost respect. He turned and opened the door of his dinged-up 4WD, bowing in welcome. "It would be an honour to drive you, boss. I know where you need to go."

Of course, he did.

Everyone here knew of our mine. They knew it was untouchable. They knew not to raid or pillage. That sort of respect went a long way in this country.

I clasped his hand in thanks. "You'll be repaid. But I expect you to drive fast."

"No problem." He smiled broadly. "I know how Hawks fly."

I curled my hands, unable to ignore the ticking time bomb in my chest. *Nila.*

Glaring at my driver, I ordered, "Do whatever it takes, but I want to be at *Almasi Kipanga* before sunrise."

Nila

"LET HER GO."

Daniel dropped his hold.

I spun to face them. I didn't know why; I knew what was about to happen and should hide. Hide deep, *deep* inside. Hide from everything they would do to me.

However, I preferred to stare at the devil than go into this blind. I would rather pay attention, so I knew that I fought. That I'd won against whatever Cut had made me drink. That he hadn't taken my refusal away from me.

I won't let myself submit.

I vibrated and throbbed. I still begged for a release.

The drugs from the bonfire ran rampant in my veins. Cut had let me dance. He'd cut the rope from around my wrists and sat beside the fire and watched. At times, I caught him pressing a fist between his legs; others, I thought I witnessed affection on his face.

Every step, I succumbed more and more to the drugs. Every drumbeat, my pussy clenched. If Jethro had touched me, I would've dropped to all fours and begged him to fuck me.

I wouldn't have cared about people or fires or watchful gazes. I would've given myself completely in to the fantasy and thrown myself into every debauched act imaginable.

But he wasn't there.

And buried beneath lust and shameful wetness, I remembered enough to be disgusted at my urges. Below the tremors of salaciousness, I hung on with fingernails so I didn't double cross every moral I had left.

The more I danced, the more the fire chased away the chill of the night sky, coating my skin with dew.

The sweating and heat helped.

Perspiration helped shed a little of the drug's claws, bringing me back from untamed animal to a woman I vaguely recognised.

I'd won.

Against the hardest battle of my life.

But now, all that existed was desire and the knowledge there was nowhere for me to run.

Not this time.

No Kestrel to fake it. No Jethro to save me.

Just Daniel, Cut, and me in this flimsy fabric tent.

Drumbeats pounded outside, the occasional whoop and incantation fading into the starlit sky. I'd never battled myself so hard. Never tried to cling to right and wrong when faced with impending doom and wanting so fucking much to give in.

Sex.

They wanted sex.

And whatever they'd given me made me want it bad, too. Terribly bad. Stupidly, fearfully *bad*.

But I couldn't.

I couldn't forget. I *wouldn't* forget.

And so my body split further into two, quaking and twitching, demanding I give in.

Cut came closer, cupping my cheeks with his rough hands. My skin sparked beneath his touch and I hated, hated, *hated* myself for the way I swayed closer, focusing on his mouth and heat and charred smell from the fire.

He chuckled softly, running his thumb over my bottom lip.

It took everything, absolutely everything, inside not to open for him and suck his finger.

"You're still fighting, little Weaver. I suggest you give in."

Never!

I moaned as he kissed me, encouraging me to just let go. Cut no longer played by whatever ancient rules that'd bound him. He played a different game. He seemed younger, softer...and the occasional similarity between him and his eldest son shot confusion into my brain like the worst vertigo attack.

He's not Jethro.

He's not!

I might've given in to the music and danced. I might've become one of the clan as I cavorted around the burning blaze. But now I would control myself, even if it meant shackling everything my body wanted and ensuring I was taken against my will.

Rape would destroy me.

But willingly participating...I would rather die a thousand times on the threatened guillotine.

"Do you need me to go into details, Nila?" Cut ran his nose along my jaw. "You know what happened to our ancestor. He was buggered from one a.m. to one p.m. He was shared. There were no rules on what could be done to his body. He was given as a debt."

I swallowed hard.

The terrible tragedy of what'd befallen his relative helped fortify my resolve.

I leaned away from his touch. "No, you don't have to. I remember."

Jethro...

God, I wished he was here.

Kestrel...

He'd saved me last time. He'd remained true and honest and so damn selfless—I'd wanted him in that moment.

I wanted him now.

The drugs made me want anyone as long as I earned pleasure and an end to the incessant drive for a release.

I balled my hands. "Whatever you gave me—I won't give in to it."

My eyes glazed as Cut grabbed his cock. "You sure about that?"

Animalistic primal urges overrode my humanity. I was sick. Sick, sick, *sick* to want this murderer. The man who'd slaughtered my mother. The man who killed my lover and his brother—his very sons.

No!

A wash of clarity helped me stand firm. "Get out! Get *out*. I won't enjoy this. I won't. No matter what you do, I won't welcome this. You want me to give myself willingly? You want me to love you like I love your son? But I won't. I never will. You're a twisted bastard who deserves nothing more than death!"

Silence smothered us as my outburst hung loudly in the tent.

Daniel ran his hand over his face, chuckling. "Oh, fuck, Weaver. Now, you've done it."

Cut didn't say a word, but the loose enjoyment on his face tightened with rage. Lashing out, he grabbed my hair, jerking my head back. "Love my son? I think you meant to say *loved*, my dear. He's dead."

Shit!

I forced desolation into my gaze, burying the truth deep inside.

Cut's gaze probed mine, searching for my lies. "You're strong, I'll give you that. Stronger than your mother. Do you want to know how she begged me to fuck her? Want to know how wild she was? How she confessed she loved me and would die happily after the night we had together?"

Lies. All lies.

My heart formed a callus, a scar, thickening against his taunts. "I don't believe you." The diamonds on my throat pressed heavily on my larynx as Cut yanked me harder.

"You think you'll fight us, but you won't. The minute I lay a finger on that wet pussy of yours, you'll be screaming for more." Letting me go, I stumbled backward.

Cut prowled to a small table where a decanter of cognac had been delivered. His white shirt clung to his lanky body, almost translucent with sweat from the ceremony. His skin glimmered with dampness and his eyes glowed with sickness as he turned with a poured shot in his hand.

If only he *was* sick. If only he caught a disease and died.

He raised the goblet in a toast. "To the Third Debt, Nila." Throwing back a large mouthful and tossing away the glass, he came forward. Reaching into his pocket, Cut pulled out a one pound coin. "Heads or tails, Dan."

My heart ran wild.

My breasts tingled.

Arousal battered at my hatred, urging me to bow to the false euphoria. I wouldn't be subdued or seduced by trickery. I would stand and *fight*.

I will kill you, Cut Hawk. I will kill you!

Daniel rubbed his nape. "Ah, shit. Um…heads. Gimme the queen."

Cut flicked the coin into the air. Catching it on its downward sweep, he slapped it on the back of his hand and revealed it. His lips pulled back. *"Fuck."*

Daniel punched the sky. "Fuck, yes." Darting forward, he lassoed an arm around my waist. "I guess that means you and I get the first round, Nila." Possession leaked through his pores.

No!

A bone-deep sob tried to claw free.

Pointing at the tent flap, Daniel growled, "Come back when the screaming stops, Pop. I'll make sure to leave her alive for you."

Everything inside me withered like a flower in autumn, dying, dying, dead.

Cut ran a hand over his face. "Motherfucker." His golden eyes turned dark, but he snarled reluctantly. "Fine." Storming toward the door, he looked back one last time. "See you in a little while, Nila. Remember what I said—the minute I touch you, you'll be on your knees begging me to fuck you. Don't let Daniel steal everything. Save some of your strength for me."

And then, he was gone.

Leaving me alone with an insane Hawk who deserved to be torn apart and devoured by wolves.

Stay strong. You can do this.

My lungs ceased to work. I wanted the earth to open up and consume me.

"Ready for some fun, Weaver Whore?"

I gritted my teeth, refusing to look at him.

Daniel came closer, capturing my chin, raising my eyes to his. I hated that his touch felt good. That my body craved more. That whatever drugs in my system chipped away my strength, my panic...just waiting for weakness to consume me.

"Don't touch me." I tried to remove my face from his grip, but he only pinched me harder.

"Ah, don't be shy. Now isn't the time to be shy. Not when I finally get to see what made my brother such a fucking idiot over you." Trailing his hand down my cleavage, he muttered, "Don't like your small tits. Perhaps it was your pussy that drugged him, huh?" Pushing me backward, he laughed. "Let's find out. Shall we?"

I screeched as he shoved me toward the bed.

No torments or games. No history lessons or delays.

He wanted me. He would have me. And then his father would. And I'd be mentally, physically, spiritually broken.

Tears sloshed inside me like a storm upon a sea, smashing against my ribcage.

Don't give in.

Time sped up as unsteadiness latched onto my brain, throwing me to the side. My skin crawled. My blood boiled with misplaced disgusting lust.

Being in this place, this awful foreign place, imprisoned me worse than Hawksridge.

I'm all alone.

Even my body was a traitor as it hummed and melted, ignoring my demands to remain frigid and fighting.

"Get on the bed, whore." Tossing me onto the mattress, Daniel cackled. The alcohol he'd consumed glazed his eyes, turning his touch sloppy and cruel.

I bounced on the soft bedspread, shaking my head to rid the imbalance. The tent parried and pirouetted, refusing to remain in one place.

Daniel threw himself on top of me. The air erupted from my body with his heaviness.

Instantly, fire exploded through my system. "Get *off* me!"

"Oh, yes. Scream all you want. No one will care." His hands fumbled with the waistband of my jeans, tearing at the zipper.

"*No!*" My voice broke as the scream tore my throat.

"Fuck, that makes me hard." Daniel licked my cheek, spreading disgusting saliva. "I'll make sure you prefer me to my father, you can count on it." His hand soared over my ribcage, latching onto my breast.

I squirmed and kicked and screamed and *thrashed*.

"Goddammit, you're wild."

I kept fighting. My petrified fear buried beneath lawyers of rapidly failing courage. "Stop. *Stop!*"

Daniel only laughed. "Tire yourself out. There's a good fucking bitch." He shoved my shoulders against the mattress, pinning me down. His legs spread over mine. "Been waiting for this day for months, little Weaver."

His fingers tweaked my nipple and heinous pleasure shot through my system.

Lust.

Desire.

Pleasure.

No.

I could handle fighting. I could handle battling for my life. But I couldn't handle wrestling with my body. That was supposed to be on *my* side. Mine. Not his.

Mine.

A surge of power swatted the drug's effects away; I soared into life. My knee shot upright, colliding with soft balls and hard cock.

Daniel crumpled in slow motion, a guttural groan tearing from his mouth. His skin shot white as pain-perspiration decorated his forehead. Gasping for breath, he fell to the side, releasing me to hold his precious equipment.

Writhing away, I flew to my knees and rolled off the bed. "I hate you! *Hate you!*"

Somehow, Daniel fought through the agony, hurling himself after me to grapple around my legs.

We tumbled to the tent floor, pricked by twigs and debris beneath the canvas lining.

Daniel turned red. "You fucking bitch!"

His fists pummelled my side, stealing the oxygen from my lungs. I squirmed and kicked, but the liquor in his blood muted whatever I managed to land on him.

Stumbling to his feet, Daniel kicked me in the belly. "That's for hurting my dick, bitch."

Agony radiated out as fast as lightning. I groaned, sickness dousing every inch. I curled up, holding my stomach, cursing him in every religion. Somehow, I compartmentalized the pain and lashed out with my foot. My toes hooked around his heel, sending him toppling to his knees.

He grunted, but it didn't stop him from punching me again in the thigh. "Plenty more pain where that came from. Like it? Do you like it when I kick you like the bitch you are?"

I moaned in torture as he rolled me onto my back. "You're not going anywhere, whore. Not this time."

The tent turned fuzzy as the drugs made everything so hot. My muscles were weak from lack of food. I wouldn't be able to win the fight.

You can win.

I growled, aiming for his nose.

He deflected my hand as if it were nothing more than pollen.

I can't.

I tried again, slapping his cheek, connecting with his hot flesh.

I can!

Daniel snarled, his fingers fumbling with his belt. "That's the last time you'll hit me." His head came forward, cracking his forehead on mine.

The mutual pain crested through my skull, rendering me numb and lost. Swimming through it, I did my best to scramble backward, kicking him. "Leave me alone!" Somehow, I got free of his putrid embrace, crying in fleeting triumph.

"Fuck!" He grabbed my ankle.

"No!" My skin tingled, awoken by the drugs from the fire. I moaned as another flush of heat and hatred became bedfellows in my heart. Every inch of me was swollen and wet with desire. I'd never wanted sex so much but fought so hard to avoid it.

The awful contradiction stole every last dreg of energy.

He yanked me back, a morbid chuckle on his lips. "Getting tired yet?"

"Never."

Yes, so much yes.

Tears torrented down my cheeks even though I didn't permit myself to cry. My body bypassed synapses, defending, slipping into preservation. "I'll kill you. You're nothing. *Nothing.*"

"I'm nothing? I'll show you fucking nothing." Rearing upright, Daniel cocked his fist and ploughed it straight into my cheek.

Stars.

Galaxies.

Lions and tigers and bears.

I lost consciousness.

How long, I didn't know. I floated in an ocean of affliction, vaguely aware as cold air licked around my hipbones, then arse, then thighs, then toes.

Lucidity slammed back as the rotten feel of his fingers on my pussy jerked me awake.

I came to with my jeans ripped away and my knickers wrenched to my knees.

The room spun as my cheekbone shrieked in pain. "No…"

"Yes." Daniel grinned. "I'm going to show you punishment. I'm going to teach you a lesson you'll never forget."

The sound of belt buckles and zippers rapidly gathered my wits.

Fight, Nila.

Time had run out.

Daniel would rape me on the floor of a tent in the middle of their diamond empire. I was alone. If I didn't win, Cut would take me next, and I would crave the day I paid the Final Debt as I wouldn't be able to live with myself.

Please…

Sobs wanted to take over rather than fight. I'd burned through everything I had.

How can I win when I have nothing left?

Daniel shifted, jerking down his trousers, freeing his red-angry cock.

"We're in fucking Africa." Daniel breathed hard, his breath reeking of liquor. "Know what happens in Africa?"

I didn't respond. I never liked his answers. I *hated* his answers. Instead, I wriggled, trying to get free.

I'm done.

It was over.

It's not over!

Memories of altered garments and sewn weapons flooded my mind. How could I forget?

My vision narrowed, searching, flying around the tent.

My jeans.

They rested an arm's stretch away. In the leg, I'd hidden a scalpel.

The scalpel!

My heart catapulted in my chest with joy. The hidden blade would be my guardian. My saviour. Grunting, I stretched my arm out, fingers fumbling with the denim.

Daniel didn't care about my attempt to grab discarded clothes. His fingers latched around my collar, shaking me with frustration. "You know, this would be a lot more fun if you played along. Answer me. What happens in Africa, Weaver?"

Spit welled in my mouth—partly from grey sickness and partly from vile disgust. My fingers stretched harder.

I can't reach.

"Fuck, answer me!"

"I'll answer you." Turning my head, I spat in his demonic face. "Shut up! There? That make you happy, arsehole?"

His features contorted, but he didn't move away. "That's the last fucking straw. You pushed too far. Gonna do what I've wanted for months." His breathing turned sporadic. "I'm going to break my promise."

My heart stopped.

What?

I was torn between straining to reach my jeans and paying attention.

Get them. Before it's too late.

"I promised Cut I'd leave you alive for him. But after that—" He chuckled coldly, his eyes darkening into golden blackness. "After that blatant disregard, I'm going to fuck you dead, you hear me? I'm going to make you scream and cry and beg and pray for motherfucking *death*."

He smiled, showing perfect teeth that only childhood braces could deliver. "Get on your knees, bitch."

Before I could respond, he hooked his fingers tighter in my collar. The thick filigree and impenetrable diamonds were the perfect lasso to jerk me up and flip me over.

No!

My jeans were no longer in reaching distance.

The moment I was on my knees, Daniel spread my legs and grabbed my hips. "Shit, yes."

I screamed as he dug fingernails into my skin so hard he drew blood.

I gave up trying to reach for help. I gave up trying to remain human. The drugs buzzed in my blood, twisting me with horror and desire. But the desire was no longer for sex or pleasure. Oh, no. This desire was for *murder*. To rip out his entrails and stuff them in his bleeding mouth. To slice off his cock and present it to Cut as my trophy. This desire was my ignition.

This desire was my *annihilation.*

Clearheadedness settled into every cell, even as Daniel yanked me back and fisted his cock to thrust inside. Purity and precision slowed my breathing. Certainty and courage stopped my shaking hands. And proficient power guided my fingers to the hem of my hoodie.

I forgot.

But now I remember.

The knitting needle.

The one implement I'd stroked and caressed since leaving Hawksridge. I didn't need a scalpel. I had something better.

A thirty-five centimetre, single-pointed metal spear.

Closing my eyes, I conjured everything I loved, everyone, every reason why I would survive and Daniel wouldn't.

Jethro.

Vaughn.

My father.

I would survive for them.

No matter what it takes.

I gave myself over to bloodlust.

I did the one thing I was born to do.

I carried out my promise to my ancestors.

My fingernails were blades as I sliced through the loose stitching and pulled free my weapon of choice. My life might be over. I might be alone. But I wouldn't die without taking a Hawk with me.

Daniel grunted, lining himself up to rape me.

My skin went cold. My heart went calm. And I fisted my knitting needle.

"You ready for this, Weaver? Ready to be fucked?"

I didn't reply as his knees touched the back of mine.

I didn't move as his thighs pressed against mine.

I didn't flinch as the tip of his cock entered me.

I waited.

I hunted.

I swallowed my tears and fears.

Another inch inside me.

His awareness faded, focusing entirely on sex.

Weaker...weaker...

And still I waited.

Another centimetre of my enemy's cock inside me.

I paused for the perfect moment.

Now.

I attacked.

Rage stole everything.

I wasn't afraid of repercussions or consequences.

I wasn't afraid of getting hurt or dying.

All I cared about was ending this monstrosity before he took my soul.

"Fuck you!" Throwing myself to the side, his cock slipped out and Daniel's hold fumbled. The ground kissed my shoulder, rattling my teeth as I flipped onto my back beneath him.

For a moment, I drank in the final image I would have of Daniel. He stood poised on his knees, his cock swollen and hungry, his face rageful and surprised. A simple man turned into a despicable creature. He was no longer human. Just the mistake. The unwanted.

I did the world a favour.

I did the only thing I could do.

"Goodbye, Daniel."

Sitting upright, I hugged his shoulders, lining my trajectory for perfect aim. I wrapped my fingers around the needle; I pressed my face into his throat. Energy exploded. Righteousness detonated. I bared my teeth and bit his neck as my arm soared up, faster and faster, guided by the divine, flying with ghosts of my family, winging with the precision of fate, and pierced my mortal enemy.

The sharpness of the knitting needle slipped as easily and as cleanly as a knife slipped through expensive steak. Up and up, puncturing through his ribcage, slicing through his lung, and finally, finally, *finally* perforating his heart.

Time stopped.

The world ceased to spin.

Daniel turned from rutting animal to shocked puppet.

His eyes popped wide as the softest cry tumbled from his lips. His gaze met mine. His hand flew to where the knitting needle lanced his side. He was no longer my adversary but merely thread, welcoming my needle, ready to be transformed into a seamstress's masterpiece.

And then, he toppled.

Falling, falling, *falling* to his side.

Vertigo teased as death swooped across *Almasi Kipanga* and whipped into the tent. My wrist twisted as I fell with him, never letting go of the needle. I rolled, straddling him, forcing the weapon further into his heart. I almost lost my grip as he bucked and lurched, but I didn't let go. Using two hands, I pushed down. Harder. Harder.

Die, Daniel. Die.

I'd researched how to take a life while existing at Hawksridge. I'd read articles, watched examples, planned the perfect murder. To puncture a heart didn't guarantee death. A 'stiletto' type perforation could be survived.

I had no intention of letting Daniel survive.

Locking my knees either side of his chest, I ripped the needle free.

An agonising groan came from his chest as blood oozed from the hole.

Daniel's stupor fell away. His hands reached for my throat, his fingers shaking and weak as his blood pressure dropped from the orifice gushing in his chest. His brain starved for oxygen the longer his heart bled. He only had seconds before the machine of his body shut down.

His arms flailed. His palm struck my cheek, desperate to hurt.

Tears spurted and pain smarted, but I didn't move. I wouldn't have the power to fight him if his body hadn't turned traitor, poisoning him from the inside out. But right now, I had all the power in the world.

"You fucking cu—" He coughed, his fingers slipping in their attempt to curl around my neck, grasping my collar instead. The impenetrable diamonds kept me safe from being throttled as I arched my arm and prepared to complete my final strike.

"Die." The needle glistened with dripping crimson as it hurtled through the air and kissed his skin again. The wickedly sharp point crunched its way through flesh and fat, returning to lodge in his most important organ.

Daniel howled, his torso thrashing, face straining. He hit me, struck me, tried to knock me over. But I had an anchor—the needle. I held on, pushing down with all my might driving the end home.

"You can't stop me."

He bellowed as the needle tip slid deeper, deeper, past gristle and bone, impaling my victim inch by inch. He twitched and bucked, his fingers unable to snare as his nervous system shut down.

The wet squelch of my needle ripping another hole in his heart brought rushing nausea, but I didn't falter. All masterful killers knew to make the result permanent, dedication and desire had to be invoked.

I was dedicated.

I desired freedom.

I would finish this.

Holding the base of the needle, I twisted it like a corkscrew.

"Ah!" Daniel jerked. His arms fell to his side, scrabbling at the needle, but it was too late. Adrenaline would keep him animated for another few seconds, but it was already done.

I took his life, not with horror or regret, but with no mercy and complete acceptance.

A life for a life.

He owed me that.

Watching him succumb iced my blood, turning me into a ruthless executioner. His golden eyes met mine, gasping for hope and help. His motions turned languid and dull, a broken pawn, never to live again.

"How does it feel, Daniel? To know you've lost?" I gasped, but my nerves remained calm. "How does it feel to know a Weaver took your soul?"

He never had the chance to answer. His face froze of vitality. His breath wheezed, his heart stopped, and in those final seconds before his soul leapt free, he snarled with sinister hate.

Then...emptiness.

There were no longer two people in my tent, only one. Just me.

Just me.

I killed him.

As if the universe rejoiced in one less monster breathing its air, a lion bayed on the dawn's horizon. Daniel's blood slowly seeped in an odd little trickle around my needle. Weeping wetly and warmly, staining his chest like spilled wine.

He twitched.

I rejoiced.

I'd killed my first Hawk.

Daniel...

...

was dead.

THE LUMINESCENT glow of imminent dawn welcomed me to *Almasi Kipanga*.

I knew the compound well and ordered the driver to wait a kilometre from the perimeter. He obeyed because he trusted my family's name. And I trusted him because I hadn't paid him yet. I had no intention until I found Nila and had her safe in my arms.

He was my ticket to freedom, and I would reward him handsomely for it.

Jogging through the long grass of the plain surrounding the encampment, I hoped the dried blood from my side wouldn't attract unwelcome predators. I'd stepped into a world where teeth and fang were much more dangerous than bullet and gun.

The camp sat like a giant growth in the centre of nothing. Armed guards patrolled the fence line but I knew another way in that would go unnoticed. I'd used it when I was young, when hanging out with too many people overwhelmed me. Kes had found it—the unfortified entrance—kindly giving me an escape route to find silence and sanctuary.

Keeping low, I avoided the main entry and dashed to the service area and staff quarters. Keeping my footsteps light and breathing shallow, I pulled on the loose wooden panel and slipped into the latrines. Either the guards had never found the perimeter's weakness or they had no intention of doing repairs while breathing in the stench of excrement.

Animals avoided the scent of human waste, and men who wanted to rob us didn't think to follow the malodour for a way in.

Smoke from a dying bonfire crackled in the centre of the camp. Fast asleep tribesmen and their families slept in lean-tos while some preferred to dream in the elements beneath the stars. My lips curled, remembering the ceremony that'd almost incapacitated me emotionally.

I'd been fifteen.

I'd been an unwilling participant.

But that hadn't stopped them from forcing me to ingest the drug-liquor, consuming me in their drumbeats and chanting.

It'd fucked me up worse than normal. I'd never felt so unhinged and aroused, turned on by the tiniest touch, overwhelmed by the simplest emotion. The entire camp had become an orgy, and I'd run far and fast.

I'd barricaded myself for twenty-four hours, remaining alone and far away from rutting sex-crazed humans. But it hadn't stopped me from pleasuring myself or spilling orgasm after orgasm on the dusty African plains.

Holding my breath, I wrapped my arm around my painful side. Every heartbeat activated the wound, highlighting my lack of rest and fever. I wouldn't have the strength to fight many men if they woke up.

Tiptoeing through the scattered sleeping forms, I calculated where Nila would be. The faster I could get in and out, the higher our chance of survival.

But at least we would be together again—regardless of what happened.

One particular woman moaned and rolled over in her sleep, hugging a black-skinned man beside her. The one blessing of the drug was insane lethargy. After the passion and demands of animalistic behaviours, they'd be out cold until the heat from the African sun forced them to move indoors or incinerate.

My heart remained in my mouth as I weaved around tents and shipping containers. Cut's sleeping quarters were across the compound, upwind and in a prime location. Daniel's rested four tents away which left the guest one beside it.

My gaze shot to the fabric A-frame in question.

Lights.

The only one with lights illuminating the inside like a trapped firefly in a jar.

It took a few minutes to skirt around the edge, stepping through shadows, avoiding open spaces. I listened for noises. I hoped to God Nila hadn't been harmed. And I wished for a gun to protect her.

A noise sounded inside the tent. A gentle thud followed by a female moan.

Nila!

I couldn't wait any longer.

Surprise would be on my side, but I hoped righteousness and fate would be, too.

Ducking beneath the entrance canopy, I charged inside.

My heart stopped.

My mouth fell open.

It couldn't be.

"Nila…"

Her head shot up. She looked as wild as the animals of this country. She crouched beside my brother, her hands covered in blood, her hoodie hanging off one shoulder, and her legs bare and exposed. Bruises marred her porcelain skin, scratches and blemishes hinting at a fight I was too late to stop.

She jerked to the side, wielding a long red weapon. "Don't—" Her eyes focused, then love poured from her. "Jethro? It can't…it can't be true."

I staggered toward her, glancing between my half-naked woman and my dead brother. His cock was still hard on his belly. My skin crawled even as my heart stopped beating. "How…how did this happen?"

Her skin was white as milk, her frame shaking with adrenaline. My eyes drifted to her naked pussy and rage unfurled inside me.

"Did he rape you?" My hands curled as I stood over my brother's corpse. "Did that motherfucker touch you?"

She shook her head, throwing down her weapon and wiping bloody hands on her hoodie. Her eyes flashed, hiding the truth she didn't want me to see. "No." Standing, she huddled into me.

My arms automatically wrapped around her, protecting her, even though I begged her to be honest with me.

He'd touched her.

That motherfucking animal touched what wasn't his.

My embrace became shackles as I dropped my head in despair. Inhaling the softness of her scent and sharpness of spilled blood, I trembled with rage.

Nila let me hold her, her arms returning the furious hug.

I'm sorry.

So fucking sorry.

Her emotions collided with pride and purgatory. She'd killed him and hadn't processed what his death would mean.

I hugged her harder.

I'm here.

Her voice whispered into my shirt. "He didn't rape me, Jethro. I swear. I'm sorry…sorry…so sorry."

Liar.

I understood why she'd lied. Even now, even with death on her hands and fear in her heart, she still tried to save me.

I was the one who'd let her down.

I was the one who made her return to the Hall.

This was *my* fault. "I did this."

Her quaking arms wrapped tighter, hurting my unhealed side. "No. Don't blame—"

"If I don't blame myself, who can I?" I pressed my face into her throat, the short ends of her hair tickling my cheeks. "I sent you back. I fucking sent you back to be raped and—"

She struggled in my arms. "He didn't—"

I pulled back, anger cresting. "Don't lie to me! You can't lie to me, remember?"

Her lips pursed; she battled between looking at the floor for privacy and fighting me like she'd fought my brother. "Don't. Don't get mad. I'm only trying to save—"

I bared my teeth. "Save me? That's my fucking job, Nila. Not yours. Don't you get it? I should've been the one to protect you. Not the other way around."

She didn't reply, her eyes burning black holes into my soul. There was no judgement in her gaze, only forgiveness for making her leave when she'd begged me to reconsider.

"Fuck." My back rolled, and I grabbed her close again. "I'm sorry. Shit, I'm so sorry."

Her arms twined around me, her love giving me somewhere to hide from my own fucked-up emotions. "I know. It's okay."

It wasn't okay. None of this was okay. But I wouldn't press it further. Not here. Not now.

Whatever had happened before my arrival spilled out of her, lapping around our feet.

Her fingers dug into my spine, reliving what she'd done. "I wanted to kill him. But now…now, maybe…I didn't. God, I killed him, Kite. I—I took a life." She hugged me impossibly harder as she lost herself to tangled thoughts. An odd overtone layered her emotions the longer I held her. The sensation of need and desire so strong it superseded her misery at killing.

I winced at her strength but didn't care about the pain. All I cared about was her. About taking her far away from here and protecting her like I should've done from the start.

I crushed her in my embrace, holding her so fucking close. "It's over now. Whatever happened, it's over." I kissed the top of her head, her brow, her eyes. "Are you okay? Don't lie to me. I need to know you aren't hurting." My eyes trailed over her injuries. Daniel had done more than touch her, he'd hit her, possibly kicked her.

Her hair stuck up in places, and her cheek flamed red from a slap. She'd been to hell and back, but she'd left my brother in damnation.

I'm so fucking proud of her.

She nodded, breathless and broken. Tears washed down her face. I'd never seen her so primitive, focused only on survival and death. "I'm okay. I'm okay. I am. Truly. I'll be okay." The same shadow of lust tainted her voice. I could understand sudden joy at winning over an enemy, but lust?

Taking a few steps back, I pulled her away from Daniel. He lay on his back, blood clotting on his side, a blue tinge already creeping over his lips.

I didn't want her to look. I'd been around death before. I'd been the instigator of taking another's life. It wasn't easy to stare into the eyes of your victim once it was over. Especially when self defence forced your actions.

"Don't look. Forget what happened. I'm here now, and I'm never leaving again." I kissed her hair, so, so thankful I had her back in my arms.

Nila squirmed, disobeying me and looking at Daniel's corpse. Her muscles locked; a haunting hollowness entered her eyes. "He deserved it. So why do I feel like such a monster?"

I clamped my hands on her shoulders. "He *did* deserve it. Don't second-guess. You did what you had to do."

"Did I? Was there no other choice?"

I shook my head firmly. "None. It was the only way."

Nila bit her lip, her eyes overflowing with liquid. "But…he was the youngest. He couldn't help that Bonnie and Cut called him a mistake. He couldn't stop being ridiculed or believing in what he'd been told."

What?

What did she know about our upbringing and who Daniel had become because of his childhood? I'd caught him hurting for fun, killing animals for a rush. I'd told him off for being so egotistical and crude. Kes dealt with Daniel's fuck-ups more than I did because being around him was too hard. I'd slowly feed off the nastiness inside him. But because of my condition, I could wholeheartedly say he deserved what he got. Nila hadn't killed him. Karma had.

"Putting tragic tales to villains is a sure way to destroy yourself when they force you to do something cruel in order to survive, Nila."

Nila clenched her jaw, ready to argue. To judge herself into torment. Yet again another ripple of need, completely out of context to the situation, polluted the air.

Forcing her to twist and look at me, rather than Daniel, I cupped her cheeks. "Nila, listen to me. Don't look for redemption in those who don't deserve it. If you hadn't fought back, he would've raped you and possibly killed you. You don't know him—not like I do. And I can safely say, he deserved it."

She sniffed, dropping her eyes. "I'm so sorry, Jethro."

"Sorry?" My heart thundered. "What for?" Letting her go, I marched toward the bed and whipped the sheet free. Wrapping her bottom nakedness, I guided her further away from the body. "Why the hell are you apologising?"

I'm the one who should.

I'm the one who left you on your own.

Her body quaked as she looked over her shoulder, unable to stop staring at Daniel. "Because...because I just killed your flesh and blood."

I grabbed her waist, holding her tight. "I'm *grateful*. Not mad. Did you think I would care? Nila, I love you. Ever since you replied to my first text, my heart has put you above everyone in my family. *I love you.* And you're killing me by hating yourself for doing what was needed."

Softening my voice, I tucked her short black hair behind her ears, rubbing away her tears with a thumb. "Nila...he deserved to die. You need to trust me on that. You can't hold his death inside you. You can't feel responsible. I'm glad you ended him because if you hadn't, I would've made his demise a lot fucking worse. You did the right thing—that's all you need to know. Promise me that's all you'll remember?"

She sucked in a breath, leaning into my touch. "But—"

"No buts."

My heart cracked at what she was going through. I wished I'd arrived sooner. Been the one to stab him and wear his life on my soul, pinned there for eternity. Anything to prevent her from feeling the pain of aftermath. However, I hadn't been. And knowing Daniel had hurt her—taken something that didn't belong to him—that was my punishment to bear.

I shook as my own hurt surfaced. I had no right to ask. Not now when she struggled. But I couldn't stop the question falling from my lips. "Please...tell me one thing...and be truthful."

Her eyes met mine. "Anything."

I swallowed hard.

I swallowed again.

I lost courage but spoke anyway. "I know he touched you, Nila, you can't hide that from me. But how badly did he rape you? How much do you hate me for letting that happen?"

I hated my question. *How badly did he rape you?* Were there gradients of rape? Every form, no matter how long or brutal, were equally as terrible.

Christ!

I wanted to kill myself for being so useless.

But I had another question. One I didn't want to ask. Why did I feed off her overwhelming desire for sex? Why did she have such powerful thoughts when the current predicament was so inappropriate?

A slight pause, another lie formed. She shook her head. "I could never hate you. And I already told you. I stopped him—before..."

My shoulders sagged.

She rushed. "Jethro, don't torture yourself. Let me keep some secrets. Let me choose which ones to tell you and which ones to let die." Her voice cracked. "*Please*...you don't need to know. Just...leave it. I'm sorry..."

I died a little as my condition flared into full reception. Her emotions told me everything I needed to know. He'd been inside her. And she'd defended herself the only way she could.

Fuck.

How could I ever forgive myself for this?

Would she want me now? Would she trust I could protect her?

My arms latched around her, crashing her face to my chest. "Goddammit, Nila. You put me to shame. For the rest of my life, I'll make it up to you. I'll keep you safe. I'll stop all of this because I'm never letting you out of my sight again."

She kissed my shirt, moaning in gratefulness as she finally allowed me to take some of the responsibility. Her fingers fluttered over my hips, questing more than just a hug...more violent affection.

Her thoughts begged me to give in. To grant her some relief from the intensity in her mind. But I couldn't. Now was not the time.

"It's over now. It's done. You're safe."

For a moment, she let me soothe her. Her lustful taint gave way to sobs, and she crumpled deeper into my embrace. Together, we fell to the floor—me to my knees and Nila in my lap. I rocked her. I kissed her. I promised so many, many things.

Time ticked onward, putting seconds then minutes between her and taking Daniel's life. Nothing else would be able to fix her—only time and distance.

Finally, the shock of killing left and her eyes opened to focus resolutely on Daniel. Any hint of desire disappeared with clear-headed determination. "Cut will be back for his turn soon." Her voice shook. "What do I do, Kite? What do I do with the body?"

"You?" I laughed harshly. "You aren't doing anything. You've done too much already." I ran a hand through my hair. "I should've been there for you and I wasn't. I'll deal with this."

Her skin turned frigid beneath my fingertips. "No, you have to go. If Cut sees you—"

"I don't fucking care if he sees me." Pushing Nila off my lap, I stood. Marching across the tent, I tore through her open suitcase and threw fresh knickers and leggings her way. "Put these on. And shoes. I'm going to get rid of Daniel and you're coming with me."

"But—"

I cut my hand through the air. "But nothing, Nila. I'm not letting you out of my sight. Got it?"

"But Jasmine and Kes. You have to think of them. Cut can't know you're still alive, he'll—"

Kill me. Yes, I know.

But my life was worthless compared to hers. I would willingly trade it if it meant she walked away from this with no more bruises or battered memories. She'd already endured so much. She wore the marks of war, and I refused to let her endure more. I'd tried to save too many people. Kes would understand, and Jaz would expect me to do what was right.

This was right.

Nila was my only choice.

"Don't worry about them. I know what I'm doing." I glanced at my dead sibling, feeling nothing but relief. His cock taunted me with what he'd done to my woman. If he wasn't already dead...he would die with severe mutilation to purge myself of the wrath in my blood.

"So...how will we dispose of the body?" Nila whispered.

My mind ran with scenarios. "We could cover him in liquor and make it seem like he drank himself into the grave."

Nila swallowed. "Is that believable?" She looked at the floor where the long bloody weapon stuck to the tent covering. "I stabbed him in the heart with my knitting needle. The two wounds are small, but there. They'd know it wasn't self-inflicted."

She killed him with a needle?

An awed smile lit my face. "You're so fucking strong."

She glanced away, despair still prominent.

I rubbed my face, willing tiredness and pain to fade so I could come up with a solution.

Think.

Where could I put him that Cut wouldn't find him?

The diamond mine!

The idea sprang from schematics to doable. "We can make it look like an accident. I can bury him in the mine. Make it look like he fell."

Nila paused, tasting my plan, nibbling at it for flaws.

"Shit, that won't work." I shook my head. "I couldn't get him there without someone hearing the Jeep." My eyes narrowed, rushing forward with a new idea.

Then, it came to me.

Africa would take care of it for me.

I snapped my fingers with decision. "I know what to do."

Nila opened her mouth to argue, but I stormed across the room and grabbed her face. I couldn't help myself. She was so fucking courageous. Her emotions so clear. Her love so deep. Her passion so pure. Not one inch of terror or hate that I hadn't been there for her. Not one smidgen of hostility or judgement.

She's so damn selfless.

I kissed her.

The instant my lips touched hers, it was if a nuclear explosion mushroomed inside her. The lust I'd gleaned in her mind erupted into full force, drowning everything. Her tongue snaked into my mouth, decaying my resolve not to touch her.

Dropping the clothes I'd given her, she groaned long and low, her mouth tempting mine to give more. The sheet fluttered from her hips as her naked leg twined around my hip, grinding against me.

"Fuck..." I stumbled forward as she turned crazed with desire. I'd never felt such passion pouring from her. "Nila...wait..."

Her tongue shot swifter, sexier into my mouth. Kissing. Licking. *Demanding* I respond.

"Nila..."

"No, Jethro. Give me this. I *need* this." Her lips recaptured mine, pulling me under.

"Shit." It all suddenly made sense. The clouded residue on her thoughts. The flowing undercurrent of something stronger than death and pain. She wanted sex. She *needed* sex.

They'd drugged her.

They'd given her the same thing they'd given me when I was fifteen. Something so potent and heady no one could say no to the aphrodisiac power.

Goddammit.

My gut twisted into a knot as her tongue licked and flicked. I forced myself not to listen to her tainting thoughts—I didn't want the urgent need to fuck to consume me. But my cock thickened, drawn to her even as I tried to battle the rapidly building need. "How—how did you fight it for so long? How did you stop?"

Her hands flew up my t-shirt, skirting over my wound, dancing over my skin like compelling butterflies. "Stop talking. Please…give me what I want. I need to feel alive. I need to take back what Daniel tried to steal. *Please*, Jethro. Please, fuck me."

The memory of our first kiss in her room—the way she'd chopped my resolve to pieces with her demands to kiss her, fired into lustful flames.

Kiss me.

Fuck me.

She'd fought him; she'd killed him, even while under the influence. If she were anyone else, she would've willingly submitted. She would've enjoyed whatever Daniel did because her body would've given her no other choice. The drugs were beyond powerful, but somehow she'd been able to fight them along with fighting my brother's advances.

I don't deserve this woman.

This Weaver. This answer to my wrongness. This salvation to my condemnation.

"Jethro…please." Her kiss deepened.

"Goddammit." In a vicious yank, I plucked her into my arms and stalked to the bed. Her hands flew into my hair, tugging as her mouth danced over mine.

Our breathing grew laboured. Our skin slick and sensitive.

My entire body stiffened. The tent crackled with lust so painful it crippled us.

How much time do we have?

We were tempting fate. Beyond stupid to give in.

There's a dead body…

It was macabre.

It was wrong.

But I'd failed her in so many ways.

We didn't know what awaited us.

We didn't have the luxury of time.

She wanted this. It was the least I could do to obey.

Throwing her onto the bed, I stood over her. Her jaw-length hair fanned out on the white bedding, her legs spread, and her hand dipped to her pussy. Her fingers weren't shy as she rubbed her clit.

My lungs refused to operate. "Shit, Needle."

"Take me, Kite. I need you to take me." Her finger smeared wetness around her entrance, her stomach tensing with pleasure. "I fought him. I managed to stay true to myself and not let the lust take control. But I'm tired. I'm empty. I can't—I can't fight it anymore." Tears glittered on her eyelashes. "I need it. I need a release. I need to forget, for just a little while. I need to live, to remember, to be happy, to be free. *Please*." Her fingers swirled faster, her skin flushing with need. "Oh, please…*please*."

I couldn't speak.

I was hypnotised by her.

My hands shook as I wrenched open my belt. The idiocy of fucking her when Cut could return at any moment had no power over us. Common-sense died on the pyre of desire and all I could think about was filling this stunning creature and claiming her over and over and fucking over again.

Her eyes met mine, and everything that'd happened the past few months fractured. *This* was all that mattered.

Making love. Connecting. Merging into one.

She was my all and only.

My world.

Her tongue licked her bottom lip, her teeth biting as her finger dipped inside. "Jethro...please!"

"Shush. You have me. I'm here." My heartbeat drummed in my erection as I shoved down my jeans and boxer-briefs.

Nila's eyes hooded as I fisted my cock, stroking hard and fast. "Tell me." My voice was guttural.

"Tell you what?" The diamonds around her neck refracted light.

"My cock...how do you want it?"

A seductive smile lit her face. She moaned low and full of invitation. "Hard and fast. God, so hard. So fast." Her hands skated to her nipples through her hoodie, twisting cruelly. "I've never felt like this before. This unhinged. This horny. God, please don't make me wait any longer." Her spine arched off the bed. *"Fuck me."*

Fucking hell.

I lashed out. My hands captured her hips, yanking her toward the edge of the bed. "You want me? You can fucking have me."

She cried out as I forced her thighs wide, presenting her pussy to me— glistening and perfect. I bowed and bit her knee, running my hand up her thigh and pressing a finger deep inside her.

She screamed.

I slapped a hand over her mouth. "Quiet!"

She was my punishment and penance all in one.

Her eyes rolled backward as I forced another finger inside her. Her hips rocked dangerous and demanding. She was liquid and heat. She didn't want foreplay. She wanted to be fucked, used, abused, *claimed.*

My mind shattered; I couldn't stop.

Her breathing turned ragged as I strummed her clit. My cock wept at how fucking beautiful she was. How needy and fierce.

"I'm going to take you." I thrust my fingers hard. "I'm going to claim you. I'm going to give you everything because you deserve fucking everything. You deserve to be worshipped and praised. You deserve to be loved every damn day of your life."

She gasped, her skin sticky with sweat.

Withdrawing my fingers, my heart filled to bursting.

Nila panted, whimpering beneath my hand.

She looked so fragile and delicate, but I knew that was a lie. She was stronger than anyone. And I wanted to bow at her feet for the rest of eternity.

Keeping one hand over her mouth, I rubbed my fingertips together, slick from her desire, and grabbed my cock to position at her entrance.

I sucked in a gasp as her body heat cremated me.

I slammed inside her.

Stretching.

Fisting.

Tight.

Tight.

Tight.

"Goddammit, Nila." My blood boiled with feral hunger.

My mouth watered to bite her throat.

Her hands latched around my wrist as I held her silent, her lips parting wide beneath my palm. I sank deep, so fucking deep. She spread her legs, her body yielded, and I sheathed into my soul-mate.

For a second, we paused. Heartbeat to heartbeat. Desire to desire. Sex turned to saturated connection, and I couldn't stop the words spilling from my lips.

"I love you, Needle." My hand fell from her mouth as I slammed my palms on either side of her head on the mattress, rocking into her. My toes curled in my shoes, my jeans tightened around my thighs as I stood over this goddess and fucked her like she begged.

"I…love…you…" Her pants destroyed her voice, but I didn't need the words to know. Her emotions screamed it louder than anything. My condition swam in her contentment and affection, and I knew there would be no going back from this.

This was the moment she became totally mine.

And whatever happened afterward, we would be together forever.

I couldn't live another moment without her bound to me. Without knowing this creature belonged to me for every day after, every year, every decade.

I *needed* her.

"Marry me."

Nila gasped, her body flinching with shock. "What?"

I grabbed her legs, wrapping them around my hips. Her shoulders remained on the bed, arching into my hold. Her pussy fisted my cock, giving me an answer to my question.

The most important significant world-changing question.

"Marry me. Become mine."

I groaned as I rocked harder, fucking her with everything I had. My knees bashed the bed, my balls smashed against her arse. Emotions and feelings and sensations grew out of control. "I need you so much."

Her breasts bounced as my pace turned crazed.

"I need you forever."

My hips bruised against her inner thighs as I rode her so hard.

"I need you as my wife."

A release snarled into being, hungry, savage in intensity.

My heart twisted as Nila licked her lips. "I…I—"

Everything else faded.

I drove into her over and over again. Our eyes locked and we fucked into promises. "Say yes…. Fuck, please say yes."

I lost myself to the rhythm, sinking my fingers into her thighs.

Her pussy clenched; her head thrown back as her body prepared to release. Her eyes glazed as the pain of riding her and the pleasure of her building orgasm turned our connection into an almost unbearable fight.

I couldn't think straight. I was lost, owned, *consumed*.

I couldn't get enough oxygen. My arms trembled as Nila finally gave me the greatest gift I'd ever earned.

"Yes...Yes, I'll marry you."

"Christ." My heart shattered into fractals.

I gave up.

Our rhythm turned frenzied, fucking, rutting, taking everything we could.

"God, yes. I'm coming...I'm *coming*." She cried and laughed and cursed as she drowned under the crest of her release. Her gaze locked with mine and midnight irises consumed me as fireworks turned into catastrophic detonations.

"Yes," I hissed. "Yes. Shit, yes." Electricity charged through my toes, my quads, my balls, my dick. Spilling deep as I pounded inside her, delivering every last drop of bliss. Pleasure I'd never experienced stampeded with a thousand heartbeats.

She was mine as much as I was hers.

Now and for always.

Alive or dead.

We were one.

Nila

"THIS WON'T WORK."

Jethro shushed me, inching through the wonky panel hidden in the toilet block. The wretched air almost made me gag.

The moment Jethro had come, he'd made me dress, and hoisted Daniel's carcass over his shoulder.

His eyes blackened with nerves and resolution as he ignored me. "It will." Under his breath, he added, "It has to."

Another shiver darted down my spine. The millionth shiver since I'd arrived in Africa.

It felt like an eternity had passed since I'd claimed a life, pierced my needle and taken someone's last breath, last gasp, last thought. It felt like eons since I'd finally succumbed to the raging lust in my bloodstream and forced Jethro to take me.

But in reality, only forty minutes had ticked past.

How long would Cut give Daniel to rape me? An hour? Two? Or would he wait until Daniel tired and went to tag him for his turn? Either way, time was finally on our side—for now.

Every step, I couldn't stop the remembrance of Daniel's heart giving way to my needle point. Every breath, I couldn't stop reliving the final moments of victory, followed by a canyon of regret.

I'd killed someone.

I've murdered.

I no longer had the right to heaven or angels or eternal paradise. In order to win against the devils, I'd had to become one. Before, I was willing to make that sacrifice, but now…now I knew what a weight it was to value my life above another's. And I wasn't so sure. Did I have the right? Did anyone—regardless of circumstance?

I kept seeing the trickle of blood, oozing and pooling on the floor— unwilling to leave its host, copper and crimson…slowly turning to unwanted rust.

Dirt to dirt.

Ashes to ashes.

Daniel had been raised with diamond spoons and diamond toys. Would his body eventually fuse with the earth, transforming from bone and becoming the sparkling gemstones his family coveted?

Reborn.

Into the one thing his family treasured the most.

Was that karma?

Or serendipitous endings?

Stop it.

You heard what Daniel said. He would've raped me until death.

If I had died, he wouldn't be moping about mourning my loss or regretting his decision.

Straightening my shoulders, I stopped thinking about the murder and dealt with the aftermath.

Jethro moved silently and stealthily. I refused to look at Daniel's sheet-wrapped body. A bloom of blood was the only sign that beneath the burden existed something sinister.

"Jethro…" I whispered, cursing the remnants of the drug-liquor still hammering my heartbeat. My orgasm had been blistering and explosive, but it hadn't nullified the urge entirely.

He looked up, stepping through the fence opening, leaving the encampment for the free world. "What?"

"I—I—" I didn't know what I wanted to say. I'd apologised for killing his brother. I'd let him console me when really I should console him for losing yet another member of his family.

He hasn't lost Kes…not yet.

I felt responsible. I should be the one to destroy the evidence, not him.

"I want you to go. If Cut—"

His teeth bared. "*Don't* bring that up again. I'm. Not. Leaving. I don't fucking care if he sees me. I'm here for good. I'm with you *for good*. Got it?"

His gaze entrapped me; I sucked in a breath. The magical question he'd asked filled my mind.

Marry me.

Marry me.

Marry him?

I'd said yes, but nerves tap-danced on my ribcage. I wanted him as mine more than anything, but there was so much we had to defeat before we were free.

Looking over my shoulder, fear tiptoed through my shadow, terrified Cut would find us.

Repositioning Daniel on his shoulder, Jethro held the panel wider. "Come on." Perspiration and strain etched his forehead. "We have to hurry."

I didn't hesitate again.

Ducking through the fence, I stayed by his side, crunching through long grass, keeping my eyes wide and wary. We were no longer in the den of Hawks but entered a much larger one of lions and hyenas. I'd never been to a place where humans weren't on the top of the food chain. It made me very aware of how vulnerable and edible we were.

A few hours ago, the plains had been shrouded in darkness so thick, my eyes were completely blinded. Now, the black turned pinky-grey, slowly yawning as daybreak appeared.

We had to hurry.

Hurry.

Jethro had to hide.

We have to run.

Trailing in his wake, I didn't ask about his plan. I trusted him. However, being so exposed out here—visible to both man and beast—I didn't like it.

I had to pinch myself to believe he was truly here. When he'd run into the tent, I thought I'd finally snapped. That whatever drugs Cut had given me had consumed me whole.

But then he'd touched me and the repellent desire in my blood became an incinerating demand. His arrival was a miracle. And I'd appreciated that miracle by making him fuck me.

He'd helped me forget for just a tiny moment.

The further we travelled, the more numb I became.

Shock was a weird thing.

It had the power to anesthetize even the most horrifying situation. It could dull the most excruciating pain and make it liveable. But it could also abolish instinct and make a bad idea seem good.

Was this a good idea? Or terrible?

Jethro stumbled beneath his dead brother's weight.

Dashing forward, I reached out unthinkingly. My hand touched cooling flesh. I swallowed the urge to retch. "Let me help."

Jethro shook his head, pain scrunching his face. "I can manage. Just stay close." Blood trickled down his side where his gunshot wound had torn. The heat in his eyes wasn't just from rage but fever. As much as he would deny it, he wasn't fully healed and should be resting.

Instead, he's out here…saving me.

We were both in pain. The kick from Daniel throbbed and the hits and scratches didn't appreciate being ignored. Even the slice on my palm from the ceremony still stung. We both needed to be held together with stitches and bandages.

"Jethro, please, you're not well. Let me help. We're in this together. Don't carry this burden on your own." By burden, I didn't just mean Daniel's death, but the entire situation.

He smiled softly. "Nila, I can feel your urge to help. I feel your love, your fear, your uncertainty." He sighed. "I even feel your confliction about saying yes to marrying me."

I sucked in a gasp. His condition gave me no room to hide. No secrets.

"I'm sorry. I can't—"

He moved forward again, his knees kissing the long grass. "I know you can't help it. But don't ask me to lean on you when there is so much I made you survive on your own." His jaw clenched. "I *need* to do this. And I would appreciate it if you didn't interfere."

"Interfere?"

"You know what I mean."

"Jethro—"

"No!" He slammed to a halt. "Nila. Stop. Just stop. Be quiet in both voice and thoughts and let's get rid of him."

I looked down, rubbing my fingers together, hating the sticky residue of Daniel's blood. I hadn't even washed my hands after stealing a life. A life he didn't deserve but still a life.

The terrible crime would shade me forever.

Who am I? Who have I become?

"Please, Needle," Jethro murmured when I didn't respond. "Be quiet. Just…focus on happier things. It will help me immensely."

Forcing a door closed on my thoughts, I nodded. "Okay." If blocking my feelings was the only way I could help him, I would do it.

"Thank you." Jethro's back bunched as he slowly moved ahead with his slain sibling.

A rustling sound shot my head up. Every thought dispersed like the wind while fear squatted heavily on my spine. "Jethro…"

"Shit." He froze.

"Shit?" I couldn't breathe. "What—what is it?" My ears strained for more noise while my eyes frantically searched the thigh-high yellow grass.

Jethro took a determined step forward. "Don't look. Just keep moving. We need to get a little further."

I disobeyed, locked into a statue.

A chilly morning breeze rustled the grass, making it dance and weave. But there was something else…something other than plant life…something very much alive.

Stalking us.

Hunting us.

"It's watching us…" My voice barely escaped.

"Do as I say. Don't run. Don't panic. Just stay calm."

Something glided, hunting closer and closer.

Jethro slowly turned to face me, his eyes narrowing on a spot to the side. Daniel's arm escaped the sheet, hanging loosely over his shoulder, his frame morbidly sprawled.

Jethro tensed. "Fuck."

My heart rate exploded. Instincts ordered me to run. But I couldn't unlock my knees.

Never tearing his eyes from the speck in the grass, Jethro very gently, very methodically slid Daniel off his shoulder. His legs, hips, torso, arms, until finally Daniel lay on the ground. The moment he was down, obscured partly by foliage, Jethro tore off the sheet, threw it away, and paced toward me.

Stupidity made me speak. "People will find him. It's too close to the camp."

Jethro shook his head. "Believe me when I say, they won't." He backed up, splaying his hands as if showing no threat to whatever hunted us.

I knew why.

Don't ask why.

"Why?"

Ignoring me, his voice dropped to a whisper as his face skittered between fear and fight. "Nila…back away. Return to the camp. I need you to run, understand?"

My mouth fell open. I gulped terrified breaths.

Jethro came close enough to touch me, swivelling my shoulders until I faced the fence. His voice burned my ear as he growled, "Run. *Now!*" He shoved me hard. "Run!"

His command was a gun and I became a blur of motion. My knees shot high, bouncing over the tall grass; my hair flying in all directions.

Movement immediately exploded beside us, disrupting the peace of the plain.

Shit!

Run.

Run.

Run, run, run.

I wanted it to be explainable—grass stroked by the breeze. But it wasn't. There was no wind anymore.

Prickles on the back of my neck had nothing to do with the cold morning. Basic instinct knew what this was—why I ran for my life.

I was prey in the middle of a hunt.

My legs sprinted harder.

My lungs burst as we covered the distance back to the base in seconds compared to minutes.

We collided with the fence, Jethro grunted as he wrenched open the panel. "Get inside. Quick." Shoving me through, he was rough and aggressive, before tearing inside behind me and slamming it shut.

I buckled over, planting my hands on my knees as I inhaled air and life. The whiff of ammonia and excrement hung thick in the space, but I didn't care.

I'm alive.

I'm alive.

We made it.

Jethro didn't move. He pressed his face against the crudely made fence and stared.

That was when I heard it.

Not a howl or grunt or purr. But a loud *crunch*.

"Oh, my God." I sidled up beside him, staring through the slats to the plains beyond. Daniel had disappeared in the grass, the sheet caught on the stems, fluttering in the breeze. But he wasn't alone.

Two lionesses had found him. Their tails flicking in greed, tan coats camouflaging them perfectly, and muzzles covered in Hawk blood.

"Oh…" My stomach roiled as the larger feline ducked and grabbed Daniel's throat, hauling his carcass into view. I slapped a hand over my mouth as she tore through his jugular, ensuring I'd done the job correctly and he was dead.

The other lioness swatted her companion, taking a bite of Daniel's shoulder.

Jethro vibrated beside me, silent but merciless.

We didn't say a word as the cats gnawed a snack from the man I'd lived with, a brother Jethro grew up with. They ate a few large mouthfuls before grunting with triumph at the dawn sky.

With tan fur rippling, the head huntress snarled over Daniel's gashing throat and with powerful muscles, carted her trophy away. The black tuft on her tail bounced back and forth as the evidence of my murder slowly disappeared.

His death to give life.

His evilness to feed purity.

We watched until there was nothing to see. No lions. No Daniel. Nothing.

Finally, Jethro pushed away, swiping a hand across his face. His shoulders rolled as he battled and segmented whatever emotions had risen. His voice was gruff as he said, "That's why."

I blinked, ignoring the stench of toilets and smarting realness of what had just happened. "What?"

He smiled sadly. "Out there, you asked me why he wouldn't be found."

A shudder stole my nervous system. "They'll eat him?"

He nodded. "I doubt there'll be any remains. And if there is…it's the perfect alibi. Daniel got drunk after raping you and stupidly went for a walk to clear his head." He grabbed my shoulders, holding me tight. "Promise me you'll only remember that part, Nila. You didn't kill him. He didn't touch you. He didn't rape you. And you didn't have to defend yourself. Wipe it from your mind. It will help you live easier. He had it coming—even nature agreed with you."

I cupped his cheek. "Is that what you're worried about?"

His face tensed. "It's what I feel from you."

"Really?"

Dammit.

He was too in-tune, too perceptive.

He sighed, nudging my forehead with his. "I sense what you're not saying. I know he went further than you want to tell me. I know you're in pain—most likely from the slap to your face and kick to your stomach—and I know the drugs in your system from the ceremony made fighting that much worse."

How—? He'd picked up on not just emotional but physical woes, too.

"I'll never get used to you doing that."

His arms wrapped around me. "Well, you agreed to marry me—unless you're having second thoughts—so I guess you're going to have to get used to it."

My body suddenly burst into a blistering sunrise. "I did, didn't I?"

"Did what?"

"Agree to marry you."

Jethro shuddered. "Fuck, I love hearing that."

"That I'll marry you?"

He smiled. "No, that you'll be my wife."

I did my best to squash the pessimism that we might never be granted something so precious. That the Final Debt might still come to pass, no matter he wouldn't leave me again.

I used to be such an optimist…now…it was hard after the past six months. I smiled and kissed his lips. "You'll be my husband. How did I ever get so lucky?" I did my best to project confidence and joy. However, I couldn't hide anything from him.

Pulling back, he ran a hand through my hair. "We'll win in the end, Nila. You'll see."

I sighed. "I know."

I hope.

"We will. I promise." Taking my wrist, he pulled me toward the panel. "Come on. Let's go. I've got a driver waiting a kilometre away. We can leave."

My heart galloped. "Wait. Through *there*? No. No way." I tugged on his hold. "That fence is the only thing stopping us from being breakfast to the pride that's already taken Daniel."

Jethro frowned. "They have food. I doubt they'll come after us."

Food being his brother.

Knowing Jethro could see into the souls of others made a smidgen of relief settle. He didn't care Daniel was gone. In fact, he seemed more than okay with it.

That said something.

I looped my fingers through his. "I'm not willing to take that chance. We're together now. No lion or Hawk will take you from me."

Pacing away, he looked like a wild animal trapped against this will. "I could run ahead. Get the driver and come back for you."

Slamming my hands on my hips, I shook my head. "There is no way you're leaving without me again. No way. You promised. Will you renege on that so soon?"

He exhaled heavily. "Agreed. I was wrong to leave you at Hawksridge. If I'd listened to you, none of this would've happened."

I softened. "If you'd listened to me, then your sister and Kes might have been hurt." I snuggled into him. "You did the only thing you could."

He groaned, gathering me close and kissing the top of my head. "I don't deserve you. Not after what Daniel—"

I kissed him. "Shut up. I won't let you think that way."

I would never verbally tell him I let Daniel enter me—just a little—to ensure my trap was sprung before killing him. He didn't need to carry such knowledge. It was a price I willingly paid. Jethro didn't need to know how repulsive those few inches had been, or how much I loathed myself for letting it happen. I couldn't stop him from sensing what I refused to say. But they were my thoughts and I wanted them to remain unspoken.

His lips grazed over mine. "You're right. Let's get out of this hell hole."

"That's a good idea."

"Stay quiet and follow me." He twisted to leave, a painful hiss escaping his lips.

I yanked him to a stop, inspecting his side. "Are you okay? You need a doctor." Pressing the back of my hand on his forehead, I whispered, "You're burning up, Kite. You need medicine."

He scowled. "I'm fine. Don't worry about me. Just focus on getting out of here. Then we can both heal and relax once we've won."

I didn't ask how we would do that. But I did ask, "Are we going to the driver a kilometre away?"

"No. You're right. It's too dangerous." His eyebrows furrowed, thinking of a new plan. "The Jeeps that the workers take to the mine aren't far away. I know where the keys are stored. If we stay hidden, we can get there in time to leave when the employees do."

"What about Cut?"

"What about him?"

"Will he have come looking for me by now?"

A harsh look filled his gaze. "Cut will leave you to Daniel. Call it training. Like a lion leaves its cub to maul its dinner before stepping in and killing it. He wants Daniel to use you. He won't interfere with that."

I wasn't so sure. The way Cut had looked at me spoke of rage that his youngest son got me first. He'd hated Daniel had won the coin toss.

Stepping away from the smelly latrines and into fresh, morning air, I squeezed Jethro's hand. "I trust you."

His golden eyes glowed with their own daybreak. "I'll make sure to finally deserve your trust, Nila."

Tugging me forward, he smiled. "Now, let's go home."

Jethro

I HID MY fear as I held Nila's hand and guided her through the camp.

She didn't need to know I had no fucking clue how to keep my promise. She didn't need to hear my worries or concerns about this new plan. What she did need was for me to be strong and get her out of this mess.

And I would do it.

Gritting my teeth, I pulled her faster. I'd told her Cut would wait until Daniel had had his fill, but that was wrong. Cut had a fascination of claiming everyone for himself. His tolerance for time would've ended by now.

I had no doubt he would be on his way, if not already pissed at waiting so long.

Bird-song and awakening animals heralded in the new day. The calls and chirps sent chills down my back. Daniel had deserved to be devoured. Nature had taken care of it. But it didn't mean it was easy to watch.

Flashbacks of him growing up, of him chasing Kes and me, of the rare times we got along all unspooled in my head as pieces of him were sliced and disappeared down lionesses' throats.

Guilt for not trying to understand or help him festered and I wished for a moment that I'd been a better brother to all my siblings.

But I couldn't change the past. I barely had power over my future.

I had to pay attention to the present so I could save the woman I'd chosen above my family.

"Stay low." I jerked Nila behind a shipping container, sticking to the darkness and shadows. The workers and guards who'd been sprawled unconscious after a night of debauchery had disappeared. The dusty footprints signalling the camp might still be quiet, but people were awake, in their homes, cooking breakfast, readying for work in a few short minutes.

We need to move faster.

Nila trotted beside me, her breathing shallow. She mimicked me without noticing, ducking when I ducked, scurrying when I scurried.

She wasn't stupid. She knew what was at stake. And for some goddamn reason, she trusted me to lead her to safety.

I almost got her killed by the lions.

For the tenth time, I berated myself for taking her onto the plain with a body oozing blood. I knew the predators would come. That was my plan—for them to cart Daniel off and turn his body into animal shit—but I hadn't planned on them coming so soon.

"Stay hidden." My voice barely registered as I guided Nila down a small alley, bypassing the open paths and doing my best to remain unseen.

However, I knew it wouldn't be enough.

Eventually, we would be spotted…it was just a matter of time.

We need to be closer to the Jeeps before that happens.

Nila tugged on my hand, pointing to the side where the fire had burned itself out and the strewn men and women had disappeared.

"I know." I narrowed my eyes. "Stay quiet."

She nodded.

My side panged with agony as I twisted around to continue our perilous journey. My fever gradually made me weaker, draining my system of reserves. Nila was right about needing a doctor. We both did.

I couldn't stomach looking at her bruises without wanting to repay like for like. My short-term goals included getting her on a plane where I could assess how badly hurt she was and how much she'd hidden from me. My next plan was to secret her away where she couldn't be touched while I went back to Hawksridge and finished what I should've finished years ago.

I refused to leave Jasmine in Bonnie's clutches any longer. Especially now Bonnie knew the depth of Jasmine's deception. And I needed to see Kestrel. To touch him and encourage him to wake from his coma and come back to life.

The Hawk children were down from four to three.

I didn't want any more of us to die.

Nila stumbled, hissing through her teeth. I pulled her upright, matching her hiss with one of my own. I chuckled morbidly. We were both running on fumes.

Our footsteps made no noise as we moved forward. For all intents, the camp wasn't large—housing upward of thirty to forty people. But this morning, it seemed as if we crossed the Serengeti with hyenas on our heels.

We ducked and froze, scampering across an open distance to the cover of another container.

We're close.

Squeezing Nila's fingers, I motioned with my chin that we were almost there. The parking lot was just around the corner.

Pointing at the ground for her to stay put, to stay safe, I untangled my fingers from hers and prowled forward to the edge of the fence line. I didn't look back, but I sensed her annoyance with me leaving her.

It's only for a moment.

No one.

Nothing.

Only vacant property between me and the first Jeep.

Could it be that easy? Had fate finally decided to let us win?

My eyes danced from guard box to guard box. Last night's ceremony was a special occasion where the rules on security were loosened. However, there should be at least one guard.

No one.

It wasn't uncommon, but it didn't ease me. It only made my condition fan out, seeking any emotional sway to signal humans were there just unnoticed.

My attention fell on the single cabinet bolted to the ground in the middle of the parking lot. The lock box housed the keys to the twenty or so Jeeps waiting to take the freshly slept workers to replace the night shift.

The cabinet didn't require a key but a pin code.

And I knew the pin code.

My mother's birthday.

Waving at Nila to follow, I dashed across the dirt and quickly fumbled with the tumbler.

Please, don't let it be changed.

That would just be my fucking luck.

It took three long seconds before the padlock sprang open.

Thank God.

My hands shook as I grabbed the set labelled with the closest Jeep's license plate.

So close.

Please, let us get out of here.

My thoughts became prayers, paving the way to hopeful freedom.

Waving for Nila to dash from her hiding spot, I shoved her toward the car. "Go."

She didn't hesitate.

Together, we bolted around the vehicle and I unlocked the doors. Throwing myself into the driver's side, I swallowed the gasp of pain from my side. Nila leapt in the passenger side and I shoved the key into the ignition.

Nothing happened.

I stomped on the gas, twisting the key.

Again, nothing.

"What the fuck?" My eyes flew between the dead dashboard to the rapidly cresting sunshine.

We're running out of time.

I tried again, shoving the pedal to the floor.

Start. Please, fucking start.

The engine suddenly sputtered into life, coughing.

Then the worst sound imaginable.

It backfired.

The loud crack ricocheted through the quiet morning, ripping through silence, announcing to the world where we were.

"Fuck!" I pounded the dash with my fist. My heart stopped beating.

Nila huddled in her seat, panic glistening in her eyes. "What do we do?"

I wanted to tell her this wasn't the end. That we still had a chance. But I didn't have the breath.

I tore my gaze to the entrance gates.

Shit.

A guard appeared, bleary eyed and not doing his duty. He jogged to his post, raising his weapon, searching for the threat.

I didn't wait for a bullet or an invitation to leave.

This was the only chance we had.

"Hold on!" Wrenching the gear stick, I forced the old Jeep into gear and shot forward.

Nila squealed as we fishtailed and pebbles pinged below us. The tyres chewed up dirt, snarling faster and faster.

The guard aimed.

"Go!" Nila screamed, gripping the dirty fabric of her chair. "Go. Go.

Go!"

I forced the car faster. It lurched forward, squealing in a cloud of dust.

The guard dropped his arm, ducking out of the way as we careened over the half-way point, swerving around parked cars.

Closer.

Closer.

Come on. Come on.

He fisted a walkie talkie on his vest, his face bouncing between shock and surprise.

Yanking the steering wheel, we hurtled straight for him. I wouldn't let him gather forces. Not now. Not when we were so close.

The gate and final freedom rose before us, promising happiness the moment we barrelled through it.

"We'll make it. We'll make it," Nila chanted, holding the dash with white fingers.

I stomped harder on the gas, preparing to ram the entry. "We will. Almost there."

My heart chugged and hope unfurled with joyous frissions at the thought of finally, *finally*, saving Nila and living up to my promises.

Only…

Fate wasn't on our side, after all.

The gates swung wide and a barrier of men appeared from either side, marching in perfect combat, weapons drawn and armed.

"No!" Nila yelled, her voice mixing with the screaming engine.

What the hell—?

And then a man in a white shirt, goatee, and glistening colourless hair stepped pride of place in the line-up. He stood with his legs spread in the middle of his henchmen and pointed a finger right into my soul.

Motherfucker.

I was right. Cut hadn't waited.

He probably gave up waiting the same time we left with Daniel.

While we gave the lions breakfast, Cut had amassed a counter-attack.

"Fuck, fuck, *fuck!*"

"No!" Nila cried as I stood harder on the gas. "Don't stop. Please, Kite. Do. Not. Stop. I don't care. I don't care if they shoot. Just…don't stop!"

Feral ferocity exploded in my veins. "I won't."

They were in my way. I had a car. They didn't.

"Put your belt on. Now!" I downshifted, granting more power and more screams to the angry engine. Our trajectory turned from hurtling to flying.

I would kill every last guard barricading my way. And I would do it gladly.

Nila's eyes bugged, but she did as she was told. Trembling hands grabbed her seat belt, securing herself tightly. I did the same, juggling between belting myself in and steering the old Jeep.

I gritted my teeth against the influx of emotion pouring from the men before me. Their bodies might form a wall, but their emotions did, too. Fear, obligation, unwillingness to get hurt regardless of what threats Cut had delivered.

My heart skipped a beat as the youngest of the men—just a boy—stepped from the line and raised his gun.

He aimed.

I drove faster.

He fired.

The explosion hurt my ears as the kid recoiled, his arm soaring upward from the kickback. Nila screamed as the bullet pinged off the bonnet.

"Get down!" Grabbing her neck, I forced her to bend over her knees.

"What about you?!" She looked sideways, frantic terror in her eyes.

"Don't worry about me."

Worry about them.

I swerved, placing my side of the car more prominent than hers. If anyone was going to get shot, it was me. I'd already survived one bullet. I could do it again.

"Jethro!" Nila disobeyed my orders and looked up. "Watch out!"

We stared down the barrels of guns. Machine guns. Shot-guns. All types of guns. Armed and cocked and ready to—

They fired.

We didn't stand a chance.

The wheels blew, the metal carcass became pockmarks and mangled debris.

The car kept flying, but not on the ground. The front end crunched as the axis buckled, sending us tumbling through the sky.

Slow motion.

Loud noises.

Utter carnage.

The last thing I remembered was skidding, smashing into a boulder, and flipping end over end over end.

Then...

Nothing.

I LIVED IT all.

Jethro fighting with the wheel.

The rain of gunfire.

The buck and kick of the Jeep as its nose ploughed into earth and sprang upward into the air. I witnessed Jethro's head snap sideways, his temple crunch against the windshield, and the bone-shattering landing when air turned to ground and the Jeep morphed from car to flattened sandwich.

Vertigo had affected me all my life. But this…the flipping, ricocheting, swerving nightmare was ten times worse. The hurl, the roll, the loop de loop forced our bodies to forsake our bones and turn into cartwheels of flesh.

Down was up. Up was down. And fate had well and truly abandoned us as we came to a teeth-chattering stop upside down.

I hurt.

I throbbed.

The engine wouldn't stop whining. The shattered glass rained like fractured crystals. Blood stung my eyes, but I refused to tear my vision from Jethro.

Jethro…

Tears clogged every artery. Panic lodged in every vein.

We'd been so close…

He hung unnaturally still. Blood dripped from his temple, splashing against the roof of the car with morbid artwork. His side bled a rich scarlet while the gash on his forehead oozed almost black-red. His arms dangled, wrists bent and lifeless on the roof.

No…no. Please, no…

He couldn't be dead.

He couldn't.

Life wouldn't be that cruel.

It wouldn't bait hope before us and then yank it away as we reached for it.

It can't be that cruel!

Jethro…

I wanted to reach out and touch him. I wanted to speak and assure him. I wanted to pull him free and drag him far, far away.

But my brain had no power to send the message to bruised limbs.

So I hung there—a broken marionette held up by strings.

My lungs suddenly demanded breath. I gasped and spluttered. My seatbelt hugged me too tight, cutting my ribcage, keeping me pinned upside down. My hair hung around me, droplets of my blood tracing their way over my forehead, like incorrectly flowing red tears joining Jethro's on the roof below.

"Ki—Kite…" I groaned as the word ripped me in two. I begged my arm to move to him, to see if he was alive.

But I couldn't move.

Jethro didn't move.

Nothing moved apart from the spinning tyres and settling dust, cocooning us in a cloud of yellow ash.

Blinking away blood, I sucked in another breath, willing the oxygen to knit me back together and revive me.

Come on.

We weren't safe. I couldn't remember why. But we weren't safe.

Lions?

Hyenas?

Footsteps crunched closer. The click and snap of weapons being disarmed echoed in my skull. Instructions given in a language I couldn't understand.

I suddenly remembered.

Hawks.

Someone tried to open my door, but it wouldn't budge. I didn't look at them. Keeping my eyes trained on Jethro, I wordlessly told him everything he deserved to hear.

I love you.

I trust you.

Thank you for coming for me.

I'll follow you.

I'll chase you.

This is not the end.

Horror that he might've gone forever consumed me. I'd watched him die twice. *Twice.*

I knew what it was like to survive without him. If he'd died, I wanted to go, too.

Tears streamed from my eyes, joining the blood dripping from my forehead.

More footsteps.

More crunching and conversation.

"Jethro…" I battled against the pain and misfiring synapses and managed to force my arm to move. Inch by inch, cripple by cripple, I reached for him.

When my fingertip touched his elbow, I burst into ugly tears. "Please…wake up."

He didn't twitch.

I poked him.

He didn't flinch.

I pinched him.

He only hung there like a butchered corpse.

The windshield suddenly shattered. I screamed as a rain of safety glass pebbled in a waterfall.

My arm wrenched back of its own accord, sheltering my head instinctually. The butt of the gun came too close to my face.

Then a human replaced the gun. A dark-skinned masculine human. His gaze met mine. "Alive, boss."

I squeezed my eyes. Outside, the view mocked me. We'd managed to soar free of the compound before succumbing to bullet fire. We'd been free. We'd made it past the fence.

But now…I would be dragged back and Jethro…I doubted reincarnation would happen a second time.

I drifted in and out of consciousness; half pictures and stuttering images showed me a story of African workers, slowly making sense of the wreck. Someone reached inside and undid my seat belt.

Instantly, gravity yanked me into its embrace and folded me in two on the roof.

A moan tore past my lips, aching with pain.

The moment I was undone, someone grabbed my ankles, yanking me through the jagged hole where the windshield used to be and into the bright morning sunshine. Sharp shards of metal cut me as they pulled me free. Sand burned my bleeding skin as they dragged me across the dirt.

"No!" My fingers latched onto the bullet-riddled car. "Not without him. No!"

No one listened.

Instead, arms plucked me effortlessly and carried me away from the Jeep. They put me down, spreading me onto my back. My spine creaked and stretched, my brain rapidly cataloguing pain, agony, and excruciating discomfort.

My body had been through so much in such a short amount of time.

I hurt, but it didn't matter anymore.

Pain was only temporary as I focused on more important things.

While part of my brain catalogued my injuries, I looked at the destroyed Jeep. Everything bellowed, but I could move in small increments. I didn't think anything was broken.

The man who'd dragged me from Jethro left me alone. However, his sunburned silhouette was replaced with the man I hated the most.

His shoes crunched as he stood over me like a devilish avenger. "You were leaving before the best part, Ms. Weaver." Cut spread his legs, placing his hands on his hips. "I can't permit my guest to leave before the festivities are over."

I had no more to give. No more to fight with.

Ignoring him, I twisted my head to stare at the 4WD. My heart leapt as Jethro was dragged from the wreckage.

I didn't look away as the man who'd carried me placed Jethro's inert form beside mine on the ground. His head lolled to the side. Dirt and grease smeared his handsome face, braiding with the blood on his skin.

Cut nudged me with his toe. "So…you were telling the truth when you said you 'love' not 'loved' my son." Squatting, he poked Jethro in his broken side—the side where he'd shot him.

My arm flailed with uncoordinated projection. "Don't—don't touch him."

Cut smiled, placing his hand on his son's throat. His forehead knitted together, searching for a pulse.

I bit my lip, begging him to find one while at the same time hoping he wouldn't, so Jethro would be free of more torture.

Slowly, Cut's lips spread into a grin. "Well, well. He's still alive."

Thank God.

Thank you, thank you, thank you.

Softer tears fell, enjoying the moment even knowing the future would be anything but happy.

Cut's fingers landed on my cheek. I swallowed back rage, pushing unsuccessfully off the ground to get away.

"I'm so glad to see you're in one piece." His fingers latched angrily around my chin. "However, you have a lot of explaining to do before I let you stay that way."

"Let's start with a few easy questions, shall we?" His other hand smeared blood from Jethro's forehead. "How is he here? How is he alive? Where the fuck is Daniel?"

Gritting my teeth, I used every avenue of energy and shoved Cut's hand away from my lover.

You can touch me, you bastard. But not him. Never him.

"I'll tell you everything if you let him go."

"Let him go?" Cut chuckled. "Why on earth would I do that? It's not every day a ghost comes back from the grave."

I tried to crawl closer to Jethro, to place myself between him and his father. He was alive but unconscious. Cut could kill him so easily, and he would never know until his soul untethered and became homeless over the African plains.

"Stop it. Leave him alone."

Cut dropped his hand, his smile deepening. "You're telling me what to do now, Weaver?"

"Yes."

His eyes glowed. "And what do I get in return?"

My heart clanged and the pits of Hades opened up beneath me.

Marry me.

Yes.

Husband.

Wife.

None of that would come true now.

But I had the power to keep Jethro alive. I would do whatever it took.

"Me, you get me. Just...let him go."

Cut stood upright. "No. I have a better idea." Snapping his fingers, he ordered a guard closer. "Bind his hands."

The guard nodded. Dropping to his knee, he rolled Jethro roughly onto his stomach, not caring his bloody face squashed into the dirt. Efficiently, the guard wrapped the same coarse rope that'd bound me in the mines around his wrists.

It physically hurt watching them maul him while he couldn't defend himself. Then again, it was better this way. This way, he couldn't antagonise his father or somehow manage to get shot a second time.

Please, wake up.

Please, don't leave me.

Selfishness rose. It would be better if he left in peace. If he slipped quietly away. But I couldn't stomach his loss.

Whatever Cut had planned would make both of us wish we'd died. The belief that we'd get out of this intact and alive was left in the disfigured Jeep, crushing our dreams into African soil.

Cut wiped his hands on his jeans, glaring at the workmen. "Has anyone seen Daniel?"

Men scuffed their boots, fiddling with their guns. None of them made eye contact.

Finally, someone found a backbone. "No, boss. Not since last night at the ceremony."

Cut scowled, running a hand across his face. "Well, find him. He can't have run off too far." His glare landed on me. "Unless you have something you want to share with me, Nila?"

I glared right back, silent.

"Fine." Pacing, Cut growled, "Search the compound, head to the mine to see if he was stupid enough to go there, and check the plains around the camp. I want him to be a part of the afternoon plans, and he doesn't get to skive off just because he has a fucking hangover."

My lips twitched. I'd won in some small measure against Cut.

Daniel was suffering the worst hangover of his life.

In *pieces*.

The workers nodded, fanning out in levels of importance to carry out Cut's orders.

When only a few men remained, Cut said quietly, "That damn son of mine has to learn a thing or two." Pointing at the man who'd rescued me, he ordered, "Take them to cave 333."

"Yes, boss." The man ducked to collect me.

Cut grinned, stepping closer, blotting out the sunshine with this evilness. "I think it's time you learned a few secrets, Nila, and for my eldest to learn that nothing he does can stop me."

I wanted to scream. I wanted to kill. But I bit my tongue and stewed. I'd had my chance to leave. We both did. We'd done what we could, but it wasn't good enough.

Now, we would pay yet another price.

Another debt.

Another toll.

My entire body howled as the worker hoisted me to my feet. My imbalance threw me sideways, turning the world into a broken jigsaw. I groaned as I gave up trying to find an anchor and swam in vertigo.

"Carry her, for fuck's sake," Cut snarled. "She won't make it otherwise."

"Yes, boss." The worker's arms scooped me up, holding me firm. I squirmed, looking drunkenly over his shoulder as he carted me away.

Bye, Jethro…

I didn't relax.

I didn't cry.

But I did die inside as another worker hauled Jethro into his arms and together we were thrown into a Jeep and taken to perpetual hell.

The stickiness of Daniel's blood stained my hands as his father paced before me. Luckily, it threaded with the blood from my sliced cheek and grated legs from the car accident, hiding my sins.

We were no longer above ground but below it.

Cave 333.

Deeper than the caves Cut showed me. Bigger than the sorting or paraphernalia storage caves by the surface.

My bruised body craved sunlight. To beg the sunshine to grant me its healing power so I could run.

But in here…with dampness and rankness and darkness—I was already dead and buried.

There would be no exhuming into daylight. No one to disembalm us when Cut had finished his morbid chores.

Cut dragged his hands through his hair, never stopping his pacing. His white shirt stained and jeans dust-smeared. "Answers, Ms. Weaver. I expect them. This very fucking second."

I bit my tongue, glancing at the earthen walls, wrapping around us with a cold, moist welcome, swallowing us whole like a greedy giant.

This wasn't a cave. It was the giant's stomach. Its entrails.

"You have exactly three seconds to tell me what I want to know. Otherwise, I'll stop treating you as my guest and hurt you as my prisoner instead."

I snorted. "The past six months was you treating me as your guest? Last night with the coin toss? This morning with the gunfire? That's typical behaviour for your *guests*?" Flames smouldered in my belly, suppressing my injuries and allowing me to focus on staying alive.

Cut spun to face me, stalking quickly to slam his hands on the armrests of the wooden chair he'd tied me to. "Six months in my house and haven't I kept you fed and content and given you free rein to explore? Last night, didn't I give you something to make the Third Debt more bearable? I let you dance, smile. You had *fun*, Nila. You can't deny that." His voice lowered to a hiss. "You had fucking fun and you cannot say otherwise."

I trembled. "You want to continue thinking of yourself as a gentleman? A maverick making sacrifices for a good cause? Go ahead. Fulfil that fantasy by letting Jethro and me go. Then I'll answer any question you want. Give me your word we're free to go and I'll tell you everything."

Not everything.

Because the moment he knew about Daniel, there would be no guillotine or Final Debt. He would wring my neck within seconds. He would avenge his youngest because he hadn't been the one to decree it should be over.

Pushing off from the armrests, he resumed his pacing. "Let's begin with the elephant in the room, shall we?" He pointed at Jethro. "How the fuck is he alive and here?"

My heart cracked, taking in Jethro's beaten form. He slouched unconscious in an identical chair. However, the ropes holding him in place were triple mine. Twine snakes licked around his thighs and torso, gluing him to the chair. His wrists hung lifeless, trapped behind him while his ankles were locked against the chair legs with yet more rope.

There would be no escape. Not even if he was a magician with every spell in the world.

My mind raced with ideas on how to get free, but so far…I had nothing. Blank. Zero. Zilch.

"I shot him. He died on the rug at my feet. He's meant to be dead." Cut's face turned red.

I flinched but held his gaze. "Just let us go. No one else has to get hurt."

His eyes narrowed. "No one else? You say it like someone just got hurt, Nila. Was it Daniel?" He soared forward, his fingers biting into my cheeks. "Where is he?"

Survival kicked in. I'd never been a good liar.

"No idea." Keeping my chin high, I aimed to be honest but obtuse. Forthcoming but mysterious. "Why would I know where your despicable son is?"

"It seemed you knew where my oldest was, even while living under my roof." His face etched with fury. "You ate my food, slept in my rooms, and lied to my fucking face."

"No, I didn't."

Cut laughed coldly. "Don't be a bitch. You knew. All along, you knew."

"I didn't!" I swallowed back my shout. "I thought he was dead. Same as you." Granting him a smidgen of truth, I added, "I only found out a few hours before you put me on the plane."

Cut glared. "How? How did you find out?"

What could it hurt? Jethro was here. Whatever plans he had, they wouldn't come to fruition. "He told me himself. He came to get me."

Cut's mouth fell open, a surprised cough falling free. "You're telling me he *willingly* came back to Hawksridge, had you to himself for however long, and then left you again?" His eyes glowed. "Wait, *that's* where you were when Daniel found you outside your quarters."

I didn't respond. He already guessed with conviction. "What a fucking idiot." He shook his head. More shadows darkened his soul.

Shoving aside the new knowledge, he said, "Speaking of Daniel. Let's get back to what's important. Jethro is alive. I'll need more information on that. But for now, Daniel is more pressing." His eyebrows knitted together. "You were the last one with him. What did you do?"

"Me?" I scoffed. "How could I win against Daniel? I wouldn't stand a chance."

"Did he rape you?"

Blood flowing over my needle.

Oxygen leaving a corpse.

Lions chewing on flesh.

"Yes."

He tried.

"You're lying."

"No."

He paced around me, standing behind my chair so I couldn't study his face. "I find that very hard to believe."

I sat taller in my imprisoning seat. "Why?"

Cut's voice licked over my nape, stroking my dust-blanketed hair. "You're bruised and bleeding, but I don't know if that's from the car crash or my son. You're hurting but not broken. Not exactly encouraging if Daniel had his fill of you." He sneered, "I think you're lying because you're still alive." His fingertips glided down my throat to my breasts. "You can walk. Talk. Answer back. I know my son, Ms. Weaver, and if he'd taken you the way he planned, you wouldn't be sitting there with rebellion in your eyes." His hands fisted my hair, jerking painfully. "You'd be in fucking pieces."

Shit.

Tears pricked as he moved to stand in front of me again. His hands on his hips, he towered like judge, jury, and executioner. "You're lying to me."

"No." I fought my shivers. "I'm not."

Cut bowed, his face to my face. "Tell me the truth. *Now.*"

"I *am* telling you the truth."

His eyes blackened. "One last time. One more chance and then you'll get a painful reward for each lie."

My heart flung itself against ribs. "I'm telling you the truth. Daniel took what he wanted."

"Implausible." His hand curled. "There is no proof and my son is suddenly missing."

Lie better.

Fight smarter.

Taking a deep breath, I snapped, "I didn't say he took what he originally wanted."

Cut froze. "What do you mean?"

Please, let him believe my lies.

"After you left, he—he changed his mind."

Cut raised his fist. "I don't believe you—"

"Wait!" I tucked my chin, tensing against his strike. "The drug-liquor you gave me. He'd had it, too. He said he thought he wanted me to fight and struggle, but then he decided he'd rather I participated."

Cut paused, never dropping his fists. "Go on."

Words tumbled in a rush, tangling with bullshit and storybooks. "I kissed him and said I would willingly submit. That I wanted him because of what you'd given me. That I found him so sexy and I wanted him so, so much."

Filth.

Trash.

Scum.

"He didn't need to hurt me. I participated. I happily gave him pleasure because I earned pleasure in return."

Soap.

I desperately wanted soap to wash my mouth.

Silence fell, cloying and sticking to the cave walls. I hoped my lie wasn't so farfetched to believe. The past few months at Hawksridge gave no hint to who Daniel truly was. He was awful, but I did understand what it would be like to be rejected from birth, told you were unwanted, stripped from human connection. *Love.* He'd never had unconditional love.

Was it too hard to imagine that with his guard down and happiness in his veins, he wouldn't want togetherness rather than rape? Jethro and Kes were kind-hearted and loving—beneath the bullshit layered on them by Cut. But at least they'd had some semblance of family. Their mother had cared for them. They'd been raised in a marriage not a regime.

Daniel hadn't been so lucky. Was that why he'd never evolved past a spoiled brat? Did he lack everything that made him human because he'd never been given tenderness and mothering? Had I gone too far by hinting in my arms he'd found sanity for a change?

"I gave him more than he asked for. I gave him affection." My eyes narrowed with anger. "I gave him what you were never able to give."

Cut froze. His entire body locked down as if I'd stripped back his shell and revealed a grotesque truth inside him.

Oh, my God.

Was that Cut's issue, too?

Lacking love from his own mother?

Bonnie…how much had she warped her son?

His lips pulled back, revealing glistening teeth. "Where is he then? If you gave him a night of fucking wonder, why wasn't he in your bed? Why were you fleeing with Jet? Why does every word spewing from your motherfucking mouth reek of horseshit?"

I stiffened, curling into myself for protection. "I've always said I would run if I got the chance. Jethro gave me that chance. As for Daniel, he left after he finished. I assumed he went to fetch you."

My mind grabbed a new idea.

"Perhaps, he found another woman to spend the remainder of the night with. Perhaps, he got too drunk and is sleeping it off in the shade." I kept my voice level, even though it begged to wobble with uncertainty and plead Cut not to hurt me. "I don't know where your son is. And no matter how many times you ask me, my answer won't change."

Cut swiped a tired hand over his face. A tiny part of me wanted to shout so loud my admission would echo in every cave within the mine.

It was me.

Me.

I slaughtered your offspring.

I was the one who took his life before he could take mine.

And I'll take yours before we're through.

But I swallowed it back, letting my rage rejuvenate me.

Cut snarled, "You're lying. Stop fucking lying and tell me the truth."

"I'm *not* lying."

He grabbed my hair in a feral fist. "You had something to do with his disappearance. I know it. You can't spin it away, Nila. I'll tell you what I think happened." Cocking his chin at Jethro, he growled, "Kite arrived and together you killed him. You plotted this and—"

"No!"

He yanked my head back. The diamonds around my neck bruised my larynx. "Tell me the truth then. Where. Is. My. *Son?*"

I gasped. "I didn't do anything."

"Liar!"

"No!" My eyes flew to Jethro. "Besides, it doesn't matter now. Your firstborn is back from the dead. He's your original heir. He can be again." My injuries all flared in time with my raging heartbeat. Fighting against his hold, I did my best to cajole. "You know in your heart Daniel wasn't fit to rule your empire. But Jethro is. You groomed him. He's—"

"Shut up!" Cut's palm smashed against my cheek.

Stars.

I groaned in pain; my head hanging heavily as he let me go.

Cut breathed hard, pacing away.

Trying to tilt my chin and blink through grey and black, I willed Jethro to wake. I didn't want to be alone anymore. I didn't want to face whatever would happen by myself.

I'm selfish.

Wake up. Please…

Jethro didn't move, slumping in his matching chair, barely breathing.

Cut continued pacing, his boots kicking up diamond dust and soil. "I don't care if Jethro is back from the dead. You're forgetting I wanted him hurt. He betrayed me—with you, no less. I shot him on purpose."

"No." I shook my head. "That's not true."

Cut paused, his eyebrows shooting upward.

I rushed, "You shot Jasmine, but Jethro protected her." My heart raced, doing my best to touch some sort of humanity before it was too late. "I don't think you wanted to shoot Jethro. You've never understood his condition, but you're proud of how strong he is—how loyal he is to your family. How much he endured to be everything you ever asked him—"

"Shut the fuck up." Cut reared backward, wiping his hands on his trouser leg. "You have it all wrong."

"Enlighten me then. Tell me your secrets. You said you would. You told me I was entitled to know everything." I couldn't suck in a proper breath with fear. "I want to know. I have questions. So many, many questions. Tell me the truth of what happened when you claimed my mother. Did you love her? Did you ever feel anything for her to stop from killing her?"

A cold smile spread his lips. "Out of everything, *that's* what you want to know? Unpractical, stupidly romantic things?"

I nodded. "Yes. Because those stupidly romantic things will show me if you ever had a soul."

He chuckled. "Oh, I have a soul, Nila Weaver."

"Show me."

"What do you want to know?"

"Everything."

Keep him talking. Keep stalling.

"Tell me your story, Cut. Before you end this, make me understand."

Cut didn't reply. Instead, he strolled over to an empty table lining the wall and stroked a finger in the thick dust. "I can see through your ploys. I know what you're doing, but it so happens your request falls in line with my intentions."

A chill sent fearful frost down my spine.

Throwing me a smile, Cut changed his path and headed toward the crudely made wooden door. The only entrance and exit. "Seeing as extracting truth from you is proving tiresome, let's move onto more exciting things, shall we?"

I couldn't speak as terror cloaked me.

I'd tried to stall and now Cut had twisted my agenda with his. I had a feeling I would've preferred a fist to the jaw every time I lied rather than what he planned now.

Grabbing the door handle, Cut wrenched the entrance wide. Immediately, two men marched in. Men I hadn't seen before. The whites of their eyes glowed in the darkness of their skin; yellow dirt stained their skin with war paint while their clothes of jeans and dirty t-shirts marked them as workers inside the mine.

"Put it on the table." Cut sidestepped, moving out of the way as the men pushed a cart across the cave to the mentioned table.

I couldn't look away as they placed random but terrifying things in place. A rubber mallet. A bucket full to the brim with water. A square shallow container. A ziplock bag with black pouches which I assumed were diamonds. A packet of something with medical jargon on the front, scissors, gauze, and lastly a small stick.

What does all of that mean?

None of it made sense, but my stomach twisted with percolating horror.

Once the workers had emptied their cart, Cut motioned for them to leave. "That will be all for now." He followed them to the door and locked it behind them.

I hated how similar his gait was to Jethro's. Powerful, no-nonsense, a masculine stride. As much as I loved the son, I would never care for the father.

Tearing my gaze from Cut, I looked at the cave ceiling. If I died down here, would my soul find its way from the mine and into the heavenly sky? Or would I sink further into the ground toward hell for murdering Daniel?

A droplet splashed into my eyes, leaving its entourage of teardrops above, balancing precariously until finally giving into gravity's beckons. The occasional splash on the top of my head and the tiny ding as droplets hit plasticware and containers added another dimension to the cave-crypt.

Cut smiled, coming back toward me. "Before we begin, I think my son has slept long enough. Don't you?"

My heart hurled itself into my mouth as he stalked toward a large barrel in the corner full of silty water and grabbed a small pail. With liquid sloshing over the sides, he beelined for Jethro. With a savage smile, he tossed it over him.

Jethro burst into life.

His mistreated body lurched as he gasped and choked, shaking in his shackles. His face drenched and dripping, his tinsel hair plastering against his head.

Tears shot to my eyes as his head flopped backward, gulping air as if he'd been drowning forever. His lips parted wide, his eyes squeezed closed as he rallied.

Watching him come back to life was a miraculous thing. To be so close to death, so inert and broken, and be able to wake up astounded me.

The cave echoed with sounds of his crippled gasps. His head lolled to the side, fighting the weight to take in his surroundings. His eyes glowed wild and worried, drinking everything in at once.

I didn't need to suffer his condition to understand his thoughts. He saw the cave, his father, and then me.

Me bound to a chair with the saddest smile on my lips.

He shattered internally and I heard every smash.

His shoulders flopped further, his soul slipping deeper into a grave. He couldn't move thanks to the rope, but even if he was free, his weakness at hurting kept him tethered.

"It's okay…" I murmured, fighting tears. "It's alright."

Nothing is alright.

Nothing went to plan.

We never got free.

His own eyes glassed with longing and fury. Apologies and unconditional love blared toward me before slipping into hateful rage at his father. The longer

518

he was conscious, the stronger he became. His back straightened, forcing energy to keep him tall rather than slouched.

He coughed again, convulsing with heavy chokes.

My body begged to go to him, to help him breathe. At the very least, to brush aside his dripping hair and dry his face.

Cut didn't do a thing, letting his son fight through the pressure of pain.

Jethro's chin landed on his sternum as he did his best to calm his wheezing and gather a nourishing breath. Finally, he swallowed and glared at Cut beneath his brow. His eyes sparkled with tears from suffocating, but his temper snarled with peril. "Le—let her g—go."

Cut clasped his hands in front of him, letting the pail fall to his feet. "Suddenly, you're in the position to give me orders?"

Jethro groaned and spat on the floor, clearing his mouth from filth and water. "I'll do what—whatever you...want." His voice resembled sandpaper on a skill saw. "Just le—leave her out...of this."

The irony. I'd said exactly the same thing.

Wasn't that true love? The conviction of self-sacrifice in the face of your loved one's agony? It was the greatest selfless act anyone could do.

"I have a better idea." Cut snatched my face, imprisoning it in nasty fingers. Looking at Jethro, he squeezed me until I flinched with pain. "Instead of letting her go, I'm going to have some fun."

Jethro groaned, still breathless and gasping. "Please...do whatever you want t—to me but forget the de—debts. Forget whatever it is you th—think she's done. Just let her go...Father." His voice slowly smoothed, pronouncing words more clearly.

Cut paused at the term of endearment. "Do you hear that, Nila? He wants me to be a better man and hurt him instead of you. What do you think?"

I swallowed, wincing in his hold. "I think you should let him go. He's suffered enough. Let him leave and I'll stay in his place."

Jethro spasmed in his ropes. "No!"

Cut let me go. "You're both as stupid as the other. Seeing as you refuse to save your own skin and prefer to be fucking martyrs, the only course of action is for me to oblige you."

Stalking around my chair, he sawed through the rope holding me against the wooden seat and hoisted me to my feet. I swayed with wobbliness but blinked it back. The incurable illness had been my gaolers, my prison guards for too long. I refused to be weak while Cut destroyed me piece by piece.

"Let her leave." Jethro's gaze bounced between Cut and me. He smothered a cough, his face blazing. "Nila, run."

My wrists remained bound but being free from the hard wood granted a false sense of freedom.

Cut clucked his tongue. "She's not running anywhere. Are you, Nila?" Capturing my elbow, he dragged me to the centre of the cave. "Stand there."

"For fuck's sake—" Jethro's words tore short in a vicious cough. "Le—let her go!" He fought the rope around him. The chair legs wobbled, creaking with pressure. "Stop. Nila...don't be an idiot."

It hurt so much watching him struggle to protect me when he hurt himself so much.

"Leave, Nila. He doesn't care about you and the debts. Not now I'm here to take his anger out on." His eyes glowed golden and sad. "Please, you ha—

have to let me save you."

Tears tracked silently down my cheeks. I wanted to give him what he wanted. I wished I was able to turn my back on him and value my life above his.

But I'd done that with my hated enemy, and I'd almost buckled under the right and wrong of taking his life.

I wouldn't survive if I sentenced Jethro to death when I had a small chance of preventing it.

"I'm sorry, Kite." I dropped my eyes, unable to look at him. "While you're here, so am I. I'm not leaving you."

Cut slung his arm over my hunched shoulders. "It's too depressing in here. It's time for some fun."

I shuddered.

"Let. Her. Go!" Jethro's voice vibrated against the cave walls, threatening an avalanche of dirt. A cascade of soil kissed the top of our heads, a verbal earthquake.

Cut growled, letting me go to prowl behind Jethro's chair. "She's been a part of this since the day she was born, Jet. The sooner you understand that she *will* pay the Final Debt and there's nothing you can do about it, the easier your life will be."

Jethro stiffened, his nostrils flaring with the urge to fight. "What do you mean, my life? I thought I was dead."

Cut bowed over his son, wrapping his arms around his shoulders in a sinister hug. "I mean, I've reevaluated my decision to kill you. Haven't you found it strange you're alive and not currently being gnawed on by hyenas?"

I bit my lip.

His hypothesis was eerily close to what'd happened to his third-born son.

Three boys.

Three heirs.

All gone in different ways.

Only one actually killed.

It was the perfect murder.

And I got away with it.

Jethro shivered with disgust. "Stop with your games. Spit it out."

"Fine." Cut pulled out a dirty rag and duct tape from his pocket. "I mean I'm not going to kill you."

I sucked in a gasp. Thank God! Had he decided to reinstate Jethro as his heir, after all? Had I got through to him in some small way?

You don't believe that.

The tiny voice undermined my hope, tainting everything with sloth-like anticipation.

With measured motions, Cut held Jethro's cheeks and unceremoniously stuffed the rag into his mouth. Jethro thrashed, shouting around the material. His nostrils flared, fighting once more for hard to earn oxygen.

Cut didn't stop. His fingers manhandled his son until he'd forced the gag into Jethro's mouth. Once done, he roughly stuck duct tape over his lips sealing his mouth and gluing to five o' clock stubbled cheeks.

Jethro twisted and squirmed, searching for a way free. But it didn't stop the inevitable. He was silenced, bound…stuck.

"I mean I'm going to grant you a long life, son. After what happens today, after watching what I do to the girl you've fallen in love with, your fate will be worse than death."

Patting Jethro's cheek, he moved toward me. "Much, much worse."

"Don't come near me." I backed away, eyeing up the door to run. Even if I did manage to flee, I couldn't open the door with my wrists tied. And I couldn't fight countless workers scurrying around the mine like mice.

"I'm going to do more than that, Nila." Cut caught me, dragging me close. "Remember the dice throw back at Hawksridge?"

I gulped.

Heretic's fork.

Vaughn.

Kissing Daniel.

I knew, but I played stupid. "I have no idea—"

"Yes, you do." He stroked my arms with threatening fingers. "You rolled the dice and I claimed the roll was to be paid once we got to *Almasi Kipanga.*" His voice dropped to a deep baritone. "Well, we're at *Almasi Kipanga.* And if you refuse, your brother, Vaughn, will be hurt. It doesn't matter that we aren't in the same country. All it takes is one little phone call."

I *hated* him.

I threw myself sideways in his hold, trying to get free. "No!"

Cut didn't let me go, giving me enough leeway to tire myself out but not run. His voice lowered with mirth. "Not only will your brother pay for your refusal but Jethro will, too."

He paused, letting the warning sink into my blood.

Jethro growled, gagged and furious. His bleeding body twisted and jerked in his ropes.

I tore my eyes away. I couldn't look at him. "What—what do you want?"

"I'm going to give you a history lesson, then take what you owe me from the dice game. The Third Debt might once again be elusive, but I have a better idea." Cut's eyes flashed. "Once I've taken my fill, you'll pay the remainder of the Fourth Debt...the Fifth Debt as it were."

Moving me so I stood directly in front of Jethro, Cut murmured, "And my son will watch it all. He'll remain alive, but his soul will die knowing he couldn't help you. And then, once I've taken what I'm going to take and done to you what needs to be done, he's going to continue living with that agony eating him away day after day. I'm going to leave him here, alive, knowing he can't stop me from carrying out the Final Debt. That I'll fulfil the prophecy because he was too much of a chickenshit to do it. And he'll live with your death forever."

Kissing my cheek, he sighed. "That is what I want from you, Ms. Weaver."

It wasn't a happy sigh or even satisfied he'd won—more like a weary, ancient sigh speaking of a man who showed nothing but violence. "My son loves you, Nila, and not a day will go by he won't remember this cave or your death. That is your legacy to him."

Wrapping his arms around me, he whispered, "Don't worry, I'll give you time to say goodbye."

Pulling back, he smiled at Jethro. "Now we all know what to expect, let's begin."

Jethro

I'D LOVED HER for months.

Yet it seemed like my entire life.

I'd fallen for her as an adult.

Yet she'd intrigued me as a child.

She'd been born for me.

I'd been born for her.

We were linked. Joined by fate and history and destiny. Star-crossed, doomed from the start, absolutely forbidden lovers.

Bound and gagged and utterly fucking helpless, I faced the truth head-on. I'd entertained fantasies of living a normal life. Creating my own family, putting an end to grief and wretched revenge.

But I think I'd always known that no matter what we did, no matter how hard we fought, no matter what we sacrificed, there would be no other ending than the one signed in blood by my ancestors.

I'd said I'd loved her.

I'd proved I'd loved her.

I'd vowed to love her forever.

But the Debt Inheritance was too strong.

It wanted what it'd been given time and time again. Fate marched us faster and faster, stealing everything we'd promised.

Not many people had lived in hell. Not just visited for a while, but actually slept and ate and breathed there. As I watched my father manhandle my woman, the girl I wanted to marry, I set up home in hell. I breathed its sulphur air. I ate its brimstone hate. And I gave my soul over to the devil because what good was righteousness when only evil prevailed?

I was a demon's son.

The demon's son.

Wrought in fire and moulded by sins. My blood forged with terror; my body formed from mistakes and wrong turns. Debts. Contracts. Vengeance.

And no matter how I raged to be free, to end my predetermined inevitability, I couldn't find a way to triumph.

Nila had fixed me.

She'd helped me escape my purgatory.

She'd been the nebula of perfection. The freedom of flying with no wings. Granting wind to a kite with untethered strings.

I'd soared. I'd rejoiced.

And now, I'd fallen.

Whatever Cut would do, whatever he would make me witness and Nila endure, I wouldn't walk away intact.

I would breathe, but I would die.

I would blink, but I would be soulless.

I would vanish inside.

My heart would split open, veins slashing bloody substance all over a life I no longer wanted.

I knew what hell was.

As I fought the rope and begged for salvation.

As I blinked back tears and resigned myself to living the worst day of my life.

I knew what hell was.

I knew...

Because I was there.

Nila

"THE BEST WAY to tell the full story is to start at the very beginning."

Cut left me standing in the middle of the cave, pacing around me pompously. His nose elevated with smugness, arms crossed with self-confidence. Each footstep, he slipped into the history lesson that Jethro ought to deliver. I preferred Jethro's eloquence. His raspy, delicious voice. His melodic accent. His love pouring through every syllable.

But Jethro was gagged, and I had no choice but to hover where I'd been placed and listen.

"You've read the Debt Inheritance," Cut said, "You understand Frank Hawk was whipped for stealing, which you repaid in the First Debt. You know his daughter was killed for witchcraft, which you repaid in the Second Debt. You know Bennett Hawk was sodomized, which I still don't believe you paid with Daniel for the Third Debt, and you understand the mother did anything necessary to keep her family alive. That particular sacrifice was touched on at Hawksridge but will be fully repaid while you're here."

I balled my hands, trying to stop my mind racing with scenarios of what he would make me do.

Cut spun around, pointing a finger like a professor teaching a vital lesson. "Here's where it gets complicated, Nila, so pay attention. Bennett Hawk despised what the Weavers did to his family. He ached constantly from the rape and time moved forward where daily atrocities were delivered. As much as he hated it, his family continued to work for the Weavers. Indebted to them with unpayable taxes and outstanding warrants. They could never leave the Weaver's employ, thanks to a bribed police officer.

"More years passed where no hope of being saved seemed possible. Until Mabel Hawk, the mother who saved, not only her family but her bloodline, did what she had to do to repair their future."

Cut smiled broadly. "She thought outside the box. She used whatever assets she had and fought against society and social standing." He shook his head, almost in awe of his ancestor. "She took out a loan, Nila. Not just a loan, but a carefully plotted move and effortlessly executed design. Once her husband, Frank, died of sickness, instead of giving up, she blossomed. She approached a wealthy earl and bedded him. She'd learned the art of seduction thanks to Percy Weaver raping her every night and put that training to good use. Through sheer determination, she earned the good graces of the earl, who agreed to grant her money for revenge.

"His heart grew fond of her. After her tale of what the Weavers had done, along with evidence of her nightly terrors, husband's death, and her son's troubles, he agreed to take the Hawks in and helped them with legal counsel and the drawing up of the Debt Inheritance.

"Bennett Hawk was mentally unstable from his tragedy when it came to signing the Debt Inheritance. However, it didn't stop the document being lodged with the crown thanks to the earl who'd become mesmerised by Mabel Hawk. On the day of the signing, Bennett didn't have an heir but Mabel circumnavigated that problem by writing an unborn son called William Hawk into the binding contract. She thought of everything, never resting as she prepared to overthrow the Weavers. It didn't matter to her there would be an age gap. She had bigger plans than taking Sonya's life.

"In a few short years, she'd earned the affection of a powerful gentleman, all for her own ends, protected her family, and ensured retribution to those that'd hurt her."

Cut stopped pacing. "But it wasn't enough."

He ran a hand through his hair. "She was on her own with no husband or help. If she failed, the Weavers would ensure she'd be arrested and rot in jail for ever daring to leave their employ. The Debt Inheritance was flimsy at best. She had no wealth to back up her claim. No court on her side. No crown to defend her. She'd done all she could with the earl's help, but she needed more. More money, more power, more protection.

"As it was, living in the earl's house, she and Bennett were untouchable for a short time. She worked tirelessly, never failing in her quest to bring the Weavers down, but despite the earl helping her, his small amount of power wasn't enough to ensure the Debt Inheritance would be enforced.

"A few years passed and the threat of the Debt Inheritance kept the Weavers from coming after her. However, Sonya grew older and Bennett still had no heir. The ages to be claimed would become void, and Mabel wasn't getting any younger. So she put the next part of her plan in place.

"Despite her hoodwinking the earl in the bedroom, he wouldn't do anything more. He wouldn't publicly announce his involvement with her— relationships outside classes were forbidden—and she grew tired of being yet another secret and burden.

"Instead, she set her sights higher. Her family had their freedom—for now—and were the proud owners of a document stating Bennett Hawk's heir could claim Sonya Weaver to extract the debts his family had endured. However, Bennett refused. His fight was gone and he slipped into sickness and depression.

"Mabel noticed her son fading and did what any mother would do to immortalise her family's lineage. She hired a girl off the street—a whore she knew in passing, a girl who'd fallen for the malicious sins of the upper class. She interviewed this girl, got close to her, and ensured she was good stock to breed the perfect offspring. Only once she was sure she was strong and untouched by disease did she get her son drunk enough to make love to her night after night until she was pregnant with a new heir."

Cut pursed his lips. "What was the name of that heir, Nila?"

Despite the sudden switch from storytelling to questioning, I remembered easily. "William Hawk." A firstborn son. Fate smiling kindly on a family who'd endured so much. How different would history have been if he'd had a girl instead?

He nodded, satisfied. "Yes, exactly."

Breaking eye contact, Cut continued to roam the room, unable to stay still. Jethro followed him with his gaze, like me. While Cut talked, we were safe. However, the moment the lesson was over…we wouldn't be.

I didn't want to listen. I wanted to plot an escape. But Cut's voice dragged me back under his tortuous spell.

"Bennett sprang to life when the whore gave birth to his son, but it wasn't enough to completely drag him from his demons. He lived a little longer, enough to see his son grow up from toddler to young boy, before succumbing to the sweating-sickness that plagued London with no warning.

"Instead of mourning her son's death, Mabel Hawk kept it a secret and summoned a meeting with Sonya Weaver. She had already hit maturity and was old enough to understand her place in society. She was of claiming age, but William was still too young. However, that was never Mabel's intention, and it didn't stop her from setting things into motion. Things she'd planned for years now she had an heir to fulfil her prized future.

"Waiting until Sonya was away from her family with a new lady's maid in the park, she approached her with the contract. The girl tried to deny it, but she was old enough to know what went on in the household. Smart enough to know Mabel had been hurt by her father and crimes such as those had to be answered for.

"No doubt Percy Weaver had told her about the preposterous contract, laughing with his wife at such a thing. But Sonya, in her wise young way, saw the Debt Inheritance as something strict and serious rather than a joke.

"She didn't scoff or run when Mabel uttered, 'The time is nigh to pay your debts,' and passed her a sealed and signed copy of the agreed contract.

"Sonya didn't believe she had to answer for her father's sins and tried to refuse—as anyone would—but she'd witnessed what her family had done. She'd heard Mabel's screams while lying in her bed. She'd been too young to stop it but not young enough to stop the guilt festering inside for not trying to help."

"Even as a young woman, she was a good person," I interrupted. "Not all my ancestors were cruel. You can't hate my entire bloodline for two rotten people."

Cut tutted. "No but the same cruelty that ran in your ancestor's veins runs in yours. No matter how small. We merely keep it at bay by making you pay for what you did." Marching away, Cut slid back into his tale. "Mabel knew she ran a risky game by approaching Sonya. For weeks, she sat on edge, waiting for Percy Weaver to storm into her sanctuary and drag her from safety. She didn't venture outside; she didn't let William leave to play with his friends. He was all she had, now her son was dead, and waited with worry. However, nothing happened. Sonya hadn't told. She'd proven a worthy martyr and there was no need to enlist the help of her quiet benefactor the earl."

I rolled my wrists, spinning in place as Cut patrolled the cave. Jethro's eyes glazed with pain and vexation, the gag and duct tape stretching his cheeks. He looked half in this world and half in the other, fading before my eyes.

No matter his story dragged out Jethro's discomfort, Cut continued, "In that fateful meeting with Mabel and the first indebted girl, a new deal had been struck. Unbeknownst to Percy Weaver, the new bargain was in favour of everyone involved."

"What?" I bit back the question, hating I'd become involved in Cut's story.

He smiled. "Sonya would be spared the long and agonising death by debts if she did two things." He paused for me to ask him what those two things were, but I refused. He'd tell me without me playing his twisted game.

Cut sniffed. "Those two things bound the women together as another year ticked past. Mabel endured living with the earl even though his affection came with more and more bruising fists, and William grew up, faster every month.

"Mabel was prepared to wait however long it took for Sonya to fulfil her promises. However, she didn't have to wait as long as she feared." Cut grinned. "Item number one for Sonya to achieve, to ensure she would be spared, came true without much trouble."

Cut spun, running his hand over his chin. "The silly girl fell in love, and in a night of passion, ruined the life Mabel agreed to save."

I shivered. "What do you mean?"

"I mean, the first condition was fulfilled. Mabel wanted Sonya to get pregnant, to give birth to many offspring for William to inherit. He would never be of age to inherit his original indebted. But there would be others. Amendments to be made. New rules to be scratched into parchment. Sonya wasn't married, but had stupidly gotten with child from her secret lover. Mabel immediately ensured the earl took care of the dowry and married the pair.

"Percy Weaver stood by in shock as his daughter accepted the terms because her name would be disgraced if news got out she'd slept around. He hated that his ex-housekeeper and sex-slave had left his employ and was now protected by a man he couldn't touch. Mabel wasn't stupid; she didn't antagonise the Weavers without putting solid foundations down first. And with the one good deed of marrying Sonya to her lover, she held her life in her hands.

"That very life she offered to give back to her on one condition." Cut paused for dramatics.

The rhyme of his words wrenched to a stop, leaving the silence in the cave eerily cold. My eyes landed on Jethro. We shared a silent conversation.

I love you.

I love you more.

Whatever happens, I'll find you.

Whatever happens, we'll be together.

"What was that one condition, Nila?" Cut asked, coming close enough to run his fingers through my hair.

I shook my head, dislodging his hold. "From what I'm beginning to learn of Mabel, the one condition would be their deaths."

Hurry up.

I'd listened long enough. I didn't want to become consumed with past rights and wrongs. I always ended up feeling hatred toward my own flesh and blood and unwillingly on the Hawk's side.

Despite that, I needed to know. I would never have guessed the story was so tangled or full of deceit and double-cross. I ached to think of Bennett Hawk living such a sad existence only to die unhappy and tormented by his past.

Cut smiled, his goatee bristling. "You're a fast study. Good girl." He continued his journey around the cave. "Exactly. Sonya would live a full life with a husband and children...if she agreed to kill her parents."

My heart raced. *A hard bargain but, dare I agree, a justified end?*

"Sonya sullenly agreed, and Mabel found a woman in the ghetto selling potions and poisons. The same witchcraft that her daughter was killed for thanks to the Weaver Wife. With money from her earl, she purchased two vials of deadly poison and gave them to Sonya."

Cut's voice sped up, reaching the end and rushing toward other things. "Two weeks later, Sonya met Mabel in their agreed meeting place. There was a new wedding band on her finger, a growing baby in her stomach, and the news that both her parents—the very same ones who'd raped, mutilated, and killed the Hawks—were dead from fatal poisoning."

"Did the police not investigate?"

Cut laughed. "No. The authorities didn't get involved. Weary from the paperwork and previous nightmares caused by the Weavers, they stayed out of it. The Weavers' standing within the community was tarnished and nobody really cared about a suspicious death when it solved so much propaganda and ill will."

Cut clapped his hands. "So there you have it. Mabel Hawk single-handedly ensured the continuation of the Weavers by Sonya's pregnancy, made it so her mentally broken son impregnated a whore, and the two people who'd been the crux of her pain were dead.

"Unfortunately, Bennett had died before her triumph. Her revenge came years after his brutal rape, but it didn't dampen the pleasure in knowing she'd won the first battle."

My voice replaced Cut's deep one. "That doesn't explain how she became so wealthy or how the Hawks crushed the Weavers. A scandal like that would fade in time. My ancestors had a skill. They worked for the crown. Even if Mabel married the earl, her title wouldn't be enough to be highly influential in court—not to mention she was a commoner, regardless of marriage."

Cut smiled, savouring the rest of his secrets. "Don't rush the story, Nila. I never said she married the earl. In fact, quite the opposite. After a time, she faded from his affection, and he tossed her out on the street. He finally saw she'd used him and wanted nothing more to do with her. Over the years, he'd become a drunkard and a wife-beater, ripping apart what they could've shared.

"Mabel went from living in a nice abode to begging for scraps on the street. The only possession she took with her was her grandson, William. The boy had just turned twelve and was a troublesome child."

Moving closer, Cut whispered in my ear, "And that leads to the next part of the tale. The part where the true rise to diamond power began.

"The part that destroyed your family, once and for all."

Mabel

TOO MANY YEARS had passed since my family fell apart thanks to Percy Weaver and his hellish family. So many years since he'd raped me for the final time. Excruciating years since I secured our lineage and ensured my son's heritage was passed to another.

My daughter was dead, drowned for lies of witchcraft. My son was dead, raped and mentally broken. And my husband was dead, leaving me to defend our legacy on my own.

The hate toward the family who'd taken my everything never ceased—bubbling, billowing, wanting so much to deliver revenge.

And now, I had a way to extract that revenge.

In the days before we worked for the Weavers, I'd been a hopeful girl looking for love. I'd met Frank young and fell pregnant within months. For years, I thought our troubles of living on the streets, of begging and stealing, would be the lowest point in our lives.

However, we hadn't met the Weavers yet. We hadn't entered into their employment. We didn't know how bad things could get.

I wanted to rest. I *needed* to rest. But I couldn't.

For a time, things had been good with the Earl of Wavinghurst, but then I ran out of energy to perform and beguile. He had an issue with his fists, and although I willingly paid for my freedom from the Weavers with a little pain, I'd reached my threshold.

It was mutual—the day he asked me to leave.

I had nothing of my own, only my precious grandson, and traded the staff quarters of his manor for the slums of the London poor.

The Weavers were dead.

Sonya gave birth to a boy followed by twins—a boy and a girl—a year and a half later. The firstborn girl had been delivered, and in order to claim the Debt Inheritance and finally balance the karma scales, I had to find more power and immeasurable wealth so William was in a position to claim his birthright.

In the meantime, I had to find a way to put food in my grandson's belly. I didn't want to, but I had no choice—I returned to what I'd become with the earl. I sold my body; willingly giving the only asset I had left to stay alive.

William's mother—the whore I'd interviewed, given to my son, and bought her child—helped me gain employment with her current madam. And I was grateful. William was growing well. He wasn't sickly and grew strong. He would make a fine Hawk someday. All I had to do was provide for him at his youngest, so in turn, he would provide for me at my oldest.

We moved around a lot that first year, living up to the last name Hawk given to us by the court. Hawks were scavengers, predators, always ready to swoop and steal. I'd never liked the name, until now. Now, I embraced it and nurtured my grandson. All his life, I'd told him bedtime stories of what the Weavers did. I took him to the neighbourhood park where Sonya would walk her children and show him the daughter who would soon belong to him.

He watched that little girl with untold interest, begging me to introduce them, to play with her. It took a lot to ignore his requests. I didn't know what would be better. For them to meet as children or as adults. What would be easier to carry out the terms?

More years passed and I picked up work in sculleries and markets. Along with the occasional trick in a dark alley, we had enough to get by. We made do. William continued to grow, his interest in our history and what the Weavers had done increasing as the years rolled on.

However, he took matters into his own hands when it came to meeting Sonya's daughter. On his fourteenth birthday, I gave him a few coins and told him to head to the local market to pick up whatever he wanted for his birthday treat.

Only, he came back with the money and a story of meeting a Weaver girl who asked to be called Cotton, even though her name was Marion.

Time had sped up and soon both firstborn children would be of age to begin the Inheritance. However, I often caught William doing strange things. He was strong, oh yes. He was well-spoken, kind-hearted, and hard-working, but there was an oddity about him I couldn't explain.

I would lay in bed at night pondering why he was so different. Why he was so aware of others' plights, why he would often give our hard-earned money to those deserving, or soothe random acquaintances in the street.

As he grew older, he couldn't handle crowds as well as other young men. He'd shake and sweat, striking fear into my heart that he would fall ill with the sweating-sickness like his father.

I did everything I could to shelter him. I saved every penny and prepared for a better life.

And finally, that better life arrived.

Our new existence began one evening at the local brothel, where a share of my nightly profits provided a mouldy bed. After work, I headed back to the temporary home I'd found thanks to a local baker's kindness.

William looked up, covered in flour—as usual—working all hours of the day for the baker and his customers. He preferred this job—away from people, hidden in a kitchen with only his thoughts for company. He'd bloomed into a delightful, handsome man.

I couldn't believe he would turn twenty-one next month.

I was proud of him. Proud of myself for never quitting, even when life became so hard.

Dropping my shawl on a flour-dusted chair, I said, "I heard something, Will. Something that will get us far away from here and somewhere better."

My grandson, my darling grandson, looked up. His golden eyes, courtesy of his father glowed in his icing-smeared face. His hands kneaded the fresh dough, and his smile warmed my soul.

Every time I looked at him, my heart broke remembering my daughter and son. Despair and fury never left me alone—they fed me better than any other substance, and until I got back at those who'd wronged me, I would remain alive and deliver vengeance.

William wiped his hands on a tea towel, sitting on the roughly-sawn stool by the oven. Moving to the bucket of water, I rinsed my arms and neck wishing I could cleanse my body from the foul stench of men who'd used it.

I might have a grandson, but I maintained myself. I looked better than most of the whores downtown.

"What did you hear, Grandmamma?"

I smiled. "The street criers said the man from Genoa—the explorer, Christophorus Columbus—has set out on his second journey. They say not since the Vikings has anyone been so brave to risk the dangerous seas and commit a voyage to new worlds." My voice rose with eagerness. "His successful first journey has inspired many ship merchants to follow in his stead. Exploration is the new wealth, William. Those who risk will come back with untold treasure and knowledge."

My heart raced as I recounted what I'd heard on the streets this morning. News from Europe travelled fast, spreading like a disease to infect those who listened. "He took three ships last time. Seventeen this time. Can you imagine, William? Seventeen brave boats to find out what's yonder over the horizon. He left this morning." I wished I could've seen the departure of such a fleet. To have travelled to Spain and waved a white handkerchief in good luck.

William smiled indulgently, his cheekbones slicing through his short beard. "Grandmamma, you need to give up these fantasies of leaving. We live here." He stood, using the tea towel to pull out handmade bread from the crackling fireplace. "I know you don't like it here. I know you and your family didn't find happiness. But it's all I know."

William took after his father. And just like Bennett, he was a quiet soul. He preferred to be gentle and kind, rather than battle and wage war on what was rightfully his.

"We might live here, but I refuse to die here." I crossed my arms. "I'm leaving this country one way or another, and you're coming with me."

He shook his head, smiling softly. He was used to my rambling of finding a better life, a better world. I would give anything to move. To seek what we were owed after such tragedy.

"It's a nice idea. But this is our life." He winced as he sat back down—his body already overused even at such a tender age. I didn't want him labouring to an early grave when I had the gumption to find a way to deliver a splendid upper-class life.

Standing, I fumbled in my skirts for my one saving grace. I'd worked for decades to acquire such a sum. I never went anywhere without it and hid it within my petticoats.

Money.

Enough for two passages on the next boat leaving port.

Moving around the table, I handed him the meagre purse that offered so much. "We're leaving this place, William. There won't be any arguments. We're going to make our fortune and only then will we ever come back."

Eight weeks and counting.

Almost half of those passengers who'd boarded and paid for a hammock in the rat-infested bowels of the ship, *Courtesan Queen,* had died. My gums bled. My stomach wouldn't hold food. And my eyes only saw blurs and shadows rather than vibrant pictures.

But England was far, far away from us.

The ship had no final destination. No advice on where they would deposit us. But I hadn't cared. I believed in fate, and would rather die chasing my dreams than sitting at home never brave enough to try.

True to my word, I'd bought us passage on the next departing boat. The seafarers had seen Christophorus Columbus' triumphs and raced to chase him. When I offered money and my body in exchange for a safe journey, the captain had agreed.

We'd left the very next day. No belongings. Nothing but hope in our hearts.

I'd either condemned us to die at sea, forever lost beneath the waves, or set us free for a better future.

I just wished seasickness hadn't made my new life such a misery.

Groaning, I grabbed the pail again, retching as another swell rocked the creaking vessel.

Twelve weeks.

Even more of us had died. Storms had come and battered the crew and ship. But still we bobbed and travelled.

Sunshine broke through the clouds, granting nutrition in the form of its heated rays. William lost weight. He looked like a walking skeleton, but I was no better. My ribs had become so sharp, my skin bruised where they stretched my sides. I'd lost teeth due to rotting gums and my vision sputtered with useless blurs.

But hope still blazed.

We were owed happiness. I had no doubt we would be paid.

Fourteen weeks after leaving mother England, my hope was justified.

Land.

Sweet, life-giving land.

The next few days gave new energy to the ship and its remaining inhabitants. Celebration ran rife and excitement levels gave us the final push to reach salvation.

The first steps on terra firma lifted my heart like nothing else could. I'd made it. I'd left hell and found heaven. Here, my grandson would find a better life. I owed him that.

Only, I didn't know how hard this new world would be.

For three long years, we lived in squalor and hardship. Our newfound existence turned out to be no better than England. Instead of buildings, we lived in huts. Instead of food, we had to hunt and kill. And instead of streets, there were dirt tracks and violence.

However, every day William thrived. He shed the shy baker from England and transformed into a warrior matching the courage of the black-skinned neighbours of our new home. They taught him how to track and trap. They taught him their language, and eventually, adopted us into their tribe.

Once accepted, we made the choice to return with them to their home. We had nothing holding us in the port town and agreed to make the pilgrimage to their village. It took weeks of travelling by foot. My old age slowly caught up with me and eating had become a chore with very few teeth from bad nutrition on the boat over. My body was failing, but I hadn't achieved what I'd promised.

Not yet.

I had to provide for William. He had to go back and claim the Debt Inheritance before he was too old. My to-do list was still too long to succumb to elderly fatigue.

William was a godsend, helping me every step. He held my hand. He carried me when I collapsed. He helped the shamans break my fever when I was sick. He never stopped believing with me that one of these days we would find what we were owed.

And then one day, five years and four months after leaving England, we finally found it.

My eyesight had deteriorated further but every night at twilight, William would take me for a walk around our adopted village. He'd guide me to the riverbed and guard me from local predators while I washed and relaxed.

However, that night was different. A hyena appeared, laughing and hungry, and William chased it off with his spear. I stood in the middle of the water, not daring to leave but unable to see my brave grandson.

He wouldn't respond to my calls. No sound gave a hint that he'd won. Tears started to fall at the thought of losing him. If he'd died, I couldn't keep going anymore. Why should I? My stupid hope and blind belief that something good would happen would no longer be enough to sustain me.

However, my worry was for nothing because he returned. Blood smeared his bare chest as he dragged a hyena carcass behind him. He looked as wild and savage as our ebony-skinned saviours. He dropped the carcass and waded into the water directly to me. My animal hide skirt danced on the surface, lapping around my thighs as he held out something large and glossy and black. Black like a nightmare but an ultimate dream come true.

"What is it?" I whispered, my heart rate climbing. I didn't know what I held, but it felt right. It felt true. It felt like redemption.

"I don't know, but the stories they tell us around the fires might be based on truth. Remember they sing of a magical black rock? I think this might be it." He kissed my cheek, hefting the weight of the suddenly warm stone. "I think this is worth something, Grandmamma. I think this might be the start of something good."

I'd like to say I lived to see the good arrive, but I'd done all I could for my grandson. A few months later, I fell sick and remained bed-ridden as he found more black stones, digging with spears and hipbones of lions, slowly sifting through soil and rock. Black stones gave way to white stones, clear stones, glittering beautiful stones.

Our tribe gathered and hoarded, filling bushels and burying them safely so other clans didn't rob us. William gathered a hunting party to return to the bustling port and trade his magical stones.

I remained behind, clinging to life as hard as I could.

My body had done its task, but I didn't want to leave…not yet.

We'd heard tales of a gold trader who made a fortune in saffron and bullion. That same trader took William aside and whispered in his ear that he might've found a rare diamond.

Diamond.

I'd never seen one up close. I'd heard of them on the king's finery but never been lucky enough to witness.

The night William returned from port, he told me he'd traded enough clear stones for passage back to England. And that was when I knew the tides had finally turned. The Weavers had ruled for long enough.

It was our turn.

By candle-light, we negotiated his plan upon returning to the United Kingdom. I gave him my elderly wisdom and what I'd learned the hard way. In order to become untouchable, he had to buy those who would protect him. He had to give the king everything to purchase his trust. He had to spend money to make his fortune last longer than fleeting.

I hoped he'd heed my advice.

Unfortunately, I never knew.

I died two weeks before William named a handful of trusted warriors the Black Diamonds and booked passage on the first boat back to England.

I never got to see him strip and destroy those who'd ruined us.

I never got to see the fruition of my sacrifice.

But it didn't matter.

I loved him with all my heart.

I'd given him everything.

I'd finally set him free.

Nila

"COULD YOU FEEL her loyalty, Nila? Her unfailing spirit toward her beloved family?"

Cut's voice tore me from the hypnosis of learning about Mabel Hawk. She was the only reason the Hawks had become the superpower they were today. Without her, without her determination and willingness to do whatever it took, the Hawks would've remained poor and unknown.

I rolled my shoulders, forcing myself to snap out of the trance he'd put me in. I couldn't forget I stood in a dank mine—the very mine William Hawk started so many centuries ago. Cut wasn't telling me history for the fun of it— he gave me a prelude to the debt I would soon have to pay.

Listening to Mabel's tale, I couldn't figure out what the payment would be. Mabel had given up everything for her grandson. What a strong, commendable woman she was. Even if she was the reason for my pain.

"Yes." I nodded. "She did so much." My eyes met Jethro's. His nostrils flared wide, sucking in damp air, unable to talk with the gag lodged in his mouth. My heart overflowed with love and affection. I fully understood Mabel's drive to save someone she loved.

She saved them.

I smiled sadly to think two things in both our families had been passed down from generations. One, my family had always had the tendency to breed in multiples. Twins were common and triplets a regular event. And Jethro…his empathy had come from William. Mabel wouldn't have understood his plight, but listening to the characteristics of her grandson, I had no doubt he suffered what Jethro did.

"Can you see how everything we are is owed to that woman? That she is, without a doubt, the bravest Hawk." Cut paced in front of me.

Yes, I can see.

I asked a question of my own. "Why don't you have her portrait up in Hawksridge? You have so many men hanging in the dining room, where is Mabel—considering she is the founder of your family's fortune?"

Cut paused. "There is a portrait, or as close to her likeness as William could make it. When he returned and created a new life for himself in England, he did his best to describe his grandmother to a local artist. The poor couldn't afford painters, Nila. And she died before she had the means for such frivolous items."

"Where do you keep her painting?"

Cut's lips twisted into a smile. "It's interesting you should ask that."

"Why?"

"Because you'll see, soon enough. You'll see her portrait, along with many other Hawk women before the Final Debt is paid."

Jethro growled, struggling in his binds.

Cut chuckled. "Don't like me mentioning your girlfriend is on borrowed time? I'm glad I gagged you. It's nice being able to have a conversation and not have you interrupting us."

Jethro's eyes glowed with rage.

Turning his back on him, Cut gave me his full attention. "Now you know how we found the diamonds. Let's continue with William's story when he returned to England."

I didn't approve or deny as Cut moved around me, his voice taking on a story-time timbre. "William grieved his grandmother's death, but he knew she would want him to reach the heights she'd dreamed. So he left on the boat with his Black Diamond warriors and returned to England without his grandmother.

"When he reached English soil, he went directly to the king. He didn't try and find someone to value the stone or seek backhanded deals. He knew that was a sure way to get himself killed.

"Instead, he announced he'd been on a voyage and had returned with a gift for the king. It took him four months of hanging outside court, following dukes and duchesses, and slipping through the king's guard before the king finally agreed to an audience.

"In a meeting attended by courtiers and advisors, William presented the black diamond. The stone was the largest ever found at the time and the king immediately gave him authority to return with a fleet of ships to collect more on his behalf.

"William remembered what Mabel told him. He was willing to give up the wealth he'd found, pay exorbitant taxes, and lavish gifts upon the crown in order to have the most powerful monarchy behind him."

Cut ran a hand through his hair. "Imagine that. Giving up every stone you'd found, returning home richer than the king, and leaving penniless once again."

I kept my chin high. I had to admit it would be a hard decision to swallow but smart at the same time. No king wanted a richer subject than he. This way, the crown became insanely wealthy and the Hawks cemented a lifelong partnership, ensuring better things than money.

Friends.

Allies.

Kings in their feather-lined pockets.

Was that how the crown became so rich? Were the jewels on their garments and diamonds on their scepters all thanks to the Hawks?

I gasped, my mind running away with the new angle of thoughts.

Every war. Every triumph and takeover of other countries—had they been possible and financed entirely by the Hawks?

Cut interrupted my epiphany. "William returned to Africa and found yet more diamonds. His Black Diamond warriors increased in number, his mine and village became the most protected piece of dirt in Botswana, and he returned to England with far more than before.

"The king once again welcomed him with open arms. He granted William a title, land, property—anything he wanted. He agreed to the terms that all Weavers—related to Sonya or not—were no longer favoured in court and banished them to Spain. He also approved the Debt Inheritance to be binding for future years.

"By his third trip, the young Hawk boy had become an untouchable aristocrat. He'd grown in wealth and power and wore his self-worth like the expensive tailoring he commissioned. The fleet of ships given to him by the king grew until the crown jewels filled to bursting with diamonds of all shapes and sizes."

"What about the Debt Inheritance?" I tried to do quick arithmetic. "He would be nearing his thirtieth birthday—if not older. What about claiming Marion?"

Cut's forehead furrowed. "Don't rush me, Ms. Weaver. I'm getting to that." Jamming his hands in his pockets, he continued with his tale. "It was almost a decade before William found another black diamond that trumped even the one he'd given to the king, the one he'd named his entire brethren and brotherhood in honour of. This new one…this black monster found beneath the soil of the African plains, made the one the king owned pale in comparison. To this day, it sits carefully guarded in our safe at Diamond Alley."

Diamond Alley?

My eyes flew to Jethro's.

Oh, my God. He'd shown me. He'd allowed me to hold the menacing stone that'd become the most treasured item in his family history.

Jethro scowled, shaking his head slightly. *Don't mention it.*

I bit my lip. *I won't.*

"For years, the arrangement with the king prospered but then an aspiring courtier tried to kill William and take his trade routes and diamond mine for himself. The man ambushed the boats journeying home. His entourage robbed the crates of gems when they arrived at port. And they killed members of William's Black Diamond brothers in order to weaken the wealthy Hawk importer.

"William obviously didn't put up with such behaviour and fought his enemies by becoming a smuggler."

I rolled my wrists, encouraging blood to flow into my fingertips. "How?"

"The mines at *Almasi Kipanga* gave many ranges of diamonds. Some of low grade. Some of high. The lower grade, William mixed with quartz and other invaluable gemstones, pretending the shipment contained millions worth of invaluable cargo. He'd allow the hijacking and sacrifice the haul without losing anything of value.

"The king was aware of the ruse and allowed him to create tales and fiction of robberies and bankruptcy. But what the thieves didn't know was, William had found better ways to transport. He lost his reputation of respectful decorum and embraced a notoriety of strict and fearful.

"His trusted warriors ensured his mystery increased, killing those who opposed him, creating a formidable empire no one could take down. Not even the king."

Cut stopped before me. "That wealth started our dynasty and the power that ensured we were above the Weavers, even though they'd been the court seamstresses and royal designers for decades. It was the same power that made the Weavers run like vermin, hiding in their new Spanish home, believing they were safe from any other claimant on the contract."

I frowned. "So William never made Marion pay the Debt Inheritance? He let her live?"

Cut smiled. "There's something you didn't know about William. Something Jethro shares with his great-great—too many great ancestor."

I smiled, happy I'd seen within the lines of his story. "I think I know what that is."

Cut narrowed his eyes. "I suppose, after being so close to my son, that would make sense. For the purpose of full disclosure. What is it?"

My arms ached to hold Jethro. My heart throbbed to be with him, away from this place. I held my lover's eyes as I muttered, "He was an Empath, too."

"Exactly." Cut nodded. "An unfortunate trait that runs in the family. It wasn't diagnosed or even recognised as a condition. But records and voyage logs give hints into William's emotional perception. His disease prevented him from hurting the one girl he was owed."

Cut moved toward me, his body heat defiling mine. My feet moved for every one of his, moving in a slow waltz around the room.

"Because William was so weak emotionally, he felt the brunt of inflicted pain. He'd endured discomfort in his merchant world. He'd seen things, done things, and lived through things he couldn't shake when having to deliver agony firsthand. Unfortunately, the thought of carrying out the same punishment, of whipping her for his grandfather and ducking her for his aunt, and raping her for his father—he knew he couldn't do it."

Cut's story achieved two things. One, it showed that although my ancestors had been conceited and cruel, Sonya had been compassionate and kind. And even though the Hawks were insane today; back then, they sounded upstanding and courageous.

Cut's voice cut through my musing. "Instead of taking her for his own, William let Marion marry and breed. He married himself and accepted the gift of land from the crown to build our home, Hawksridge Hall."

Cut stopped moving; I stopped backing away.

His white hair flickered with the electric lamps around the room. His voice turned raspy from delivering such a long tale. "Unfortunately for William, his firstborn, Jack Hawk, was nothing like his father. Jack willingly accepted the Debt Inheritance when he came of age."

I finally understood why, through so many generations, only a select few inheritances had been claimed. There would've been more Hawks like Jethro—especially if it was a common trait. And my family didn't take the threat seriously because the claiming wasn't strictly enforced.

Cut didn't speak again for a minute, letting history fade around us, allowing ghosts to settle back into their coffins.

Taking a deep breath, he finished, "So you see, Nila. We had our own hardships. We knew what it was like to rise from the gutter. And the Weavers couldn't stop us."

I squirmed in my ropes, hating he'd come to an end—knowing it meant only one thing. I'd enjoyed the lesson, but I wanted to run from whatever debt he would make me repay. "But you have so much. Why bother hurting others when you no longer need to?"

Cut scowled. "Why do politicians lie? Why do the richest families in the world create war? Why do those who have the power to fix global poverty choose to exploit and murder instead?" His fingers kissed my cheek. "Nila, the world is black beneath the skirts of society. We aren't any different from others."

"That's not true. I don't believe that."

"Don't believe what?"

"That other men do this. Hurt others."

Cut laughed loudly. "Don't you pay attention to the news? Do you not see between the lines of what a corrupted, blackmailed globe we live in?"

I looked away.

Jethro continued to wriggle. Nervous sweat beaded on his forehead while wildness glowed in his eyes.

We both understood time had run out. Cut was ready for the next part of this sick and twisted game.

"I do agree some families control every earthly asset." I stood tall and defiant. "I agree death to them is as simple as a signature or a whispered word. What I don't agree with is *why*. *Why* do you have to do this?"

Cut marched quickly and gathered me close in his arms. "Because I can, Nila. That's all." Letting me go, he prowled to the table where items I didn't want to look at rested. "Now, enough history. I've rambled on long enough, and it's starting to get boring. Let's get to the exciting part, shall we?

"Let's pay the rest of the Fourth Debt."

GET YOUR FUCKING hands off her.
Don't touch her.
Let her go.
Leave her alone, goddammit!

Every thought hurricaned around my head, blistering with outrage but not able to spill thanks to the rancid gag inside my mouth.

I wanted to kill him. Motherfucking slice his godforsaken head off his shoulders.

Every inch of me cried with agony—from the gunshot wound to the fever to the pounding headache and potentially cracked ribs from the car crash.

Yet nothing hurt more than listening to Cut deliver the story of Mabel and William—the same tale I'd heard over and over again—and counted down the minutes of when it would be over.

Nila paid attention, rapt beyond her will, absorbing my family's history. To hear it for the first time would've answered so many of her questions but I had my own about William Hawk. Along with Owen, I felt most connected with him. I had documents of when William was inducted into the House of Lords while building Hawksridge. I had countless notes of his rise to wealth and the ledgers from his ships.

He was the keystone to my family, just like Mabel. He'd managed to deliver our rightful happiness without spilling any more Weaver blood. I liked him. But I hated what'd happened after his time had passed.

Nila struggled in Cut's control. "I paid the Fourth Debt at the Hall."

Cut laughed. "You paid one element of it, that's all. This is the main part and must be completed for the contract to be appeased."

Snatching her tied wrists, he stroked her tattooed fingertips. "You've only earned two tallies. You need two more marks before the Final Debt can be paid."

Nila snarled, "If you think you can etch your name into my skin, I won't let you. Jethro's initials are what I bear. Only he can tally me. Only he can claim me as per the Inheritance rules."

Cut let her go, tutting under his breath. "As you no doubt have figured out, Ms. Weaver, I'm not exactly playing by those rules any longer."

Another wash of crippling pain from my headache dulled their voices. My shoulders ached from flipping in the car and my sockets bellowed from being wrenched behind my back.

They continued to argue as I grappled for coherency.

I willed them to continue talking. Every extra stolen minute could help.

Gritting my jaw, I struggled with renewed force. For the past half hour, I'd done everything I could to get free.

My fingernails sawed at the rope; my tongue pushed on the gag. But Cut hadn't tied me with half-measures. He'd tied and triple tied.

All I achieved was more pain and tiredness. Despite my bitterness and hatred, I'd become helpless. All I could do was sit there like a fucking arsehole while my father tortured Nila with anticipation.

The Fourth Debt.

Originally, the debt ensured ultimate pain and a quick delivery to the Final Debt. Not many would've survived for long—especially a few centuries ago when anaesthetic and disinfectant weren't used. The Fourth Debt was the last to be claimed and the most barbaric.

Missing body parts.

I shuddered, breathing hard through my nose. My innards crawled with what would happen, what Nila would endure, what I would witness.

I have to find a way to stop it.

Thankfully, Nila wouldn't be subjected to Cut's surgery skills. Not in this day and age. The debt had evolved a little since then. But it would still be painful. It would still be brutal and cruel.

I twisted in the ropes, wishing for just a small loosening that I could use. But the twine only gathered tighter, rocking the chair legs against the floor as I writhed.

Cut glanced at me, his eyes narrowing. "I'd save your strength, Jethro. You have a new task, remember?"

I threw every inch of hate into my gaze. If only looks could kill. I would've ripped his motherfucking head off with one glance.

"Your fate is no longer death." Cut came toward me, calm and collected. He acted as if this was a business meeting discussing new terms of the estate. "Your destiny is to stay alive, missing her when she's gone. Forever alone with memories of her death."

Nila swallowed a cry, her eyes darting to the exit. "That doesn't have to be the case. He's your son. I'm in love with him. Let us go and be a father rather than tormentor." She could run, but her hands remained tied—without her fingers to open doors and arms to defend, she was as trapped as I was.

Cut ducked to my eye level. He hid so much of himself but throughout my childhood, I'd seen parts of him in direct contradiction to the man before me now. Was there any goodness left inside, or was he nothing but a black shadow, a grim reaper of Weaver souls?

Don't hurt her!

Don't do this.

He didn't need words to understand what I begged. If the ropes didn't lash me to the chair, I'd fall to my knees and plead. I'd give him anything—my life, my future—*anything* to save Nila from what he would do.

With a smile, he patted me on the head. "Keep your eyes open. Nila agreed to do a certain something for me back at Hawksridge. It's time to see if she'll obey." Leaning closer, he whispered so Nila wouldn't hear. "If she does it, it will rip out your fucking heart but she'll remain intact. If she doesn't, she'll be loyal to you but will pay the price with pain."

Taking a step back, he grinned. "Let's see what she chooses, shall we?"

I looked directly at Nila. How could I tell her to behave and do whatever Cut asked? How could I tell her to choose between two horrendous things?

Her eyes widened, confusion settling on her face from my scattered questions.

Trying to calm down, I did my best to silently share a message. *Do what he asks.*

She flinched. *Never.*

Please.

Don't ask me to do that.

Her emotions waked around the space, tainting the walls and air. I couldn't turn my condition off, and I wouldn't survive feeling Nila's agony.

My muscles bunched as I struggled harder. I choked on saliva, sucking on the disgusting gag.

Cut placed himself in front of Nila with his back facing me.

I couldn't see.

I can't see.

I strained to the side, seeking a better vantage, but I couldn't see around Cut's large frame.

"Now, you've heard the history, so let's focus on the present." Cut's voice echoed in the cave. "But first, you owe me from the dice throw in Hawksridge. I won't tell you what you'll avoid if you obey, but I will tell you if you don't, worse pain than you've endured so far will be delivered."

His hand landed on her cheek, brushing aside glossy black hair. I *hated* his hands on her. I *hated* I couldn't see Nila's reaction or read her face. I hated, hated, *hated* he'd already stolen so much from her—her long hair, her happiness...her smile.

She looked nothing like the young seamstress from the runway show nor any hint of the sexy, shy nun in her first text messages.

Together, my father and I had stripped her of everything she'd been and created this new creature. A creature being led to the slaughter.

No!

I growled.

Cut looked over his shoulder, rolling his eyes. "A growl? That's all you have to say?" His gaze landed on the duct tape over my mouth. "Like I said, Jet. Save your energy. All you need to do is watch."

I'll fucking watch.

I'll watch wolves tear apart your carcass.

I'll watch demons suck your soul into hell.

My breathing crescendoed until my ribs creaked and my head swam.

Nila trembled in place. Her emotions stuttered, fading a little as she locked down internally. I'd felt it happen to many people. When stress overloaded the system, a human's natural response was to go quiet. To focus. To numb. To delete every distraction.

I'm here with you, Nila.

I'm with you every step.

Nila's voice was a blade as she replied, "If I refuse, will you hurt Jethro?"

"No, my son isn't going to participate in this next part."

She sniffed. "In that case, you can't inflict worse pain than I've already endured. The day you shot him and I believed he was dead is the worst you can ever do." Her tone strengthened until it shone with steel. "So do your worst, Cut Hawk, because I can survive you."

Cut didn't reply, but his hand lashed out to wrap around her waist. "We'll see about that." Jerking her elbow, he spun her around to face away from him. "If that's how you want to play this." Letting her go, he pulled out a switchblade from his back pocket.

My heart splattered into my toes.

Stop!

I growled and struggled, but it was no use.

Shit!

Maybe I was wrong. Maybe the Fourth Debt would still include slicing off a limb or appendage. I had to stop him!

Don't!

Don't fucking touch her!

With a flick of his wrist, Cut sliced through the rope around Nila's wrists and spun her around to face him again.

The relief at no blood being drawn layered my shoulders with heavy relief. I slouched, breathing hard, fighting through the *thump-thump* of my headache.

Thank fuck.

Tucking the knife back into his pocket, he smiled. "Now you've had time to think about your lies, Nila, let's try again. Where is Daniel?"

Black hair flicked as she shook her head. "I've already told you. I don't know."

"You do know."

"I don't."

Cut gathered her close, wedging her body against his. "When I find out the truth, you'll understand I can deliver pain outside of the original debts to be claimed." He ran a hand over her chin. "If I find out you've hurt or somehow killed my youngest, you'll wish to God you died in the car crash today."

Pacing away, he gathered his temper. His boots scuffed the earthen floor.

My eyes immediately latched with Nila's. Now Cut's body didn't block hers, I shot as much love and pride that I could.

I'm so fucking in love with you.

She smiled sadly. *I know.*

We'll get through this.

Her body folded with depression. Her eyes didn't return a response.

Cut moved behind Nila, folding his arms around her in a rotting embrace. Locking eyes with me, he whispered in Nila's ear.

I couldn't hear, but the change in Nila faded her heartbeat by heartbeat.

Christ, I wanted to stop this. Hadn't he done enough?

My tongue pulsed against the gag, doing my best to curse and yell.

Her spine rolled, her cheeks whitened, her hands opened and closed by her sides. When Cut finished whispering, she bit her lip and shook her head.

He murmured again, his breath disturbing her short hair.

Once again, she shook her head, gritting her jaw against the sudden sickness rolling from her. Not sick from a malady but sick to the stomach with hate and disgust.

What did he say to her?

What happened at Hawksridge with the dice?

Cut whispered harder, his voice hissing like a snake. Again words were non-existent but his tone was insistent. He pointed a finger at me, his lips forming rapid threats.

Don't listen to him.

Whatever he does to me, I'll take it.

If it means you're safe, I'll do anything.

Nila looked up, her dusky skin as white as the clouds far, far above us. She studied me. Decisions fluttered then shredded. Conclusions formed then discarded with revulsion.

I sensed her battle but wanted to howl when she finally nodded.

Don't...don't...

Whatever it is...don't.

"Fine."

Cut smiled. "Good girl."

My eyes bugged as Nila willingly spun in Cut's embrace, facing him in the cage of his embrace. Her back blocked what her hands did, but the muscles in her spine rippled beneath her clothing.

My stomach knotted as she sucked in a breath; her hands moved to Cut's belt.

No. Fuck, no.

I tripled my efforts, my head roaring, my ribs screaming.

I growled and grunted and groaned. I sounded like a wild beast fighting for its life.

No!

Her elbows moved as her fingers flew over his belt and fly, undoing both effortlessly. I hated her skills with zippers and buttons. I hated her gorgeous hands and strong fingers and how they disappeared into Cut's trousers.

My voice garbled around the gag, swearing in every dialect as Nila swallowed a moan and touched my father where she should never have to touch.

Cut's eyes darkened as her hand wrapped around him.

My gut clenched, appalled and outraged he'd forced her to do something so wrong.

"Good girl," he murmured as her hand worked up and down. I didn't need to see what happened to have foul images splash across my mind. She touched him. She fucking stroked my father's cock.

The chair creaked and splintered as I shook—fighting, *fighting* against the ropes.

Nila stiffened as Cut whispered loud enough for me to hear. "That's it. Make me hard. The drugs from last night might've left your system, but I'll make you scream while you pay my part of the Third Debt."

Fuck, he was going to rape her in front of me?

He was going to emasculate me and kill me all over again by stripping Nila of her rights as a woman.

I won't.

She can't.

Throwing myself to the side, the chair legs buckled. Gravity latched on, slamming me sideways to the floor. Pain radiated through my shoulder, but I didn't care. My feet kicked, trying to unravel the rope from around my ankles. I stretched, slowly inching the twine down the chair legs.

I gave everything I had.

I ignored the splitting headache. I forced bruised muscles to gather power beyond normal limits. I turned rogue as Nila continued to stroke Cut.

Stop!

Don't touch him.

Cut smiled, wrapping one arm around Nila as she did what he commanded. But his eyes never left mine. They gleamed with triumph. Knowing this would break me worse than any bullet, better than any guillotine.

Soil smeared against my cheek as I rolled on the floor, doing my best to get free.

You won't get away with this, you bastard!

Flashbacks of Emma, Nila's mother, being in Cut's embrace merged with the present. She'd tolerated my father. She'd played him better than he knew. But I'd known all along her true thoughts. I'd felt her repellent dislike for him, even while she smiled affectionately and let Cut believe she was in love with him.

She'd done what Nila had attempted to do; only Nila fell in love with me. Emma never fell in love with Cut. And that'd only layered to his fundamental issue.

No one loved him. No one cared.

People respected and feared him, but it wasn't the same as being completely devoted through affection. And he knew that.

Nila cried silently as her hand worked harder. What had he threatened? Why had she agreed to touch him?

I knew Nila. It wouldn't have been anything toward her. Her own pain she faced far too easily. No, he would've threatened me—even though he'd said I wouldn't be used in this debt. Bastard. Utter fucking *bastard*.

Nila!

The shout warped unintelligently around the gag as Cut dropped his face into the crook of her neck and inhaled.

Her shoulders quaked; tears making her tremble and shake.

I would've killed countless innocent people if only I had the power to stand and shove a dagger into Cut's heart.

Tears stung my eyes at being so fucking helpless.

Cut brushed aside Nila's hair, kissing the diamond collar. "God, that feels good. I hope you're wet for me, Weaver. Because I can't take much more of your teasing."

Everything changed.

Nila's hand ceased stroking. Her shoulders stopped quaking. And the room turned stagnant with possibility.

"I—I can't—" Ripping her hand from his trousers, she shoved him hard. "I won't!"

Cut wobbled from her push, his legs spread and jeans undone. The shadow of his erection tightened the fabric. His voice was blackness personified. "Think wisely, my dear. Are you sure?"

Nila nodded, frantically wiping her right hand on her leggings. "I won't. I won't grant you pleasure. No matter what you say. I won't!"

Storm clouds covered Cut's face. He lowered his jaw, glaring at her beneath his brow. "Have it your way." Marching toward her, he grabbed her wrist. "This way, please."

Nila looked over her shoulder. Her eyes widened, taking in my change of sitting upright to lying on the floor. Her features contorted with sorrow and guilt. *I'm sorry.*

I shook my head, dispelling ancient dust. *Never. There's nothing to be—*

Cut forced her to turn, stealing our private moment.

Her feet stumbled as he threw her against the table at the perimeter of the room. Yanking out a chair, he shoved her into it. "Sit."

She breathed hard, red spots of fear and fury on her cheeks. "Cut...please, whatever you're about to do—don't. *Please.*"

"You're getting repetitive, Ms. Weaver." With an angry swipe, Cut shoved the paraphernalia the mine workers had brought in and cleared a spot on the dirty table.

His hands shook as he rearranged his cock and zipped his jeans. His belt buckle clanked as he fumbled to do it up. "You could've paid the Third Debt without pain. I wouldn't have hurt you. I would've even granted you pleasure."

Nila spat on the floor. "Pleasure? Rape would never be pleasure. Your touch is grotesque."

I sucked in useless air through my nose. Her strength astounded me but also pissed me off. Answering back would only deliver worse things. As much as it would've butchered me to witness the love of my life submit to my father, watching this...whatever this was...would be worse.

At least Nila would be intact.

You don't believe that.

Her strength came from answering back and standing up for herself. If she let Cut willingly strip her of sexual rights and permit him to take her...I doubt her mind would remain so rebellious and untouchable.

Christ, I'm so sorry, Nila.

I wriggled on the floor, trying to get closer, doing my best to get free. Every inch of my body worked against me, slowly draining with every sordid breath.

Cut panted hard as he brushed back his hair, centring himself. "Give me your arm."

Nila froze. "What? No? I won't touch you again."

"I didn't ask for your *hand*, Nila. I asked for your arm."

She slowly shook her head, crossing her arms defiantly. "You ask and I deny. No, you may not have my arm."

"You're wrong. I didn't ask to begin with. I said *give.*" Cut's anger rose to the surface. I was surprised he'd let Nila's outbursts last as long as he had. No matter how he would deny it, Cut had feelings for Nila. Feelings he still nursed for her mother. He wanted her. He wanted to keep her. But it fucking killed him that the daughter fell in love with his son when the mother cursed him to hell the day he took her life.

He'd given her a choice...

My mind skipped back to the private conversation I hadn't meant to overhear. A week before the Final Debt with Emma, Cut had admitted to his Weaver prisoner he loved her too much to kill her. He wanted more from her. More time. More togetherness. He was willing to hold off the Final Debt indefinitely if she agreed to be his completely.

Marry him.

Submit to him whenever he desired.

His one condition for her life—she was forbidden from seeing Tex or her children ever again.

It was a testament of Emma's love for her family and husband that she turned him down and chose death instead.

"For fuck's sake, give me your bloody arm." Cut lashed out; snatching Nila's arms and breaking the hold she'd formed. She struggled but was no match for Cut's strength.

Slamming her forearm on the table, he growled, "Did you listen to the part of the story about smuggling diamonds?"

Nila wriggled in Cut's possession, doing her best to take her imprisoned arm back. "Yes. I listened."

"In that case, you'll understand what the rest of the Fourth Debt entails." She stopped breathing. "No…I don't…"

He chuckled, fighting her tugging, keeping her arm against the table. "Yes, you do." Holding her down with one hand, he reached to the side with the other. Plucking a narrow stick from its resting place, he pressed it against her mouth. "Open wide."

Her face arched away from the offer. "What? No."

Cut pinched her arm. The shock stole her attention, parting her lips. Taking advantage, he slipped the stick inside her mouth so the ends stuck out either side of her cheeks. She looked as if she'd been bridled.

Turning her head to spit it out, Cut held the stick in place. "Ah, ah, ah. I wouldn't do that if I were you."

Her eyes glared daggers.

"Bite down." Cut slowly removed his hand, daring her to dispel it.

Nila paused, the stick remaining lodged in her teeth. Her eyebrow rose with questions as Cut slowly picked up a black rubber mallet. A type of mallet used for hitting unwilling pieces of timber or coaxing nails into holes. A hammer that would bring untold pain.

She sucked in air around the stick, her struggles renewing. "No!" Her voice wavered around the obstruction.

"I told you, bite down." His fingers latched tighter around the mallet. "This will hurt."

No!

My heart lurched as I twisted and bucked. "Stwrop!" I despised not being able to move, to talk, to shout, to help. "Nwoooo!"

Nila.

Fuck, I'm so sorry.

"What—what's—" Nila couldn't tear her eyes away from the mallet. Her entire body went on lockdown. "Cut…don't." The stick remained in her teeth, her tongue forming words with care.

His eyes glinted. "When William's reputation of priceless diamonds made its way around the city, more and more people tried to rob him. Opportunists and pirates all wanted a piece of his good fortune even when he'd paid so much for it. Thieves. Cheapskates. They all deserved to hang."

Nila whimpered, fighting his hold as Cut braced his legs, preparing to deliver the Fourth Debt.

My heart bucked, smashing against bruised ribs, leaping into the throbs inside my head. From my angle on the floor, the world tilted sideways, my mind straining to stay with her, to find a way free.

"William constantly had to come up with new ways to smuggle his cargo into the country. He started with the obvious: the orifices of his men. The switch and ruse. The fake packaging ploy. But after time, each one would fail as word got out of the latest scam.

"Even in the last few decades, we suffered our own setbacks. Our smuggling mules would swallow the diamonds or wrap small quantities around their stomach and legs, and fly in sweating guilt and terror—guaranteed to have the shipment ceased upon arrival. Or they'd shove them in arseholes and pussies but that's become too widely used by drug traffickers and with tighter border security, not practical. So…we came up with a new plan."

His voice thickened. "Know how we solved this problem?"

Nila shook her head, black hair sticking to sweaty cheeks, tears cascading in streams.

"Sewing into flesh."

She sucked in a horrified breath, the air whistling around her stick.

Cut frowned. "The sewing was rather barbaric and didn't have such satisfactory results. A doctor would cut a mule in the least invasive place, insert a few packets of diamonds, and sew them back up. Once the traveller arrived at their destination, the wound was reopened, diamonds removed, and their sum paid. However, the risk of infection and hospitalisation was too high.

"So…we came up with a better idea."

He twisted his wrist, dragging Nila's attention back to the black mallet in his fist. "We don't cut anymore, we break. We offer legitimate disabilities while using the fracture as the perfect alibi." He grinned. "Understand what I'm saying, Nila?"

Shit.

I gave everything I had left. My wrists soaked with blood as I fought the rope. My back splintered with every wriggle. I couldn't watch. I couldn't prevent what Cut would do. I couldn't do a thing as he broke her and dressed her in diamonds.

I yelled profanity, choking on the gag. I wanted to talk to her. Comfort her. I didn't want to fail her all over again.

Shock electrocuted her system. She spat out the stick even though she'd need it to ride the upcoming pain. "You can't be serious."

"I'm deadly serious." Cut's smile twisted his face into horror. "You had the choice to make me hard and deliver pleasure with your right hand. You had my cock in your fingers, your future in your grasp, yet you threw it in my fucking face. Well, your right arm will pay, Nila. It now has a different task."

Nila fought harder, scratching at Cut's hold with her free hand. "No, let me go. Let me—"

"You really should've bit down like I told you. Too late now." Cut didn't soften, raising the mallet above his head. "Do you repent? Do you take ownership of your family's sins and agree to pay the debt?"

"No! Hell no!"

"Wrong answer." Cut prepared to strike.

"No. Wait!"

His jaw clenched.

"Stop, please!"

"With or without your ownership, I won't stop."

His gaze glowed.

His arm sailed down.
The mallet became a black boulder of agony.
"This is going to hurt."

Nila

THE MALLET SOARED downward.

No!

The whistle of wind heralded imminent agony.

Please!

The small cry was my soul escaping.

Don't!

The silent scream from Jethro was my undoing.

* * *

The crack of impact.

Pain.

The loud splinter of skeleton giving way.

Torture.

The wave of sickness as mallet defeated bone.

Torment.

The cloud of unconsciousness that numbed everything.

* * *

The room spun and tilted.

I'm crippled.

The agony swelled and crested.

I'm mutilated.

The mallet left my burning broken bone, resting innocuously beside my wrist like a fallen executioner.

I'm in pieces.

I'm in splinters.

I'm broken.

I threw up.

* * *

There were two worlds.

The one where I'd existed only moments ago—intact, whole, afraid but complete.

And now, this new one. The one where I shook with excruciating pain…was in pieces…destroyed.

A delayed scream fell from my lips as I cradled my shattered forearm.

I screamed

and screamed

and *screamed.*

It hurt.

God, how it hurt.

I'd broken pieces of myself in the past. How could I not living a life with vertigo? But I'd never felt it coming. Never seen the pain unfolding. Never heard the agony delivered.

I moaned, battling wave after wave of deep throbbing pain.

Please...make it stop!

Gentle arms cradled me, embracing me, fingers wiping tears from my cheeks. "Told you it would hurt," Cut murmured.

I couldn't look at him. I couldn't breathe around him. I couldn't stay alive in a world where he existed.

No!

Shying away from his touch, I bit my lip hard enough to bleed. My intact fingers wrapped around my broken arm, soothing the burn, wanting to erase the damage. The flesh turned red and swollen, bloating with pain. It wasn't disfigured or deformed but the hot swell hinted he'd done the damage he'd intended.

He broke it.

He hurt me.

He did this!

Noises clanked beside me.

I didn't look. I let my hair curtain the outside terrors. I didn't glance at Jethro. I didn't blink. I didn't care.

All I cared about was nursing my battered body and surfing the tsunami of suffering.

Time ticked onward, dragging me further into this new world where I hugged a broken limb. He broke me. He struck me. And all for what? So he could use the wound as a suitcase for his disgusting diamonds.

"Give it to me, please."

Cut's voice cut through my horror.

I curled tighter around my injury. "Fuck you." Tears shot to my eyes. Not again. *Please, not again.* I couldn't handle that pain twice.

I should've agreed to the hand job. I should've got on my knees and performed the blow-job he'd commanded. I should've let him fuck me—even if it meant Jethro would forever remember my willingness to be raped.

That was what Cut whispered, what he'd promised. He'd vowed I would enjoy it. That if I gladly made him hard, if I obediently removed my clothing and spread my legs, he would make me come, moan, beg for more.

I didn't believe him. How could I ever do that? How could I ever betray myself in such a way? But I couldn't trust he wouldn't play my body better than I could control it. I couldn't know if the drug-liquor had left my system entirely, and I wouldn't give in. My options had been submit and let Jethro leave Africa unhurt and alive. Or not agree and watch Cut rip him apart once he'd raped me anyway.

What good were options when they only offered one conclusion?

I'm sorry, Jethro.

He'd come to my rescue only to find Daniel had touched me and I'd touched his father. What a fucked-up situation to be in.

Cut leaned against the table, his fingers tucking my hair behind my ear.

"It's a simple fracture, Nila. You should be thankful I didn't slice you open and insert my diamonds directly into your bloodstream." His touch dropped, tracing an outline on my wrist. "You've kept all limbs. You've retained your precious body. This is merely a means to the final end."

I looked up, shaking with anger. The pain plaited with rage as I stared him down. "One day, someone will do to you what you've done to others. Someday, your crimes will come back to visit you, and I hope I'm there to tell you to be *thankful.*"

Cut scowled. "If that day ever comes, Ms. Weaver, I can safely say you will not be in attendance." Holding out his hand, he snapped, "Now, don't make me ask again. Give me your arm."

I twisted my body away, hugging my broken limb. "No."

"I'm not going to hurt you."

"You already did."

"What does that tell you?"

I didn't reply.

He growled, "It tells you I'll rectify the pain I've caused. I have no doubt after each debt Jethro would've tended to you. Am I right? He would've fixed his wrongs and ensured you were healthy to continue."

My mouth fell open. "You're sick."

I couldn't stop my eyes flying to Jethro. In my haze of pain, I hadn't given him attention. I hadn't seen him thrashing on the floor, desperately trying to get free. I hadn't witnessed him covering himself in mine dust, furious tears tracking mud down his cheeks.

Oh, Kite.

My heart hurt almost as much as my arm.

Cut pointed to the equipment on the table. "Open your eyes, Nila. What do you think this stuff is?"

Despite myself, I looked closer. Before, the items made no sense...now, they began to.

Gauze, water, padding, and medical packets with jargon stating their contents as plaster strips.

A cast.

He's going to make you a cast.

I sniffed, fighting back another wash of agony. "If you're honestly going to set my arm, I want painkillers first."

I expected a scoff and refusal. But Cut merely nodded and opened a small plastic case. Popping out two tablets from a blister foil, he handed them to me with a bottle of water. "They're codeine. You're not allergic, are you?"

I bared my teeth. "Why? You going to care if I have a reaction?"

He frowned. "Despite what I've just done, I want you to remain well. We have a long journey ahead of us, and your pain needs to be managed accordingly—minus any allergies."

I swallowed my fear. "Long journey?"

Cut nodded as I threw the tablets into my mouth and drank. The water slipped down my parched throat like liquid life. I hadn't eaten or drunk in so long. *Too long.* The water splashed in my stomach, reminding me how empty it was.

"I didn't break your arm for fun, Nila." Cut shoved away the plastic container, ripping open a packet of plaster strips a moment later. "I told you.

We smuggle diamonds. We're going home, and I want to take a few high-quality stones with me. They're larger than normal and rare. I want to keep them with me at all times."

"With *you* at all times? Me, you mean?" Another wave of pain made me hiss.

Cut dumped the plaster into the fresh bucket of water. Steam gently rose from the surface.

"Yes, you." He busied himself with opening packets and preparing to set my broken bone. I didn't know what to think. He'd pre-empted this. He'd sat down logically, cool-headedly, and planned to break my arm then gathered enough supplies to fix it in the same location.

Who does that?

The answer dripped with sarcasm. *A Hawk.*

Once his supplies were in order and the plaster reaction had ceased, Cut held up a plastic splint. Three sides, smooth and well formed, with little compartments hidden where my arm would rest.

"Now you know I'm not going to hurt you, will you give me your arm?"

I hugged my wrist, looking at Jethro rejected in the dirt. "Let him go."

Cut looked over his shoulder before glancing back. "No. Now, give me your arm."

Shakes stole my body, shock trying to erase everything that'd happened. "Please, at least untie him."

Jethro looked in pain, squashed on his side. I dreaded to think how he coped with my internal and external screams when Cut broke my arm.

Had he felt it?

Had he lived through it like Vaughn used to whenever I fell and hurt myself?

Shit, Vaughn.

He always knew when I'd broken something. Twin intuition. Would he ache in his right arm in sympathy? Would he terrorize England trying to find me, or worse, stampede Hawksridge Hall trying to save me?

Cut laughed. "Why? So he can stupidly attack me and get himself re-killed in the process?" He rolled his eyes.

It was such a juvenile, simple thing to do that it sent chills scattering down my spine.

His temper thickened. "I won't ask again, Nila. Arm. Now."

The painkillers already siphoned into my blood thanks to no food delaying the absorption. I had no other choice but to let Cut fix me.

Not that there was any fixing me. Not after the past six months.

Gingerly, breathing hard through my nose and hissing through my teeth, I gently laid my arm in the three-sided cast.

Cut tutted. "No, not in there. Not yet." Slipping it free, he opened the opaque ziplock bag and pulled out multiple black velvet pouches. Holding one up, he smiled. "In each of these parcels rests over one million pounds worth of stones—total of five million." His eyes landed on my diamond collar. "Almost as priceless as the gems around your neck."

Meticulously, he slipped the parcels into the sections cut out of the plastic splint. "They'll be hidden. They're not metallic, so they won't set off the alarm, and they won't be inside you, so they won't show up on the body scanners."

Alarms?

Body scanners?

He's going to fly me home and force me to lie to airport security.

A terrified lump lodged in my throat. "They'll catch me."

Cut shook his head. "I have full belief you'll be fine. The nervous sweats will be blamed on the new break. The waxy pallor of your cheeks on overwhelming pain. They might ask you questions, but they won't find anything untoward with the cast. You'll see."

Tears prickled my eyes at the trials I still faced. My lips twisted with hate. "You could've just put me in a fake cast. No one would know the difference."

Cut cupped my face, holding me firm. "Wrong. People can tell. Liars are spotted easily in airports. And besides, we'll have an extra arsenal that will prove our tale isn't false."

I ripped out of his hold, gasping at more pain. "What's that?"

Cut inspected inside the bucket, lifting out the plaster strips to rest in a plastic tray. "We'll have x-rays stating your accident, evidence of the fracture, and time and date."

My eyes widened. "How?" I scoffed at the dirty cave. "You're telling me you have a state of the art x-ray machine down here, too?" A half-crazed, half-diabolical laugh escaped me. "Not only a diamond smuggler but doctor, biker president, and doting father as well. Is there anything you can't do?"

Cut narrowed his eyes. "Careful, Nila. Just because you're in pain, it doesn't mean I can't discipline you. I demand respect at all times. You'd do well to remember that while we travel home together. When you go through security, I'll be with you. When you board and land, I'll be beside you. You won't be free and you'd be wise to hold your tongue." He pointed a finger at Jethro. "Otherwise, he doesn't live like I promised. Obey me, and he survives. Pull something stupid and he dies." He shrugged. "Stupidly simple."

Stupidly simple?

How about I kill you on the plane?

That would be stupid as I'd end up in jail for the rest of my life. But so simple because Cut would no longer be breathing.

I laughed sarcastically. "Sounds as if you've thought of everything."

His forehead furrowed, but he didn't respond. Instead, he ignored me in favour of inserting the diamond packets and layering soft padding over the compartments. Even if airport security shone a light or poked a stick in my cast, they wouldn't find the stones.

Cut held up the tampered cast. "*Now* you can place your arm inside."

My heart raced, but I did as I was told, breathing a sigh of relief as the gentle cushioning helped soothe some of the pain.

Cut grinned. "See, I told you I'd make it right."

My voice transformed into scissors, cutting him into pieces. "Just because you're tending to me now doesn't mean I forgive you for before."

Jethro groaned, dragging my attention to him. His beautiful golden eyes were dull and anger-filled. Love linked us together, forged stronger despite such adversity.

He'd proposed to me.

I'd say yes to him.

Yet, horribly, time was running out.

Once Cut had immobilized my injury, I had no doubt we wouldn't be in Africa much longer. He would want to get home. He would want to finish whatever else he'd planned.

Will he carry out the Final Debt before he partakes in the Third?

I shuddered. How wrong was it that I hoped he would kill me instead of rape me? I should value my life over anything my body was subjected to. But having Cut inside me wouldn't just be physical; it would be mental and spiritual, too. It would mess me up completely knowing he'd been with my mother and killed her. Then done the same with me.

I'll kill him before that happens.

The memory of stabbing Daniel in the heart granted me a much-needed boost. I'd been terrified of him. Yet, I'd won. I could do the same with Cut.

Cut pressed down on my arm, making me cry out with pain. I flinched, trying to pull away. "Stop!"

His strong fingers ceased tormenting me. "Just making sure you're wedged comfortably."

"Bastard." The curse fell beneath my breath.

If Cut heard me, he didn't retaliate.

Letting me go, he layered another lot of padding on top of my arm, followed by the gauze. He wrapped it around and around, binding my arm into its new prison. Once it was secure, he placed surgical gloves on his fingers, and pulled out a strip of plaster from the drying tray.

"Don't move."

I didn't respond as he industriously wrapped warm, wet plaster around my broken limb. The chemical reaction offered hot comfort to the throbbing ache, and I relaxed a little as the painkillers worked their magic.

It didn't take long. In the past, the doctors would wrap three or four layers of plaster around my cast, ensuring no way could I break or damage myself further. However, Cut only wrapped two layers, finishing off the top with a gauze sleeve, smoothing the plaster with wet fingers.

"There. Don't twist or move your arm for sixty minutes while it hardens."

I wanted to laugh. He knew how to apply basic medical help. But his bedside manner was atrocious. No doctor had ever caused his patient's injury in the first place.

Sitting upright after leaning forward for Cut to work on my cast, I held it away from me to dry but wanted to hug it close. For some reason, a hug—even from me—helped the pain fade.

My eyes soared to Jethro. His face was red and furious; his eyes glassy with sorrow.

I'm fine.

You're not.

I'll live.

You better.

I smiled at the last silent message. I would live because I deserved to. Jethro, too. We would find each other again—even with imminent separation about to tear us apart.

Washing his hands in a fresh bucket of water, Cut smiled at his handiwork. "All done." His eyes glinted. "How does it feel to be a millionaire with so many diamonds against your skin?"

I tapped the collar condescendingly. "Like I've felt ever since Jethro put the Weaver Wailer on me."

I looked at Jethro shooting an apology. *I didn't mean that in a bad way.*

He squeezed his eyes, flinching against the memories of our fucked-up beginning.

Cut nodded. "That's a fair comment. You've worn more diamonds than most Hawks in their lifetimes." He cocked his head at Jethro. "Did you notice Kite's lapel pin? That two carat diamond was handed down for generations. I gave it to him on his sixteenth birthday when he assured me he had his condition under tight control. I wanted nothing more than to believe him." His voice softened. "I know you can't comprehend it, but I do love my son, Nila. More than you'll know."

I snorted. "Did you love Kes when you shot him? Or Daniel when you let him grow up believing he was an unwanted mistake?"

Cut froze. "What do you know about that?"

Unwittingly, I handed weight to my previous lie. "I told you. We shared the night together. He shared a little of his past. He opened up to me because I gave him what he needed."

Jethro didn't move on the floor.

For the first time, Cut paused. His eyes narrowed as his brain mulled over my answer. He looked unsure...contemplating it might be the truth, after all.

I doubted he would ever find Daniel's remains. I might get away with his murder, all thanks to a hunting party of lionesses.

I never knew nature can be such a competent alias.

"Regardless, when Daniel is found, I'll learn the truth and shall decide on your punishment." Cut dried his hands and ran both through his white hair. "Now the Fourth Debt has been paid, it's time for us to depart."

Striding across the cave, he squatted by Jethro and swatted his son's dirty cheek. "Make yourself at home. I'll give the staff instructions to release you once we've been at Hawksridge for a few days and there's no way for you to interfere." Standing, he smiled at me. "All you have to do, Nila, is get through security with my diamonds still in your possession and your lover will remain alive. That's not too much to ask, is it?"

I slid off the chair, wobbling a little with vertigo and residual pain.

Moving toward Jethro, I ached to hug him, kiss him, tell him I loved him and always would. But Cut stopped me half way, planting a stern hand on my breastbone. "No. Say your goodbyes from a distance."

I shook my head. "Why can't I touch him? What harm can it do?"

Cut clenched his jaw. "More harm than I'd like."

"You know I have no weapons to give him." My temper surged. "You know I have a broken arm and am suffering a serious case of shock. Let me say a proper goodbye. You *owe* me that."

Cut breathed hard, preventing my path. But slowly, he nodded. "Fine."

The minute he'd cleared my trajectory, I rushed forward and landed on my knees. My good hand tugged at the awful duct tape around Jethro's mouth. "Breathe." That was all the warning I gave him.

With a quick rip, I tore the stickiness away from his five o' clock shadow and yanked out the disgusting gag.

He hacked and spluttered, sucking in a noisy breath.

Cut stomped forward, towering over me. "Nila fucking Weaver—"

I glared at him, balling the sodden gag and throwing it at his face. My left arm never had strong coordination, and the toss ended up soaring past his cheek. "He can barely breathe. Shut up! Letting him talk won't change things, you monster."

"Needle—" Jethro coughed, spittle landing on his chin.

Needle.

The name I'd asked him to call me so many months ago when I didn't know he was Kite007. Tears sprang to my eyes. "I'm here."

I wished I could sit him upright, but he'd broken the chair and without cutting the ropes, I couldn't help him.

God, I hate this. All of this.

Jethro smiled, grimacing with pain. "Fuck, Nila, I'm—"

I placed a shaking finger over his dried lips. "Don't. I know."

We shared an endless look, weighted with past and present. The unsaid words sank into my soul like a heavy anchor, lodging itself in my heart forever.

Bending over him, I brushed my lips against his temple. His bloody temple from the car crash. How badly was he injured? His forehead still burned from his fever and the gunshot wound on his side hadn't scabbed.

He needs help. And fast.

Glancing at Cut, I begged, "Please, bring him with us. He needs a doctor."

Cut crossed his arms. "He'll stay here until I say."

"But—"

"No fucking buts." Holding out his hand, Cut snapped, "You've said goodbye. Time to go."

"No!"

Cut towered higher. "The longer you deny what will happen—regardless of your willingness—the longer Jethro has to go without medical help." He cocked his head. "Does that encourage you now? Knowing you have the power to get him much-needed attention by behaving?"

I hated I had the power to save the man I loved by obeying the man I hated.

Gritting my teeth, I looked down at Jethro one last time. "I have to go."

He shook his head, his lungs rattling and wet. "No."

"I love you, Kite."

His eyes glossed with fear. "Nila…don't. This isn't the end. I don't care what he says. I'm coming after you. I'll stop the Final Debt. I promise." He shook hard in his binds. "I fucking promise, I'll stop it. You're mine. I won't let the Debt Inheritance have you. I won't!"

His pouring unhappiness and despair cracked my heart. I couldn't let him drain himself of whatever reserves he had left. Cupping his cheek with my good hand, I guided his face to mine.

I never closed my eyes and neither did he as I kissed him.

His lips parted, his tongue threaded with mine, and we agreed he would fight for me. He would chase me. And who knew, maybe he would save me one last time.

Cut shattered our moment, yanking me away from Jethro and dragging me toward the exit. My arm bellowed, but it was nothing compared to the internal shattering at leaving Jethro behind.

At the door, Cut pulled me closer and I staggered in grey imbalance, imprinting Jethro on my soul forever.

His chin cocked, keeping me in his sights for as long as he could. "Don't give up, Nila. It's not over."

Silent tears dripped from my eyelashes as Cut shoved me out the door and separated me from my soul-mate.

    The door closed behind me.

    Tears fell faster.

    Pain billowed thicker.

    And all I could do was whisper, *"Goodbye."*

Jethro

"FUCK!"

The door closed. Nila was gone. I remained crumpled on the floor like a discarded fucking prisoner.

I'd been in worse binds.

Have I?

I liked to think I had and overcome them. That I would overcome *this*. But how?

My stomach hadn't unknotted since Cut started his creepy history lesson and worked up to the most horrendous thing I'd ever witnessed.

The slam of the mallet on the love of my life's arm. The scream as her bone broke.

I shuddered.

It won't remain the worst thing you've ever witnessed if you don't get your arse off the floor.

The Final Debt.

Jasmine had said Cut planned to carry it out before the week was finished. The moment he returned to Hawksridge, Nila would be dead.

Ferocity spread through my veins, and for the millionth time, I wriggled and struggled, trying so fucking hard to get free.

The ropes around my ankles had slid off the chair legs, but my wrists and torso remained tight.

Think. There must be something you can do.

Forcing my breathing to calm, I glanced around the cave. The table with remnants of cast-making equipment was too far away. I might be able to shuffle with the chair attached to my body, but it would waste valuable time and energy. Besides, Cut hadn't used any sharp implements and the knife he'd utilised to slice Nila free had disappeared with him in his back pocket.

Kes.

It was times like this—when I'd fucked up and couldn't see a way free—that he'd come to my rescue. He always came. Always answered his phone if I'd had a relapse, or shared a beer with me when I needed his welcome support.

Kes was the only one I knew who could regulate and calm his emotions to the point of soothing rather than a battering ram. I didn't know how he did it but being around him was the opposite of being around others.

I miss you, brother.

The door opened.

My eyes shot to it, my heart leaping with hope.

Nila...

Only, it wasn't Nila.

Marquise stomped inside. His burly size and Black Diamond leather jacket blocked the exit as he turned and relocked the door. He didn't say a word, merely raised an eyebrow in my direction and sat in the chair Nila had when Cut broke her arm.

He. Broke. Her. Arm.

Motherfucking *bastard.*

I'd felt her pain, bewilderment, and terror as the mallet crushed her. I'd felt her fear that she wouldn't make it through airport security with the bushel of diamonds in her cast.

I wanted to tell her to scream when she boarded the plane. Let the pilots know she had contraband and ought to be detained. If she was caught, they'd hold her, possibly convict her, and she'd remain alive in prison until I could figure out a way to free her.

If she was locked up, Cut couldn't kill her, and I could hire the best attorneys to dismiss her case. I could show the entire world what my family had been up to. I could rip open the truth and finally, *finally* show what money could do.

What loyalties it could buy.

What sins it could cover up.

How happy middle-class families were duped by the few who held the wealth of the globe.

If it meant I'd go to jail, so be it.

At least my conscience would finally be clear and Nila would be alive.

And Cut would rot right beside me in an eight by eight cell, never seeing his precious Hawksridge or diamonds again.

The daydream shattered as I twisted to glare at Marquise. I couldn't get free on my own. But he could help me.

"Free me and I'll pay you two million pounds." I tugged on the ropes around my wrists, inhaling hard against the bruising binds across my chest. The car accident battered me and my vision hadn't stopped spluttering with the massive headache. I hadn't kept my promise to pay the driver who'd brought me here, and I hadn't done what I'd vowed by rescuing Nila.

This entire trip had been one big fuck up. However, I would trade ever feeling whole again, every good thing I'd ever done, if I could rewind time and stop Cut from breaking Nila's arm.

Marquise grinned. "Your grandmother has paid me far more for my loyalty." Crossing his arms, he glared. "Stop talking. I won't let you go for any amount."

"What about a title? An estate of your own? Shares in our companies?" I spat the lingering taste from my tongue thanks to the awful gag. "Everyone has a price. Name it."

Marquise inspected his ragged fingernails as if he was a fucking king on his throne. "I'll get all of that if I remain true to Bonnie." He sniffed. "So shut the fuck up."

I exhaled heavily. For now, he wouldn't budge, but he would. I just had to find his weakness. Everyone could be bought. We'd learned that prime example through years of bribery and control.

My mind returned to Nila and Cut, keeping count of time and distance slowly separating us.

I have to get free.

A shrill tune ripped around the cave.

Marquise slouched and pulled out his phone. He stabbed the screen, holding it to his ear. "Yes?"

Silence as he listed to instructions.

"Still on the floor and tied up. Yes, will do. Got it."

He hung up, a sinister smile spreading his lips. "Looks like you should get comfortable, Hawk. Got orders not to let you up until the Prez is on a plane. And then…he wants me to give you an extra special surprise."

Of course…

I didn't expect Cut to let me survive—not after trying to kill me. He might have a sick fascination with making me survive in a world where Nila didn't exist, but he understood the moment I was free, the moment I had a chance, he would be dead.

It was only a matter of time if he let me live.

He won't let me live…

I clenched my jaw. "What's the surprise?"

I already know.

Pain and then death.

Cut wasn't overly original.

Marquise clenched his fists, showing scabbed knuckles and ropy forearms. "You'll see."

CUT GRIPPED MY unbroken arm tighter, hauling me faster through the airport.

He'd manhandled me and corralled me ever since we'd left Jethro in the mine and flew by Jeep to a small doctor's surgery on the outskirts of Gaborone.

While the African doctor nodded and smiled and arranged my arm for x-rays, Cut had washed his face and changed his clothes, discarding the dirt-smudged jeans and white shirt in favour of black slacks and shirt.

The doctor didn't remove my cast, and he didn't show me the x-rays once the decrepit machine had whirred and snapped grainy pictures of what Cut had done to me.

Once the large black and white images were tucked safely into his briefcase, Cut allowed me five minutes to wash as best I could in the surgery's small bathroom. The blood from Daniel and the car accident siphoned down the plug hole, revealing scratches and bruises in their colourful glory.

I had no makeup to cover the marks and no choice but to change into whatever clothing Cut had grabbed from my suitcase on the way out from *Almasi Kipanga*.

Unfortunately, he hadn't selected any of the clothing I'd artistically amended, leaving me without scalpels or knitting needles, leaving me vulnerable.

The one good thing about the doctor's surgery was the sweet-eyed man gave me a homemade honey muesli bar—either noticing the way I ogled his sandwich sitting on his desk as he x-rayed me or the wobbles of weakness as Cut dragged me outside.

I didn't think much of his practice, considering he didn't check if my arm was set correctly, or there was nothing majorly damaged inside, but I inhaled the food offering before Cut could snatch it away.

With Cut's timeline, he envisioned my head in a basket within a few days. Who cared if my arm was set wrong? It wouldn't be needed much longer.

That's what you fear.

But it isn't what will happen.

I curled my fingers, testing the pain level of the break. My grip was weak, and it burned to move, but I still had mobility. My fingers still worked, which I was thankful for. I couldn't stomach the thought of never being able to sew again or hold intricate needles and lace.

Cut had stolen so much—he couldn't steal my entire livelihood and skill, too.

"Hurry up." Cut pulled harder.

I staggered beside him, breathing hard as every footstep jarred my aching arm. The pain resonated beneath muscle and skin, a hot discomfort stripping me of energy.

The moment we'd arrived at the airport, Cut had abandoned the Jeep in a long-term car park and only bothered to carry his briefcase. At the time, I wondered if we'd be questioned for suspicious behaviour travelling long-haul with no luggage. But I'd rolled my eyes and hid my snort.

This was Cut Hawk.

This part of Africa *belonged* to him—no doubt the airport security would belong to him, too.

"For God's sake, Weaver." Cut slowed, forcing my half-trotting, half-lagging footsteps to fall in line with his. "We'll miss the plane."

Fresh throbs brought scratchy tears to my eyes.

"I want to miss the plane. I want to go back for Jethro."

The entire travel I couldn't stop thinking of Kite. Of him bleeding and feverish tied to a chair. Of him having no choice but to watch as I was taken.

The muesli bar I'd eaten roiled in my stomach. "You'll keep him alive…won't you? You'll keep your promise not to hurt him."

Cut smiled coyly. "I wouldn't worry your pretty head about it. Soon, trivial things like that won't matter to you."

The veiled hint at my death should terrify me. I should fight and scream and act like a terrorist to prevent boarding the plane. But the fear of interrogation and imprisonment kept me silent.

Cut was insane, but there was only one of him. One beating heart to stab. One life to extinguish. If the police took me, I wouldn't know who or how to fight. I'd be alone.

Yes, but you might stay alive.

Perhaps in England I would cause a fuss. But not here. I didn't trust the Hawk's power in Africa. Cut might have the means to murder me even in the custody of the law. Buy a cop—arrange a convenient suicide in my cell.

No, I'll wait.

I would return to England, to my home, to a land I knew and could gamble my life with better odds.

Checking us in, Cut never let me go as the agent handed over our passports and boarding passes. Dark-skinned security and airport personnel didn't look our way as Cut guided me roughly through customs and immigration to the baggage x-ray.

The closer we got to the metal detector, the more my heart galloped.

Don't think about the diamonds.

Cut whispered in my ear, his fingers digging into my bicep. "If you bring unwanted attention or do anything stupid, I've given Marquise strict orders to make Jethro pay."

I shivered, joining the queue to pass through the detector.

My heart permanently relocated into my mouth as my turn fast approached and I held my broken arm protectively. I didn't know if I hugged it for the pain or the illegal diamonds. Either way, the flush and wax of my skin played right into Cut's masquerade that I was under the weather from agony rather than smuggling.

The woman officer smiled, waving me forward. "Come through, ma'am."

I shuffled through the arch, cringing as it beeped.

"Stand there." The woman came closer, waving her wand over my front and back.

I squeezed my eyes, expecting her to detain me. Terrified she'd find the millions of pounds worth of diamonds and sentence me to death by hanging.

What would be better? Hanging or guillotine?

What kind of morbid thought is that?

Cut stepped through without setting off the alarm and gave me a smirk as he collected his briefcase off the x-ray belt. He stood close by, not interfering as the woman did one more pass and the wand failed to beep.

She dropped her arm, waving for me to go. "Have a nice flight."

"Uh—uh, thanks." I scurried forward, sweat dripping down my spine with nerves. An itch developed on my forearm beneath the cast, slowly driving me mad as Cut placed his hand on the small of my back and guided me into the departure lounge.

"See, wasn't so bad, was it?" He spoke quietly, not making eye contact as we dodged travel-weary passengers.

My uninjured hand ached from holding the cast. I wished I could keep it close to me but not have to hold it. Wait…

That was what was missing.

I stopped in the centre of the duty-free shop we'd cut through. "A sling. I need a sling."

Cut frowned. "What?"

I held up my arm. "It hurts. I need to keep it close so it doesn't bump or dangle, but my other shoulder is sore from the car accident. I need a sling."

When his lips curled with dismissal, I rushed, "Besides, a sling will only add evidence to the break. It doesn't have to be much. Just something to give me some relief."

Cut scowled, his throat working as he swallowed. "Fine." Storming toward a bookshop, he quickly bought me a canvas tote bag and asked the sales clerk to cut it straight down the centre.

Guiding me from the store, he quickly cradled my arm with the sliced tote and knotted the handles around my side and shoulder, creating an imperfect but practical sling. The ease and quickness in which he'd done such a tender thing made me freeze.

If I was honest, I hadn't expected him to listen, let alone *help* me.

"You—you—" I looked away, hating him but grateful. "Thank you."

Cut stiffened, his golden eyes meeting mine. "I wouldn't thank me, Ms. Weaver. You know I didn't do it out of concern for your well-being."

Now that my other hand was free, I pushed hair out of my eyes and relaxed a little. "No, but you can't hide there's more to you than just a crazy man hell-bent on ruling everyone."

He smirked, the skin by his eyes crinkling. "You might have figured out Daniel, but you'll never figure me out, so don't bother." Stepping closer, we formed a little island as flowing passengers darted around us. The fear for Jethro and the nervousness in my gut layered my aching muscles, but I didn't move back. I didn't show a weakness that Cut's proximity irked and irritated.

His gaze fell to my lips. "You're strong, Nila. I'll give you that. You remind me so much of Emma that it's sometimes hard to remember you aren't mine. That you aren't *her*. You might think it would be a good thing for me to think of you kindly, but it wouldn't, believe me." He lowered his voice. "Your mother ripped out my heart before I cut off her head. And nothing will give me more pleasure than doing the same to Jethro and you."

My lungs stuck together, unable to gather oxygen.

Cut cocked his head, smiling at my dumbfoundedness. "Why does that continue to shock you? Why do you, even now, still look for the good in others?" Patting my hand, he looped his fingers through mine and pulled me back into motion. "You should know by now no one is what they say they are, and everyone deserves to pay for something. People have been covering up or blaming their mistakes on others for centuries. I take control of mine. I do the best I can to better myself and I refuse to let you or anyone else stand in my way."

I didn't speak—what could I say to that?

We moved through the large departure gate, heading toward the plane.

Cut smiled as he pulled out our documentation for the gate staff. His gaze met mine. "This is the easy part." Handing over the boarding passes, Cut guided me down the air bridge, keeping me close to him, controlling me at all times. "It's the stress of landing that's the hard part."

Landing.

English security.

Maximum penalties for lies and incorrect declarations.

Marching onto the plane, we moved down the aisle, through first class, through business, right into the dregs of economy.

Cut pushed me into a row with a window and aisle seat. "Sit."

I sat.

Stretching, he placed his briefcase in the overhead lockers before sitting smoothly and unhurriedly beside me.

The moment he settled, I asked, "Why a commercial airline? Why not the private jet we flew in on?"

"Why do you think? Because the private plane would be far too easy. This way is much harder."

My eyes widened. "Harder?"

"Harder on you." His voice lowered into a threat. "This way you have to sit with hundreds of strangers, wondering if they suspect you. You'll have to hide your fear when we land and lie through your teeth when they question you. The stress of being watched, of being surrounded by countless people, of having to lie—it's to show you how hard it is to transport a secret. You'll value the cost so much more."

Reclining, his long legs spread out in front of him. "You'll learn what it's like to protect something so precious by any means necessary."

I swallowed. "You forget I don't care about your diamonds. I don't care if they find them."

His eyes narrowed. "It's not the diamonds I'm talking about, Nila. It's my firstborn rotting in *Almasi Kipanga* watched over by Marquise. You fail, and he dies in the most horrifying ways. You win, he lives even when you die. It's a fair trade—don't you think?"

I bit my lip against the torrent of hate and helplessness.

I couldn't reply. It would be an explosion of retorts and profanity.

Reaching between our wedged hips, he yanked out one end of my seatbelt.

"Now, buckle up, Nila. You can never be too safe."

"I'll never be safe as long as you're alive."

I will kill you.

I'll find a way.

His eyes darkened. "Careful."

"Why are you doing this?"

Cut smiled, looking the perfect distinguished gentleman travelling on business. "Because William Hawk smuggled his wealth numerous times. He completed his grandmother's legacy, but despite his hard work and terrible history, the king wasn't satisfied with taking half of his profits, he wanted it all."

Cut gathered tension around him, suffocating me. "So William went one step further. He gave the king his dues, he paid taxes, indulged in bribery, and ensconced himself in the good graces of the court, but he managed to keep the exact location of our family's mine a secret.

"And the stones, well, he used extra ships he purchased to smuggle quantities the king could never contemplate. He sacrificed millions in order to cement his place, but he also saved untold wealth by being smarter than the pompous arse on the throne."

Another flush of agony washed over me from my arm. I hugged the cast, slipping it free from the sling to rub the gauze, wishing I could rub the pounding break beneath. "I don't care what you think. I don't care how much money or power you have. One day, karma will catch up and make you pay."

Cut ran his hands through his hair, smoothing the white strands into snow perfection. "You can make empty threats all you want, Ms. Weaver, but the truth will forever stand."

"What truth?"

"The truth you can't make someone pay when they're completely untouchable."

I tore my eyes from his, glaring out the window.

Oh, but that's where you're wrong.

Your son was a prince to your empire, untouchable, unkillable—a Hawk.

Yet, I touched him.

I killed him.

I murdered him.

And I'll murder you, too.

One hour into the flight.

I groaned in agony as the pressure of the cabin swelled my broken arm.

* * *

Two hours into the flight.

Food was served. Some overly microwaved rubbery concoction with salad and a slimy strawberry cheesecake. I devoured the entire tray, even the hard-as-a-brick bread roll. Food helped replace a small piece of the emptiness inside me.

* * *

Three hours.

I squirmed beside Cut dying for pain-killers. He barricaded me in, sitting in his aisle seat like my jailer. My bladder protested and my thoughts swam with

Jethro.

* * *

Four hours.

I lost my promise not to cause issues and pressed the button for an air-hostess. Cut glowered when the woman with coiffed red hair appeared. Ignoring him, I begged for some Panadol, some Advil, anything to lessen my pain.

She looked at Cut.

He shook his head.

I never did get my painkillers.

* * *

Five hours.

I stared out the window, counting stars, following wisps of clouds and pleading with the universe to keep Jethro safe.

"Stop fidgeting." Cut narrowed his eyes at my tapping fingers and dancing legs.

"Let me walk the cabin. I need to stretch."

And use the bathroom.

His jaw twitched. "Five minutes, Nila. If you're any longer, or I suspect you're disobeying me, I'll give you a taste of Diamond Dust."

"Diamond Dust?"

His lips curled. "You remember...the drug Jethro gave you from Milan? The magical substance that turns you mute and obedient while you can scream all you want in the inside?"

I gulped.

I completed my stretches and a bathroom break in four minutes.

* * *

Six.

Seven.

Eight.

Nine.

Ten hours.

Clammy sweat broke out over my skin. Adrenaline drenched my system the closer we flew to England. The cast itched with hot imprisonment, eerily heavy with its tormenting cargo. Lack of sleep clouded my mind and I swore the facets and sharp edges of diamonds burrowed their way into my flesh, gnawing me like a worm gnawed an apple.

* * *

Eleven hours.

The captain announced our upcoming arrival. Breakfast was served and cleared away in record time. Cut smiled and patted my hand. "Almost there, my dear. Almost home."

I cringed, looking out the window.

I just want this to be over.

* * *

Eleven hours and forty minutes.

The plane left clouds for earth, flying me toward my greatest challenge and worst debt yet. It wasn't my pain on the line. It wasn't Vaughn's like the night with the dice. It was Jethro's.

The man I'd willingly given my heart to. The man I said I would marry. The man who needed me as much as I needed him.

If I failed, he would die.

And not just die but be tortured until he begged for death.

My ears popped and my arm distended as the airplane tyres skimmed the horizon before skidding onto tarmac.

I didn't speak as we taxied to the gate. Cut filled in arrival cards, running his fingers possessively over my passport.

My stomach performed circus tricks and trapeze stunts as the air-bridge attached and the flight attendants announced we could disembark. Passengers exploded into action, grabbing cases, children, and blocking the aisle in their rush to leave.

None of them were aware of what a monumental task sat before me.

Stay calm.

Don't think about what's in your cast.

Cut grinned, standing upright and holding out his hand. "Ready, Nila?"

I longed to scream and tell the truth. I wished I could tell everyone what I smuggled. If they knew, perhaps they could take away the worry that I wouldn't make it.

Jethro.

Think of Jethro.

You'll do this because of Jethro.

Standing, I took Cut's hand for balance and followed the other passengers onto English soil.

"Miss?"

Shit. Shit. *Shit.*

I turned slowly, doing my best to swallow my nerves. "Yes?"

"You don't have any hand luggage to put on the x-ray belt?"

I blinked, holding up the line waiting to go through the body scanner. The new equipment did a better job than the metal detector in Africa. Upgraded facilities, shrewd airport staff, and suspecting officers kept my heart permanently lodged in my throat.

"Oh, no. No bag."

The middle-aged security guard wrinkled his forehead. "No luggage on a long-haul trip?"

My stomach hurled itself against internal organs, knotting with kidney and spleen. "Well, I—"

"She's with me." Cut slung his black briefcase onto the conveyor belt, raising his eyebrow as if daring him to deny it.

I froze.

Why had he come to my rescue? Wasn't it his intention to make me sweat? To give him reasons to hurt Jethro? *Not that he needs a reason.*

The man eyed Cut, taking in his expensive clothes and white hair demanding respect. "Okay…" He glanced back at me, beckoning me to step into the round chamber with its curved glass and two footsteps painted on the floor. "Hold your arms above your head and wait until I tell you to move."

Tears sprang to my eyes. Tears of fear. Tears of pain.

I pointed to my tote bag sling. "I—I just broke my arm. I can't—"

The man behind me snapped my forearm with a mallet.

He's going to kill me when we return to his home.

Help me…

No sympathy glowed in his eyes. "Do the best you can."

Jethro.

I still had his fate in my hands. I couldn't falter.

Swallowing my racing heart, I slipped the cast free and raised my arms as best I could. Blood pressure throbbed in my fingertips and shooting pain bolted down my forearm. A terrible image of diamonds spilling out the end of the cast had me swallow a gasp-cough.

Closing my eyes, I waited as a two large sensors swung around me with the whirring noise of rotor blades.

"Thank you. Come out, please."

I obeyed, forcing my legs to remain firm and not buckle. Standing beside the man as the screen lit up with an image of a nondescript person, he frowned as black splotches appeared on the screen where my cast, my bra, and diamond collar were.

The officer cleared his throat. "Miss, you'll have to undergo a pat down." Looking behind him, he said, "Jean, can you help this lady?" He sidestepped, giving room for the female staff member to move into my personal space with her rubber gloves and judgemental stare.

"Do you wish to go into a private room?" Her voice screeched across my nerves.

A private room.

I could tell her what Cut did. I could inform her of what I carried. I could destroy not just my life, but Jethro's, too.

Cut met my eyes through the scanner. He hadn't gone through yet. He didn't say a word, crossing his arms, waiting for my decision.

I bit my lip. "No, here is fine."

"Alright." Clasping her hands, she ordered, "I need you to spread your legs and hold your arms out to the side."

Other passengers milled around, slyly watching as they grabbed their bags and slipped into shoes and jackets.

I did my best to comply, but my arm burned. God, how it burned.

Without asking for permission, she swept swift hands from my wrists to my shoulders and down the front of my chest. My white jumper with a unicorn in the same grey colours of Moth gave way beneath her touch. Her fingers pried at the underwire of my bra, ensuring there was nothing hidden. Skimming my leggings, she returned to my chest and slipped her fingers beneath my diamond collar.

I held my breath, forcing myself not to choke as she tugged a little, running her touch right around my neck.

She pursed her lips. "You'll have to take the sling off. I want to x-ray it."

I awkwardly shrugged out of it, passing it to her one-handedly.

She placed it onto a tray and gave it to another guard to run it through the x-ray machine.

"I'll also need to see inside your cast." Pulling free a torch from the arsenal on her belt, she said, "Stand to the side and hold out your arm."

Air suddenly turned to soup.

Tears pricked as I handed over my broken limb, throbbing with the crime of diamonds.

Cut was wrong.

A cast didn't offer sympathy these days. Perhaps in the past it had. Once upon a time, the sign of weakness and pain might've allowed a trafficker free range to import whatever they wanted by tucking a parcel of contraband in a fake cast. But not anymore. People had no empathy these days. High on their careers and pompous on their commitment to protect the borders—any shred of compassion had disappeared beneath strict training and no-nonsense.

I stiffened as the woman bent closer, her torch illuminating the inside of my cast. Could she see? Did the sparkle of diamonds glitter through the plaster?

Cut came through the body scanner, cleared by the male officer. He never took his eyes off me as he collected his briefcase and my sling from the conveyer belt. Coming closer, he pulled free the envelope the African doctor had given him before we boarded. "I have the x-ray if you need it. She's my daughter-in-law." Yanking out the images of my abused arm, he shoved it at the woman currently peering down my cast.

She pulled back, frowning. "I didn't ask for evidence. The signs of pain are obvious."

Cut smiled smugly. I knew his thoughts—they glowed in his eyes. *I told you people could see a faker from the truth.*

Dropping her torch, she inspected the x-ray quickly. The light of the airport showed what Cut had done to my arm with clear precision.

Stupidly, I'd hoped Cut had been wrong. That the mallet had only severely bruised me. That the snapping sound I heard wasn't an internal structure giving way, merely a movement of the table.

However, the image clearly showed a clean break on one of the two bones in my forearm. The two pieces hadn't separated, but the large shadow was enough to make me faint. Cut obviously had practice. The fracture would knit together, eventually.

Won't it?

He'd broken me, and I hadn't had proper doctor care.

Would it need to be reset? How long did something like that take to heal? I squeezed my eyes. *Will I die with this fracture?*

"How did you hurt your arm, Miss?" The officer pursed her red-painted lips.

My heart fluttered as fear ran amok. "I don't—I'm not—"

Jethro.

Lie better.

Cut crossed his arms, crunching the x-ray in his grip.

"I—I fell." Standing taller, I sucked in a breath. "My father-in-law and I were on a safari. One of those open top, no door Jeeps. I didn't listen to the guide and we went over a gully and bounced quite hard." I dropped my eyes. "I fell out of the car and broke my arm."

Cut laughed. "Kids. Can't teach them survival skills these days."

Annoyance painted her face. "Sir, I'm going to have to ask you to step back." The woman pointed toward baggage claim. "Your daughter-in-law will catch up with you when she's finished here."

I narrowed my eyes.

Morbidly, I didn't want him to go. I didn't want to give him any reason to hurt Jethro. He'd bolstered my tale, given x-rays with evidence. I wasn't delusional to think it was to keep me from breaking my promise to Kite.

All he cared about were the diamonds stuffed in my cast—smuggling his own wealth to avoid taxes and government thresholds.

My stomach twisted.

He would cut off my head before Jethro managed to find a way to chase me back to England. And Jethro would have to live every day knowing that he failed.

That fate was worse than death.

My shoulders slouched as a rogue tear escaped my control.

The airport officer softened. "It's okay."

Cut moved a few steps away, always watching, always controlling.

"Is there anything you want to tell me, Miss?" The woman widened her eyes. I guessed she tried to come across as sympathetic and helpful, but it only made her more duplicitous.

I shook my head. "No, I'm just in pain, that's all."

Holding up the sling Cut had passed back to me, I asked, "Can I put this back on?"

She paused for a long moment, eyeing up my cast while chewing on the inside of her cheek.

She's going to arrest me.

She's going to lock me up and Cut will hurt him.

Finally, she nodded. "I hope you get better soon." Turning off her torch, she waved me through. "Go on. Get home and sleep. You look positively drawn out."

"I will."

Unfortunately, I had no idea how many hours I had to breathe. I wouldn't sleep...I wouldn't waste a minute. After all, I wouldn't wake from death—the longest sleep imaginable.

I gave her a watery smile, trudging in Cut's footsteps toward the exit.

I've won but at what cost?

Cut's diamonds had entered England undetected, and I'd just condemned Jethro to a life of hell when I paid the Final Debt.

Jethro

NO MATTER WHAT I offered Marquise, he didn't bite.

He flat-out fucking ignored me, tapping on his phone, sitting like a troll in the corner. I hated he had reception down here. It used to be that being metres beneath the ground there would be no signal, but that was before technology and routers and modems.

My shoulder screamed for mercy like it had for the past few hours. My neck ached from lolling on the floor and my headache flickered with hazy tiredness.

I wanted to sleep but couldn't.

If I were concussed—which I feared I was from the car accident—I couldn't afford not to wake up. I had to keep going. Keep trying.

Blood slicked my wrists from trying to get free. I'd hoped, once I broke the skin, that the crimson lubrication would help me. If anything, it'd just clogged the twine and wrapped it tighter.

Nila.

Was she on a plane now?

Had Cut helped her through security?

"What time do I get my surprise?" My voice tore through the stagnant silence. We hadn't talked since Marquise informed me of Cut's final plan.

I had no doubt my time was running out. I would remember the pain I was currently in with fondness once Marquise started delivering.

Marquise looked up from the glowing screen in his hands. "Eager to begin?"

"Eager to leave." I cleared my throat, desperate for some water. Not that I'd ask him for some. He'd only taunt and torture. "Come on. Name your price."

He chuckled. "You don't have a clue, do you? You think you're in charge. You're not. I know the way your family's wealth moves. Bonnie is the one with full jurisdiction and she's the one I work for. You have no money—it's controlled by your tiny grandmother, and I bet that pisses you the fuck off."

I clenched my jaw. "She's old. How much longer do you think she'll last?"

Marquise shrugged. "Alive or dead, it doesn't matter. I'm written into her Will. Loyalty is what she bought and loyalty is what she'll get." His eyes dropped to his phone. "Now shut the fuck up and prepare yourself for all the fun we'll have."

I fell silent. Not because he told me to, but because my energy levels were dangerously low. I had to be smart. I had to find a way out of this godforsaken crypt before it was too late.

Something shuddered above us. A sprinkling of dirt shivered from the ceiling, merging with the dirt below. I twisted, looking up, squinting as another dusting landed on my face.

What the—

Then a boom sounded. Low and echoing and terrifying.

Shit!

An explosion or cave-in.

When I was young, Cut had brought Kes and me to visit for the first time. I'd rather liked the oppressive tunnels. The thickness of earth and loneliness so far beneath sunlight appealed to my chaotic, oversensitive brain. But I'd explored too far. I'd got lost.

I'd tried to find my way out, only to crawl and get trapped in an unused part of the mine. A section of wall had caved in, partially blocking my exit. Luckily, a worker had come to reinforce pretty quickly and found me.

I'd laughed off the experience and Kes had used my tale as a fascinating story of diamond warfare, but I never forgot the instantaneous terror at being buried alive.

Another reverberation travelled through the walls and floor, shivering like a beast waking up.

Marquise shot upright, his phone clutched in his hand. "What the fuck was that?"

That isn't normal.

The mine was sturdy, despite its ancient age. The rarity of a continual yield in diamonds after so long was another reason why the shafts and cylindrical passageways were well maintained. No one wanted to destroy a never-ending wealth creator, especially after centuries of collecting.

I flinched as another curtain of soil landed over my tied-up form.

Marquise charged toward the door. We humans were alike in that respect. We craved oxygen and sunlight. Put us underwater and claustrophobia could kill you better than any shark. Put us underground and fear could drive you insane.

My heart charged out of control as another smaller cannonade sounded.

Fuck.

If Marquise didn't kill me on Cut's behalf, it looked like *Almasi Kipanga* would.

The mine shouldn't behave in such a way. The tunnels dived deeper and deeper as the years went on, but the workers knew how to reinforce. Their lives were on the line. They didn't cut corners.

Yet another boom. Louder. Stronger. Closer.

The cave walls trembled, scattering earth over the table and medical supplies Cut had used.

I raised my eyes, fearing cracks and sudden crashing of rock and earth.

"Fuck this shit." Marquise grabbed the handle and wrenched open the door.

Armageddon broke out.

Gunfire.

It ricocheted into the room with a sudden spray of bullets. Flashbacks of Jeep metal crumpling and crash landings swarmed my mind. I pressed my face into the ground, curling up the best I could while tied to the chair.

What the hell—

Whizzing bullets and the dull thud of their pockmarked landing ratcheted my heart rate until I inhaled dirt from the floor. Terror lacerated my blood, setting up residence in my pounding head.

My system had a healthy dose of fear when it came to lead projectiles. When Cut shot me, I'd reacted instinctually. I wasn't thinking about pain or death but saving my sister's life. I didn't know how it would feel. But now I knew what happened to a body in the path of a mortally wounding weapon.

It fucking hurts.

I didn't want a repeat.

Fighting the ropes to protect myself, I couldn't stop my mind doing a mental cleanse, saying goodbye to everyone and everything I ever loved.

Nila.

Jasmine.

Kestrel.

Even Wings.

My life story flickered pitifully lacking and empty of experience.

And then…it was over.

As suddenly as the gunfire began, it ceased.

The silence was almost as deafening as the shots.

A howl replaced the bullets, growing in decibels as the seconds ticked on.

I looked up.

Marquise.

He lay on his back, his hands glued to his chest where multiple red spots bloomed on his t-shirt. I couldn't unravel what'd happened. It was just us in the room. No one entered. No more firing.

I looked at the open door. The wooden frame had dings and splinters from a spray of firepower, but the exit remained empty. Within the depth of the mine, feet pounded, guns erupted, and the sounds of a battle exploded out of nowhere.

What the fuck is going on?

Marquise's howls slowly turned into moans. The soil beneath him accepted his blood like a tree accepts fresh rain, sucking it deep into the ground.

I put up a blockade between him and me. I didn't like the guy, but couldn't help sharing his pain as he died in front of me. Death was private, and I had no intention of participating in his final moments.

Somewhere in the mine, a war had broken out. I didn't know who was on what side. I didn't know if it would work in my favour. But I did know I'd been granted a second chance; I wouldn't waste it.

Kicking, I somehow managed to rock sideways, propping myself awkwardly on a fulcrum of brittle chair leg. My shoulders sagged in relief, but the way I repositioned put immense pressure on my chest and ribs from the ropes.

I couldn't suck in a deep breath as I jerked and twisted. The chair cracked and groaned, fighting against my encouragement to break.

Footsteps suddenly sounded closer, scuffing pebbles and belying numbers.

I froze.

Sweat dripped off the end of my nose as I squirmed harder. If they were new enemies, I couldn't be there still fucking tied up when they—

They entered the cave.

Five men poured inside, blocking the exit. Their dark skin sucked the meagre light from the lamps, the whites of their eyes hell-bent and focused. The rifles in their hands were old but still capable of murder.

I glowered, drinking in their warrior thoughts and violence. One of the men moved forward, scuffing the blood-soaked dirt where Marquise lay.

Marquise erupted to life, pulling a pistol from his pocket and firing. His aim struck one of the men in the heart.

No!

Everything happened at warp speed. More workers poured through the door, launching themselves at the mountain of muscle, swatting his pistol, slamming his hands onto the floor.

He hollered like a beast attacked by insects, but in sheer numbers, he was overwhelmed.

Another man entered, this one wearing the patch of manager on his dirty t-shirt. He was older, more Cut's age, and full of authority as he stood over Marquise. Without flinching, he hacked at his neck with a machete.

One moment, Marquise was alive, keeping me from Nila. The next, he was gone to the underworld. Gruesome to witness but humane to put him out of his misery. He was a dead man already…this way…the pain had gone—even if he didn't deserve such compassion.

Bonnie will need to buy someone else's loyalty.

If she survived what I would do to her when I returned home, of course.

If *I return home.*

A man moved toward me. My muscles stiffened as he cocked his head. Up close, he appeared younger. His skin unblemished and pupils as dark as his skin. Without a word, he went behind me.

I swallowed hard, waiting for a knife to slice my throat or a bullet to lodge in my brain.

The swish of a blade being drawn from a scabbard set my heart racing but then the pressure around my chest suddenly vanished.

I toppled sideways, freed from the chair, ropes trailing after me. The sawn ends landed on the floor like decapitated snakes. The moment the chair no longer held me captive, the young man grabbed my wrists and sawed through the remaining twine.

I couldn't understand…why?

Why had they done this?

The man helped push me into a sitting position. My head thundered with pain, but I blinked and stretched my spine. It felt amazing to sit up and roll my back without stiff wood holding me in place. My ribs complained and the wooziness of my vision didn't help, but I could move, I could breathe, I could survive.

Pearly white teeth, almost as bright as diamonds, appeared in the gloom. He smiled, speaking rapidly in Afrikaans.

My memory of their language was rusty, but I let my condition and the few remaining words I recalled give me a hint of what he said: *We save for you save.*

It made no sense.

The worker who'd cut me free gave me a hand. Without hesitating, I clasped fists, staggering to my feet. I stumbled sideways, finding yet more injuries now I stood upright. My right kneecap ached and a large bump on my thigh swelled with a new bruise.

The weakness from lack of rest and nutrition caught up with me as the room spun.

Holding my elbow, the worker didn't say a word as I blinked and forced myself to be stronger.

Pushing the help away, I brushed off damp mud from my clothing with shaking hands. The movement helped remind my body how to react, fresh energy filtered, and the pain faded a little. Looking up, I glanced at the men all watching me. "I don't understand."

The manager came forward. His once white shirt was now stained a rusty ore from digging all his life. His skin glistened while his eyes shone with vengeance. His hand shook around the machete—still glistening with Marquise's blood—as he raised it to my heart. In English, he repeated, "We saved you so *you* could save *us*." His blade wobbled as he breathed hard. "We've taken care of the guards. We're in control of the mine now. We thank Kestrel Hawk for his help, but the guards obey the bossman's orders and our conditions are no better."

Temper strained his voice. "We have had enough of being treated like slaves. Tonight we rise. So answer me honestly, diamond son, or share their fate." His weapon shook as he pointed at Marquise and back to me. "Are you like them? Or are we right in thinking you are not like your family?"

I rubbed my face, forcing myself to focus on conversation not bodily pain. All Kes's work here had been for nothing? Had none of his generosity and deals behind Cut's back been delivered?

Injustice for our men and my brother's cause pissed me off. "You're asking if I'm not a Hawk?"

He shook his head. "No, we're asking if you're like them."

I didn't move. "Why? Why ask this now?"

The young man who'd freed me said, "We saw you."

My eyes landed on Marquise's corpse, unable to look away from the gash in his neck from the sword. "Saw what?"

"Saw you drag your brother's body and the lions take it. You killed your own flesh and blood."

Fuck.

I froze.

I didn't think now was the time to mention Nila had killed him. I'd just helped tidy up.

The manager moved closer, his fingers tightening around his blade. "You killed him because you don't agree with his practices, yes?"

I frowned, trying to keep up. How long had they hated my family? How long had they waited to overthrow us? My heart thundered with their combined hurt and hope. They'd killed in order for me to help them.

We were on the same path.

Bracing myself, I banished myself from my family, vanquishing any relation. I let myself be true with the men who'd saved my life. "No, I don't agree with his practices. If I'm honest, I never did."

"We can tell." The manager smiled. "We watched you while you were younger. You are not like them."

He didn't know he'd just given me a compliment I would always remember. All my life, I hated the fact I wasn't like my family, that I was an outcast, a disappointment. But now...now, I couldn't be more fucking thankful.

It just saved my life.

I pressed a fist over my heart. "I'm forever in your debt."

Debt.

Indebted.

It seemed Nila wasn't indebted any more, but I was. A Hawk owing a debt. I rather liked the responsibility of paying them back after something so unforgettable.

The manager lowered his machete. "You'll help us?"

I nodded. "I give you my word."

He grunted under his breath. "Good."

"I promise I'll change everything you are not happy with. But first...I really need to go after my father. I need to save—"

"The woman. Yes. I know." The manager sidestepped, waving at the exit. "A Jeep is waiting at the top of the mine. The driver will take you to the airport."

I couldn't stop the swell of gratitude. Moving toward the ziplock bag Cut had left behind after loading up Nila's cast with as many diamonds as he could fit, I scooped out a handful, stuffed them into my dirty jeans, and handed him the remains.

Inside rested countless jewels to be included in the next shipment. Hundreds of thousands of pounds worth of stones. "Please, call me Kite. Spread this out amongst your men. I'll be back as soon as I've controlled the situation at home."

He grinned, taking the diamonds. "Thank you, boss."

I shook my head. "No, thank *you*."

Moving a few paces, my legs argued and my gunshot wound protested, but I had bigger things to worry about.

I had to get home.

I had to fly.

Looking one last time at the manager and workers who had changed my future, I stalked from the room as smoothly as I could. I ignored my headache. I dismissed the pains and discomfort in my muscles. I charged through the earthen labyrinth and exploded outside.

Fresh air.

New beginning.

Blinding hope.

This is it.

This was my true inheritance.

I'd earned the loyalty of men by remaining true to who I was.

Now, I would make the world a better place and end those who didn't deserve to survive.

A worker beamed, revving a Jeep with the Hawk crest on the side as he waited for me to climb inside.

The moment my door slammed shut, we tore off toward the airport.

Nila

"AH, SON, I'M so glad you're home."

My eyes wrenched upward as Cut threw me inside Hawksridge Hall.

Bonnie.

She stood with prideful smugness as I stumbled over the threshold.

A Black Diamond member had collected us from the airport. Cut hadn't said a word to me on the drive back, preferring to type furiously on his phone the entire journey home.

Home?

Hawksridge was never home.

Not without Jethro.

He was my home.

I hugged my cast harder, trying to push away the fears of Jethro's safety. I had double terror now I was back in the one place that would steal my life.

How many breaths did I have left?

How many heartbeats and moments?

Bonnie inched forward, leaning heavier than normal on her walking stick. When I first arrived, she'd refused to use her stick, moving around without any aid. Now, she seemed to have aged decades in the months I'd been her prisoner.

I smiled slightly. The trouble I'd caused had withered her—trading her youth for my longevity.

If I died, at least she wouldn't be far behind me.

My fingers curled with defiance, activating the break in my arm. It'd taken almost an hour for the adrenaline to leave my system after dealing with airport security. I'd burned off what food I'd eaten on the plane and felt shaky and sick.

However, there was one silver lining to being back in the rat's nest.

We'd returned to Hawksridge minus a Hawk.

Daniel.

His body was now lion shit turning to dust on an African plain.

Was that what Cut was emailing about? Trying to find his wayward son?

I'd been surprised Cut left without waiting for news of him. Leaving his offspring behind seemed callous, but I supposed he'd done worse. What was a departure without a note in the scheme of what he'd committed?

Bonnie seemed to sense my thoughts. Her hazel eyes narrowed on me. "Where is my grandson?"

Cut stormed forward, pecking his mother on her cheek. She stood in the grand foyer of the Hall, where Jethro and I had guided the *Vanity Fair* interviewers for our photo session in the grove.

Her skirts hung regally, her chin tilted just so, offering a royal welcome.

"I'd like to know that, too." Cut gave her another peck. "Hello, mother." Turning to face me, he growled, "Nila knows something. She's not talking currently, but she will. Have no doubt about that."

I gulped as Bonnie turned frigid. "I see." Shuffling forward, her eyes landed on my cast. "Despite that blip of bad news, I understand the Fourth Debt went okay."

Cut nodded. "Yes. No one suspected." Marching toward me, he grabbed my good wrist and yanked me toward Bonnie. "I'll leave you to remove the cast and retrieve the merchandise. I have to attend to something." His eyes glittered, filling with secrets. "Ask me what I have to attend to, Nila."

I clamped my lips together. I didn't need to ask. He'd threatened me for too long.

The Final Debt.

There would be no more dallying or delays.

No more reprieves or hope things could end differently.

I'm not going down without a war.

Fisting my hair, he kissed my cheek. "I have an old friend to dust off and prepare for its latest victim. You have a date in the ballroom tomorrow, my dear."

"Tomorrow?"

My heart splintered. Was this how prisoners felt on death row? Having a date for their execution? Wishing for more time all while begging it to slow?

"Tomorrow." His mouth pressed against mine.

I squirmed, but he held me firm. "Daniel might've made you pay the Third Debt but don't for a second think I've forgotten that I didn't. You chickened out at *Almasi Kipanga*, but you won't have a choice tonight."

I refused to let him see my fear. "I fought you then. I'll fight you now."

Cut chuckled. "We'll see."

"I'll die fighting. I'll fight every second for Jethro."

"Jethro?" Bonnie snapped, full attention brimming. "What about that traitor?"

Cut smiled at his mother. "Long story. I'll tell you later." Turning his gaze back to me, he whispered, "Jethro will know you'll fight. His imagination will run rampant of images of me doing all sort of things to you now we're home." He kissed my cheek again. "The eyes paint an awful picture, Nila, but the mind is far worse."

Letting me go, he strode off, saying over his shoulder. "When you're dead and Jethro's been taught a lesson, he'll no doubt try to find a way to kill me. What he doesn't realise is, I'm one step ahead of him. I'll hurt him. I'll ruin him. And I'll tell him word for word what I did to you and watch it break him apart."

Rounding the corner, Cut's voice sailed back with promise. "He won't kill me because he'll be ruined before he ever gets the chance."

FINALLY.

Finally, fate decided to throw me a fucking break.

The captain hesitantly accepted my pocket full of uncut diamonds, swiping a hand through a bushy moustache. I'd never met him, but he'd heard of me——like everyone in Botswana. "You want to leave *now*, now? Like right now?"

I nodded, anxiety pinging in my blood. "Yes. Like this very fucking minute."

Nila…

He frowned. "Just you?"

I nodded.

"To Turweston Airport, England?"

I nodded again.

We'd been over this, but I felt his confliction. He wanted the diamonds. He wanted to fly me. He just needed a moment to let the magnitude of logging a new flight plan and departing the moment he landed from a previous contract compute.

Lowering my voice, I encouraged, "I know you've just arrived with another client. But I need to go this very moment. If that's not a possibility, then I'll have to look elsewhere."

I held out my palm, requesting the return of the glittering stones.

The captain clutched his fist where the diamonds lay. He bit his lip, slowly working out what tiredness was worth compared to an instant fortune. Amazing how such simple stones could corrupt even the most innocent.

"I didn't say I couldn't take you."

I crossed my arms, wincing a little at the aches in my body. "Decide. We need to leave."

His eyes darted to the private jet sitting serenely by the hangar. After arriving at the airport, courtesy of the worker who should've been a racecar driver rather than a diamond digger, I'd found there were no commercial flights for thirty-six hours.

That was too long.

It wouldn't work.

I fucking refused to go through the nightmare of flying economy while fearing for Nila's life. Last time, I'd arrived late. Daniel had touched her and

Nila had to defend herself by taking a life.

I won't let that happen again.

But the gods of fate had finally smiled at me as the captain I now propositioned had walked through the terminal with his flight bag and weary eyes ready for a nightcap and bed. He paused, eavesdropping on my conversation with another pilot offering all number of things if he'd charter a plane and get me to England tonight.

He'd interrupted and guided me outside where no other ears would hear.

The moment it was just us, I'd pulled free the pocketed diamonds and given him my terms. There were a few missing—I'd paid the worker a big bonus for driving me so quickly before sending him back to the mine to find the guy who'd driven me last night. I'd promised my previous ride two thousand pounds. Who knew if he still waited by the gates, but he deserved to be compensated for his loyalty.

I would never take people's willingness to help another ungratefully again.

The pilot rolled a clear stone in his fingers, a decision solidifying on his face. Finally, he nodded. "Fine. Let's go."

"Good choice." I wanted to fucking kiss him. Instead, I prowled toward the aircraft and prepared to face my father one last time.

I checked the clock above the cockpit for the millionth time.

Almost there.

By my calculations, I was only a couple of hours behind Nila and Cut. Their international service had been delayed—I'd seen the departure board at the terminal—and their airliner travelled at a slower speed.

Also, once in England, clearing customs would've taken a while depending on Nila's acting skills.

Even though I was so close, chasing Nila through the skies—it wasn't quick enough.

Come on. Fly faster.

The air-hostess, who hadn't looked happy when the pilot asked her to pull a double shift, came forward. The co-pilot had also grumbled, but nothing a few bribes and promises couldn't fix. Both the flight attendant and the crew had assumed they'd finished for the day. But they'd agreed. Everyone agreed for money. Even if tiredness and common-sense told them otherwise.

We were all running on fumes, lethargy and stress slowly polluting the interior of the plane. Mile after mile we travelled and I drank coffee after coffee, refuelling on pre-packaged sandwiches and fruits stocked in the plane's galley.

My stomach was no longer empty and with edible vitamins came healing. My body knitted together enough to get me through the day. My vision stabilised and my headache receded. My fever remained, however, staining my hope with an unwanted film.

"Another drink, Mr. Hawk?" The air-hostess with her plaited dark hair was pretty enough but held nothing compared to Nila.

God, Nila.

I'd never been so attracted to someone both physically and emotionally. The shared text messages had made me proud of her, pissed at her, lusting for her. She'd become a friend...then lover. But mostly, she'd become everything I ever needed.

Clenching my hand, I rubbed at the sudden ache in my heart.

I fucking miss you, Needle.

I shook my head. "A phone. Do you have an in-flight phone I can use?"

She nodded. "I'll get it for you." Disappearing down the back of the aircraft, she returned with a satellite phone.

The moment I turned it on, I forgot all about her and focused on rallying every plan I'd put into place before Jasmine called to say Nila had been taken to Africa.

How long ago was that?

A decade? Two?

Shit, it felt like an eternity.

The first call was to Tex.

He answered on the first ring, almost as if he sensed the magnitude of the situation and the peril his daughter was in.

"Arch speaking."

"It's Jethro."

His voice turned sharp. "You said you'd call me hours ago, Hawk. What the hell happened?"

"Change of plan." I swiped a hand over my face. "Look, they took her before I could put everything into place. It's happening right now. You need to gather whoever you've been working with and get to Hawksridge this very fucking second." My heart charged with gunpowder. "Can you do that?"

"What the fuck happened? Is my daughter okay? Tell me what the hell you did!"

"She is for now, but she won't be if we don't move fast. Get ready. I'll meet you outside the gates to the estate in—" I checked the clock. Landing was in two hours. The local airport I'd ordered us to land in was closer to Buckinghamshire than Heathrow. Every extra minute I gained on my father counted. On a commercial service, Cut would've had no choice but to land at Heathrow.

Local time would place my arrival at late morning.

I'm closing in.

Working out the time differences, I said, "Meet me at eleven thirty a.m. Bring everything you have. I'll tell you what we need to do when I'm there."

"Jethro—"

"No, I don't have the time to console or repeat myself—just be there." I hung up and dialled the next man on my list.

Kill answered on the third ring.

"Speak."

"Kill, it's Hawk."

"About time you fucking called. Been sitting in this damn bed and breakfast waiting for the green light to move."

"You're in Buckinghamshire?"

"Where the fuck else would I be? I said I'd come. I came. Brought three of my best men with me, too."

I slouched in my seat with gratitude.

Thank God for friends in random places.

I took a deep breath. "I need you to get to Hawksridge as soon as you can. Sneak onto the grounds. Hide. If you see anything threatening Nila Weaver's life, you have full permission to do whatever's necessary." My voice faded. "Just keep her safe for me. I'm almost there."

"The woman I met at your diamond warehouse?"

I pinched the bridge of my nose. "That's the one. My father will have her, or possibly my grandmother. I want to deal with them on my own so keep them alive if possible. But above all, do whatever you need to keep Nila unharmed—even if it means slaughtering them."

Kill's voice grew cold and calculated. "You have my word. We'll leave now. See you soon, Hawk."

Hanging up, my fingers shook as I dialled the final number.

"Flaw speaking."

"Flaw…it's Kite."

It didn't escape my notice I'd made three phone calls and used three names. Was that who I'd become? Three facets of myself? How would I choose which was the better side of me and settle into one person after so much strife?

"Shit, man. Cut just arrived ten minutes ago. Bonnie has Nila up in her quarters. Where the fuck are you?"

Shit!

"I'm on my way. I've sent reinforcements, but I need you to do something for me."

"Name it."

"I'm making you vice president of the Black Diamonds. I need you to gather those you trust to take down the members loyal to Cut. Fracture and Cushion should swear allegiance to you. Colour might, too—he was friends with Kes and not a bad guy. But the rest, I'm unsure of. You'll have to work out who to trust and who to peg for a rebellion. You think you can do that?"

Silence before he gulped. "You want me to start anarchy?"

"I'm asking you to get the brothers out of the way. The war is happening right now. It's going to end tonight. I can't have the club getting in the way."

"I know which members will stick by you and which won't. Leave it with me. I'll make sure to keep them out of the way and deal with those who won't behave."

I smiled with thanks. "Appreciate it. I'll be there soon. Help will arrive with me. I have reinforcements. Just stay low and get ready."

"Been born ready, my man. This is yours. Don't fucking care it's not your thirtieth or you haven't inherited the estate yet. This became personal when that motherfucker shot Kes in cold blood."

Leaning against the window, I sighed. "It's personal. And it's almost over."

Flaw growled, "Let's finish this for him."

The ache returned to my heart—this time for my brother.

I fucking miss you, Kestrel.

"For Kes." Hanging up, my eyes fell on the clouds and world far below us.

Up here, I was closer to my brother. Closer to his untethered soul.

If you can hear me, brother. Don't leave. Not yet. Things will be better after tonight. You'll be safe. Jaz will be safe. We can have the life you always dreamed.

Turbulence hit the plane, bouncing us like a skittle.

I liked to think it was him…telling me he'd heard and wouldn't give up.

Stay alive. Give me a little more time.
And then wake up and come home.

Nila

"COME HERE, CHILD."

All I wanted to do was escape, to be alone so I could drop the mask of defiance and indifference. It took every effort to come across contrite and fearful but not guilty and sinful.

Daniel's death glowed inside me, giving me power. But I couldn't deny I was tired. I needed to rest...in case I said something stupid and escalated my death from tomorrow to today.

Jethro...keep breathing.

Every time I thought of him, the image of dank mines and oppressive walls came back. I hated him trapped down there, alone, hurting.

I knew so much now. I knew about Mabel and William. I knew a secret both Bonnie and Cut didn't know.

The secret burned a hole in my soul because what good was a secret if I died with it—especially when it would grant pain to hear it.

If I tell her, I could kill her before she tells anyone else...

My heart skipped.

Yes, I like that plan.

Bracing my shoulders, I moved toward Bonnie. She'd escorted me into her quarters, ferrying me into the lift I assumed Jasmine used to move around. I'd never been in the silver box and hated travelling even a small distance with Bonnie in such a tight space.

Jasmine.

Does she know I'm back?

Could she sense her brother's predicament? Was she like Vaughn and in-tune with her sibling's well-being?

Vaughn.

Could he tell I'd been hurt? Where was he? The entire drive from the airport, I'd feared he would be at Hawksridge, firing cannons and charging with some fictional cavalry to rescue me.

But he wasn't.

I was both glad and heartbroken.

Jethro couldn't save me this time. I would do my best—I wouldn't die without a fight—but what if it wasn't enough? I was more alone here than I was at the mine. At least there I was surrounded by strangers. Here, I was surrounded by enemies.

Stop that.

It took every last reserve, but I shoved my fears deep, deep inside and embraced antagonising pompousness.

Bonnie expected me to be as broken as my arm.

She was very much mistaken.

Cocking my chin, I pranced toward her. "Did you miss me?" I eyed up her quarters. "Last time I was in here, I seem to remember I taught you seamstresses are better than flower arrangers."

Bonnie's rouge-painted cheeks whitened. "And I seem to recall I showed you what happened to Owen and Elisa and proved Jethro played into the hands of fate. He's dead because of you. Congratulations."

Goosebumps darted over my skin. I probably shouldn't but Cut would tell her. I wanted to be the one to deliver the news. "He's not dead. He's alive and coming for you."

Wishes were free. Threats were cheap. I could taunt her even knowing Jethro remained bound to a chair and lorded over by Marquise.

She fisted the top of her cane. She didn't break decorum, merely looking a little ruffled and a lot annoyed. "I highly doubt that. How is he still alive? What exactly is the meaning of this nasty business?"

I glided forward. "You don't deserve to know." The pictures of Owen and Elisa still graced the walls. The overwhelming perfume of her flower arrangements poisoned the air.

My skin crawled with how much I despised her.

Die, witch. Die.

Bonnie came closer, her cane sinking into the carpet, her red lipstick once again smeared on pencil thin lips. "You look at me as if I'm the devil. You're such a stupid child. Go on, you have my permission. What do you see when you look at me?"

My mouth parted, sensing a trap.

She waved her stick. "Go on. I want to know."

I balled my hands, rising to her challenge. "Fine. I see a twisted, old woman who's controlled her son and grandsons with no mercy. I see a soulless creature who doesn't know the meaning of love. I see a scorned hate-filled Hawk who never understood the true value of family." My voice lowered to a hiss. "I see a walking dead woman."

She chuckled. "You have more perception than I gave you credit for." Sniffing, she looked down her nose. "You're right on some accounts. I *have* controlled my son and grandsons because, without me, they wouldn't have the discipline required to maintain the Debt Inheritance and future responsibilities of this family."

"When you're dead, your legacy will die with you."

"Yes, perhaps." She smiled. "But you'll be dead long before me, Ms. Weaver. Perhaps you should remember that so you don't forget your place." Stabbing her cane into the carpet, she sneered. "Now, enough, what do you have to say for yourself?"

My hands fisted. I stared at the flower arrangement on the trestle by the door. I'd had to stand there and listen to her high-class airs and demands, seething while she speared lilies and roses into oasis foam.

I hated the perfection of lilies. I *despised* the bright red of roses.

My temper swirled out of control. "I'll tell you what I have to say, old witch."

Bonnie froze. "*What* did you just say?"

If I did this, there would be no turning back.

I would die tomorrow.

But I could live today.

I could achieve more in one act of cruelty than I ever could in a coffin.

No one knew when death was coming.

I supposed I was lucky in a way—knowing the grim reaper waited for me gave me a certain kind of freedom. The knowledge gave me power to face my nightmares rather than run.

Plucking the vase with my good hand, I held the bushel of flowers as a weapon. Petals fell by my feet, dripping slowly in the heat of her boudoir. "You make me sick."

Her eyes flared. "Put that down this instant."

Tucking the arrangement haphazardly into my sling, I stalked closer. Wrenching the head off a red rose, I threw the petals in her direction. "You set a bad example for all grandmothers around the world."

She stood taller but stepped backward. Not wanting to give up ground but wary at the same time.

I threw another destroyed rose in her direction. "You've polluted this earth for long enough."

She lost to my invasion.

Her cane tapped for traction as she scuttled backward.

The door soared open and a Black Diamond brother came in.

Shit!

I breathed hard, fistful of petals and a standoff with Bonnie Hawk.

Instantly, Bonnie's face transformed into feral confidence. "Ah, Clarity. Good timing." She pointed her stick at me. "Kindly remove the vase from Ms. Weaver's control."

"Right away, ma'am." I had no hope of holding onto it one-handedly as he snatched it from my sling. He was smaller than Marquise but had the same evil glint and malicious satisfaction. His bald head shone with the sconces around the room.

He didn't look at me again as he placed the flowers back on the trestle. "You summoned me?"

Bonnie nodded, smoothing fly-away hairs from her chignon. "Go and fetch the Dremel and a bucket of water and vinegar."

He cocked his head in my direction. "You okay alone?"

"I'll be fine. Go."

Clarity nodded. "On it." He left, closing the door behind him.

I *hated* she trusted she could be in the same room with me—even after my outburst. I hated I came across so weak that she didn't feel she needed protection.

Make her regret that.

"Trust me alone with you now?" I tilted my head. "Rather a stupid thing to do, don't you think?"

My hands curled as thoughts of killing her ran wild. I had nothing to lose anymore. Jethro was in Africa. I didn't know where Jasmine was. V was hopefully back with Tex. And Kes was in the custody of doctors and nurses. We were scattered to four corners, no longer touching but still linked.

I could kill Bonnie before Cut killed me.

Bonnie smirked. "Child, you have a broken arm, most likely a fever, and death looming on your horizon. I have no need to fear a guttersnipe like you. You just used whatever energy you had. You can't deny it. You're positively dripping with exertion and fatigue." Turning her back on me—showing just how little she viewed me as a threat—she snapped, "Now, after that highly inappropriate incident, return to the subject. What about Jethro?"

"What about him?"

She cleared her throat angrily. "Am I correct in assuming he's still alive?"

Rage spread like wildfire through my system. I might not have knitting needles or scalpels, but I couldn't stomach this old bitch any longer. "Yes, as a matter of fact. He *is* alive, and I was telling the truth. He's on his way to kill you all."

She flinched, unable to hide her sudden suspicions. "I don't believe you."

I shrugged. "You don't have to believe me for it to be true."

For a second, silence was a third entity in the room before Bonnie laughed. "Cut would've mentioned such a thing. You're lying. Didn't your mother ever tell you liars go to hell?"

"Was she supposed to tell me that before or after you killed her?"

Bonnie tensed. "You're getting mighty bold for a Weaver about to die."

I drifted forward. "Bold enough to kill you before I go?"

Say no so I can prove you wrong.

One Hawk soul tallied my own. I wanted two. No, I wanted three before I was through.

The door sailed open, shattering the tension between us. The Black Diamond brother strolled in and placed a bucket of water, sour smelling vinegar, and a power tool on the flower-arranging bench.

Glancing at Bonnie, he wiped his hands on his jeans. His bald head caught the rays of late-morning sunshine.

My body clock was so screwed up; I didn't know if it was meant to be night or day, sleep or awake.

"Need anything else, ma'am?"

Bonnie pursed her lips, glancing at me with a mixture of wariness and disdain. "Yes, stand by the door. Don't leave."

I laughed softly. "Afraid of a Weaver, after all."

Bonnie snapped her fingers. "Shut that trap and come here. I have work to do."

Damn.

Now I had an audience; my plans shifted slightly.

Be patient.

She'd grow cocky again and send the brother away. And when she did…

Playing along, for now, I moved toward the table. "What are you going to do?"

She didn't reply as she shuffled toward a chair, dragged it closer to the bench, and perched on the padded seat. "What do you think, you stupid girl? You're carrying our money. I want those diamonds. Your arm is currently worth more than your entire family history."

"I don't believe that. My family earned its wealth through skill and hard work. Weaving and sewing for dukes and duchesses. We didn't lower ourselves to smuggling stones and calling it hard work."

She spluttered. "Soon that tongue of yours will no longer be attached."

"Why? You plan on cutting that off along with my head?"

She smiled coldly. "Such a temper."

I smirked back. "I've learned from the best."

I would never bow to her again. *Never.*

Bonnie huffed, busying herself with an attachment for the small power tool. "Stand here."

Looking over my shoulder, I calculated how much time I would have before the brother managed to stop me. If I slashed her throat with a pair of scissors, would I have enough seconds or not?

Mulling the problem of murder, I moved to where she pointed.

"Don't move."

I didn't move; too consumed with my own ideas to care about hers.

Bonnie grabbed the Dremel in shaking, arthritic hands and switched on the battery-operated machine. A loud buzzing filled the room as she ordered me to remove my sling and place the cast on the table.

The ache in the broken bone had faded a little, or maybe my body had become fed up with letting me know it was hurt. Either way, I did as she asked. Obeying for now—purely biding my time.

How should I do it?

Cutting shears to her jugular?

A fire poker to her heart?

My fingers around her throat, strangling, *strangling?*

I flinched as the sharp teeth of the Dremel chewed through the cast, removing the heat and itch. It didn't take long for Bonnie to slice from wrist to elbow. Her hands shook, trying to pincer it open—her age not granting enough power to break the mould.

"Open it," she commanded, growing weary. A sheen of sweat covered her brow, a grey tinge painting her skin.

My heart skipped to see her struggling. Her heartbeats were numbered. My mind started a countdown.

One beat.

Two beats.

Three beats.

Four.

My hand was steady as I cracked open the cast, almost as if contemplating murder worked wonders for my peace of mind. I winced as the cast fell away, destroying whatever support I'd had.

Once the pieces hit the table, Bonnie immediately scooped them into the bucket. They sank into the water and vinegar mixture.

Air bubbles popped on the surface, faster and faster.

She caught me looking. "Allow me to teach you a few things before your final hour. The vinegar dissolves the plaster. Once it's reduced to nothing but sludge, the water will be sifted, any wayward diamonds scooped from the bottom, and washed in preparation to go to Diamond Alley for processing."

She snapped her fingers. "Give me the rest of the cast. I know the pouches are hidden in the padding."

Fifteen beats.

Sixteen beats.

Seventeen beats.

Eighteen.

Pain amplified as I slipped out of the cushion and handed over the plastic tray. My arm held marks and indents from the padding, red from the cast's itch. However, the swelling hadn't gone down. An angry bruise already marred my skin, black and purple and blue.

Immediately, she scooped the diamonds out and placed them beside the bucket. "Once they go to Diamond Alley, then where do you think they go?"

Nursing my arm, I tested my fingers. They worked but with no power or grip. If I had any chance at killing her, I'd have to work through the agony and force my limb to obey. Otherwise, I wouldn't stand a chance.

"Well, Ms. Weaver?" Bonnie slapped the table. "I asked you a question. Answer it."

"Oh, I'm sorry. You mistook my disinterest for attention." I rolled my eyes. "I don't care."

"You should." Prodding my vulnerable break, she hissed. "Hurts, doesn't it?"

Flinching away, I fought the pain as I grabbed the edge of the table. A horribly frustrating and terribly timed vertigo wave attacked me. I hung my head, anchoring my feet to the floor, riding out the vicious swell.

She chuckled as the greyness subsided, leaving behind the serendipitous knowledge that Bonnie's flower shears rested only a finger breadth away.

Scissors.

Blood.

Death.

She didn't notice my sudden hope and fascination with the weapon within reach.

Wrapped up in her own importance like a fluffing peacock, she looked at the brother by the door.

She pointed at the bucket and pouches. "Take those downstairs and make sure each diamond is accounted for." Her eyes narrowed. "I'll know if any go missing and you'll be subjected to a cavity search once the diamonds are bagged and labelled."

The man came forward, cringing a little at the thankless task and the reward he had to look forward to once completed. "Yes, ma'am."

I held my breath.

The brother grabbed the items and departed through the door.

She made him leave.

We're alone.

Thirty.

Thirty-one beats.

Thirty-two.

Thirty-three heartbeats.

Stupid, stupid Hawk.

Slowly, I fisted the shears with my unbroken arm, wrapping tight fingers around the handles.

Bonnie didn't notice, so consumed with her own self-importance as she stood and brushed plaster dust from her blood-red skirt.

Blood-red.

The same colour she wore at the dice game a few days ago.

My fury fired and I held up the twin blades. "You asked me before if my arm hurt. I'll now ask you a similar question. Do you think this will kill you if I lodge it in your heartless chest?"

She scooted off her seat, shuffling backward. "Drop it, Ms. Weaver."

I advanced, brandishing my weapon. "No."

Her mouth opened to scream.

Fifty-two.

Fifty-three heartbeats.

I'd lost my opportunity last time.

I'd been too slow. Too weak.

I had no intention of screwing this one up.

I charged, stopping her before she could make a sound.

I slammed my palm over her mouth, tackling her. My break bellowed and my good fingers weakened around the pilfered scissors, but I didn't let her go. She tripped, but I managed to right us. Bolts of agony and shards of pain drenched my nervous system from my uncasted arm.

"Ah, ah, ah. I think silence is better in this newly developed situation, don't you?" My vocabulary mimicked hers, thriving off the power of manhandling the wicked Hawk witch.

Bonnie's papery breath fluttered over my hand as her nostrils flared.

She struggled. But her brittle bones were no match for my rage. Her eyes tried to hurt me with unspoken curses, but I wouldn't put up with it anymore.

In a burst of power, she ripped out of my hold, swatting my broken arm.

I groaned in agony as she sucked in a breath for help.

I had two choices. Let her scream, give into the overwhelming pain, and let this end without victory, or fight through everything and win.

I fought.

Tackling her again, I didn't care about my arm as I wrapped the broken one around her tiny waist and slapped my other hand over her lips.

Seventy-four.

Seventy-five.

Seventy-six heartbeats.

She folded as delicately as her beloved flower petals, crashing to the floor. I didn't try to protect myself. I didn't relish the impact or brutal pain.

I fell with her.

Agony I'd never felt before ripped through my bones.

I bounced on her decrepit body, squashing her into the carpet. I gasped, willing myself to keep going. "Not this time, Bonnie. You don't get to win this time. This time...it's *my* turn. It ends here. Just us."

I was better than this. Better than her and all Hawks combined.

I would take this grandmother's life, and I would *enjoy* it.

She was frail, ancient—the matriarch of a power-crazed house. Yet she was just human—same as me, same as Jethro, same as every person on this planet.

She wasn't immortal or scary.

She's already dead.

She batted at my hold with wrinkled hands, her strength rapidly dwindling.

"You deserve to die, Bonnie." I pushed her further into the carpet. "You asked me when I came into this room what I saw when I looked at you. It's my turn to ask you." I held her wriggling form, breathing hard. "What do you see when you look at me?"

Your killer?

Your demise?

Not letting her answer, I snarled, "I'll tell you what you should see. You should see a girl who's reached the end of her limit. A girl who won't hesitate to kill. A girl who fully intends to survive this massacre and burn your legacy to the ground."

Her eyes shadowed with fear.

She fought me—surprisingly strong, but she couldn't defeat the cold animosity siphoning through my veins. My rage turned into something not entirely sane as I stared into Bonnie's terrified gaze. "Want to know a secret?"

Her nose whistled as she sucked in ragged breaths around my silencing palm.

"I know something you don't know." I had meant to kill her quickly, but taunting was too much fun. I wanted to do to her what she'd done to my family and me.

A dose of her own medicine.

And my secret about Daniel had to be shared. Who better than his grandmother who would soon be joining him in the afterlife?

Her hazel eyes glared into mine. I understood her silent message. *You'll die because of this.*

I giggled, hovering over her. "I'm dead already, so what does it matter if I take you with me?"

The fight left her. An eerie calm replaced it instead. Her face filled with conversation, dragging curiosity through my blood.

Dammit.

Despite my need to end her, I had an intolerable desire to hear her final words.

"Don't scream and I'll let you speak."

She nodded.

Was it stupidity or possibly insanity making me trust her? Whatever one it was, I removed my hand.

Her face turned to the side, sucking in oxygen, her white chignon falling apart thanks to the carpet.

I squeezed her tiny body with my knees. I was her death shroud. A crow hovering for murder.

One-hundred and four.

One-hundred and five.

One-hundred and six heartbeats.

"You're not stupid, child. You know you'll pay for this the moment Clarity returns. There are worse things than death. Haven't you learned that yet?"

"I know."

"Then get off me and I'll make sure they don't maim you too much." Her smile was evil personified. "However, wait another moment longer, and I'll personally tear you limb from fucking limb."

The curse fell from her red painted lips.

I smiled, cocking my head. "Not yet. I want answers first."

"I've given you plenty of answers."

"No, that was convoluted history seen through your twisted eyes."

She snorted.

"I want to know why you are the way you are. Why you're ludicrously set on an ancient vendetta. Are you just mad and passed that defective gene onto your son or did you grow into this despicable creature?"

"You stupid, *stupid* girl. I've helped keep this family together. There is nothing wrong with loving blood over others."

"Even murder?"

She grinned, showing yellowing death and bad breath. "*Especially* murder." She raised her head off the ground, bringing our eyes closer together. "Especially your bloodline's murder. You *owe* us."

"What did we ever do to you to deserve such barbaric treatment?"

"You know what!"

"No, I don't. I will never understand because there is nothing rational to understand. It's just a sickness inside you that needs to end."

She coughed, her ancient lungs rattling. "You don't know a thing about me."

"Tell me. I'm giving you the opportunity, right now." I glared. "I want to know. This is your last chance." A contorted smile spread my lips. "Call it your last confession. Purge your sins, Bonnie, because I'm sending you to your grave—secrets told or not."

No fear shone on her face, only black rebellion. "I have nothing to confess."

"Bullshit."

I don't have time for this.

I wanted to know Bonnie's tale. I wanted to try and understand why someone would go to such lengths. But I wouldn't sacrifice my only opportunity to kill her.

"You don't want to talk? Fine. I changed my mind." Gritting my teeth against another influx of pain, I grabbed her scarf—the pretty silk decoration to match her despicable outfit—and tugged it tighter around her neck. "Want to know what I promised myself when I first came to your home and was told what would become of me?"

She pushed at my hands, sending a shard of agony down my break as I slowly tightened the scarf. Her eyes bugged wider and wider.

"I made an oath to be the last Weaver stolen. At times, I didn't know how I would honour that vow. But now...I do."

She begged for air, her lips gasping. I wasn't throttling her...yet, but the fear of strangulation sent droplets of panic across her overly powdered face.

The stench of rose water and summery perfume gave me a headache, but nothing would stop me doing this.

I lessened my hold a little. "Now, before I go too far. Do you want to know what I know or would you rather die clueless?"

Are you sure this is wise?

My arm throbbed as I doubted my actions.

Daniel's death wasn't only my secret. Jethro would be implicated, too. I couldn't risk his life if Bonnie told—

Told!

I laughed out loud. *Who is she going to tell? She'll be dead within moments...*

Something corrupted inside me. Something I didn't want to acknowledge. Straddling Bonnie, I was cold-hearted and focused—more Hawk than Weaver and ready to bloody my hands for revenge.

"No, you have nothing of value to tell me. Get off me, you heathen." Bonnie tried to buck me off, but her ninety-plus years meant it was like pinning down a fluttering leaf.

I bent further. "I know where Daniel is."

She went deathly still.

"Do you understand?" I bared my teeth. "Do you get what I'm telling you?"

Her gaze narrowed, disbelief shadowing them. "You're saying you killed my grandbaby?"

"I'm saying he hurt me and paid the price."

Bonnie shifted, trying to kick beneath me. The grey tinge staining her face slowly spread over her cheeks and throat. "You're lying."

"I'm not." I laughed softly. "What if I explained a bit more? What if I told you a bed-time—? No, a *kill-time* story. And prove I'm telling the truth?"

No reply.

Digging my knees, imprisoning her skirt tighter, I wrapped her scarf around my fist. "He won the coin toss against Cut. He got first right to rape me. *Rape*. A word so abhorrent, a family should disown any offspring who would ever do such a thing. And yet, you encourage them. You like your sons and grandsons to take what isn't theirs to take.

"Well, Daniel would've made you proud that night. He hurt me. Kicked me. Knocked me out for a few moments. But he didn't understand how powerful the will to live is, or the single-minded determination sheer hate can deliver.

"He did take me—just a little—and I let him. Does that shock you? That I didn't fight the final part when he invaded my body just enough to taint my soul?"

Bonnie swallowed, her breathing erratic, her chest lurching beneath my hold.

"I let him think he'd won, but really, I guided him to his death. I'd come prepared and I had my weapon of choice within my grasp. While he focused on rape and pleasure, I turned cold and ruthless."

I tugged the scarf. "I hugged him, you'll be glad to know that. I hugged your grandson as I jammed my metal knitting needle through his heart."

Bonnie sucked in a noisy breath. "No..."

"Oh, yes. I took great satisfaction driving that needle through Daniel's soulless chest. He didn't see it coming. He was too arrogant to notice until it was too late." My mind skipped back to the tent, recalling the last breath, the final topple of his corpse. "It was over so fast."

Bonnie spluttered, "But, they—they haven't found his body. You're lying. He's alive. I don't believe you."

"You don't have to believe me. It's the truth." I smiled brutally. "Only you know what really happened. Cut suspects me, but he has no proof."

"But how..." The muscles in her neck stood out, straining against translucent skin. "How did you hide his body?"

Even on her back, with death hovering over her, Bonnie remained frosty and aloof. If I didn't hate her, I might've respected her. She was the same formidable force Mabel Hawk had been. The same invincible dowager.

I stroked her papery cheek. "I didn't."

She glowered. "Then it can't be—"

"A Hawk did." I twisted her scarf a little more.

More sweat dotted her forehead. Her fingers scrabbled at the obstruction. "The Hawk who's in love with me and is fully on my side."

Her eyes popped wide, then glared with the hate of a thousand hells. *"Jethro."*

"Yes, Jethro…Kite. The man I agreed to marry."

Sharing my secrets even to a gnarly old cow lightened my heart. In two breaths, I'd admitted to murder and marriage. Not exactly two subjects that went hand in hand.

But they do in this case.

Without murder, Jethro and I would never be allowed to get married. We'd never be allowed to live.

The deadline of my own demise tried to shred my confidence. I might be the killer currently, but soon, I would be back to being the prey.

Spittle flew from Bonnie's lips. "Impossible. Jethro is loyal. He knows his responsibilities—"

"Responsibilities?" I laughed in her face. "Your son *shot* him. That loyalty died the moment you had him killed in cold blood. We're together. Against all of you."

Bonnie shuddered. "Never. A Hawk would never work with a Weaver."

"Lies. I know more of your history now. I know that Hawks gave Weavers leniencies throughout the years. I also know there was more than one generation who tried to stop this ludicrous debt."

"You know nothing, you insolent child."

My heart raced as I shook my head. Short black hair curtained my cheeks, giving the illusion we were already in a coffin, blocked off from the world.

"I know Jethro walked in and saw his brother dead. I know he helped me clean up. I know he—"

"How that boy is still alive is beyond me." Bonnie interrupted me as if she couldn't stand to hear more. Perhaps she did care, after all. "It's an abomination of nature."

My fingers tightened. "No, I'll tell you what's the abomination. That's you. *You're* the abomination. You twisted your family into criminals."

I waved at the room, the majestic Hall, the entire Hawksridge estate. "This is more than most people will have in their entire lives. You have everything, yet you seek to destroy everyone."

I rushed my parting words. "Once Jethro arrived, he helped me dispose of Daniel. We took him outside the fence of *Almasi Kipanga*. We left him on the plains…"

Understanding etched Bonnie's grey-washed face.

"You know, don't you? You know what happened from there."

Her pallor turned sickly, her lips tinting blue. "They ate him."

I nodded. "They ate him. Piece by piece. Chunk by chunk. Daniel no longer exists. Just like you will no longer exist."

My arm pushed harder, pressing her against the carpet. "I've killed your grandson, but I haven't finished."

Bonnie tried to yell.

I clamped a hand over her lips. "Ah, no bringing attention to us. I haven't told you the best part yet."

She shook her head, trying to free her mouth.

"I'm going to kill your son. I'm going to ensure your mad family tree dies. Only sane Hawks will continue. I'm going to kill Cut. I don't know how, but I will. The only one who will pay the Debt Inheritance is *him*."

Her struggles became frantic.

I held her down, riding her like she was a bucking bronco. I waited for her to tire herself out so I could look her in the eye as I strangled her. Only…she never tired.

Her body moved inhumanely, twitching like the undead, knocking me off her with super strength. Her gaze locked with mine; she stiffened and bowed. Her right arm flailed outward and the ire in her gaze changed to terror.

My stomach tangled as her entire body scrunched up in agony.

Shit.

Four-hundred and five.

Four-hundred and six.

Four-hundred…and seven…heartbeats.

She's having a heart attack.

Seconds whizzed past as the knowledge sank deep.

No!

Fate stole her death away from me.

I wanted to take it.

Her heart.

Her life.

She *owed* me.

But the very thing I'd stabbed in Daniel was now failing in Bonnie.

Thump—thump. *Thump…*

"Damn you, Bonnie." I climbed to my feet, standing over her with the flower shears. I'd wanted to capture her soul as it escaped her body but destiny hadn't judged me worthy. Perhaps claiming Daniel's soul was all I was allowed. Bonnie's belonged to more powerful entities.

The ghosts of my ancestor's filled her chest cavity, slipping into heart chambers, blocking veins and arteries.

Her back arched as if an exorcism was performed. She reached for me. The greyness of her face slipped straight into starch white. "He—hel—help…"

"No…"

I backed away.

I wasn't worthy enough to take her life, but I would watch every moment. I would stand vigil as she passed away at my feet and would cherish the moment when she existed no more.

But then the door swung in.

The fucking door swung and Cut entered.

He stormed into the room. Summoned by deep family bond, his posture switched from confident and assured to frozen in shock. His eyes bounced between me standing over his mother with sharp scissors and Bonnie convulsing on the floor. His eyes glittered, his face arranging into symptoms of disbelief, shock, and outrage.

How long did it take someone to die of cardiac arrest?

Die, Bonnie. Die.

The mantra repeated from when I'd killed Daniel.

Die, Hawk. Die.

"Fuck!" Cut launched into action, sprinting across the boudoir and slamming to his knees beside his mother.

She rattled and chortled, breathless and wheezing. Her eyes begged for help while her heart suffocated.

"Hold on. Hold on." Raising his voice, he screamed, "Someone call a fucking ambulance!"

No one replied. No Diamond Brother's spilled into the room. No one to take orders.

I just stood there.

A morbid spectator as Bonnie faded from this world.

"Call a fucking helicopter!" Cut didn't seem to notice his orders fell on deaf ears. I'd never seen him so normal. So afraid and lost.

I paced back and forth, hugging my smarting arm, hoping no one heard his commands. An ambulance would be too slow…but a helicopter? That might be too fast.

Die faster, Bonnie. Faster.

And fate listened.

Life chose its victor.

Me.

Thump…thump-thump—*thump.*

Heartbeats failing.

Heartbeats ceasing.

Cut cradled his mother as she quickly lost the elderly crone persona and tumbled into an emaciated corpse.

My secrets dying with her.

My sins silencing with her.

However, Bonnie didn't go quietly. She gave a parting gift, granting her final breath to me, sending me straight to damnation.

"She—" Bonnie gasped. "Dan—Dan—Daniel. She—"

Cut wiped her forehead, pushing away soaked strands of white hair. "Shush, save your strength. The doctors are coming."

Bonnie spread her lips, lipstick staining her teeth. She knew as well as I did she wouldn't be living another day. Gathering every last remaining strength, she raised her quaking arm, pointed her finger, and hissed, "She kil—killed hi—him."

And that was it.

Last heartbeat.

Last breath.

Her eyes latched smugly onto mine, then closed forever.

I'd killed my second Hawk.

But she'd delivered me into terrible torture.

Her arm tumbled to her side, bouncing off her dead flesh, coming to rest awkwardly by her side.

For a moment, the room mourned its owner. Flower petals drooped and curtains twitched with a non-existent breeze.

Then Cut raised his head, eyes glittering with unshed tears, face swelling with unadulterated hatred. *"You…"*

I raised my scissors, backing away.

He didn't move, hugging his dead mother, my second victim—stolen, not at my hand, but by the poltergeists of my ancestors.

"*You* killed Daniel."

Two choices.

One future.

I was so sick of running. So sick of hiding. So sick of being *weak*.

I didn't run.

I didn't deny it.

Instead, I held my chin high and claimed all that I'd achieved.

I'd won; they'd lost. So be it if my life was now over.

"Yes. Yes, I killed him. I took his life, I disposed of his body, and I enjoyed every damn second of it."

Cut gasped.

I smiled.

We didn't move as the next battle was drawn.

Bonnie

NO ONE WANTED to listen to the story of the sinner. The bad guy. The villain.

No one truly cared about my agendas or goals.

No one could comprehend that my actions stemmed from a place of love, family, and commitment to those I cherished.

Did that make me a terrible person?

Could I not put those I cared about before a total stranger?

People did it all the time.

They murdered to protect themselves and loved ones. They willingly forgot the commandments in favour of how they viewed what was acceptable and what was not.

I was no different.

Those who knew me understood my passion and drive. And those who didn't. Well, I didn't give a rat's arse what they thought.

There were rarely two sides to every story. In my long life experience, I'd come to see the truth. There were multiple sides. Pages and pages of sides. A never-ending battle where humans picked what they believed, causing friction and intolerance. Sometimes the choices were for understandable reasons—not justified or rash or right—just...understandable.

And when I understood that magic, I learned how to create the same spell within my own empire.

There was no right and wrong.

There was no black and white.

Those two simple lessons guided me through my life forever.

My reasons for doing what I did made sense to me. They were my dreams, and I was lucky enough to have the power and authority to press those dreams on others.

Was I right? Depended on who you asked.

Was I wrong? Not in my eyes.

And really, that was all that mattered.

I believed in what I did. I loved my family. I adored the power and wretchedness my loved ones could deliver. I gave my entire being to ensuring they thrived.

It all started on the day Alfred 'Eagle' Hawk asked me to marry him. The day he went from courting to bent knee, I knew my trials at living within my place in society were over. I hated the airs and graces of stuck-up princesses at the seasonal parties. I hated dealing with egotistical jerks who thought one manor and a career slaving for others meant they could take care of me.

Idiots.

That was just a prison sentence, and I had no intention of sharing a cell with middle-class achievers.

I came from wealthy stock myself. The Warrens owned most of South Hampton and a fleet of transportation that travelled all over the world with merchandise. Mainly, other people's merchandise—a fact I didn't like. I didn't like that we helped others improve their footing in this world.

Finite resources meant me and mine had to *share*.

I believed those I loved and shared blood with should prosper and those who didn't shouldn't. A simple decision that came with so many different sides.

As I grew used to my newfound authority, I decided to forgo my first name of Melanie and rechristen myself as Bonnie.

Bonnie Hawk rose from the ashes of Melanie Warren.

And I became a true wife and supporter.

When I fell pregnant with Peter, my first child, I swore he would be the reason I worked beside Alfred and gathered more power. Hard work and dedication didn't scare me. Failure and destitution did. So I did everything in my power to make my husband great—beyond great—unsurpassable.

One night, Alfred told me of the Debt Inheritance. It took me years to get him to fully explain what it meant. Wives of Hawk men were not supposed to get involved with the so-called Indebted business, but Alfred was mine, and if it was in my power to bring him greater glory, I would do it.

I was then graced with another son, Bryan. Life smiled on us, doting on my perfect children, ensuring they would become great masters and lords of a universe I would help maintain and create for them.

However, one stormy night and a few too many cognacs, Alfred told me how he claimed a Weaver before he met me. He carried out a few debts but couldn't carry out the final one. He didn't attach the Weaver Wailer, and he lied about killing her to a save face with the history books.

He let her go. Told her to run. To hide. He buried an empty coffin, pretended he'd completed the debts, and covered up the truth on the moor.

Stupid bastard.

That kind of weakness was not tolerated. I lost all respect for him. I saw him for what he was—a wimp. So I moved out of his bedroom to new quarters. I could no longer stomach his unwillingness to deliver a perfect future for our sons. Years later when he died of lung cancer, I didn't mourn his loss. I celebrated it.

Now was my time to triumph or meddle—again, it depended on whose opinion.

Peter took after his father. A hard worker, loyal and kind. I truly hoped he would be a good replacement and heir but time slowly changed my opinion.

Bryan took after me. He had my soul, my discipline, my drive for the impossible. Peter preferred to study and donate our wealth to charities. Bryan preferred to take that wealth and turn it into even more wealth for us—not others.

We were blood, but battle lines had been drawn and as age separated my two sons, I taught the one who listened. Bryan had been my student since he was little, and he remained my student all his life.

I'd wanted more children. I wouldn't deny it. Lots and lots of children to ensure a greater probability of world domination. We traded in the most priceless of wealth. We owned countless empires in countries around the globe. I was finally in a position to ensure we were unstoppable, but I only had one son on my side. However, he was a son who was happy to oblige.

While I was busy teaching Bryan how to run the Black Diamonds with better efficiency, digging through Hawk history books and immersing myself in my new family more than I ever did as a Warren, Peter fell in love.

A woman he met at an animal shelter. He brought her home to introduce us a few months into their relationship. Behind my back, he'd asked her to marry him and she'd agreed without my consent.

Rose Tessel was everything I wasn't. Softly spoken, obsessed with dogs and cats and horses. She didn't care about Hawksridge. She didn't care about diamonds or money. All she cared about was making Peter happy and spending time at the stables with my firstborn.

That bitch completely clouded Peter's mind. As my eldest son, he had a duty to perform. His father hadn't followed the rules of the Debt Inheritance, but my son sure would. However, he left it too late. He didn't collect Emma Weaver and pretended it didn't exist—burying himself in storybook romance and stupidity.

Bryan tried to make him see sense, but Peter and Rose fought a good battle. They were so wrapped up in their own plans; they forgot we were family and family sticks together through *everything*.

It was Bryan who came up with the idea.

He was such a good son, so attentive and switched on. He made a promise that if I put him in charge of Hawksridge, he would grow the empire to ever-new heights. He would always look after me and would grace me with many grandchildren to rule.

However, he had one condition.

He wanted to claim the Debt Inheritance. He'd spied on Emma Weaver. He'd coveted what should've been Peter's and a dislike for his older brother festered deep within his heart.

I pondered my decision, not because I doubted his capabilities, but because it would do him good to stare defeat in the face before granting his dreams. Unfortunately, while he waited for my deliberation, his jealousy of Peter overflowed one drunken night.

Peter was at a business meeting in London, delayed overnight. Rose had agreed to wait for him at the estate in his quarters instead of returning to her place in Buckinghamshire. I hated having that hussy under my roof—unmarried, no less. But Bryan did something unforgivable.

He raped Rose.

He took what should've been Peter's.

But what he took, he gave back. He impregnated her with my first grandbaby.

I cursed him for that. I was disappointed in him. Disgusted in his weakness for flesh.

But after he'd taken what he wanted, he regretted the choice immeasurably. He came to me with the weeping woman and together we put her back together again. I held a meeting that very evening and said Rose could remain in my household, but she would have to marry Bryan. If she didn't, Peter would pay the price.

She refused but wisely reconsidered when I threatened Peter's life.

The next few months were fraught with drama I didn't care for. I realised too late that my eldest would never accept his love was betrothed to his brother. Peter reminded me too much of his father, and I'd had enough of his indecision and weakness to have the strength to deal with it again. So I told Bryan he could have everything he ever wanted. A family. Children. An empire. And the Debt Inheritance.

All he had to do was put an end to his brother.

And he did.

He strangled Peter while I was at a council meeting. I pretended to grieve and act disgruntled with his actions. I made it known that the incident was on his head alone. But in secrecy, I was awed he'd had the gumption to do it.

Peter's death was reported as a horse riding accident. Rose was married to Bryan. And life moved on. Jethro was born followed by Jasmine and Angus. Bryan became known as Cut as he stepped into the role I always knew he was capable of and took the Hawk name to even greater heights.

He strengthened our relationship with authorities. He befriended new royals and smoothed out age-old alliances. And then one night, he announced Rose would have another child.

Daniel.

Cut hadn't planned on more, but he'd said he'd been to watch Emma and couldn't wait any longer to claim the Inheritance. He'd used his wife to dispel some of his lust that night—even though they'd barely talked for years.

After Jasmine's birth, Rose had moved out of Bryan's rooms, living a sham of a marriage, only glued to us by her children. My dislike for her grew year by year.

Unfortunately, Daniel's birth unravelled the perfect family I'd gathered.

Rose insisted on a hospital birth—regardless that her other deliveries had been at Hawksridge with a midwife and no complications. Bryan felt guilty for his treatment of her and softened. He gave her her wish.

Stupid man.

A few days after the birth, Bryan returned to the hospital to bring his son and wife home. Only, his wife had vanished. She'd abandoned her family—the greatest sin of all. She left behind four children and a husband who would've protected her for life.

Only, she didn't get far.

For a few months, she managed to escape our notice, but then Bryan—my ever resourceful, capable son—found her awaiting an international flight. She'd willingly traded her children for freedom—an unpayable crime.

He brought her back to the Hall. He kept her by his side while the children grew a few more years. But then the incident occurred.

I didn't approve of what happened that night, nor will I ever forgive him for the slip of Jethro and Jasmine seeing what he did to their mother. But what was done was done and there was nothing more to be said.

She was finally gone.

Good riddance.

However, her death taught me one final vital lesson: even family could disappoint. In fact, family could do more than disappoint—they could destroy everything with one ungrateful action.

I wouldn't put up with any more nonsense. Jethro turned out to have the same condition plagued by previous generations of Hawk bloodline. I ordered Cut to beat it out of him until he learned that as firstborn he had responsibilities, destinies, obligations to fulfil.

Angus pleased me but only because he had a gift not many others had. He could read people and only show them what would be appropriate to the situation. He was a chameleon within my ranks, but he was family and did what he was told. So he was left to his own devices.

Jasmine listened and obeyed, but she was rebellious in her heart like her older brother. Yet she was my only girl and despite myself, I doted on her. I wanted a mini-me. It would take time, but eventually, she would see the light and mimic all that I did.

However, recent events made me see what a foolish wish that was. I didn't show how much she hurt me when she picked sides against me. She needed to be disciplined. I knew that. But…for some reason, my ruthless laws faded when it came to Jasmine. I couldn't hurt her—not when she'd already been hurt so much.

I shouldn't have been so weak toward her. It would remain my greatest regret.

And Daniel.

Well, not having a committed mother screwed him up from the start. He was a needy, attention-seeking, reckless child. Strictness didn't work with him. Time-out. Smacks. Nothing. At least he idolized his father and ensured he wouldn't turn out like Peter or Alfred. That was his only saving grace—that and the fact he was blood and obeyed me.

And now, my beautiful family—the son I'd groomed who'd pleased me so much; the grandson who'd disappointed and destroyed everything—would now have to fend without me.

My legacy was long. I was proud of what I'd achieved.

The Hawk name was who I was.

I was born to become a Hawk even if it was only through marriage.

I'd strengthened our lineage. I'd played my part precisely.

And death could never take that away from me.

Nila

"YOU!"

Cut stumbled to his feet. His fists clenched and every muscle in his body spasmed with hatred.

I forced myself not to run as he shot across the room, weaving and wobbling. I tensed for the pain of him tackling me, hitting me, delivering his sadness and rage into my flesh.

Fear of his inevitable revenge and repercussions of my actions wouldn't let my knees unlock to flee. I wouldn't look weak by running.

Not anymore.

I'd achieved two out of the three lives I promised I'd steal. Those were good odds. I might not achieve every goal before my life was done, but I wouldn't turn my back on two victories.

Cut was broken. *I* did that. I broke him. His reign over the House of Hawks still stood strong and powerful, but I was the mole beneath him. Digging through foundations, chewing on support beams, gnawing at everything he held dear.

So no.

I wouldn't run because there was nowhere to run to, and I'd earned the right to stare at my defeated before he defeated me.

Those thoughts sucked to a violent stop as Cut charged toward me.

Whatever conclusion spilled into my head must've filled his. Perhaps in the same order—the knowledge he looked upon a worthy competitor and not just a Weaver—or the newly forming plan to strip me of everything now I'd stripped him.

Either way, he slammed to a halt, breathing hard—almost as if he didn't trust himself if he touched me. Giving time to gather his scattered self and focus on so many new developments.

"You killed her."

I balled my hands. "I wanted to, but I didn't."

His breathing billowed like dragon smoke from his nose. "You did. You fucking did!"

"It was a heart attack. Her own body killed her."

"Lies. Just like you lied about Daniel. It was *you*."

My spine straightened even as I winced at what my truth would bring. "I did."

His fists shook. "You fucking bitch." He wanted to strike me—it lived in every cell—but at the same time, there was something else…relief? Traitorous gratitude instead of mournful grief?

Did he hate his mother as much as the rest of us?

Pain from my arm gave me false bravado. "Can I help that I learned from you? You killed two of your sons. I only killed one."

Cut lowered his chin, glowering beneath his brow. "They were *my* sons. Mine to do what I like. They were only alive because of me. *I* created them."

"You might've created life, but they created themselves into the men they are."

He went deadly still. *"They?"*

I swallowed.

Shit.

"Kestrel is fucking alive, too?" His eyes bugged, ignoring the death of his mother so easily. "You're telling me I didn't murder either of my children, yet you killed my youngest, the one I'd promised to make my heir?" His voice gruffed. The air tinged with…regret?

Relief and regret—two very contradictory emotions I never expected Cut to feel.

What does that mean?

Backing away, I held up the scissors. "I said nothing of the sort."

Cut prowled toward me, slower this time, as if he couldn't comprehend such blasphemous facts. "They. You said *they*. Who's *they*?" His gaze flew around the room, to the open door, to his dead mother. "What do you mean by that? Where is he? Where the fuck is Kestrel if he didn't die with the bullet in his godforsaken heart?"

Kes was anything but godforsaken. God chosen perhaps. Protected and watched over and given friends who ensured his healing and safety.

"Answer me!" Cut's hand shot to his back waistband, pulling free a pistol.

I froze, staring down the black muzzle, expecting any moment a flash of gunpowder and a cold kiss of lead. Cut bounced between so many emotions, I couldn't keep track.

Was it the pistol he'd shot Jethro and Kes with? He didn't have it with him when we cleared customs at the airport. What outstanding matters had he attended to once we returned to Hawksridge?

Despite facing a grave, I kept the truth hidden. Jethro was trapped in Africa subjected to survival only if I obeyed Cut and gave up my life. I couldn't help him. But I could help Kes by staying silent. Kestrel was safe. I wouldn't tattle on his whereabouts, and I definitely wouldn't tell Cut that both lives had been saved thanks to Flaw and Jasmine.

Flaw!

He's on my side.

The tentative friendship we'd sparked when Kes let me into his chambers at the start. The jokes and conversation around late afternoon snacks when Jethro avoided me after the First Debt was paid. Flaw had come through for me, for Kes.

Could he help me now?

Where is he?

My heart thundered with despair. Even if Flaw was close by, it wouldn't be a simple matter of screeching for help. Hawksridge Hall swallowed men whole, disappearing for days in its cavernous corridors.

He'd never hear me.

Cut suddenly stopped, leaving a few metres between us. His eyes narrowed as sorrow, anguish, and loathing crossed his face. The hand holding his gun lowered until the nose threatened the carpet and not my life. "I underestimated you, Nila."

My lungs siphoned oxygen faster. My spine wanted to roll, to give in to the sudden ceasefire, but I knew the armistice wouldn't last long.

His mother had just died in his arms. His mourning and rage fought to take ownership of what his next move would be. He was as unpredictable as a penny in the air.

"That's the first compliment you've given me."

He looked over his shoulder at the cooling, decaying body of Bonnie. "Emma was right."

I flinched. "Don't talk about my mother. You have no right to mention her name."

His eyes landed on mine with ferocity. "*I* have no right? I have every fucking right. Did you think I didn't see her playing me? Pretending to love me while all along I knew her love was for her wretched family left behind. Even when she was nice to me, she warned me what would happen if Jethro claimed you."

Chills darted over my skin. "What did she say?" As much as I hated discussing my mother with Cut, I wouldn't stop him sharing more of his weaknesses. Because Emma was definitely his biggest weakness.

His shoulders sagged as he swiped a hand over his face. For a short second, he looked defeated. As if without Bonnie, the drive to be the worst, the most despicable overlord had vanished. "She said you'd finish us."

An icy smile lit my face. "I guess you should've listened to her."

His lips spread in a snarl. "Want to know what else she was right about?"

The atmosphere switched. Cut shed his melancholy, gathering the storm of venom he so often carried. "She said you would steal the heart of my oldest and the Debt Inheritance would end with your generation."

I gasped. How had she known how the future would unfold? How much time had she spent with Jethro to understand that my soul and his would find peace with one another?

Cut chuckled. The sound sliced through the envelope of death, fast-forwarding through his grief. "I'd wipe that smug smile off your face, Nila. Because that wasn't all she told me."

Throwing the gun to the floor, his hands fisted as he pushed off the thick carpet to charge toward me.

I squeaked, stumbling back. My broken arm bounced against my body, dragging a sharp cry of pain.

My eyes flew to the door; my legs prepared to bolt.

But I'd made a vow not to run.

Besides, Cut was too fast.

His arms wrapped around me, clamping in a hellish hug. "She also told me that while your generation would be the last, you wouldn't find a happy ever after. You share the same fate as her."

I stopped breathing as Cut grabbed my cheeks. "Her fate has always been your fate, Nila. No matter what you did, who you corrupted, or how many conspiracies you planned, your fate was unavoidable."

Kissing the tip of my nose, turning something so sweet into something so sinister, he murmured, "You've taken from me and I've taken from you. Now, it's time to end this so I can repair the damage you've caused."

Slipping his fingers from my cheeks to my hand, he snatched away the scissors and carted me from Bonnie's quarters. He left his mother decomposing; surrounded by bushels of her favourite blooms, already in a tomb with flowers.

Without my cast or sling, my broken arm twinged with pain. The wooze and wash of imbalance toyed with my vision as Cut carted me down the stairs.

"I'd planned on giving you a final night of pleasure, Nila. You deserved a shower, a good meal, a good fuck before your final breath. You've robbed me, not only of being generous for your good performance smuggling my diamonds but also of my opportunity to claim the Third Debt."

The Third Debt.

I'd been granted my wish, after all.

Hadn't I whispered I would rather pay with death than rape if I had a choice?

I didn't have a choice, but the preferable ending had been selected.

My skin broke out with clammy nervousness as Cut stalked me down the main artery of the house, past rooms I'd relaxed in, nooks I'd taken refuge in, libraries I'd napped in. Turning left, we bumped into a Black Diamond brother.

His leather jacket creaked as he slammed to a halt. "Cut."

Cut yanked me closer. "Are the final touches complete?"

The brother nodded, his shaved head and mix-matched tattoos absorbing the darkness of his attire. "Yes. All ready to go, as per your instructions."

Cut sniffed, his fingers tightening around mine. "Good. I have another task for you. My mother is dead. Take her body to the crypt below the Hall. I'll deal with her remains once my afternoon is finished."

The brother nodded obediently, unable to hide his sudden shock and curiosity hearing about Bonnie. "Okay…"

Cut stomped onward, then stopped. "One other thing. Get Jasmine. I want her there. And the rest of the brotherhood."

The man frowned but nodded again. "Right you are."

He took off the way we'd come, jogging with purpose.

I squirmed in Cut's hold, wishing he hadn't thrown his gun away upstairs. If the weapon were still lodged in his waistband, I could've commandeered it and shot him point blank. There was no need to be secretive any longer. No need to hide my true intentions.

He's my last victim.

"Where are you taking me?" I skip-trotted to keep up, gritting my teeth against my pain.

Cut smiled, his golden eyes blank and cruel. "The ballroom."

Chills darted down my spine.

Ballroom.

Instead of conjuring images of finery, sweeping drapes, and sparkling dancers, I pictured a mausoleum, a morgue…the last area I would ever see.

Jethro had said a debt would be repaid in the ballroom.

Despite my courage in Bonnie's quarters, fear engulfed me now.

Debt.

The last debt…

My heels dug into floor runners, creasing ancient rugs. Cut merely dragged harder, never slowing his pace.

Hawksridge seemed to exhale around us, the portraits and tapestries darkening as Cut dragged me down yet more ancient corridors. Moving toward large double doors in the same wing as the dining room, he stopped briefly before another Black Diamond brother opened the impressive entrance.

My eyes drank in the inscriptions and carvings on the doors, of hawks and mottos and the family crest of the man who was about to kill me in cold blood.

I'd walked past the doors countless times and never stopped to jiggle the handle—almost as if it'd kept itself secret until this moment—camouflaging itself to remain unseen until the Final Debt.

Cut clenched his jaw as the large entry groaned open, heavy on their hinges and weary with what they contained.

Once open, Cut threw me inside. Letting go of my hand, he grabbed a fistful of short hair, marching me to the centre of the room.

The chasmal space was exquisite. Crystals and candlesticks and chandeliers. Needlepoint and brocade and craftsmanship. Money echoed in every corner, shoving away dust motes and proving that glittering gold was immune to tarnish and age.

The gorgeous dance floor competed with the tapestry-covered walls and hand-stitched curtains, yet it wasn't overshadowed. The glossy wood created the motif of the Hawk crest inlaid with oak, cherry, and ash.

The black velvet curtains gleamed with diamonds sewn into the fabric, and everywhere I looked, the emblem of my capturers gilded wall panels and ceiling architraves.

There was no denying who this room belonged to, nor the wealth it had taken to acquire it.

"Like what you see, Weaver?" Cut never stopped as we stormed toward something large and covered by black sheeting in the middle of the empty expanse.

There were no chairs or banquet tables. Only acres of flooring with no one to dance. Loneliness and echoing eeriness swirled like invisible threads, tainting what would happen with its chequered history.

There'd been good times and bad in this place. Wine spilled with laughter and blood shed with tears.

Goosebumps darted over my flesh, almost as if I stepped through the time-veil. Able to see previous generations dancing, hear their lilting voices on the air.

And then I saw them.

Cut grunted as I slammed to a stop, zeroing in on the portraits he'd told me about in Africa.

The Hawk women.

Unlike the dining room with its over-crowded walls of men in white wigs, chalky faces, and gruffly stern expressions, the Hawk women bestowed the ballroom with class.

Their faces held colour of pink cheeks and red lips. Their hair artfully coiled and curled. And their dresses tumbled through the artist's brush-strokes, almost as if they were real.

Cut let me look. "Beautiful, aren't they?"

I didn't reply. I couldn't. I was overwhelmed with antiquity and yesteryear.

He let me survey his family's history while I searched for the portrait that'd caught my eye. I needed to look upon the woman who started it all.

I can't find her.

Bonnie.

She found me first.

Her painting hung vibrantly, royally. She'd posed with a white poodle and an armful of lilies. Her face unlined and youthful vitality hinting at a woman of early forties rather than the ancient ninety-one-year old who'd just perished.

Up and up the family tree my gaze soared, over Joans and Janes and Bessies.

And finally, at the very top, overseeing her realm and all that she helped create and conquer was Mabel Hawk.

The shadowy sketch wasn't as intricate in detail as the rest. Her grandson, William, could only remember so much, commissioning the painting off memory. But the intensity of her gaze popped full of soul even if her features weren't drawn with precision. She looked like any other woman from the bygone era. Any other mother and grandmother. Her gown of simple brown velvet held a single diamond at her bosom while her cheekbones swept into her hairline.

She reminded me of Jethro in a way. The same potency of sovereignty and power.

"Drink it in, my dear." Cut let go of my hair, running his fingers along my collar. "This room will be the last thing you ever see."

I still didn't respond. I'd taken so much from him, and I refused to give it back in the form of begging and tears.

Time ticked onward, but Cut didn't hurry me. I let the portraits on the wall tell their story, filling me with timeworn relics, ensuring when the time came to bow on my knees and succumb to the guillotine's blade, I would be more than just a girl, more than a Weaver, more than a victim of the Debt Inheritance.

I would be *history.*

I would be part of something so much bigger than myself and would take mementoes from this life to the next.

The room slowly filled with witnesses. Black Diamond brothers trickled in, lining the walls with their black leather. Out the corner of my eye, I noticed a few with bloody knuckles and shadow-bruised jaws. Why had they fought within their ranks? What had caused their violent disruption?

The oppressive summoning from the hidden apparatus in the ballroom pressed deeper and deeper the longer I ignored it. The portraits had been studied, the room scrutinized—I had nothing left to capture my attention away from the monolithic mysterious thing.

Cut turned me to face it. "Would you like to see below the cloak?" He smiled tightly. "I'm sure your imagination has created a version of what exists before you."

I straightened my spine. "Whatever you do to me, it won't bring them back."

He stiffened.

The gentle squeak of a wheel broke the brackish silence. I looked over my shoulder as Jasmine suddenly propelled herself into the room, slipping quickly over polished wood with a horrified expression. "What the hell do you think you're doing?"

Cut turned around, dropping his touch to land on my lower back. He didn't hold me in place, but I wasn't idiotic to think I wasn't trapped and unable to move.

"I'm doing what needs to be done."

Jasmine wheeled herself right up to Cut's knees. Her beautiful face pinched with disbelief. "No! That isn't your task. It's Jet—I mean, Daniel's."

Cut narrowed his eyes, looking between the two of us. "Fuck." He ducked down, grabbing his daughter roughly by the chin. "You knew, too. You knew all the fuck along Jethro and Kestrel were alive." He shook her. "What sort of daughter are you? What sort of loyalty do you have toward your own flesh and blood?"

Jasmine chopped her hands on Cut's wrists, breaking his hold on her cheeks. "My loyalty is to the right thing. And this is not right! Stop it. Right now."

Cut chuckled. "There is so much you don't know, Jaz, and so much you'll never learn. You're a failure and no longer a fucking Hawk. The moment I've dealt with Nila, I'll deal with you. What's good about family if it's the same family that does everything possible to destroy itself?"

Snapping his fingers, he growled at the brother who'd just arrived.

The man skidded through the doors, breathing hard as if he'd been at war rather than on whatever errands the club did.

My eyes met his. Dark floppy hair and kindness hid beneath ruthless.

Flaw.

My heart leapt, hope unspooling.

I had many enemies in this room but two people I cared about and trusted might be all I needed against Cut and his blade.

"Flaw, take my daughter to the back of the room. She's to watch from a safe distance and not to leave, understood?"

Flaw glanced at me. Secrets collided in his gaze before looking resolutely away. Nothing in his posture apologised or promised he would try to prevent the future. He merely nodded and clasped his hands around the handles of Jasmine's wheelchair. "Yes, sir."

Flaw...?

What had I done to warrant his sudden coolness?

Backing away, he dragged Jasmine with him.

She screeched and jammed on her brakes, leaving large grooves and tyre marks on the elegant floor. "No!"

"Don't argue, Ms. Hawk." Flaw dragged her faster toward the border of the room.

I couldn't believe he'd abandoned me. Wouldn't he at least try to argue for my life?

Jasmine made eye contact with me, fighting Flaw's yanking, shaking her head in despair. "Nila...where is he? Why isn't he stopping this?"

Jethro.

She means Jethro.

I wanted to tell her everything, but there was too much to that question and I had no strength to answer it. She didn't need to know what happened in Africa. She had her own issues to face once I'd departed this world at the hands of her father.

I shook my head, a sad smile on my lips. "I'm sorry, Jaz. I tried. We both did."

Tears welled, catching on her eyelashes. "No. This can't be happening. I won't let it." She reached behind her, trying to slap Flaw and scratch his hands from dragging her farther. "Let me go!"

With jerky movements, he bent angrily and hissed something unintelligible in her ear.

She froze.

Flaw used her sudden motionlessness to yank her the rest of the way.

What had he said?

How could he betray us?

My heart stopped. *Has he betrayed us or did he make another oath to Kes and Jethro I'm not aware of?*

Vexatious questions came faster, battering me with final worry. Was Kestrel awake? Was he alive in the hospital waiting for his brother to visit?

I wish I could say goodbye to him.

My tummy clenched even as I tried to remain strong.

I wish I could kiss Jethro one last time.

Cut spun around, forcing me to do the same. Flaw and Jasmine's eyes seared brands into the back of my spine. Two brothers dashed forward, gripping the ends of the black sheet hiding the apparatus, looking at Cut for commands.

He snapped his fingers with regality. "Remove it!"

Their hands gathered swaths of material and tugged. The fabric slid like ebony silk, kissing angles and gliding over surfaces, slowly revealing what I'd known existed all along.

The method of my death.

The equipment I'd hoped never to see.

There was no Jethro to stop it.

No Kestrel to fix it.

No Jasmine to ruin it.

Only me, Cut, and the awful gleaming guillotine.

The lights from the chandeliers bounced off the glossy wood of the frame, suspending a single blade ensconced in two pillars of wood. A latch at the top held it in place while the rope dangled down the side, ready to pull aside the barrier and let the blade plummet to its task.

And there…below the chopping block where my head would lay was the basket that would be my final resting place.

Cut kissed my cheek, wrapping an arm around my shoulders and guiding me toward the machine. "Say goodbye, Nila. It's time to pay the Final Debt."

Jethro

I'D BEEN AWAKE for centuries.

I'd travelled thousands of miles. I'd fought hundreds of battles. I'd lived a million lives in a matter of days.

My brain gasped for rest. My eyes screamed for sleep. But my heart pushed relentlessly toward the end.

"Stop here."

The taxi driver did as I asked, pulling to a halt beside a grass verge a few metres away from the entrance to Hawksridge. As soon as we'd landed, I'd paid the crew for their fast service and hopped into a taxi.

The flight had gone as planned. Once I'd made phone calls for Tex to gather his enforcements, Flaw to sort out the brothers, and Kill to hide on the grounds and watch from a distance, I'd focused on ensuring my body would continue to obey me and the strength I'd need for the future tasks wouldn't fail.

I'd eaten and tended to my wounds in the airplane bathroom. I'd patched up my gunshot wound as best I could and added a Band-Aid to the cut on my forehead. I asked the flight crew to give me the first-aid kit and took what pills I could to lower my incessant fever and subdue the aches and pains I didn't have time to deal with.

When we finally traded air for earth, I wasn't recharged or ready for carnage, but I was better than I'd been a few hours ago.

I had enough energy to finish this…and then…then I would sleep for a fucking eternity and let others worry about the world for a change.

Nila, I'm coming.

Once she was in my arms, I was never letting her go again.

Looking through the taxi windshield, my eyes widened at the countless cars and SUVs decorating the entrance to the Hall. All of them black and threatening—waiting for commands.

I hope to fuck that's Tex and his men.

"That's ten pounds twenty." The driver twisted in his seat, pointing at the metre.

I threw him twenty quid from the bankroll the captain had given me in exchange for another diamond and climbed out. "Keep the change."

The driver nodded, shifting into gear and pulling away from the verge. As he drove off, I prowled toward the convoy, peering at men I didn't recognise.

No, that wasn't true.

I did recognise them. I recognised the ferocity in their gaze. The merciless stare of a hired killer. I felt their quiet thoughts and slipstream of emotional commitment to a job they'd been hired to do.

I wanted to grab them all in a fucking hug and thank them profusely for being on my side after a lifetime of war.

Vaughn spotted me first.

Nila's brother careened around a 4WD, pointing his finger in my face. "*You.* What the *fuck* is going on?" Gel plastered black hair away from his face; his eyes ready to slaughter me.

Not giving me time to reply, he grabbed his right forearm, shoving it beneath my nose. "What did you do to her? Why do I have an ache in my arm?" Grabbing me by the neck, he growled, "Tell me what the *fuck* you did to my sister!"

His internal thoughts flew haywire, screeching in fear and fluster.

I held up my hands, submitting to his hold. "Your fight is not with me." I held my ground as he clenched his fists, tightening his grip. "I didn't touch her. I *love* her. I'm on your side, Weaver."

"Let him go, V." Tex appeared from around another vehicle, dressed all in black like his son. They truly looked alike, whereas Nila looked very much like Emma. A true family. The only thing my family had in common was insanity and golden eyes.

Damn genetics.

Damn contracts and debts and greed.

Vaughn bared his teeth, ignoring his father. "I asked you a question, Hawk. I *said* what the *fuck* is going on? I didn't ask if you're on our side. That's debatable, and we'll make up our own minds without you telling us thank you very fucking much."

I dropped my hands, my fingers itching for one of the guns holstered to the men slowly surrounding us. Each man held an arsenal on his body, fully equipped for battle and not afraid of firepower or injury.

My back ached from bowing with my neck in a headlock, but I wouldn't fight. I refused to fight with the Weavers anymore. "Let me go."

"No. Not until you talk."

"We're going to end this." My voice sounded tired to my ears, but truth rang loud. "That's what's going on."

V shook with anger. "Where's my sister?"

"At the Hall."

"Is she safe?" Tex asked, his aging face strained but resolute. In a different world, I would've liked Nila's father. His inner thoughts were gentle and quiet—almost like Kes with the ability to switch off overwhelming hate or happiness, living a mediocre life of monitored emotions. Unlike Kes, who'd learned to hide in order to live a better existence, I doubted Textile did it for fun.

My suspicions were he kept his true feelings locked away, padlocked and buried, so he didn't have to deal with a daily drowning of sorrow and regret of losing the women of his family.

Surprisingly, there was no guilt. He'd allowed me to take Nila with no fight or fury. He should feel some patina of shame for handing over his daughter, even if he'd been trained to do exactly that. There was more to his defeat than he let on. Something lurked on the outskirts of his thoughts…wrapped up in flickering pride and solemn dignity at something he'd done where Nila was concerned.

What did he do?

Vaughn suddenly released me, pushing me away from him and rubbing his forearm. "She's hurt. I feel her—always did."

My eyes shot to his, appreciating the twin-link he and Nila shared more than he knew. He might feel her physically, but I felt her emotionally. And he was right, she *was* hurt.

Tex sucked in a heavy breath, his large shoulders rolling beneath stress. I made a note to ask him what he'd done when this was all over. I wanted to know his secrets. I had a feeling he held the answers to a lot of loose ends.

But now is not the time.

Nila.

We'd stalled enough.

Is she safe? Are you safe, Nila? Please, be fucking safe.

I shook my head. "We need to go. You're right, she's hurt. My father broke her arm, and I have no doubt he means to do more than that. That's why we have to move fast."

"*What!?*" V's eyes narrowed to slits. "You'll pay, Hawk. I'll make you pay for every injury Threads has endured because of your fucking family."

My heart pattered irregularly—my rhythm always struggled when faced with such overwhelming emotion. "I'll pay whatever you want, Weaver. But for now, we have to work together." Eyeing up the cars, I counted eight in total. At least two men to a car, so sixteen men.

Sixteen men to kill Cut and whatever brothers remained patriotic to him. I didn't relish the thought of killing club members who'd served beneath me for years, but maybe I wouldn't have to if Flaw managed to separate the loyal from the traitors.

I cocked my chin at the silent mercenaries. "They work for you?"

Tex nodded. "I told you I'd hired help. I found them before you came to take Nila."

My nostrils flared. "*Before?*"

If he had them before, why not use them to protect Nila from ever falling into my hands?

Tex swallowed, looking away. "I meant *after* you took Nila. I gathered an army. I won't let you take another of my loved ones, Hawk. I won't."

His slip-up and sudden lie to switch timelines didn't make sense. There was no one else to take. Nila was the firstborn girl. We never went after Weaver sons.

So what is he hiding?

Pushing aside my curiosity, I nodded. "I know. And you won't have to." Searching for the ringleader, discarding ex-Army and Marines by the way they held their shoulders and weapons, I ordered, "Who's in charge here?"

Vaughn stomped closer, poking his annoying finger in my chest. "We are, motherfucker."

I gritted my teeth. "Fine, if that's how you want to play it. How about you give them orders on how best to infiltrate. If you know where Cut will have Nila and how to get inside the estate undetected, be my fucking guest."

Tex growled under his breath. "Watch it. We're tolerating you right now. Doesn't mean we've agreed to be your taskforce when you've already taken so much. We're here for Nila and that's it. You hear me?"

I swiped a hand over my face. "If you're here for Nila, prove it. She's in trouble. The longer we stand here comparing dick sizes, the worse she'll need help." Spreading my arms, I snarled, "You decide. You want my insider knowledge so this goes well or would you rather do things your way and risk Nila dying and yourself in the crossfire?"

Tension smouldered between us, itching for a naked flame to incinerate.

Tex looked at Vaughn. They shared a silent conversation until finally Tex exhaled heavily. "Fine. We agree to cooperate."

"Good." I crossed my arms. "I'm in control from here on out. I'm the only one who knows where to go, how to get in, and what we need to do."

"Like fuck you are. I've stayed in your house of horrors. I know enough to guess—"

Tex placed his hand on his son's shoulder. "Enough, V. Let him. I just want my daughter back, and if he says he can do that, then…let him get her back." Twisting to face an elderly man with a black beanie on his head, Tex motioned him to come forward. "Change of plans, Dec. Follow Hawk's orders. Let's move out."

The silent journey through the estate twisted me with fear.

The driveway went on for a fucking eternity, revealing our black line of cars clearly. I just hoped Cut was busy elsewhere and didn't look out the south-facing windows onto the sweeping vista as we crept over Hawksridge.

Rolling hills and soft dirt hindered but didn't slow; we chewed up distance, bringing me closer to Nila and my dreaded birthright.

I rode with the ringleader, Declan. He'd given me his resume in a few short bullet points.

Retired military.

Awarded service.

Highly trained and skilled with the best men loyalty and money could buy.

Sitting with him, I suffered flashbacks of hunting animals for food and sport. For someone like me—someone who felt not just human emotions but even the emotions of the basest of creatures—I struggled to hunt like a normal, unfeeling being.

Cut knew that.

He'd forced me to hunt until I could switch off the panic of the prey and focus on the joy of the predator.

It'd been one of his most valuable lessons.

Focus on the hawk stalking the rabbit, not the rabbit running for its life.

Focus on the dog's infectious joy bounding after a deer, not the deer galloping from death.

Those two parallels had been so fucking hard to choose between, but I'd done it. I'd even been so successful, the predator's joy infected me enough for hunting to become almost…fun.

And now I was on another hunt. About to hurt others, about to feel their pain.

But I could do it because I was the beast, not the quarry. And I was surrounded by men who focused on the same sweet victory.

That was all I needed to know. I trusted Declan and his men. I just hoped they'd be enough if the Black Diamonds decided to fight against us.

I hope Flaw came through.

I didn't want bloodshed. The Hall had seen enough fucking death. I wanted to end terror without more of it. But I was prepared for either scenario.

Hawksridge appeared above us, watching us with its impressive turrets and spires. The ancient building had been my home all my life. The grounds had been my salvation. The animals, my lifeblood.

I'd grown up running away from this place, but now, I wanted to turn my legacy around. I would rule a different dynasty from the one Cut envisioned, and I would do it on my own terms with Nila by my side.

Pointing at a service track—an un-tarmacked path with weeds growing through pebbles, I said, "Follow that road. It'll cut across the chase and head in behind the main entrance. We might prevent being seen a little longer."

Hawksridge sat perched on a hill. The design was deliberate for times of war and protection from enemies who might try to topple the estate. No ambush could happen. No entrapment. We would be seen—it was a matter of time. I just didn't want to show my hand before we were close enough to launch an attack.

Where are you, Nila?

Was she with Bonnie on the third floor?

Was she with Cut on the fourth?

Or was she already in the ballroom on the ground floor, on her knees and about to become the latest stain in a horrendous basket?

"Step on the gas." My order lurched us forward, tyres grinding gravel, skidding around bends and hurling us closer to the awaiting battleground.

I'd deliberately chosen to travel with two mercenaries and not Nila's brother or father. I needed to keep my head clear and I couldn't do that with Vaughn's emotions bouncing kamikaze in his skull or Textile's secrets gnawing a hole in my patience.

No one talked as we pulled to a stop by the stables. A wash of homesickness crippled me. Not for the Hall but for Wings. Being around so many people set my nerves on edge. My condition flickered with intensity and numbness. One moment, I was blank from sensory overload, and the next, I'd succumb to frivolous things of what the men would do afterward, what they planned to do during.

People saw fellow humans as respectful and civilized. Only, I knew the truth.

They were as animalistic as they'd been hundreds of years ago. Inner thoughts and unspoken quips painted them as vindictive, selfish, and focused on things that should never be revealed aloud.

It almost made me happy to know I wasn't as terrible as I'd feared. I was normal. I was human. I had faults and flaws and fears, but despite all of those, I tried to be better, bolder, and braver than I truly was.

And that was what made right triumph over wrong.

Isn't it?

At least, I hoped so.

The convoy rolled to a stop, and Dec gave the order to leave the cars behind. Boots landed on gravel, and car doors quietly closed. Concentration levels of the men added to the cauldron of emotions, and I wiped away a combination of fever and sweat from trying not to listen.

Once Nila was safe and Hawksridge secured, I would need to be alone. I knew the symptoms of system failure. I knew when I'd reached my limit. A wash of nausea climbed up my gullet, and my hands shook as I wrapped fingers around the gun Dec handed me.

I was borderline.

Overtiredness and over-empathy would end up killing me if I didn't kill Cut soon.

"Come on." I waved for the men to line up behind me, a black line patrolling from the stables toward the Hall.

Leaving the cars behind, I guided the men up the hill toward the house. We stuck to the trees as much as possible, moving in short waves. Weapons were drawn as we crested the hill and made our final descent.

I didn't say a word, too focused on seeking weakness and attack points of my family's home. I searched the shadows for Kill and his men, trying to see where they hid, but spotted no one.

The closer we got to the Hall, the more my heart pounded.

V and Tex shadowed my every move and luck kept us shrouded long enough to sidle up to the ancient architecture and fan out around the buttresses of Hawksridge.

Left or right?

I couldn't decide.

Dining room wing or staircase leading to boudoirs and parlours?

The wind howled over the orchard, sounding like someone screamed.

I froze; my head tilted toward the dining room wing…the ballroom wing.

The noise came again.

Haunting.

Lamenting.

Dragging chills over my flesh.

It came again, shrill and cut short.

It wasn't the wind.

Fuck surprise.

Fuck the regimented ambush.

Fuck everything.

Nila!

I held my gun aloft and charged.

Nila

"READY TO DIE, Nila?"

Cut's voice physically hurt me as he forced me up the crudely made steps and onto the wooden foundation. My heart tore through my ribcage.

Jasmine screamed from across the room. Her cry split the ballroom apart, tears staining her pretty cheeks. "Please."

Tears of my own threatened to wash me away, but I wanted to remain dry-eyed. I wanted to remember my last few moments in perfect clarity and not swimming with liquid.

Cut wrenched my arms behind my back; I groaned with agony from my break. The twine wrapped around my wrists, bending my forearm unnaturally.

"Please. Don't——"

Cut spun me around with his large hands on my shoulders. His golden eyes glowed with apology, and at the same time, resolution. "Hush, Nila." His lips touched mine, sweet and soft, before he marched me to the kneeling podium and pressed hard. "Kneel."

"No!"

"Kneel." His foot kicked out, nudging the back of my knee, shattering my stability and sending me cracking into place. I cried out as the pain in my kneecaps matched the pain in my arm. Like a snapped needle, I lost my sharpness, my fight.

The ballroom splendour mocked me as I bowed unwillingly at the foot of my executioner.

Velvet and hand-stitched crewel on the walls glittered like the diamonds the Hawks smuggled—a direct contrast to the roughly sawn wood and crude craftsmanship of the guillotine dais.

"Don't do this. Cut...think about what you've become. You can *stop* this." My voice mimicked a beg, but I'd vowed *not* to beg. I'd seen things, understood things, and suffered things I never thought I would be able to endure. I'd been their plaything for months, their adversary for years, their nemesis for centuries. I refused to cry or grovel. I wouldn't give him that satisfaction.

I know the history of the Hawks. I know I'm stronger than they are.

"I want to live. Please, let me live."

He cleared his throat, masking any thoughts of hesitation. "In five minutes, this will all be over." Cut bent to the side and collected a wicker basket.

The wicker basket.

I didn't want to think about what its contents would be.

He placed it on the other side of the wooden block.

My heart jack-hammered, thudding faster and faster until lightheadedness made me sick.

My lungs demanded more oxygen. My brain demanded more time. And my heart…it demanded more hope, more life, more love.

I'm not ready.

Not like this.

"Cut—"

"No. No more talking. Not after everything you've done. My son. My mother. You think you've stolen everything I care about, but I'm going to steal so much more from you. From Jethro. And when I find out where Kestrel is, I'll steal from him, too." Ripping a black hood from his pocket, he didn't hesitate. No fanfare. No pauses.

"No!" I cried out as the scratchy blackness engulfed my face, tightening by a cord around my throat.

The Weaver Wailer chilled me. The diamond collar that'd seen what I'd seen and whispered with phantoms of my slain family prepared to revoke its claim and detach from around my neck.

This was it.

The Final Debt.

Cut pushed my shoulders forward.

I struggled, willing my wrists to unlock, to find a weakness in the rope to get free.

A heavy yoke settled over the top of my spine.

No. This can't be it. This can't be!

"Goodbye, Nila."

The breeze of Cut moving to the side sent goosebumps over my nape. My breath clouded the hood. My eyelashes jewelled with unshed tears.

I hunched, tensing against the painful conclusion.

I couldn't get free.

I couldn't save myself.

I hadn't won.

Cut's boots crunched on the platform, the gentle clink of rope and pulley signalling he'd reached for the release of the blade.

I waited for his last history lesson.

Surely, I should have a history lesson.

All the debts did. He couldn't have forgotten the theatrics of the debt. His story would extend my life just a little longer.

But no words fell.

Only my breathing…

My heart beating…

My tears falling…

My body living its final seconds…

I'm dead.

I curled inside, waiting to perish.

A loud bang rang in my ears.

For a moment, I thought I'd died.

In my mind, I saw the jerk of the rope. I felt the slice of sharpness. I suffered the untethering severance.

I waited for some mystical deliverance where my soul flew free, growing wings to hover over my decapitated body.

I hung in limbo waiting for pain or freedom.

But neither came.

What was death?

How would it feel?

What should I expect?

Would the blade slice through and turn me from alive to dead? Would I know once it had happened? Would I witness the end and feel the agony as my soul snipped free?

Or would it be over so fast I wouldn't even know he'd stripped my life away?

I tensed.

Nothingness...

Am I dead?

Nothing happened.

Then every sense rushed into liveliness. The hood still covered my head. The yoke still crushed my shoulders. And the burning break in my arm still throbbed.

All my discomforts returned along with noise.

So, so much noise.

Deafening noise.

Gunfire slaughtered the air as footsteps pounded the hardwood floor of the ballroom. Men hollered. Things banged and clanged and a cacophony replaced the empty silence.

Curses. Words. Promises. They were all cut short as fighting broke out all around me.

I couldn't see, but I could *feel.*

The whoosh of wind as bodies flew past. The flinch of bullets flying too close to my skin. And Cut's hand on my head as he bellowed for it all to stop. "Black Diamonds! Attack!"

More boots. More curses. More bullets.

Thank you, thank you, thank you.

My final hopes had been answered, my prayers delivered.

Help had arrived at the last second.

Who was out there?

Who fought on my behalf?

My eyes begged to see. My body twisted to know. But Cut's fingers dug into the hood, pressing my throat against the wood and the yoke tight over my shoulders.

Instead of dying, I'd entered a warzone where my vision couldn't tell me a story.

I huddled at Cut's feet, my spine curled and knees bruised beneath a guillotine just waiting for the sharp edge to plummet.

My heart lodged in my throat, terrified a rogue bullet would slice the rope and drop the blade to butcher my tender flesh.

I was alive, but for how much longer?

How reckless was the fighting?

How could they prevent an unforeseen event from killing me all while they tried to save me?

"Fuck." Cut never stopped touching me, his fingers digging into my scalp as anarchy rained. "Over there, get him!" His orders fell on the raucous, delivered to an unseen fighter.

I had no way to judge time, but the war only increased in ferocity. More gunfire, more thuds as bodies fell and fists connected with flesh.

My ears rang with gunshots. My thoughts suffocated with violence and mayhem.

Grunts and curses bounced off portraits and velvet, changing the destiny of the ballroom from dancing frivolity to carnage brutality.

Stop.

Don't stop.

Save me.

Don't kill me.

Slowly, curses switched to moans and stampeding footsteps gave way to limping.

The fight could've lasted hours or seconds. The only thing I knew with certainty was I clung to this life—the one I didn't want to leave—and the break in my arm cemented me firmly into being.

Finally, a stranger's voice crescendoed over everything else. "You've lost, Hawk. Step away from the rope if you wish to remain alive and not meet your maker."

That voice...I didn't recognise it.

Shivers stole my muscles.

Cut could still kill me.

The battle was over, but my life could be, too.

I couldn't breathe.

One second.

Two.

Three.

Disbelief and uprising perfumed the air. Boots stomped forward, the click of a bullet entering a trigger chamber the only noise in the suddenly silent ballroom.

"Let her go, Cut."

That voice I did recognise. I would know it anywhere.

Him.

I trembled in love.

I wept in gratitude.

He'd come for me.

He'd saved me.

Jethro.

"Never. Lower your weapon, or I pull. I'll do it, Jet. You know I will."

Another voice I adored joined that of my lover. "You do and I'll shoot you until you're so full of holes even the worms won't want you."

My father.

"And if he shoots you, I'll shoot you three. You'll be fucking shredded."

My twin.

Their voices pulsed with barbarity I'd never heard before.

Three men I never thought would be in the same room together, let alone fighting on the same side. How things had changed since that night in Milan.

I wanted so much to stay alive. To launch into Jethro's arms and kiss my father and touch my twin. But no one moved as I remained trapped by the guillotine.

Hope warred with defeat.

Cut could still kill me so easily and no one would be able to stop him. If they shot him and he held the rope in his hand, the guillotine would fall. If he decided to commit suicide and die right alongside me, no one could stop him from releasing the blade.

Only the final shred of decency left in Cut could stop him from doing the unthinkable and stripping me of a future I so desperately wanted.

Do something.

I didn't know what. My mind was blank.

Play him...

Cut had welcomed me into his home, he'd had moments of civility, of *normalness*—he was human beneath his devilish ways. Perhaps...perhaps there was some way to cajole him into listening.

I whispered through the hood, "I forgive you."

It sounded condescending and forced.

Try harder.

"I forgive you for everything you've done. What you did to Emma, me, your children. I forgive you. Let me live and break the indebted history."

Jethro sucked in a breath.

No one else spoke.

Everything hinged on the bond between Cut and me.

I huddled beneath the blade...waiting for his decision. Over the past few months, we'd come to understand one another. I knew he loved his children in his twisted way. And he knew I wouldn't give up without a fight.

There was hatred between us but respect, too.

If only that respect saved my life.

The whole room paused, watching history unfold.

Feet scuffled and weapons spewed rich-smelling smoke from used gunpowder, but no one moved.

My spine tickled with tears, fearing the worst.

I'd offered my forgiveness, going against everything I'd wanted to say. I'd traded my own morals for the right to keep my life. But what if it wasn't enough? What if my only value to Cut was in pieces?

"Cut..." I breathed. "Don't let her win."

The pulley clanked as Cut flinched. I didn't need to look into his eyes to know I'd hit home. Watching Bonnie die of her body's own volition had taught me something. She had been the root of all psychotic and immoral behaviour in her family. She was the one who drove her children to the point of lunacy. She was the seed sprouting such demonic petals.

And now, she was dead.

"You don't need to obey her anymore." My voice came out half-prayer, half-beg. "Free me. End this."

Once again, silence settled like a smothering pillow.

No one moved.

Cut's body heat branded my thigh, standing, just standing. *Deliberating.*

Then...finally...the clinking of rope and mechanism sounded again, only this time I didn't fear it. Cut's leg nudged me as he secured the rope, staying the blade and my death.

I didn't breathe as he squatted beside me.

I didn't flinch as his hands landed on my shoulders, undoing the yoke and helping me to my feet.

I didn't make a noise as his fingers untied the rope around my wrists and his touch grabbed a handful of hair as he tore off the hood in one swipe.

I didn't do anything to make him regret his courageous decision.

He'd saved me knowing he was doomed himself.

Was that redemption? Was it enough to be free of everything he'd done?

I trembled as the black material freed my vision, blinking as my eyes accommodated to light.

Cut didn't smile or grimace, he just stared.

I wanted some time to take stock of how close I'd been to dying. To look my potential murderer in the face and thank him for sparing me even while hexing him to hell.

But the moment our gazes met, Jethro stormed up the podium and yanked Cut's hands behind his back.

Bryan didn't say a word, submitting to his son.

I remained locked in the moment, reading so much into Cut's eyes but not understanding any of it. Rubbing my throat and the phantom slice through my neck, I nodded. "Thank you."

Cut shrugged in answer to all the questions I wanted to ask, before allowing his eldest to jerk him down the steps and throw him into my father's control.

The minute Cut looked away, my attention switched to the space around me.

I gasped.

The pristine ballroom had turned into a warzone. Blood spilled and broken men decorated the pretty floor. Men dressed in black and Black Diamond brothers both moaned and held their multiple wounds.

What the hell happened?

Who were these men?

Flaw came forward with Jasmine at his side. He gave me a tight smile as Jethro gripped my upper arms. "Are you okay?"

I flinched, drinking him in.

Was I in shock? A dream?

I couldn't make sense of how calmly I accepted that I was about to die and now...wasn't. I'd been granted a second life...and all I could do was nod in a daze and blink in a stupor.

"Fuck, Nila." Jethro crushed me to him. My broken arm wailed, but I didn't care at all. All I cared about was him.

I hugged him back, squeezing as hard as I could. "You're here."

"I'm here."

"You saved me."

"You saved me first."

"I love you."

"I love you more."

"It's over." He pulled back, kissing my lips with the softest flutter.

"Is it truly?"

Jethro smiled with the wattage of a thousand moons. "It's done."

My heart unfurled, and for the first time, I believed that.

The Final Debt would never be paid.
The Hawks had lost.
The Weavers were free.
The Debt Inheritance would never claim another victim.

Jethro

"NO, FOR THE final time, you're not coming." I pushed Nila aside. "You're not going to be there when I do what needs to be done."

Her mouth opened to argue, her uninjured arm hugging her broken one. "But—"

"No buts. You're not coming. No matter what you say. You. Are. Not. Coming." A sliver of the old me—the arsehole who'd collected her that first night—came back. That shell had long since broken, but it rapidly reformed.

And I let it.

I let it because what I was about to do would test every inch of my condition. It would kill me as much as it would kill Cut because I would feel everything my father would go through. I wouldn't be able to shut off his emotional screams nor freeze myself from ignoring his thoughts.

I would be with him for every lash.

Nila tried to grab my arm. "Jet—"

Dodging her hold, I pointed a finger in her face. "No, Nila. You're to stay. *Obey* for once. Don't make me ask again."

"You're not asking, you're telling."

"Goddammit." I swallowed hard, running a hand through my hair. I hadn't slept in days, my body hurt all over, and my mind barely functioned from dealing with so much death and agony in the ballroom. Seeing her on her knees with the hood on her face and guillotine above her head—it'd fucking crippled me.

I'd hurt so many people for her. I wore their souls like badges of worthless honour. And yet, she *still* argued.

I can't do this.

You have to.

I couldn't falter now. Not when the end was so close.

All I wanted to do was drag Nila to her quarters, tend to her arm, and fall asleep. I wanted today to be over so tomorrow could banish the past.

But I couldn't.

I had things to do, and I would not—no matter how much she fucking argued—let Nila be a part of them.

I looked at my sister as she wheeled closer. My eyes shot two messages: *Help and don't argue.* My voice sounded like I'd been smoking for decades. "Take Nila to her quarters."

Jasmine nodded slightly, understanding better than anyone what I was about to do and why I had to do it. Her fingers slinked around Nila's unbroken wrist.

Nila jerked, trying to free herself. "What? No way." Managing to shake Jasmine off, she planted one hand on her hip; the other she let hover by her waist, protected by her body.

Her gaze darted between Cut and me. "He's not worth it. Can't you see that? He isn't worth what you're about to—"

I grabbed her cheeks, rubbing my thumbs over her face. "Nila…shush. I need you to let me do this."

Tears sprang to her eyes. The diamond collar he'd almost extracted glittered in the false light of the chandeliers.

I forced myself to hide my nerves, soothing her with whispered confidence. "Don't ask me to stop. It's what I need to do to fix my family and yours—our very history."

Tears trickled over my thumbs as she fought my decision. "But—"

"There are no buts, Needle." Looking at Cut, I hardened my heart toward him. He'd done the right thing in the end. He'd let her go. Nothing had stopped him from killing Nila in front of me. Only his decency and lingering affection for Emma.

When Nila had forgiven him, I thought for sure he would pull the lever. He'd never been good at accepting charity.

But for once, he went against the actions of the man who'd raised me and became a hero. He deserved a fragment of respect for that gallant move.

But he also deserved to pay a very painful toll for every other sin he'd committed.

That was his fate.

And it was my fate to deliver it.

Nila pressed her cheek into my palm, her skin warm beneath my touch. "Kite…I—"

I understood her knotted thoughts and scrambled conclusions. "I know." My voice was a breath as I kissed her. "I understand your fear, but you have to trust me."

How many times had I asked her to trust me, only to shatter the trust she bestowed?

I won't shatter it this time.

I knew what I was doing.

Don't I?

Nila's onyx eyes glowed with rebellion, and I steeled myself against yet another argument. I sensed she only wanted to support me. For me to lean on her while I did something so heinous. But I didn't *want* to lean on her. I had to do this for me, my siblings, my past and present.

I couldn't have her there because I didn't know if I'd be able to carry out the punishment he deserved. I didn't know if I'd break and crumble and submit to his power like I'd done all my life.

It would be my biggest trial. But I'd try my fucking hardest to make Cut pay.

Dropping my hands from Nila's cheeks, I stepped back. "Just trust me, okay?"

Kill morphed from the men checking on the wounded, coming toward our tight-knit gathering.

Flaw had fetched his medical equipment and put his healing knowledge to work on those needing immediate attention. I trusted him to arrange help and take those who required more than he was capable of to the hospital without alerting a massacre had just taken place.

Killian had come through for me. He'd waited outside the ballroom where Tex, V, and our team of mercenaries poured in. He had his gun pinpointed on Cut and would've pulled the trigger if we hadn't arrived at that exact moment.

He would've saved Nila without a bloodbath, but by doing so, he would've stripped me of the right to make my father pay. It'd been risky, barging in and giving Cut the opportunity to murder Nila right before my eyes, but Cut didn't know everything that I did.

He slipped.

In Africa, I'd felt a slight thawing in him. And today, as we barged in and brought death on our heels, he looked almost...relieved. As if he expected me to show up and was grateful it was over.

I couldn't understand it. But he couldn't keep it hidden any longer. He'd finally shown the truth of how tired he was. How tired we all were.

All my life, he'd been a controlling bastard with unattainable ideals and strict rules. I'd maintained my belief that he never liked us, let alone loved us. But there was something more to him. Something I never let myself focus on as it only confused my conclusion of my father.

But I sensed it now. A deeper facet poured from Cut as Kill jerked him from Textile's arms and pinched his shoulders. My father held a lot of hate and delivered many ruthless requests, but he also held compassion and guilt.

And that guilt had steadily grown more and more dominant the longer Nila lived with us.

That was another reason why I wanted to be alone with him. I wanted to look him in the eye, drop my defences, and truly strip my father of his secrets so I could understand him for the first time in my life.

And that was why I didn't know if I'd be able to go ahead with what he deserved. because what if I found his secrets redeemed him? What if I felt something that changed twenty-nine years of believing a lie?

"Jethro..." Nila's voice dragged me back from thoughts and tiredness. My vision wavered, dancing with figments of hallucinations from lack of sleep and stress overload. The hallucinations weren't anything major, just the odd flutter of a curtain looking like a blackbird or a ripple of sunshine resembling a bumblebee or butterfly.

Innocuous things but non-existent things nevertheless.

Sleep.

I could sleep soon.

Pinching the bridge of my nose, I inhaled deeply. *Keep it together. A few more hours and I'll be free.* We'd all be fucking free, and I could rest safely for the first time since I could remember.

The minute this was over, I would visit my brother. I would tell him things were taken care of and it was safe to come home.

I missed him so fucking much.

Time to return, baby brother.

Time for me to show him I had his back like he'd had mine all my life.

"Kite...I do trust you. But you need to rest." Nila's fingers landed on my hand. "Please, whatever you're thinking of doing, it's already eating you alive." Pointing at Cut imprisoned in Kill's arms, she murmured, "You've won. The Debt Inheritance is over. Let the authorities deal with him."

I chuckled darkly. "Authorities? Nila, we *own* the authorities. No one would dare testify or incarcerate him. If you want justice, this is the only way." Cupping her chin, I smeared a strand of cotton from the hood away from her skin. "Trust me when I say this is what needs to happen. Don't try to stop me again."

Nila dropped her gaze. Her heart raced, her emotions bubbling like the hot springs beneath the Hall, but she obeyed me. She stepped back, giving me the freedom to leave.

I sighed, thanking her silently.

Cut didn't say a word—not that he could. The minute he'd submitted to my custody, I'd returned the favour of a reeking rancid gag and duct-taped his mouth closed. His nostrils flared, white hair cascading over his forehead in a tumbled mess.

Daniel was dead. Bonnie would be soon. Cut would be the next to expire.

Nila stepped back as Jasmine wheeled closer to me and grabbed my hand. "I won't try to stop you, but don't feel like you have to—"

"Don't you start, Jaz."

"I'm only worried about what—"

I laughed coldly. "What it will do to me? Jaz, you know yourself what will happen if I *don't* do this. I'll never forgive myself. He's delivered enough agony to those we love. Don't you think it's time he felt his own medicine?"

Kill didn't say a word, gripping my father tighter in his arms.

Nila bit her lip, looking down at Jasmine, waiting for her reply.

Jaz sat stiffly in her chair. I let my condition fan stronger, singling her out in the crowd. She felt the same fear Nila did. Fear that I'd never be the same if I did this. Fear that it would forever haunt me.

That might be the case, but I owed this debt. To the miners who'd helped free me. To Kill who'd had my back. To Textile for the death of his wife. To everyone involved in the Debt Inheritance.

I wasn't doing this for me. I was doing this for *them*. And it was a sacrifice I was willing to make.

Jaz smiled softly as my eyes met hers. Her emotions quieted, fading into one singular calling: closure.

I nodded, letting her know I understood her conclusion. "Thank you."

She smoothed the blanket over her useless legs. Legs that'd been payment for me. Disability given by our father who would now answer for his crimes.

Tonight was the night everything ended.

Cut's life was the full stop on his terrible reign.

Jaz nodded, too. Wordlessly giving me permission and strength. Her eyes narrowed on Cut. "I tried to be the daughter you wanted, but I was never good enough. I hope that thought alone haunts you for eternity."

Cut's chest rose with an influx of breath, repentance bright in his gaze.

She didn't give him forgiveness like Nila had. She'd suffered too much at his hand to be so selfless.

Her switch of fear for me and need for retribution drenched her. She wanted me to do this. She *urged* me to do this.

Good enough for me.

Cut swallowed, his face glowing, filling with things addressed to his daughter. The scramble of emotions from him smothered me and I deliberated removing his gag to say farewell to Jasmine.

However, my sister decided for me. Her fists wrapped around her wheels, shoving backward and granting space for Killian to move forward.

"Take him." Her voice hissed. "I don't want to see him anymore." Grabbing Nila's hand, she kept her anchored as Kill stormed forward, carting Cut toward the exit.

Nila's gaze met mine. I sent a silent message. *You understand why?*

Her lips twisted, but she nodded. *Yes.*

"I'll come find you when it's done." Turning my back on Nila's family and a room full of carnage, I stalked past Kill and snapped my fingers for him to follow.

I didn't stop to give directions. I trusted the biker president of Pure Corruption would obey. Whatever hierarchy existed, we were on equal footing. Kill knew the terms when he came to help me. I would pay him back for his help. I would honour the agreement we'd made.

Besides, his task was almost over.

While mine is just beginning.

Leaving the room of men, I sucked in a breath. The oxygen helped cleanse my system of thoughts and pain. I did my best to shut out Cut, but I couldn't completely ignore him.

We were bound together until the end. Blood to blood. Pain to pain. There would be no separating my mind from his until he was dead.

"Jethro—" Nila gave chase, following us out the exit, leaving the guillotine behind.

I spun around just in time for her to launch into my arms. Her black hair glistened like a raven wing. The afternoon sunshine mocked us after the darkness that'd happened in the ballroom.

Kill continued onward, dragging Cut away and granting a small oasis of silence. My arms wrapped around her tightly even though I wanted to push her away.

Her chest rose and fell, her embrace one-armed with her other dangling painfully by her side. "Please, Kite…just stop for a moment and—"

"Nila, you promised."

"I know, but—" Her eyes met mine, glossing with angry tears. "I'm not going to stop you. I understand. I really do. I just. I needed to—I need…"

My heart overflowed, and I grabbed her. My forehead nudged hers as I bowed over her. "I know what you need."

My mouth claimed hers and she sighed, melted, positively submitted to my kiss. Her tongue instantly met mine in a tangle of hot desire, invoking pleasure and pain and undeniable passion.

This kiss deleted the last one we'd shared in the mine as she was dragged away. That kiss had been a goodbye. This kiss was a hello. An acknowledgment we soon wouldn't have to fear tomorrow. That the future was no longer our enemy but our friend. We could be together. Our promise to get married could come true. Our heartbeats unnumbered now we'd won.

Pulling away, I kissed the tip of her nose, her eyelids, her hair. "I'll be back soon."

She arched in my hold, peppering my rough cheeks with affection. "I'll be waiting for you."

"I know."

Slipping from my embrace, her gaze travelled past me to Cut. "Do you mind?"

I stiffened but didn't stop her. "By all means."

If it granted her closure, who was I to stop her saying goodbye? Cut was no threat. Even if he wasn't bound and gagged and held by Kill, he wouldn't run. I knew he'd accepted his fate and would stand regal and defiant until the end.

His almost royal bearing made me proud for a moment. Proud that I came from such strong stock, even if madness ran in his veins. If my condition had prevented me from inheriting his drive for perfection, regardless of what sins he committed, then I was glad.

I wasn't like my family.

I was unique.

I was me.

And I'd never been more fucking grateful.

Nila padded over to Cut, her bare feet disappearing into the long grass. Kill didn't speak as she stopped in front of my father. The wind whipped her hair around her jaw, slicing and slicking, looking like oil in the breeze.

"I said before that I forgive you."

Cut shifted, rolling his shoulders in Kill's grip.

"I'm not here to take that forgiveness back. I don't even know *why* I'm here." She rubbed her face, trying to re-centre herself. "I guess I wanted to say…be thankful. Your crimes have caught up with you…and I'm there to see it." Her voice lowered as she looked back up. "I'm here to see you one last time. To know you're just human. That you were doing what you thought was right, but now you have to pay. We all have to pay, Cut. Nothing is free in this world, and you've taken enough from my family that from now on, we've paid our dues and deserve happiness. I won't celebrate your death. I won't think of you with hate or cruelty. But I *will* be free of you, and I'll be happy you're no longer there to terrorize my lineage."

Shuffling away, she smiled softly. "May God have mercy on your soul, Bryan Hawk, and for you to find redemption in whatever awaits you."

Looking at me one last time, she moved back toward the Hall.

V and Tex hugged her, kissed her, then let her go.

Flaw appeared from the exit, jogging over to Nila and slinging an arm over her shoulders, joining her family. His possession didn't spark jealousy; if anything, it granted peace knowing she would be cared for and protected while I was gone.

"Thank you, Flaw." My voice travelled on the gentle wind to the Black Diamond brother. I didn't know how much war had gone on before our arrival, but he'd managed to enlist over three-quarters of the brothers to fight on our side. I would have to debrief and investigate each member and have them swear new allegiance to me, but for now, Flaw was in charge.

He saluted me casually. "No problem."

V guarded her while Tex looked dotingly at his children.

Switching his grip on Nila, Flaw relinquished her shoulders in favour of her hand. "I'll take her to her quarters and make sure she's fed and rested. Don't worry about her."

I smiled in gratitude.

Nila didn't say a word as Flaw guided her around Hawksridge, leading her toward another entrance and avoiding the nastiness of the ballroom. Tex and V followed, smearing bloody hands on their black trousers.

I would never know if Flaw's loyalty was because he trusted me or because of his steadfast friendship with Kes. Either way, he was a good man. And his actions today had prevented yet more deaths and helped those injured with his medical help.

Turning my back on the Hall, I moved alongside Kill as he shoved Cut forward, leading us away from prying eyes and looming buildings.

We didn't talk as we traversed the lawn, circumnavigated the maintenance shed where Cut had given me the salt shaker and told me it was time for the Second Debt, and entered the woods.

Our shoes snapped twigs as we moved deeper into forest darkness.

"You sure you want to do this, Hawk?" Kill's voice grabbed my attention. He fisted Cut around the back of his neck, shoving him forward. Two of Kill's men flanked us, morphing from the trees where they'd been watching the Hall.

I appreciated the back-up, but I didn't want an audience. The minute we arrived at our destination, I would send them away.

I needed to be alone in this.

Looking at the Florida-born president, I nodded. "I know what I'll have to pay in order to get retribution. But yes, I'm sure."

Kill grinned. "When the day comes for me to claim vengeance on my own father, I'm taking it. I don't care how hard it will be to kill flesh and blood or how fucked-up I am afterward. I need closure. I understand you completely."

I didn't reply. I had no reason to. He lived the same predicament, and his approval helped fortify my resolve.

In shared brotherhood, we made our way down animal tracks and through clearings, moving ever deeper into the treeline.

The outbuilding I'd decided on existed the furthest from the Hall. This one was hidden—alone with its horrible secrets. A place I'd never been able to enter after what happened to Jasmine, no matter what Cut did to me as a child. No matter the threats and corrections. No matter the curses and pain. I'd never stepped foot into the torture chamber again, boycotting its hateful memories.

Our clothing dappled with leaf stencils, trading sunshine for shadows as we traipsed deeper and deeper. The outbuilding nestled in the woods— swallowed whole by trees doing their best to delete the terrible atrocities.

We kept moving.

Cut didn't struggle, his breathing loud and uneven around the gag.

More flickering hallucinations played havoc with my vision. Leaves danced, turning briefly into wolves. Bracken crunched, morphing into badgers.

Goddammit, I need to rest.

My hand went to my side. The fever I'd had ever since heading to Africa hadn't broken or grown worse. If anything, it granted a heightened sense of everything, muddying outside influences, letting me focus entirely on what I wanted. What I needed. But it came with a price. A price of withering energy and health.

Soon.

Soon, I can rest.

Breaking through a final thicket, we stepped into a small glen.

The building loomed tall and ancient. Two stories high with oaks and pine surrounding it in their morbid cage. The double barn doors remained locked with a large padlock.

The key was hidden.

"Wait here." Leaving the men, I ducked into the woods and searched for the tree I needed. Cut had taken me the night he'd told me of my birthday present and inheritance of Nila. He'd marched me through the darkness, filling my head with tales of what would happen and how proud he was that soon I would show him how worthy I was and finally take the place I was born for.

My eyes searched the green gloom.

Where is it?

It took longer than I wanted, but finally, my strained eyes caught sight of the symbol of a diamond and an outline of hawk wings signalling I'd found the right one.

Climbing a few feet up the coarse bark using gnarly roots and limbs, I found the knot left behind after a branch fell away and reached inside for the packet. Jumping down, I undid the fastening and tossed out the key into my palm.

A few others jangled free, landing with a hint of rusty metal. The extras operated parts of the machinery inside. Machinery I had no intention of using or ever switching on again.

Fisting them, I turned on my heel and stomped out of the brush past Cut, Kill, and his men and toward the brittle barn doors.

My breathing turned harsh as I inserted the key into the tarnished padlock.

The mechanism turned as smoothly as the day the lock was bought, the doors creaking on their frame as I shoved open one partition. The stench of dead rodents and rotting foliage mixed with time-stale dust hit my nose.

Barring the entry with my body, I turned to face Kill.

The biker came forward, delivering my father.

I held out my arm. "Give him to me."

"You sure?"

"Very sure. I want to be alone for the next part."

Kill passed over my father without another word. He didn't try to talk me out of this. He didn't have any obligation to remind me that this was murder, not revenge. That I would become as bad as those I hated if I went through with this.

Kill was not my brother or my conscience. He'd done all he needed to. His obligations were complete.

Cut didn't struggle as I latched my fingers around his bound wrists. However, his eyes glowed with golden rage. His emotions poured forth, swamping with hatred and killable fury.

"Are we done?" Kill asked, crossing his arms over his leather jacket. "Will you be okay with your own men or do you want back-up?"

Shoving Cut into the barn, I ran a hand through my hair. "No. That's it. Your task is finished. You're free to return home, and I'll make sure to repay the favour whenever you need." Holding out my hand, Kill shook it.

"We'll wait until you're done. I'll station my men at the forest edge, just in case. Once they know you've finished, they'll leave." He cocked his head, eyeing the building. "How long will you need?"

His question weighted with hidden curiosities he wouldn't get answers to.

What will you do? What's in there? How badly will he die?

I swallowed, dreading what my night would entail. "Until dark. I need until dark."

Kill grinned. "Six hours, it is." Moving away, his large boots created indents in the soft woodland. "Pleasure knowing you, Hawk. I doubt we'll see each other face-to-face again, but we'll stay in touch."

We'd come together for mutual advancement, and now, we would go our separate ways. It was for the best.

I waited for Kill and his men to disappear from the clearing before turning my back and entering the barn.

The moment I traded trees for tomb, I shed all resemblance of who I was.

I left behind my humanity.

I tore Nila from my heart.

I embraced the motherfucking ice my father had taught me.

This would kill me.

But it had to be done.

I stepped into the darkness and prepared to murder.

Nila

"HE WON'T BE able to live with himself."

Jasmine shook her head, wheeling toward me. "Yes, he will."

I sucked in a breath, looking toward the window. The same window where the bird of prey had delivered Jethro's note to meet me in the stable.

God, was that only a few days ago?

It felt like an entire lifetime.

I begged for a feathered messenger now to tell me everything was done, finished; that Jethro would return to me and nothing else could keep us apart.

Jasmine's wheels whispered over the thick carpet of my quarters. The soft bubble of the fish tank and gentle tick of the clock all screeched over my nerves.

Springing from my mattress, I paced the large room. On every surface scattered half-sewn garments, scribbled drawings, and hastily cut fabric. My Rainbow Diamond collection existed in all stages of creation, but I would burn every scrap if it would bring Jethro closure and erase everything that'd happened.

"Nila, stop. You're worn out." Jasmine stopped by the chaise, narrowing her eyes at my frantic pacing. "Sit down, for God's sake."

I glared, disobeying.

Flaw had done what he'd told Jethro. V and Tex had gone with the maids to spare guest rooms and Flaw had taken me quietly back to my quarters. He'd fetched a banquet of fruits, snacks, and vitamin rich food, and summoned a servant to help tend to my bruises in the shower.

I wanted to refuse the food, knowing Jethro was just as weak as I was. I wanted to decline the shower because why should I be comforted while Jethro had such a trial to endure?

But Flaw hadn't let me argue.

He'd crossed his arms and stood in my room while I showered away African dirt and dried sweat from the pain of my broken arm. Struggling to wash, I was grudgingly grateful for the sweet-smiling maid who helped me dry off with a fluffy towel and dress me in the black shift I'd worn when the weeping scabs on my back from the First Debt healed.

The steam and warmth from the shower helped ease my aches and injuries, conjuring sleepiness and lethargic healing.

By the time I re-entered my quarters, Flaw had a spread of plaster strips, gauze, and warm water—just like Cut used in Africa. He shuffled me over to the bench, shoved aside my needles and lace, and ordered me to eat while he gently felt my break, ensured my arm was in the correct position, and re-cast it with confident precision.

I'd wanted to ask him questions about his life. Find out how he became a smuggler when it was obvious his true calling was to heal. But once the first mouthful of delicious food hit my tongue, I couldn't stop eating.

And that was why I wouldn't stop pacing even though my arm still hurt, my knees still wobbled, and my eyes still burned with unshed tears. I couldn't sit still. I'd been on the brink of death, and now, I was alive with a full belly and the welcome numbing of painkillers.

What did Jethro have?

Nothing.

No one.

Out there, on his own, about to do the unthinkable.

Whirling around, I glowered at Jasmine. "He's an Empath, Jaz. How the hell does he think he'll make Cut pay without feeling everything he does to him? Whatever pain he bestows, it will boomerang back and hurt him in equal measure." Gripping my damp hair, I missed the length. I wanted to tug on the ends and find some relief from the rapidly building pressure of despair.

Jasmine sighed softly. "I learned early on that Jethro is stubborn—especially when he believes he's doing the right thing."

"But he *isn't* doing the right thing! He's going to kill—"

Her lips thinned. "And that's not the right thing? Tell me, Nila. How much disgrace, death, and debts does my family have to do to yours to make it the *right* thing?" She pointed at the closed door. "I bet if I found Tex and Vaughn and asked them what they thought of Cut's justice, they would dance for bloody joy."

I stormed toward her. The sling Flaw gave me kept my broken arm snug against my body, leaving me free to gesture with the other.

"I won't lie and say I don't want Cut to pay. That isn't what I'm worried about. I'm worried about what it will do to Jethro. What if this changes him? What if he can't wipe away—"

Jaz bent forward, capturing my hand. "Nila, shut up." Squeezing my fingers, her temper glittered in her gaze. "It isn't up to you. If Kite needs to do this—if he believes he has the strength to do this, then that's his call. He's waited almost thirty years to reap what his father has sowed. It isn't up to you, me, or anyone else to interfere."

I hated that she made sense.

My eyes once again returned to the window. My indignation and worry spilled out of me, dampening my desire to run after Jethro and stop him. My love for him flew out the window, winging to wherever he was.

"I just..." My head hung as I struggled to articulate what I truly fretted over. "I love him, Jaz. I love him so damn much. It terrifies me to think I've only just earned him and he might leave me. How can I help him if he returns broken? How can I piece together a future I want so desperately if he can only remember death and agony?"

Jasmine pulled me closer, forcing me to sit on the chaise. "Don't torture yourself with what-ifs, Nila." Her voice softened. "He *will* be able to live with himself, and I'll tell you why. You don't know what it was like living here since birth. You don't know the mind games we endured and the unsaid threats we were raised with."

Pointing at her useless legs, she smiled sadly. "I have a daily reminder of what our childhood was like. And Jethro…every time he looks at me, he remembers, too. I try to hide my inner thoughts when he's around because I don't want him to know how much I miss walking. How much I miss running and riding and even the luxury of leaving the estate and going to a shop to browse things on shelves that are eye height instead of unreachable from a chair."

My heart broke for her.

I grabbed her hand with my good one, granting back the support she'd just given me.

For all Jasmine's assurances that Jethro could withstand what he was about to do, I didn't believe her. His empathy would mean everything he did for himself, for his sister, for me, would ricochet with persecution.

I couldn't stomach the thought of how much strength that would take. How much courage to do something, knowing you would feel every inch in kind.

"I know he has to do this, Jaz. I just wish—I wish I could be there with him. To give him another emotion to focus on. To feel love even while drowning in pain."

Jaz tucked her hair behind her ear. "My brother knows what he's doing. He'll remember how to block it out. He'll remember how it felt when Cut taught him all those lessons."

My heart froze.

What if he doesn't remember how to block it out?

What's the worse fate? Remembering or not?

My fingers clutched Jasmine's harder. "Please, tell me he'll come back."

Jaz sat higher in her chair, pecking my cheek with a kiss. "He'll come back. And when he does, it will be over.

"For all of us."

Jethro

"YOU HONESTLY EXPECT me to believe you're going to be able to do this?" Cut spat at my feet the moment I removed his gag. His tongue worked, dispelling the taste of being silenced. "Come on, Jethro. We both know you don't have it in you."

I didn't answer.

Leaving him tied up, I moved toward the main attraction in the room.

Just like the guillotine had rested in the ballroom pride of place, the torturous device sat in this one. Dirty grey sheets covered the apparatus, looking part phantom, part ancient relic.

Cut shifted on the spot, his jeans rustling. "Jet, I'm still your father. Still your superior. Stop this fucking nonsense and untie me."

Once again, I didn't answer.

The longer I concentrated on what had to be done, the more I remembered my childhood lessons.

Silence is more terrifying than shouts.

Smoothness is more horrifying than sharp motions.

The key to being feared was to remain calm, collected, and most of all, with a finely balanced decorum where the prey believed they had a chance of redemption, only to take their final breath with hope still glowing in their heart.

He'd taught me that.

My father.

It was thanks to him I'd built a shell around myself and portrayed to the outside world I was strong and unflappable. While internally, I combusted with chaos and calamity.

Fisting the material, I yanked it off. The billow of moth-eaten fabric floated like wings as it settled elegantly on the floor. Dust shot into my lungs, dried leaves flurried in a vortex, and grit stung my eyes. But I didn't cough or blink.

I couldn't take my eyes off the implement of my childhood.

The rack.

My fingers shook as I stroked the well-worn wood. The leather buckles stained with my blood. The grooves of my heels as I kicked and kicked and *kicked.*

"No!"

"Stop your fucking bitching, Jethro."

"Dad, stop. I didn't do anything wrong."

Cut didn't listen. "You did do something wrong." His fingers bruised my ankles as he tightened the buckles. I kicked, doing my best to prevent the thick leather imprisoning me, but it was no use. Just like it'd been no use trying to stop him tying my hands above my head.

This wasn't the first time I'd been here, nor would it be the last.

But I wished so much I could finally be better so he didn't have to hurt me.

My ten-year-old heart punched against my ribcage. "I didn't. I can't help it. You know I can't help it."

Notching the leather one more loop, he patted my knee and walked toward my face. "I know, but that is no excuse."

I lay horizontally, looking up at my father. His dark hair turned whiter with each year. His leather jacket reeked of long rides and hard excursions.

"Haven't I been lenient the past few months? I tried to help you with kinder means. But that doesn't work with you." His face contorted with affection and disbelief. "Jet, you jumped in front of my gun. What the fuck were you thinking?"

"You were going to shoot it!"

"Yes, it's food."

"No, it's a deer, and it felt fear." I squirmed, wishing I could make him understand the agony of hunting, of watching an animal notice the gun, feeling it understand my father's intentions and the wrecking ball of knowledge it was about to die. Animals were intelligent, beyond wise. They knew. They felt—same as us. "Can't you feel them, Dad? Can't you see how scary it is for them?"

"How many times do I need to tell you this, son?" His fingers grabbed my cheeks. "Animals are there for us to eat. We are all disposable and huntable if we don't fight back. Screw their fear. Screw their panic." His anger drenched his voice. "You. Are. My. Son. You will block it out. You will not embarrass me."

Moving toward my head, the distinct thump of his hand hitting the lever sent blood whizzing through my veins. "Okay, I'll stop. I didn't mean it. I won't do it again. I don't want to be a vegetarian. I'll hunt. I'll kill. Just don't—"

"Too late, Jet. Time for your lesson."

The lever cranked, the leather tightened, and pain began in earnest.

The memory ended, slamming me into the present. My heart raced as fast as it had back then, making me breathless with panic.

Only a memory.

Why did I come back here? Why didn't I choose an easier place?

Because this is where it all began. It needs to end here.

Fever drenched my brow as I glared at the rack. I'd lost count how many times I'd been subjected to its binds and stretching agony. Cut would leave me for hours to think about what I'd done, all while my joints popped and cracked.

Until the day he brought Jasmine along to share my lesson, of course.

We'd just been children. Trusting, gullible children.

Motherfucker.

Spinning, I marched toward my father and grabbed him by the arm. "Even now you look at me as if I'm a disappointment. I feel you, Father. You truly don't think I'll have the strength to do this." Pressing my face close to his, I snarled, "Well, you're wrong. I'll do this because of what you did to me. Nila might've forgiven you, but I won't. I *can't*. Not until you've paid."

Cut stood taller, rolling his shoulders in my hold. His bound hands couldn't hurt me, but it didn't stop him from trying with his voice. "You always were a pussy, Kite. But if you let me go, I'll honour the inheritance. On your birthday, I'll give you what you want. I'll give you everything."

I clenched my jaw, shoving my father against the wooden rack. "I don't want your money."

He stumbled. "It's not my money. It's yours. I was just the safe keeper until you were of age."

"Bullshit." I sliced the rope around his wrists—the same rope that'd been wrapped around Nila's—and shoved him backward.

He grunted as his back slammed into the rack, his clothing smearing the dusty wood. He tried to shove off, but I pushed back. He lost his footing, sprawling over the contraption.

Without thinking, I looped the rope I'd just removed from his wrists around his neck and prowled to the other side of the single-bed sized platform. The twine hooked under his chin, forcing him to arch back, keeping him pinned and choking.

His fingers fought at the imprisonment, angry curses percolating in his chest.

I didn't give him leeway to talk. I pulled harder.

The harder I pulled, the more his emotions grew stronger. I could ignore them...for now.

"Nothing you say can save you, old man. I've learned a lot from you over the years. Let's see how much I remember."

"Wait—" Cut gurgled as I tied the rope to a hook below the rim, keeping his neck throttled. He lay awkwardly, his legs dangling off the side. Moving around to his front, I grabbed behind his knees and scooted his bulk onto the table.

He couldn't stop me, too focused on fighting the rope to breathe.

Once his body was in position, I grabbed his flailing arms. Fisting his right, I pinned it to the unforgiving wood above his head, wrapping the leather around his wrist and fastening it tightly.

"No, wait!" His voice wheezed, his fingers clawing at his throat.

He continued to pant while I remained silent, moving down the table to capture his right leg. The leather had turned stiff with age and blood, but I managed to wrap it around his ankle, shoving his jeans out of the way and fastening tight.

"Jethro—stop."

I didn't obey.

Meticulously, I drifted to the left side of the table. His left leg tried to kick as I crushed his knee against the table. I wrestled with him to buckle the strap. I panted with exertion but won.

I was weak. Tired. Sick from traipsing around the world and dealing with complications he'd caused.

Yet, I had enough strength to subdue him.

Our gaze met as I skirted the table, reaching for his left arm.

"Don't." His eyes widened as I forcefully removed his fingers from around his neck, slamming it unceremoniously against the wood above his head. Bending over him, his chest rose and fell as I threaded the leather around his wrist and finished the final binding.

All four points secured. There would be no running, no fighting back—completely at my mercy.

"Still think I don't have it in me?" I looked down at him, pitying him a little. When I was younger, I'd always hoped he'd be lenient and let me go. I held blind belief he was my father and wouldn't hurt me too much.

But Cut knew otherwise. He remembered what he'd done to me. He recalled every scream and beg. It was his turn now.

I patted his cheek.

His lips tinged purple as he sucked in a lungful of air. "Jethro...fucking obey me and—"

"I'll never obey you again." Wanting him to remain lucid for future events, I unwrapped the rope from the hook at the base of the table and removed it from his throat.

He gasped, sucking in air while an angry red line marred his bristle-covered neck.

Leaving him to breathe, I moved toward the table beneath the grime-smeared window. No reflection or view from the outside world was noticeable. The pane had turned cloudy with age, deleting everything but us and what was about to happen.

Cut's emotions built until they threatened to eclipse my own. He wasn't terrified—not yet. He still believed I wouldn't be able to do this.

I'll prove you wrong.

Grabbing the corner of yet another dusty sheet, I whipped it off to reveal a long table of nasty implements.

My heart clenched as my eyes fell on every tool. Most had been used on me. But a few had been used on Jasmine.

I shuddered, closing my eyes against the influx of memories.

"No, leave her alone!"

Cut didn't obey. He finished tying Jasmine's hands before twisting to look at me. The leather bit into my wrists and ankles, binding me to the table. But the fulcrum had been activated, switching the table from horizontal to vertical. I hung as if crucified.

I would see everything. I would feel everything. I wouldn't be able to stop anything. Jasmine's bronze eyes met mine, her twelve-year-old face glowing with grief.

"Don't. Please, don't." My voice battled with tears.

Cut marched toward the table to grab a tiny blade. "Seeing as hurting you doesn't teach you how to switch off your condition, I've come up with a better idea."

His boots clomped on the barn floor as he strode back to his daughter.

I fought. Fuck, I fought. The rack groaned as I threw my weight against the buckles. "Don't touch her." Jaz. My baby sister.

Pulling Jasmine to her feet, Cut wrapped an arm around her shoulders. Her dainty black shoes were no longer shiny patent but dusty and scuffed. I remember the day she got those shoes. Mum had given them to her just for being the sweetest little girl.

"You have the power to stop this, Jethro." Cut angled the blade against Jasmine's shoulder, slicing through her pretty blue dress, revealing a sliver of skin. "All you have to do is focus on my thoughts, rather than hers." He dragged the blade over her flesh, not hard enough to break the surface, but hard enough to make her flinch.

She bit her lip. Jasmine was quiet. When we played, she'd laugh and joke, but when she was afraid or in trouble, she turned mute. Nothing could get her to talk. Not the threat of the knife; not my pleas for her freedom. She stood there in her father's grasp and didn't say a word.

But fuck, her thoughts said so much. They screamed for me to help her. They hated me because I couldn't. She battled with love for Cut and loathing his actions. She crumpled me like a piece of rubbish, giving me no hope of focusing on anything else.

Cut dragged the knife again, only this time a little deeper.

Jasmine's flinch turned into a jerk, squirming in his arms.

"*Stop. Don't do it again. I get it. I'm not listening to her anymore. I only feel what you are.*" *Lies. All lies. But truth got me into this mess maybe falsehood could get me out of it.*

Cut cocked his head. "What am I thinking then, boy?"

My hands balled as my joints stretched beyond normal capacity. Jasmine's thoughts overpowered me. I couldn't hear him. I didn't want to hear him.

So, I bullshitted. "You like the power over her. You like knowing you created her but can take her life just as easily as you gave it." I sounded older than fourteen. Would he believe me?

For a moment, I thought he would.

Then reality dispelled that hope.

"*Wrong, Jet." Cut used the knife again. This time…he broke the skin. Tears erupted from Jasmine's eyes, but still she didn't cry out. "I hate this. I hate doing this to my children. And I hate you for making me do it."*

My fingers grazed the blade he'd used, tarnished and abandoned on the table. I could cut him. I could make him feel what Jasmine felt. But I had a better idea.

Breathing hard, I bypassed the cat o' nine tails and grabbed the large club. Resembling a billy stick the police used to carry, this one was thicker, heavier, ready to break limbs and turn bone into pulp.

I turned back to face my father. He lay prone on the rack, his eyes wide, white hair a shock of snow in the gloomy barn. "Remember this?"

He swallowed. "I remember what a fucking pussy you were when I used it."

Memories tried to take me hostage of him beating me, bruising me— teaching me lesson after lesson.

"Only fair you get to see why I screamed, don't you think?"

Cut gulped. "You knew all along I didn't enjoy what I did. I did it to try and save you from yourself. You were my children. Didn't I have a right as your father to use my flesh and blood to help my firstborn?"

I shook my head. "Using and abusing are two entirely different words."

He sneered. "And yet, only two letters separate them."

My chest hurt from breathing; my side burned from fever. I wanted this over. I'd made a commitment to make him pay, but I wasn't there to drag this out.

I wanted to finish it.

I wanted Nila.

I want to forget.

"That doesn't matter. You were still wrong to do what you did." Striding toward him, I held the club over his face. "Look at this and tell me what you feel. Don't make me work for your answers, Cut. For once in your godforsaken life, tell me the truth."

His goatee jerked as he tucked his chin into his neck, repelling from the weapon. "You know me, Jethro. You know I love you."

"Bullshit. Try again."

He bared his teeth. "That isn't bullshit. I *do* love you. When Nila returned to London and you took your medication, I was so fucking proud of you. Never been so proud. I had the son I always knew you were. Capable, courageous, a worthy heir to everything I'd built."

"I was always those things, Father. Even as a boy, I did my best to make you see that."

The wood creaked as he shifted in the buckles. "But it was overshadowed by your condition. It made you weak. It made you susceptible. I needed someone strong, not just to look after my legacy but to protect your future family. Was it so wrong of me to want to give you the life skills needed in order to fight what you are?"

"What *I* am?" I choked on a cynical laugh. "What I am is nothing compared to what you are. You talk about life skills and transforming me into a man. I call that disabling your daughter, emotionally crippling your son, and ripping apart the only people who would've loved you unconditionally."

Cut opened his mouth to respond, but nothing came out.

He stared at me, and the one thing I'd hoped wouldn't happen came true.

His emotional rage petered out, mixing with nervousness that I was right. That he'd done the wrong thing. That somehow…he'd been bad.

Gritting my jaw, my arm flew back with ferocity. "No, you don't get to think those thoughts. Not after what you've done."

The club whistled through the air, striking his thigh with sickening power. The heavy pummel and resounding aftershock made my fever crest to unbearable heights and nausea to clutch around my throat.

Cut bellowed, his body jerking in the buckles as he writhed.

Being on the opposite end of a scene I was so familiar with twisted my gut.

His agony swamped me. The unravelling sanity. The nastiness inside him giving way to fear. I wanted to vomit. I wanted to cut myself so I could focus on *my* pain and not his. I wanted to run.

But I couldn't.

If I tried hard enough, I could turn off my condition. I could return to what he'd taught me. But not today. I owed him this. I owed *myself* this. Together, we would purge everything I'd been. Everyone we'd hurt.

"Hurts, doesn't it?" I struck again, this time on his other thigh. The denim of his jeans protected him a little, but his cry boomeranged around the space.

A sour taste filled my mouth as self-hatred settled around my heart. I hated that feeling his pain meant I couldn't enjoy it. I couldn't appreciate the power as I delivered a dose of his own medicine, finally demonstrating what an awful disciplinarian he'd been.

His breathing stuttered as pain flashed through his system. I hadn't struck hard enough to break bones, but he would have a hell of a bruise.

Striding around the table, I stroked the black club. The heavy rubber was dense and threatening. There would be no escape. "What did you tell me once? That I could cry and scream as loud as I wanted and no one would hear us…?"

His eyes glowed, meeting mine. Sweat shone on his forehead. His arms fought the buckles as his knees trembled from adrenaline.

"Answer me." I struck his chest. The side of the club delivered with perfect precision against his lower belly.

"Ah, fuck!" Cut's spine bowed, his entire psyche wanting to curl up around his injuries and hide. Any sign of regret or shame at doing the wrong thing drowned beneath his sudden need for relief.

That I could deal with. Feeling another's pain had been a by-product of my condition all my life. I'd never grown used to it. However, if I stood in a room with someone dying or mortally wounded, I would eventually become numb then catatonic from their agony.

The same would happen if I continued with my father.

I had to finish what I'd started before I slipped into insanity.

He hadn't paid enough yet. He hadn't learned what he needed.

I've withstood worse.

I could stomach delivering more punishment.

Tucking the club into my waistband, I stalked around the table.

Cut gasped, his eyes watering but doing their best to follow me. "What do you want me to say, Jet? That I'm sorry? That I regret what I did and beg for your forgiveness?"

He stiffened as my hands drifted toward the lever he'd used so often. Words tumbled from his mouth. "Look, I'm sorry, okay? I'm sorry for asking so much of you when I knew you struggled. I'm sorry for hurting Jasmine. I'm sorry for what I did to Nila. Fuck, Jet, I'm sorry."

"Not good enough." Curling my fingers around the sweat-polished wood of the lever, I murmured, "I think we can do better than that."

My muscles bunched as I pushed on the mechanism. The first crank sounded like the gates of hell opening up, groaning and howling as ancient wood slipped into motion after so long.

"Wait!" Cut wriggled as the leather slowly tightened around his wrists and ankles. "Listen to my thoughts. Pay attention. I'm telling the truth."

The sad thing was he *did* speak the truth. He honestly was sorry. He burned with apologies and willingly took possession of everything he'd done.

But it wasn't enough to be sorry. He had to wish he'd never done it in the first place.

Taking a ragged breath, fighting through my weakness and fever, I cranked the lever again. The cogs and prongs slipped into place, welcoming each twist. Ducking over Cut, I pressed a little harder, pulled a little tighter. "Ready to grow a few inches?"

Cut squeezed his eyes. "Please…"

"You don't get to beg." I jerked the lever, pushing a full rotation.

The rack obeyed, separating beneath him, pulling Cut's extremities into agonising tightness. The skin on his hands and feet stretched like an accordion played to maximum, turning his flesh red as it yanked him in two directions.

Cut screamed.

I pushed again.

The table fought Cut's body, snarling against the unwilling tension, causing him to stretch beyond natural comfort.

He screamed louder.

My ears rang and my condition spluttered as too many thoughts collided in Cut's head. I felt sick for becoming this monster—a beast willingly taking my father's pain. But at the same time, I felt redeemed—as if I'd finally become the man Cut wanted me to be and only now deserved his praise.

"Tight enough for you?" My question was hidden in Cut's groans as I pressed the lever once more.

The shifting parts of the rack obeyed, slipping further apart, tearing a few ligaments, cutting into my father's flesh with its leather cuffs.

Cut didn't scream again, but a feral cry fell from his lips. His face scrunched up as his skin shocked white with agony. His back arched, his shoulders pulled tight and toes pointing. His hands remained fisted, his fingernails digging into his palms as his body fought to stay together.

I knew what he felt—not because I sensed him, but because I'd been in the exact position he had. I'd been tighter. I'd been younger. His shoulders would be the first to give out. They would pop from position in order for his joints to fight a little longer against the strain. Once the shoulders went, other joints would follow. Depending on how tight the rack stretched, knees would dislocate, tendons would snap, muscles would shred, and bones would break.

This form of torture had been one of the worst used in medieval times— and not just for the victim in the rack's embrace but for the victims watching it. The sickening rip of body parts giving up the fight. The horrifying pops of joints coming apart.

Confessions were willingly given just waiting for their turn.

Would I go that far?

Would I tear Cut slowly into pieces, tightening his noose until his limbs quit fighting and just disintegrated?

Could I be that cold-hearted and merciless?

Let's find out.

My palms drenched with sickening sweat as I pushed one last time on the lever. The table cracked, the leather squeaked, and Cut convulsed with cries. "Fuck, stop. God, what d—do you want? Stop—"

"I want nothing from you." Locking the table from loosening, I removed my hands from the rack. His sockets were at breaking point. For now.

It was amazing how nimble the human body was. An hour in that position and cartilage would slowly snap, tendons stretch, and bones bellow for relief. But once freed, the body would knit back together. It would take time to realign the spinal column and soothe the blistering tears inside, but the long-term effects would be nil.

I knew.

I was walking proof.

Cupping my fingers around the club again, I prowled around the table. Cut's question resonated in my mind. *"What do you want?"* In all honesty, there was nothing I wanted. I had Nila—she was all I needed. But I wasn't doing this solely for her. Jasmine mattered, Kestrel, even Daniel.

I did this for them.

Wrenching to a halt, I looked at my father. "You know what? There *is* something I want from you." I moved from his head to his feet.

Cut tried to look down his body, but the pressure on his shoulders and arms wouldn't let his head rise. "What...anything. Name it and it's yours. You're a good son, Jethro. We can forget this and move on."

"You're right in some respects, Father. I will forget and move on. But you lost that luxury when you stole Emma from her family and let Bonnie manipulate you for so long."

Once this was over, I would deal with my grandmother. I would make her regret playing puppet master to her own family.

"Bonnie's dead." Cut sucked in a breath, his neck straining against the pressure in his joints. "She died of a heart attack just before you arrived."

I froze.

Her death had been stolen from me. But perhaps, it was for the best. I already shook with rapidly fading courage. I already whittled beneath Cut's emotions. I wouldn't have the energy or bodily strength to take another life.

"I'm sorry." For all my hatred toward my grandmother and her strict ways, Cut did love his mother and feared her in equal measure. I let myself feel what he felt. He hurt. A lot. He was penitent and self-condemnatory but not enough to warrant salvation. Beneath his pain, he still thought he was justified.

He was wrong.

Holding up the club, I moved so the weapon was in his line of vision. "Remember who else you used this on?" I shuddered, fighting back memories of that horrible, fateful day. The day I realised he would never understand me, and I had to be strong—not for myself, but for my sister.

He'd taught me the final lesson in this place. The lesson that'd helped me remain true until Nila made me thaw.

Cut gulped. "Kite...wait."

"No, you don't get to give me orders anymore." Smashing the club into my palm, I welcomed the sting. "I've waited long enough."

Another thing about the rack—while tightening joints and stretching bones, it placed the human body into the perfect position of extra sensitivity. The natural cushioning of cartilage and fat suddenly wasn't enough to protect such an elongated pose.

Before, the strikes I delivered would've hurt him but not murdered him. The pain would've been sharp but survivable. But this...if I hit him now, the pain would be a hundred times worse. A *thousand* times worse.

Barricade yourself. Prepare.

The simplest touch could shatter a kneecap. The gentlest nudge could snap an elbow. He was the most vulnerable he'd ever been physically. It was my job to make him as defenceless emotionally.

My heart chugged. I didn't want to do this. But I would.

"I need you to know I'll be with you every step. I won't be able to turn off what you're undergoing, but I'm going to do it anyway because this isn't for me." Spreading my legs, I prepared to swing. "I'm doing this for Jasmine. You'll finally understand how your daughter felt that afternoon."

"Jet, no, don't, don't—"

Cut understood what I did: I wouldn't hold back anymore. I wouldn't be gentle or forgiving.

Before had been the warm-up.

This...this was his true punishment.

"I'm sorry."

Swallowing hard, I let loose and smashed my father's ankle with the club. The blow did what I knew it would. It pulverized his complex skeleton, shattering the talus and lateral malleolus. Biology came back; names of body parts I didn't really care about popped into my head before giving way beneath my strike.

The room seemed to explode outward as Cut sucked in the largest breath then screamed his fucking soul out.

His screams flew to the roof and bounced down.

His screams rattled the window in its ancient frame.

His screams sent me hurtling back to the day I wished I could forget.

"Stop it!" I didn't care the rack kept me immobile. I didn't care blood seeped down my wrists from fighting the leather. All I cared about was a silently sobbing Jasmine at Cut's feet. "Leave her alone!"

Cut breathed hard, swiping away damp hair from his forehead. This lesson had been the worst of them. He'd done everything he could to get me to no longer care he hurt Jasmine. He forced me to stay stoic and calm, hooking my heart rate up to a monitor so he could track my progress.

After the first few lessons, he couldn't tolerate my lying. He struggled to know if he'd made progress or not.

He hadn't.

No matter what he did to me, I couldn't stop what was so natural. I felt what others did. I couldn't switch it off. How could I when I didn't know how to control it?

So he'd upped his efforts, forcing me to hunt with him and shoot hapless rabbits and deer. He threatened to hurt Kestrel. He brought Jasmine in to watch. For a time, he didn't touch her. Just having her there made me work doubly hard.

In every lesson, she never said a word—merely watched me with sad eyes and hugged herself while Cut tried everything for me to mimic his inner calmness. To accept his ruthlessness. To become him in every way possible.

For a while, I willed it to work. I got better at lying, and Cut began to believe he'd 'cured' me. But then he hooked me up to the lie detector and heart monitor. And I couldn't bullshit any longer.

Jasmine didn't look up as she huddled at my father's feet. He'd slapped her repeatedly; he'd used his hands rather than blades, forcing me to focus on his mind rather than hers.

Become the predator, not prey.

Embrace ruthlessness, not suffering.

Become the monster, not the victim.

The pinging of the heart machine wouldn't stop shredding my hope and showing Cut just how hopeless I was. I couldn't be fixed. It was impossible.

"Please, let her go."

Cut swiped a handkerchief over his face, looking disgustedly at me. "I'll let her go when you can learn to control it."

"I can't!"

"You can!"

"I'm telling you—I can't!"

As we roared at each other, Jasmine scuttled away. The dust from the barn layered her pink dress, staining her black tights. It was winter and frost decorated the glass, billowing our breath with little plumes of smoke.

Keep him yelling.

The longer I kept him occupied, the more chance Jaz had to escape.

I glared at Jasmine, willing her to get to her feet and run. Run out the door and never come back. She nodded quickly, understanding my silent command.

Cut stormed toward me, grabbing my cheeks and shoving my face toward the out-of-control monitor. I'd always had an irregular heartbeat whenever there was too much emotion to contain. My heart felt others; it was only natural it tried to skip into their beat, to mimic their pulses.

"What the fuck am I going to do with you, Jet? Are you ever going to get better?"

My cheeks couldn't move beneath his pinching hold; I did my best to speak without spitting. "Yes, I—I promise."

"I've heard you promise before and it never comes true."

Over his shoulder, I silently cheered as Jasmine shot to her dainty legs and tiptoed toward the double-born doors. So close…keep going.

"What else can I do to make you focus inward and not be so fucking weak all the time?" Cut prodded my chest where my teenage heart thundered. "Tell me, Jethro, so we can *end this charade."*

Jasmine's hands looped around the handle, yanking on the heavy exit.

Yes, run. Go.

The wood grunted like a beast hunting in the woods.

No!

Cut spun around. His eyes bugged as he dropped his hold. I couldn't move, hanging on the rack as he balled his hands and strode to the table where things of nightmares rested. "Where do you think you're going, Jazzy?"

She plastered herself against the door, shaking her head.

"Run, Jaz. Run!" I struggled. "Don't look back. Just go!"

She didn't.

She froze as Cut picked up a black club and advanced on her.

"No!" I squirmed harder, drawing more blood, more fear.

"I'm going to teach you to control it, Jet, if it's the last fucking thing I do." Cut swatted the club into his hand, making goosebumps scatter over my body.

Jasmine trembled as Cut towered over her. "You love your sister. Let's see if you can protect her by focusing for once." His hand rose, shadowing her face with his arm.

"Run, Jaz!" I screamed, tearing through her terror and kick starting her flight. Her fear kept her mute, but a sudden resolution filled her gaze.

She ran.

Pushing off from the door, she charged around my father and darted across the barn.

Cut spun, holding the club, watching his daughter bolt from him. Only, he didn't let her go. He gave chase.

"No!" I couldn't do a thing as he stormed after his child and wrenched his arm back to strike.

"Jasmine!"

And then it was all over.

The club struck her back.

The force sent her tumbling head over heels.

Her little shoes clattered against the floor as her skirts flew over her face. She came to a stop facing me, her little eyes glassing with tears, locked on mine above her.

For a second, she just lay there, blinking in shock, cataloguing her hurt. Then, the thickest, hardest, all-consuming wave I'd ever felt washed over me. Her pain drenched me. Her agony infected me. Everything she felt—her childish whims, her hopeful wishes—they all rammed down my throat and made me sick.

I vomited as Jasmine burst into tears.

Her screams echoed around us, slipping out the door, licking around the trees and rising to the crescent moon above.

I cried with her. Because I knew what'd happened as surely as she did.

Winter had watched this atrocity. Frost hadn't prevented it. Ice had let it happen. And a blizzard began deep in my soul.

I couldn't do it anymore.

I couldn't handle my sister's agony, my father's despair, my own brokenness.

I can't do this.

And neither could Jasmine.

Her tears stopped as suddenly as they began, but her eyes never tore away from mine. Her cheek pressed on the floor as her breath puffed cold smoke from bluing lips.

And she uttered the words I would never forget.

The words ensuring I stepped into an icicle prison and gave her the key. The sentence forever turning me into snow so I never, never, never had to feel what I'd felt that day.

"Kite...I can't feel my legs."

I howled in remembered agony, hating him all over again. He'd disabled my sister. He'd broken her back, crippled her spinal column. He'd irrevocably destroyed her life all because of me.

Me.

Fuck!

Blocking out his screams, I stormed toward the head of the rack and traded the club for the lever. While Cut trembled and shook in his restraints, I punched the mechanism, cocking it another rotation.

His broken ankle and limbs stretched further, eliciting more screams, more begs. The barn filled with sounds of popping and cracking. The gristle and ligaments finally gave up, breaking in increments.

I wanted to be sick. I wanted to wade through his pain, and for once, stop wallowing in others' misfortune. But unlike the instant with Jasmine teaching me in one violent swoop to stop, I couldn't.

"Jethro—stop. Please..." Cut's voice interspersed with deep-seated groans. I wanted so much to give in and obey. But he'd committed too much. Done too much wrong.

He hadn't paid enough. Not yet.

Shoving the club down my waistband again, I sat on my haunches and grabbed the small wheel below the rack. I knew this machine so well. Too well. It'd become a regular enemy, and I'd learned how to use it from too young an age.

Cut had felt what it was like to lay horizontal while receiving pain. It was entirely a new experience to be vertical.

Spinning the wheel, I shut my ears off to Cut's string of curses and pleas as the table slowly tilted upright, transforming from bed to wall. With every inch, Cut's body shifted as the weight transformed from his back to his wrists. His spine remained stretched, his body distended, but now the new angle meant he could see me moving around. He was the messiah this time about to die for his sins, not others.

Feeling his eyes on me, I didn't look up as I made my way toward the table of horrors. Gently, I placed the club back into its dusty spot and grabbed the cat o' nine tails.

"Have you hung there long enough, Jet?"

My father's voice roused me. My head soared up even though my neck throbbed. He'd left the clock on the stool in front of me, letting me count the time. Today, I'd been on the rack for two hours and thirteen minutes. Jasmine was still at the hospital. The doctors did all they could to fix the blunt force trauma to her spine. But they weren't hopeful.

Nothing Cut did to me now would ever be as bad as watching my sister run for the very last time.

I'd made a promise never to come here again, but that was before Cut scooped me from my bed at daybreak and gave me no choice.

"Let me down." I coughed, lubricating my throat. "You don't need to do this anymore."

He came to stand in front of me, his hands jammed in his pockets. "Are you sure about that?"

I nodded, tired and strung out and for once, blank from feeling anything. "I'm empty inside. I promise."

He gnawed on his lower lip, hope lighting his gaze. "I really hope this time you're telling the truth, son." His head turned toward the table. The dreaded, hated, despised *table.*

A thought clouded his face as he strolled over and picked up a whip with multiple strands with cruel knots tied in the cords. He'd threatened me with the whip before but never actually used it.

I tensed in the cuffs. My limbs had stopped screaming, but my joints were beyond moving. Cut knew how far I could be stretched these days without causing me too much agony.

After all, it was about keeping me immobile and sensitive, rather than ripping me into pieces.

"Let's see if your lessons have been learned, shall we?" He dragged the whip through his fingers. "Call this your final exam, son. Pass this and you'll never have to come in here again."

He didn't give me time to argue.

His arm cocked backward.

The whip and its knotted tails shot forward.

The first lick shredded my t-shirt, biting sharply into my chest.

A scream balled in my throat, but I'd finally learned. I'd learned not to focus on myself or my sister or prey or hope or happiness or normalcy. I'd learned to focus on him—my father, my ruler, my life-giver.

So I did.

Every strike, I took with pride because Cut felt proud of me.

Every cut, I accepted with gratefulness because Cut finally believed he'd earned a worthy son.

I listened to him and only him.

And it saved me from myself.

I gripped the table as a feverish weakness throttled me. I couldn't do this much longer. Every part of me was heavy with sickness and toil. I'd proven my point. I'd made him suffer. I had to end this before I drove myself into a grave beside him.

Pushing off from the wood, I stalked to face Cut on the rack.

His eyes widened, locking onto the whip.

"Let's see if you've learned your lesson, Father. Let's see if you can accept what you gave me as quietly as I accepted it."

My arm shook as the whip sailed over my shoulder. I paused as the cords slapped against my back, ready to shoot forward and strike its quarry.

Cut bit his lip. "Kite…"

I didn't wait for more. "No."

Grunting, I threw every remaining energy into my arm and hurled the whip forward. The knots found his shirt; they sliced through it like tiny teeth, blood spurting from his flesh.

And finally, his emotions switched from sadistic hatred, misplaced actions, and a lifetime of incorrect choices to begging and shaming and accepting everything in full measure.

His head bowed as I struck again, tears streaming from his eyes. Not from pain. But the knowledge he'd done this to people he'd loved. He'd willingly done this to his *children*. And there was no worse crime than that.

I'd finally broken him. Finally shown him the error of his past. Finally taught him what it was like for us. He paid homage to Emma Weaver. He said sorry to Jasmine. He repented toward Nila. And finally, *finally*, he submitted to me and my power.

His apologies layered my mind.

His regret boomed in his thoughts.
He accepted what had to happen.
We were no longer father and son, teacher and disciple.
We were two men cleaning up the mess we'd caused.
Two men alone in a world we'd created.
And we would both suffer a lot more before it was over.

HE DIDN'T COME back.

Minute after minute.

Hour after hour.

Still he didn't return.

I stared out the window, imploring him to appear.

I stroked my phone, willing a message to arrive.

I glanced at my door, begging him to enter.

But nothing.

Jethro was gone.

He'd committed to what had to be done.

And I feared I might never get him back.

DARKNESS.

It fell over the estate like the gown from death itself, trickling like oil into nooks and crannies, stealing light.

Every thickening shadow devoured a little of what'd happened—blotting out the day, the past, everything that'd led to this moment.

Time had passed, changing me as a person, as a man, as a son. Cut and I had visited purgatory together, and a small part of us hadn't come back. I'd proven my point and won. And the saddest part was that the connection between us was the strongest it had ever been.

My heart wept for what I'd done. My muscles growled with tiredness. My entire body wanted to shut down.

Almost.

It's almost time to rest.

Needing some fresh air, I left the barn and stumbled outside. Every sensory output was on fire. I'd never been so exposed or naked, drenched in the feelings of others.

The moment night chill caressed my face, I raised my eyes to the moon, gulping in purging breaths.

The atmosphere in the barn was too thick, too putrid. I couldn't breathe properly after what I'd done.

Burying my face in my hands, I forced myself not to relive the whipping or clubbing or Cut's tears and begs. I'd broken more than just his ankle. I'd broken his heart, his soul, his entire belief. I'd done everything I could to show Cut how blind he'd been toward his children and empire.

"Fuck." The cuss fluttered to my feet like the autumn leaves, crunching beneath my boot. How could I have done what I did? How did I hurt my father over and over again? How did I draw his blood and break his bones?

I didn't know the answer to that. But I was still standing, and my father finally understood.

It was over.

Rubbing my aching eyes, I swatted away my thoughts and took a deep breath. The moonlight cast my bloody hands in silver-chrome, turning the red black. Shoving the evidence of my crimes into my pockets, I strode through the forest, searching for the two men Kill had left to guard the woods.

It didn't take me long. I followed the reek of cigarette smoke, encountering them on the border of the glen.

They turned to face me as I approached. Their hands curled by their sides and jackets bulky in the gloom.

I didn't bother with niceties. I didn't have the strength. "It's done. You can go."

The man with a mohawk nodded. "Right-o. See you around."

I doubt it.

I left them to guide themselves out. I wouldn't play host tonight. I still had too much to do to be a gentleman.

Leaving, I faded through the forest. Once I could no longer sense them, I sat on a rock and grabbed a final breath.

This was the last decision.

Cut had been taught his lesson. I'd hurt him enough that he bordered this life and the next. He was half dead, but did I have the right to take his life completely?

He took so many others. Emma. Almost Nila. Jasmine's livelihood. My mother's soul.

My hands curled again, sticky with everything that'd happened.

I'd contemplated all manner of things. I'd thought of, and discounted, the idea of hanging my father, drawing out his entrails and quartering him just like convicts were done in the past. I'd pondered the concept of letting him live and banishing him from Hawksridge.

I had enough of my father's blood on my hands. I'd hurt myself and him.

But I knew he wouldn't let me have the happy ending I desired if I left him alive.

Eventually, he would want vengeance. Eventually, he would forget the lesson I'd taught and come back for me—come back for Nila.

I can't let that happen.

I had to end it.

It's the only way.

Climbing off the rock was a million times harder than it was to sit down. My body seized; I tripped forward as my head swam. How much longer could I stay awake without needing serious medical attention?

Not very.

Forcing my legs to work, I left my place of solitude and returned to the barn. My fingers shook as I turned and locked the door.

Cut didn't make a sound. He'd passed out just before I'd left. Tearing my eyes from the almost unrecognisable shape of my father, I headed toward the table and selected a small knife.

No matter that history tarnished the blade, the sharpness still remained.

Moving toward Cut, his chin lolled on his chest, his arms splayed high while his legs spread wide. His arms and legs were abnormally long while his body couldn't stretch any more without skin tearing as well as bones.

Blood seeped down his torso in a crisscross lattice from the whip. Beneath his wounds, the faint lines of the Tally Mark tattoos from Emma decorated his ribcage. Emma had been the one to choose the position, just like Nila chose fingertips for ours. I hadn't seen his tally in so long; I'd almost forgotten they were there.

He had more than me and he'd carried out the Final Debt.

That was the main difference between us.

Dedication versus empathy.

Sighing, I did my best to gather my shredded power. The blade turned warm in my hand. Tearing my eyes from him, I moved to the rack and groaned as I bent in half to twist the small wheel.

Slowly, the rack reclined from perpendicular to parallel.

Cut still didn't move.

Placing the knife by his unconscious head, I unbuckled his wrists then his ankles. The ankle I'd shattered hung at an unnatural angle, mottled and black with bruising.

My heart clenched that I could ever be so cruel, battling with childhood memories and adulthood obligations. Along with his ankle, I'd also broken his arm for Nila's in Africa. I'd smashed his kneecap and rearranged an elbow.

I'd done such nasty shit to the man who made me.

Don't think about it.

Snatching back my knife, I tapped his grey-covered cheek. "Wake up."

Nothing.

I tapped harder. "Cut, open your eyes."

His lips twitched, but his mind remained asleep.

"Goddammit, don't make me get the water."

I hit him, harder this time. His face slipped sideways against the table, slowly cracking the cocoon his mind had built. Whatever chrysalis he'd formed against his agony wouldn't stop him from living through the next.

It took a few swats, but finally, his eyes opened.

For a while, confusion battered him. His gaze darted to the ceiling, coming to focus on me. I didn't move as he took note of his over-stretched joints, broken parts, and lurched with blundering pain.

I was the nail being hammered by his thoughts, deeper and deeper, harder and harder into my soul. After tonight, I needed solitude and aloneness. I needed to gallop away and never live through something like this ever again.

"Get up." Slinging his useless arm over my shoulder, I plucked him from the rack.

He screamed as I slipped him off the table. Regardless of his agony, he tried to move, but his limbs were no longer operational. His legs didn't support his weight, and he fell to the dusty floor with a cry.

I went with him.

We fell in a mass of body parts, sitting side by side, our backs resting against the rack.

He gasped but didn't try to untangle himself. Shock quickly deleted much of his overwhelming injuries, letting him rest for a moment without suffering.

The fact he found peace for a second let me find it as well.

I shared in his silence, letting the air wrap around us in a dusty hug.

For a while, I didn't speak. What could I say? Over the past few hours, I'd proven I was as much a monster as he was. I hadn't found reconciliation or closure. I'd only found sadness and cruelty.

But words weren't needed.

My father, the man who'd raised me, hurt me, and ultimately cared for me in his own twisted way, slowly laid his head on my shoulder and gave me the first righteous thing of his life.

"I'm sorry, Jethro. For everything."

My heart clamoured as tears sprang to my eyes.

I couldn't speak.

Cut didn't wait for a reply. He knew he was dying. His body was broken beyond repair. There would be no healing or walking away from this. His time on earth had come to an end, and now was the time to relinquish his sorrows and regrets.

His voice was a croaky thread, but my eyes pricked with his every word.

"I know how badly I treated my children. I know I was never entitled to what I took. I let power and bloodlust cloud me. I can't amend what I did, and I can't bring back the lives I stole, but I can ask for your forgiveness."

His head turned heavier on my shoulder, dampness soaking into my sweat-clogged shirt from his tears.

"I need to know you forgive me, Kite. I need to know you accept my apology."

Matching liquid sadness ran silently down my cheeks as I stared at the locked doors. "Why? Why should I forgive you?"

"Because you know I mean it. You sense I'm telling the truth. It wasn't just the pain you showed me or the memories I relived tonight—the same memories I have no doubt you relived as well. It was hindsight, and I've finally allowed myself to acknowledge what I never did before."

My gut knotted with everything I wanted to say. "And what was that?"

Cut sighed, taking his time to reply. "I listened to my mother for too long. Time twisted her mind. It made what we did acceptable, *expected* even. I didn't stop to think it wasn't right." He broke into a sob. It wasn't fake or forced. His emotional undoing fed directly into me and I trembled with his honesty.

Forcing himself to keep going, Cut laid his conscience at the altar of wrongness. "I'm not blaming Bonnie. I'm not blaming my past or the morals I'd been fed. I'm blaming myself for being so fucking weak to stop it. Two of my children are dead. One is disabled for life. But you came back from the grave to teach me the lesson I needed to learn."

Kestrel isn't dead.

He'll come back to me because I made it safe for him to do so.

My eyes stung thinking of what my brother would say if he saw what I'd done. Would he hate me or understand? Would he fear me or celebrate? "What lesson?"

Silence fell as Cut worked out how best to deliver his epiphany.

He forgot I could taste his confession as clearly as a drop of expensive cognac on my tongue.

"That I'm no better than a Weaver. That being a Hawk doesn't grant immunity or power over another's life. That I'm not the monster I tried to be."

Silence reigned once again.

I had no reply. He didn't need one.

I played with the knife, running the blade through my fingers. His head never left my shoulder, his arms useless by his sides.

He couldn't move even if he wanted to, but I felt he didn't want to. This rare precious moment would never come again, and we needed to touch, to say sorry deeper than words.

Ten minutes could've past or ten hours—I lost track of time. My thoughts were with ghosts of people I'd lost. Of tragedies that'd come to an end but would never be forgotten.

Finally, my father forced his head off my shoulder and smiled sadly.

"You're a good son, Jethro. I'm proud of the man you turned out to be, even after I screwed you up. I wish I could say sorry to Nila for taking the Debt Inheritance too far. I had the power all along to stop it, just as my father did, and I chose not to. I also wish I could apologise to my brother for what I did and to Rose for how terribly I treated her. So many things to apologise for." He sucked in a breath, his arms and legs like discarded puppet strings. He couldn't sit up. He could barely breathe. "So many things I've done."

I'd done that to him. I'd shown him what he'd become, and he'd finally accepted his actions were bad, but his soul...it wasn't as decayed as he feared.

Shifting, I kissed his temple. "I believe you."

His sigh expelled more than just worry but his entire scorecard of wrongdoings. He exhaled his past, living the final moments in the present. "I'm ready to go, Kite. I *want* to go. Let me die and find peace. Let me fix the wrongs our family have caused."

My heart charged faster. As awful as it'd been breaking my father, forcing him to be honest and true, I didn't think I could kill him.

Not now.

Not now we'd connected like we always should've—man to man. Father to son.

Another tear rolled down my cheek. "I accept your apology, and I grant you my forgiveness." I passed him the knife. "I don't have the power to grant redemption for what you did to Jaz or Kes or Emma or Rose or the other people you hurt, but I do promise they will know you regretted it before you passed. If they can, they will forgive you in time."

Cut clenched his jaw as I moved away.

I accidentally knocked his painful limbs to squat in front of him. "I can't kill you, Dad."

Dad.

I hadn't used that word since Jasmine's disability.

Not since the last time he'd deserved such an adoring title.

Cut smiled, his golden eyes matching mine in the darkness. "I've always loved you. You know that, don't you?"

I wanted to say I didn't. That when he shot me in the parlour. That when he hurt my sister in the barn. That every day I strived for his respect and love, I didn't know what was beneath his sadism.

But I refused to lie to a dying man.

I'd known. And that was why I trusted that eventually, one day, the goodness inside him would win. That he wouldn't remain as awful as he had.

A childish hope and finally, it had come true.

Only for him to die.

"Kite...before I go...I want to do something to right my mistakes." His voice ached with sorrow. "Something to protect you all from the instructions I set beyond the grave."

If I didn't sense his sincerity, I wouldn't have believed he could feel so much regret. But he did—mountains of it. Chasms of it. He truly hated what he'd done. To everyone, not just to Jasmine and me but also to Nila and Kes and Daniel. And Rose. Most of all Rose.

I stared at him. He wanted something...something to...

"A piece of paper? Is that what you need?"

Cut smiled crookedly. "You always were a mind reader."

"Even when you tried to beat it out of me."

The truth in our words was just that. *Truth*. Not judgement or accusation. Just a statement of what was.

Cut nodded. "I'm sorry."

"I know." Climbing wearily to my feet, I moved toward the large table with implements of destruction and opened a rickety draw. Inside, I found a mouse-chewed notepad and a gnawed-on pencil.

Taking both back to my father, I sat back down and passed them to him.

He tried to take them, but his arms wouldn't work. The tendons failing to transmit instructions.

He sighed. "You'll have to do it."

He didn't lay blame. Just spoke the facts. He accepted his punishment and didn't hate me—if anything, he was grateful to have paid for his trespasses.

"What do you want me to write?"

He took a deep breath, thinking.

Finally, he recited, "I, Bryan 'Vulture' Hawk, do solemnly pledge my death is justified and accepted. I renounce all former decree that if my death is judged as murder that my firstborn heir, Jethro 'Kite' Hawk, is cut from my will. I revoke the agreements in place to send him to Sunny Brook Mental Institute and rescind all further instruction dealing with my daughter and other inheritors."

His voice hitched, but he forced through his body's shortcomings to relay his final message. "On this day, I draw forth a new Will and Testament with Jethro Hawk as my witness and true heir that all lands, estates, titles, and fortune pass to him upon my demise. This is binding and unchangeable."

A ball lodged in my throat as Cut shifted awkwardly. "Hold the paper and help me grab the pencil."

Swallowing hard, I wrapped his fingers around the pencil and hovered it in place on the newly written Will. I didn't know if it would stand up in a court of law, but we had paid lawyers on our side. Marshall, Backham, and Cole would ensure the paperwork would be lodged and executed. And then I would destroy their practice so they would never serve law to monsters such as my family again.

Cut grunted in agony as he signed his name; his signature almost illegible. Remembering what else lived in this barn, I hauled myself to my feet for the second time. "Wait there."

I returned with a handheld video recorder and new battery that'd been stored in the safe away from vermin. I didn't let myself remember why there was a recording device in here.

Ripping open the battery casing, I inserted it into the device, and turned it on.

The first thing that came up was the last filmed event.

Me.

Stored in this tiny recorder was what happened once Jasmine's back had been broken. I remembered the day in crystal clarity. It was never Cut's intention to hurt his daughter so much.

The video unspooled, crackling with sound.

Jasmine looked at me. "Kite...I can't feel my legs."

Instantly, Cut shed his pompous strictness of emperor of our estate and become a terrified parent instead.

He rushed to release my binds, not caring I crunched into the dirt once he'd loosened the leather. Once, I was free, he scooped up Jasmine and darted toward the exit.

"We'll go to the hospital, Jazzy. Fuck, I'm so sorry."

All he cared about was fixing what he'd done.

But I didn't let him get far.

I snapped.

I became like him. I craved his pain after what he'd done to my baby sister.

I wasn't proud of what I'd done. My hands trembled as the video-tape showed a devil-child leap onto his father's back and beat him over and over and over again with the club he'd used on Jasmine.

I stared transfixed as the tape continued, transforming me from abused to abuser as Cut fell on the floor, covering his face and hands.

I could've killed him that day and I would've if Jasmine hadn't screamed for me to stop.

Hearing her terror wrenched me from the blood cloud I'd swam in, putting her first rather than making my father pay.

I'd scooped her in my arms and charged to the Hall. I'd been the one to get Jasmine to the hospital all while Cut lay unconscious in the barn.

"Turn it off." Cut closed his eyes, cringing against the scratchy noises of the recording.

I couldn't breathe properly as I fumbled with the machine and switched it from memory card to fresh start.

Neither of us mentioned what we'd just seen or the past feelings of the incident. We knew who'd won that night and as a kid I'd expected harsh retribution. But Cut hadn't punished me. He'd pretended nothing had happened even while bruises marked his skin. He'd continued with my lessons but didn't hurt me any more than normal.

It was as if he wanted to be hurt for what he'd done to Jaz.

Clearing my throat, I held up the lens and pointed it at Cut.

The screen bounced in my hold, but it would have to do.

This was my insurance policy.

Cut understood immediately and dropped his head to the notepad I'd tossed in his lap. He fortified himself from our strained relationship and read my scrawled writing—for Jasmine and Kes and future heirs of Hawksridge Hall.

Occasionally, he looked up, reciting his pledge while staring into the camera. More often than not, his eyes remained downcast, reading his Last Will and Testament quickly.

My hands only shook harder the closer he got to finishing. My fever fogged my eyesight, and his voice threatened to put me in a trance.

I needed to rest and fast.

Finally, he finished.

Once his declaration was verbalized, I turned off the camera and placed it beside me for safe-keeping.

I looked at the same speck he stared at, unable to move forward but knowing I had no choice. "Thank you. Not for me, but for Jaz and the workers we employ. You've kept them in their homes and jobs."

A thought pricked me.

I'd planned on dismantling the diamond smuggling ring once Cut was dead, but his unselfish act of preserving the company and giving back my birthright reminded me it wasn't a matter of shutting down something just because I wanted to. We had people relying on us. I had to do right by them. I couldn't steal their livelihoods.

"Take care of those you love, Jethro." Cut coughed. "Don't ever let corruption turn you into me."

His words said one thing, but his heart another. He'd done what he'd been taught. But now, he wanted to go. He wanted the pain to stop, and I wouldn't deny him that.

He'd done what any human would do on their death bed. Apologised for past transgressions and accepted forgiveness for those he violated.

His soul was no longer burdened.

Picking up the knife once again, I placed my hand over his, squeezing his useless fingers around the hilt. His tendons and ligaments were no longer attached to signals from his brain. Completely disabled for the rest of his short life.

His eyes met mine. "You'll do it, after all?"

I shook my head, guiding his hand to hover over his heart. "No."

"Then what?"

"I can't kill you, but I can't allow you to live in such pain any more." My own bones howled in sympathy. My spine ached and brain overwhelmed with agony.

"You'll help me?"

I nodded.

"You're a good son, Kite." His head fell forward, using up the last of his energy. His lips landed on my forehead and kissed me.

I sucked in a breath, fighting against everything that'd passed between us. I accepted his kiss. His blessing. We held an entire world in a silent conversation.

I wished there was another way. I wished I didn't have to do this.

But Cut nodded, signalling he was ready.

Who was I to deny his final wish when I'd taken so much from him?

Without breaking eye contact, I leaned on his fist, puncturing his heart with the sharp blade.

So much pain to make him see.

And now, a quick death to make him free.

His forehead furrowed as the knife sank into his chest. He groaned as I twisted the hilt, tearing through the muscle and killing him as fast as possible.

He'd already suffered enough. I wanted him to leave without pain.

His forehead touched mine as I bowed over his dying form. His pulse thundered in his neck. His soul clung tight to his perishing body. And as the final gasp left his broken chest, I closed my eyes and kissed his cheek.

"Goodbye, Dad."

I did what I could never stomach and tethered myself to his last flickering thought. I held tight as he slipped into the afterlife. I lived his final farewell.

His eyes shot their message as well as his heart. *"Take care of those you love, Kite. Don't ever doubt I was proud of you. So, so proud."*

And then…he was gone.

It didn't take long to source enough kindling and set up a small pyre inside the barn.

All I wanted to do was rest. To sleep. To forget. But I wouldn't leave my father's corpse undealt with. That would be sacrilege. His immortal soul was free. His mortal remains had to be, too.

It took the last of my energy to move his dead body into the middle of the barn and rest it on top of the kindling. Once his hands were linked on his chest, and his broken limbs placed straight and true, I worked on building a last goodbye.

Moving as quickly as I could, I wedged more tinder around his lifeless corpse. Trudging from forest to barn, I built up enough fuel to create a fire that would last all night, a fitting send-off for my cruel father.

Once I'd buried Cut in branches, I hauled the rack closer, scooped every torture device off the table, and scattered them around him. After the fire, I wanted no remains or reminders of what went on in this place.

Stepping back, I checked my handiwork before moving toward the utility cupboard storing bleach and gasoline. The bleach had been for blood and the gasoline for the bonfires we'd occasionally had out here to cull a few trees.

Fighting the dregs of energy in my system, I poured the sharp smelling petrol over my father's corpse, the rack, the floor, the very walls of the despicable barn.

Only once every item and inch of the place had been drenched did I strike the match.

Taking the camera and Cut's last confession to a tree a safe distance away, I returned to stand by the doors and fling the sulphur rich flame onto the slick trail of gasoline.

Nothing happened.

The flames didn't catch. They went out.

Fuck.

My hands shook hard as I struck another match—letting the fire chew some of the stick before tossing it to the glistening floor.

This one worked.

The sudden whoosh of heat and orange exploded into being, rippling along the liquid path I'd set, eagerly consuming the tinder I'd given.

The cold night warmed as I stood in the entry and let the fire take firmer root. I didn't move as the crackle and singe of my father's skin caught fire. The smell of human remains burning and the whiff of smoke didn't chase me away.

I stayed vigil until the woods glowed red with heat and the air became thick with soot.

And still I stood there.

Smoke curled higher in the sky, blotting out the moon and stars.

I stood sentry like the oaks and pines, watching the fire slowly eat its way along the floor and walls, devouring everything in its fiery path, deleting the barn and its history.

Watching my father char to ash, I couldn't fight the memories of what I'd done. Of the stretching and breaking and pain I'd delivered. I buckled over, vomiting on the threshold. The intensity of what I'd lived through suddenly crushed me. I had no reserves left to ignore it.

I'm sorry.

I'm not sorry.

He deserved it.

No one deserved that.

Stumbling away from the burning barn, I tripped and jogged through the forest to the lake where Nila had been strapped to the ducking stool. There, I fell to my knees, willing the past to fade.

My body purged itself. Daniel's death. Cut's death. My mother's death. Kes's coma. Jasmine's disability. And Nila's torture.

It's all too much.

Even from my sanctuary by the water, I could still smell smoke. The aftertaste of my father burning coated my throat, and my eyes smarted with ash.

Throwing my head back, I glowered at the moon.

I'd never have another birthday where I feared the cake was laced with cyanide.

I'd never be sent back to the mental institute and kept prisoner in a straitjacket.

I'd never have to worry about Jasmine being tossed from the Hall and left to fend alone.

I'd never again bow to the wishes of a deranged family lineage.

I'm free.

Cut's free.

Those I love and fought for are free.

Feeling more animal than human, I had no control as I crawled on all fours to the water's edge. My hands squelched through the mud, moving like a beast. I gasped as I traded land for icy water. Waist deep then chest. I kept going until the mud switched to silt, welcoming rather than preventing.

I kept going.

Leaving ground and gravity, I slipped into weightless swimming.

I didn't try to stay on the surface. The moment I couldn't feel the bottom beneath my shoes, I let go. I sank below, dunking into the cold darkness.

I ran from everything, hiding in the pond.

Holding my breath, the freezing temperature stole my pain and hunger, soaking through my blood-saturated jeans and cinder-coated jumper.

With water above and all around me, I opened my mouth and screamed.

I screamed and screamed.

I screamed so fucking loud.

I screamed for my father, my mother, my sister and brothers.

I screamed for myself.

Bubbles flew from my mouth.

Salty tears mingled with fresh water and frogs sped away from my emotional unravelling.

I screamed and yelled and cursed and shouted and only the depth could hear me.

I poured forth my despair, my guilt, my condition, my fever, my battle-worn body.

I sank deeper and deeper, permitting my liquid-logged clothes to take me to the murky bottom. Plant fronds tickled my ankles, bubbles erupted from my shirt, and my hands hovered in front of my face, white as death and just as cold.

Hovering, I focused on my heartbeat—the only noise in the cavernous body of water. As seconds ticked on, it slowed…it steadied; it finally found its own rhythm away from tonight's atrocities.

Down there, I found something I'd been missing.

Forgiveness.

Only once my lungs burst for air did I kick off my shoes and push off the bottom. The rush of water over my skin washed me clean—not just from tonight but from everything. I hadn't done it out of fun. I'd done it out of loyalty to those who needed to be fought for.

I wasn't vindictive or spiteful.

I was *justified.*

I was baptised anew.

Breaking the surface, I gulped in greedy breaths, feeling a sense of rebirth. My tiredness faded, my wounds numbed, and I swam to look back the way I'd come.

There, on the horizon, the angry reds, yellows, and ochres of a raging fire danced in the dark night sky. Smoke stole the Milky Way and fire cleansed Hawksridge.

I hung in the snowy embrace of the water, just watching, always watching.

I shivered. My teeth chattered. And I craved warmth and bed and Nila.

I'd done what I needed to even though it almost broke me.

I had nothing left to fear.

Looking at Hawksridge Hall, my eyes found Nila's bedroom. The light burned in her window, a lighthouse for my drowning sorrows, a beacon leading me back to her.

I kicked toward the shore.

I need you, Needle.

I need you so fucking much.

She would put me back together.

She would understand what I'd done and accept me with no questions or ultimatums or tests.

She would love me unconditionally.

My heart calmed.

My mind quieted.

And finally, finally, *finally*, I found peace.

Kestrel

THERE WAS A saying that humans were capable of knowing only one thing.

One thing of ultimate, undeniable conviction where everything else—our thoughts, opinions, careers, likes, dislikes—even our entire lifespan of choices, were open to interpretation and amendments.

Only one thing was irrefutable. That one thing was: *we exist.*

We knew as a species—as an intelligent race of culture and history—that we lived and breathed and *existed.*

Nothing else outside of that was fundamental, only the knowledge we were alive. It evolved us from animals because with our existence came awareness for what a gift life was.

Some of us squandered it.

Others muddied it to the point of no redemption, but most of us appreciated the small present we'd been given and were grateful for it—no matter how lowly or high, rich or poor, easy or hard.

We existed, and that was a wondrous thing.

I'd never truly understood just how grateful I was.

But I did now.

As I lay in an in-between world where pain, death, or even time couldn't reach me, I had endless space to evaluate and understand. I'd existed as more than just a man, more than a brother, or friend, or son.

I'd existed because I made a difference to those I loved.

I cherished my sister.

I helped my brother.

And I did my best to remain true to the soul inside me rather than outside influences trying to change me.

I existed truthfully and that was all that mattered.

I wouldn't lie and say I didn't miss him. I missed the relationships with those I cared about. I missed my home, my possessions, my future. I missed worldly items because I knew I'd never see them again.

Jethro hadn't been easy to love. He'd been the cause of my sister's pain, my hard childhood. He'd been…difficult. But he'd also been the most loyal, loving, coolest brother I could've ever asked for.

He'd earned forgiveness for his issues. And I liked to think I'd played my part in helping him become a better person—a person who could live an easier life with his condition.

My time was over; my existence almost done.

And although I was sad to go, I wasn't afraid.

Because I *existed*.

And because I existed, I could never un-exist.

I would move on. I would transcend. I would grow and change and magnify to the point of whatever new experience awaited me. I would see those I loved again but not for a while.

And that was okay, too.

So I waited in my in-between world, listening to silence, hovering in nothingness, just waiting for the right time. I didn't know how I would know. I didn't know why I waited. But something kept me tethered to a world I no longer belonged to.

Until one day, I felt it.

The snip.

The silence turned to sublime music, the nothingness turned to warmth, and contentment blanketed with permission to leave. I knew he would be okay. I knew she would be okay. The family who persevered would be okay.

My father was dead.

Bonnie was dead.

Daniel was dead.

Evil had finally perished in my house.

And Jethro no longer needed me.

It took no effort, not even a sigh or conscious thought.

I just…let…go.

He had her.

He had her.

He had his very existence.

Nila would be there for him now.

He no longer needed my help.

I smiled, sending love to both of them, goodbye to everyone, and so long to a world that'd been briefly mine.

Jethro has found his reason for breathing.

It was time for me to find mine.

Goodbye…

Nila

JETHRO CAME FOR me at daybreak.

His icy touch woke me, trailing over my cheek to my lips.

I'd waited for as long as I could. I'd remained vigil by the window, imploring him to return. I'd paced thick grooves into the carpet, forcing myself to stay awake.

But I'd failed.

Jasmine left around midnight, and my body shut down soon after. Even opening the window and enduring the chilly gale couldn't fight sleep from claiming me.

After the fourth stumble and micro nap almost plummeting me to the floor, I reluctantly climbed into bed and slipped instantly into dreams. Good dreams. Bad dreams. Dreams of death and destruction then love and liveliness.

"Nila..."

His voice slinked around my soul, yanking me from slumber and delivering me directly into his control. My eyes shot wide, drinking him in. The dawn light barely illuminated my room, shyly warming the carpet and windowsill with promise of a new day.

I sat up on my elbows, cursing the sudden swirl and lack of sleep fogging my reflexes. For a moment, I couldn't see him, then his form solidified beside me.

Physically, he was in one piece. Tall and strong. Vibrant and majestic.

He stood silently, gazing intently. His eyes became fireworks in the gloom, sparking over my skin.

My gaze fell from his strained face over his chiselled chest to his half-hard cock. He stood naked. Not in a sexual manner but stripped back, bared, undressed and nude. Laying his horror, harrowing evening, and every haggard emotion at my feet.

His skin gleamed a white alabaster—looking as if he'd become a nocturnal being, an immortal monster.

Tears leapt to my eyes, understanding the brink of where he stood. He'd done things he wasn't proud of. He'd done things he *was* proud of. And ultimately, he'd come to me with nothing, leaving the past behind, asking me to forgive, forget, and help grant absolution he so desperately needed.

Sitting higher in bed, I nodded at his silent requests.

Why is he wet?

His discarded, sodden clothes stained the emerald carpet; his chest rising and falling as if he'd run a marathon. His eyes were wild. His hair wet and tangled. And his smell spoke of everything he'd done and done alone.

Copper for blood.

Soot for fire.

Metal for weapons.

And salt for sadness.

We didn't speak.

He was on the precipice of breaking.

I was the strong one in this dawn-lit moment. I was the one who had to save him.

I've got you.

Soaring upward, I scrambled out of the covers and kneeled before him. Silently, I wrapped my arms around his quaking shoulders. I'd removed the sling before falling asleep and my cast rasped against his soft skin.

I hadn't taken my shift off and the iciness of his body thawed into mine, delivering snow storms and blizzards the longer I held him.

He's so cold.

I hugged him harder, begging him to respond.

But he just stood there, trembling, shivering, his breath scattering hot and cold into my hair as I nuzzled against his chest. "It's okay. It's okay. I'm here."

Pressing warm lips against his frigid shoulder, I crawled on my knees closer to his marble-like form.

A gasp escaped him as I smoothed back his hair, kissing my way up his neck to his ear. "You're with me now. Feel how much I love you. Concentrate on how happy I am that you're back."

I never stopped kissing him, stroking him, willing him to come back to life. "Jethro, focus. Forget everything. Let me in."

Suddenly, his back bent, and he sagged in my hold. His arms flew around me, crippling me against his hard muscles. I didn't speak, but his soul screamed for help.

I let him hold me. I let him shake and shudder.

Time held no meaning as we existed in each other's embrace and fed each other with love and togetherness. I would hold him for the rest of my life and ensure he never felt anything but acceptance, adoration, and unconditional love.

"It's okay." My voice hung around us, glittering like fireflies, warming up his ice-ridden body. "I love you. I'm here for you. Feel what I feel. Live in how much you mean to me."

With a loud groan, Jethro scooped me from the bed. His arms bunched around me, cradling me gently as he carried me toward the bathroom.

My broken arm rested in my lap as I permitted him to do whatever he needed. I wouldn't fear him. I wouldn't question him or give him any reason to sense hesitation or unwillingness.

He wasn't well. His strength had reached depletion, but something drove him onward. Something he needed to abolish to find peace.

I was his. He was mine.

I would be his everything until he'd gathered his scattered psyche and returned to me.

Silently, Jethro traded the room for the shower. The same shower where he'd caught me with the water jet between my legs. The same bathroom where I finally knew I was falling for him, despite everything.

Silently, he turned on the hot spray and walked directly under it.

My dress became instantly sodden, but I didn't care. All I cared about was reanimating my lover, protector, husband-to-be by any means necessary. Cupping his nape, I pulled his face toward mine.

He didn't fight me as our lips met.

He sucked in a tattered breath as I licked his bottom lip, worshipping him sweetly. His eyes closed, his arms gathered me closer, and the world became just us, water, and steam.

Opening his mouth, his tongue met mine hesitantly, apologetically.

I hated that he'd forgotten our promises and commitment. That he didn't trust my vow to marry him. That he wasn't sure I could love him after tonight.

Holding his neck tighter, I pressed our lips together harder.

He groaned as I tasted his sadness, licking away his worry, replacing it with welcoming passion.

Slowly, he responded. The ache inside him unfurled, the pressure and stress siphoning down the drain as more droplets cascaded over us. Our heartbeats communicated in-tune with worded confessions.

"I killed him."

"I know."

"I hated him."

"I know."

"But I loved him, too."

"I understand."

His tongue teased my bottom lip. His heart cracked open and poured everything he'd done.

"I hurt him."

"He deserved it."

"I liked it."

"That's okay."

"I loathed it."

"That's okay, too."

"Did he deserve it?"

"Yes, he deserved to pay."

"He asked for forgiveness."

"Did you give it?"

"Yes.

"Oh, Kite..." I kissed him harder, our lips turning from dancing to fighting.

"He apologised."

"He should."

"He regretted his actions."

"Good."

"In the end, he was the father I always knew he could be."

"It's over now."

Jethro dropped me to my feet, crushing me against the tiles. My cast was drenched, but I had no concerns apart from Jethro. My dress clung to me, highlighting straining nipples, and the fact I had no underwear on beneath the shift.

Jethro tore his lips away from mine, staring at me. In my hold, he slowly came alive, shedding the holocaust and returning to me. He fell forward, trapping me between the tile and his nakedness.

The moment our tongues met again, our hearts shouted louder and louder. The more our souls conversed, the more violent and awake he became.

"I miss him."

"You can miss the man but not the monster."

"I shouldn't have hurt him."

"He hurt you."

"I should've been stronger to save you."

"You did save me."

He groaned as my hands shot into his hair, jerking hard. I didn't want him spiralling into self-hatred. Cut wasn't worth that. I'd set aside my hatred; I'd granted forgiveness. But I wouldn't let Cut's shadow ruin Jethro's hard-earned future.

I touched him. "You saved my life. More than once."

"I was almost too late."

"But you weren't. You made it."

"I should've saved you the first time I saw you."

"You *did* save me."

"How?"

"You fell in love with me."

His hands coasted up my sides, tearing at my drenched clothes. My hair plastered to my cheeks as his fingers tore at the neckline of my dress, ripping it down the centre.

Dropping to his knees, he yanked the material down my wet body until we stood naked under the steaming stream.

We hadn't turned on any lights and the window barricaded the watery attempt at dawn. Our bodies were Braille as our fingers tracked and touched.

His skin glowed white in the grey morning. His eyes such a vibrant bright.

Standing, Jethro grabbed my hips and guided us under the spray. His mouth claimed mine—desperate, hungry.

We drank water and each other, kissing, always kissing. Touching, forever touching.

There was no soap, but his hands covered every inch of me, washing away the past, the murder, the last few hours.

I repaid the favour, massaging his tense shoulders, his rigid spine, the knots in his lower back. I sluiced water over his bruises and cuts, willing the warmth to knit him back to whole.

My broken arm nullified any pressure I might've granted with my fingers, but I refused to let it hang uselessly by my side.

I forced every inch of me—parts unhurt and parts in pain—to heal him, love him, bring him back into the light.

Tugging his hair, I pulled his lips from mine.

His eyes narrowed but he didn't speak.

Tracing his mouth with my fingertip, I smiled as he nipped me gently.

Dropping my touch from his face, down his throat and chest, I didn't stop as my fingers traced muscles, dipping between his legs.

The moment my hand latched around his cock, a guttural growl tumbled from his lips. He reached for my cheeks, to kiss me, devour me, but I shook my head and dropped to my knees before him.

My broken arm rested on my thigh while my strong hand stroked him, encouraging his cock to swell and harden.

His stomach tensed, every muscle shadowed with need. His mouth fell open as his head fell back and he gripped the tiled wall for balance.

My attention fell to his stiffening erection. The fact his thoughts swam with desire pleased me so much. He gave me power over him. He let me take the memories and replace them with us.

Not only would we wash away whatever he'd committed tonight, but also the blood of the past, the unjust repayments of debts, and the dusty plains of Africa.

His cock fully swelled as his thoughts switched from self-preservation to sex.

I smiled, taking his long, thick length into my mouth.

His hand fell heavily on my head, fingers threading through my hair as I swallowed more of his cock, welcoming his musky heat onto my tongue.

I worshipped him, giving him everything that I was. My tongue swirled, teasing and adoring. His balls tightened, gathering closer to his body as I gave him what he needed.

He needed to know I was okay. That we both were. That he would find no judgement here. That he was loved just as deeply as before.

His hips pulsed in time with my bobbing head. My hand twisted and stroked, smearing saliva and shower water over his shaft. His hand gripped my hair harder then relaxed as if remembering to be gentle.

I didn't want him to remember anything. I wanted him so far gone, so in lust and consumed by desire he let go completely.

I wanted to *rule* him.

My pace increased, my tongue danced, spearing the sensitive crown and swallowing the saltiness of pre-cum.

Slowly, his breathing changed from ragged and sad to tortured and turned on.

His fingers jerked my hair, granting pleasurable pain as his other hand slapped loudly against the wall behind me, slipping and sliding, holding himself up while his hips worked faster into my mouth.

My heart burst, knowing he'd finally found some relief from his thoughts.

I closed my eyes and let him use me. I let his groans slip into my heart. I let his tugs and thrusts fill my soul.

I didn't know how long we stayed that way. Me at his feet and water raining all around but the tearful rage Jethro suffered finally faded, complex and unsolvable but faded nevertheless.

My jaw ached; my tongue throbbed.

However, I didn't try to bring him to an orgasm. I only tried to keep him centred on me. Consumed by bliss and able to find happiness after a nightmare.

His hand suddenly left the wall, slinking with the one already in my hair. Looping fingers under my chin, he broke my mouth's suction, pulling me away from his cock.

His gaze obliterated me with such love and affection, I couldn't breathe.

"Nila…" His hands tucked under my arms, tugging me to my feet. "I need you." His cock bounced against my lower belly as he hoisted me into his arms. He stumbled a little but kept me protected. His mouth captured mine, and for a blistering moment, he kissed me so damn hard, so damn feral, my core twisted with the beginnings of a release.

His tongue was magic, granting me the same gift I'd tried to grant him, ensuring all I thought about, all I needed was *him*.

Breathing hard, he tore his lips from mine and swayed weakly from the shower.

I didn't say anything.

There were no appropriate words as he reached back to turn off the spray and grabbed a towel from the rail. Placing the fluffy towel over my body, he hoisted me higher and marched back into the bedroom.

A trail of dampness turned the green carpet almost black as he plopped me on my feet beside the bed and reverently placed the towel over my shoulders.

The dawn gave way to weak sunshine. In the ever-brightening light, the scars of our trials became more apparent. My skin looked like a mismatched carousel: the bruises of Daniel's kick and punches. The scratches from glass and car carnage. The shower-drenched cast of my arm.

And Jethro.

His body held shadows and secrets of what he'd survived to get to me. His hair covered the injury on his temple. His skin, now it wasn't cold from trauma, radiated heat with the fever he needed to break. The gruesome red wound in his side was no longer hidden. The puckered skin where stitches had come undone wept, needing a doctor and healing.

We each had our craters and defects from war.

But we would wear them with pride because we'd won.

And the moment our bodies had reconnected, I would find Flaw to help stop Jethro's fever. I would call a doctor to sew up his side. And I would hire the best team to ensure he had no long-term damages from the car accident in Africa.

Jethro's lips twitched. "I love feeling your thoughts. I love knowing you want to heal me even while your body demands I take you first."

I shivered as his husky voice layered the air.

Ever so gently, with his eyes full of love, he dried me off from the top of my head to my toes. Once I was dry, I took the towel and repaid him. It took me a little longer and more awkward not having full use of two arms, but by the time I tugged his cock in the towel, he didn't care about a few remaining droplets on his shoulders.

Guiding me by the wrist, he stalked to the head of the bed and ripped back the sheets. Swooping me off my feet, he placed me gently on the mattress and tucked me tight. Moving to the other side of the bed, he climbed in and immediately grabbed me, spooning my back against his warm chest.

A huge sigh escaped him. For a moment, we just were. Just lived and relaxed and hovered in the anticipation of sex while soothed by the happiness of connection.

His cock remained hard, wedged against my lower back. His feet stroked mine, twitching like the tail of a predator.

"I don't know who I am anymore."

"I do. You're mine. You're Kite."

"I'll never be able to tell you what happened tonight."

"I know. I don't expect you to."

His arm squeezed my middle, and I arched into his erection.

Breathing faster, he turned me to face him, pressing his nose against mine.

His eyes delved past my soul into the epicentre of who I was. He sought answers to his fearful questions. He hunted for any lie that I didn't love him as much as I said I did. That I regretted any inch of what'd happened.

I wasn't afraid.

He would find no such farce or hidden secret.

Only once he'd searched every facet did he relax a little. Only once he fully accepted I loved him with no lie tainting the truth did he touch me. Truly *believe* me.

"I've done so much to you. I've hurt you so terribly." His hand cupped my cheek. "I don't deserve you or your forgiveness, but I give you my vow, Nila. I will *never* hurt you again. I will never put you in harmful circumstances. I will never ask more of you than you can give. I need you to be strong for me. Like I told you the night after the Third Debt, loving a creature like me is hard work. I'll drain you of every reserve. I'll feed off your love. I'll crave everything you can because you save me from life itself. But I vow that whatever I take from you, I'll give back a hundred-fold. I entrust my heart, my wealth, my very fucking soul to you forever."

His voice dwindled, fading to an almost-whisper. "I will never be able to discuss what I did, and I will never do anything like it again. I can't promise I won't have bad days. I can't assure you I won't need space or time if emotions get too strong to bear. But I *will* promise I will never love anyone as much as I love you."

His gaze entrapped me. "Can you live with that? Can you be so fucking selfless to take me at my worst, my best, my messed-up self and stand by me even when I break?"

I swallowed tears, pressing my cheek deeper into his hold. "I can."

He didn't speak, letting me gather my thoughts because I had more to say...I just didn't have the words in which to say it. "You'll never be on your own, Jethro. You never have to fear I won't understand or I'll push you away. You'll never have to run because I suddenly stopped loving you. I accept your promises and give you my own.

"I promise that no matter what happens in the future, we will work it out. I vow that no matter how life goes, I'll be by your side. I'll always love you because I've seen the worst of you and I've seen the best, and I know just how lucky I am to have met my perfect match."

The room seemed to solidify and melt as he surrendered. "I fucking adore you. I'd lay down my life—"

My good hand shot up, my fingers pressing against his lips. "No more talk of dying. Not now." My eyes drifted to his mouth; my fingertips warming as the pinkness of his tongue licked me gently.

The air between us changed.

Rapturous ecstasy replaced my blood as Jethro gathered me closer. My hand fell from his lips as his head tilted toward mine. His body heated, scalding me, drugging me with unspoken words and fleeting fondles.

I needed him.

He needed me.

We needed each other to wipe away a lifetime of conditioning and destinies. *This* was our new destiny. Right here. And no one—not debts, family, or contracts—could take that away from us.

His eyes flashed gold-bronze with brutal intention as his head bowed the final distance. His lips caressed mine before his tongue fluttered over my bottom lip. "Nila…"

My muscles turned limp, reacting to the desire in his voice.

I kissed him back.

Our lips danced, turning primal, taking, giving, wet, *consuming*. He sucked on my tongue, gruff sounds of lust and possession vibrating in his chest.

He tugged my hair, forcing my head back. With my neck exposed, he kissed his way down my chin and throat, over my collar, to my breasts. He never let go of my hair as his mouth settled over my nipple.

I cried out as he pulled hard and deep, tugging on the invisible cord between breast and core. My womb clenched, wetness wept, and I opened my legs with blatant invitation.

Rolling me onto my back, he slipped his hard body over mine. His hips fit perfectly between my open thighs, and he sighed heavily as his cock nudged erotically against my delicate flesh.

Securing my head with fistfuls of my hair, he kissed me deeply, his flavour making me drunk. Satisfaction, relief, desperation—they all had a flavour. Musky, smoky, sweet. He gave me everything. His fear. His happiness. His regret. His hope.

The kiss was a kaleidoscope of tastes, weaving us closer together.

"Thank you," he murmured, kissing my cheekbones and eyelashes. "Thank you so much."

I struggled to understand as his hands trailed down my belly. "For what?"

His mouth never left my skin. "For trusting me, even when I gave you no reason to do so. For giving me everything, even while I took more than I deserved."

My eyes remained closed, my body hovering in his masterful spell. My voice was the softest melody. "You can feel that?"

He nodded, his hair tickling my ribcage. "I feel everything when I'm with you, Nila."

I gasped as he captured my nipple again. His teeth threatened, slicing deliciously around the sensitive skin.

I turned rigid in his arms. *More. Bite me. Mark me.*

My fingertip tattoos burned with his initials. I wanted more. I'd paid the debts and survived the final one. I wanted the marks to prove it was him who saved me. He who decimated the contracts and war.

"I'm so fucking grateful for you." His slow smile was pure truth. "So awed you've fallen for me." He worshipped me, submitting to me in the most endearing male way. "You kill me every day because I can't believe how lucky I am."

"Stop. You don't need to—"

He kissed me again. "But I do. I need to make you see it isn't empty words or shallow promises. It's the honest to God truth."

My heart skipped. He'd given me so much, and he didn't even know.

The mattress cushioned me as his bulk pressed me deeper into the covers. His sculpted arms trembled as he stroked me. His fever still glowed in his skin, and injury slowed his movements, but he never stopped. Never gave any reason not to take me.

For once, I'd like to make love without fear or regret. I wanted to surround ourselves in happiness and pleasure and shut out the world.

I ran my hands over his chest.

He quivered, his muscles hot and tight beneath my touch.

"I need you, Kite." I pressed my lips into the hollow of his throat. "I need you so much."

"And you have me. Now and forever." His voice slipped from gruff to husky. He slid higher over me, dropping his head, his teeth biting my shoulder. Gathering me closer, he aligned our hips, pressing his full length against me.

Being in his arms was divine. A timeless world within a broken one. Untangling my arms from around his, I swept back salt and pepper hair, staring into his eyes. "You're beautiful."

He sucked in a breath.

"Beautiful inside and out."

"You don't know how long I've wanted to feel worthy of that. To like myself. To be able to live with what I am."

"You don't have to live with yourself anymore. You live with me. Let me love you enough for both of us."

His arms flexed, squeezing me so damn hard. "Fuck, Nila." Rolling me onto his front with a fluid show of masculine power, he hugged me as if he wanted to shatter every bone in my body. Then, as if the glued contact of our skin and overwhelming tenderness of the moment was too much, he rolled me again, pressing my shoulders onto the mattress.

He hovered over me, eyes heavy with lust, his jaw shadowed with sexy stubble. The attraction between us throbbed to unbearable levels.

We'd lived through more than anyone would in their lifetime. And despite all the wrongs we'd endured, the delicious provocative taste of danger still lurked around us.

Jethro was dangerous. He would always be dangerous—not because of his lineage or wealth but because of what he was. However, he was also the gentlest person I'd ever met, building walls and mechanisms in order to live in a world of overstimulation and noise.

He was also the strongest person I'd ever known. If I dealt with physical imbalances upsetting me daily, I couldn't image the strength it took to stay true to yourself even when there were so many avenues in which to disappear.

His hands gripped my hips. His mouth parted, pressing against mine. Tilting his head, he deepened the kiss, sending me spiralling in his arms. His lips were soft but demanding. His tongue silky but possessing. There was no escape from such control.

I sensed him everywhere, all around me, inside me. His flaws. His triumphs. But most of all his selfless love. He loved me enough to do what he did to his father. Enough to follow me around the world. And enough to put an end to the six-hundred-year-old feud between Weavers and Hawks.

I skated my hands over his taut spine, tracing his hips to grab his cock. The heat of him was still damp from our shower.

"Ask me again. Now that it's all over."

Jethro frowned, his pulse thundering. "Ask you—"

Then understanding filled his gaze. He kissed me sultry and sweet. "Nila 'Threads' Weaver…will you marry me?"

The intensity in his voice burst my heart.

I nodded. "Yes. A thousand times yes."

"Everything you feel for me, Nila. It's so intense. *Too* intense. I need you to never take that way from me. I don't think I'd survive if you did."

"I promise."

A lazy smile—the first I'd seen in weeks—stole his lips. "I'm going to make you keep that promise."

The melancholy disappeared as the dawn switched brighter into daylight. "Oh? How so?"

His hand slipped down my body, moving between my legs. "By claiming you every day for the rest of our lives." His gaze hooded as he stroked my clit with sensuous fingers. Everything about him was wicked and wild and so shamelessly real. "Help me, Nila. Help me show you how much I love you."

I didn't need instructions.

Opening my legs, I let his touch drop downward, stroking my entrance, slowly inserting a finger.

My hand stroked him in return, rippling over the velvety stone of his erection.

My back bowed as his thumb pleasured my clit, effortlessly playing me into a ballad of pleasure.

I cried out as his one finger turned to two. The pressure became indescribably decadent.

With his free hand, he caught my hips, holding me as I rocked on his hand. "God, you're beautiful." His voice was desperate, his fingers fucking me almost leisurely but completely possessively.

Uncurling my fingers from around his cock, he pressed his erection against my thigh. "Feel me. Feel how much I want you—not just now, but for the rest of our lives."

My hands flew downward again, recapturing him, working him faster, harder.

He groaned, driving his fingers inside me, matching my vicious beat.

A ripple of bliss caught me; I moaned as his thumb continued strumming. "Jethro…"

He stopped. "Don't come. I don't want you to come. Not yet." His teeth caught my ear as his harsh breath sent delightful goosebumps over my skin. "Not until I'm inside you and claiming your body as well as your heart." His voice held a warning, growling with bite.

"Jethro…take me, please."

His lips fell into a stunning smile. His fingers withdrew, and he smeared my wetness around my throat where the diamond collar rested. A slight shadow clouded his eyes. "You'll wear this for the rest of your life."

"I know."

"I'll try to find a way to take it off."

I shook my head. "No, I like it." Holding up my hands, I showed him my tattooed fingertips. "Just like I like these. Our beginning didn't start the way a romance should, but I wouldn't part with any memento. Including the Weaver Wailer."

His forehead furrowed. "Let's not call it that. It needs a new name." His hips rocked, joining his puzzle piece with mine. His face darkened as the tip of his cock found my entrance. Without looking away, he sank inside me, impaling me slowly. His jaw clenched as my body welcomed him.

The slowness and friction of his penetration drove me mad.

I gasped as he pushed past the barrier of comfort, sinking his entire length inside me. Only once he sheathed completely and could speak through echoing pleasure did he whisper, "How about Hawk Redeemer?"

My core clenched around him. "I like it."

"Me too." The rasp of his voice drugged me as he rocked once, twice.

"Oh..." My eyes shot closed; all I focused on was where we joined. I'd never grow tired of sleeping with this man. Never cease loving him.

"Fuck, I love when you think those thoughts." His eyes gleamed with awe. "They're so strong and pure—it feels as though I'm reading your mind and not just your emotions."

"I have nothing to hide from you." My head fell back as he thrust into me again, driving deeper, changing the angle of his direction. My body accepted him in one smooth glide.

We fit together so well. We always would.

"Shit, Nila." His head fell forward. "You're so tight, so amazing, so fucking precious."

Words abandoned me as I accepted his every thrust. His cock throbbed inside, so hard and thick.

Jethro kissed me. Hard and fast. His lips trailing to my ear. "I want you forever and always. Like this. No lies. No falsehoods. Nothing between us but honesty."

"Nothing." I wriggled beneath him, craving more. "I promise."

The delirium he caused in my blood sent my thoughts scattering. I needed to come. I needed to shatter and be reborn from everything that'd happened.

"I don't think I can wait," Jethro growled, rocking his cock so the base of him rubbed against my clit. I gasped as yet more blood incinerated.

"Then don't." Holding onto his nape with my good hand, I begged. "Please...give me what you want. I need it, too."

Heat misted across my skin as he thrust harder, fucking me, adoring me, driving me up the cliff of ecstasy. Heat flushed until it was an inferno, turning me sick with sex-fever, demanding medicine in the form of an orgasm.

"God, yes. More. Please."

Jethro slammed his fists into my pillow, using the bed as an anchor as he rode me. His cock drove in and out.

I accepted every punishment, cresting higher and higher, wrapping my legs around his hips, begging, loving, soaring faster and faster toward a release.

His forehead met mine, warmth enveloped us and his pace turned frantic.

I couldn't...I couldn't handle it any longer.

Ecstasy turned to euphoria. Tingles shot from my toes, crackling through my legs, detonating in my core.

Explosion and bands of bliss.

I came. "Yes. Yes. God, *yes.*"

My pussy fisted him, clutching desperately with waves of pleasure.

Jethro cursed, but he didn't come. He hovered above me, giving me a gift, all the while watching me come apart. It made my release so singular and special—turning our moment into something so intimately vulnerable.

Only once I'd wrung myself dry did he fist the pillow and wedge his face into my throat. His guttural groan as he came undone sent another flash of intoxication through my system.

"Fuck, I love you." His growl dripped pure sexuality and unrestrained reverence.

His orgasm quaked his body, wringing him dry as he spurted inside me. I hugged him, letting him splash with his release.

We stayed clinging together long after his hips stopped twitching. Our heartbeats thundering to the same beat.

Slowly, he raised himself on his elbows and cupped my head in his hands. The intimacy between us caused sudden tears to spring to my eyes.

"You're everything I've ever needed, Nila." His voice was hoarse and deep. "Through every day, every text message, every awful debt, I gave you my heart." He nudged my nose with his. "And now, you own all of it."

My nipples tingled against his chest as my uninjured arm wrapped around his muscular waist. There was no space between us. His heart pattered against mine and I never wanted him to leave. My pussy quivered with aftershocks of our orgasm—milking Jethro's erection still inside me.

He chuckled, causing his cock to jerk. "Eager for another round, Ms. Weaver?"

I gasped, shivering with a mixture of happiness and distress at my last name. "Always."

Tilting his head, he breathed, "Kiss me, Needle."

My heart leapt into my mouth as I kissed him with everything I had left. Our lips met hot and wet, the crackling lust of sex mixing with the erotic promise of more.

My fingers disappeared into his hair, holding him like he held me. Our hearts once again spoke silently as his kiss turned demanding and infinite. His cock thickened inside me as his tongue drove in and out, fucking my mouth just like he'd fucked my body.

I couldn't love him anymore than I did. I couldn't ask for any more than I'd been given.

Whatever he'd done tonight still tainted the air around us. The undercurrent of death and destruction hadn't dissolved, but the allure of a bright and untwisted future grew stronger every minute.

It would take time for us to move on. But we *would* move on.

All of us.

Because we deserved it.

With him inside me, we were inseparable.

Now and forever.

He'd proposed.

I'd said yes.

We were each other's.

For eternity.

Jethro

MY HEART COULDN'T handle any more stimuli.

Not after yesterday's rush of terrible highs and morbidly low lows. And yet, I had no choice but to endure more.

In my right hand, I held my sister's. In my left, I held my fiancée's, unknowingly passing emotional messages as natural as breathing.

Last night, we'd become more than two people beneath the spray. We'd become one.

Things had changed between us.

There was a new layer to our connection. A deeper, unbreakable bond—an indescribable friendship.

And as much as I wanted to deny it, I needed Nila's friendship and support more than anything today.

Today.

I swallowed hard, hating the word.

I would forever remember this day. I would forever *despise* this day.

The morning had been blissful. After fucking Nila, I'd tumbled into a sleep so deep, I entered a black hole of tiredness. I didn't wake until late lunch and only because the gnawing pain of hunger drove me to service my other needs now my brain wasn't shredded with lethargy.

Once Nila and I had raided the kitchen for roast chicken sandwiches and crisps, Flaw found us and demanded we follow him to his newly created triage in the east wing.

There, he'd redone Nila's soggy cast, and stitched up the tear in my side. He'd also checked my vitals, and given me antibiotics for my fever. Afterward, he'd given me strict instructions to head for a proper check-up with my doctor at the hospital and assured me he'd taken care of the injured from the ballroom and had the aftermath well in hand.

I normally didn't give employees such trust. But Flaw was more than that now. He'd proved himself capable and loyal. If he said he had things under control, I would believe him while I focused on more important things.

Things such as healing and shedding the memories of what had happened between Cut and me. Every time I thought of my father, my heart ached with torment. Was I right to do such things? Was I wrong to regret them after everything he'd done?

I sighed, squeezing my sister's and Nila's hands. I couldn't think about that.

Not here.

Not now.

Not when the very building I stood in stripped every reserve I had, poisoning me with sadness, grief, and insurmountable helplessness.

Kestrel.

Goddamn you, brother.

My eyes burned as I focused on my best friend.

Flaw had gotten his wish. I'd returned to the hospital. However, I stood in the basement of a facility dedicated to healing and keeping the injured alive, breathing in the stench of death. Above, the living still clung to hope. But down here…down here, we stood in a morgue.

A crypt where soulless bodies froze on ice, waiting for their loved ones to determine their fate. A terrible, terrible place where the lingering emotions of destroyed relatives and broken-hearted lovers said goodbye for the final time.

I don't want to say goodbye.

Nila squeezed my hand as I swallowed back a growl, snarl, curse…sob. I didn't know how to react. I couldn't unscramble my thoughts from Jasmine's or Nila's.

In the car over here, I'd had to screech to a stop, scramble out, and sucker punch an innocent tree on the side of the road.

Jasmine.

She hadn't told me.

After Flaw patched me up, I'd searched for Nila. I'd dealt with my hunger and sickness, all I wanted to do was return to bed and spend days hiding from others, wrapped up in the love Nila had for me.

But that was before the phone rang.

That was before Jasmine called and told me to join her at the hospital.

The motherfucking hospital.

The same place I'd almost died and my brother…

My head bowed as I tugged my hand from Jasmine's, squeezing the bridge of my nose.

Jasmine had received the call earlier. The one conversation no one wanted to have. She'd enlisted Vaughn's help to take her to the hospital.

She'd gone without me.

She'd deliberately left me in the dark that my goddamn brother had fucking died.

Jasmine's hand landed on my elbow, her sniffs quiet but distinct as she cried. "I'm sorry, Jet. So sorry. I came to get you. Truly. I entered Nila's quarters and watched as you slept in her arms."

Her touch fell away; her eyes on Kes, her words directed half at him, half at me. "You looked so happy, so peaceful. After everything you've been through, I couldn't. I couldn't wake you up."

Nila let me go, moving to Jasmine's side and wedging herself where Vaughn kept a subtle touch on my sister's shoulder. Nila smiled at her twin, wrapping her arm around Jasmine. "We understand. Jethro isn't well. He needed to rest. You did the right thing—"

I turned on both of them. "The right thing? How *dare* you decide what's the right thing when my fucking brother is dead! I should've been here for him. I should've held his hand and said goodbye. I should've had the freedom to tell

678

him just how much I loved him. How much he helped me. How much I appreciated his friendship even when I pushed him away."

The pain at his passing crumpled my heart like a dirty piece of paper, screwing it into a tear-stained ball. "I should've been there."

Jasmine's skin waxed white with grief. "He was already dead, Kite. He passed when you were with Cut." Her eyes popped wide. "Forget that. I wasn't going to tell you. Forget—"

"*What?*" My spine rolled. I punched myself in the chest, seeking relief from the slowly fermenting agony. "You're telling me while I hurt our father—while I did what I thought was right—my brother *died*! Is this life's cruel joke? I stole a life. Therefore, they stole his in return!?"

I faced my brother, grabbing his ice-cold hand with mine. "Is this my fault?"

Jasmine's wheels creaked as she rolled closer. Nila came with her, moving to my side, wrapping me in her sadness and despair.

"He was my brother too, Jet. Don't you think I wanted to say goodbye? I would've given anything to be there. But we weren't." Her voice turned fierce. "And it isn't your fault."

Vaughn didn't say a word, backing away a little, never taking his eyes off Kestrel.

"Kes knew how we felt about him. He knew he was loved and wanted. He didn't die without knowing how much we'd miss him." Jasmine couldn't continue; her tears turned to sobs, and my heart cracked with her pain.

I curled my fists, pressing nails against my palm, wanting to draw blood. I needed to hurt myself so I could focus on a singular discomfort rather than a room full of tragedy. I needed my blade. I needed to cut open my soles and activate age-old salvations so I could get through this.

But I had nothing with me.

And I couldn't leave Kestrel.

Nila curled into me, wrapping her unbroken arm around my waist, pressing her head against my shoulder. She didn't say a word, but she didn't have to.

Somehow, she pushed aside her grief at Kes's death and focused on her love for me. Standing in a room full of crippling unhappiness, she gave me a cocoon of togetherness.

Unknowingly, my body relaxed a little. I leaned into her, kissing the top of her head. "Thank you."

She didn't look up, but she nodded.

Having a moment of peace, I sucked in a heavy breath and turned to hug my sister. My back bent, gathering her crying form from her wheelchair, murmuring in her ear. "I'm sorry, Jaz. I had no right to yell at you."

She clung to me, crying harder. "I shouldn't have made the decision to let you sleep. I should've woken you. I'll never forgive myself. But I haven't moved from his side, Kite. I stayed with him until you arrived. I kept our brother company."

Pulling away, I brushed aside her tears. "Thank you."

The moment I let Jaz go to touch Nila, Vaughn placed his palm back on my sister's shoulder.

My eyes narrowed.

He glared.

I didn't want to feel what he did, but he gave me no choice.

He liked her.

He wanted her.

He hated she was hurting and would be there for her whether I liked it or not.

The complication of Vaughn developing feelings for my sister pissed me off but there was too much to focus on. And there was another person much more important to fret over.

Ignoring him, I faced Kestrel once again.

He lay stiffly on the metal table. His skin looked fake, his hair dull, his form unwanted. His arms remained dead straight beside him, the inked kestrel on his flesh glowing morbidly under the lights, while a white sheet covered his nakedness.

He still looked like my brother, but at the same time, completely different. His skin was no longer warm and pink but lifeless and cold. The pure heart inside him and huge capacity to forgive, heal, and protect had moved onto a different form, leaving us but not forgetting us.

He'd been so strong. So brave. I'd taken him for granted, expecting him to be there beside me as we grew old and grey.

Yet, now he'd forever remain young. Frozen in time, immortal to the end.

I wanted to collapse to my knees and confess everything to him. I wanted to tell him what I'd done to Cut. I wanted to purge my sins and have him carry them for me.

But I couldn't.

I would never speak to him again.

And I couldn't grieve.

Not yet.

Not after the destruction of yesterday.

And in some strange way, I felt as if Kes already knew what'd happened in the barn. As if he hadn't died because I'd taken a life and another Hawk must forfeit. But because he sensed he no longer had to fight against our father.

He was free to go.

Free to be happy.

You'll always have my gratitude and friendship, Kes. No matter where you are.

A ball lodged in my throat, but I didn't break down. It took all of my remaining strength to stare dry-eyed at my brother and whisper farewell.

"He died without pain," Jasmine murmured. "The doctor told us his heart gave out from his injuries. He was still in a coma…he wouldn't have felt it." Jaz looped her fingers with Kes's lifeless ones. "He's at peace now."

My back locked as Kes remained unmoving. His bird tattoo didn't jerk, no feathers quivered over his muscles. I kept expecting his eyelids to flutter, his lips to twitch. His laugh to explode and an elaborate hoax to be unveiled.

But unlike his prankster illusions from his childhood, this wasn't a deception.

This was real.

He was dead.

He's truly gone.

I hugged Nila closer. "He didn't die alone. You're never truly alone when you know you're loved by another."

Jaz's tears wouldn't stop, and I wouldn't force her to dry her eyes until she was ready. I'd purged and sewn myself back together in the lake after coming apart with my father's death. Today, I would help my sister do the same thing.

Nila cried quietly beside me. Her heart sorting through so many memories, so many complexities even though she'd known Kes only a short while. They'd bonded. They'd loved each other. They would forever be linked by their own relationships as well as the family tie Nila would form by marrying me.

I'm sorry, brother.

I looked at his face, his cold body and vacant shell, and said a private eulogy.

I'm sorry I wasn't there to say goodbye, but this isn't goodbye; it's just a postponement. I'll miss you, but I won't mourn you because you were too good a friend and brother to remember with sadness.

Time lost meaning as we all stood beside Kes one last time.

The moment we left, we'd never see him again. The only way we would look upon his face was to stare at pictures from happier times or watch videos trapping his soul forever.

None of us wanted to leave.

So we stayed.

The room quieted from emotional strain until we all hovered in the same thoughts. We relived our special times with Kestrel. We rifled through memories; we smiled at antics and shared childhoods.

"What are you doing here?" I looked up as the locked door to the prison cell swooped open. I'd been at the mental institute for two nights and couldn't stand another fucking minute.

Kes slinked through the darkness. "Busting you out." Holding out his hand, he grinned. "Time to leave, big brother. Time to make a run for it."

He'd tried to help me escape that night, just like he'd helped me escape so many times in our childhood.

"Now, what are you doing?"

"Focusing." Kes sat cross-legged on the floor of his bedroom, his hands on his thighs in a yoga pose.

Throwing myself beside him, I rolled my eyes. "It's not working. Your thoughts are just as horny." At seventeen and fourteen, our hormones had kicked in, and Kes was a terrible flirt.

His laugh barrelled through the room. "Least I can talk to girls."

"Yes, but I can feel them."

"Not in an interesting way, though." He winked. "You feel their silly concerns while I—" He flexed his fingers "—I feel their tits."

I punched him in the arm, so damn grateful he was my brother.

God, I would miss him.

He was gone.

It was time for us to go, too.

Moving for the first time in hours, I placed my fingertips on Kes's icy forehead. His skin seeped my warmth, stealing it the longer I touched him.

Pulling away, I had the incredible urge to touch life after touching death. To hold onto something real. Gathering Nila closer, I hugged my sister and nodded at Vaughn. Flaw would come to pay his respects tomorrow. He was close to Kes; his death would be hard on all of us.

Somehow, two Hawks and two Weavers had come together in shared grief, mourning a man who died far too young.

But that was life.

It was cruel. Unjust. Brutal. And dangerous.

Good people died. Bad people lived. And the rest of us had to continue surviving.

A week passed.

In that week, things changed a lot and none at all.

My fever finally broke, my wound healed, and my strength slowly returned. My body was still exhausted but every day, I pieced myself back together.

Nila had a lot to do with that.

The day after seeing Kestrel's body, I returned to the hospital on my own. I sought out the nurse who'd brought me the cell phone while I healed and paid her a thousand pounds for her trouble. She'd gone out of her way to give me the means to contact Nila. The least I could do was compensate her.

While there, I submitted to a full examination and the doctor's instructions to take it easy. I was cleared of any concussion or long-term maladies. I also singlehandedly arranged the transfer of Kes's body to the crematorium. As part of Cut's meticulous upbringing, all his children had Last Wills and Testaments.

Kes was no different.

I'd found his file amongst the others in Cut's study. The bones of his dog, Wrathbone, lay in the coffee table as I scattered paperwork and skimmed through Kestrel's final wishes.

I already knew he wanted to be cremated and scattered on Hawksridge grounds. We'd shared many a late night conversations as young boys about how unappealing the thought of being buried and eaten by weevils and worms sounded. We were both slightly claustrophobic, and I understood his wish to be sprinkled as dust, prisoner to the breeze, and weightless as the sky.

I wanted the same ending.

However, what I wasn't expecting was a note addressed to me—penned almost five years ago. The strangeness of holding a letter from the grave clutched my stomach.

There was also one for Jasmine and Daniel.

My heart suffered thinking of Daniel's remains. He wouldn't be buried or cremated, but perhaps, he would be happier away from Hawksridge and on his own with no delinquent comments of unwanted belonging.

Respecting Kestrel's privacy, I burned Daniel's letter. Never to be read. The words remaining between two dead brothers forever.

I delivered Jasmine's to her room, leaving her to read on her own. And I took my envelope onto my Juliette balcony off my office where I'd spied on Kes and Nila as they'd galloped across the meadow.

Squinting in the winter sunshine, I slipped out the rich vellum and read my brother's parting words.

Hello, Jet.

I'm guessing if you're reading this, bad things happened.

I must admit, I didn't see myself dying before you. After all, you're the old bugger, not me. But if I died to protect you or help in some small way, then I'm glad. If I died from sickness or doing something stupid, then so be it. At least I'm free from whatever pain I was in.

I do need to ask something of you. And I need you to do it, Jet. Not just nod and pretend you will. I truly need you to do it.

Don't mourn me.

Don't think of me gone, but imagine I'm still with you because I am. We're brothers and I have no intention of leaving you. I've been your support for too long to leave you in the lurch.

So even though I'm physically gone, I swear to you I won't leave spiritually. Scatter my remains on the estate and whenever the wind blows, I'm there telling you a joke. Whenever it snows, I'm there covering you in frost. Whenever the sun shines, I'm there warming your chaotic soul.

And when you finally meet a girl worthy of your love, I'll exist within her. I'll teach her how to help you. I'll guide her how to protect you like you'll protect her. Because you're the best goddamn friend a brother could ever ask for and whoever the girl is who steals your heart, I know she's worth it.

I love her already. Just like I love you.

Never forget that friendships are forever.

I'll see you again, Kite.

I'll always be around.

I didn't cry, even though my soul raged at the unjust and loss. My hands shook as I folded the letter and placed it carefully into its envelope. Kes had written the note before we claimed Nila. He'd sat alone one night and penned a letter to be delivered after his death.

How had he managed to pour so much into a few short paragraphs? How had he known exactly what to say?

If only he'd written it after he met Nila.

He would know what he predicted came true.

Nila was my everything.

She'd replaced Kes as my crutch, and I would never take her for granted like I did him.

Never.

The breeze blew gently, smelling sweetly of hay from the stables.

I closed my eyes and just rested in the moment. No thoughts. No concerns. I let life exist around me and stole a few short seconds to connect with my dead brother.

You're still here, Kestrel.

I feel you.

Another few days passed and life found a new rhythm.

The Black Diamond brothers sorted out their own hierarchy. I put Flaw in charge as temporary president and he culled the members who didn't want to walk on the right side of the law. Those we paid handsomely, made them sign non-disclosure agreement guaranteeing hefty punishments if they spoke out of turn, and let them leave the club.

As our membership was always about diamonds and business, no one had to be unpatched or excommunicated from the brotherhood. They were just employees searching for new work.

One night, once we'd all eaten—Weavers and Hawks sharing a table in the red dining room where so much pain had occurred—I took Nila by the hand to our quarters. Once upon a time, my rooms had been called the bachelor wing, but now, they were our matrimonial suite. A honeymoon before I made her my wife.

We entered the wing. However, instead of taking her to bed, I gave her a key.

Standing at the base of a small staircase leading to a storage floor above, her black eyes met mine with confusion. "What's this?"

I smiled softly, wrapping her fingers around the key. "The past week I've managed to put some of my past behind me. It's time for you to do the same." Gathering her in a hug, I murmured, "Time to let the past go so we can all move on and heal."

I didn't want to think about what she'd find up there. She had to face it. Just like I'd faced Cut.

She let me hug her, her desire for me building the longer we touched. I couldn't put this off anymore. I'd already put it off too long.

Pulling away, I let her go, dragging a hand through my hair.

She frowned, twirling the key in her fingers. "What does it open?"

Something you won't want to see.

Climbing the first few rungs of the steps, I held out my hand for her to follow. "I'll show you."

She silently chased me up the twisting stone staircase, nervousness layering her thoughts the higher we strode.

We didn't bump into anyone. There was no fear of being caught by snooping cameras or hiding from madmen with death threats. Just an ordinary house and an ordinary night. About to do a very unordinary thing.

Nila slowed the higher we climbed. "Where are we going?"

I didn't look back. If I did, I'd second-guess the intelligence of what I was doing. It wasn't my choice to decide if this was wrong. It was Nila's. "Almost there."

When we arrived on Cut's third floor, she faltered. "Tell me."

Grabbing her hand, I tugged her down the plush carpeted corridor. Up here no artwork or embroidery decorated the space. These rooms were the unseen part of the Hall. The place where secrets were stored and debts were hidden for eternity.

"You'll see." I led Nila further down the corridor, stopping outside a room she hadn't been permitted to enter. This wasn't just a room but a tomb of memories. There were still so many unexplored parts of the Hall. She'd only visited a fraction of my home and most rooms were welcoming and just like any other.

But not this one.

This one housed nightmares.

The storage mecca of every debt extracted.

The carved door depicted roses and tulips, similar to the awful flower arrangements Bonnie had enjoyed. The moment the contents were cleared, I would destroy the door, too.

Taking the key from Nila's suddenly shaking fingers; I inserted it into the lock and opened the door. The soft *snick* of the mechanism made me swallow hard. I felt as if I trespassed on things I shouldn't, entering a realm not meant for me. "After you."

My heart thudded at the seriousness on her face. "What—what's in there?"

I looked briefly at the carpet, forcing myself not to drown in her sudden fear. "An ending of sorts, or a beginning, depending on how you look at it. Either way, you need to see and decide for yourself."

Straightening her shoulders, holding onto non-existent bravery, she brushed past me.

Her eyes widened as I switched on the light, drenching the wall-to-wall cabinets of files. In the centre were a large table, a TV, VCR, and DVD player. Everything she'd need to read and witness decades of hardship.

Nila covered her mouth as realisation came swift. "It's all here. Isn't it?"

I nodded, steeling myself against her sudden outwash of rage. "It is."

"I can't—I don't...." She backed away. "Why did you bring me here?"

Stalking forward, I opened the one cabinet where I'd seen Cut deposit all things relating to Emma.

Nila stepped again, her bare feet tripping with a sudden wash of vertigo. I rushed to her side, but she pushed me away, balancing herself with practiced ease. "Jethro...I don't. I don't think I can look."

"I'm not saying you have to. I'm giving you the option if you wish, that's all." I moved back to the filing cabinet and grabbed the largest file. Carefully, I carried it to the table. "It's your call, Nila." Heading to the door, I murmured, "I love you. Remember that. Come find me when you're ready."

"Where are you going?"

I smiled sadly, hating leaving her but knowing she had to do this on her own. She needed to say goodbye, consolidate the horror of what my father did, and work through her hate to come back to me. "Tomorrow is Kes's funeral. Tonight, we should have one for your ancestors. Send the dead away all at once, eradicate the estate of the ghosts living in its walls."

For the longest moment, she stared. She didn't say a word. She looked as if she'd bolt or fly out the window. Then, finally, an accepting tear rolled down her cheek. "Okay."

I nodded. "Okay."

It was the hardest thing I'd ever done, but I turned and closed the door behind me.

Heading down the stairs and away from the Hall, I disappeared into the woodland and gathered branches, kindling, and twigs for the largest bonfire Hawksridge ever seen—minus the barn that'd wiped Cut from existence.

I enlisted the help of Black Diamond brothers and carted every torture equipment and vile method of pain onto the lawn, ready to be burned.

The Iron Chair, Scold's Bridle, Heretic's Fork, Ducking Stool, whips, thumb screws—every mortal thing.

I didn't want such heinous items living beside us any longer.

Hawksridge Hall would evolve with us; it would embrace happiness and learn to accept sunshine rather than darkness.

Nila might be in a room full of ghosts.

But I intended to purge them free with fire.

"DO YOU ACCEPT the payment for this debt?"

Cut's voice echoed in the room, sending chills down my spine.

Silent tears oozed down my cheeks as the old video played footage of my mother and him. She stood in a pentacle of salt beside the pond. The ducking stool hovered in the background and the white shift she wore fluttered around her legs.

The memories of the day I'd paid the Second Debt merged with the horrifying scene before me.

She held herself like I had that day: hands balled, chin defiantly high.

"No, I don't accept." Her voice was lower than mine, huskier and more determined. She'd said in one of her diary entries that I was a stronger woman than her.

I didn't agree.

My mother was royalty. She might not wear a crown and blue blood might not flow through her veins, but to me, she was so queenly she put Bonnie to shame.

Bonnie was younger, her hair not quite white and her back not as bent. She clasped her hands in front of her, watching the altercation between Emma and Cut. The way Cut stared at my mother belied the lust he felt for her. His fingers grew white as he fisted, regret shadowing his gaze.

Regret?

Cut turned out to have so many avenues and trapdoors. I'd always believed he was mad. A barking, raving lunatic to do what he did. But what if he became who he was because of circumstance? What if he fell for my mother just like Jethro fell for me? What forced him to take Emma's life if he loved her?

"Get on with it," Bonnie snapped when Cut didn't move.

He flinched, but it was Emma who forced Cut to obey.

She scrunched up her face and spat on his shoes. "Yes, listen to the wicked witch, Bryan. Do as you're told."

Acres of unsaid tension existed between them. They had a connection—strained and confusing—but linking them regardless.

Cut cocked his head. "You know your orders don't work on me."

My mother balled her hands. Her perfect cheekbones and flowing black hair defied the whistling wind, hissing into the camera like a thousand wails. "Do your worst, Bryan. I've told you a hundred times. I'm not afraid of you, of your family, of whatever debts you make me pay. I'm not afraid because death will come for all of us and I know where I'll be."

She stood proudly in the pentagon. "Where will you be when you succumb to death's embrace?"

Cut paused, the grainy image of his face highlighting a sudden flash of nerves, of hesitation. He looked younger but not adolescent. I doubted he'd ever been completely carefree or permitted to be a child.

Bonnie ruled him like she'd ruled her grandchildren—with no reprieve, rest and a thousand repercussions.

"I'll tell you where I'll be." Cut stormed forward. His feet didn't enter the salt, but he grabbed my mother around the nape. The diamond collar—

My fingers flew to the matching diamonds around my throat.

The weight of the stones hummed, almost as if they remembered their previous wearer.

—the diamond collar sparkled in the sunlight, granting prisms of light to blind the camera lens, blurring both her and Cut.

In that moment, something happened. Did Cut soften? Did he profess his true feelings? Did my mother whisper something she shouldn't? Either way, he let her go. His shoulders slouched as he looked at Bonnie.

Then the sudden weakness faded and he stiffened with menace. "Accept the debt, Emma. And then we can begin."

My hand fumbled for the remote control, my cast clunking on the table-top.

I can't do this.

Once Jethro had delivered me into the room, I hadn't been able to move. My feet stuck to the floor, my legs encased in emotional quicksand. I couldn't go forward, and I couldn't go back.

I was locked in a room full of scrolls and videos.

For a second, I'd hated Jethro for showing me this place. I knew a room such as this must exist. After all, Cut told me he kept countless records and their family lawyers had copies of every Debt Inheritance amendment.

But I hadn't expected such meticulous documents.

Stupidly, I thought I would be strong enough to watch. To hold my mother's hand all these years later and exist beside her while she went through something so terrible.

In reality, I wasn't.

These atrocities didn't happen to strangers. These debts happened to flesh and blood. A never-ending link to women I was born to, shared their hopes and fears, ancestors who donated slivers of their souls to create mine.

But I had to stay because I couldn't keep them shut in the dark anymore. If I didn't release their recorded forms, they'd be forever locked in filing cabinets.

Pointing the controller at the TV, I stopped the tape as Cut ducked Emma for the second time. I'd been with her while Cut delivered the history lesson. I'd hugged her phantom body as she awaited her punishment. But I couldn't watch any more of her agony. I couldn't sit there and pretend it didn't shatter me. That while my mother was almost drowned, I'd been alive hating her for leaving my father.

Forgive me.

Forgive me for ever cursing you. I didn't know.

Leaning over the table, I ejected the cassette and inserted the tape back into its sleeve.

I'd gone through her file. I'd watched the beginning of the First Debt and fast-forwarded over the whipping. I'd spied on security footage of Emma strolling through the Hall like any welcome guest. I held my breath as she sewed and sketched in the same quarters where Jethro had broken, made love to me, and told me what he was.

I couldn't watch anymore.

Whatever went on in her time at Hawksridge was hers to keep. It wasn't right to voyeur on her triumphs over Cut or despair over her moments of weakness. It wasn't for me to console or judge.

My mother's presence filled my heart, and in a way, I felt her with me. My shoulder warmed where I imagined she touched me. My back shivered where her ethereal form brushed past.

I'd summoned her from the grave and held her spirit, ready to release her from the shackles of the catalogue room.

I have to free them all.

Shooting out of my chair, I rubbed my sticky cheeks from unnoticed tears and rushed to the other filing cabinets. Each one was dedicated to an ancestor.

I couldn't catch a proper breath as I yanked open metal drawers and grabbed armfuls of folders. Working one-handed slowed me down. I dropped some; I threw some, scattering them on the table.

Cursing my cast, I lovingly touched every page, skimmed every word, and whispered every sadness.

Time flowed onward, somehow threading history with present.

Jethro was right to leave.

As a Hawk, he wouldn't be welcome.

The longer I stood in that cell, the more I battled with hate.

Folder after folder.

Document after document.

I made a nest, surrounded by boxes, papers, photographs, and memorabilia from women I'd never met but knew so well.

Kneeling, I sighed heavily as their presence and phantom touches grew stronger the more I read. Their blood flowed in my veins. Their mannerisms shaped mine, their hopes and dreams echoed everything I wanted.

No matter that decades and centuries separated us, we were all Weavers taken and exploited.

My jeans turned grey with dust, my nose itchy from time-dirtied belongings.

Lifting images from the closest file, I stared into the eyes of an ancestor I didn't recognise. She was the least like me from all the relatives I had. She had large breasts, curvy hips, and round face. Her hair was the signature black all Weaver women had and looked the most Spanish out of all of us.

So much pain existed in her eyes. Trials upon trials where the very air solidified with injustice and the common hatred for the Hawks.

I didn't want to sit there anymore. I didn't want to coat myself in feelings from the past and slowly bury my limbs in an avalanche of memories, but I owed it to them. I'd told my ancestors I would set them free, and I would.

Tracing fingertips over grainy images, I worshipped the dead and apologised for their loss. I spoke silently, telling them justice had been claimed, karma righted, and it was time for them to move on and find peace.

My fingertips smudged from pencil and parchment, caked in weathered filth. The video recordings ceased the earlier the years went on. Photographs lost pigment and clarity, becoming grainy and sepia.

I hated the Hawks.

I hated the debts.

I even hated the original Weavers for condemning us to this fate.

So many words.

So many tears.

Reading, reading, reading...

Freeing, freeing, freeing...

There wasn't a single file I didn't touch.

The eerie sense of not being alone only grew stronger the more I opened. The filing cabinets went from full to empty. The files scattered like time-tarnished snowflakes on the floor.

I lost track of minutes and had no clock to remind me to return to my generation. I remained in limbo, locked with specters, unwilling to leave them alone after so long.

Eventually, my gaze grew blurry. The words no longer made sense. And the repetition of each woman paying the same debts merged into a watercolour, artfully smearing so many pasts into one.

By the time I reached the final box, photographs had become oily portraits. The last image was cracked and barely recognisable, but I knew I held the final piece.

The woman who'd started it all.

The original Weaver who'd sent an innocent girl to death by ducking stool and turned a blind eye to everything else.

She didn't deserve the same compassion as the rest of my ancestors—she'd condemned us all. But at the same time, enough pain had been shed; it was time to let it go.

They all deserved peace.

The small space teemed with wraiths of my family, all weaving together like a swirling hurricane. The air gnawed on me with ghoulish gales from the other side.

Taking a deep breath, I re-entered the land of the living. I moaned in discomfort as I stood. My knees creaked while my spine realigned from kneeling on the floor like a pew at worship, slowly working my way through a temple of boxes.

I didn't believe in ghosts walking amongst us but I couldn't deny the truth.

They were there.

Crying for me. Rejoicing for me. Celebrating the end even though they'd paid the greatest price.

They loved me. They thanked me.

And it layered me with shame and ultimately pride.

Pride for breaking tradition.

Pride for keeping my oath.

They'd died.

I hadn't.

I lived.

I found Jethro outside.

The sun had long ago set and winter chill howled over the manicured gardens, lamenting around the turrets and edges of Hawksridge Hall.

I'd had the foresight to grab warmer clothes before embarking on finding fresh air and huddled deeper into my jacket, letting the sling take the weight of my cast. Tugging the faux fur of my hood around my ears, I wished I'd brought gloves for my rapidly frost-bitten fingers.

Jethro looked up as my sheepskin-lined boots crunched across the gravel and skirted the boxed hedgerow. Wings and Moth stood in the distance, blotting the horizon, cloaked in blankets.

As I'd made my way through the Hall, I'd seen silhouettes of people outside. I'd recognised Jethro's form. I wanted to join them—be around real people after dusty apparitions.

And now, I'd not only found Jethro but everyone I loved and cared for.

On the large expanse of lawn stood my new family. Jasmine, Vaughn, Jethro, and Tex. They all stood around a mountainous pile of branches, interspersed with the Ducking Stool and Iron Chair and other items I never wanted to see again.

Ducking my head into the breeze, I patrolled over the grass. My hood whipped back, and I caught the eye of Jasmine.

She gave me a smile, holding out her hand.

I took it.

Her fingers were popsicles, but she squeezed mine as I bent over and kissed her cheek. We didn't need to talk. We understood. She'd lost her brothers and father. I'd lost my mother. Together, we would stand and not buckle beneath the tears.

In the distance, the south gardens glittered with rapidly forming dew-frost, glittering like nature's diamonds on leaves and blades of grass.

Jethro skirted the large tinderbox of firewood, pausing beside his sister with a large log in his hands. His eyes glowed in the darkness, his lips hiding white teeth. "I won't ask what happened. And I won't pry unless you want to share. But I built this for them. For you. For what lives in that room."

He dropped his gaze, awkwardly stroking the log. "I don't know if you'll want to say goodbye this way, but I just thought—" He shrugged. "I thought I'd make a fire, just in case."

I didn't say a word.

I let go of Jasmine, flew around her chair, and slammed into his arms.

He dropped the wood and embraced me tightly. I didn't care my brother and father watched. All I cared about was thanking this man. This Hawk. Because now he'd let himself be the person I always knew he could be, I couldn't stop falling more and more in love with him.

His lips warmed my frozen ear, kissing me sweetly. "Are you okay?"

I nodded, nuzzling closer, inhaling the pine sap and earthy tones from collecting firewood. "I'm better." I gathered my thoughts before whispering, "When you left me in there, I couldn't move. I truly didn't like you very much. But you were right. Thank you for giving me that time. For knowing what I needed, even when I didn't."

He hugged me harder. "Anything for you, you know that."

I shivered as another howl swept over the treetops. The night would be bitterly cold, but soon there would be something to warm us.

Pulling away, I smiled at my twin standing with his arms crossed and a bitter look on his face. Eventually, I would have to talk to him and tell him Jethro would be his brother-in-law. He would have to accept him. Tex, too.

I asked far more than they could offer—to love the son of the man who'd stolen Tex's wife and our mother—but that was life.

The heart had the incredible capacity to heal wrongs. And I wouldn't apologise for betraying my family name with Jethro. I'd chosen him. And if they couldn't accept that...well, I didn't want to think about it. Not tonight.

Jethro tucked flying hair behind my ears and pulled up my hood. "Are you ready?"

I rested my face in his palm, reaching on tiptoes to kiss his wind-bitten lips. "I'm ready."

Taking my hand, he kissed my knuckles. "In that case, let's put the past behind us."

It took us an hour and a half to lug the boxes from upstairs to the bonfire outside.

We formed an assembly line, a never-ending factory of willing hands to transport.

Jethro joined me in the room, respectfully gathering files and packing them into boxes. I'd left the space in a mess, but together, we created neat piles so Vaughn and Tex could carry them downstairs.

Jasmine stayed on the lawn, willingly accepting the items on her lap and wheeling them across the grass to the unlit bonfire.

The last box to go down was full of my mother's time at the Hall. I blinked back tears as I handed it awkwardly to my father.

He knew with one look what the paperwork entailed. His face echoed with heartbreak as he cradled the heavy package and took it downstairs himself. He didn't transfer it to Vaughn. He didn't let go. Hugging his wife's spirit one last time.

Once he'd gone, and the room stood empty, Jethro popped into the corridor and spoke to V.

"Can you give us a minute?"

Vaughn looked past him, his black eyes meeting mine. "You okay, Threads?"

I came forward, my heart beating faster. "I'm okay. I'll see you down there." I gave him a half-smile. "Don't start without us."

He scowled. "You know I wouldn't."

I sighed. We had a long way to go to be able to joke with one another again without a filament of mistrust and pain cloaking everything. "I know, V. Stupid joke." Brushing past Jethro, I gathered my twin in my arms.

He buckled, his spine rolling and strong arms wrapping around me. He shuddered as we stood there and squeezed. The past ten days had been good for us. We'd spent time together, skirting true issues, but I had a feeling after tonight, we'd have nothing keeping us apart and could finally talk through the events and find our closeness once again.

Letting me go, he smiled. He'd let a slight beard creep over his chin, dark and rich, making him seem exotic and untameable. "Love you, Threads."

"Love you more." I patted his chest. "I'll see you in a bit."

Vaughn nodded and disappeared down the staircase. Once he'd gone, I entered the room and waited while Jethro silently closed the door.

My heart went from fast paced to flurrying. "What are you doing?"

Jethro grimaced, striding to a filing cabinet and shoving it to the side. "There's one more box you haven't seen. One I hid."

I ghosted forward. "You hid it? Why?"

Dropping to his knees, he ran his fingernails around a wooden panel in the wainscoting. Popping open a hidden compartment, he shuffled back to pull out a dust-smeared box. This one didn't match the other drab brown ones. This one was white and narrow with the initials E.W. on top.

My heart flew into my throat.

Jethro stood up, supporting the box and swatting at dust motes on his jeans. "I hid it because I was asked to by someone I cared about."

Moving toward the table, he placed the offering in the centre. "She asked me to give this to you. She knew I'd come for you once she was gone, but she also knew I was different."

I couldn't move. I couldn't take my eyes off the carton. "Different?"

"She caught me one day. She caught me before I had the chance to have another lesson. She didn't fully understand what I was, but she guessed enough that it made her trust me. I wanted to tell her not to be so stupid. I was still my father's son. But she didn't give me a choice.

"She told me I would fall in love with you. She told me you would win. She also told me that if I let you help me, everything could be different."

A tear glassed my vision then spilled over. Talking about my mother, learning new memories I didn't share was wondrous as well as bittersweet.

I didn't notice I'd moved forward until my fingers traced her initials. "She told you all of that?"

Jethro chuckled quietly. "She told me a lot of things. She also told Kes. I think she preferred him over me—he was the one everyone fell in love with—but she trusted us with different tasks."

I finally met his eyes, tearing mine from the box. "What did she make you do?"

Jethro nodded at the table. "She wanted me to keep this safe for you. She said one day, I would find the right time to give this to you. And when I did, she hoped it meant things hadn't gone the way they had for her. That you'd won.

"At the time, I almost hated her for being so cocky and sure. I hated I'd come across weak enough that she dare predict my future. But at the same time, I loved her for seeing things in me I hadn't even permitted myself to see. I loved she thought I was worthy of your love. I loved that she wanted me to take you because, ultimately, she knew I'd lose and you'd win and together we'd fight."

I struggled to breathe as more tears joined the first. I wanted to ask so many questions. I wanted Jethro to regale me of every time he'd conversed with my mother. I wanted to hoard his memories as my own and build a picture of her strength after she'd been taken from us.

But I didn't want to rush something so precious. Another time. Another night. When people weren't waiting to say goodbye.

Sucking in a breath, I asked quietly, "And Kes? What was his task?"

Jethro's face tightened with pain. "You already know. He completed his promise within days of you being with us." His eyes narrowed, willing me to recall.

What had Kes done apart from taking me into his quarters? He'd given me sketching paper. Become my friend. Laughed with me. Entertained me and granted normalcy while I swam in bewilderment.

"He was to become my friend."

Jethro nodded. "Your mother knew no one could replace Vaughn. You'd grown up together. You loved each other so much. But she also knew not having that connection would be one of the hardest things you'd have to face. So she asked Kes to be your brother while your true one couldn't be there."

My stomach knotted as I wrapped arms around myself. Kes's friendship had been invaluable, but now, it'd become priceless knowing every touch and joke had come out of respect for my mother.

In a way, it could've cheapened Kes's kindness to me—knowing he'd been asked to do so—but I didn't see it that way. I saw it as a selfless deed, and I was confident enough in our mutual affection that he hadn't just done it for Emma. He'd done it for himself, for whatever bond blossomed between us.

Jethro came closer, moving behind me to envelop me in a hug. My back fell into his chest, my head tilting to the side for his kisses to land on my neck. "She also asked him to give you the Weaver Journal. I knew you thought that was a tool for my family to spy on your thoughts. That we were the ones to create such a tradition. But we didn't."

His lips trailed lovingly over my collar to my ear. "That was a Weaver secret and at least one Hawk in every generation kept it hidden. Kes was tasked to give it to you. But he wasn't asked to tell you why he'd given it. It was yours to do what you wanted—write in it or not. Read it or ignore it. The choice was yours."

How could I learn so much in such a few short sentences? How could I fall in love with the dead even more than when they were alive?

Spinning in Jethro's hold, I pressed my face against his chest. "Thank you. Thank you for telling me."

His embrace tightened. "Thank you for making your mother's premonitions come true."

We stood still for so many heartbeats, thanking the dead, reliving the secrets, rejoicing in the rightful end.

Finally, Jethro let me go. "Open it. And then we'll join the others."

I looked at the box. The air around it seemed to throb with welcome, begging me to look inside.

Jethro shuffled, moving toward the door.

I held out my hand. "Wait. Don't go."

He halted. "You don't want to be on your own?"

"No." Shaking my head, I smiled. "I want you beside me. She would want you to be here."

Biting his lip, he returned to my side.

Wordlessly, I pulled the box closer and slid off the lid.

A puff of lint flurried with the opening pressure, scattering onto the table-top. My heart stopped beating as I reached into the tiny coffin of memories and pulled out the letter sitting on top.

"It's addressed to me."

Jethro looped an arm around my waist, trembling with everything I felt.

The confusion.

The hope.

The sadness.

The happiness at hearing from her one last time.

"Open it."

The glue on the envelope had weathered and unstuck, gaping open as I turned it over and fumbled with my sling to pull forth the note.

Dear my sweetest daughter,

I've promised myself I would write this letter so many times, and every time I begin, I stop.

There is so much to say. My mind runs wild with guidelines and tips for all things you are yet to enjoy. First love, first heartbreak, first baby. I'll never get to see those things. Never see you grow into a woman or enjoy motherhood.

And that upsets me, but I know I'll be proud of the woman you became because you're part of me, and through you, I shall remain alive, no matter what happens to my mortal body.

There might also be a chance you won't achieve what I hope you will. That you'll fall to the guillotine like me. That we'll meet far too young in heaven.

But I'm not thinking those thoughts.

If you live at Hawksridge while Cut is still in power, remember two things. That man is violent, unpredictable, and cruel. But beneath it, he can be manipulated. A man who has everything has nothing if he doesn't have love. And he's never had love. I pretended to give him that. I hoped my false affection could prevent my end, but I didn't have it in me to love him true. I love your father. I can never love Cut while I have Arch in my heart.

And that was my downfall.

Anyway...

Before I prattle on about nothing, I have to tell you two things. I've hoarded these confessions for far too long.

First, I need to tell you about your grandmother.

I know by now you will have seen the graves on the Hawk's moor. You'll have seen her name on a tombstone. But what you won't know is...that grave is empty.

Like you, I believed she died at the hand of Bonnie's husband.

But that was before Cut told me the truth.

He viewed his father as weak because that was what Bonnie fed him. However, I see Alfred Hawk as one of the bravest men. He succumbed to tradition and claimed my mother. He completed the first two debts, but his affection for her—the love he could never give Bonnie—meant he couldn't attach the collar or kill her.

So he did the only thing he could.

He pretended to end the Debt Inheritance. He buried a fake corpse and set her free. He gave her a second chance but with the strictest of conditions: never contact her Weaver family again—for her sake and his.

She kept that promise for many years. I grew up believing she'd died. However, one night, I received a phone call from Italy. She was alive, Nila. She'd watched me from afar, celebrated when I had my children, and lamented when I was claimed. She would've fought for me—I know that. But she died before she could.

Now...Nila...this is the hardest part to write. The second secret I've kept my entire life, and I honestly don't know how to tell you. There are no easy words, so I'll just have to swallow my tears, beg you to understand, and hope you can forgive me.

My children.

I loved you. All of you. So, so much.

I let my fear get the better of me just before they took me. I begged your father to hide you. But we both knew this was our only chance. Arch didn't want to go ahead with my plan. Don't hate him, Nila. It was me. All me. I take full blame, and even though I'm dead and you can't berate me, know I died with regret and hope.

I regret you living in my path, but I'm full of hope you'll achieve what I couldn't.

I always thought a letter like this would be long and full of tears, but I know now (after so many failed attempts) that I can't over think this. I can't write everything I want to say because everything important you already know.

You know I love you.

You know I'll always watch over you.

And I know when Jet comes to collect you, you'll win. You'll win, darling daughter, because you're so much more than I ever was. You're the strongest, bravest, most brilliant daughter I could ever ask for, and that's why I sacrificed you.

Does that confuse you?

Does that make you hate me?

If it does, then I won't ask for your forgiveness. But know I believed with all my heart you had the potential to do what I couldn't. I chose you over her—over Jacqueline.

I made that decision. Right or wrong. I'll never know.

After watching you grow up, I just know you have the power to end this. And it was a risk I was willing to pay. You were the one I pinned all my hopes on. You were the one to save us all.

I love you, Nila, Threads, my precious, precious daughter.

Forgive me or not, I'll never stop caring for you, never stop watching.

Please, try to understand.

I gambled both our lives to save so many more.

Thank you for being so brave.

Love,

Your mother.

JACQUELINE?

Who the motherfucking hell is Jacqueline?

Nila dropped the letter. "What does she mean? She *sacrificed* me?" Her emotions swelled in one huge wave of question marks. "What does that *mean*?!"

Jacqueline.

Jacqueline.

Who the fuck is Jacqueline?

Snapping out of my trance, I pulled Nila away from the table, the box, the condemning note. "Nila, it's okay. Don't—"

Her black eyes met mine, wide and horror-filled. "It's *okay*? How can you say that? All this time, I hated my father for letting you take me, but I just found out my mother was the one who orchestrated it? He wanted to hide me, Jethro! And she stopped him! She was supposed to protect me. Tell me how any of this is *okay*? I don't understand! First, I find out my grandmother was never killed, and now, I find out I have another...what? *Sister?*"

My fingers pinched into her elbows, but she tore out of my hold. "No! Don't touch me." Her cast blurred through the air as she shoved off her sling and grabbed her hair. "What does this mean? Jacqueline? Am I supposed to know who she is? What. Does. This. *Mean?*"

She whirled on me. "Who is Jacqueline, Jethro? Tell me!"

I stood there, buffeted by her emotional turbulence, wishing I had the answers.

But I didn't.

I didn't have a fucking clue who Jacqueline was.

I spread my hands in defeat. "I wish I knew, Needle. I'm sorry. My family had yours under surveillance for decades and not once has anyone called Jacqueline come up."

Nila breathed hard, her tears drying as anger filled her instead. Her eyes flew to the window where the barely-there outlines of our combined family stood around the wooden pyramid.

Her hands balled, pain flashing over her face from her break. "I know who will have answers."

My heart stopped.

I took a step toward her, trying to grab her before she did anything reckless. "Nila, listen to me. Calm down. You can't go out there like this. You can't—"

"I can't, can I?" She stomped forward, avoided my grasp, and scooped the box off the table. The letter crumpled inside as she slammed on the lid. "My mother just cleansed her soul by dumping decade's worth of secrets. It's not fair. How could she do that to me?" She sniffed, ice filling her black eyes. "I won't let her get away with this. I want answers and I want them now."

"Nila...don't. Wait until later. Stop—"

She bared her teeth. "Don't tell me what to do, Kite. She was my mother, and this is my fucked-up history. I deserve to know what she meant."

I stumbled to grab her. "You shouldn't, not tonight—"

Crushing the box, she glowered. "Watch me."

Turning on her heel, she bolted from the room, leaving me standing all alone wondering what secrets we shouldn't have uncovered.

Damn Emma.

Perhaps the tales of the dead should remain dead.

Did I do the right thing?

Had I just kept a promise to a ghost and stupidly destroyed our carefully perfect world?

I won't let that happen.

"Nila!" I charged after her, careening down the staircase and erupting onto the grass.

Her treadmill running days gave her a good sprint, and I didn't reach her in time.

I couldn't stop her slamming to a halt in front of her father.

I couldn't prevent her throwing the box in his face.

And I couldn't halt the torrent of questions spilling from her soul.

Nila

"WHO THE HELL is Jacqueline?"

I stood trembling in front of my father, fighting a vertigo wave.

Tex was almost comical as he froze, gaped, and swiped a shaking hand over his face. "How——how did you hear that name?"

Ducking, I ripped out the letter from the box at his feet and shoved it into his chest. V drifted closer, drawn by the air of animosity and questions. "Mum just told me."

Tex gulped. "What? *How?*"

Jethro came jogging over the lawn, sternness on his face. "Nila...perhaps now is not the best time."

I whirled on him. "If not now, when?" Pointing at the ready-to-blaze bonfire, I snapped, "I think now is the perfect time. Closure, Jethro. That's what this is and that's what my father owes me."

Ripping my eyes from Jethro's, I glared at Tex. "So, tell me. Who the hell is Jacqueline?"

"Threads...what's going on?" Vaughn nudged my shoulder with his. "What's gotten you so upset?"

My father didn't look up as he read the same letter I'd just devoured, his pallor shifting to a sickly yellow.

My voice throbbed as I looked between my twin and father. "Mum left a note." I pointed at it, rippling in the breeze in Tex's fingers. "That one. She not only told me our grandmother was never claimed by the Debt Inheritance, but I was *sacrificed* over a girl named Jacqueline. So my question is...*who is she?*"

"Holy shit. What the fuck?" Rubbing his jaw, V glanced at Tex. "Well? I think we deserve to know."

Taking a huge breath, Tex finished reading. His eyes darted to Jethro before locking on me and V. "She's your sister."

I'd already guessed as much, but it still hurt. "Older sister?"

The eldest who should've paid the debt. The sister who should've protected us by being the chosen one, not the saved.

Jethro came closer, barricading me against the wind. "I think you better spit it out, Tex."

Tex nodded, fighting ghosts and things I never knew. How could he keep such a secret? How could my own father be a complete stranger?

Picking up the box, I hugged it, waiting for knowledge.

His body tensed, thoughts filing into collected streams, ready to tell me the truth. "There isn't much to say. Your mother and I met young. We never planned on getting pregnant—she was averse to the idea of children right from the start. But the pill failed. When we found out, we agonised for days what to do. We couldn't abort as my parents were very religious and had recently died, making me loathe to destroy new life. But we also couldn't keep it.

"We were too young to make the choice, so we decided to let life do that for us. We got married because we loved each other, not because Emma was pregnant, and we set up life while she grew with you. However, instead of it being a happy time, it was fraught with secrets and tension. I didn't care about any of it—the strangeness of taking her name. The oddness of her family empire and unspoken obligations.

"By that point, I was happy to start our family young. Emma...she wasn't. She came from Weaver money. I'd been inducted into the business and we were financially secure. We could start building our own family—regardless if we hadn't planned it so quickly.

"Early on in the pregnancy, we found out she was carrying not one, not two, but *three* babies. The shock quickly faded into happiness, and I was glad she came from a bloodline that tended to give birth to multiples. I transformed my home office into a large nursery with three cots, three bouncing tables, three singing mobiles. Three of everything.

"But no matter what I said or how excited I became, Emma shut me out. The closer to delivery, the more she'd cry, need space, and push me away. I was told by our local doctor to leave her be—that some women required time to come to terms with their body changing and the uncertain future.

"So, I gave her time. I was there for her, I left her notes telling her how amazing our life would be, how perfect our children would be, and how happy I was to grow old with her—"

Tex stopped, wiping his eyes with the back of his hand. He stared at the awaiting bonfire and rushed onward. "She disappeared. I remember it so clearly. We'd just come back from our latest check-up and I'd left her in the lounge to make her a cup of tea. When I came back...she was gone. The front door was open, her shoes by the welcome mat. Just gone.

"She was seven months pregnant and padding barefoot around London. Winter was close, and the air was freezing. Terrified, I hopped in the car and patrolled the streets for her. It took me hours before I found her sitting in the cathedral where we were married.

"There she told me the most awful thing, the curse on her family, the debt she must pay. She tried to divorce me, telling me she'd made a terrible mistake. She tried to convince me to give up the children for adoption the moment they were born and let her run far away.

"Of course, I didn't believe her. I thought she was tired and stressed from the pregnancy. I murmured and soothed and took her home to bed. She didn't mention it again, and I stupidly thought it was over. Only, then the birth came around, and I rushed her to the hospital.

"Jacqueline was born first, then you, Vaughn, followed by tiny Nila." His eyes glistened with paternal love. "I held you all in my arms. Three small bundles with tiny red fingers and squished up faces. I fell madly in love with you within seconds.

"I kissed Emma and handed over my newborn triplets for the nurses to weigh and measure. I trusted everything was right in my world."

Tears welled in his eyes as he cleared his throat. "However, after forty minutes, when the nurses didn't come back, I began to worry. I tracked them down only to find my three children had become two."

My heart lurched, imagining such a tragic revelation.

"I rushed back with you and V, demanding an explanation from Emma. She merely shook her head and said she'd told me what happened to the firstborn girls of her family, and she wouldn't let that happen to Jacqueline.

"Behind my back, she'd arranged a private adoption; she'd bribed the nurse and doctor to wipe all record of ever having triplets and listed her delivery as twins. She did it all. She stole one of my daughters to protect her, and for a time, she believed you would be safe, Nila. She said you wouldn't be claimed as technically Vaughn was firstborn and not you.

"However, that plan showed its flaws when Cut came to collect her. She was my wife, but she had so many secrets from me. She'd told me you would be safe, but she knew better. She sacrificed you. She let them take you. And I did nothing to stop it."

Silent tears tracked down his face. "I'm so sorry, Nila."

I couldn't move.

My mother had always been a perfect memory. I'd hated her for a time for leaving my father with no explanation, but then she became a saint when I found out the Hawks murdered her. She'd been a hard woman to love. And Tex had been there for her. He'd loved her so much even when she left. He lied for her. He did everything she asked. And he'd honoured her wishes and let them take me.

I had so many questions, but I couldn't formulate them clearly. My brain remained fuzzy, slow to grasp the magnitude. All I could think about was—

"We have an older sister…" Vaughn murmured, stealing my thought. I leaned my head on his shoulder, slipping back into my body after living the past with Tex. Having my twin back and sharing the same thoughts was like wearing a favourite pair of slippers. I'd taken our ease for granted, and having him by my side while we learned something so monumental was a blessing.

My hand slipped into Jethro's. He hadn't moved. He stood on my left while my twin stood on my right.

I was the only female in an all-male gathering—apart from Jaz.

I'd been the only female for most of my life.

To find out there'd been another girl? A *sister*? A potential best-friend who had been robbed from me…it hurt. But excited, too.

I have a sister.

I could find her.

Swallowing, I asked, "Where is she now?"

Tex sniffed, reaching for the box in my hands, willing me to give it to him. I did, handing over the pieces of jewellery Emma had been wearing and whatever other knickknacks she'd treasured.

They belonged to Tex more than me. It would've been Emma's wish for her husband to possess her last trinkets. "I don't know. I've never known."

"You never tried to look her up?" Jethro asked.

Tex shook his head. "I wanted to. But Emma made me swear I wouldn't."

"But you said you hired the mercenaries *before* I came to take Nila. What did you mean by that?" Jethro was deceptively calm, as if he'd been planning to ask that question for a while.

Tex swallowed. "You caught that, huh?" Sighing, he added, "You're right. I'd enlisted the help of a P.I and protective team to track her down. I kept it a secret from everyone—even the men working for me. They didn't know why they were searching for a girl with my strict criteria. They just hunted.

"Emma said if I ever tracked Jacqueline down and the Hawks found out, they'd take both my daughters. So I kept it secret—half of me wanting them to find her so I could love her from afar, and half of me hoping she remained lost so she stayed safe." His eyes narrowed. "Is it true you would've taken both? If I'd found her?"

Jethro pinched the bridge of his nose. "In all honesty, if Bonnie was still in charge, probably. But now, you have nothing to fear. If you want to track her down, I think you should."

Tex looked at me. "Nila...what do you think? Do you want to?"

The question was too large to answer so quickly. I bit my lip. "Yes...no...I—I don't know."

"I vote yes," Vaughn piped up.

How would a girl who'd been given up for adoption, stolen from her heritage and family's legacy, ever slip into our world?

"Imagine it from her point of view," Jasmine said, wrenching our attention to her. "You two grew up together. You've been best friends all your life. She didn't have that. She might've felt like she was missing something but didn't know what."

She smiled sadly at Jethro. "I know I loved having more than one brother. It's natural to want similar people to share your life with."

Yes, but we didn't have a similar upbringing.

Vaughn chuckled, sharing my thoughts again. "You think anyone could enter our life and not want to run away? Especially once we told her what happened and why she was given up?"

Tex ran a hand through his hair. "You have a point."

"Shouldn't she be given that choice though?" Jasmine rested her hands on her lap. "I think you should find her."

We all slipped into silence, mulling over the idea. There was still so much to say but not tonight. We'd all been through so much. Jacqueline had been missing from our family for so many years. Another few days wouldn't make a difference.

Tex straightened his shoulders, looking a hundred times lighter even after recounting something so hard. "I didn't realise how much that secret weighed me down." His eyes glittered. "Every time I look at you both, I remember Jacqueline. I wonder if she looks like you, has the same habits and fears. I hate that I was glad my parents died, so I didn't have to break their hearts by stealing a grandchild."

He sighed. "I'm not one to complain; I loved your mother. But she did leave me so alone. Stranded with secrets and missing a wife I could never have."

Unthreading my fingers from Jethro, I went to my father. I'd held a grudge against him for so long, believing it was his fault for not protecting me. But I hadn't known the full story. There was no black and white—for any of us. We'd all made choices on half-facts and uncertainty. If we couldn't forgive, then what was the point in any of it?

Wrapping my arms around Tex, I hugged him hard. His arms were imprisoning jaws, squeezing me tight. "Will you ever be able to forgive me for not saving you?"

Vaughn joined our hug. "She already has, Tex."

I nodded. "He's right."

Tex hugged us even harder. "I'm so glad I have you both. I love you so much."

As we healed each other through touch, Jethro moved to the pyramid and drenched the branches, torture equipment, and boxes full of records with gasoline.

The pungent whiff of chemicals laced the night sky, and our hug ended with much needed closure. It hurt to hear the truth, but it patched up a hole inside me I didn't know I had.

My heart knotted as Jethro diligently thought of everything, making sure tonight would be a perfect end. I hated the fact I'd just gained a sister I didn't know, while he'd lost a brother he loved. Life was never fair.

Jasmine wheeled closer, touching my hand. "I know what you're thinking, and he'll be okay."

"I know. It's just so hard to say goodbye to good people."

"He was the best."

We shared a smile as Jethro held out a box of matches. His half-grin fluttered my heart, and my lips ached to kiss him.

Taking the offered box of matches, Jethro cupped my cheek and kissed me softly. "It's all yours."

Tonight, when we were alone, I would show him how thankful I was for everything he'd done.

I moved away and stood beside the kindling. The bonfire would burn for days with the amount of fuel Jethro had gathered.

Stroking the matchbox, I closed my eyes and said a prayerful goodbye.

This is to find your perfect freedom. The Debt Inheritance is gone. It's over.

Stepping to join me, Jethro's gaze glowed with love and support. Holding out a folder, he murmured, "This isn't the original—I'll get that from the lawyers next week and burn that too—but this should be destroyed with the rest of what we've done."

Taking the folder, I opened it. Tears sprung to my eyes. Inside were the pieces of Debt Inheritance I'd been given after each round of the table along with the amendment I'd recently signed under Jasmine's duress.

"Thank you. This means a lot." Holding the folder, I struggled to open the matchbox to set it alight. It would be the first piece to burn. The catalyst to decimate everything else.

A flick of flint and glow of flame appeared in my peripheral. Jethro held out a monogrammed lighter. I'd seen it the night he'd dragged me into his office and made me sign the Sacramental Pledge.

"The wood is drenched in kerosene, so it will catch easily." Holding the lighter to the corner of the Debt Inheritance folder, he waited until the paper caught fire. Taking a step back, he smiled. "Whenever you're ready."

I looked at my brother and father. They stood like two sentries against the darkness. Hawksridge loomed behind them, leering over all of us as no longer foe but friend. A few of the windows gleamed with golden lights, spilling rectangle wedges of illumination across the grass.

Jasmine sat primly in her chair, her eyes reflecting the smoking flame in my hand. The folder rapidly dissolved into leaves of blackened char.

Evil had vanished. Only happiness remained.

With no hesitation, I threw the burning paper onto the bonfire and watched with soul-singing satisfaction as the entire thing erupted with orange heat.

The icy air was battered back as flames whipped into existence and my mind quieted from thoughts of Jacqueline, my mother, and secrets. My family stood all around me, cementing me in a brand new world where nothing could separate us.

There was nothing else to say.

The flames spoke for us.

The smoke purged the past.

And the crackling spoke of a future where no debts existed.

SOOT TAINTED MY mouth.

Smoke laced my hair.

And my eyes still burned with sparkling orange and yellow from the bonfire. We'd stayed vigil for hours. Nila and Vaughn were the only ones who threw the documented debts onto the flames.

The rest of us paid our respects and supported them silently.

I didn't save any evidence. I didn't put aside valuable proof to incarcerate the men who'd hidden my family's secrets. Partly, because their sins were our sins and it would be hypocritical to lay the blame at their feet when we all shared the crime. And mostly, because I wouldn't use others' pain as a bargaining chip.

I had more respect than that.

If the lawyers wanted to play and proved to be a problem when sorting out the final paperwork, then I had other means in which to hurt them. More *just* means. We'd dealt outside the law for so long, a few more 'loose ends' could be managed in the same way.

Tex had stared ahead, his hands clasped and face hard. If I let myself feel what he went through, I'd suffer a clout of shellshock. He hugged Emma's last remains, twirling her engagement ring from the box as if he could invoke a spell to bring her back.

But nothing would bring her back.

Nothing could undo what Emma had announced.

And I feared what Nila would do once the wounds of tonight had been tended to and she'd had more time to think about the sudden revelation of having a sister.

I hid my derisive snort. Daniel had been right, after all. His stupid joke in the car about stealing the wrong sister——he'd meant nothing by it——a stupid ploy to unsettle Nila even more.

But somehow, he'd guessed the unthinkable.

There'd been another Weaver.

A firstborn girl hidden from us.

Jacqueline.

A few minutes older than Vaughn. A few minutes older than Nila.

The love of my life had been sacrificed to a fate that wasn't hers to bear.

Did that make me happy or sad?

Happy she'd become mine?

Sad I'd put her through so much?

Who was Jacqueline?

What did she look like? How would she have reacted?

My hands balled.

One thing I was certain of—whoever Jacqueline was, she wasn't Nila. I wouldn't have fallen in love with her. I wouldn't have broken my vow or bowed at her feet.

Jacqueline wouldn't have changed history.

Succumbing to torrenting thoughts, I remained silent, locked where I would stay for the rest of my life—beside Nila.

I didn't leave as she threw paperwork and audio and video into the raging flames. Every time Nila looked my way, I kissed her. I passed her file after file, delivering my family's crimes into her hands to dispose of.

Only once the grass was empty of history did we disperse our separate ways. The fire would continue to rage on its own while we retired to different corners to rest, revalue, and regroup.

Textile was the first to disappear, wordlessly hugging Emma's box and disappearing into the orchard grove.

Vaughn rolled Jasmine toward the Hall, her wheels sucking in the mud of her tracks from carting so many files earlier in the evening.

Nila and I—we headed back to my quarters.

Her cheeks smudged with ash and charred pieces of paper decorated her hair and lined her jacket hood. She looked as if she'd been in a battle. She looked endlessly tired.

Entering the bachelor wing and my bedroom—*our* bedroom—I shrugged out of my jacket and draped it over an ancient sideboard.

Nila drifted to the middle of the carpet, staring blankly at the bed.

My heart clenched. All I wanted to do was take away the weight of decision and grant her peace. Moving behind her, I unzipped her jacket and slid it off her arms.

The scents of fire and fresh air licked around her.

"Do you want a shower?" I asked softly, massaging her shoulders.

She jumped, startled by my voice after only the crackle of fire as conversation. Turning to lock herself in my embrace, she shook her head. "I don't need a shower." Her voice echoed with need for something else. I didn't need to ask what she needed—I already knew.

I knew far more than I should.

However, I was respectful of granting some semblance of boundaries.

Nila had a lot to sort out internally. I wouldn't make it worse knowing she couldn't pretend she was okay when I knew completely she was not.

So even though I didn't need to, I asked anyway, "What do you need..."

Her head tilted up, her black eyes flashing with ebony fire. "You." She stood on tiptoes, pressing her lips to mine. "I need you."

My cock thickened; my heart raced.

I needed her, too. So fucking much. More now than ever as she was currently lost to me. She didn't know how to take her position within this life. She didn't know how to admit to herself that if she hadn't been chosen over Jacqueline, she would never have met me. Never have fallen for me. And I would never have fallen for her.

I groaned as the true worry of her thoughts rose.

I didn't want to pry, but I couldn't let her think such incorrect things.

"I wouldn't have loved her, Needle."

She gasped, her kiss stalling.

I parted her lips with my tongue, feeding her the truth. "Only you. I don't care she was supposed to be my inheritance. I don't care you took her place. In fact, I'm so fucking glad."

Her breath hitched as I kissed her harder, crushing her to me. "I'm so happy it was you because you cured me, fixed me. I love you, Nila. Not her. Not anyone else. *You.*"

Her arms, both good and broken, slung around my neck, pulling me hard against her mouth. I let her guide me to bed. I let her control the kiss. I let her grab my shirt and pull me down upon her. And I let her control whatever she needed.

I'd give her anything she ever wanted.

I'd spend the rest of my life ensuring she never had to doubt my feelings for her.

She was it for me.

It didn't matter if lies brought us together.

Fate had decided we were matched.

And we'd fulfilled that prophecy by falling head over fucking heels.

I WOKE UP the same way I'd fallen asleep.

By Jethro making love to me.

We'd remained wrapped in each other's arms for a few vacant hours of sleep. I didn't dream. I didn't fret. I just slept and recharged after such a long emotional day.

Jethro roused me with kisses and touches, bringing me to a soft release before carrying me into the shower to wash.

After the bonfire, the sun had already risen on a new day.

The day.

The day we said goodbye to Kestrel.

I feared I'd be tired as Jethro and I dressed quickly, slipping into jeans and jackets and boots. I feared I'd be muddled with sleep deprivation as we ate a quick lunch in the kitchen and strode over the gardens to the stables.

But I didn't need to fear.

The time with Jethro had recharged me better than sleep.

During the bonfire, I couldn't think about my mother without wanting to howl at the moon and demand her explanation. I wanted to kick and punch my father for holding such a terrible secret my entire life. And I wanted to hold Vaughn because it wasn't just me this news affected.

We'd been raised as each other's everything. Twins. Best friends. Confidants.

To find out we were actually only two-thirds of a complete sibling set—it hurt.

Jacqueline.

Tex said he would continue to track down the adoptive family. He hadn't been strong enough until now to find the truth.

Then again, maybe strength kept him away.

I was third born.

I should never have had to pay the debt.

But I had, and I'd ended it.

Jacqueline owed her life to my parents for saving her. But her future children owed me their safety.

Jethro took my gloved hand as we stepped from the sun's glare into the musky world of the stables. "Are you ready?"

Cobblestones and hay welcomed along with memories of Jethro tenderly cutting my hair, putting me back together again with the same implement that'd destroyed me. Stable hands bustled about, gathering saddles and bridles, tending to the horses.

My heart leapt as I noticed Moth.

Kes's horse.

My horse.

The bridge between us I'd always cherish.

Squeezing his fingers, I nodded.

His lips smiled, but his eyes fought tears.

Today would be hard for him. But I would be there. I would *always* be there.

He sucked in a deep breath. "Okay, then."

Together, we prepared to say goodbye to Kestrel Hawk.

Jethro

"YOU SURE YOU want to do this?" I eyed Jasmine as Vaughn manhandled our gentlest horse from its box. The grooms had already combed, saddled, and prepared six mounts.

I'd planned this day for the past week.

I wanted it to be perfect.

"Stop asking me that. Yes, I'm sure." Jasmine wheeled herself awkwardly over the cobblestones, her wheels catching and stalling on the uneven surface. But she didn't complain. Not once did she curse or lament. Her disability had finally been accepted and she no longer hid away in the house, regretting the life she would never have.

Her acceptance had come from a multitude of things. Vaughn Weaver's unwavering attention had been one of those things but so had Kes's death. His passing at such a young age shook all of us. Yes, she'd lost the use of her legs but she hadn't lost her life like our brother.

"Lead her over there." I pointed V at the already erected platform I'd had the Hawksridge carpenters create.

Originally, I'd planned to put Jasmine in a carriage, safely protected by walls and wheels. But the moment I told her the plan, she argued. She used to ride a lot with Kes and me when we were younger. She wanted to share one last ride with him…before he was gone.

I'd done my best to persuade her but she was damn stubborn when her mind was set.

I didn't interfere as Vaughn did his best to guide Claret to the mounting block. However, the Roan had other ideas—hay being her main focus.

Vaughn cursed under his breath, doing his best to yank the mare forward. "Come on, you bloody animal."

Christ, at this rate we wouldn't get out of the stables until dark.

Nila laughed as I stormed forward and grabbed the reins. Taking responsibility for the horse, I pointed Vaughn to a new task. "Help my sister up the ramp. I'll move Claret into position."

Tex entered the stable. His eyes darted from the horse to Jasmine in her chair. He wisely didn't mention her safety and focused on his own discomfort instead. Rubbing the back of his nape, he said, "You sure I have to be on a nag? Can't I follow on foot?"

Nila went to her father and looped her arm through his. "Kes would've

wanted us all there. Please, do it for me. We need to honour his final goodbye."
Pecking his cheek, Nila smiled, completely winning over her father within moments.

Try saying no to her.

Hell, I couldn't.

Hiding my smugness, I let my condition fan out. Tex still confused me. He'd stood up for his daughter in the end. He'd helped put an end to our family's madness, but inside, he still wallowed in self-hatred and guilt. That guilt ate at him like acid. If he didn't find a way to forgive himself—he'd be dealing with his own mortality in the form of sickness.

Tearing my eyes from Nila and her father, I marched forward. Swatting the mare with the tips of the reins, she plodded onward, submitting to my direction as I led her around the newly-erected ramp.

Vaughn grabbed Jasmine's chair. Almost shyly, he tucked her jaw-length hair behind her ear before hurtling her like a fucking rocket up the ramp.

Goddammit.

"Shit!" Jasmine grabbed the handrails, ferocity etching her face.

"Just thought I'd make sure you were awake." Vaughn chuckled.

"Yes, well, I'd like to keep awake and not dead for as long as I possibly can." Her fake anger couldn't hide her enjoyment that Vaughn didn't treat her like a china doll.

Unfortunately, her emotions couldn't lie. Her heart skipped a beat whenever that damn Weaver was around.

Nila came to stand by me, her delicate hand landing on my wrist. "Stop scowling. I know what you're thinking."

I didn't look at her. The more time she spent with me, the more she could read me. She might not be able to keep secrets from me, but I couldn't keep them from her, either. "I don't know what you're talking about."

She smiled. "Yes, you do." Her eyes shouted: *My brother likes your sister.*

I clenched my jaw, ignoring her.

Claret stomped, tossing her head as Vaughn bumped her going around to the front of Jasmine's chair. His eyes locked on Jaz's. "Remember the last time you asked me to be your legs?"

Jaz cocked her head, her gaze flickering to me. "Yes."

"Did I drop you?"

She frowned. "No."

"Good, so you trust me?"

Her tongue swept over her bottom lip. Fuck, she was flirting with him. "Perhaps."

"That's good enough, I guess." Bending, he smiled. "Put your arms around my shoulders."

My stomach knotted, wanting to tell him to be careful, but Jaz immediately looped her arms around him and allowed him to scoop her useless legs from the chair.

I'd never seen Jaz so open to trusting someone she hadn't vetted and investigated within an inch of the law before. Yet she accepted Vaughn so easily.

Holding her in his arms, he completely forgot about the rest of us and the over-packed stable.

I coughed deliberately.

Vaughn grinned not giving an arse what I thought. Murmuring in her ear, he carefully placed Jasmine on Claret. Her useless legs wouldn't straddle the horse, but Vaughn held her aloft so Jaz could grab her jodhpurs and sling herself into position.

Once Jaz sat on the horse, she nodded. "You can let me go now."

V did as she requested, looking at me for instruction.

Leaving Nila, I climbed the ramp and checked the girth was tight, Jaz's legs were anchored and buckled to the custom saddle, and her balance was correct. The pommel came up extra high and the back of the saddle cradled her back with cushioning and a seatbelt.

She'd have to be careful of sores and bruises as she wouldn't be able to feel but she was as safe as she could be on a beast.

"Ready for your first ride?"

I'd never seen Jaz's eyes so bright. The thought of doing something she'd given up granted a smidgen of magic on this melancholy day. "Never been more ready."

Fighting my brotherly protectiveness, I passed her the reins. "You sure?"

Her lips pursed as she stole the leather. "Positive."

Giving her a dressage whip, I climbed down the ramp. The whip was longer than a hunting version and meant she could encourage Claret to move without having to kick or twist.

Moving toward Wing's stall, I stopped dead as Nila came out of Moth's enclosure already sitting on the dapple grey.

So many times in the past fortnight I'd thought of Kes. Pictured him still living and joking and teasing. *Laughing.* Filling the holes of our lives with antidotes only he could.

But my brother was gone and his horse, who he so generously gave to Nila, remained.

My heart skipped a beat as Nila pulled to a stop, her eyes drowning with love. For me. *Love…* something I never thought I'd earn.

I marched to the side of the large dapple and grabbed her wrist. "Kiss me."

The one sentence that started it all. The command that broke my every resolve.

Nila smiled softly. "When you ask so nicely, how can I refuse?" Bending in her saddle, I stood on my toes to reach her delicious mouth.

It wasn't a slow kiss or even erotic. Just a quick affirmation we belonged to each other and always would.

Reluctantly, I let her go. Vaughn had managed to help Tex climb onto a large Clydesdale called Bangers and Mash, and a stable hand in turn helped V clamber on top of a newer addition to the stables called Apricot.

"Head on out, everyone. I'll catch up."

Jaz obeyed, flicking her whip and urging Claret forward. A procession disappeared out the barn. Tex followed gingerly, his hands tight on the reins while V chuckled, shaking his head at his father's nervousness.

Their lack of skills was what happened when you worked in a factory all your life.

Now Nila was mine, I intended to share.

I wanted to show her Hawksridge.

I wanted to teach her how to play polo.

I wanted her to help me run the empire of diamonds and run so many facets of my world.

I also wanted to enter hers.

I wanted to travel with her on her runway shows.

I wanted to watch her sew and spend hours just sitting beside her as she crafted exquisite designs from nothing.

I want everything.

Moth snorted as Nila prevented her from following the others into the sunshine. "Do you want me to stay?"

My insides glowed with affection. "No, I'll only be a minute."

Swatting Moth on the rump, I sent Nila out to join our family. Retrieving my important requirement, I headed to Wings and secured the saddlebag to the pommel. "Ready, boy?"

Wings snorted, his eyes black and endless.

"I'm not, either." I pressed my forehead against his silky neck, just like I had whenever my condition got too bad and needed space from life. "I don't want to say goodbye but at least this way, he's still with us."

Swinging my leg over his immense side, I kicked him and followed the others.

"This is the place." I pulled on my reins, bringing Wings to a stop.

For an hour, we'd trekked through woodland and glens over chases and riverbeds of Hawksridge Estate. The moment Kes's Will had been read, I'd known what his instructions would be.

We'd had such happy times here. Away from our father and obligation. Away from even our sister. Just us and the wilderness.

"It's stunning." Nila came up beside me. Moth's breathing caused plumes of condensation in the chilly winter air.

Jasmine encouraged Claret to move further up the ridge, looking down the valley to where a small village rested in the distance. Hawksridge Hall couldn't be seen from here. That was why Kes and I had liked it.

Sitting at night, wrapped up in sleeping bags and roasting marshmallows on a fire, we used to watch the twinkling lights of the village and conjure stories for what each person did.

We pretended we lived hundreds of years ago. Discussed and argued what sort of career we would've had. I was adamant I would've been a horse farrier or black-smith. There was something about hammering hot metal until it submitted that appealed to me. Kes, on the other hand, wanted to be a carpenter. Not because he liked to create things from trees but because he reckoned women preferred a man who knew how to use his wood.

I laughed under my breath, remembering his quips.

"You're such a moron." I fired a flaming marshmallow his way.

Kes ducked, swatting the gooey mess into the ground. His shaggy hair glistened with moonlight, while the horses munched contentedly on grass behind us. "Whatever, Jet." Holding up his hands, he smirked. "These puppies were on Selena's tits last week. She told me I had good hands."

I rolled my eyes. "She's probably never been touched by a guy before and had no one to compare you to."

Kes scoffed. "I might only be sixteen, but I know how to please a girl."

Sighing, I reclined in my sleeping bag, looking at the stars. "Well, she'd be lucky to have you."

Kes shuffled closer, the crackle of the bonfire wrapping us in safety. "Same with you. You'll meet someone who doesn't just think of shopping and teenage girl idiocy one day. You'll see."

Lightening the mood, I snorted. "Perhaps, I should become a carpenter, too, so I know how to use my wood."

We burst out laughing.

My heart filled with history as I left the past and returned to Nila. "Kes will be happy here."

Nila nodded, her eyes glassing a little.

More horse hooves thudded over the hill as Tex and Vaughn finally caught up. They'd handled the trek well, allowing their horses to follow us.

Twisting in my saddle, I opened the bag and collected the urn that held my brother's ashes.

Jasmine moved closer, her lips twisting against the urge to cry. I smiled, reminding her to be happy and not dwell on what we'd lost. "Do you want to say it?"

"No. You. I think you should be the one."

Taking a deep breath, I unscrewed the lid of the copper urn and held it aloft. "To our brother. Every wind that rustles, we'll remember you. Every leaf that falls, we'll think of you. Every sunrise, we'll recall the times we shared. And every sunset, we'll value all that we've been given. This is not goodbye; this is a 'see you soon.'"

My hands shook as my chest compressed with sadness. Nila wiped away a tear and Jasmine swallowed a sob. Their emotions swelled with mine, threatening to avalanche with despair.

Needing to say a private goodbye, I kicked Wings forward and shot into a gallop. The ridgeline spread before me as I let my horse fly.

I let him gallop as fast as he could.

I let him carry me away.

And, as the thunder of his hooves blotted out the black hole of grief, I tipped the urn and sprinkled Kes's last remains.

The grey dust clouded behind me, whirling in the breeze, spiralling in the wind.

Goodbye, brother.

The wind picked up, encouraging the grey cloud to plume and soar down the valley, becoming one with the countryside.

My family had owned this estate for almost six-hundred years. It held many souls. Had seen many events. And witnessed many evolutions. My brother would remain its watcher and warrior—guarding Nila and my new family forever.

As Wings slowed, I looked at the sun and smiled.

The urn was empty.

Kestrel was gone.

From bone to ash.

From blood to dust.

His body had vanished, but I knew he still lived.

And we would meet again.

We would laugh again.

We would be brothers again.

Nila

"WHY DID WE come here?"

Jethro grabbed my hand, leading me from the Ferrari and through the car park at Diamond Alley. "You'll see."

Four weeks had gone by.

Four weeks of adjustment and simplicity.

I'd had my cast removed and my arm had knitted together, erasing Cut's crime. My father and I had discussed the revelation of Jacqueline many times, and V and I were both keen to track down our triplet and stare into the eyes of a lost relation.

Every day brought different experiences. Kes was gone. It was hard to get used to—especially as he deserved to enjoy the changes we slowly wrought on Hawksridge Hall—but time ticked onward, dragging us forward without him.

After staying with us for a few weeks—to clear the air and spend time together as a new puzzle-fitted family—my father moved back to London to oversee a busy part of the year with fabric deliveries and demands.

Vaughn stayed most weekends, chatting quietly, slowly letting go of his animosity about a past he couldn't change. Instead, he focused on a future so much brighter.

During the week, my twin spread his time between his penthouse and Hawksridge. He and Jaz spent a lot of time together, and Jethro and V talked more and more.

I'd caught them chatting over cognac beside a roaring fire in the gaming room. The room no longer tarnished with gambling debts and almost-rapes but a place where my lover and brother found friendship.

Tinsel hair brushing dark hair, discussing the world's problems and hopefully seeing eye-to-eye on most subjects.

I'd also seen them chuckling over something juvenile in the dining room, slowly switching from enemies to friends.

I'd stop and watch, hidden by shadows, and allow residual fear to flee. The gaming room was no longer the room where the Third Debt was almost repaid, the octagonal conservatory no longer where the First Debt was extracted, and the lake no longer where the Second Debt had been delivered. They were blank canvases ready for new memories.

Hawksridge slowly shed its antiquity of brutality and pain, relaxing into a gentle ceasefire.

And now Jethro had brought me to another place I'd already been.

Diamond Alley.

The fascinating warehouse where I'd met Kill for the first time.

Arthur 'Kill' Killian had returned to Florida after the final battle and the day I almost lost my head. We had a future because of him. We had a life to look forward to because of what those men did that day.

Knocking the same door we'd passed through last time we came here, a small pang hit my heart. Kes wasn't with us today, and he wouldn't be any other day, but his presence never left. Jethro didn't bring him up often, but I knew he thought about him.

The nine-digit password was accepted and the door opened.

Immediately, Jethro handed me a pair of sunglasses and pulled me into the large diamond building. The incredibly bright spotlights warmed my skin like a tropical sunshine while tiny rainbows danced on the black velvet sorting pads of the tables.

The diamond collar I wore hummed to be amongst its kinsmen and I willingly clung to Jethro's hand as he dragged me down the corridor toward the door I'd once thought was a janitor's closet.

He didn't say a word as he opened it and entered the code to the large safe and spun the dial. Once the armoured entrance hung open, Jethro bowed. "After you, Ms. Weaver."

I grinned. "I can imagine Cut is turning over in his grave seeing Weavers stay happily in his Hall and touch his diamonds on display."

Jethro hadn't told me what'd happened in the outbuilding, and I hadn't pried. That was his trauma and triumph to bear.

Bonnie had been buried on the estate, in the catacombs beneath the house. Her sarcophagus had already been crafted as per the custom of burial rights for rich lords and ladies.

At first, I hated to think of Bonnie beneath my feet as I roamed the Hall, but after a while, I didn't mind. I'd won. She hadn't. It was her penance, not mine, to witness life move on for the better while she rotted below.

Daniel's body had never been found. His bones gnawed on and flesh devoured by predators. The Hawks had taken so much from the African soil. Karma had seen to pay that debt with his flesh.

"I don't think he would've minded as much as we think." Jethro moved toward the safety deposit boxes. "In the end, he truly was sorry for what he'd done. Without him revoking the conditions on his last Will and Testament, all of this would've been lost. We would've spent years in legal battles trying to claim our birthright and Hawksridge would've been torn to pieces by the state."

I looped my fingers, listening quietly. Whatever passed between Jethro and Cut that day was their own affair, but I was glad Jethro got closure. Cut hadn't died with hate in his heart as I'd expected. He'd died with an apology and sorrow. I hoped he was at peace, wherever he was.

Standing in the middle of the safe, I waited as Jethro pulled out the long gunmetal grey drawer.

My heart beat faster.

I know what's in there.

The last time he'd shown me the original black diamond, he'd hinted at what he was. He used the stone as an example of his condition—absorbing light and emotions rather than refracting and preventing them from entering. The analogy was perfect for him.

Moving closer, I placed my hand on his forearm. "I should've guessed that day. I should've known what you were and convinced you to run away with me."

He chuckled. "Running was never an option, Needle. But you're right. Those drugs really fucked me up. I'd hoped you'd guess and slap me out of it."

I smiled. "I seem to remember I did in the end. I marched into your bedroom and forced you to listen."

"You'll never know how much your strength helped. How your tenacity to make me feel broke my unhappiness." His lips touched mine as his hands pulled out the black pouch.

"This is for you." He pushed the soft material into my grip.

I jerked backward. "What? No. There is no way I can accept that!"

He grinned. "Yes, you can. By accepting me, you've accepted it already. It's yours and I want you to open it."

"Jethro…"

He placed the ribbon in my fingers. "Open it."

My hands shook as I opened the velvet. My eyes narrowed. I expected one large stone tenderly nestled in padding. However, something didn't look right. Inside rested more parcels wrapped in delicate tissue paper.

Jethro crossed his arms, smugness decorating his face. "Go on. Keep going. You haven't opened it all yet."

Placing the pouch on the table, I plucked out the first packet. My fingers trembled harder as I pushed aside crepe paper. As soon as I unwrapped it, I almost dropped it. "Oh, my God."

Jethro didn't say a word as I pulled out the most stunning bracelet I'd ever seen. "This…it's…you made this from the single black diamond?"

The one stone that'd started it all. The priceless gem that'd raised his family to riches and tainted glory so long ago.

Jethro nodded. "Yes." Taking the dangling bracelet, his fingers traced the filigree pattern where gold licked around clusters of black diamonds, steadily growing bigger to one large rock in the centre of the design. "Give me your wrist."

Speechless, I held out my arm.

Jethro very gently secured the jewellery. Of course, it was the perfect size. "You had this made for me?"

"How could I not?" He kissed me again. My heart transformed into feathers wanting to take flight. "You're the reason I'm alive and happy. I want to give you everything, Nila."

Running his fingers over the uniquely shaped diamonds, he added, "This cut is called a kite. It's rare—not many jewellers remember the art." He smirked. "I thought it was rather fitting to use in the design."

I couldn't stop staring. "More than fitting. Now I have a Kite in my heart and kites on my wrist."

"For the rest of your life, I hope."

Not letting me answer, he looked at the pouch again. "There's more. Open the next one."

I couldn't pull my eyes away from the one he'd already given me. It was too much. Far, far more than I ever expected. The blackness of the stones sucked the light, glowing like an otherworldly charm.

Unable to speak, I pulled free the next crepe paper present. Tears glossed my eyes as I revealed what rested inside. "Jethro—"

Before I could kiss him or pounce in gratefulness, he dropped to one knee before me.

Stealing the black diamond ring, he grabbed my shaking left hand and smiled tenderly. "I've asked you to marry me twice. And each time you've said yes. As far as I'm concerned, you became a Hawk the moment you answered my first text. But I couldn't steal you away for the rest of your life without doing this properly."

I gasped as his voice broke. "Nila 'Threads' Weaver. Will you do me the absolute honour of accepting this ring, this man, this future? I offer you everything that I am and will become. I promise to adore you with every heartbeat and will forever protect you like I should've done from the day we met. Will you agree to be my best-friend and partner for the rest of our lives and continue to be so selfless with your love and kindness?"

He cleared his throat, forcing himself to continue. "In return, I promise to always love you, always protect you. I'll be the anchor you need and will never do anything to hurt you again."

I dropped to my knees before him. Knee to knee. Heart to heart. "I do. I accept and I promise you the same thing. I will never lie to you, hurt you, or keep things from you. I will always be there when you need me most."

His lips crashed against mine. My fingers dove into his salt and pepper hair. Everything I'd been through was in order to deserve this. *Him.* The greatest trophy, gift, and reward I could ever have dreamed of.

With his lips on mine, Jethro slipped the engagement ring onto my finger. Snug, perfect, never to be removed just like my collar.

I'd turned from seamstress to diamond heiress with the amount I now wore. The huge stone glittered menacingly in a cushion cut with baguettes on either side.

I didn't want to guess how many carats the ring held.

Breaking the kiss, Jethro murmured, "There's something else in there. Something that isn't for you, but I want you to see it."

My eyebrow quirked, but I reached upward and plucked the pouch from the table. With the weight of my new engagement ring, I fumbled with the crepe.

Once it was unwrapped, I couldn't stop the tears this time. I huddled over the necklace where a teardrop black diamond had been fashioned with gold scroll work and the wings of a hawk and a needle with thread in the fixings. It wasn't just a necklace; it was a joining of our two houses. A gift for someone who would be treasured above any diamond or estate. A priceless necklace for a priceless child.

"You made this for our daughter."

Jethro sucked in a breath. "How did you—"

I smiled, liquid glassing my vision and heart. "I know because I know you." Stroking the diamond, I breathed, "You want a daughter over a son?"

His arms banded around me. "Nila, I want whatever you give me. But a daughter, if she's firstborn, will be the end to everything. The debts will never take place again. She'll be part Weaver, part Hawk, and I wanted her to have something to symbolise what a new beginning she will represent."

"I love you." I grabbed his cheeks. "I love you so damn much."

His entire body melted in my hold, his adoration for me glowing in every facet. "I know. And I'll never ever deserve it."

Climbing to his feet, he helped me upright. Tugging me into an embrace, he kissed me softly. "There's one other place I'd like to take you to, if you'd let me?"

My body curved into his like a comma. "I want to go wherever you want to take me."

His gorgeous face lit with a sexy smile.

Thoughts of sealing our engagement with more than just a kiss crossed my mind.

When Jethro had bundled me into the car this morning and driven off the estate, I thought it was to complete a few errands or to stand beside me while I visited my assistants at Weaver Enterprises and give feedback on an up-and-coming design line.

Our life had become somewhat normal with work and businesses to run. I loved the normalcy but loved the magical alone times, too.

I would never have expected something as spellbinding as this to happen.
It is spellbinding.

We'd made promises in the heart of Diamond Alley to love, honour, and treasure each other for the rest of our lives. What else existed if those vows weren't classified as a spell? A forever kind of spell. A spell that would keep our souls joined even after death.

My eyes fell on the large diamond on my finger.

I couldn't stop looking at it. Flashing the black gemstone, revelling in how thoughtful and incredible my future husband was.

I ran a finger over the glossy surface. "I'll never be able to thank you for what you've given me, Jethro. More than just an anchor. You've given me a home in your heart and made me belong."

He grabbed my hand, squeezing my fingers tight. "I feel exactly the same way. Now, let's go, so I can show you the next part of my plan."

"The next part?" I laughed. "Careful, you might spoil me."

He smirked. "You don't know where I'm taking you yet. It might be an awful place."

"I highly doubt it." Tossing my hair away from my face, I smiled. "Tell me then. Where do you want to take me?"

Guiding me from the safe, he grinned. "You'll see."

"In here?" I looked over my shoulder as Jethro nodded.

We'd left Diamond Alley and driven into a bustling local town where knickknacks and tourists decorated the streets.

"Yep." Jethro bit his lip to stop from smiling.

"You want me to go into a coffee shop?"

He moved past me, pushing on the door until the chime above welcomed us into the decadent smell of coffee and sweets.

"But I don't even like coffee. You know that."

He smirked. "I know."

"Then why—?"

"Stop asking questions and get in there." Grabbing my wrist, he dragged me over the threshold and beelined for a tatty couch in the coffee shop window.

The couch.

The coffee.

Oh, my God.

My heart stopped. "This…it's similar to the café in Milan where I tried to kiss you when we first met."

He nodded. "Exactly."

I frowned, even as my heart thundered with love. "Why…why did you bring me here?"

He patted the couch, sinking into the soft cushions.

I followed, our knees touching as we faced each other. The softness of the settee cradled me as Jethro stroked my ring, his face alive and pensive. "That night I told you so many lies and hid so much from myself. I wanted you so much. I wanted to run the other way, to hide you, to never return to Hawksridge. But I didn't. I let a lifetime of conditioning control me, and I made the worst mistake of my life."

Looking around the tiny café—at the grandmother feeding a teacake to her granddaughter and the barista serving a couple—he added, "I've known you for months, Nila, and I haven't once taken you out on a proper date. Never been to see a movie or eaten at a restaurant."

My entire soul overflowed with affection. "You're saying you want to do that?"

"Of course." His back straightened. "I want to explore the world with you. I want to show you off and let people know I might've planted evidence saying you ran away with me at the start of this mess—that the media believed we'd had an affair well before we did—but now, it's true, and I value you enough not to keep you all to myself."

His golden eyes darkened to bronze. "You're no longer indebted. You're free to go wherever and whenever you wish; I want to be by your side for every experience you find. I want to be the reason you smile every day and the man you hold every night."

Quick flashes of the doctored photographs and Flaw's handwritten note to the press the night Jethro stole me entered my mind. I no longer suffered any hurt or annoyance because, in the end, that was life's plan. To give me to Jethro so I could steal him in return.

My voice stayed soft, inviting. "What are you saying?"

"I'm saying, I'll be beside you no matter what you want to do. If you want to return to sewing, I'll be there holding the fabric. If you want to travel and help me with diamonds, I'll be there carrying your bags. As long as we're together, Nila. I don't care where we are."

My heart galloped with longing and love and overflowing lust. "Kite…" Leaning closer, my eyes latched onto his mouth. "As far as I'm concerned, you come first. I might not be indebted anymore, but I have no intention of running far from you. I don't care what we do as long as we do it together."

He relaxed a little. "I'll never get tired of hearing that."

"Never get tired that I love you or that I won't run?"

His smile turned into a sinful invitation. "If you run from me, I have the means to chase you. I'd find you and make you mine again."

My legs twitched as my belly fluttered.

Inching closer to me, Jethro ran the pad of his thumb over my bottom lip. "Now, if you don't mind, I believe I need to do something that I should've done that first night."

My breathing stopped. "What should you have done?"

His breath fanned over my lips. "Kissed you. You owe me the kiss you so naively offered me moments after we met."

"Naively?" My heart pounded as my core grew wet. The tension between us swirled and sparked. "Don't you mean stupidly? I remember you calling me that a few times."

His hand cupped my cheek; his thumb skimming from my lip to my ear. "Like I said. I told a lot of lies that night." His eyes drifted to my mouth. "May I? May I take back that first wrong and make it right?"

I couldn't breathe.

I nodded.

"Fuck." His body fell forward, his mouth met mine.

I parted for him, welcoming his taste and control. Scooting closer, his arms banded around me, his knees bruised mine, and the coffee shop faded into obscurity.

I moaned into his mouth, melting into his embrace. I'd never been kissed so deeply or so selflessly. He poured the past and present down my throat, rewriting history and revoking everything that'd happened. In his arms, I only remembered how happy I was and not about the sadness still clinging to us.

My diamond ring weighed on my finger. My diamond bracelet decorated my wrist. And my diamond collar locked me forever as his. So much had happened. So much pain and debts and death.

But this.

A simple kiss in a simple coffee shop in a simple world.

This made it all worth it.

This made it all *priceless*.

His tongue danced with mine, slowly pulling away from me, leaving me needy and desperate for more.

Letting me go, Jethro reached into his jacket pocket and pulled out a folded piece of parchment. "It's fair to warn you, Needle, that after that kiss I'm fucking rock hard and need you more than I can stand. I doubt I'll have the self-control to order a coffee or watch you eat a piece of cake without needing to be inside you, so I'm going to show you this before I yank you out of this place and find a dark place so I can fuck you. Then, when the violence in my blood is sated, I'll reward you by making love to you and showing how my love can both be a punishment and a play."

My mouth fell open. His torrent lapped around me, licking my nipples with promise. "We can leave now. This very second."

He shook his head, fanning out the parchment on the low coffee table. "No, we can't. Not until I show you this."

His eyes met mine, dark and delicious, his lips glistening from our kiss. "I never told you this, but the Sacramental Pledge I made you sign the night of Cut's birthday—the one you signed after breaking in my office—I burned it before I came to get you in London."

I shivered, remembering that night and what happened afterward. He'd kissed me. He'd fucked me. He'd let me win after watching me come apart.

"Why?"

His fingers stroked the inked words. "Because I didn't want the burden of owning your soul when I'd taken it so cruelly." Spreading out the parchment further, working the kinks from the centre, he dipped into his pocket again and grabbed a fountain pen.

Holding it out for me, he said, "It's not a quill, but this will have to do." Sudden nervousness covered his features. "Would you? Will you sign another, now you know everything that I am?"

My eyes fell on the paper. *That's what this is?*

A new Sacramental Pledge? A new contract trumping the Debt Inheritance and everything it stood for?

I took the pen without hesitation. "I've already agreed to marry you. I'll agree to anything that puts your heart at rest and grants me you for eternity."

He sighed, his knee rubbing mine. "You're far, far too good to me."

"And you gave me everything I ever wanted." Kissing him gently, I whispered, "I'll sign whatever you want me to sign, Kite. But…can I read it first?"

He chuckled, tucking fallen strands behind my ear. "Of course. I want you to read it. I want you to know what I need from you."

Plucking the parchment, I held it within slightly trembling hands. The night of Cut's birthday came back. The way I broke in his office. The cuts on my back killing me from the First Debt. This was so different. Our first 'date.' Our first normal outing together as lovers rather than debtor and debtee.

My eyes landed on the gorgeous calligraphy of Jethro's writing. The words were so similar to the other pledge I'd signed but at the same time so different.

Jethro Hawk, firstborn son of Bryan Hawk, and Nila Weaver, firstborn daughter of Emma Weaver, hereby solemnly swear this is a law-binding and incontestable contract.

Nila Weaver revokes all ownership of her free will, thoughts, and body and grants them into the sole custody of Jethro Hawk. In exchange, Jethro Hawk renounces his free will, thoughts, and body and grants them entirely to Nila Weaver to do as she pleases.

The previous incontestable document named the Debt Inheritance is void now and forever. No debt nor family decree will ever befall these two houses. This new agreement brings two enemies into one family where bygones are bygones and the future is bright for all.

Both Nila Weaver and Jethro Hawk promise neither circumstance, nor change of heart will alter this vow.

In sickness and in health.
Two houses.
Two people.
One contract.
One lifetime marriage and commitment.

I looked up.

My heart showered with countless droplets of adoration.

I kissed my future husband. "How is it possible that you keep making me love you more each day?"

His face shattered into tenderness.

Before he could reply, I scrawled my name and accepted everything—the past, the present, the future. The triumphs and tragedies. The deaths of good people. The demise of bad. The pain that'd ruled us for so long. And the treachery that allowed madness to rule.

But not anymore.

This was our new chapter.

Our new story.

And we would write every sentence together.

Nila Weaver.

Jethro Hawk.

Two houses.

One future...

...

One family.

Continues in INDEBTED EPILOGUE

"Life after death…love after debts…is it possible after so much pain?"

Find out in the bonus edition: INDEBTED EPILOGUE

THE ENTIRE SERIES IN THE INDEBTED SERIES ARE OUT NOW!

You don't have to read **Indebted Epilogue** *if you do not wish to. It's a bonus book for Jethro and Nila to show life after the Debt Inheritance.*
There is also a Question and Answer session in **Indebted Epilogue**, *sneak peeks into* **Unseen Messages, Sin & Suffer**, *cover reveal for* **Indebted Beginnings** *(yes, you heard that right), along with a couple of deleted scenes from Final Debt including a sex scene that didn't make it into the published copy.*

Playlist

Avicii Hey Brother
Madonna Ghost Town
Paloma Faith Only love can hurt like this
U2 With or without you
Adele Skyfall.
Jarryd James Do you remember
Stan walker Holding You
Rhiana Dimaonds
Imagine Dragons Roots
Avicii Addicted to You
Bruno Mars I'd catch a grenade for you
Halo Starset
Chris Isaak Wicked Game
Sam Smith The Writings on the Wall.
Adele Rolling in the Deep
Avicii Wake me Up
Shawn Mendes - Stitches

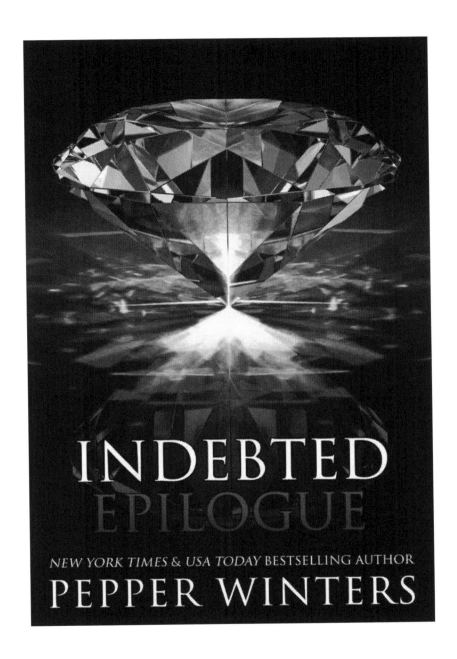

INDEBTED
EPILOGUE

NEW YORK TIMES & USA TODAY BESTSELLING AUTHOR
PEPPER WINTERS

KITE007: *COME TO bed.*

Needle&Thread: *I'm working. Almost finished on this dress.*

Kite007: *I don't care. Come to bed. My cock is hard. My arms are empty. I want to fuck you.*

Needle&Thread: *So bossy.*

Kite007: *And you're back to being a tease with your naughty nun outfit.*

Needle&Thread: *I'm neither a tease nor a nun. For your information, I've been designing a very important outfit tonight.*

Kite007: *Teasing again. I might have to come down there and spank you.*

Needle&Thread: *You can spank me, but not here. You're not allowed to see.*

Kite007: *Now I'm hard and pissed off. What are you hiding from me?*

Needle&Thread: *My wedding dress, oh so impatient husband-to-be. Or did you forget about our marriage next week?*

Kite007: *Fuck. Say that again.*

Needle&Thread: *What? Marriage? Wedding Dress? Husband-to-be? I'm going to be your wife soon; you have to stop being so demanding by text message. Otherwise, I'll just delete your number.*

Kite007: *Your teasing is driving me insane. I'm touching myself, Needle. I want you lips where my hand is and my tongue between your legs.*

Needle&Thread: *I want that, too.*

Kite007: *Come to bed.*

Needle&Thread: *I have a better idea. Come find me. Come claim me. Come fuck me as your naughty nun before I become your wife.*

Kite007: *Your wish is my command…better start running, little Weaver. I won't be gentle when I find you.*

Three Months Before…

HAWKSRIDGE HALL REMAINED the same but slowly evolved as more minutes passed. Furniture that'd seen countless generations bound by contracts were no longer clouded with debts and ill wishes. Drapes and tapestries that'd witnessed countless days of sadness, suddenly looked upon freedom. Weavers lived with Hawks and no debts or screams collected.

Rooms were transformed, Bonnie's parlour renovated, and the drab and dreary aura dispelled.

Bonnie had done a lot of wrong, but training Jasmine was not one of them. My sister's lessons were exemplary and together we took on the mammoth task of running the estate.

I was heir but I willingly shared the role. Primogeniture and old-fashioned standings had no bearing on us anymore.

Together, we patched up the Hall and put bygones with bygones. However, there was one thing I had to do myself. The hastily-written Will and video declaration from Cut superseded the previous ruling of his death ever being suspicious. I travelled on my own to a new lawyer firm. Not the ones who'd looked after my family's interests and debt catalogue for generations. I had plans for that firm. I would deal with them soon enough.

In the meantime, I wanted new contacts—above board and legal.

After shadowy background and vague description of my father's wishes, I lodged the updated version with them with their assurances they would ensure Hawksridge and my future wouldn't be harmed.

One more thing off my list, but so many still to go.

I also strengthened our alliance with the local authorities to ensure no more nasty misunderstandings and assured them Vaughn's prank with social media and public nuisance wouldn't happen again.

Returning to the Hall, I sought out Nila for comfort.

Whenever we were apart, dealing with life and difficulties, I missed her. Without even realising it, she'd become my world, my salvation, and my heart never stopped skipping whenever she was close.

My quarters were empty without her. My arms were useless without her in them.

The past couple of months, I'd grown used to having her in my bed, showering in my bathroom, and leaving her half-finished creations in little heaps around the room.

She had quirks I found endearing. Habits I adored.

I fucking loved her.

Everything about her.

My condition hadn't grown easier to bear. Leaving the estate and dealing with strangers was the hardest part. Listening to emotions I had no right to listen to. Feeling arguments and worry from people I didn't know stripped me bare, ensuring I drained Nila when I had her back in my arms.

I couldn't watch TV or relax with a movie. I barely tolerated music.

But Nila tolerated me.

For some reason, she didn't mind when I told her to be quiet and just let me hold her. She didn't argue when I took her silently to bed and teased her mercilessly so I could settle into the lust and desire she felt for me.

She gave me everything with nothing barred.

She made me more whole and centred than I'd ever been.

She made me...better.

Nila

THREE MONTHS HAD passed since everything ended.

Three months since Kestrel died.

Three months since Jethro stopped his birthright and the Debt Inheritance.

Jethro dealt with lawyers and other estate business. Jasmine ran the household. My father helped clear away evidence of the ballroom bloodbath and paid the mercenaries who had helped save my life.

We were all busy, traipsing onward, living…

Hawksridge was no longer a mausoleum housing smugglers and psychopaths—its halls were now light and airy, its rooms full of tentative laughter and love.

Spinning my black diamond engagement ring, I smiled. We hadn't set a date yet but life had been good to us. Tex had renewed his efforts to find Jacqueline, and Vaughn had been a regular visitor to see Jasmine. We'd all found a place within this new world.

A gentle tap on the greenhouse octagon door wrenched my head up.

Jethro had left me for an hour to deal with more paperwork. The requirement of running such a large estate was never ending.

I would be lying if I said entering the muggy warmth had been easy. The scars on my back twinged. The crack of the whip as Jethro hit me for the First Debt hovering in the stagnant air.

Orchids and white jasmine perfumed the air, granting peace where before there'd been only pain. I hadn't been back since that day, but it didn't give me nightmares with unresolved issues.

I found closure by trailing my fingers on the post where Jethro had tied me. I smiled softly as I weaved old memories with new—knowing my plan of making him care had worked.

We'd begun this as enemies, fighting against each other.

But we'd ended up as partners, stopping the war side by side.

The tapping noise came again, hidden by foliage on the other side of the octagon.

I stood up just as Jethro stepped into the room, his golden eyes more amber honey in the gentle sunshine of the glasshouse.

"I looked for you in our wing." Jethro's gaze narrowed on the whipping post in the centre of the octagon. Newly budded flowers and juvenile vines helped hide its original occupation. "I never expected to find you in here."

Moving toward me, his touch landed on my shoulders, digging deep with need and love. "You okay?"

Sunlight highlighted his silvering hair, glittering like some expensive thread. His cheekbones cut shadows, his brow etched with contours. And his lips...his lips were slightly parted and damp from his tongue.

Ever since Cut had taken his last breath, Jethro had changed. Not significantly but enough to notice subtle evolutions. He held himself higher, not proud like the rightful heir to his fortune, but like a man no longer crippled with negativity and hatred seeping from the air.

He looked younger, wiser, calmer, gentler.

I smiled softly, lifting my hand in invitation. "I am now you're here."

His fingers slinked through mine, sending arcs of electricity into my heart. He squeezed, bending his elegant legs to sit beside me, dragging me back to the bench.

I sat willingly, melting into his side, inhaling his unique scent of woods and leather.

Hip to hip, thigh to thigh, our hearts beat to the same rhythm.

Sighing contentedly, I snuggled into him, kissing his throat as his arm wrapped around my shoulders, gluing me tighter against him. "What are you thinking about?"

I closed my eyes, letting the gentle warmth of late spring's sunshine eradicate any leftover history. "You can't tell?"

Jethro shook his head. "It's scrambled. You're sad but not. Happy but calm." He pulled away, looking into my eyes. "You're focusing on too much too fast."

My lips twitched. "Ah, finally a way to fool you. I was beginning to think I'd never be able to keep a secret."

His face darkened. "You promised there would be no need for secrets." Anxiety stiffened his body. "Is everything...okay?" He waved at the room. "Did you come here for a reason? Do you still hate me for that day? For hurting you so much?" His voice lowered with regret. "Fuck, Nila. I'd give anything to rewind the clock and—"

"Shush." I cupped my hand over his mouth. His five o'clock shadow rasped beneath my palm. "Everything is fine. I'm just...sitting still. If that makes sense. I'm letting my thoughts wander without thinking, finding ends to things that need to be finished."

Imprisoning my wrist with his fingers, he tugged my hand away from his mouth. "That makes perfect sense."

His fingers drew lazy circles on my inner wrist, sending delicious shivers over my skin. Looking at the blooming flowers and exotic breeds, he fell silent.

For a while, we didn't say anything, both of us lost in our own thoughts. Every breath I took scattered rainbow-diamonds over our laps. My Weaver Wailer—or should I say Hawk Redeemer—was the last piece, the final symbol that the past few months weren't a nightmare but real.

And I'd survived them.

Even if there was a way to get it off, I didn't want to. I'd grown accustomed to the weight. I wore its fracturing rainbows with pride, and I liked the thought of the diamonds being my friend instead of my enemy, gracing my body until I took my last inhale.

Jethro kissed the top of my head. "I have something for you."

"Oh?" I pulled away, looking into his gorgeous face. "Do I need to be worried?" My thoughts filled with teasing. We'd all been so serious; it was time to play again. My lips spread as I asked, "Is it time for another de—"

"If you ask me if it's another debt, I'll put you over my knee right here and spank you." His voice flirted with gruff and sexy.

My eyes flittered to the post, a coy smirk widening. "You know you could spank me on the pole and replace the First Debt with a better ending."

His throat contracted as he swallowed. "What better ending?" His eyes flashed dark. "If I remember rightly, I almost raped you after that debt. I felt sick to my fucking stomach for ever thinking that way, let alone being turned on by hurting you."

He looked away, shaking his head in disgust. "I don't understand how I got off on that. How I could ignore your pain and find anything remotely erotic about it." He curled his lips. "You called me a sadist, remember? I refuted it, but once I'd finished tending to your back, I wondered if you were right. How could someone like me—someone who's gone his entire life absorbing other's thoughts—suddenly be turned on by another's agony?"

My heart fluttered. I hadn't given it much thought. But the more I studied Jethro's abhorrent self-confession, the more an answer unfurled inside my mind.

He felt what others did. He had no choice. And yet he'd still been under the influence of Cut's conditioning just enough to block out avalanches of sensation.

Would it make sense he'd picked up select thoughts? Drank in my desire for him, my aching, burning need when he'd taunted me with history and barely-given kisses?

I looked at my fingers, twining together in my lap. "I think I know why."

His eyes shot to me, his eyebrows raised with questions. "Know what?"

"Why you were turned on that day."

He tensed. "It was a sick thing to do. Out of everything I did to you, masturbating on your back still fills me with shame. I wish I could take it back."

Twisting to face him, I stroked his cheek. "Before you berate yourself, stop and think. Did you never question why you desperately needed to come? Why you wanted me so badly?"

He froze.

I laughed. "Come on, Kite. You know your condition inside and out, and you're telling me you can't figure what caused that minor incident?"

He growled, "It was hardly minor."

Not waiting for me to reply, he soared upright, untangling himself to pace. "I don't understand. What are you saying?"

I stood too, smiling as if I had the secret to everything—which, in a way, I had. I thought he'd figured it out that day. That was why he'd been kind to me afterward, why he'd softened even when he was told not to. "You enjoyed hurting me that day because of me."

"Yes, because of you," he snarled. "I got so fucking hard over you. And I hated you for it. You made me enjoy your pain when I normally run from feeling anything remotely intense."

"Exactly."

Jethro slammed to a stop. "You're not making any sense. Spit it out."

I moved toward him. "You felt what I felt. Yes, it hurt. Yes, that whip was my worst nightmare and the lashes felt like a bazillion bees stinging my back, but before it grew too painful, I wanted you. God, I wanted you. I was so wet. If you'd stopped after a couple of strikes, I wouldn't have fought you. I would've willingly spread my legs and taken you because all I could think about was how much I needed you."

Jethro's mouth fell open. "You're saying I fed off what you were feeling that entire time?"

"Toward the end, I'll admit I hated you. I wanted more than anything for it to stop, and when you tried to take me, it was the last thing I wanted to happen. But, Jethro, before that. I genuinely craved for you to touch me. I begged for it. But you never cracked. You wouldn't even kiss me."

"Fuck." He dragged a hand over his face. "I honestly thought I'd lost it. For months, I feared who I'd become because of what happened that day. I stayed away from you for weeks afterward, because I didn't trust myself. I thought I'd get off on hurting you more. I was fucking terrified I'd finally turned into Cut."

My heart beat harder for him, wishing I'd known so I could've comforted him. Then again, we weren't exactly friends yet. He'd suffered on his own, but perhaps that was the way it had to be for him to finally realise there was something rich and deep and undeniable between us.

"I guess there's a lot of things we need to go back over and put to rest."

His arms lassoed around me tightly. "I think you're right." Nuzzling my hair, he murmured, "How about we go to each place where the debts were completed and replace them with a happier memory."

I hugged him back. "I'd like that."

Sex to replace the First Debt.

A lakeside picnic to replace the Second Debt.

My mind skipped to the Third Debt—the debt that would've broken me if it weren't for Kestrel protecting me by being such a gentleman. At the time, I'd been conflicted, hurt Jethro wasn't there, confused as to my body's reaction to Kes.

But now, I was glad we'd had that moment together. I loved Kes. I couldn't admit it before as I didn't fully understand it, but I loved him more than a friend but less than Jethro. A friend who would always have my heart.

Jethro sighed, knowing where my thoughts were without me having to vocalize.

His condition truly took any secrecy out of our relationship. I would never be able to hide anything, and in some ways, it annoyed me. I would never be able to sulk behind white lies or indulge in a cold shoulder if we ever had a fight.

But at the same time, it was refreshing to know there would never be anything between us because his gift worked both ways. Yes, he could feel what I felt, but at the same time, I could read him better than he knew. His eyes, his face, his body—they all told me what I needed to know.

Jethro cupped the back of my nape, running his fingers along my throat and collar. "I know what Kes did to you that night. At the time, I fucking hated him for it, but now...I'm actually glad you had that with him. You deserved to know how much he cared for you."

I nodded. "Me too. It was wrong in a way but right as well. It doesn't mean I love you any less, but there'll always be space for Kes in my heart."

Jethro smiled sadly. "As it should. He was part of me, my only true confidant. I'm glad you'll miss him as much as me." His head tilted, lips coming to meet mine.

We stood still as we kissed softly.

His tongue licked my bottom lip, and I opened for him. Inhaling his soul and taste, I slipped into bone-sated happiness knowing I belonged to this man and he belonged to me.

I was no longer alone.

I would never be alone again.

We'd bound ourselves together and become family.

I WON'T SAY it was easy. Because it wasn't.
I won't say everything became fucking puppies and rainbows. Because it didn't.
The pain was still there.

The knowledge my father was broken, my mother murdered, and an unknown sister given away at birth.

But things did get easier.

Tex slowly grew used to Threads and Jethro together. He'd watch them touch and whisper and even he couldn't deny their love was pure.

Jethro had been a cocksucker; he'd hurt my sister and almost destroyed my family, but he'd done everything in his power to fix his wrongs and ensure he earned the right to forgiveness. It helped that he loved Threads so fucking much. He lit up around her. He became *more* around her. He breathed because of her.

In a way, I was fucking jealous. He'd stolen her from me completely. They shone around each other, and when I caught him watching her, the aching adoration in his gaze made me admit Nila was lucky.

She would never be alone or unloved again. She'd met the one who would be there for her through night and day, happy and sad, bad and good.

He would be there for her even when death came for them.

I, on the other hand, grew restless living on someone else's turf. I loved patching my family back together and enjoyed the night chats I had with Jasmine. But I missed the magic of London, the thrill of running the company—the real world.

I returned to my apartment in the city a couple of weeks after Kestrel's funeral. Tex moved back to the family home, returning to the factory as if nothing life-changing had happened. Jethro had given me an open invitation to come and stay at the Hall as often as I liked. And Nila said she'd miss me but her place was now with her Hawk.

I was fine with all of it.

However, it was Jasmine who shocked everyone.

She admitted she wanted to leave Hawksridge and explore a new life.

Jethro had almost fucking passed out hearing his baby sister, a self-confessed recluse, wanted to leave the estate.

She wouldn't tell me the story of how she lost the use of her legs, but I knew it had something to do with her brother and father. I wanted to know her secrets, but then again, so much was in the past that it was best to let it go and move forward.

The argument about Jasmine's living arrangements had lasted a full night before Jethro conceded he couldn't keep his sister prisoner—no matter how much he would fret over her safety.

I'd almost spat out my tea when Jaz calmly turned to me and asked if she could move in with me for a time.

Fuck.

I'd gone from a bachelor flirting with the sister of the man about to become my brother-in-law to inheriting a live-in girlfriend.

I'd be lying if I said I didn't put the moves on Jasmine. I'd kissed her. I wanted her. But she wouldn't let me go any further. I knew she was a virgin, and she was worried about her body and disability. But I didn't care about that. Fuck, all I cared about was hearing her laugh and making her come with my tongue.

As for her request, I didn't have to think about it. Of course, I agreed. And the next day, we moved out of Hawksridge. I stole a Hawk to share my home.

Luckily, I had a penthouse in downtown London. Lifts serviced the floors and the extra-wide corridors proved to be the perfect environment for her to get around.

We became friends.

Great friends.

More than friends.

I wanted her every evening we spent ribbing each other watching crap TV. I needed her every day we argued over which model would be best to showcase Nila's show pieces. My cock hardened constantly around her, yet she never insinuated sex and I didn't want to scare her by pushing.

For months, we lived together and never crossed the line.

I honestly didn't know if she could even have sex. Would she be able to feel me? Would she even want me to see her naked, to bring her pleasure and fulfil the prophecy she herself had decreed the night she'd rolled into my life and demanded my help to save her dying brothers.

She'd said one day I would belong to a woman other than my sister.

At the time, I'd wanted to rip out her fucking heart for ever suggesting such a thing. I was a Weaver. Loyal and true. But what she'd said was right. Life moved on, we grew up, and eventually, we all replaced our blood families with chosen ones.

And somehow, Jasmine became my chosen one.

She enticed me more and more.

I wanted her more and fucking more.

If only she would give in to me. If only she trusted me that I wanted her because of her mind and soul and not just her body.

She wouldn't submit…not yet.

But I wouldn't stop trying.

And the day she finally gave in…she would make me the happiest fucking man in the world.

Three Months and One Week Later...

LIFE WAS FULL of moments and this was the biggest of all.

Today was the end of my godforsaken life and the first day of a pristine existence.

For three months, I'd found the happiness I never dared dream of. Hawksridge Hall came alive with companionship and friendship rather than lust and greed. Flaw managed the Black Diamond brothers with ease. Our smuggling was no more; we'd opened the lines for proper trade with diamonds, ensuring our mines and workers were well compensated.

Nila and I had returned to *Almasi Kipanga*. We'd given every worker bonuses, set up fair work practices, and arranged a proper building estate to be erected to house those who wanted to stay.

Once completed, we sent word to our other mines: emeralds in Thailand, rubies in Burma. The other Black Diamond factions changed their practices to better suit our loyal workers.

The new regime was named after the man who'd planned all along to improve our employees' conditions: Kestrel.

While in Botswana, we also overturned Cut's commands that any worker injured in the mine had to leave. We tracked down those employees and rehired all those he'd fired and rehabilitated those who'd lost limbs in tragic accidents. We also compensated the families who'd lost loved ones working for us. Money couldn't bring back their family, but it could make their future a little easier.

Vaughn and Jasmine officially announced they were together, and Tex had finally started to shed some of his guilt.

Together, the Weavers worked to find Jacqueline. Only last week we were told there might be a lead on a woman matching Nila and Vaughn's birthday living not far away in Cornwall.

Things were healing. And Nila had healed me in return.

And now...she'd given me the best gift she could ever do.

Married me.

My hands fisted as she appeared at the top of the aisle. All around us, the ocean glistened as the sun set on the most spectacular day.

This had been V's idea. He'd seen the photos I'd doctored when I first stole Nila. The ones of me hugging her on a private yacht and kissing her at sea. He'd jokingly said a couple of months ago when we set the date that our nuptials would have to be on a boat to honour the almost futuristic prediction of those photographs.

I couldn't agree more.

My heart thundered as Nila drifted forward. Her father clutched her tight while his face glowed with pride and love. Her dress was the one she'd refused to let me see the night she didn't come to bed.

She'd somehow conjured exactly what I envisioned. After making love to her that night, the strangest thought popped into my head and never left.

The black gown I'd torn from her when I threw her on my motorcycle had always haunted me. I'd felt what that dress meant to her. The countless hours of hardship and skill she'd poured into the fabric creation. I hadn't let her see how much her despair affected me that night but I wanted to somehow change that memory—just as we'd changed all the others.

Either she'd sensed my desires or I'd picked up on her thoughts of what she busily created—either way, she drifted toward me in the mirror image of the dress, but instead of black, she glistened in silver and white.

My eyes smarted, drinking her in. This was the first time I'd seen the gown but not the first time I'd been teased with it.

Once she finished the dress, she'd called George and Sylvie who'd done the *Vanity Fair* article when Nila had returned to Hawksridge. As promised, they were offered an exclusive release, hiding the gown from me but preparing the four-page spread for the world.

I glanced over at the two reporters, snapping pictures and taking notes on our wedding. Part of the arrangement included coverage of the ceremony so the last nasty rumours were put to rest—along with every other transgression and hardship of the past year.

Vaughn apologised for causing the social media backlash, but I didn't accept his apology. He'd done what he could to save Nila. He was a pain in my arse most days, but he loved his sister, and in turn, I loved him because of that.

George waved his pen in my direction, smiling in his tuxedo.

They were the only invited non-family guests at this wedding.

We'd kept it small—partly because of my condition, but mostly because a marriage was private. Really, it was between two people and that was it. A spectacle didn't need to be made when all we needed was a celebrant, a ring, and a shared vow.

My back straightened as Nila ghosted closer. She looked like a princess, a queen—*my* queen.

White and soft grey feathers covered her cleavage, sewn with immense skill to transform from feather to gemstone further down the bodice.

The hooped skirt swept like a bell as Tex brought his daughter closer to me, gifting her to me in an age-old tradition.

The first time I'd stolen Nila, I'd threatened him and taken her without his approval. This time, he willingly gave her to me to safeguard because he knew without a doubt I would die for her, I would fight for her…I would change history for her.

The sea breeze caught the edge of her veil, fluttering the lace around her face, activating the large diamond secured in her hair to drench her in rainbows.

The diamond collar gleamed like fire, picking up the orange of the sunset and the flash of white heels peeked under the layers of skirts with every step. The only thing on her that wasn't white was her engagement ring and bracelet.

The black diamonds sucked in what the white diamonds glittered off. The onyx gem absorbed the emotions and celebration of such a day, storing deep within its priceless heart, kept safe forever.

"You're a lucky son of a bitch." V's whispered words came from beside me.

Glancing at him, I grinned. Today was bittersweet. I never thought I would get married. And if I ever found the one to take me on, I envisioned my brother as my best man. Kestrel wasn't there in body, but he was in spirit. I felt his pride on the sea air. I saw his smile in the sunset. And my new brother stood in his place. My brother-in-law.

"I know. Believe me, I know."

Jasmine sat opposite, in the maid of honour position. Her eyes reflected the colour of her beautiful bridesmaid's dress of purple and black. Nila had designed the gown, as well as my suit and V's best man's outfit. We all matched. A family.

The soft music stopped playing as Nila ended the procession within touching distance.

Tex wiped away a tear as he hugged his daughter. He'd lost the weight he'd carried ever since I'd taken Nila and looked like the distinguished gentleman from the night I stole her.

We'd had a private chat a couple of months ago. I'd apologised to him for what my family had done and sworn on the graves of my ancestors that Nila was forever safe in my arms.

Nila stood before me.

I blinked, drinking in her incredible perfection.

Her tiny hands slotted into mine, and I squeezed her so damn hard.

The celebrant I'd hired clasped his fingers together, looking at the small congregation. There weren't many of us. Flaw represented the Black Diamonds. Tex represented Nila's family. There were no business partners or friends, no assistants or organisers.

Just the people who mattered.

"Do you have your own vows or would you like to repeat after me?"

Nila smiled softly. "We've already said what we needed to."

I nodded, thinking about the newly framed Sacramental Pledge hanging in my office. The figurines from my boyhood and the contract for my happiness as an adult, side by side.

"Go ahead with traditional. The sooner she's my wife, the better."

The celebrant smiled, his dark hair catching the sunset as it kissed the ocean. England was behind us. The Greek isles and Santorini nestled us, floating on the turquoise ocean.

Our honeymoon would be spent here. Relaxing on the beach and making love in the moonlight. V and Tex had planned to source some local cotton and silk, while Flaw had meetings with jewellery shops to stock our diamonds.

Work and pleasure.

A perfect combination.

"Do you, Jethro 'Kite' Hawk, take this woman as your lawfully wedded wife, for now and forever, in sickness and in health, for as long as you both shall live?"

I didn't need to think. "I do." *A thousand times, I do.*

"And do you, Nila Threads Weaver, take this man as your lawfully wedded husband, for now and forever, in sickness and in health, for as long as you both shall live?"

Nila shook her head.

Shook her head? *What the fuck?*

Smiling, she murmured, "I take him now and forever but not for as long as we both shall live." She squeezed my fingers, her eyes glinting. "Far beyond that. For eternity."

I couldn't wait for the 'you may kiss the bride' part. I grabbed her shoulders and yanked her forward. My lips met hers, and I forgot about the world and witnesses. I forgot about everything but soldering my soul to this woman who'd captured me as carefully as a net captures a hawk.

Speaking into her mouth, I whispered, "Seeing as you changed the rules, I have another one to add to your vow. I swear to love you forever. You are no longer indebted to me. I'm indebted to you. My heart is in your debt. My happiness. My very life is yours."

Nila melted, holding onto me as I dipped her and deepened the kiss.

Laughing, the celebrant spoke to the gathered crowd. "Seeing as you just sealed your vows, I now pronounce you husband and wife."

The cheers crested, and for the first time in my life, being in a crowd didn't hurt. The overwhelming sensation of everyone's emotions was of happiness, fulfilment, and joy.

Tex enveloped us in a hug. "Welcome to the family, Hawk."

I grinned. "Thank you for having me."

Tex kissed his daughter. "I guess you're no longer a Weaver, Threads."

Nila sighed. "I'll always be your daughter, Dad, but for now, I belong and have willingly become a Hawk."

He nodded as if it made perfect sense that his daughter married the son of the man who killed his wife. It was a twisted world, but somehow, Nila and I had found a way to untangle it to the point of acceptance.

My fingertips tingled from our tally tattoos and I made a note to ask Nila if she'd like to finish the marks now we'd cemented our lives together. Ten fingers, ten tattoos. A lifetime of happiness.

Somehow, we'd found life over death.

Chosen freedom over debts.

And I would never take my future or my wife for granted.

Nila

JETHRO LOCKED THE door.

The yacht rocked beneath our toes, sedate and savage in its sea-cradle.

The curtains had been drawn across the balcony, the bed turned down by well-trained staff, and all the guests remaining on board were a floor below.

We were the only bedroom on this level.

Private.

Alone.

Swiping a hand through his slicked back hair, Jethro traversed the distance between us. We didn't speak as the air intensified and love poured from his heart to mine.

The white gold wedding band I'd had fashioned along with a few black diamonds I'd sourced at Diamond Alley graced his finger—absorbing the light rather than sparkling—sucking its life inward, protecting its secrets.

The matching ring hummed on my finger. The large midnight stone grew heavier the closer Jethro came.

"We did it." His voice teased with disbelief. "We're married."

I nodded, a little breathless and a lot nervous. "We are."

"You're mine."

"I'm yours."

"There are no more debts. No more threats."

I moved toward him, stepping onto the silver rug he stood on. Our bodies swayed as a current rocked the yacht, but our eyes never unlocked. "We're free."

Breathing hard, Jethro reached for me. His arms wrapped around me, gathering me toward him so the white silk of my gown rippled over my skin and floor.

Stars and moon above were the only elements invited into our room. The skylight above had a ladder granting access to the private deck. The nose of the boat was out of bounds to anyone. We could make love down here with the sky as company or make our way upside and fuck with the air licking our skin.

We could travel the world.

We could kiss and touch and never have to hide our happiness from anyone.

We have so much to look forward to.

Jethro's gaze drifted to my collar. His tongue swept over his bottom lip as the faint sparkle of diamonds kissed his chin. "You should know something."

I froze in his arms, my heart rate spiking. "Know what?"

He shifted me in his embrace, cupping my throat with gentle fingers. His thumb ran along the diamonds. "You admitted you didn't want me to find a way to remove this. You'll never wear another necklace as long as you live. No matter where you go. No matter what you do, this collar will be with you every step."

"I know. I want it to be that way." Resting my hands on his hips, I frowned a little, trying to understand his point. "You put it on me, Jethro. It will stay on until I die."

His back tightened, the muscles either side of his spine bunching beneath my fingertips. "That's how I view what happened today."

"What do you mean?"

His forehead furrowed, shadowing his golden eyes. "I mean—marriage to me isn't a simple ceremony and celebration. Marriage is like your collar. A one-time deal. Never to break, binding us together until death do us part. Just like there will never be another necklace, there will never be goodbye between us. No opportunity to sever what we've found."

My tummy twisted as flutters entered my core. "That's how I view it, too. It wasn't a meaningless vow, Kite. I willingly said the words."

"But do you fully comprehend that this is it? No other men. No flirtations or dalliances. *Me*. I'm the last you'll ever have." His head dropped. "Is that enough for you?"

I laughed softly. I couldn't help it. "You're seriously asking me if you're enough for me?" My heart overflowed. "Jethro you're *too* much. You're everything I could ever hope for. Why are you feeling insecure?" I snuggled closer, pressing my cheek on his lapel, avoiding the diamond pin through the fabric. "After everything we've been through, everything we said today and yesterday, you're afraid I'll divorce you and run?"

Jethro didn't respond. His chest rose and fell, his arms binding tighter as if he didn't trust me not to vanish.

I let silence and the creaking of the yacht ease some of his fear before murmuring, "I suggest you remember the day I ran from you after the welcome luncheon because that's the one and only time I'll ever run away. I chose you with my eyes open, Kite. I know what our connection will mean for you and the struggle I'll sometimes have to keep giving you what you need. But I'm not a little girl. I'm a woman who's chosen her soul-mate. I'm strong enough to love you unconditionally. I'm smart enough to know some days will be good and some days will be bad. And I'm brave enough to solemnly swear that we will be together until the end.

"I don't want anyone else. You're my best friend, my rescuer. You're the man I was born for as decreed by six-hundred-years of pacts. Don't doubt what we have on the eve of what could be the happiest time of our lives."

Jethro suddenly groaned, wrapping his arms so tight he bruised me. "Fuck, I'm sorry. I don't know why I doubted."

"I know why."

He raised my chin with a fingertip. "Why?"

I smiled, loving the way the moonlight highlighted the silver in his hair, making him look part god, part majestic sculpture. "Because everything is so good now. It's hard not to suspect it will all vanish after a lifetime of having everything you loved stripped away."

He paused, biting his inner cheek. "You're right."

"Of course, I'm right."

His lips tilted crookedly. "To this day, I don't know what I did to deserve you, but I'm never letting you go."

"Good." Standing on my tiptoes, I whispered, "Now, enough talk of divorce. Let's enjoy being married first. Stop speaking and take me to bed, Mr. Hawk."

He jolted, a growl escaping. Letting me go, he grabbed my wrist, yanking me toward the towering mattress and turned down sheets. "It would be my pleasure, Ms. Wea—" His mouth shot closed, his eyes clouding.

I knew his thoughts. Mine had already been over the technicalities. My father had changed his last name to match my mother's as per the rules of the Debt Inheritance. By right, Jethro should become a Weaver.

However, I had no intention of stripping the heir of Hawksridge his name. The very name he'd always strived to earn and change for the better.

Sitting on the bed in a shower of white lace, I patted the mattress beside me. "I think the term of address you're looking for is *Mrs. Hawk*."

His eyes shot bronze. "Are you sure? You don't have to take my name. You can keep Weaver if you want—"

"What I want is to belong to you. I want the world to know it. I want the ghosts who battled together for so long to hear it. I want us to become one." Taking his hand, I yanked him beside me. "Try again, only this time, use the right name."

Pressing my shoulders, he slowly guided me onto my back. His breath skated over my mouth as he lowered himself beside me. "I'm going to love you until my heart stops beating and then beyond...Mrs. Hawk."

I shivered. "I'm glad. Because I had the exact same plan, Mr. Hawk."

He grinned, bowing his head to kiss me.

My heart raced as his tongue slipped past my lips, seducing me with slow licks. His fingers slinked into my hair, pulling free pins and clips, letting the black strands cascade into a mess on the sheets. Once every decoration and slide was free, he massaged my scalp, dislodging a few remaining petals from the rice and flower confetti.

"As much as I love you in this dress, I think it's time it disappeared, don't you?"

I nodded.

Jethro was mine in every possible way. He would continue to need me. I would continue to need him. We were no longer on our own but a partnership, lovers...a family.

The stress of the wedding left my bloodstream, relaxing my shoulders into the springy bed.

His hands slipped behind me, rolling me onto my stomach as he set to the task of undoing fifty-two pearl buttons down my back.

The panels of lace decorated my skin, revealing the muscles of my spine and risqué glimpses beneath. I didn't think I'd have time to sew something so delicate, but it'd been cathartic for me to sketch and create something so stunningly simple but intricately beautiful.

Goosebumps erupted as Jethro's knuckles brushed my skin, slowly releasing me from the gown. Half-way down my back, he swallowed a groan. "Goddammit, I want to rip this off you. This is taking far too long."

I laughed into the sheets. "You rip it and I'll make you fix it. Patience is a virtue, husband."

His touch halted. "What did you call me?"

I looked over my shoulder. "Husband." Loving the way his eyes hooded, I breathed, "That's what you are now. Husband. *My* husband."

His mouth parted, dangerous darkness stealing over him. "Say it again."

I didn't care my dress was only half undone, I rolled onto my back, slipping beneath his inert hands. "Husband."

His gaze dropped to the front corset of my gown. "That word makes me hard."

The spaghetti straps slid off my shoulders, tickling my skin. "How hard?"

"So fucking hard."

"Show me."

He gulped. "Show you?"

I nodded, reaching for his tented slacks. "I want to see."

Darting out of my grip, he climbed off the bed, a slow burn building in his gaze. "*Why* do you want to see?"

Coyness slipped into my blood. He wanted to play? I could play.

Sitting up on my knees, I struggled against the imprisoning nature of the silk layers and licked my lips. "Because it's mine and I want to see what my marriage has bought me."

His hands fisted. "*Bought* you?"

"Uh huh." The conversation turned anchor-heavy with want, sinking through the yacht to the seabed below. I'd never been so needy, so ready for sex. I wanted him desperately, but at the same time, I loved the anticipation, the building joy that we could touch whenever we wanted but chose a little self-denial.

Jethro's hands flew to his belt. Never taking his eyes off me, he unbuckled the clasp, slipping the black leather from the loops. "If you get to see me, I want something in return."

"Oh?" My knickers grew shamefully wet. "What's that?"

Taking a step back, he crooked his finger. "Get off the bed."

Without a word, I obeyed.

My bare toes hit the soft carpet. My high heels had fallen off as Jethro carried me down the gangway to our room after leaving the party.

"Take your dress off." Jethro's left hand looped his belt tight around his fist while his right one disappeared into his black boxer-briefs.

The train of my dress resembled a wake of lace, the undone buttons giving me enough room to slink out of it and let the combined corset and overlay slip to the floor.

I stood before him in the sheer teddy I'd had Jasmine order for me online. She'd hidden it for me so it would be a surprise on our wedding night.

Tonight.

We're married.

The words sporadically kept popping into my head like toys on Christmas morning.

I'm a wife.

I have a husband.

There was nothing more erotic than that. Nothing more tantalising or desirous.

Grabbing his cock, Jethro swallowed hard. "Christ, you're beautiful."

The intensity in his eyes stripped me bare. I struggled to keep my hands by my side and not pluck at the garter belt attached to the unsubstantial G-string or run my prickling palms over the silky pantyhose.

I let Jethro drink me in because I had every intention of doing the same. My eyes were selfish. My body greedy. My soul hungry.

"I want to bite every inch of you. I want to rip off your lingerie and take you hard. I want to bury you in my arms and never let you fucking go."

Jethro's voice mimicked a tidal wave on sand, velvet and soothing but rough and wild.

His hand worked harder, his quads tensing beneath his slacks. The action alone made my nipples throb with need.

"I can't stop staring at you." Jethro's jaw clenched as he stroked faster. "Nothing else matters knowing you're mine and I can touch you, taste you, fuck you however I want."

The urge to touch him overwhelmed me. I wanted to consummate our marriage.

Now.

However, Jethro drove me to breaking point. The least I could do was return the favour. Drifting my hands from my throat to my breasts, I tweaked my nipples through the sheer teddy. "I love knowing you're mine. That your fingers belong inside me, your cock was made to pleasure me, your mouth designed to kiss me every day."

Jethro stumbled. "You have no idea. Every day, Nila. Every fucking day I'm going to give you those three things."

The room swam with lust, inviting the ocean below to transform air into liquid and oxygen into molten heat.

Dropping my hands to my pussy, I fingered myself through the lace. "I want to see you. I want to see your hard, long cock. I want to get on my knees and suck you. I want to feel you shatter and lick up every drop."

"Fucking hell." Jethro broke first.

My heart leapt with triumph as he stalked toward me, wrenched his hand from his trousers, and grabbed mine to replace it. His other hand latched around my nape, the buckle of his belt clinking against my collar. "Touch me, Needle. Fucking feel how much I want you."

My fingers instantly obeyed, stealing his invitation and invading his underwear. The moment my touch met velveteen steel, his stomach rippled with tension.

Grabbing a fistful of my hair, he growled, "I want your lips around my dick. I want your tongue lapping what I give you. But for now, now, I can't fucking think straight. I can't do this anymore. I need to be inside you. *Immediately.*"

His lips smashed against mine, his groan slipping deep into my chest. I battled his tongue, hints of violence and danger unravelled my decorum faster and faster.

The kiss turned fatal, killing off any last worries or maladies.

The ignition between us turned viperous as our past was suddenly deleted. The lid on our previous lifetimes snapped closed with finality. And a blank new page spread out before us. We were the quill and ink ready to pen a new chapter.

"Nila—" Jethro's touch turned savage, his tongue making mad love to mine with unscripted synchronicity. His touch became a Ferris wheel of caresses and demands, pushing me onto the bed again.

Splaying my hips, he stepped between my spread legs. The moment I rested on my back, he ripped at my knickers, yanking them down my legs. The garter belt fastenings pinged away, relinquishing the pantyhose and leaving me bare.

I couldn't breathe. I could barely stay within the boundaries of my skin as Jethro slammed to his knees and yanked me closer to his mouth.

His breath seduced me first, breezing over my clit, followed by filthy, delectable words. "I have no doubt we'll fight and make-up. We'll spend every day sharing a different experience, but this...this is the best part of today." His fingers danced over my entrance, teasing me with distraction. "I'm going to eat you, Needle. I'm going to lick and fuck you with my tongue before I fuck you as my wife."

His fingertips flew to my pantyhosed thighs, holding me down. "You're the sunbeam to my black diamond..."

My heart billowed at the poetic confession. "Jet—"

My hands dove into his hair, looping through the strands. He lived in my heartbeat, my breath, my thoughts. And now, he lived in my soul because we'd traded one for the other with our vows.

His tongue touched me first, a tentative lick—followed by the wet heat of his mouth. I bucked, my fingers clutching his hair for an anchor. Dizziness took me hostage; I didn't know if it was vertigo or Jethro's mastery.

He kissed my clit, moving to my entrance with a pointed tongue. The first quest inside me wrenched a moan from my chest. A very loud moan.

I craved more, more, *more*.

Tugging on his hair, I arched my hips, demanding what I needed.

Jethro chuckled, turning my world topsy turvy. "Not enough for you, greedy wife?"

His head ducked, his tongue pushing inside me... *deep* inside.

"Oh, God." My entire body contracted, begging for everything he wanted to give. The first ripple of an orgasm made me gasp. Yes. *Yes, yes, yes*.

"No, not yet." Jethro stopped, ending the ladder of bliss.

I growled, pushing my cheek into the bedding. "Tease."

He blew on my pussy, drying his saliva and activating a whole other world of enslavement.

"I don't want you coming. Not until you're screaming."

My eyes met his. "I'll scream. I'll do whatever you want."

He grinned. "I'll remember that next time you're arguing with me over some mundane thing."

"Our life will never be mundane."

His gaze clouded a little. "You're right. You've shackled yourself to a VEP."

Smiling, I stroked his bristled cheek. "Wrong, I shackled myself with a diamond heir who I share six-hundred-years of history with. That alone means our future will never be drab."

His head tilted in my hold, his glistening lips pressing against my palm. "You're right."

Tearing his face from my touch, his mouth landed back on my pussy.

"Let's start rewriting history right now."

His tongue dived back inside me, tearing away comprehension.

I writhed as the promise of a release built quickly and sharp. A violent crackle of lust doused my system as his tongue thrust so deep, I convulsed on the covers.

Gone was the patience of making me wait. Gone were the threats of wanting to make me scream. It was no longer a threat but a promise.

He would make me scream—with or without my permission.

A release, as well as the sharpest cry, percolated in my heart like bubbling champagne ready to escape the bottle of my body.

"Will you scream?"

His tongue penetrated again, destroying every last wall and filling up every remaining crevice inside me. I became whole as his groans vibrated against my slippery flesh, the physicality of sex turning into an emotional reward the longer he licked.

Pleasure built and built and *built* as his rhythmic sucking destroyed me.

"Scream, Nila." Two fingers suddenly replaced his tongue, spearing deep, tearing my orgasm from eager into existence.

I had no choice.

I came.

And came.

And *came*.

Two fingers became three, twisting me open, dragging far more pleasure than I thought possible.

I rocked and thrashed and screamed.

I screamed for Jethro. For our future. For every day of our lives unwritten.

"Fuck." Jethro's five o'clock shadow sandpapered my inner thighs as he granted me such a delicious release. "Again."

Every inch of me burned and tingled. "There's no way."

Jethro took my denial as a challenge. "There is a way." He blew hot air over my swollen pussy. The warm breeze did nothing to temper raw and throbbing nerves.

My legs trembled to close. I wanted to rest. I *needed* to rest.

The tip of his tongue licked my folds, granting tenderness after a feral finishing. "You will come again. You'll come as many times as I command. After all, tonight is our wedding night, and I love watching you come apart. I love knowing I bring you pleasure. I love hearing you pant and moan. I love the way your cunt clutches my fingers as if afraid I'd ever leave you."

His three fingers slowly moved in and out of me, spreading my wetness, forcing my body to spindle into another climb.

He didn't rush me this time, taking every second and stretching them until my satedness gave way to hunger. The steady gathering made me breathless, my body tightening and quickening under his erotic conducting.

"Come for me."

My toes curled as he increased his pressure, but I wanted something more.

"I can't…I need—"

"What do you need?"

I rocked my hips, giving myself over to the creature he'd made me. "I need your cock. I need you riding me. I need to feel you claim me completely."

His teeth nipped my clit, a rumbling growl spilling from his mouth.

"I need you to come with me, Kite."

In an effortless move, he leapt from knees to feet. His cock was a javelin, proud and hard, while his slacks hung precariously on his hips.

His face set into a sexual scowl; his eyes demonic with need as his fingers grabbed my arse and arched my spine. His features set into stone, skin lashed over bone far too handsome for my heart. His golden eyes glowed with grey shadows, dilating with the need to break all boundaries, embrace every want and no longer limit himself with control.

He'd made me come. He'd ensured my body would accept his size with no hardship. He wouldn't hold back.

I didn't *want* him to hold back.

My mind segmented. Part of me paid attention to this incredible man about to fuck me and part turned animalistic. Spreading my legs, I welcomed him closer.

The bed jerked as his knees hit the edge. I went to scoot higher so he could climb on, but he stopped me, yanking my hips upward.

"No. Like this."

With gritted teeth, Jethro bent his knees, and in a seamless move, the tip of his cock found my drenched entrance.

My gaze riveted to his fully clothed body. The sheers of my pantyhose wrapped around his hips, the crumpled silk of his white shirt and the diamond pin glinting on his blazer.

Our eyes locked as he slipped inside me.

My mouth fell open as his immense length hit the top of me and stretched me wider than any finger.

I shivered; goosebumps sprouting as he sheathed himself balls deep. So possessing, he stole any remembrance of who I was.

Staring into his eyes, I knew he would take me hard and fast. My fingers clutched the sheets, preparing myself for how he would use me.

When he didn't move, I licked my lips, rocking my hips a little.

His head fell back, the tendons in his neck stark and tense. "Christ…"

"Fuck me, Kite." I moved again, enticing him to take. "I want you to fuck me."

Anticipation hovered like a curtain waiting to be shredded.

Temper swelled and I wrapped my legs tighter around his hips. "Fuck me, Jethro. Fuck me. Please, fuck—"

He didn't let me finish. Pulling out, he slammed back inside, penetrating in one fierce thrust.

I gasped as shooting stars arched out from where we joined. The connection was far too intense. Far too deep and demanding. He was so big, so hard, so *so* deep.

He'd taken me with everything. Nothing bared. I'd never felt him so open, so completely controlled but treasured at the same time.

Jethro's domination of my heart and body exploded my desire until I begged for another release. I needed another orgasm, and I needed it while we were both raw and wounded by love.

I clenched around him, proud and smug at having him inside me. He'd taken me, but I'd taken him. I held him in my body. I was his home.

His fingers switched to hands, holding my hips as he thrust again. And again. His strokes stretched nerve endings until the fluttering wings of another release begged to form.

His entire body hardened, his arms trembling, his suit whispering with every thrust.

Pulling out to the very tip, he rammed hard inside me. Over and over. Sweat decorated his forehead from being fully dressed as he let euphoria claim him.

His groan was primitive and so low; it slipped into my chest, wrapping around my heart. "Christ, you feel so incredible."

His hold tightened as his thrusts turned to fucking. The bed moved with his knees and my breasts bounced from his furious claiming. Every hot drive nailed me to the bed as he fell over me—turning from standing to squashing.

Having his body blanket mine, having his cock scatter my thoughts, turned me molten.

Pleasure rippled through me again and again. Keeping time with his fucking, pushing us up and up.

I gave myself over to ecstasy.

Harder.

Harder.

Long, invasive strokes.

Every second I came undone, losing my sense of self.

Burying his face in my neck, Jethro held me so tightly, he almost stopped my breathing. Our torsos glued together, but our bottom half worked harder, faster. We fucked each other to heaven.

"I've never been so hard." His lips found mine, his tongue driving into my mouth. "Never been so fucking deep."

He pounded into me, never breaking his pace.

I mewled and begged and said things I would never remember.

I was helpless.

I was powerful.

I was desperate.

I was sated.

My orgasm switched into a storm, drenching me with raindrops, turning me into a river.

Holding my hair, his thrusting turned vicious. The crown of his cock stroked my inner walls, stretching my ache, coaxing my orgasm to teeter on the final pinnacle.

"Come, Nila." His teeth captured my bottom lip as he groaned long and low. His own orgasm started slow, thrusting inside me with calculated possession.

His back arched; the base of his cock rubbed my clit perfectly.

The first splash of his cum set me off.

I climaxed in one quick unravelling, wave after wave, milking him as he came. The release magnified as Jethro kept fucking, kept claiming.

His arms suffocated me, his body pinning me as his hips continued to pump until he spent every drop of his desire.

Minutes and heartbeats became uncountable as we lay there, hot and sticky but more in love than ever. His lips whispered over my jaw to my ear. "I married a goddess."

I chuckled. "No, you married a Weaver."

He nipped my lobe. "And now she's a Hawk." The flash of his grin stopped my heart, then like a defibrillator, restarted it in this new world he'd given me.

Rolling onto his side, we both winced as his cock slipped out, lying spent on his lower belly. Following him, I rested my head on his chest, letting the heavy *thud-thud* of his heartbeat rearrange my own.

My arms and legs quivered with residual pleasure, melting me boneless onto him. "Did we really just consummate our marriage?"

Jethro's arm banded around me. A kiss landed on the top of my head. "I think fucking each other close to death is more the correct term."

Raising my eyes, I smiled. "Well, your destiny was always to kill me. If you do it by orgasm, I won't complain."

His eyes narrowed, filling with past debts and things I no longer wanted to think about. The love he held for me couldn't be denied as he gently kissed my lips. "My destiny might've been to kill you, but I've rewritten fate. Now, I'm going to do everything in my power to make you immortal."

My heart skipped at the passionate vow in his tone. "How will you do that?"

He nudged my nose with his. "By turning our duo into a family.

"By making you a mother."

Six Weeks Later

MARRIAGE WAS BETTER than any other gift, wealth, estate, or luck combined.

Being married to Nila made my life, my very fucking world, complete.

The past six weeks had been a chaotic mess of building new goals, guiding our dreams forward, and slipping into new patterns of normalcy.

Tex had found Jacqueline.

Nila and Vaughn had stared at the photo of their sister for days before deciding to set up a meeting.

They'd all agreed to meet somewhere neutral. A restaurant two weeks from now.

I feared how fraught everyone's emotions would be that night, but I would be beside her every step.

Not a day went by where I wasn't fucking awed by Nila. She handled her sister's reappearance, her new world, and my need for her emotional comfort with ease. She guarded my condition when we were out in public. She knew exactly how to treat me so I felt loved but not mothered.

And she let me do everything she did for me in return. She allowed me to provide a home for her, deliver gifts in both physical and emotional capacity.

Together, we'd found a new happiness, and I lived in its bubble every second of every day.

After our wedding and honeymoon in Santorini, Nila had returned to her craft with passion. She sewed late into the night while I completed ledgers and created new loyalties. We would often work side by side, sometimes in the Weaver quarters where all her fabric, supplies, and mess still lived; sometimes in the front parlour where I liked to drink up the sunshine, and sometimes in bed. A lazy afternoon where we stayed hunkered in warm covers and did the bare minimum of adult responsibilities so we could play beneath the sheets for the rest of the day.

And today, all that hard work had come to fruition.

My heart burst as roses spewed from all around us, kissing our feet.

Nila clung to my forearm, breathing hard, combating any vertigo spell she might endure.

I'd done my best to find a cure for her. I'd scoured website after website, consulted doctor after doctor. Some said it was an iron deficiency, so I stocked her up on vitamins and minerals. Some said the brain would eventually cease granting dizzy spells as it grew to equalize. However, seeing as she'd had it all her life, I didn't see that happening.

The best solution I'd found so far were a series of exercises called the Canalith technique. It helped, but hadn't fixed her.

But we had time, and I wouldn't stop trying.

For now, I would be her anchor, holding her close in a sea of tilting worlds.

"They adore you, Needle."

Her face met mine, painted with camera flashes. "They adore the collection. Not me."

I shook my head, looking over the carpet of journalists, photographers, and celebrities.

Fashionistas and reporters from all over the world had come to witness Nila's Rainbow Diamond Collection. The collection she'd started when she'd stood naked on Hawksridge lawn about to run for her life through the forest.

She'd told me being naked that day and wearing only diamonds had given her the strength to run. It'd also been the inspiration to create her best showpieces and couture designs yet. Her brand, *Nila*, graced not just the high fashion world but shops and local department stores, too.

I'm so fucking proud of her.

Tonight, she hadn't shared the limelight with any boutique or label. The entire two-hour production had been piece after piece she'd created at Hawksridge and a few pieces she'd saved from Bonnie's wardrobe made courtesy of Emma and her ancestors. Those vintage pieces were heralded as a fashion comeback and the words 'Victorian lace' and 'crinoline skirts' wafted on the warm air inside the theatre.

"You did it. Be proud." I nuzzled into her neck. My teeth ached to bite, but I restrained myself. Tonight. Tonight, I would bite her and show her just how fucking proud I was.

"I couldn't have done it without you." She leaned into my embrace, bringing her scent of vanilla and orchid perfume.

"That's not true, but thank you all the same." I kissed her ear, careful not to disrupt the intricate up-do Jasmine had helped her with. The past few weeks had flown by and the shorter cut I'd given her in the stables had grown, thick and glossy—the perfect length to fist while her mouth fitted around my cock.

I hardened, remembering her swirling tongue last night.

We'd arrived two days ago in Milan—in the very same theatre where I'd stolen her all those months ago.

Time had its own strange irony.

I'd ended her life in this place.

And yet she'd come back to life here, too.

A year ago, I'd come to steal her from the limelight and prevent anyone from enjoying her creations. Now, I shared her with those who valued her skills and fought each other for the prestige of wearing her art.

All around us stood the models from tonight's show. The Rainbow Diamond collection truly was spectacular. Pastels, pinks, purples, teals, yellows—an array of fabrics Nila had educated me on and cuts and gathers and fancy needlepoint she'd explained every time she worked.

Standing beside her, I couldn't for the life of me remember a single stitch's name. All I could remember was how much I loved her and how stunning she was in a gown made of bewitching smoke.

Obviously, it wasn't smoke but silk and tulle and any number of materials she forced me to recall. But the panels of midnight down her tiny waist and the glitter of black beads down the front made her the crown of the show, the black diamond of her empire.

Every time she swished in front of me, I wanted to throw my tuxedo jacket over her shoulders to hide the scrumptious line of her spine and the swell of her arse below.

I appreciated the skill and design of the dress, but I didn't appreciate the way men gawked at my wife.

One of the boutique shops that'd already bid at auction and won Nila's new collection climbed on the stage and presented her with a bouquet of white roses. The dark-skinned man kissed her cheek, smiled at me, and faced the audience to reinvigorate the clapping.

For once, I didn't mind being in a crowd this size. Not because Nila was beside me and I'd become accustomed to tuning into her thoughts when in a gathering such as this, but because everyone had one focus: impressed awe.

Nila waved at the cameras, bowed—hiding the little wobble by digging her fingernails into my cuff—and turned to leave.

Not so fast.

I held her a second longer. I wanted to bask in the moment. I wanted to absorb every thought and feeling because tonight was special for Nila but special for me, too.

Tonight was my thirtieth birthday.

I'd made it.

Nila wasn't beheaded, her body wasn't rotting on the moor with her ancestors, and I wasn't dead at the hands of my father.

We'd turned evil into benevolence and lived a life worthy of deserving.

"Come on, it's time to go." She tugged on my hold, swaying in her stupidly high heels.

I cupped her elbow, turning her to face me. Unfortunately for her, she couldn't keep surprises and I knew tonight she'd already planned a birthday party for me. I didn't know where or what it would entail but I felt her excitement at surprising me and her enjoyment at celebrating such a huge milestone. A milestone we both feared would never come to pass.

However, there was something else, too.

Something she guarded and protected. Something that meant a great fucking deal to her and she hadn't told me.

For the past couple of weeks, I thought it was the collection. The fact she'd finished the entire wardrobe of twenty three dresses and other apparel was a huge feat.

But now...now, I knew it wasn't that because the secret still glowed bright inside her.

Nila looked once more at freedom, sensing my determination to make her tell me. I hadn't meant to trap her on the runway and force her to spill in front of the world of fashion. But where else was she the most vulnerable?

I held her up. I kept her imbalance at bay. The least she could do was—

"I have a secret and I can't keep it any longer." Nila sighed, fighting a smile. Camera flashes continued to go off along with the stray rose thrown as the models paraded one last time behind us.

I let out a breath. *About bloody time*. "I thought as much." Bending my knees, I stared directly into her eyes. "You've done a good job at hiding it from me."

I froze as she raised her hand, brushing aside my salt and pepper hair, showing the world the utmost affection between us. We were private in that respect. After the *Vanity Fair* article at our wedding, we avoided all mention and interviews.

I sucked in a breath as she cupped my neck, bringing me closer. "You haven't been able to guess?"

I shook my head, my hair mixing with hers. "No." I let myself dive deeper into her thoughts, searching for the answer to her hoarded truth. Her emotions were murky, mixed with bone-deep contentment and a sense of quiet achievement for all that she'd done tonight.

She swayed a little in my arms. "Is this truly the first time you can't guess? You don't know what I'm about to say?" Her lips pursed. "Because I already know you figured out my surprise about your birthday party tonight."

I laughed. My body relaxed, melting into her the more we spoke. I forgot where we were. I ignored the thousand other thoughts and human psyches. It was just us. Needle and me.

My wife.

"Instead of teasing, how about you put me out of my misery?"

Her eyes glittered, mimicking the diamonds around her throat. "I rather like having a secret for once. I think I might enjoy it a little longer."

I growled, wrapping my arm around her waist. The rustle of her skirts sounded loud over the murmur of the audience. "Tell me…. Otherwise, I'll have to use more forceful means the moment we're in private."

She licked her lips. "Promise?"

I rolled my eyes. "You're really going to drive me mad, huh? Fine, the moment I've blown out those bloody candles on whatever cake you bought—"

"I'm pregnant."

My mouth fell open.

Everything paused.

I couldn't move, speak, think.

Pregnant?

Fuck, she's…pregnant.

My mind scrambled, trying to make sense of the word. My heart bucked, squeezing every drop of oxygen from my lungs.

Nila chuckled at my lack of intellect. Her fingers looped with mine, pressing against her belly. "Pregnant, Kite. As in…I'm going to have your child."

My legs gave out.

I crashed to my knees on the stage in front of thousands of fucking people.

Tears shot to my eyes as I stared at her flat belly. The skirts and petticoats of her smoky gown hid any flutter or growth, but my heart sprang with knowledge. "You're—you're…" I couldn't finish.

The crowd went silent as I wrapped my arms around her legs and hugged her close. I kissed her stomach. I swore on everything I owned that I'd do whatever it took to be worthy of this new gift.

Pregnant.

She's pregnant.

I glanced up, drinking in her glowing face. "Ho—how?"

She curved over me, her eyes darting between me at her feet and the crowd. "Get up, they're all watching."

"I don't care. They can see what true love looks like. I'm not ashamed to worship you, especially after you tell me something as life changing as this." Pulling her down to me, she kneeled in her dress, eye to eye.

"How? I thought—"

She shook her head, smiling wide. "The contraceptive you gave me before the Third Debt wore off months ago. I meant to tell you I wasn't on birth control, but then I thought...we have everything we could ever need. We won over seemingly impossible odds. Why wait? We're young but wise. We've proven we know what's right and wrong."

Her hand cupped my cheek, shaking a little but so damn strong. "I want to have your children, Jethro. I hope you don't mind I made the decision for both of us."

"Mind? Why the fuck would I mind?" I crushed her to me, crumpling her feathers and rhinestones, messing up her elaborate hair with kisses. "This—it's more than I could ever ask for." Cupping her face, I kissed her deep.

I poured my heart and thankfulness down her throat. "How—how long?"

She sighed, holding onto my wrists. "I'm not sure. A few weeks...possibly a month or so."

A stupid grin spread my face. "Do you know what it is yet?"

A girl.

Please, let it be a girl. Just like Nila.

A child I didn't have to worry about facing such horrendous debts. A firstborn daughter who would survive and not be made to pay for historic crimes.

She shrugged. "I don't know. But whatever it is, I know you'll love it and me, and we'll fill Hawksridge with the sounds of laughter."

I couldn't stop myself.

Clambering to my feet, I swooped her into my arms. The train of her dress rippled over my arm as I stood in the centre of the stage with so much fucking pride I could fly.

Glaring into the ever-invasive cameras, I announced, "My wife is pregnant."

The theatre erupted into applause.

I didn't care.

All I cared about was getting somewhere private so Nila and I could have our own celebration.

Turning my back on the world, fading out the claps and happy conversations, I kissed my wife. "I love you. I love you so fucking much."

Nila laid her head on my heart, making me wondrously complete. "I know."

Three Years Later...

"GOOD NIGHT, GOOD NIGHT, DON'T let the bed bugs bite."

The squeal echoed merrily around the room as Jethro blew raspberries on the belly of our child. Our firstborn. Part Weaver, part Hawk.

The past few years had gone by so fast. We became a true family—working together, loving together, learning and evolving and laughing.

My pregnancy had been easy. Thanks to my fitness from running, I remained supple and able to work until the day I delivered. Jethro would often find me in the Weaver quarters, sewing and sketching with my belly ballooning as the days stretched on.

He never told me to stop. He supported whatever I wanted to do. He held my hand when I walked the estate and commandeered the kitchen at all hours to concoct my ridiculous cravings.

He absolutely doted on me, and I fell deeper into love with him. I hadn't known there were so many layers to love. Sweet and sparkling then lusty and desiring, evolving into bone-deep and endless as the years slipped by. And the longer we lived together, the more we became soul-mates in every sense of the word.

He knew my thoughts without me verbalising.

I knew his concerns without him having to speak. We became in-tune with body language and heart-code...listening with more than just ears.

The further I progressed in my pregnancy, the more my father visited. His fear for my health grew until I resembled a blimp, soothing the scars of our past. He begged for the right to help decorate the nursery and almost singlehandedly bought London out of every nappy, cuddly toy, and cute baby clothes.

My twin was less impressed. He ribbed me constantly of the weight I'd gained—taunting me like a brother was allowed. On the nights he came to visit, he'd pat his washboard stomach and poke my humongous one, laughing good-naturedly. He even joked he'd buy me a few lessons with a personal trainer once I'd popped to get back into shape.

Jethro had not been happy. His eyes flashed with jealousy as Vaughn played up the angle of some beefed-up jock helping me stretch and train.

The night had ended with drinks for the boys and giggles for me.

I'd never been so contented.

And the day I'd given birth had once again changed my life. I'd been terrified—not that I told Jethro. My heart bucked and the fear of dying in labour stole all enjoyment of bringing life into the world.

But Jethro had been my prince, keeping me anchored, rubbing my back when vertigo struck and driving me calmly to the private hospital we'd arranged for the delivery.

The birth hadn't gone perfectly. I'd been in labour for twenty-four hours. The baby had turned the night before and faced the wrong way. An emergency caesarean had to take place after Jethro roared for the doctors to take away my pain.

For every one of my contractions, Jethro felt it. He sweated beside me. He trembled in sympathy. He almost threw up when the agony threatened to rip me apart.

But when the first screams of our child shredded the operating theatre, Jethro had slammed to his knees. His shoulders quaked in silent sobs as he let himself feel another conscience for the first time.

Not mine.

Not the doctors and nurses.

Our baby.

His.

Our son.

The moment the doctor cleaned up the newborn and swaddled him in Jethro's arms, he'd irrevocably changed. He became more than lord and master of Hawksridge. He became more than lover and friend.

He became a father. A protector. A single piece in a jigsaw of never-ending history. The look on his face when he stared into the eyes of his heir fisted my heart until I couldn't breathe.

It'd been the singular most awe-inspiring moment of my life.

And I'd done it to him.

We'd done it together.

We'd created the squalling new life wriggling in his embrace.

He'd found his peace.

His centre.

Our son cooed as I brushed his bronze-black curls off his cherub cheeks. To begin with, I'd been terrified of making a mistake—of being the worst mother imaginable. But once I returned home to the Hall, the cooks and cleaners all came to welcome their new inhabitant; granting snippets of their own experiences, and filling me with courage I could do this. I could raise this little person. I could teach him how to be moral and kind and wise. I'd been able to break the Debt Inheritance. I could raise a baby boy, no problem.

Jethro touched my hand from the other side of the cot, looping his pinkie with mine. Our son wriggled in his bed, grabbing our joint fingers and squeezing them tight.

My heart glowed as Jethro strained across the crib, kissing me softly. "I love what we've created."

I smiled. "I'm rather glad about that."

The chubby fingers around ours pinched, demanding more attention.

"Okay, okay, demanding little thing." Jethro let me go, bending over to kiss his son one last time. "It's time to go to bed."

"No!"

"Yes."

The little boy shook his head, loving his favourite game.

I stood quietly, watching son and father interact. The name we'd chosen couldn't be more apt.

Kestrel.

Kestrel 'William' Hawk after Jethro's original ancestor and closest brother.

Jethro sighed dramatically. "If you don't go to sleep, you won't get to enjoy tomorrow."

"Yes. Tomarrooww."

I smothered my chuckle. Kes was beyond intelligent for his age. He'd learned to talk far earlier than normal, but his little accent cracked me up.

"No, if you don't go to sleep, there is no tomorrow." Jethro grinned, blowing another raspberry on Kes's neck. "Know why?"

Kes frowned as if the question was incredibly important. "No."

"Because if you don't sleep, tomorrow can't come because you're still in today. That's why we sleep, Kes. So today can pass and our dreams can conjure a new beginning. You don't want to ruin that tradition, do you?" Tucking the sheets tighter around him, he smiled. "After all, Mummy and I will be in the future, living tomorrow while you're stuck in the past living today. We're going to go to sleep. That means you should, too."

Kes suddenly froze, his inherited golden eyes latching onto me. "True?"

"Very true." Pressing the button of his nose, I murmured, "Go to sleep, little one, so we can have a good day. We'll go riding. Would you like that?"

He yawned wide, finally letting tiredness take him.

"Good boy." Removing my hand from the cot, I moved quietly toward the door. Jethro remained, bending to give Kes another kiss. Patting his son's tiny chest, he checked the nightlight was secure and the baby monitor switched on and synced to his phone.

The little boy who looked exactly like his namesake with cheeky golden eyes and floppy dark bronze hair snuggled in his covers, already falling into dreams as his father sneaked across the room to me.

"You do know he manipulates us to drag out as many minutes before bedtime as possible, right?"

I laughed quietly; stepping into the corridor of our wing, I left the door open a crack. "Did you sense that or just parenting 101?"

His arm snaked around my waist. "A bit of both. If we're not careful, he'll have us completely wrapped around his little finger."

"Eh, I think that's already happened."

Leaving the nursery, we padded down the corridor of the bachelor wing. Not that it was the bachelor wing anymore. We'd transformed many of the rooms into playrooms, media rooms, and revamped the bedroom with soft whites and greys rather than overbearing brocade and maroon leather.

It'd been the only part of the house we'd renovated and removed the symbolism of Hawks on plasterwork and architraving. The rest of Hawksridge was a monument to architecture and history. It wouldn't be right to tear apart something so rich and detailed.

The thought of heading to bed to do more than sleep crossed my mind.

After Kestrel's birth, I'd returned to running. It wasn't a chore. I ran for freedom, for peace. I ran because it was something I enjoyed. The baby weight came off, and I returned to designing gowns for my figure. The caesarean scar was just another mark on my body proving I'd lived a life and won. But unlike the many others scars I'd earned fighting an age-old debt, this one I wore proudly because it'd been given to me by the greatest gift I could imagine.

And soon, I would have another gift.

I had another secret.

A secret I'd managed to keep far longer than the first. Sneakily hiding my growing bump with excuses and masquerades. I'd kept my surprise hidden for two reasons. One, I wanted to see how long it would take Jethro to sense my news. I constantly expected him to suddenly drop the dishes or stop doing paperwork and announce what grew in my belly.

But ever since Kes had come into our lives, his condition had mellowed. He now had two of us who loved him unconditionally and didn't walk a razor blade of hypersensitivity—he didn't need to. All he needed to focus on was happy thoughts and contentment.

Before Kes was born, I'd catch him having a stressful day and try to soothe his condition by giving all the love I could share. I'd grant him sanctuary in our connection and hold him as long as he needed. Being in crowds was still too much for him. Dealing with company travel didn't often happen as his need for silence hadn't diminished.

At the start of our relationship, when he'd told me how much he would drain me, how much he would rely on my love for him, I hadn't fully understood the ramifications of what I'd agreed to.

But now I did and it was the least I could do.

He'd given me so much. On a daily basis, he gave me more of himself than I could ever ask for, and to be able to help cure him after a long day dealing with people granted me power and connection.

But our son.

Well…he was the true cure.

Jethro only had to hug Kes and the stress in his eyes would melt. The strain in his spine would vanish, and the need for simplistic silence came from holding the two-year-old in the tightest embrace.

Two years.

I couldn't believe we'd had Kestrel Hawk II in our lives for two years.

My mind returned to my secret, subtly stroking the growing bump.

The other reason why I'd kept it from him was I wanted the moment to be special. I wanted to whisper in his ear and give him a treasured present after he'd given me so much.

Spinning my black diamond engagement ring, I remembered Kes's first week at the Hall. Jethro had disappeared for a day, telling me to rest and all would be revealed upon his return.

I couldn't believe it when he returned with a foal.

Tears had spilled as he clutched the halter of such a delicate little pony and pranced him proudly through the Hall to Kestrel's nursery.

There, the adorable dapple grey colt stuck his nose through the bars of the cot, snuffling at the baby, building the first stone of an unshakable bond between horse and rider.

We'd agreed to call the foal Gus—labelling the colt with yet another name from the man who watched over us. It wasn't for a few weeks until I found out the origins of where Gus had been sourced.

Jethro had returned to the breeder who'd given his brother Moth—creating yet another circle of fate, buying pedigree from excellent stock.

My heart overflowed; I came to stop in the corridor.

Jethro raised his eyebrow. "You okay?"

"I want to tell you something."

He paused, his nostrils flaring. "Tell me what?"

"Not here. I want to go somewhere special. Just the two of us."

He frowned. "You're scaring me. Tell me." His hands latched around my hips walking me backward to the wall. Pressing me against the fancy tapestries, his mouth latched on my throat. "Don't make me torture you to learn what you're hiding, wife."

I melted as his tongue and hot wetness of his mouth sent needful flurries through my core. "Perhaps a swim? I could tell you in the hot springs?" My mind filled with happy moments, splashing with Kes in the hot water and making slow love to Jethro once our son was in bed. The springs beneath Hawksridge had become a regular part of our lives. And I happened to know Jasmine took Vaughn down there a number of times to not only ease her atrophied muscles but also to indulge in…other things.

His lips kissed their way over my neck to my mouth. Tilting his hips, a rapidly hardening erection nudged my lower belly.

I moaned, accepting his invite.

His breathing quickened as his tongue danced with mine. Kissing me slowly, savagely, sweetly. The Hall swam, and my leg itched to hook over his thigh, hitch up my skirt, and welcome his body into mine.

Planting his hand by my head, he held himself over me. His voice trembled with lust. "I won't let you distract me. I want to know what you're hiding, and if you want it to be somewhere special…I have a better idea."

"Oh?"

Pushing off from the wall, he took my hand. "Yes. You want somewhere priceless. Let's go for a walk on the grounds. The very land we own and safeguard for our son. That's the most special I can think of."

I couldn't agree more.

Our fingers linked as we moved through the house, nodding at Black Diamond brothers and waving at Flaw as we crossed the foyer. It wasn't late, about nine p.m., but the summer sky teased with dusk. The sun had gone, cooling the outside temperature, but my ankle-length skirt and gypsy blouse would keep me warm enough for a small excursion.

Our footsteps disturbed gravel and leaves as we left the Hall and meandered down the driveway.

Passing the orchard, my mouth watered remembering the juicy fruit we'd picked the day before. Jasmine did her best to teach me how to have a green thumb like her, but I wasn't interested; not when I had baby clothes to sew.

It hadn't escaped my notice the way Jasmine held little Kes. She wanted one. We'd had a late-night conversation once about her getting pregnant with Vaughn.

For a long time—too long—she hadn't let Vaughn touch her. She couldn't get over her fear that someone could love her, no matter how stupid such a notion was. They'd been together for over two years, and she'd confided it took her almost a year just to allow him to sleep with her.

"Where are you taking me?" I asked as we left the driveway and cut into the woods. Together, we followed the path where we'd been for a run, skirting past the graves of my ancestors.

My heart clenched, recalling the day we'd tended to the awful moor and made it a better resting place. After discussing the graves with my father and brother, we all decided to leave them where they were buried. However, we re-blessed the ground, had new tombstones engraved, and ensured the hilltop only held good manifestations rather than ill will.

It was fitting that both Weavers and Hawks were buried on the estate and had followed through with legalities for a personal graveyard permit, so we were fully within the law. I didn't visit often, but had no intention of hiding any of our history from our children when the time came.

Including Jacqueline.

I'd begun to tell her about our shared lineage but hadn't gotten very far. We'd met five times over the past two years.

To begin with it was awkward and confusing to stare at a stranger who'd shared a womb and birthday. But slowly, we turned from polite acquaintances to pleasant friends. We had plans to take Kes to see her next month up in Cornwall.

She didn't have children of her own and had only just married her long term partner, Joseph. She was my sister...but it would take time to become family.

"Somewhere special." Jethro smiled in the dark. "I thought we'd walk off dinner...that okay?"

"Of course, more than okay." My mind raced with how to tell him the news.

A snuffling sound came from the undergrowth. I froze, peering into the bush, searching for a hedgehog or badger.

Squirrel came bounding out of the undergrowth, weaving around Jethro's legs.

"Bolly, what the hell are you doing out of the kennels?" Jethro scowled. "How the devil did he get out?"

I grinned, dropping to my haunches to hug the dog. He'd adopted me on my first night at Hawksridge and was still my favourite of the foxhounds. Jethro no longer hunted, but every now and again, we would gallop across the estate with the baying dogs at our heels.

The dog yipped, coming to lick my hand. "He can come with us."

"We'll take him back to the stables afterward." Jethro snapped his fingers. The hound heeled obediently.

Silence fell as Jethro and I moved further into the woods. The moon only illuminated so much, but our eyes adjusted. Following an animal path, we popped out in a little clearing where a few ferns and foxglove bowed in sleep.

I turned to Jethro to tell him my news, but his mouth landed on mine, hushing everything I wanted to say.

"Would you play a game with me, Mrs. Hawk?"

I grinned, his skin silver in the moonlight. "A game? What sort of game?"

His teeth nipped their way to my ear. "A game to replace bad memories with good."

We'd done that with every debt. The octagonal greenhouse had become a favourite place for kinky sex and the lake shed its stigma of the ducking stool and became a prized picnic spot. We'd rechristened Hawksridge Hall with so many happy memories over the past few years.

My heart raced. "You have me intrigued. Go on."

He chuckled. "Remember that first day? When you ran for your life to the boundary? I told you to run. That I would chase you. And when I found you…you gave me the best fucking blow-job of my life."

I shivered. "I remember."

"I want to chase you again, Nila."

My eyes widened at the naughty, delicious thought of what he would do to me when he caught me. "Naked or dressed?"

His eyes flashed. "Run while you're dressed. It won't stop me from claiming what's mine when I catch you."

I panted, backing away from his arms. Already breathless, I had no idea if I'd be able to run very far. Not that I wanted to. But the sheer thrill of running from the man I loved, knowing what he would do when he stopped me, sent my blood racing. "How much head start do I get?"

"A few minutes." He bent and grabbed Squirrel by the scruff. "I'll have my friend here to help me. Just like I did that day." His lips twisted into a sexy smirk. "I suggest you run fast, Needle. Otherwise, I'll have you on the ground and my cock between your legs before you've gone a few metres."

Swiping my hair into a ponytail, I secured it with an elastic. "Okay." My nipples ached, and I grew shamefully wet. Walking backward, I smiled coyly. "Bet I get farther than you think."

"I suggest you stop taunting me and start running…"

"Let's see who will win." Pirouetting, I took off. My ballet flats flew, hurtling me away from Jethro.

The intoxication of being able to play and laugh bubbled in my blood. The moment he caught me, he'd take me. And once he'd claimed what was rightfully his—what would *always* be his—I'd tell him my news.

Leaping over a fallen log, I darted through the undergrowth, not caring I crunched twigs or crashed through large leaves. He would find me. And I wanted him to.

True to his word, he gave me a few minutes head start before Squirrel's howl sounded on the night sky, signalling his chase.

I ducked and parried around trees and roots, doing my best to get far. But instead of fear, I sparked with laughter and love.

"Are you running? Because I'm chasing." Jethro's baritone whipped through bracken.

I ran faster, my hair tie coming loose and ebony strands cascading down my back as I tore through a small everglade and into dense woodland.

I hoped I'd get farther. But Squirrel found me first.

His paws thundered behind me, reminding me he'd ruined my hiding place up the tree that fateful day. Puffing, I ruffled the dog as he ran beside me. His tongue lolling and black eyes bright with excitement. "Even when you were being a traitor, you had my back, didn't you?"

Squirrel yipped. I'd never get used to calling him Bolly. That wasn't his name—not with the bristly tail he had.

Breathing hard, I entered another small clearing. This one had a few saplings straining for the sky. I went to dash forward, but a hand lassoed around my wrist, yanking me back.

"Caught you, little Weaver."

I shivered, my core clenching with need. "Unhand me, Mr. Hawk. Otherwise, I promise I'll make your life a living hell."

"Never." He backed me swiftly against a tree, slamming my wrists above my head and biting his way along my collarbone. "I've wanted to do this all day."

My breath turned into moans as his tongue licked its way down my throat, over my collar, to the dip between my breasts. "Do what?"

"This." Spinning me around, he pressed my front against the tree and bent to gather my summery skirt. My skin goosebumped as the sound of his zipper coming undone sent wetness pooling.

"All day I've stared at you. I grew hard for you while you hugged our son. My mouth watered to lick you as you sipped wine at dinner."

My throat tightened as Jethro's hands skated down my body, following my contours, latching onto my hips.

"You're so fucking perfect."

My back arched in his hold. The hot steel of his erection nudged between my legs. "Open wider, pretty Weaver. I need you, and I need you hard."

I jolted with the thickest, quickest desire I'd ever felt. My feet spread as Jethro tugged my skirt up.

"Jethro…"

"Let me do this."

"I'd let you do anything."

"Christ."

Lifting one foot, I allowed him to yank down my knickers and stepped out of them, moaning as he wedged me against the tree again, thrusting his hips against my arse.

I struggled to get my hands free, reaching behind me to stroke his side. "I need…I need to touch you."

"No, you need to let me fuck you."

"Do it, then. Take me. I'm all yours."

"Shit, Nila." His hands shook as his fingers dug into my skin. "I'm going to take you. Right. Fucking. Now." Grabbing my hips, he slammed inside me.

"Oh, my God." My head shot back as Jethro's large length took possession of everything I was. He wasn't gentle. He wasn't kind. He was a man taking what he wanted.

I had no thought of the gift inside my womb. I had no thoughts at all but him inside me and the feral way we joined.

I'd never felt such bliss or baser desires. We were two animals fucking in the middle of a forest. All alone aside from the moon and stars.

Grabbing my wrists again, he held them above my head as his teeth clamped around my throat. He groaned, thrusting hard, impaling every inch inside me.

"Fuck, I love you." His voice poured more fuel onto the already blazing lust and my core fisted his length, begging for more, fearing how hard he would take me.

"Oh, God, it's so good. You feel…" My eyes snapped closed as he rode me. His pace was furious and brutal, the pleasure sharp and overwhelming. "Don't stop. *Please*, don't stop."

His breath slinked down my spine as he pulled away to fuck me harder. "I have no intention of stopping."

Angling my chin with demanding fingertips, his mouth landed on mine, sucking, slippery. His kiss stole whatever facets of humanity I had left, and I completely gave in to him. I gave myself to the wild wetness of his tongue. I moaned as he made love to my tongue while fucking my body.

His free hand waltzed over every curve, greedy and firm, twisting my nipples, grabbing my entire breast in his hold.

"You love this."

I nodded, gasping around our kiss. "So much."

"You love it when I take you nasty and rough."

"Yes."

"You love it when I take you tender and sweet."

"Yes."

"You love me."

"A thousand times, yes."

I cried out as his cock hit the top of me, heralding an orgasm to spindle and gather. My knees wobbled and the bark of the tree rasped my cheek. But I wouldn't change a thing. Not one goddamn thing.

The rhythmic strokes of his tongue matched the claiming strokes of his cock.

"Feel me, Nila. Feel my cock deep inside you."

My nipples ached as more wetness gushed around his penetration. "I do. I feel every inch."

"Feel how fucking hard I am. How much I fucking love you."

I spread my legs wider, arching my back for more. "Kite..."

"Think how much you love me now, when the last time you ran from me, you hated me."

His voice added another layer to my orgasm. I wanted him so much. I wanted to come, but I didn't want this to stop.

"Think about how much we've overcome to deserve what we have."

I loved him losing himself in me. My soul echoed with his need. My body begged for his release. I felt him everywhere—in the air, the tastes, the sounds, the very heart of me. He was more than man; he was heat and power and forever.

He'd given me a child. He'd saved me from the debts.

He'd made me more than just human. He'd made me immortal. Immortal in his love. Immortal in his passion.

"Fuck, Nila. Whatever you're thinking about. It's driving me to come."

"Then come."

"Not yet."

His pace turned frantic, our breathing mingling in echoing gasps. His hand landed on my nape, holding me in place as he drove harder, faster. We were locked completely in each other's spell—a bombardment of rapture.

"Please," I begged. "More."

"I'll give you more." His fingers shot down my front, landing on my clit.

I moaned as delicious shards of lightning crackled beneath his touch. I was a second away from detonation. A single breath from—

I came.

The lightning turned to a supernova, unspooling with the speed of light, exploding through my chest, heart, and soul. My entire body clenched and rippled, cradling me in euphoria.

"Goddammit." Jethro's forehead landed on my nape and he lost himself completely.

His cock jerked in and out, his stomach hitting my spine with every thrust. His groan cascaded down my back as the first spurt of his release shot inside me.

I didn't move as he filled me, found pleasure in me. I trembled with satisfaction even though I still ached from my orgasm.

The moment his release ended, his hands roamed over my back, massaging kinks, showering me in a perfect blend of gratefulness and submission. He'd taken me dominantly, but he'd given me everything for safekeeping. That was real power. The stuff that came after sex.

He pulled out, breathing hard. The slick trickle of his cum marked my inner thighs.

Twisting in his arms, I smiled at the affection and awe in his eyes. We'd captured a miracle and lived in a fairy-tale.

"Come here." His voice was hoarse and deep. Curling his arms around me, he embraced me with all the love we shared. The sex had been furious, but this was the epitome of tenderness.

My breasts pressed against his chest as my arms looped his waist, deleting all space between us.

We held each other for a long time, regrouping from coming undone so spectacularly.

Pulling away, Jethro's eyes latched onto my mouth. "Thank you." Bowing his head, his lips tickled mine. "Kiss me, Nila."

Those two little words had become my absolute favourite.

I kissed him.

The dance was hot and wet, an erotic fusion of past and present with a lick of unforgettable futures.

Once we felt more human and not as raw and exposed, Jethro let me go. Pulling a handkerchief from his pocket, he gently wiped his pleasure from my thighs and ducked to slip on my knickers.

I held onto his shoulder as he pulled the lace up my hips, hiding my nakedness. Letting my skirt fall back into place, I couldn't tear my eyes from him as he tucked his still hard cock back into his jeans and buckled up.

Squirrel bounded from the undergrowth with perfect timing, almost as if he'd given us privacy. He yipped, wagging his tail as Jethro tossed him a stick to chase.

I smoothed down my clothing. "Now you've just ravaged your wife in the middle of the forest, do you want to know why I wanted to go somewhere special?"

His lips twitched. "Of course, I do—"

He froze, his forehead furrowed. "Oh, my God. You're—you're—"

I rolled my eyes. "Seriously, did your condition steal my secret? After all this time, you guess right before I tell you?" Stamping my foot with mock anger, I growled, "I can't surprise you with anything."

Jethro didn't move. "So you are..."

I beamed. "I am."

He charged forward. His hands—the ones that'd been so sexually demanding and rough now held me as if I was spun glass. "Nila…hell, I can't believe it. What did I ever do to deserve this?"

Holding his cheeks, I kissed him.

I kissed him for every day we'd been together and every day we had coming.

My heart overflowed with joy. "I'm pregnant, Jethro. And this time…it's a girl."

Jasmine

WHAT DO YOU say to a brother who was the cause of so much pain, but also so much happiness? What do you say to a life that gave so much, yet extracted so much in return? What do you say to a dead sibling, a deceased father, a slaughtered mother, a deranged grandmother?

What do you say to life?

Sitting in my favourite spot in the Hall, I smiled as Vaughn slapped Jethro on the back, coming in from checking on matters around the estate. They'd become closer as time went on, each learning different worlds and responsibilities, sharing Weaver and Hawk secrets.

I didn't have the answers to life's questions, and I didn't have the wisdom to use what we'd endured for greater good. All I knew was we'd *survived*. We'd been given a fresh start, a happy future, an unsullied second chance. And I was sick to fucking death of not grasping it completely.

Nila had taught me something. She'd brought Jethro to life and Vaughn had stolen my heart in return.

For a while, I fought it. I ignored his advances and betrayed my desire for him. I didn't believe he truly wanted something so broken. However, day by day, week by week, he'd shown me what a fool I was.

Yes, my legs had been stolen from me. Yes, I hated my loss and some days couldn't shed my self-pity.

But now…now, I was stronger, smarter, and more adult than child. Yes, I couldn't run. Yes, I couldn't stand or dance or skip. But who cared when I could kiss and love and hug and exist? Exist in a far superior world than most, enjoy far more enjoyable experiences than most, and adore far more deeply than most because I knew what it was like to lose.

I was lucky.

So terribly, terribly lucky.

We all were.

Life was far too short. History had taught me that. And Vaughn had given me the strength to be brave and embrace it—hardships and all.

I loved my family—both alive and dead, both evil and kind. I loved my lineage—both revengeful debts and righteous ending. I wasn't ashamed of my bloodline, but I had full intentions to make my future mean something. I wanted to dabble in charities. I wanted to give back what we'd taken. I wanted to make a *difference* with my life.

It was time to embrace every heartbeat because each was numbered, each was accounted for, and each was wasted by being fearful.

I'm no longer fearful.

I was sister to a lord. A powerful mistress in her own right. And matriarch to a six-hundred-year-old estate.

I had the means to make a difference.

I would never take life for granted.

And Hawksridge Hall would guard over all of us...just like it had for centuries.

Five and a half years later...

"HAPPY BIRTHDAY TO you. Happy birthday to you!"

Emma clapped her hands, wriggling in her chair to blow out the candles. "Stop singing! Now. I wanna blow now!"

Clamping hands on her tiny shoulders, I held her squirmy form in place. "So impatient."

Nila smiled, snapping the happy moment with the camera. The same camera Tex bought us for our wedding anniversary last year. At the time, I was grateful but not overly-excited.

In my world, photos and videos had been a reminder of bad things. I'd prefer not to catalogue such recollections. However, that was before I thumbed through a stack of prints Nila had taken of me playing unaware with Kes and the foxhounds one afternoon.

I'd frozen. So sure the man she'd captured was a total stranger. I didn't see the guy in the mirror staring back every day when I shaved. I looked upon a man who knew his place, *loved* his place, and was happy. *Truly* happy.

My heart glowed as my wife clicked and imprisoned special portraits of Emma's fifth birthday. That camera—something so small and simple—had become so precious, capturing irreplaceable memories, colouring moments of treasured time.

In my spare time—not that I had much between running the Hawk empire and raising two demanding children—I dabbled in film exposure. I'd transformed one of the many parlours in the Hall into a dark room. I preferred the old-fashioned way of developing. I got to touch the faces of my children, be the first to witness my wife's stunning smiling lips as the chemicals morphed her from nothing, to black and white, to vibrant colour.

Almost like how she'd brought me to life with her love, breaking me free from my self-imposed prison and granting magical pigment to my world.

Kestrel grabbed the edge of the table, throwing his head back dramatically for the birthday song. "Happy birthday to Velcro Smells. Happy birthday to you!"

I rolled my eyes as Nila bopped him on the head. "Don't call your sister that."

Kes rubbed his tussled hair. "What? She does."

"I do not." Emma stuck her tongue out. "You smell. You stink like, like, like…a *hedgehog*."

Nila bit her lip so she didn't laugh.

I couldn't stop myself. My eyes met Jasmine's, and she burst into giggles. "A hedgehog? What the hell?" My sister looked at my wife. "Where have you been letting them play? I had no idea hedgehogs even had a smell?"

Vaughn bent over, coming back from the kitchen where he'd pilfered a few of last year's brew. This mix wasn't thistle and elderberry like at my father's birthday so many years ago, but lavender and honeysuckle. The liquor was strong, but I doubted I'd ever grow a palate where I would crave it. I preferred the expensive cache of cognac we had in the cellar. Not that I needed alcohol to be happy.

Thanks to Nila and my children, I lived in a state of bliss. Even when Kestrel and Emma were cranky and tangled with childhood emotions, I still basked in their love. I learned how to let my condition have full control of me because I had nothing to fear by soaking up the feelings of my beloved family.

Nila put down the camera and came to stand beside me. Her hand landed on her daughter's fuzzy black hair. Her face tilted toward mine, and we shared a brief kiss. Her eyes shot a silent message. *I'm having you the moment it's appropriate.*

My gaze hooded. *I'm having you regardless of appropriate time or not. The minute this cake is cut, you're mine.*

She sucked in a breath.

Forcing myself to look away and remain tethered to the room full of people, I smiled at the family and friends celebrating Emma's birthday. It drained me—so many people in one space all at once—but the afternoon of medieval games with jousting, dress-up, bouncy castles, and even a re-enacted sword fight had been worth the emotional strain. All day we'd had a child's dream out on the front lawn with water pistols and a petting zoo—combining old-world charm with modern simplicity.

Emma and Kestrel had explored every secret I'd set up for them and my chest warmed with pride to think I'd given them more than a childhood day of fun—I'd given them a happy childhood, and that was immeasurably priceless.

Merged voices rose together, singing the final line of the song. "Happy birthday to you!"

The burly men of the Black Diamonds—the ones vetted, vouched, and commanded by Flaw all clapped and cheered. V hipped and hoorayed, waving his arms and stealing a giggle from Emma while Tex shoved the five candle cake closer toward my daughter.

Five years old.

Fuck, time flies fast.

My heart twinged like it always did on big occasions. Small occasions, too. Every moment when I stopped and took the time to wonder how I got so fucking lucky. In those same seconds, I often thought of Kes. I remembered my brother, I missed our friendship, and I ached to share what I'd been given.

The guilt of his death still coagulated my heart. He shouldn't have died. If anyone deserved to survive during the massive purge of evil in my family, it was him. Nila knew how I felt, how I struggled to be deserving that I lived and he didn't.

She helped me accept it. And time helped soothe it.

Kes might not be with us physically, but sometimes, I'd get a sense of his quiet humour as I wandered around the Hall. I liked to believe a part of him remained with us, watching over us until our time came to join him.

"Make a wish." Nila bent over, holding Emma's hair from catching fire as she jumped up in her chair and puffed her tiny cheeks. The little hellion planted her hands on the table, about to face plant into the pale pink icing of the castle cake.

"Wait." Nila shook her head. "Before you blow, did you make a wish?"

My ears pricked. I wanted to know what my daughter wished for so I could make it come true. My entire existence was to make sure every desire materialized. Within reason, of course. I wouldn't raise a spoiled brat.

Emma pouted, her eyes locked on the cake. "I made one already." She bounced in her frilly pink tutu. "*Please,* can I blow? I wanna blow. I made a wish. This is taking *forever.* I want cake!"

Kes laughed. "She's crazy."

I pinched his arm. "Don't call your sister crazy."

He slapped my hand playfully. "Whatever. You're crazy. Mums crazy. We're all crazy."

Well, I couldn't really argue with his logic.

"Muuuumm!" Emma squealed. "Let me blow!"

Nila laughed, letting her go. "Go on then, make sure you blow all five out at once. Otherwise, your wish won't come true."

Emma froze, soaking in that vital piece of information. She glared at the cake as if she'd wage war on the frosting rather than eat it.

She's so damn fierce.

I smiled.

She took after her mother.

Nila's black eyes met mine. She whispered under her breath, "Do you think she wished for a prince, a pony, or one of those silly flying fairies she saw last week at the store?"

I wrapped my arms around her middle, pulling her back to my front. I kissed the soft skin of her throat above the diamond collar. "I don't care. I'll make sure she has every one."

Her heart thudded against mine. "Even the prince?"

I reared back. "Hell, no. As far as I'm concerned, she's the next Rapunzel. Hawksridge has plenty of towers to keep her in."

Nila giggled. "Good luck with that. She'll just scale it and run."

"Run?" I nuzzled the back of her ear. Two words never failed to get a rise out of me. Run and Kiss. 'Run' because it reminded me of Nila being brave enough to try and escape, and 'kiss' because it was the moment she broke me and made me hers.

Emma had inherited her mother's bravery and exceeded even her brother in tree climbing acrobatics. I didn't know where she got the skill, but she loved being in the treetops more than on the ground.

A sudden memory of Nila hiding naked in the trees filled my mind. Blood siphoned through my body, swelling my cock. I subtly pressed my hips into her arse. "Talking of trees and running…"

She tensed then melted. Her arm looped up and behind her to secure around my neck. "If you bring a plaid blanket, I'll make sure to give you what I gave you then."

Kissing her cheek, I breathed, "Done." Lowering my voice even more, I whispered, "You really have to stop using those words. It's highly inappropriate that I'm hard at my daughter's birthday party."

Nila swivelled in my arms, planting her mouth to mine. Her lips fed me kisses as well as barely audible conversation. "You really have to stop making me love you so damn much." Her eyes met mine. "Can you feel it? How overflowing I am? How I don't know how to contain it tonight? I just...I need you."

The rest of the room faded—the world always did when Nila touched me. "I do. I feel it."

She cocked her head. "What does it feel like?"

I glanced at Emma, who still hadn't decided how to blow all the candles out at once. "It feels like slipping into the hot springs beneath the Hall. Warmth and contentment lapping around me with a slight edge of pain from being too hot. But, unlike the hot springs, I don't have the discomfort of knowing I'll have to climb back into the cold and leave the warmth behind. You give it to me constantly."

Nila kissed my cheek. "You'll never be cold again." The double meaning of her words—that I would never be unloved again—throbbed.

Clearing my throat, I pushed her away and invited the room back into my attention. "Keep saying things like that and we won't see the rest of the party."

Nila half-laughed, half-scowled. "I'm torn in which I want more." Turning, she faced the table and Emma.

Kes rolled his eyes, never looking away from his sister, waiting impatiently for dessert. "Come on already."

"Pushy." Emma grinned, puffing out her little cheeks. Her lungs expanded and she blew raspberries rather than air but managed to get the flames to turn into curling spirals of smoke.

The room erupted into claps and cheers.

Emma didn't acknowledge the bikers or billionaires, secure in her place within their adoration. However, she did squeal and dance uncoordinatedly on her chair.

Nila grabbed Emma's tutu, just in case she toppled over. "Good girl. I have no doubt all your wishes will come true."

Kes stood by, his mouth watering. He didn't care his sister's spit just ended up all over the cake with her blowing attempt. All he wanted was sugar. Kid turned high as a damn kite whenever he had sweets. In that respect, he didn't remind me of his namesake. My brother had never truly let himself go—never been crazy or adolescently stupid.

At the time, I thought it was just him, but now, I think he did it for me. If he'd let himself get carried away, I wouldn't have had any choice but to be carried away, too.

Letting Nila go, I slipped my hand into my back pocket and squeezed the hidden box. Nila had seen this gift, but Emma hadn't. It would be the last present but the most valuable.

All day Emma had gratefully accepted gifts. I loved that she genuinely appreciated everything—from socks and sherbet to a new swing-set and pony. Her young emotions filled my heart to bursting, and in an odd way, I was able to relive my childhood through her, replacing unhappy times with excellent ones.

"Down. Down. I want to get down." Emma pointed at the floor.

Nila calmly plucked Emma from the chair, placing her on the travertine. "Don't go anywhere. I believe Daddy has a present for you while I cut the cake."

Nila's black eyes met mine. We'd been together for such a short amount of years, yet it felt like she'd been mine for eternity. I would never grow sick of waking with her in my bed, or sharing my breakfast with her by my side, or helping her sew late at night even though her needles drew more of my blood than I liked.

I love you.

She beamed. *I know.*

Tearing my gaze from hers, I dropped to my haunches and motioned Emma to come closer. It was surreal to protect and raise children named after two people who had meant the world to us; two people who'd died in the war between our houses. Kestrel had adopted some of my brother's quirks, but not all, and Emma doted on Textile in a way that made me wonder if she suffered a little of my condition.

There was no avoiding the avalanche of love and underlying despair from Tex that his wife wasn't there to see her grandchildren grow. Emma would hold his hand and sit quietly on his lap, plastering up his hurt with quiet affection.

Taking my daughter's hand, I looked toward the outskirts of the room. My sister-in-law, Jacqueline, lingered in the background. She'd come for a few days to celebrate Emma's birthday but couldn't shake the wariness the Hall invoked in her. Hawksridge had not been kind to the Weavers, and she hadn't accepted her lineage that easily.

Nila and Vaughn had gone out of their way to welcome Jacqueline into their midst, but she'd been raised differently. She'd been a single child in a stuck-up family. She didn't know how to handle large gatherings—and in that respect, I could relate.

We had happier times when we visited her in Cornwall—where Jacquie lived with her husband. There, on her own turf, her emotions were relaxed and confident while she lavished her little niece and nephew with love and antidotes.

She was a good aunt. However, her spiky black hair couldn't be any different to Nila's river of ebony. She shared the same eyes, same figure, same liquid grace, though.

Nila and Vaughn grew up believing they were twins; to find out they were triplets had taken some getting used to. However, the underlying history and mystery kept a moat from forming an intricate bond just yet.

In time, it would form. Nila would eventually warm her sister and help her dispel the remorse that she wasn't there to help. Shame was a powerful thing and Jacqueline couldn't shake the regret that she'd been firstborn by a few minutes, yet she hadn't paid the debt.

She didn't even fully understand the ramifications of the debt. Didn't care to dive too deep into history.

My heart thundered. If Jacqueline hadn't been secreted away and hidden, she would've been mine, not Nila. And the end to the Debt Inheritance might've been completely different, because even though I tolerated Jacqueline, I didn't connect with her. Her emotions were scatty and undeveloped compared to her sister. She would never have had the power to reach into my ice and shatter me from its hold.

My arms itched to hug Nila again. To thank her. To love her for being her.

So I did.

Straightening from my crouch, I quickly embraced my wife before dropping back to my haunches in front of Emma.

Nila accepted my hug with a soft smile, almost as if she'd followed my thoughts.

Emma smelled of cheese puffs and sausage rolls from the special treat for her birthday dinner. "Did you enjoy riding Hocus Pocus today?"

Emma clapped her hands. "I did. She's amazing. Can I go again? Right now?"

I swam in her infectious energy. "Not tonight. Tomorrow. We'll all go for a ride over the chase."

"Can we bring the birds? And the hounds? And Nemo?"

"Nemo?"

Emma looked at Nila. "You said you'd ask, Mummy."

Nila rolled her eyes affectionately. "Nemo is Emma's name for a kitten we saw advertised in the village. I told her we had more than enough pets." Ruffling her hair, she smiled. "You just got a pony. That's enough animal presents."

Emma pouted. I tensed against childish demands, but she balanced her emotions with such maturity, that pride washed through me.

"I know. Hocus is amazing." Leaning in, she pecked my cheek. "Thank you, Daddy."

My heart shattered with love.

It'd taken almost a year to source the perfect foal for Emma. I'd ordered a filly from the breeder who'd given me the colt for Kes.

At almost eight years old, Kes had become a proficient rider and rode with me daily, trotting beside me, cantering with courage, exploring the borders of Hawksridge as I taught him the value of land and heritage. Now, Emma could join us on her midnight filly called Hocus Pocus.

Letting Emma's sticky hands go, I reached into my back pocket for the box. Passing it to her, the room quieted as I kissed her soft cheek. "This will mean more to you when you're older, but I wanted you to have it now. Promise me you'll take great care of it and never lose it."

Her black hair bobbed as she nodded furiously. "I promise."

I laughed softly as she grabbed the red box and cracked it open. She had enough experience opening jewellery boxes. One of her favourite places was Diamond Alley and raiding Nila's precious collection. She said she wanted her mother's collar—even tried to pry it off one day with a nail file. Little did she know that it would've been on her little neck if she'd been born to another man in another time with the Debt Inheritance still in affect.

She was a Weaver girl. But now that name didn't come with such a curse.

Her little mouth parted as she took in the black diamond necklace I'd shown Nila the day I officially asked her to marry me.

Nila caught my gaze, twirling her engagement ring, letting me know her thoughts were with mine. She didn't need my condition to understand me—that came from unconditional love and a lifetime of listening to each other.

Helping Emma remove the chain from inside the box, I dangled the teardrop in front of her. "This is very special. Do you recognise the stone?"

"Yes." Her black hair bounced.

I'd never met a brighter child. She could memorize and recite diamond cuts and their flaws and attributes. She'd learned a few words in Swahili last time we were in Africa and even given the kids at kindergarten clothing advice from watching Nila effortlessly pin and style simple calico into a glorious gown.

She was a perfect blend of both of us. A magical piece of Nila and me.

"Where did you see the stone?"

She pointed at Nila's left hand. "Mummy's ring and bracelet."

"That's right. And now you have one, too."

"Because you love me as much as her?"

I laughed, gathering her in a hug. Kestrel moved in grabbing distance and I squeezed him in a group hug. "Because I love both of you as much as her. I love you all."

Nila subtly wiped sudden dampness from her cheeks, busying herself with cutting the cake. Jaz rolled closer, helping stack paper plates and take those full with pink frosting to a few of the Black Diamond brothers and family.

Once the room had received their piece of confectionary, Jaz wheeled toward me and handed out the plates of cake on her lap to my children.

Pinching Emma's nose, she said, "Now the present giving has ended, how about some cake? I want to eat your wish, little Velcro, so I can make sure it comes true."

Kes slung his arm over his sister. With boyish fingers, he grabbed the icing and smeared a huge handful into his mouth. "About time."

The room laughed.

And my world was perfect.

I was drunk.

Not on liquor or intoxicating substances but on happiness.

Pure, unadulterated happiness.

Such a cliché expression: *I'm drunk on happiness*. But for the first time in my life, I could positively say it was true.

"Hey, man, we're gonna push off." Vaughn clasped my shoulder, squeezing tight.

The last few hours had passed in good company and gentle conversation. The crowded parlour had dispersed after the cake had been devoured and Tex and Jacqueline had gone to their guest rooms while Nila and I retired to the newly decorated den with the children. Jaz and Vaughn had joined us, pulling out Twister and other silly games to tire Kes and Emma.

"You're safe to drive? You guys can just crash here." I smirked. "It's not like we don't have the room."

Jaz smoothed the blanket over her legs, reclining beside Nila. "V has the clothing line reveal tomorrow. We want to get back tonight." Her eyes landed on Vaughn. The intimacy and tenderness between them layered my happiness.

I never thought my sister would leave Hawksridge, let alone find love and support her chosen partner in the limelight, where her disability was questioned and discussed. But she had and she'd never looked better.

The fireplace crackled warmly, the burgundy drapes ensconced us away from the rest of the world, and the scattered bean-bags and toys on the floor painted Hawksridge in a completely different light than the one that'd existed for so long.

"Do you need any final adjustments?" Nila asked, running her fingertips casually through Emma's hair.

My daughter's energy level dwindled. She remained awake, playing Legos with Kestrel, but the long day finally sneaked closer to sending her into slumber.

Vaughn waved dismissively. "Nah, I'm fine. You've given me enough of your time making the men collection perfect."

Nila glowed. "Anything for you."

Vaughn beamed. "Ditto, sis."

Over the past eight years, V and I became fast friends. He was prickly and opinionated, smug and sometimes arrogant, but he adored his twin and was besotted with my sister. He adored the ground Jasmine wheeled over and treated her with the utmost care and respect.

His friendship soothed the hole left behind by Kes, giving me the comradery to share a beer at a local pub or just discuss meaningless things, but he'd never be able to fill the emotional void left by my brother—nor did I want him to.

I enjoyed V's company, but he didn't control his thoughts around me like Kes could. I knew far more than I needed to about how much he loved Jasmine, how much he found the power in her forearms from wheeling herself around a turn on, and how much he longed to cradle her in his arms after a long day at the Weaver factory.

I shifted in my wingback, nursing the small amount of cognac I'd poured. "Well, I wish you the best of luck for the reveal."

"Thanks."

Taking a sip of amber fire, I asked, "You up for clay shooting next weekend?"

V rubbed his hands together. "Damn right, I am. Gonna kick your arse after the last beating you gave me."

"Come up for the weekend." Nila ran a hand through her long hair, loosely draping the strands over her shoulders. She'd slipped into a knitted jumper, and her hair weaved with the wool. I loved that the length was the same as the day I claimed her.

Jasmine smiled. "Sure. Sounds good. We'll come up on Friday and spend a few days with you guys."

"Sounds like a plan." Glancing at Vaughn, I pointed a finger. "However, if you're up here to shoot clay and play with your niece and nephew, then no sleeping in until midday."

Jasmine swallowed a laugh.

V simpered. "Hey, blame that on your sister. She likes mornings and things that happen in the *morning*."

Nila clamped hands over Emma's ears while Kes looked up with a confused glance. "V!"

He laughed, shrugging. "What? I won't get blamed for sleeping in when it's not my fault."

I tossed back the rest of my drink. "Gross. I don't want to hear thank you very much."

V chuckled louder, ducking to slug my bicep. "Figured you'd knocked up my sister, might as well try to return the favour."

I choked on a mouthful of cognac. "Excuse me?"

His eyes gleamed as he glanced across the room at Nila and Jasmine, sitting side by side on matching bean-bags. Jaz used her chair, but V had become her legs. He seemed to know when she wanted to move, lifting her effortlessly from her chair and placing her wherever she wanted. Sometimes, he'd just randomly pluck her from wherever she was and march out of the room, only to return thirty minutes later with wind-pinched cheeks and swollen lips.

As much as I ribbed Vaughn for stealing my sister, I couldn't be more grateful. He'd given her a new life. He'd expanded her walls, given her a fresh world, and I'd never seen her so happy.

In summer, she had a tan from V pushing her through sunshine fields and carrying her to nap in the orchard. In winter, she sported a red nose—the only thing exposed seeing as V went out of his way to bundle her up so tightly.

For someone who'd never left the Hall, she now travelled with him on buying trips for his company, laughed more, and lived her life rather than just existed.

Vaughn looked at the picture-perfect scene before us. His joking switched to solemn want. "You have rugrats. Wouldn't it make sense for them to have cousins to grow up with?"

I frowned. They'd taken a long time to make that decision and I didn't think it was from lack of wanting children but Vaughn's fear that Jasmine wouldn't cope being pregnant.

I tried to block out the prying ability of my condition, but kids had been on their minds for a while. They'd either figured out the issues causing them grief or had finally decided to let nature take its course.

Nila looked up, making eye contact with me across the room. The rugrats V mentioned sat in front of her and Jaz. Two black and bronze-haired demons I wouldn't change in the slightest. The thought of filling the ancient Hall with laughter instead of tears was a perfect goal.

Clinking my empty glass with Vaughn's knuckles, I smiled happily. "Deal. Make Kes and Emma a few cousins but first…marry my damn sister and make an honest woman out of her."

V laughed. "Believe me, I've been trying. She accepted my ring but won't set a date."

I caught Jaz's eyes. I knew why. She tried to hide it, but her thoughts were always broadcast on a loud frequency. She didn't set a date because deep inside, she still didn't feel deserving of Vaughn when she wasn't 'complete.'

I didn't care I would sound stupid and let on just how many secrets I harboured, I whispered, "Jaz, you *are* complete. You're more than any other woman I know besides my wife."

She sucked in a breath, her eyes glittering with flames from the fire. "Thanks, Kite."

Vaughn paused, letting the random sentences fade before joking, "Besides, are you sure you want a Hawk to become a Weaver? What happens if some tyrant tries to claim our firstborn Weaver daughter in a few years?"

My heart panged, watching Nila and loving her so much it hurt. "They wouldn't take yours. They'd come after mine. I was the one who was supposed to change his last name, remember? But I didn't and the curse is broken. It's finished. Done. Over."

Vaughn sighed. "My mum would be proud of you, you know? Proud of how you stopped it and saved Nila."

I remembered Emma and her iron-gentle spirit. I'd grown to care for her during her short stay and looked up to her for how strong she was. "I should've saved her."

"We all agreed not to live in the past, remember?" Stepping away from me, Vaughn headed toward the women and two little ones by the fire. "We have a new future to enjoy."

Without conscious thought, I stood and followed him. Nila smiled as I stood over her, looking down at the two dark heads of our children. Her fingers wrapped around my bare ankle. "I missed you."

My heart swelled and cracked, pouring with adoration and contentment. "I missed you, too."

Dropping to my haunches, I positioned myself beside her and dragged her from the bean-bag and into my lap. Nuzzling her neck, I kissed her diamond collar and then her petal-soft skin.

She moaned under her breath, "I think it's bedtime...don't you?"

My eyes dived into hers, telling her without words that I needed her so goddamn much.

A small hand tugged on my jeans. "Daddy, story?"

I sighed. So much for bedtime.

I rolled my eyes dramatically. "And why do you think you deserve a tale, tiny Emma?"

Nila reached out and tickled the little girl who looked exactly like her. Same cheekbones, chin, and lips. However, Emma had my eyes—Hawk eyes—a trait so strong every single sibling of mine shared. "Where are your manners, Velcro?"

Emma giggled at Nila's nickname for her. On her second birthday, she'd fallen into a basket of Velcro teeth ready for invisible zippers. Her soft cotton jumpsuit latched onto the plastic thorns, ensuring untangling her took a lot of tugging and cursing. The damn child now had an addiction to pulling apart Velcro; she loved the noise.

Kestrel abandoned his Legos, shuffling closer to lean against my thigh. "Can we have a story? Just one. *Please*?"

I couldn't help myself. Looping an arm around his small shoulders, I hugged him. Nila on my lap and Kes and Emma wedged against my sides—what could be more perfect? "You want a story?"

Emma bounced up and down, but Kes merely nodded. His thoughts sweet, steadfast, and protective. He adored his little sister. And if she wanted a story, he would make sure she got a story.

His golden eyes locked with mine, pleading. Goosebumps darted down my arms, wondering, if in some small way, my brother and best friend might've found a way to communicate via my son.

Kes wriggled in my embrace. "Tell us a story. Just one. Then bed. Promise."

Nila laughed. "How often have we heard that?"

Kes smirked, a lock of hair curling on his forehead. "Promise. Hope to die. Cross my heart."

Jasmine giggled. "Got that back to front, Kessy."

Kes stuck out this tongue. "Daddy knows what I mean."

I laughed softly as Vaughn slid to the carpet, resting his back against the chaise and scooping Jasmine into his lap. "You're right. I do know what you mean."

Kes clapped his hands. "Good. Gimme the story then."

"Story! Story!" Emma curled up, cocooning all of us in a family bubble.

This right here.

This was happiness.

And I was no longer drunk on it.

I was *infested* by it.

This was my family.

My new chosen family.

We won.

Nila's thoughts washed over me in an influx of honey and serenity. Her heart swelled with love.

Squashing my two children, I grabbed my wife and kissed her hard.

Kes pretended to vomit, and Emma squealed. Jasmine and Vaughn just groaned, "Get a room."

Nila broke the kiss, her onyx eyes glowing with tenderness. "I guess we owe these demons a story."

"I guess we do."

"I've got a story." Vaughn tickled Kes. "A story about a dragon and a little boy who got gobbled up."

"No!" Kes struggled, scrunching up his face and trying not to laugh. "I like Daddy's stories."

My eyebrows rose. "My stories?"

I didn't understand. Nila was the story queen. She'd trawl the internet for every Disney animation, picture book, and tale she could find. I'd just linger in the dark, listening to her sultry voice and grow drowsy with the two infants before she put me to bed and used her mouth in other ways.

"Yes, we want the story of you and Mummy!" Kes looked at his sister. "True story, right, Em?"

Emma clapped her hands. "True. True!"

Vaughn muttered under his breath. "God, I think you're a small statistic of parents who should never tell their kids how they met. It's not like you shacked up at some bar and made a drunken mistake—that's a bad enough tale to have, but mentioning a beheading for a debt from the 1400's...kind of far-fetched."

I chuckled. "It is far-fetched...but perhaps that's what makes it a good story?"

Jaz narrowed her eyes. "How do you mean?"

"I mean life isn't meant to be generic and follow a pre-approved script."

Nila murmured, "If it did, where would the adventures be...the dragon-slaying knights and unicorn-riding princesses?"

"I'm a princess," Emma announced, poking herself in the chest. "I am. Me."

I grinned indulgently. "And what sort of princess are you?"

She suddenly shot to her tiny feet and soared around the beanbags in her pink tutu with her arms stretched wide. "I'm a Hawk princess."

Nila grabbed her mid-run, tickling her and blowing raspberries on her neck. "A hawk, huh? Not an eagle or a kite or a vulture?"

Emma wrinkled her nose. "No, silly. A hawk." Pointing at me, Nila, and Kes, she said, "We're all Hawks."

Nila's thoughts tangled between marrying me and taking my last name and the fact that Jasmine would soon become a Weaver. We'd swapped roles. Blended our bloodlines.

Gathering my family closer, I said, "Okay, you want a story? I've got a story."

Instantly, the children hunkered down, their amber eyes locked on me. Jaz, V, and Nila placed me in the centre of attention, waiting for me to spin something crazy and fantastical.

But I wouldn't do that.

I wouldn't dishonour my children by lying to them, and I wouldn't discredit the past and not learn from history. They wanted to know the story of how Nila and I met? Okay, they'd hear the truth, and it was up to them to deem fact from fiction.

My children would be the opposite of what I'd been groomed to be. They would be kind and helpful; they'd never want for anything, but they would know how to help others less fortunate. They would be *better*.

"Once upon a time, there was a seamstress named Needle and Thread."

Emma sighed, snuggling closer to Nila. "She's like you, Mummy."

Kes shook his head defiantly. "She *is* Mummy."

My heart fisted with love. "That's right. Now, stop interrupting." Taking a deep breath, I hugged them harder. "One night, Needle had the largest party of her life. Kings and queens came from everywhere to see her magical creations with lace and cotton. She'd worked for years to create something so perfect and a dress that defied all beauty. A dress with feathers and diamantes and silk."

"And the naughty prince ripped it off her." Nila kissed my cheek, granting the secret words directly into my ear. "He threw her on his gallant steed and stole her into darkness."

Placing her head on my shoulder, she breathed, "But he was already in love with her, so he'd lost the fight before it'd begun."

Kes and Emma couldn't hear what my incredible wife whispered, and I fought the urge to steal her away again and show her just how much I wanted her for eternity.

I fought the urge while my children waited for me to continue. But I couldn't tear my eyes away from Nila. "I was, you know."

She tensed, her eyes meeting mine. "You were? The text messages? They were enough to fall—"

"Fall in love with you? I think I fell in love with you when we met the final time when you were thirteen."

"I don't remember that."

"You wouldn't. I was supposed to say hello, but I couldn't ruin your day. You looked so happy. So I watched you in the park and gave my heart to you without even knowing it."

"Story! You're forgetting the story." Emma tugged on my sleeve, her face open and eager. "Please…"

Nila shifted in my arms, kissing me gently. "I loved you when you were Kite007. I loved you when you were Jethro Hawk, and I loved you when you finally became mine."

"Ewww." Kes stuck his tongue out.

With my soul about to split open with joy, I forced myself to ignore my wife and continue with the tale. Once the children were in bed and Jaz and V had gone, I'd spend the rest of the night showing Nila just how much I adored her and how glad I was that our story existed.

My voice threaded around the room, plaiting with the crackle of the fireplace. "Where was I? Oh yes, that's right. The dress Needle and Thread created was the most incredible thing anyone had ever seen. People offered to buy her castles and paradise for the chance to have her sew for them.

"Everything seemed right in the world, but Needle didn't know that a monstrous prince was coming for her. That he'd lied to her for months, sent secretive messages, and stolen her heart without her knowing." I paused for dramatics, squeezing Kes and Emma tight. "He'd been sent to *hurt* her."

"No!" Emma squeaked.

"Oh, yes." I nodded sadly. "His task was to hunt her, hurt her, devour her."

Kes balled his tiny fists. "But you didn't let the bad prince take Mummy, did you?"

I lowered my voice, turning grave. "I did."

"No! Why?"

"Because...*I* was the bad prince. I'd been given a task to prove I was royal enough to inherit the realm and faraway castles, but no matter how bad I was, Needle had a magic I couldn't fight."

I settled into the soft bean-bag, diving committedly into the tale.

I wouldn't sugar-coat.

I'd tell them of the debts and pain. I'd gloss over things too old for their young ears, but I would ensure the message behind the history remained.

I believed everyone had a tolerance for darkness because life wasn't just light. Life wasn't rainbows and bunny rabbits nor good luck or easy fortune. Real life was hard. There was mess and lies and heartbreak. They deserved to know they'd suffer tragedies as well as triumphs. They needed to be equipped to deal with losing as well as winning. Because that was what made an empathic human over a monster.

And no matter how twisted and terrible our story had begun, our belief in love and tenderness turned fate's plan. Our dreams came true and were even more precious because of what we'd survived in order to earn it.

"There's darkness inside all of us." I glanced at my children, making sure they paid attention. "Some of us let it rule us. Some of us let it destroy us. And some of us rise to the challenge and fight it.

"All it takes is for that one person to believe that they're worthy. That we won't bow to poverty or hate or greed. That our life can be better than the shadows we let creep over it."

Emma nodded, but Kes turned sombre, turning over my words, soaking in the wisdom beneath.

Nila had won because she fought against the darkness.

And I'd won because I'd embraced my truth.

All it takes is for one of us to be brave enough to turn on the light.

"So the bad prince hurt Needle?" Emma whispered.

"Yes, he gave her to the trolls in the forest to extract tolls and payments

---

782

for things she hadn't done."

"If she hadn't done them, then why could they do that?"

"Because they thought they were better than her and she owed them."

"That's mean." Emma pushed out her bottom lip. "Stupid trolls."

"I know," I agreed. "Very unfair and against every law of the land they lived in."

"So...what happened?" Kes asked, his face alight with interest.

"Yes, Kite, then what happened?" Nila brushed her lips across mine, her soul sewn completely to mine. "If the story started so cruelly, how does it end?"

I had the perfect answer.

The *only* answer.

The most brilliant thirteen-word reply ever uttered.

Kissing my wife and hugging my children, I murmured, "The only way such a tale can end...

. . .

They lived happily ever after."

Indebted Beginnings

COMING SOON

William Hawk's Tale & the Origins of the Everything...

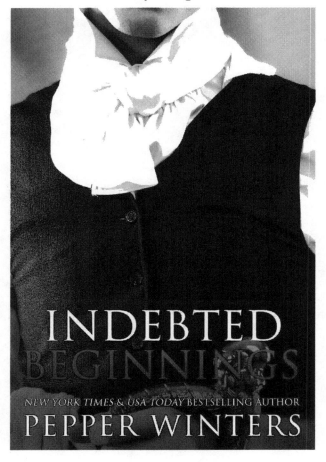

"It all began with greed and gluttony and ended with diamonds and guillotines. Debts were incurred, contracts were written, and a curse landed on the firstborns from both houses."

William Hawk was born into a family with vengeance rather than blood flowing in his veins. Against all odds, he transformed himself from pauper to Lord of Hawksridge. He became a smuggler, king's ally, and ruthless businessman. But he had flaws as well as triumphs.

It was those flaws that ruined his inheritance. Those flaws that saved him from himself. Those flaws that brought him the greatest wealth of all.
Her.

Do you want more Hawks? Do you want to know the deeper questions to the Debt Inheritance? Well, you've read Jethro and Nila's tale, now go back to the very beginning and read William's in INDEBTED BEGINNINGS.

About the Author

Pepper Winters is a New York Times and USA Today International Bestseller. She loves dark romance, star-crossed lovers, and the forbidden taboo. She strives to write a story that makes the reader crave what they shouldn't, and delivers tales with complex plots and unforgettable characters.

After chasing her dreams to become a full-time writer, Pepper has earned recognition with awards for best Dark Romance, best BDSM Series, and best Dark Hero. She's an #1 iBooks bestseller, along with #1 in Erotic Romance, Romantic Suspense, Contemporary, and Erotica Thriller. She's also honoured to wear the IndieReader Badge for being a Top 10 Indie Bestseller, and recently signed a two book deal with Hachette. Represented by Trident Media, her books have garnered foreign and audio interest and are currently being translated into numerous languages. They will be in available in bookstores worldwide.

Her Dark Romance books include:
Tears of Tess (Monsters in the Dark #1)
Quintessentially Q (Monsters in the Dark #2)
Twisted Together (Monsters in the Dark #3)
Debt Inheritance (Indebted #1)
First Debt (Indebted Series #2)
Second Debt (Indebted Series #3)
Third Debt (Indebted Series #4)
Fourth Debt (Indebted Series #5)
Final Debt (Indebted Series #6)
Indebted Epilogue (Indebted Series #7)

Her Grey Romance books include:
Destroyed
Ruin & Rule (Pure Corruption #1)

Upcoming releases are:
Sin & Suffer (Pure Corruption #2)
Je Suis a Toi (Monsters in the Dark Novella)

Unseen Messages (Contemporary Romance)
Super Secret Series
Indebted Beginnings

To be the first to know of upcoming releases, please join Pepper's Newsletter (she promises never to spam or annoy you.)

Pepper's Newsletter

Or follow her on her website
Pepper Winters

You can stalk her here:

Pinterest
Facebook Pepper Winters
Twitter
Instagram
Website
Facebook Group
Goodreads

She loves mail of any kind: **pepperwinters@gmail.com**
All other titles and updates can be found on her **Goodreads Page.**

Acknowledgements

(Deleted Sex Scene from Final Debt is after this section. Xx)

There are a few things I'd like to say now this series is complete. One, thank you for reading with me. For following Jethro and Nila through six books (really seven with the Epilogue) and (hopefully) enjoying their tale. As you've noticed, there is a lot of backstory and a rich world beyond their lives. I deliberately concentrated on Jethro and Nila's side of the story, so as not to get too confusing.

However, the longer I wrote *Indebted*, the more the past wanted to be told.

After writing Mabel and William's side when Cut is in the mine with Nila, it's made me want to revisit the beginning and truly dive deeper into the trials and hardships endured by both sides.

Indebted Beginnings will follow William as he builds Hawksridge, sets up an empire, and falls into his own pitfalls of life. I don't have a release date yet but can't wait to write his tale and answer any other questions you have about the series.

Now that's out of the way, let's talk about other things.

The stabbing with Daniel and the knitting needle.

Believe it or not, that is based on a true fact. In my family line—I won't say if it's my lineage or my husband's side—a wife killed her husband using a knitting needle. She was tried and convicted of manslaughter after a long case of confusion. The puncture to his heart was barely noticeable and most doctors back then thought it was a heart attack. (Just in case you thought that wasn't possible, it's based on fact.)

There are also a few other things in the story that are real. I, myself, suffer from vertigo. Not nearly as bad as Nila, but I know first-hand what her symptoms are like.

Now, onto the acknowledgments.

Thank you so much to Amy K Jones for being so likeminded as me. Yaya for being so honest. Tamicka for laying her thoughts out so concisely. Melissa for printing off Final Debt and reading in paper form. Vickie for keeping me going with awesome messages. Skye for being my daily writing partner for over two years. The ladies in FUNK who are the most inspiring bunch of women I know. Lisa for arranging my blog tours and handling PR. Kellie for the epic boxed set covers for Indebted. Ari for the awesome single covers for Indebted. Celesha for making some incredible teasers for this series. Jenny for her quick editing skills. Ellen for her fast proofreading. Erica for her eagle-eye proofreading. Selena for running my groups and my life so well. Katrina for her wealth of industry titbits and knowledge. My husband for sticking with me and encouraging me to write even when the beginning was rocky. And to every reader who gave this saga a try and enjoyed—to every reader who gave it a try and didn't. To every blogger, reviewer, friend, and confidant. Your messages and help and kindness truly make my life so much more rounded and happy.

I know I've forgotten people but my brain always goes on the fritz when doing these acknowledgements, hence why I don't do them often anymore as I'm terrified of leaving people out.

Lastly, I thought I'd answer a few questions that had been asked over the past year while writing the Indebted Series. Now that it's finished, I can shed light on any last minute questions and spend a little longer in the Indebted world.

Do you love knowing that you reach your fans on such a deep level when they read your books?

Yes, I'm beyond awed that I'm able to create an emotional response through words. I'm constantly grateful for messages saying they truly felt a scene or character. Nothing means more to me than that.

Will we get spinoff stories/prequel to this AMAZING series?

Yes, *Indebted Beginnings* will be released soon (no date as yet) and I might do a few more if the story strikes me. The history is very rich and a lot of avenues to explore.

Who did you vision as Nila and Jethro?

I don't have an actor or actress in mind at the moment. But if you have someone in mind, email me and show me.

Who was your favourite character to bring alive? Who did you hate most?

My favourite was definitely Jethro as he had such a multifaceted character to bring out. Hate? Hard to tell because even if the characters were evil in the book, their strong opinions made it easy to write. I guess…Daniel was the hardest as I actually felt sorry for him and how he was treated.

Will there be audio books coming?

Yes, these are being created as we speak and will be out in early 2016, you can listen to a snippet **HERE**

Will you do signed paperbacks of this series?

Yes, you can order them from my website **HERE**. I'll also have limited edition boxed sets. Debt Inheritance, First Debt, Second Debt in one edition, and Third Debt, Fourth Debt, Final Debt, Indebted Epilogue in another as there are too many pages for one complete book.

Who was the toughest character to write about? Who was the easiest?

I sort of answered this above but Jethro was easiest because I always knew who he was. Maybe the hardest was Kestrel because I fell in love with him and always knew his fate so it was bittersweet.

Can you please create a lineage of all Hawks and Weavers back to when the Hawks were given the document by the Queen. Would like to see the whole family tree - even if there are mysteries.

Yes, I'll work on something like this to insert in *Indebted Beginnings*. I won't share yet as if I do spinoffs I don't want too many spoilers revealed too early.

This story is EPIC! Why is HBO or Starz not working on the TV show already!!? Seriously!

I would LOVE to see this as a TV Series. If I can make it happen, I will.

What do you have coming next, can you share with us?

I have a LOT coming in 2016. *Sin & Suffer* will be released on the 26th January 2016 and will complete the Pure Corruption Series. It will be in book stores and online. *Unseen Messages* will be my next release which I'm DYING to show you the cover and blurb. On the 20th December, I'll reveal the insanely beautiful cover on my website. In January, I'll also release the blurb and cover for the Super Secret Series I'll be publishing in 2016. I'm BEYOND excited to share and have already fallen in love with these characters. Je Suis a Toi will be coming in 2016, too.

Will you be at any signings in 2016?

Not at this stage. I'm going to be focusing on writing as much as possible and building a home with my husband. I hope to travel again in 2017.

You mentioned a deleted sex scene from Final Debt, where is that?

Keep scrolling. It's a few pages away from here.

If you have any other questions please email **pepperwinters@gmail.com** or join the **Indebted Group Read** on Facebook to share with other readers.

I haven't forgotten that I promised sneak peeks into **Unseen Messages** and **Sin & Suffer**…here is a little taster:

Unseen Messages

LIFE OFFERS EVERYONE messages.

Either unnoticeable or obvious, it's up to us to pay attention.

I didn't pay attention.

Instinct tried to take notice; the world tried to prevent my downfall.

I didn't listen.

I will forever wonder what would've happened if I did pay attention to those messages. Would I have survived? Would I have fallen in love? Would I have been happy?

Then again, perhaps just like messages existed, fate existed, too.

And no matter what life path we chose, fate always had the final say.

I didn't listen but it doesn't mean I didn't live.

I just lived a different tale than the one I'd envisioned.

Away from my home.

Away from my family.

But I wasn't alone...

I was with him.

And he became my entire universe.

Sin & Suffer

HE WAS A BULLY.

Ever since his voice deepened he'd mean and short-tempered. Mom told me that he was at a point in his life where he had to lose himself to find himself. I had no idea what she meant. I just…I just really missed my best-friend. —Diary entry, Cleo, age nine.

* * *

AMNESIA.

A curse or a blessing?

Memory.

A helping hand or hindrance?

The things I'd forgotten and remembered had been both enemy and friend—solace and pain. They'd been constant companions, fighting over me for years. Amnesia traded my first life for a new one—with new parents, new sister, new home. But then the boy with the green eyes brought me back— showed me the path to my old world and a destiny I'd forgotten.

For eight years I'd struggled, always fearing I'd left loved ones behind. I'd hated myself for being so selfish—knowing my brain had deliberately cut them out in an act of self-preservation. I'd always wondered what I would do when I finally remembered everything…*if* I finally remembered.

I didn't have to wonder anymore.

Even after the consequences of following a mysterious letter, the snake pit of lies, the confusion of blended pasts, the rough way Killian had treated me—I wouldn't change a thing.

Those trials were a worthy payment for my broken memories. I was whole again…*almost.*

As a final note, I'd like to say thank you again for reading. I'll never stop being awed that this is my career and forever humbled that people enjoy my work. I write for you and hope to deliver many more books for decades to come.
THANK YOU.

(Keep reading for the deleted sex scene from Final Debt)

Other Book Blurbs & Reviews

26th January 2016
Sin & Suffer (Pure Corruption MC #2)

"Some say the past is in the past. That vengeance will hurt both innocent and guilty. I never believed those lies. Once my lust for revenge is sated, I'll say goodbye to hatred. I'll find a new beginning."
Buy Now

2016
Je Suis a Toi (Monsters in the Dark Novella)

"Life taught me an eternal love will demand the worst sacrifices. A transcendent love will split your soul, cleaving you into pieces. A love this strong doesn't grant you sweetness—it grants you pain. And in that pain is the greatest pleasure of all."
Buy Now

Early 2016
Unseen Messages (Standalone Romance)

"I should've listened, should've paid attention. The messages were there. Warning me. Trying to save me. But I didn't see and I paid the price..."
Get Release Day Alerts when this Book is Published

Early 2016
Super Secret Series Starting Soon

Please keep an eye out for the blurb and cover reveal early 2016. I'm beyond excited about this series and hope to deliver another epic tale.

*"He has millions, but without her he is bankrupt.
And he'll spend every dollar and penny to get her back."*
Get Release Day Alerts when this Book is Published

Tears of Tess (Monsters in the Dark #1)

"My life was complete. Happy, content, everything neat and perfect.
Then it all changed.
I was sold."
Buy Now

Quintessentially Q (Monsters in the Dark #2)

"All my life, I battled with the knowledge I was twisted... screwed up to want something so deliciously dark—wrong on so many levels. But then slave fifty-eight entered my world. Hissing, fighting, with a core of iron, she showed me an existence where two wrongs do make a right."
Buy Now

Twisted Together (Monsters in the Dark #3)

"After battling through hell, I brought my esclave back from the brink of ruin. I sacrificed everything—my heart, my mind, my very desires to bring her back to life. And for a while, I thought it broke me, that I'd never be the same. But slowly the beast is growing bolder, and it's finally time to show Tess how beautiful the dark can be."
Buy Now

Destroyed (Standalone Grey Romance)

She has a secret.
He has a secret.
One secret destroys them.
Buy Now

Ruin & Rule (Pure Corruption MC #1)

"We met in a nightmare. The in-between world where time had no power over reason. We fell in love. We fell hard. But then we woke up. And it was over . . ."
Buy Now

Deleted Scene from Final Debt

Deleted Scene taken from Final Debt *after the bonfire of burning torture relics and Weaver files. Instead of leaving it forever on my hard drive, it's here for you to read if you wish.*

Hope you enjoy...

MY COCK SWELLED as her hands grazed my chest, disappearing to unbuckle my belt. I didn't pull away as she undid my jeans and reached into my boxer-briefs to fist around my rapidly hardening length.

I groaned as her thumb smeared over the crown, pressing with perfect pressure. "Nila..."

"I need you, Kite." Her lips never left mine. "I need you to remind me I'm alive after so many of those we love are dead."

I pulled back.

Her face tracked with tears, shattering my heart. This was supposed to be a happy time, and yet we'd all been sucked into sadness.

Looping my fingers in the strands of her smoke-laced hair, I whispered, "Anything. Tell me how to make you come alive and I'll do it." I kissed her. "I'll do anything you need."

Her face darkened with desire so furious, I sucked in a breath. "That night you taught me how it was for you. The intensity lesson and the way you made me focus on the simplest of things."

My lips twisted even as my heart leapt in lust. "My whip?"

She bit her lip, nodding. "I want that again. I want to remember we're still here. That our love is still real and no matter what, we won. I need reminding we have our entire lives to spend together. It doesn't matter how we came together; nothing can ever tear us apart."

I couldn't help myself. I kissed her excruciatingly hard. "You're a witch, I swear. Or maybe a HSP yourself. "

She frowned. "How do you mean?"

"I need the same thing." I smiled, tracing her bottom lip with my finger. "I feel like I've lost you a little. That you doubt what we have is true. I need to make you focus. To accept nothing else could match what we've found. And in a way, I need to punish you for ever doubting that."

I stared at her with a mixture of awe and worship. Had she picked up on my silent wishes as I picked up on hers? Last week, while dealing with Bonnie's funeral and lawyer documents, I'd had the sudden compulsion to fight such grief with blistering dirty sex. I wanted to ravage and fuck. I wanted to remind myself that no matter what I'd done to my father, I was still me and still deserving of Nila's love.

I hadn't asked her to give me what I needed as I hadn't wanted to hurt or upset her.

But here she was asking for the same thing.

"You're fucking perfect." I kissed her.

"And you." She kissed me back.

"Will you let me have control tonight? Let me do what we both need?"

Her head fell back, submitting to me. "Anything, Jethro. I'm yours for the night. Do anything you want."

"Just the night?"

A sly smile spread her lips. "You want more than that?"

The growl built in my throat. "You know I do."

"In that case, you better prove to me you can love me enough to last forever."

More than forever, Needle.

I didn't hesitate.

Letting her go, I shot to my drawers and pulled out two ties. Both silver with diamonds spilling down the fabric.

Nila didn't take her eyes off me as I prowled to the head of the bed and snapped my fingers. The old hint of authority sent a shiver down her spine. "Come here, Ms. Weaver."

She obeyed faster than any order when I'd been deadly serious. My lips quirked.

Seems sex is more wanted than debts.

My heart tripped.

If she reacted so defiantly and strong when facing something she didn't want to face, what would she be like in our future? Would she be eager to do things I could guarantee she'd love? Could we finally have the trust I'd always begged her to give me so I could live entirely in her feelings for me?

Biting my lip, I ran the two ties through my fingers. "You're making it very hard to remember I should be punishing you and not rewarding you."

She smiled as she lay back, placing her hands above her head. Licking her lips, she never took her eyes from mine. "Perhaps, I want both."

I swallowed hard, climbing on the bed and hovering over her. Slinging my knee over her hips, I straddled her.

We didn't stop staring; my mouth watered, my cock hardened, and the shitty night faded. Somehow, she even managed to stop me thinking about Kestrel's funeral in a few hours, about the mammoth task before me of culling the mine and granting peace to a scarred nation, and all the loose ends I had to tie up now I was heir.

I'm heir.

I never thought I'd say the words.

Hawksridge is mine.

Once upon a time, that was all I wanted because it offered freedom for my siblings and me. But now...I could walk away from it tomorrow because Nila was my true freedom and I loved her more than any estate or bank balance.

Dropping over her, I kissed her quickly, forcing myself not to get carried away. Her hand swooped up to my cheek, caressing me with love and lust.

Pulling back, I dropped the ties to the mattress and tugged on the hem of her glittery blue jumper. "This needs to come off."

Sitting up in one sweep like a ballerina, she let me pull the fabric over her head. She didn't say a word as I removed the small tank top underneath and unhooked her bra.

Once I'd revealed her breasts, her nipples instantly hardened, begging me to bite and suck.

I deliberately brushed my knuckles over them, granting her a smidgen of pleasure.

She gasped, her black eyes turning into empty galaxies just waiting for me to give her an orgasm and fill them with stars.

My cock twitched, begging to take her. But I had something to do first.

Picking a single tie from beside my knee, I growled, "Put your hands together."

She stiffened with anticipation but obeyed. Her elegant fingers latched together, presenting them to me like the perfect surrender.

Taking her wrists, I gently wrapped the silver tie around her, securing it tight but not too tight. Guiding her arms back to rest on the pillow above her head, I kissed her brow. "Keep them there. Do not move. Understand?"

Her pulse echoed in her throat, dancing beneath her diamond collar. "I understand."

"Good girl."

Resting back on my knees, I turned my attention to her trousers. I tapped her hips. "These need to go, too." My voice no longer resembled a distinguished lord, more like a feral sex-starved man who desperately wanted to fuck.

"Of course." Nila arched her back, holding herself with suburb muscles as I unbuttoned and unzipped her jeans. A soft pant fell from her lips as I wrenched the denim down her legs, followed by her lacy knickers.

Naked.

Was there anything more fucking perfect than Nila naked, willing, and wet in my bed?

Fuck.

She looked positively decadent.

My hands curled, forcing myself to find some restraint from fucking her that very instant. Tracing my finger along the inside of her thigh, I murmured, "Now, Ms. Weaver…what, oh what, should I do with you?"

Her skin flushed as her eyes dropped to my fully dressed body. "I want to see you."

I shook my head. "You have to deserve that. I think you need to do a few more things for me before that, don't you?"

Her midnight eyes darkened impossibly further. "Like what?"

"I can think of a few things."

Climbing down her body, I placed my elbows on the bed, settling myself between her spread legs. My chin hovered over her cunt, my eyes locked on hers. "I'm going to taste you, Nila. I'm going to make you explode and show you you're alive and with me and safe. Foreign sisters don't matter. Mother's secrets don't matter. All that matters is *us.*"

Nila panted as I bowed over her and breathed hot on her clit. My breath misted her delicate skin, heating her core, making her moan.

She bucked in my arms. "Oh, my God." Her bound hands flew to her chest, struggling against the knotted tie.

Grabbing her silk-covered wrists, I clucked my tongue. "Put those back above your head."

She gasped, struggling to obey when every nerve ending existed in her pussy.

Slowly, she rested her arms back on the pillow. Smirking, I lowered my mouth, licking her quick and sharp.

"Oh..." She shuddered.

I licked her again, absorbing her taste, struggling with my own resolve to grant her pleasure when all I wanted was to climb inside her. "More?"

Her head tossed back, another moan responding in answer.

My muscles stiffened. My cock ached in my jeans. I wanted to forget all pretence and just fuck this woman. Claim her as mine. But she wanted to come alive. I would do everything in my power to make that happen.

I'd make her cry with hysteria. I'd make her laugh at how good it felt to breathe and let me control her pleasure.

Slipping fingertips between her legs, I traced my way upward. Every sweep of my tongue and inch of my fingers, she trembled and tensed.

The higher I got, the more her legs forced to close, clamping around my shoulders.

Shaking my head, I speared the tip of my tongue into her folds. Grabbing her legs, I slammed them open, pressing them into the mattress, ensuring she was bared, exposed, and entirely vulnerable to whatever I wanted to do to her.

"Stay, Needle. Otherwise, my tongue will become teeth."

She groaned—it echoed through the bed, hypnotising me.

Her pussy glistened, so wet with need.

Dragging a finger though her slickness, I murmured, "You want me so much, Ms. Weaver."

"You know I do."

"Tell me."

Her voice was a husky whisper. "Tell you what?"

"Tell me how much you need me."

She gasped as I inserted the tip of my finger inside her. "So much. Too much. Way, *way* too much."

Her muscles leapt beneath my touch, both externally and internally.

In our bedroom, there was nothing else to think about. Here, it was just us. A place devoid of people. We were in our own world. A world filled with love and lust and a connection so strong, I could come just from her thoughts. From living her pleasure and what I did to her.

It was the strangest, most surreal sensation.

The intimacy of the moment swamped me with everlasting joy. Her feet rubbed on the sheets as my tongue landed on her exposed core. Her hands opened and closed in the binds, her hips rocking into my mouth.

My only goal was to please her and show how much I fucking adored her. Not just for tonight or tomorrow but every night and day in our future.

I sucked her clit, unsheathing my teeth to nibble. My hips pistoned, pressing my hard dick into the mattress, seeking relief as her taste exploded through my veins.

"I'm so grateful for you, Nila."

Her head thrashed as my voice resonated through my tongue and into her pussy. "I'll spend the rest of my life making sure you know how damn grateful I am."

My hips rocked harder, fucking the bed as desire built swift and demanding in my blood. Sliding over her, I licked her nipple, sucking the hardened flesh into my mouth.

She cried out, her skin flushing with sweat. "Jethro—"

"What do you want?"

"I want—I want—"

Then a thought popped into her head, and I caught it. I caught the explosion of desire, asking me to do something she daren't verbalize. Lucky for her, I sensed what she needed.

I obeyed.

Baring my teeth, I bit her nipple.

Hard.

She moaned loudly in reward, telling me without words that I understood exactly what she wanted. Tonight, she didn't want sweet or soft. Tonight, she wanted to be marked and ridden. To feel human and come alive with aches and love-bruises and the knowledge she'd wake up tomorrow with memories of what we did in the dark.

I would oblige her completely.

Starting from her lips, I kissed her hot and deep. My teeth captured her lip, biting down so she would feel my kiss long after I left to bestow attention on other parts.

Trailing from her mouth to her throat, I bit her.

From throat to collarbone, I bit and licked and loved.

Every inch of her body, I bit.

Leaving indents of my teeth for a few seconds before her flushed skin absorbed the erotic pain, begging for more.

"I love your tiny breasts, you know that?" I swirled my tongue around her nipple remembering the first time I saw her. The awful things I said to her. The barely delivered lies about needing a woman with bigger breasts and more confidence.

I'd been enthralled with her from the very first moment. I'd just done a better job of hiding my true desires back then.

She laughed, her skin quaking beneath my tongue. "I'll have to go back over what you've said to me and see how much was real and what was fake."

I chuckled, biting my way down her stomach, nipping each rib, ensuring every inch of her was tasted. "Most was a lie. When I told you I couldn't stand you, I really meant I loved you. When I said you drove me mad, I really meant I wanted you more than I could breathe."

Her eyes met mine, liquid with love. "Jethro…"

I smiled lopsidedly. "You had to have guessed how insanely hard I fell for you? Those first texts, the First Debt. Fuck, Nila. It took every willpower not to steal you away then and there."

Tearing my gaze away, I bit her particularly hard on her hipbone, dragging a strangled cry from her lips. "I'm going to punish you for that. Reprimand you for the power you've always held over me."

She moaned as my mouth latched over her pussy again, only this time, I didn't just lick; I fucked her with my tongue, lavishing her with my teeth.

Her fingers clenched in the tie, her back arching for more. Planting a hand on her lower belly, I kept her in place as I licked and laved, forcing her to peak fast and hard.

"Oh, shit!"

Her legs locked. "I'm...I'm—"

Her belly fluttered. "Don't stop. Don't—"

"Fuuuck." Her pussy rippled around my tongue.

Her orgasm sparked from nothing, exploding with fireworks. My tongue drank up every clench, and I didn't stop until she fell limp against the bed.

My chin and lips smeared with her pleasure as I stared up her svelte body, smiling at her wanton happiness. "Are you feeling alive yet, Ms. Weaver?"

She wriggled, her skin flushing. "I'm starting to."

"Only starting to? I better increase my efforts."

Climbing up her body, I hovered over her. Impossibly, I fell even more in love with her. Tucking hair from her eyes, I undid the tie around her wrists. "Now, what do you suggest I do with you?"

Her black hair tangled on the pillow as she shrugged, rolling her wrists in their newfound freedom. "Anything your heart desires."

A grumble sounded low in my chest. "Giving me carte blanche is a dangerous thing."

"No, it's not."

"Why?"

"Because I trust you, Jethro. I trust you with my heart and soul."

Gritting my jaw, I looked away. She understood me so fucking much. Closing my eyes, I gathered my control. If I let myself give in, I'd be inside her within seconds before we had a chance to fully embrace the alchemy between us.

I groaned as Nila shifted onto her knees. "I know what else you can do." With fluttering hands, she undressed me like I'd undressed her. Her fingers kissed my lower belly, gathering the hem of my black t-shirt and ripping it over my head. "You can make love to me, so I can return the favour you just gave me."

Tossing the material onto the floor, her expert touch descended on my jeans. "I want to touch you, fuck you, and keep you forever." Her talent as a seamstress undid the fastening faster than I ever could, her hands hot on my hips as she shoved my jeans and boxer-briefs down in one go. "Move so I can get rid of these."

I didn't speak, lapping up everything she gave.

Rolling onto my back, I copied what she'd done and arched.

Her tongue came out, licking her bottom lip as her eyes locked on my hard dick, slipping my clothing off me and to the floor.

Naked.

Both of us this time.

Time stopped ticking onward. The new day paused. And Nila and I just stared.

Our promises of intensity and taking it slow hovered like scripture, slowly disintegrating the longer we breathed.

I wanted her so fucking much.

Her hand landed on my cock.

And that was it.

I couldn't do it anymore.

I didn't know who moved first.

One second, I was on my back, the next, my hands were full of Nila's hair and my mouth connected with hers.

We threw ourselves together.

Our bodies slammed into one.

Nothing else mattered but joining.

The whip and ties would have to wait for another time. This...this didn't need props or toys. This was pure undulated passion.

The sheets tangled around my legs as I imprisoned her on her back.

Her chest rose and fell, her breasts squashing deliciously against my chest. "God, Kite..."

Words.

Words weren't allowed when all I wanted was emotion.

She could talk to me but in silent form. She could beg me but only in her mind. I would hear. I would understand. And I would fucking deliver every command she decreed.

My lips captured hers again. My mind focused on nothing but the rhythmic strokes of her taste, her fingernails slicing down my spine for more.

Somehow, our legs entwined, our arms plaited, our entire bodies fought to get closer. Her legs spread wider, her knees nudging mine as she cradled me between them.

I wanted her like that.

I wanted her rough. Gentle. Safe. Dangerous.

But in that second, I needed her brutal.

She needed me to bite her?

Well, I needed to fuck her.

Shooting upward, I grabbed her hot skin, flipping her onto her front. "Tell me now if this is going to be a problem."

Sitting on her knees, she arched her spine, standing on all fours. The dip of her spine blew my fucking mind, the crack of her arse leading the way to the hottest wettest cunt I'd ever had.

Looking over her shoulder, her lips burned bright red, swollen from our kisses. Her face flushed pink from her orgasm and her thoughts...they gave me complete freedom to take her like this.

She wanted it.

"You want to be ridden?"

She bit her lip, her teeth indenting the red flesh. "More than anything."

Swallowing a possessive growl, I clamped one hand on her hips and the other around my cock. Yanking her backward, I positioned myself to line up perfectly.

As her entrance locked over the crown of my cock, I couldn't see. My eyes short-circuited as insane bliss catapulted down my dick and into my balls.

I had her in my arms, and yet, somehow, I still expected her to vanish.

She was everything I ever dreamed of. I couldn't help fearing she'd be gone when I woke. I'd find she never existed and this was all a terrible fantasy.

But then she rocked backward, sliding her pussy down my length. Her spine rolled, her head folding toward the bed. "More."

Shit, I'd give her more.

I'd give her everything.

Thrusting upward, her body offered no barrier as I filled her completely. Her previous orgasm slicked and prepared her. I didn't have to worry about being gentle or slow. I could climb inside and take everything she offered.

Leaning forward, I wrapped my arm around her chest. My hand grabbed her dangling breasts, squeezing the weight. My mouth found her spine, kissing the beads of her bones, thrusting again and again.

Opening myself to every thought of Nila's, I felt her gratitude, her love, her desire. I felt her happiness, her singular concentration on me inside her, and the quietness that being together brought.

Biting her waist, I continued to thrust upward. My hips rocking to a punishing rhythm, forcing Nila to match my pace, slamming us together, keeping our bodies joined.

"Fuck, you feel so good." I kissed and bit her, driving myself insane with sensation. "I want to come all over you. In you. On you. I want you like this for the rest of our lives. I want you to know you belong to me. I need you. Shit, I need you."

Her voice wobbled, breathless with our pace. "Don't stop."

My balls tightened, building with bubbling pressure. My cock grew thicker and harder, impaling her, spearing her, diving into her over and over and *over*.

My hands roamed over her back and waist. I couldn't stop touching her. Fisting her short hair, I rode her hard and fast. Degrading but respecting. Cruel but loving.

"I stole you from everyone. I snapped the collar around your neck and made you mine. Every scream you uttered is mine. Every moan you've made is mine. Your heart beats for *mine*. Fuck, Nila."

Her neck curved backward as I kept tight hold of her hair. "Yes. God, yes."

My legs trembled, my knees glued to the mattress as I thrust again and again.

My release gathered in every cell, electrifying together, surging into my cock.

Sweat misted my hairline as I continued to ravage. My fingers bruised her hips as I yanked her back again and again. "I'll never stop needing you, Needle. I want to know your every secret. I want to grow old with you. I want to be the reason you smile and hurt those who make you cry. I want you by my side when I finally do something worthwhile, and I want to enjoy every fucking second we have left together."

Nila's flesh bounced, her thighs cracking with mine as I hurtled toward the finish. Reaching between her legs, I strummed her clit, forcing her to climb to the heights of where I was.

I wanted to come. Fuck, how I wanted to come.

But I wanted her there with me.

A short cry fell from her lips as her back stiffened. Her fingernails dug into the mattress, forcing me to fuck her harder, touch her faster.

"Yes, yes…yes."

The pleasure was too great.

The pressure too demanding.

I couldn't wait.

Plastering my sweaty skin on hers, I hollowed my cheeks, sucking her skin, kissing her, biting her. My fingers worked her clit as my hips spasmed in a brutal finish.

Shards of pain erupted up my legs morphing into the sharpest bliss I'd ever had as the first spurt splashed into her.

"God, Nila."

I reared up, throwing my head back as another wave erupted. And another. And another. Goosebumps decorated my skin as every rapture transferred from me to my woman.

Nila came.

Her screams merged with my grunts. Her pussy milking me as my orgasm crested.

We continued rocking long after the adrenaline and intensity of shared releases faded. We didn't speak as I let go of her hair, massaging her shoulders, running my fingers over her spine.

Together, we flopped to the side, letting the mattress cradle us.

I didn't withdraw and the combined heat and wetness inside her bound us even more.

Spooning Nila, I grabbed the covers and tugged it over us. Her skin chilled quickly after the heat of sex. Nuzzling her from behind, I cupped her breast and sucked in a huge gust.

"Come closer." My voice was hoarse; my touch gentle after being merciless.

She snuggled backward, her head on my arm as I became her pillow. "Any closer and I'll be inside you."

I sighed. "You already are."

"Tell me again."

My eyes closed, sated and emotionally drained. "Tell you what?"

She waited, feathering out her thoughts for me to catch. In a strange way, I would be her very own dream catcher, sorting through her wishes while she slumbered, doing my best to make them true while she was awake.

My body quivered with residual spasms. The aftershocks of pleasure were almost as enjoyable as the finale. "You're so stunning." I kissed her shoulder.

"Not that." She squirmed, laughing softly.

"You're so dirty in bed."

"Not that, either." Her head turned; the slice of tiny teeth marked my wrist.

"Ow." I squeezed her, chuckling. "Kiss me and I'll tell you what you want to hear."

Slowly, she turned her head. Her hips arched, curving into me. My cock remained hard inside her, wanting to take her all over again.

Her lips sealed over mine, her tongue slipping soundlessly into my mouth. The joining was erotic, sated, promised, free. I held her there. Kissing her, breathing her, communicating without messy sounds.

For now and every moment in our future, we were inseparable.

My teeth sank into her swollen bottom lip, granting what she wanted. "I love you."

Her eyes opened, black and glowing. "How much?"

"As much as the universe but not as much as infinity."

Her forehead furrowed. "What does that mean?"

"It means infinity states a reference of time, regardless if it means never ending. I like to think there is no linear equation or quantifiable way to love you.

So I love you as much as love itself which really has no assessment."

She smiled. "You're so strange."

"You've only just noticed?"

She laughed. Her pussy clutched my cock, sending a wave of need into my balls. "Oh, I've noticed. I also noticed you're completely insane, mad—bonkers even. What did I call you? A loony toon?"

"I think you called me a Nutcase Hawk."

"That fits, too."

"I did warn you not to call me crazy."

"Turns out, I'm the one who's crazy."

My lips curled, knowing where she was going but happy to oblige the punch line. "Oh?"

Her hand drifted to mine, looping our fingers together, sighing happily. "Crazy in love with you." Kissing my knuckles, she settled into the bed and my arms. "We can be mad together, Kite. Because together it's the best form of insanity there is."

Thank you so much for reading.

Made in United States
Troutdale, OR
11/19/2024

25078185R00447